Love's Shadow

Left alone Christine dropped on to the stool before the mirror, staring at her face pale with fatigue, her unpinned hair falling in tangles around her shoulders. Was it possible for a few hours to change one's whole life, she wondered, and then knew it wasn't just the last few hours, it was the culmination of all those long summer days, the hours spent with Daniel, the feelings that had run between them, unexpressed but ever growing, needing only a spark to set them alight, and slowly, out of the tangle of the last few weeks, she began to wonder if after all she had been wrong. With a slow tide of bitter humiliation she wondered if she had fallen hopelessly in love with a man who had rejected her for what she still thought were insufficient reasons. And then there was Gareth . . . she stared at the ring on her finger and then slowly drew it off . . . dear God, what was she going to say to Gareth?

Constance Heaven is the author of sixteen previous novels and is a past winner of the Romantic Novelist Award. She lives in Middlesex.

CONSTANCE HEAVEN

Love's Shadow

Mandarin

A Mandarin Paperback
LOVE'S SHADOW

First published in Great Britain 1994
by William Heinemann Ltd
This edition published 1995
by Mandarin Paperbacks
an imprint of Reed Consumer Books Ltd
Michelin House, 81 Fulham Road, London SW3 6RB
and Auckland, Melbourne, Singapore and Toronto

Copyright © Constance Heaven 1994
The author has asserted her moral rights

A CIP catalogue record for this title
is available from the British Library
ISBN 0 7493 1698 5

Printed and bound in Great Britain
by Cox & Wyman Ltd, Reading, Berkshire

For Bettie and Ernest
and all my friends
in London and Overseas.

All other things, to their destruction draw,
   Only our love hath no decay;
This, no tomorrow hath, nor yesterday,
Running it never runs from us away
But truly keeps his first, last, everlasting day.

       The Anniversary John Donne

PART ONE

Christine

1851

Chapter 1

On a brilliantly sunny day in the June of 1851 Christine saw Daniel Hunter for the first time, never dreaming that from that chance meeting would spring so much anger and pain, so much ecstasy and disillusion.

It might never have happened if it had not been for her brother. They had been finishing a late breakfast in the morning room at Bramber when Harry suddenly looked up from buttering the last piece of toast.

'You don't need the dog cart today, do you?' he asked, reaching for the marmalade and spreading it lavishly. 'I thought of driving over to the Midsummer Fair at Chichester.'

'Whatever for?'

'Just for a lark. Must do something while I'm down here.'

'It could be fun,' said Christine slowly, 'and I've nothing much to do. Would you mind if I came with you?'

'Oh Lord, Chris, it'll be very hot, dusty and crowded. Not at all the thing for a fashionable young lady who has just made her curtsy at a Court garden party.'

'Oh stop grinning at me, you jackass! The less said about that the better.'

'Why? Did you trip up and land in Her Majesty's lap?'

'No, thank goodness, but it was the most boring affair possible. We had to stand and stand and stand. One girl fainted dead away. Let's forget it. What about the fair?'

'Well, I don't know,' he went on teasingly. 'Mamma wouldn't like it above half.'

'When has that ever bothered you – and she's not here, so

she won't know. Oh go on with you, Harry, don't be such a pig.'

'Oh well, come if you must but I give you fair warning. There's going to be a boxing mill. Rob Sayer, the Sussex champion, is going to take on all comers and the first village lad who gets him down wins a stake of twenty guineas put up by Jim Bates of the Three Tuns. Should be rare sport.'

'Sport indeed! Sounds more like the slaughter of the innocents!'

'Don't be so squeamish. You've bloodied more than one nose in your time.'

Christine giggled. She would be twenty in a matter of weeks, but she still remembered happily the long country days when she had run wild with Harry and Gareth and their friends. Sadly such carefree hours were long over, as her mother continually reminded her.

'When do we leave?' she asked, getting up from the table.

'Soon as you're ready and don't spend the morning prettying up, it's not a royal garden party. You won't want to bring Betsy, will you?'

'Heavens, no.' Betsy was Christine's maid and usually deep in her mistress's confidence. 'I have an idea she has a follower in the village. She asked me for a few hours off this afternoon and now I know why. Give me fifteen minutes and I'll be with you.' She turned back at the door. 'You're not thinking of meeting up with one of your floozies, are you?'

'Good God, no!' he said, shocked. 'What do you take me for?'

Christine laughed and disappeared. Harry had been sent down from Oxford a few weeks before the end of term owing to a rather discreditable episode linked with a young woman from the town. If their father were to find out, there could be the very devil to pay.

In her room Christine looked critically in the mirror and decided that her black and white striped morning gown with an edging of lace at the square neck would do very well for a country occasion such as this. She shook her dark curling hair free, brushed it out quickly and tied it back with a black ribbon.

Thank goodness Mamma was safely in London otherwise an expedition such as this would have been out of the question. Lady Clarissa, daughter of an Earl and wife of Everard Warrinder, whose successes at the Bar had made him one of the most admired and sought-after barristers in London, was always very conscious of the dignity of her position and certainly would not have approved of her daughter romping off to a vulgar country fair even in the company of her brother. Just now she was vastly enjoying herself in the preparations for her elder daughter's wedding, a most delightful round of dressmakers and shopping with endless arguments as to the merits of corded silk or slipper satin, the exact shade of pink for the bridesmaids' dresses and whether her daughter should go on honeymoon in powder blue or silver grey. It was from all this tedium that Christine had thankfully escaped on the plea of spending a few days with Grandfather who had not been so well during the winter. Not that her excuse had much validity. Lord Warrinder, a judge of some standing who had recently retired from the Bench, had been greatly surprised by the arrival of his granddaughter full of solicitous enquiries after his health.

'Never felt better in my life,' he said. 'Not that it's not always good to see you, m'dear, but won't you be bored down here with only an old codger like me for company?'

'Oh no,' she said, 'if you knew how terribly bored I had begun to feel in London with Margaret still so starry-eyed over her Freddie and her wedding dress, while here I have the horses and the dogs and you, darling Gramps. What more could I ask?'

But although she was very content to be free of the whirlwind of society, she was still pleased when Harry turned up looking somewhat shamefaced and swearing her to secrecy as to why he had come down from university so much earlier than expected. Harry and she had always done things together. He was her twin, the longed-for son and heir, welcomed with rejoicing, and fifteen minutes later she had slipped almost apologetically into the world to the dismay of her mother and the gratification of the attendant physician who had always prophesied twins.

Christine had been the unwanted one and a girl to boot, diminished already by the arrival of her brother. She had been fed, clothed, carefully reared, but never at any time really loved, a sad truth she had been aware of from a very early age.

'A surprise packet, that's what you were, my girl, and no mistake,' the under-nursemaid had said, turning from Harry, bathed and cherished, and dumping her in the bath, 'and a very unwelcome one,' she had muttered under her breath.

There was Margaret, three years older, so pretty, good and obedient, a charming little girl. There was Harry growing bigger and more handsome every day and hopelessly spoiled, his father's pride and his mother's darling, and then there was Christine, small, dark, not like either of her parents, difficult, shy and far too clever, given to bursts of inexplicable rage that had taken her many years to bring under control, always at odds with everyone except Harry who strangely enough had been far more attached to his difficult twin than to Margaret, so placid and good-natured.

Betsy put her head around the door and said in a penetrating whisper, 'Master Harry's waitin', Miss, and in a fair tizzy over it.'

'I'm coming, I'm coming,' said Christine, snatching up a silk shawl in a deep rose pink and swinging her straw bonnet by the ribbons as she ran down the stairs to where Harry was impatiently waiting by the dog cart. He helped her into it, sprang up after her, took the reins from Tom and they were off.

Bramber Grange had been bought by a certain Roger Warrinder, an astute and successful lawyer, back in the days of good Queen Bess and had been considerably improved and enlarged since by his successors, following him notably in the legal profession. Their portraits, bewigged and richly dressed, hung on the walls of the long gallery. Beyond the extensive flower gardens there was a stretch of parkland and a belt of woods bordering on the prosperous fields of the home farm. They reached the park gates and drove out into the lane, presently joining the highway and moving into the steady stream of vehicles all making towards the fairground. Farm carts, wagons, brakes crowded with country folk in their Sunday best, a few stately carriages, curricles and riders on horseback, all converging on the vast stretch of open fields.

'I'm afraid we'll have to do some walking, Christine. Hope you're wearing the right shoes,' remarked Harry turning skilfully into the yard of the Three Tuns and helping his sister to alight. The grandchildren of Lord Warrinder were well known there; an ostler sprang forward to take the horse. They could safely leave the trap in his care till they returned.

The fair was spread over a wide area of grassland and as they moved towards it through the inn yard they were met by a roar of sound. The town band, tin whistler and the thunder of drums mingled with the voices of a hundred showmen shouting their attractions, a steady hum of voices and laughter mixed with shrieking children and bawling babies, but all redolent of life, fun and entertainment. Christine's strict governesses would never at any time have allowed their charge anywhere near anything so vulgar and she clung to Harry's arm and went boldly into it prepared to enjoy everything.

Every imaginable type of freak was on show that day from an enormously fat woman to a man with pale skin stretched over bones like a living skeleton and a pig-faced boy, snout and all, which Harry swore *was* a pig dressed in nankeen trousers and blue shirt. There was a lady with two heads that nodded to each other very knowingly, a goat that danced, mind-reading dogs and performing horses. A group of acrobats tied themselves into indescribable contortions while Morris dancers with flowers in their hats capered around a horse-headed figure that made little darting rushes into the crowd who shrieked and scattered with mingled fear and delight. They paid their pennies for the flea circus which Christine watched with fascination till Harry pulled her away.

'Come on, for God's sake, I'm beginning to itch already.'

There was a huge gilded roundabout with gaily painted horses, swinging boats that made you giddy just to look at them and booths selling hot mutton pies, twisted sticks of barley sugar, long black straps of liquorice, brandy balls and delicious newly baked gingerbread. Christine stared at it so hungrily that Harry bought her a slice and she walked on biting into the rich sticky cake and thinking wickedly that Mamma would probably die of shock if she were to see her now.

After a time it became obvious that the boxing bout was going to be the prime entertainment during the afternoon. The crowd, consisting mostly of men, was already making its way steadily towards the big tent set up at the end of the field. She did wonder for a moment whether she should allow her brother to go on alone but she knew what he would say. 'Chickening out, are you, Sis? Thought you'd not have the bottom for it,' and she wasn't going to allow that. She had never shirked anything in the old days and wasn't going to start now. She walked on resolutely beside him.

Fights between rival champions were not popular with the police since they more often than not ended in riots, with the spectators fighting among themselves, but this was not one of the great championship battles but only a country affair. However the tent was still crowded to the doors. Looking around her she could see there were very few women and certainly none like herself. Good-naturedly some of the men moved back a little, permitting them to get nearer the crude platform set up at the end of the tent. Never having attended such a thing before, she took a deep breath, prayed that the stifling heat wouldn't make her feel faint and thought she could always close her eyes if she found the sight of two men battering viciously at each other too gruesome to watch.

Presently, when not another person could be squeezed into the enclosure, Rob Sayer himself stepped on to the platform to a roar of applause. She looked at him curiously. He was of medium height with a round, bullet-shaped head crowned by a fuzz of reddish hair. Naked to the waist, with skin-tight trousers on short powerful legs, he looked immensely formidable. He waved his hand to the audience, exchanging ribald jests with them while waiting for his first victim. The hopeful village lads, their eyes fixed on the promised twenty guineas, came up one after the other. Most of them were mere boys stripping off their shirts, some of them sunburnt and brawny, some pitifully puny, but one and all they leaped up on to the platform full of spirit, squaring their fists and facing up to their opponent bravely, only to be knocked down like ninepins in the first few minutes. A good many of them landed on their backs in the very first bout but now and again, to add to the fun and make it appear more equal, Rob would play them along, letting them get in a hit now and again and then, when they grew over-confident, laying them out almost contemptuously with a few well placed blows, while the spectators both hissed and applauded.

It went on for some time and began to grow monotonous. The crowd was already becoming restive when a young man came pushing himself through from the back of the tent. Most of the would-be champions had been local and had been greeted with shouts of advice and encouragement but this one was a stranger. There was a momentary hush as he stepped up on to the platform. He was taller than Rob Sayer but looked almost laughably slender in comparison with the hero's powerful torso.

'Who are you?' demanded the referee who was also the manager, and had been masterminding the whole affair ready to take charge if any trouble arose.

'Daniel Hunter's the name,' said the young man. 'Any reason why I can't try a bout?'

'You're not from these parts?'

'No. Does that matter?'

'What d'you say, Rob?'

'Why not?' The champion stared at the newcomer very sure of himself, legs apart, thumbs tucked into his waistband. 'The more the merrier, I say. Strip off your shirt, lad. Let's see what kind o' stuff you're made of.'

The young man obediently peeled off his shabby leather waistcoat and pulled over his head the clean but well-patched shirt. Then he kicked off his worn leather boots and stood balancing easily on his stockinged feet. One stocking had been clumsily darned at the toe with wool of a different colour, which Christine found somehow touching, and she surprised herself by hoping that this one would put on a better show and not be knocked out in the first few minutes.

To start with it didn't look as if her wish would be gratified. Rob Sayer, as if sensing a challenge that had not existed in any of the others that afternoon, set about the newcomer in grim earnest, but the young man, despite his appearance, possessed a wiry strength and showed a considerable resilience. Thrown to his knees, he was up again in an instant and succeeded in putting in one or two shrewd blows that aroused shouts of encouragement from the enthralled audience. Christine had never watched anything like this before. She wanted to cheer with the others when he held his own against the pounding he was receiving. She trembled with anxiety when he stumbled and fell, lest he would not scramble to his feet again in time. Both men were running with sweat, their chests heaving with the exertion. A blow from Sayer had split open the young man's forehead above his eye and the blood trickled down his cheek. Once a blow sent him spinning off the platform but before Sayer could snatch at his triumph, Daniel Hunter was back on his feet with a lucky hit that sent his opponent sprawling into a corner. The noise around her was terrific. Men were craning forward, giving advice, shouting encouragement, fighting the battle for him, Harry among them.

'He may not be scientific, Chris,' he whispered, 'but by Jupiter that chap's got guts!'

The end came with unbelievable speed. Daniel had been flung to his knees, his face ran with blood and sweat, his chest was covered with bruises and contusions. For an instant it seemed he was done for and a great sigh ran through the breathless, watching crowd, then suddenly he was on his feet again. Through the blur swam a girl's face, dark hair, lips just parted, glowing eyes fixed on him. It was the impetus he needed. He pushed the sweat-soaked hair out of his eyes and, with lightning unexpectedness, caught his opponent a smashing uppercut that spun him across the platform and over the edge, where he lay stunned and did not move. Amazingly Daniel had won. For a moment there was silence. He stood panting, head bowed, utterly exhausted, then the spectators went crazy, cheering themselves hoarse. Rob Sayer had been hauled to his feet, none too pleased, but he accepted the knock-out blow with grudging grace while Daniel picked up his shirt. He was dazedly pulling on his boots when the delighted crowd seized him, carrying him off, shoulder high, to the Three Tuns where his victory could be properly celebrated with mugs of ale and he could be presented with the twenty guineas.

Harry put his arm around Christine as the crowd jostled, pushed and shoved their way out of the tent.

'Are you all right?' he asked a little belatedly after all the excitement. 'You're not feeling faint, are you?'

'No, of course not,' she said indignantly, but she was glad of his arm all the same as she had to come to terms with the shocking fact that she had just witnessed a bloody fight between two men in all its raw ferocity, and, what was worse, had found herself enjoying it.

Outside it was a relief to breathe the fresh air. The heat had begun to abate now, a slight breeze had sprung up and they walked close together while the fair still went on merrily around them.

'Had enough of it?' said Harry.

'I really think I have, but I'm terribly thirsty.'

'We'll walk back to the Three Tuns and sit in the garden.'

'Isn't that where they have taken that young man?'

'Oh you needn't worry about that. They'll be in the tap-room. As a matter of fact I wouldn't mind having a word with that chap. I wonder if he's in training. Has the makings of a champion I should say.'

Noise and laughter flowed out from the bar room of the inn, but at the back where the wife of Jim Bates grew a few flowers and herbs, it was cool and shady. Christine sat down at one of the tables and Harry disappeared into the inn in search of something to drink.

Presently the innkeeper's wife came out herself with a plate of cakes and a glass of lemonade.

'You drink that down, Miss,' she said putting the tray on the table. 'The water comin' up from the well is real icy so it'll be nice and cool.'

'Thank you. It looks wonderful.'

'You and your brother will be staying with your grandfather, I dare say.'

'Yes, for a few days,' Christine sighed. 'Then I must go back to London for my sister's wedding.'

'Aye, I heard about that. It'll be a grand affair I'm thinkin'. I expect you'll be gettin' wed yourself, Miss, before long.'

'I don't know about that, Mrs Bates.'

A great wave of shouts and laughter surged out from the bar and Mrs Bates frowned as she took up the tray.

'That lot in there will be drinkin' themselves silly before long, I shouldn't wonder. Good for business, but as I told Jim when he put up the money, it en't right or fair on our lads when a foreigner comes like that and takes the lot.'

Christine smiled. Anyone coming from only five miles away was a foreigner in Mrs Bates' eyes.

'Do you know where he comes from?'

'Never set eyes on him before today. He comes in here early on and it was then that he heard about the fight and was off like a shot. Twenty guineas is a temptation to a youngster like that, I'm thinkin'. Well, I mustn't stand here chattin'. When Jim gets a few drinks inside him, good sense flies out o' the window and that doesn't do.'

'Will you tell my brother that it is growing late and we should be thinking about driving home?'

'I will that. Don't you fret, Miss Christine. I'll see he don't stay too long.'

She went in but time passed. Harry didn't come and Christine sat on, pleasantly cool and rested, with the evening scent of mint and lavender all around her. Jim's old sheepdog lumbered over and flopped at her feet. She bent to pat him and saw that someone had come through the back door, stood still for a moment as if glad of the coolness and then rather unsteadily dropped on to the bench on the other side of her table and she saw that it was Daniel Hunter.

He had washed his face but it was horribly bruised, the mouth badly swollen at one side. Blood had begun to ooze again from the cut above his eye and trickled down his cheek. He didn't seem to notice it and after a moment, obeying an almost irresistible impulse, she leaned forward and dabbed at it with her handkerchief.

'You should have a dressing put on that, you know.'

'What!' He seemed to realize suddenly that she was there and backed away a little. 'It's nothing.'

'But it is. Gareth says that damage to the forehead like that bleeds more than anywhere else.'

'Who's Gareth?'

'He's a doctor.'

'I've never had much to do with the likes o' them.'

'You must be very pleased with yourself. You were the only one this afternoon to stand up to Rob Sayer.'

He turned to look at her then, taking in the glossy dark hair, the elegance of the striped gown, the gold locket and chain on the white neck, the rich silk of the shawl carelessly draped around her shoulders. This was the girl he had glimpsed watching so avidly, and she was one of the class he most despised, the parasites leading their indulgent lives with no knowledge or understanding of anyone else, one of those who take everything and contribute nothing.

'You were watching then?'

The wealth of contempt in his voice drove her into self-defence.

13

'I was with my brother. He was very interested. He said you had the makings of a champion of the ring.'

A sharp resentment rose up in him at the patronising voice.

'That's not what I'm after.'

'Why did you do it then?'

'For the money o' course. What else?'

'Twenty guineas isn't very much.'

He stared at her for a moment and then looked away.

'My mother worked in a mill twelve hours a day for seven shillings a week and kept herself and two children on it till the machine killed her.'

'Killed her?' Christine was shocked.

'The machine caught her dress. There wasn't much left of her by the time they got her out.'

Christine stared at him appalled at what her unthinking question had provoked.

'How old were you then?' she asked in a stifled voice.

'Eleven and my sister were six.'

He got up from the table and walked away from her, staring across the garden to the field beyond, where two horses grazed peacefully in the cool of the evening, and wondered why he had spoken of such deeply intimate things to this unknown girl who meant nothing to him, who came from another and alien world.

'It must have been terrible for you,' said Christine gently.

'Oh no, they were all very kind. That's what orphanages are for, didn't you know?' he went on with a savage irony. 'One for me and one for my sister. So now you see why twenty guineas can seem like a fortune to the likes of us.'

'I'm sorry,' she murmured helplessly.

He swung round, not looking at her, and made for the back door of the inn, colliding with Harry who was coming out and muttering something as he pushed past him.

'Was that chap pestering you?'

'No, of course not. I just said a few words to him about the fight.'

'Rum sort of fellow. Couldn't be persuaded to take more

14

than one drink and not a word of where he comes from, only that he is on his way to London and on foot, I guess. Poor devil! I don't envy him. It's a long tramp.' He picked up the bloodied handkerchief. 'Is this yours?'

'No,' she said quickly, 'no. Leave it and let's go.'

The dog cart had already been brought out and the horse harnessed. Harry helped her in and they were off at a good trot and if Christine was unusually silent, Harry thought nothing of it. It had, after all, been a tiring day.

Shortly after they had driven away, Daniel came out of the back door carrying his pack and ready to move on. He paused at the table for a moment and then picked up the handkerchief. It smelled faintly of some expensive perfume and he was still looking at it when Mrs Bates bustled out to pick up the glass and cakes.

'Is that Miss Christine's handkerchief you've got there?' she asked.

'No, no,' he said quickly and put it in his pocket.

'She's a very pleasant young lady, not like some I could mention. Treat you like dirt under their feet some of 'em do.'

'Who are they? She and her brother?'

'Their grandfather is Lord Warrinder. A famous judge he was, retired now, lives at Bramber Grange over near Steyning.'

'Warrinder?' he repeated thoughtfully. 'Any kin to Everard Warrinder?'

'That'll be his son. he's made a big name for himself up in London so they say.'

'I see.' So she was Everard Warrinder's daughter, was she? What a fantastic coincidence! He hoisted up his pack. 'Well, I must be on my way.'

'Walkin' to London, are you? Why not wait till morning, lad? It's a long way to go and you don't want to lose that gold in your pocket to some night robber.'

He laughed. 'I'll be safe enough and it's a fair night. I can put in a good few miles before dark. Thank you for the bread and cheese. You've been very kind.'

'Ah well, you remind me of my brother. He was just such a

15

one as you, always must be on the move, couldn't settle quietly at home, till bad luck struck him. Died of a raging fever he did, caught in a winter snowstorm. See nothing like that happens to you, young man.'

'I will.'

She watched him walk through the gate and out on to the road. Then with a sigh she took up the tray and returned to the inn where a bar full of rowdy customers were already making merry. More than likely there would be a few broken heads before the night was out and Jim wasn't one to deal with emergencies. She braced herself and went in, closing the door after her.

Harry was coming up the drive at a brisk trot when they both saw the carriage at the front door and the tall figure descending from it.

'Oh Lord, that's Father,' exclaimed Harry. 'What the devil is he doing here? I thought he was in court all this week. He can't have heard about me, can he? Look here, Chris, you drive. I'm going to do a disappearing act till I find out what's up.' And before she could protest, he had slowed down sufficiently to thrust the reins into her hands, leap down and vanish into the shrubbery.

By the time she pulled up, the carriage was already moving off, the door had been opened and her father was on the steps. He turned to look at her in some surprise.

Tom had appeared and gone to the horse's head. She climbed down very conscious of how she must look in her father's fastidious eyes, hot and sweaty, her hair windblown, her hands grubby, her dress crumpled and untidy.

'Is that you, Christine?' he said frowning. 'Wherever have you been?'

'I spent the day at the fair, Papa.'

'The fair and dressed like that! Really, child, have you no sense of what's fitting and of who your grandfather is down here in the country? I'm not surprised that your mother sometimes despairs of you.'

16

She was accustomed to her father's disapproval. Whatever she did, however hard she tried, she never seemed able to please him and it still hurt, though for a long time now she had done her best to shrug it off.

'It was hot and very dusty, I'm afraid, but great fun all the same,' she said sturdily. 'Why are you here, Papa? There is nothing wrong with Margaret or Mamma, is there?'

'They are both in excellent health,' he said rather acidly. 'Not that you have shown very much concern for them, I must say, running away down here when they are so concerned with this wedding.'

'They don't need me,' she muttered.

'They seem to think they do, especially Margaret. I am here because I have something I wish to discuss with your grandfather. You had better return to London with me in the morning.'

'Very well, Papa, and now if you will excuse me, I think I ought to go upstairs to wash and change before we dine.'

'The sooner the better I should say. Off you go, child. I'll give you the messages from your mother and sister later.'

Unexpectedly, he smiled. It softened and warmed the coldly handsome face and, as had happened before, she longed to throw her arms around his neck and hug him. But she had tried it once and been repulsed, so never again. She hurried up the stairs and hovered on the landing till she saw her grandfather come out and the two men disappear together, then she crept down again and found her way to the stables where she felt certain she would find Harry.

'It's all right,' she whispered hurriedly. 'It's nothing to do with you. There is something he wants to talk over with Grandfather. We can say you only arrived yesterday instead of a week ago and Gramps is a sport. He won't give you away.'

An hour or so later, clean and very correctly dressed, they sat at dinner, quiet and decorous under their father's eye, answering when spoken to, but not venturing any remarks of their own, only now and again exchanging a covert glance of gratitude when Lord Warrinder, who was a kindly man and remembered his own youth, took pains not to give away Harry's arrival a full week and more before he should have left Oxford.

Dinner over, Christine was left alone in the drawing room, her father being closeted with Lord Warrinder in his library and Harry off on some excursion of his own. It was barely nine o'clock and the long summer evening stretched before her. She could have taken up a book or played the piano or worked at her embroidery which was all too often sadly neglected, but it had been a disturbing day and she couldn't settle to anything. The room was warm and stuffy but outside the cool night air beckoned. She suddenly made up her mind, ran up the stairs to fetch a shawl, called Benjie, her grandfather's elderly black retriever, and went out into the garden.

The air was filled with the scent of the roses which had been her grandmother's passion, and had been meticulously kept in order though she had been dead these five years.

She walked slowly, enjoying the coolness after the heat of the day, with Benjie ambling happily beside her. The few words she had exchanged with that unusual young man at the fair had stirred up the rebellion inside her, something she had been vainly trying to subdue all this past year, a revolt against the life which she and so many other young women of her class were condemned to lead. A silly, stupid, *useless* life, she thought, when so much in the world needed to be set right. She seemed to have been fighting her father about it all her life. When she was six, she had begged him to let her share Harry's tutors; when her brother went to Eton, she had implored her father to allow her to attend Queen's College, the new school for girls set up in Harley Street; when Gareth started on his medical studies, she asked if she could learn about medicine too.

'I've never heard such nonsense in my life,' her father had said, smiling at the ridiculous idea. 'The Society of Apothecaries would think you crazy. Are you out of your mind, child? You'll be wanting to be a doctor next. If you can learn to be as good a woman as your mother, look after your husband, manage his house, care for his children, you will have done very well. What more suitable career is there for any young woman?'

'Suppose I don't want to marry?'

'Don't talk rubbish. Of course you will marry,' said her father. 'Look at Margaret. Isn't she happy and contented? Why can't you be the same?'

'Because I'm not Margaret,' she had said defiantly.

'More's the pity,' said her father bleakly and that was the end of the matter. It was useless appealing to her mother. She had always backed him in every particular.

It was maddeningly frustrating. She must talk to Gareth about it. He would help. Dear Gareth, she had not seen him for nearly a year. He was a doctor now, but, as he had said, still with a great deal to learn, and had been taking a special course at a hospital in Edinburgh. Gareth had been a source of God-like wisdom and strength since she was six and he was ten.

Gareth Fraser had lost his parents at a very early age and had been mainly brought up by his great-uncle who was nearly eighty but still possessed all the raffish elegance, wit and slightly risqué charm of the Regency. Gareth's father had studied law with Everard Warrinder at Oxford. They had been called to the Bar in the same year and had remained friends to the last, so that Gareth often spent his holidays at Bramber Grange and had been neither too proud nor too grown-up to enjoy the company of Harry and an adoring little girl who would have much preferred to be a boy; and the affection and trust between them had grown with the years. She would write to him tomorrow, tell him her problem and ask his advice.

Deep in thought, her feet had carried her across the shaven grass under the cedars and brought her to the edge of the woods when the evening calm was broken by the sound of loud, angry voices. There was a thud followed by furious barking. Benjie pricked his ears and shot off like an arrow towards the sound and Christine raced after him stumbling a little in her thin sandals.

She came through the trees and into a little clearing. A stocky man in green coat, cord breeches and stout leather gaiters was just struggling to his feet while Daniel Hunter stood glaring down at him, held at bay by both dogs, not barking now but growling at the back of their throats and regarding him menacingly.

'It's Finch, isn't it?' she said quickly, recognising the man who had now scrambled to his feet, rubbing his bruised jaw and bristling with righteous anger. He was the gatekeeper who lived at the lodge and regarded himself as guardian of all Lord Warrinder's lands. 'What is it? What happened to you?'

'You may well ask, Miss Christine,' said the keeper in an aggrieved tone. 'I meets this young man marching through his lordship's woods large as life and when I tells him this is private land and he's no right here, he ups and shouts at me that no property is private, no one man has any prior right to it and so he and anyone else can go marching through it whenever they please. And when I pointed out that might be all very well where he comes from, but down here these woods belong to Lord Warrinder so he best take himself off before I set Rover on him, he flies out at me like some wild beast.'

'Did you threaten to shoot him?'

'I never so much as raised a finger to him, Miss, and that's God's truth,' he said virtuously.

'I see.' She looked from him to Daniel's sullen face and guessed that Finch could be pretty foul-mouthed and might easily have hit this touchy young man on the raw. 'Well, Finch,' she went on pleasantly, 'I happen to know this person so you can leave him to me. I'll see him safely off my grandfather's land.'

'If you say so, Miss, though I don't hardly like leaving you alone with a saucy young malapert like this one. I don't know what his lordship would have to say, I'm sure.'

'I'll deal with my grandfather. You needn't concern yourself. He won't do me any harm.'

'Very well, Miss.'

He picked up his fallen gun, called Rover, gave the young man a threatening stare and reluctantly marched off.

'I'm afraid you've damaged his pride, Mr Hunter,' she said as the footsteps died away. 'This is private land, you know. He was in the right. What made you knock him down?'

'I didn't like the names he called me,' he said sullenly.

'Are you one of those radicals?'

'What d'you mean by that?'

'A rebel, a revolutionary, cutting off heads like they did in France?'

'That were fifty years ago and I've never wanted to cut any heads off.'

'I'm glad to hear it.'

He frowned at her. 'Are you laughing at me?'

'A little. Do you mind?'

'It would be all the same if I did, wouldn't it?' He picked up the pack he had let fall to the ground. 'I'd best be goin'.'

'I think you had and I'd better show you the right path before you fall into worse trouble.'

'There's no need,' he said gruffly.

'There's every need. This way.'

She went before him along the narrow path. Under the trees it was growing dark but her white dress of some filmy material swayed before him like some wraith of the twilight. She had twisted up the dark hair into a knot on the top of her head and now and again, in the fading light, he saw the glitter of the small diamonds in her ears. He wondered if his sister Kate would look anything like her. She'd be eighteen by now and all he remembered was a thin child with terrified, tear-filled eyes when they had taken her away. It wouldn't be long now before he knew.

At the edge of the wood Christine stopped and turned to him.

'My brother told me you were on your way to London.'

'So I am.'

'This is hardly the most direct route.'

'I lost my way.'

21

She thought that was probably a lie. Maybe someone had told him who they were and he had been curious to see where they lived.

'Well, you can't miss it now. When you go through the gate there, turn left and in about half a mile you'll hit the turnpike and then you can't go wrong.'

'I'll go then.' He paused and then said grudgingly, 'I suppose I ought to thank you.'

'Perhaps you should. You might have ended up in front of the bench for assaulting a keeper.'

'In front of Lord Warrinder, I suppose.'

'Very likely. Goodnight, Mr Hunter.'

He moved away and then turned back. 'He called me a dirty bastard and my mother a damned whore.'

'I wonder you didn't kill him.'

'I wish I had.'

He hoisted his pack to his shoulder and set off along the dusty path.

A difficult young man with an outstanding chip on his shoulder, she thought, as she watched him go. She wondered if she should tell Harry about it and then decided against it. He might think she had been too lax in letting him go, and yet there had been something oddly appealing about him. It made a fitting end to what had been a queerly unsettling day. She sighed, called Benjie from his rummaging in the undergrowth, and walked thoughtfully back to the house.

Chapter 2

The small boy stood beside his mother in the midst of an enormous crowd of stalwart citizens and vagrants selling birds in cages, goldfish and rat poison, along with jugglers, conjurors, shoeblacks, crossing-sweepers, women with flower baskets, a hurdy-gurdy man with his monkey, dung collectors with shovel and bucket, girls in gaudy dresses looking for a customer when all this was over, all part and parcel of the hundreds who thronged the streets of the capital every day, all jostling one another, pushing forward, gazing up expectantly at the gaunt walls of Newgate prison, where, high up, could be seen the wooden platform where the grisly business would soon be played to the finish.

The boy's short legs ached. It had taken over a week to make the journey from the north and it had been a long tramp for a seven-year-old that morning, all the way from Lambeth, over the river and through the wet muddy streets. He shivered in the raw cold. Hot-pie men and chestnut-sellers, the nuts hissing and spitting over the glowing brazier, were doing good business. He stared at them hungrily but his mother shook her head impatiently and gripped his hand more tightly.

A huge sigh seemed to ripple through the waiting crowd and they began to sway forward. A door had opened. The governor of the prison appeared, an imposing figure, and with him came a clergyman in white cassock, clutching his prayer-book, scanty grey hair blown by the wind. He was followed by the warders and then by the man they had been waiting for, his hands tied behind his back and his head raised, proud, unyielding, defying the law to do its worst because he died for a cause he believed in with a certainty that in the end they would win through to a better life for the crushed, the exploited, the sick and the hopeless. The boy's heart swelled till he thought it would burst. It was his father up there, the father who told him stories of magic and adventure, who had encouraged him to read, who had said to his little son, 'Never forget, it's for you to carry on where others have left off.'

He wanted to shut his eyes against the dreadful moment to come, but his mother's whisper, harsh and fierce, prevented it.

'Look, Daniel, look well and never forget. They say your father killed a man but it is a wicked lie. Remember that and remember the injustice that has brought him to this hideous death . . .'

Daniel saw the hood put over his father's head, the noose placed around his neck. He saw the sudden heart-rending jerk, the contorted body, then he gave a great cry and shot up in the bed, running with sweat, still caught up in the nightmare, still shaking, until gradually the outlines of the attic room took shape around him. He could see the tiny window where the eaves sloped down almost to the floor. He saw the wooden stool, the chest in the corner, the tumble of his books on the floor where he had unpacked them and he fell back against the pillow with a long sigh of relief. He had not suffered that particular nightmare for a long time now. It must have come from what they had been talking about last night.

At the mill the factory bell had clanged at five-thirty, calling all hands to work, but now he was his own master and could luxuriate for another hour. He still found it hard to believe that he was here in London at last. It was early yesterday morning when, footsore and weary, he had caught his first glimpse of the enormous stretch of houses spreading out like some gigantic web from the hub at the centre. Confused and bewildered he had limped his way through street after street, lost himself over and over again, and at last found the river and thankfully followed it till he came to Westminster Bridge and the enormous spread of the Houses of Parliament, recently rebuilt after a disastrous fire, and stood staring at the great building. Would the day ever come when he himself would enter those impressive portals, would take his seat on the padded benches amongst those who made the unjust laws and tell them boldly where they were going wrong? A part of him was overawed, amazed at his own daring, at the absurdity of such an ambition, and another part, small but grimly determined, held on to it like a star that beckoned him on, if only he had the courage to follow after it.

By early evening he had reached the Tower and gazed at the great fortress full of grim and bloody history. He stopped there at a stall selling hot pies and bought one, sitting on the parapet of the river to eat it. He was deadly tired, aching in every limb, but he was there, in London, and an exultation ran through him as he got stiffly to his feet. He found his way to Whitechapel, through the heart of the city, impressed by the great buildings and the crowded streets until at length, and with the help of passers-by who stared curiously at the tall country lad with his tanned face, his huge pack and dusty boots, he arrived at his destination, the Methodist Chapel, whose address he had been given with his precious letters of introduction.

A prayer meeting was in progress and he sat at the back, dropping wearily on to the hard bench. A voice droned on through exhortation and prayer and he was almost asleep when the resounding closing hymn woke him up and brought him unsteadily to his feet.

Mr Glossop, the preacher, gaunt, dark and fiery, and Mr Brown, small, plump and short-sighted, who ran the business side of the community, had been warned by their colleague in the north of Daniel's coming and they had looked at the tall, travel-stained young man who stumbled up the bare, austere room towards them with a good deal of caution. They were in fact badly in need of recruits. The ragged school they had established last winter, where the children gathered for

25

a penny a week to learn their letters, needed a new teacher badly, the last one having absconded with the month's paltry takings. They exchanged a glance and thought that this Daniel Hunter looked brawny enough to withstand the onslaught of a bunch of difficult, unruly youngsters, who had little desire to learn anything but whom they hoped to capture from a life of infamy and shame.

Charity towards others was part of their code. Mr Brown, a family man, took Daniel home, fed him, found out that he could read and write, knew how to figure and was filled with a proper respect for Methodist aims and ideals.

Not that Daniel told him everything that night. He toned it down, slid over the hellish years at the orphanage. Children could be horribly cruel and they had all known about his father. The authorities had made sure of that. It marked him out. Hangman Dan, they had called him, and Gallows Boy, and worse names. He had survived them, as he had the rope slid round his neck with the push down the stairs that nearly strangled him, the dead rat that hung obscenely over his bed. It had made him tough, self-reliant, silent under stress, wary of any kindness lest it be simply a trap. He had kept himself aloof, made no friends, kept his hurts, his bruises, his bloody battles to himself, scorning to complain or to show how much he cared.

Sent to the cotton mill, unskilled, woefully ignorant, he had been given the most menial tasks, crawling between the great looms with the huge bales of cotton, scrubbing floors, sweeping up, breathing in the cotton dust till his lungs felt choked and sometimes he could scarcely breathe. His few pence a week bought him a corner in an underground cellar where he had slept with a dozen other boys like himself, but he preferred, whenever he could, to spend the nights in the open air, no matter how cold, glad to escape the fetid stench, the crawling horror of lice and bedbugs, the touch of the filthy bodies that crept closer and closer for warmth. While others died around him, he had survived by sheer force of will, till the accident that changed his life.

Mr Brown, with his wife and daughter, Elspeth, had listened avidly as Daniel described how at the very end of a twelve-hour day, choked by a heavy cold and staggering through the looms under the weight of a huge bale of cotton, he had stumbled and fallen sideways. His ragged sleeve was caught and his arm slashed from shoulder to wrist. The cry forced out of him, the welter of blood, the screams of the women, brought people running, including the overseer. Momentarily he had fainted and came round to find himself lying on the floor, his head in someone's lap and a raging argument going on over his head. Slowly, in the midst of pain and fear and exhaustion, he had realised that the woman who was busily staunching the blood was one of the workers. Prue Jessop was one of their best workers and in charge of that particular floor. The factory owner would have liked to dismiss her years ago for her outspoken way of upholding the women's rights and privileges, but she had proved herself to be too valuable, and factory owners, hedged by new rules, were not quite so powerful as they had been twenty years before. The heated argument had ended with Prue taking Daniel home with her instead of sending him to the infirmary and caring for him herself till he was well enough to return to work.

'I owe everything to Prue and Sam Jessop,' Daniel said earnestly, leaning across the table, his eyes glowing, his weariness forgotten. 'It was only with them that I learned to live again.'

'Aye,' said Mr Brown, nodding wisely, 'Sam were always a good, kind fellow. He and I grew up together, you might say. Many's the crack we've had together in the old days and though we went our separate ways, he staying up where he were born, and me coming down here, we've always kept in touch.'

Sam and Prue Jessop were in fact good, honest, hard-working people, loyal to their chapel and living austere lives that still held a few pleasures, if of a strictly serious and intellectual kind. Sam was a member of the Workers' Association, borrowed precious books from their scanty library, encouraged

Dan to read them and though his religion forbade him to use any kind of violence, he held very strong views on the rights of the working man. Dan's father had become something of a martyr in the eyes of Sam and his wife, a victim of class injustice and prejudice, so together they were determined to do their best for his son. It had been a hard life and in some ways a narrow and joyless one, but simply to have two good friends, to have a home, a place of refuge, no matter how poor, seemed like heaven after the last desolate years. Daniel learned to trust again, grew physically and mentally and with it grew his ambition and that secret resolve one day to confront the man whose brilliant prosecution had sent his father to the gallows.

The Great Charter, for which so many had fought so stubbornly, with its demands for workers' privileges, for a vote for all men, for properly established trade unions, might have been temporarily defeated but was still very much alive in the minds of workers, was still discussed at their secret meetings, was still a burning issue. Daniel had been twenty when the Workers' Association in London had sent members to the Midlands, violent inflammatory speakers whose words had set him ablaze.

'When I came home, I told Sam over and over,' he went on passionately, forgetting where he was, leaning towards his hosts, thumping the table, 'I told him the only way we'll win is by getting a member into the Parliament who's one of us, a worker, not one of those gentlemanly radicals who have never once soiled their lily-white hands, but one like Sam with a lifetime of hard work behind him, one as has come up through the mill, who has known what it is to work till you drop if you'd not see your children starve.'

'Someone like you, boy, is that what's in your mind?' said Mr Brown a little drily.

'Well, one day perhaps.' Dan had sat back suddenly abashed, afraid he was making a fool of himself.

'Don't be ashamed to admit it. We wouldn't get far without our dreams now, would we? I had 'em once too. Your father had too many and they hanged him for them, but you're flying high, Dan. It's a long, hard road you'll have to travel.'

'Mebbe it is,' he muttered, aware he was being gently laughed at, 'but I've never been afraid of hard work.'

'And there's another thing,' went on Mr Brown. 'Times are changing, Dan, you must realise that. We've achieved a great deal in the last year or so and there's some of us whose fighting days are over. We're looking for a quiet life nowadays.'

It was true of course. Daniel looked around him. The house was small and unpretentious but it was well furnished and comfortable. The supper table showed the remains of a good pork pie, thickly buttered bread, a rich plum cake. Mr Brown owned a grocer's shop that sold all kinds of provisions and catered not just for the ordinary folk but for the richer shop-keepers, the union officials and steady workers and he was ambitiously looking to open another in the near future. He'd not wish to jeopardise any of his hard-earned prosperity for a doubtful cause that had already conspicuously failed.

An immense weariness swept through Daniel, but he could not give in, not yet. He went on stubbornly.

'I tell you one thing that I told Sam. When the time comes, and it will come, when I sit in that Parliament House and make my opening speech that's going to shift some of those fat bottoms right off their seats, then I hope that he and you and all the others who think I'm crazy even to dream of it, will be there to hear it.'

'That'll be the day,' said Mrs Brown putting a motherly hand on his and patting it as if he were still only five years old, 'but it's a long way off yet, Dan. Now you eat up your tea, you're going to need all your strength if you've a mind to making grand plans like that.'

'Aye, that's true enough but in the meantime you'll be wanting some sort of a job, I'm thinking,' said Mr Brown. 'Put some water in the pot, my dear, we'll all have another cup while I tell Daniel about the school.'

Daniel had been prepared to take any kind of work for the time being, but this offer of a post as teacher in the chapel's ragged school was an unexpected bonus. It would give him a status, a place from which he could rise.

'Well, there it is,' went on Mr Brown, 'I've told you the worst of it and the money's not much. You'll have Elspeth to show you the ropes. She's been taking the little ones. Catch 'em young, I say, and they'll come back for more. With Mr Glossop's approval, we'll give you a trial till the end of the year. It's up to you to make a go of it. Don't decide now,' he said as Daniel opened his mouth, 'sleep on it and come down to the shop tomorrow and tell me what you think about it. Sam's recommendation goes a long way with us, so make sure you live up to it.' He put down his cup and got to his feet. 'Now that's settled, we must find you a lodging and I think I've got the very thing. Come on, lad, better not leave it too late. You'll be wanting your bed, I shouldn't wonder.'

'It's very good of you.'

Dan struggled to his feet, suddenly very conscious of how desperately weary he was. He thanked Mrs Brown for a delicious meal, said good-night to her and Elspeth, heaved up his pack and followed his host out of the house.

Mr Brown found him an attic room on the top floor of a lodging house run by one of the chapel members. Ma Taylor, five feet tall and thin as a bedpost, was a fierce upholder of law and order.

She had looked him up and down critically before she said, 'Mebbe you'll do, but no drinkin' and no goings-on, understand?'

'Aye,' he said meekly.

'Good, up you go then and mind you keep your room decent. I aren't climbin' them stairs every day in the week, you know.'

The room was scrupulously clean, the bed hard but spotless and after some of his experiences on the road, Daniel realised how lucky he was. Weariness overcame him almost before he had unpacked his few possessions and he fell thankfully into bed. The next morning, the grip of his nightmare gradually fading, Daniel felt immensely alive and filled with eagerness to make a start on his new life. Jumping out of bed, he peered from the attic window and could see only an endless stretch of roofs and chimney pots, but high above the streets the air smelled sweet and fresh. There was a jug and basin for his use, so he washed and dressed quickly. Then he put everything away tidily, picked up his leather waistcoat and found the bloodied handkerchief still buried deep in one of the pockets. He stared down at it for a moment – fine cotton, lace-edged, with a monogram in one corner. A faint perfume clung about it still. He saw her in his mind's eye, in her filmy white dress, diamonds glittering in her ears, laughing at him in the shadow of the trees – Everard Warrinder's daughter . . . damn him and damn her! He crumpled the handkerchief fiercely and would have thrown it away but there was nowhere to throw it. With an angry gesture he pulled open a drawer, thrust the handkerchief inside and slammed the drawer shut.

Outside in Paradise Alley he realised again how fortunate he was. Lace curtains shrouded the downstairs window, the front steps gleamed white in a row of mainly decrepit dwellings whose broken windows were hung with filthy rags or patched with brown paper. There were doors without handles or locks, and gutters running with stinking water. Daniel had been accustomed to the slums of the Midlands but had not expected to find them in London and it filled him with a helpless rage that an uncaring government allowed such places to exist.

Ma Taylor had given him a cup of tea and a plate of porridge from an iron pot that had simmered over the kitchen stove all night through. It was tasteless but hot and sustaining so he ate it thankfully and then went in search of Mr Brown's grocery store.

He found it easily. Once a small shop on the corner of the road, it had now doubled in size and seemed to stock every possible household article, from tin baths to all kinds of foodstuffs, down to slabs of toffee still made by Mrs Brown and her daughter over the kitchen fire, and sold at a half-penny a bag. One part of the shop was stocked with a range

31

of rather more expensive goods, and there he found Elspeth carefully entering items in a large ledger.

'Pa's out in the yard helpin' with the unpackin',' she said, giving Daniel a shy smile and since it seemed he was going to have to work with her, he smiled back. It lit up the rather serious face.

'I'll go through then,' he said.

She stared after him thinking how much better looking he was than the previous schoolmaster, whose pushing manners she had repulsed furiously. She was a plump girl with mouse-brown ringlets which she religiously tied up in curl papers every night. Her hand flew to the rash of spots on her chin and she surreptitiously pushed aside the piece of chocolate she had helped herself to from the shop that morning.

'Can't get school started in the summer,' said Mr Brown as Daniel gave him a hand with the sacks of flour and oatmeal and other dry commodities. 'They're off to Covent Garden some of 'em, picking up the bruised fruit and vegetables and peddling them down here. The stall holders don't like it and neither do I come to that, but you can't stop the little devils. Some families push across the river into Kent, potato lifting or strawberry picking. It's starvation money, but the kids like it if the sun shines, which it don't more often than not.' Mr Brown was apt to take a gloomy view of life.

The schoolhouse was an ugly building in a leprous yellow brick. The Methodists, who firmly believed that cleanliness was next to godliness, were having it whitewashed and scrubbed out with carbolic, a job with which Daniel had offered to lend a hand.

He found two teenage boys already at work, one with bucket of whitewash and the other with mop and pail of strong-smelling disinfectant. They eyed him warily when he introduced himself and in the space of five minutes had contrived to knock the pail over his feet and splash him with a great daub of whitewash. They both got a light box on the ear for their pains and honour being satisfied, Daniel told them genially that if they finished scrubbing the floor, they could cut off and he'd finish the whitewashing himself. It made him wonder how he was going to control the unruly youngsters he had already seen in the streets, but during the past two years the factory owner had been forced by law to provide an hour's schooling each day for all children under twelve and Dan, who had occasionally substituted for the man in charge, had discovered, to his own surprise, a certain capacity for enforcing discipline.

The money he had won at the fair would stand him in good stead, Daniel thought, till the school reopened, and he would have a few weeks in which to find his feet in this bewildering city which seemed to stretch out in a jungle of mean streets, without a tree or a blade of grass to be seen anywhere. He would also have time to find his sister. While Daniel slapped on the whitewash his mind went back to that appalling day when his mother lay dying, when he had crouched beside her bed in the bleak infirmary and listened to her whispered voice.

'Take care of Katie, Dan, she has no one in all the world but you . . . and there's something else, something I've told no one but now is the time . . .' she went on, her voice so low he could scarcely catch the words, words he was almost afraid to believe, revealing a secret that horrified his eleven-year-old mind, burning a name – Everard Warrinder – into his consciousness. He had kept the secret hidden away for years, only now and again fearfully acknowledging it.

It was years now since he had known he must find his sister. She was all the family he had. With Sam's help, Daniel had traced Kate from the orphanage to which she had been sent, six years old, torn from his arms and weeping fit to break your heart. From there, aged twelve, she had been sent into service as housemaid and the orphanage thankfully washed its hands of her. With infinite trouble they had traced the family to which she had been sent and received a curt and indignant reply. The wretched girl, Katie Hunter, had taken it into her head to run away after every care and kindness had been lavished on her. Traced to a company of common players, she had stubbornly refused to leave them and before an order could be obtained to have her forcibly removed, the whole wretched crew had decamped during the night, taking the wicked, ungrateful girl with them.

'And that's the end of it, Dan boy,' Sam said looking at him sadly, 'you'll never trace her now and I'm right sorry. Them pomping folk wander all over the country, they could be anywhere, and the devil knows what could happen to her in such company.'

To Sam and Prue theatres were anathema and actors on their way to damnation.

But Dan refused to give up. He tramped to fairs and shows, to inn yards and barns where these 'pomping' folk set up their booths, asking questions, but one and all shook their heads regretfully until just a few months before he made the final decision to pack his bag and chance his luck in London. News had drifted in of a company of players at a small town some few miles away.

'It's a wild goose chase,' said Sam warningly. 'A chance in a million and it's a good ten miles across the moor.'

'I have to try. I'll go on Saturday, as soon as work stops after midday.'

Daniel was possessed with a queer certainty that this very day he might meet his sister, his own flesh and blood, and the thought of it kept him going on the long tramp, stopping only once to take a drink from a farm pump and eat the packet of bread and cheese Prue had thrust into his pocket.

The play was half way through by the time he reached the large barn with the painted placard outside and squeezed himself on to one of the benches at the back. It was a great cavernous place with a platform stage at one end, a makeshift curtain and smoky lamps set up all around it. Daniel knew nothing of plays or theatres and his reading had never run to poetry or fiction. Most of the acting was crude, the costumes brightly coloured but tawdry. It took some time before Daniel could make head or tail of it. It seemed to be a violent drama about a black man married to a white girl and wildly jealous because he suspected her of sleeping with his own lieutenant. Most of the time Daniel was, frankly, bewildered, but now and again the grandeur of the lines got through to him. The leading actor, though the black paint on his face and hands occasionally rubbed off on the white gown of his wife, achieved a kind of dignity and power. As for that bounder who was leading him on – Daniel had met men like that in the factory, cocky devils, always out to make mischief simply for their own amusement, anyone could see what he was after, the dirty tyke.

The audience was noisy, chatting and laughing, tucking into pies and cakes, cracking nuts and munching apples, but gradually, to his own surprise, Daniel was swept into a kind of spell and when it came to the last, when the black hands hovered over the white throat, when he heard the lines:

> 'Oh perjur'd woman! Thou dost stone my heart
> And mak'st me call what I intend to do
> A murder, which I thought a sacrifice . . .'

He found himself standing up and shouting out 'Stop, you damned fool! Can't you see she's innocent!' and then he sat down again with a bump, feeling a fool, but still gripped by the tragedy of it as it swept on to the bitter end, the villain unmasked, Othello falling on his own sword before the flimsy curtain was pulled across.

The audience clapped, hooted and shouted boisterous greetings to the line of smiling, bowing actors and then pushed their noisy way out into the evening, but Dan sat on, still in a dream, still wondering what his little sister could possibly be doing in a company such as this.

After a few moments Daniel stood up, walked down to the stage, ducked through the curtain and found himself in the midst of a sort of ordered chaos. The company was moving on that night and everyone knew exactly what they should be doing. No one took any notice of him except to push him aside if he got in their way, until at last Daniel caught one of them by the arm and asked if he could speak to the manager.

'The manager? You must mean Roddy – Roderick Crowne, that is. He'll be in there,' and the man pointed to where a torn red curtain hung over a little alcove at the side of the stage.

Rather hesitantly Daniel pulled the curtain aside and walked into his first theatre dressing-room, no bigger than a cupboard but boasting a spotted mirror with a small table loaded with all kinds of pots of colour and powder, together with a large tankard of ale. Conditioned by his upbringing to believe all actors creatures of the devil on their way to hell fire, Daniel found himself staring curiously at a tall grey-haired, rather handsome man, who had already pulled off his wig and wiped the black from his face and hands but still wore the multi-coloured robes.

'Well, young man,' the manager boomed in his deep musical voice, 'what can I do for you? As you can see we are moving on, travel by night as a rule when the roads are clear, but I daresay I can spare you a minute or two.'

A little overawed by his grand manner, rather like a king granting audience to a commoner, Dan stammered out his story and was stopped in mid flow by a majestically lifted hand.

'Katie Hunter,' the man repeated, 'little Katie Hunter, and now she is your sister! How strange and unfathomable are the powers that rule our lives! For more than three years she was with us. We picked her up one winter's night some ten miles south of Bradford, and a wretched time we'd had of it, a miserable audience, no soul, no ear for the finest poetry in the world! I tell you sometimes it makes me wonder what I am doing spending the best years of my life throwing pearls before swine! But you don't want to hear about that. The child was starving and near dead with the cold and my wife, whose heart is so tender she'd not abandon a hungry kitten, insisted on taking her with us in the cart. When she recovered she told us she was running away from some brutal household where she had been subjected to the cruellest treatment and indeed there were bruises on her face and lacerations on her back that would have moved the hardest heart to pity. And she had talent, my dear sir, a very real talent. Before we knew where we were she was imitating some of our actors and she had a singing voice, sweet as a little bird, quite untaught, but an ear for a melody that was quite remarkable . . .'

'But what happened to her?' Dan asked desperately, thinking that this flow could go on for ever if he didn't stop it. 'Is she with you now?'

'Alas, no. How often I've regretted that we let her go. It was over a year ago and we were playing in Southwark – that's in London, you know, where the Globe Theatre stood and where Burbage of immortal memory first brought Shakespeare's heroes to life . . .' To Dan's despair Mr Crowne seemed to be going off into a dream again, then he suddenly pulled himself out of it. 'Ah, my dear boy, those were the days! But you mustn't let me run on. You want to know the fate of your sister. Well, one night we were playing *Romeo and Juliet*, a special version of my own and she was a sweetly pretty Juliet. I think I may say that, since it was I who taught her all she knew of the art of acting; and a man came round from the audience in raptures saying he could put her in a play up in the West End of London. She was dazzled of course. She saw fame and fortune beckoning and what could we do but let her go. She wept when we parted, promising to write but, alas, when you are constantly on the move, it isn't easy to keep in touch.'

'You've no idea where she is now?'

'No, but you might perhaps find out in London at the Princess Theatre. She was to act in the company of Charles Kean, not a patch on his great father of course. I tell you, boy, that when Edmund Kean played Richard III, the hairs rose up on the back of your neck. But all the same, Charles is a very worthy company manager. She could have done worse.'

It was some time before Daniel could get away, but he thought about it all the long way home, greatly heartened by what he had heard and full of hope, though Sam did his best to make him realise that a year was a long time in so uncertain a profession, and he would be wise to fear the worst.

Tomorrow, Daniel thought as he finished the whitewashing, put away the bucket and brush and locked up, he would find his way to the Princess Theatre. He took the key to Mr Brown, refused the offer of supper and went back to the attic room that was already becoming home. There were plenty of cheap food shops within easy reach. He bought a saveloy with pota- toes for twopence and Ma Taylor was always willing to give him a cup of tea from the pot that simmered on the hob most of the day. He settled down with his supper and buried himself in Tom Paine's *Rights of Man*, a tattered copy he'd picked up for a penny on a second-hand stall. It was old-fashioned, but still full of food for thought, but he couldn't concentrate as easily as he usually did. Now and again a tremor of apprehen- sion ran through him. What would his sister be like? Would he know her after all these years? Would she have made a life for herself and resent his intrusion into it?

Daniel tried to put these thoughts out of his mind when he set out the next morning in his best checked shirt and red neckerchief and prepared to tramp from Whitechapel through the business part of the city and into the more fashionable streets where he could ask for the whereabouts of the Princess Theatre. It was a long walk, but an interesting one, and he marvelled at the contrast between stately man- sions, handsome churches and filthy back alleys lying side by side. The crowded streets, alive with elegant carriages, costers' carts, huge drays loaded with barrels of beer, hansom cabs and a variety of sporting equipages, all jostling, pushing, and it seemed to him shouting at one another, together with an infinite variety of street pedlars calling attention to their wares, were endlessly fascinating and it was only after several wrong turnings that Daniel arrived at his destination at last and found himself staring at a theatre where tattered bills blew in the breeze, announcing not a play but a variety show whose delights apparently included horses, camels and a troupe of dancing dogs.

A supercilious manager told him that Charles Kean's com- pany was on tour for the summer and he had no idea when they would be returning. It was a severe blow after all his hopes and Daniel was walking slowly away, wondering what to do next, when someone plucked at his sleeve. The stage doorkeeper was an old man with a brown wizened face like an old monkey.

'Wot was you after, Mister, eh?' he whispered. 'Did I 'ear you mention Katie Hunter? She was 'ere just a few months gone, pretty little thing, always 'ad a friendly word for old Arthur. Not like some. Run you orf your feet some of them actors would, given 'alf a chance. She wouldn't go on tour, told me as how she'd been asked to sing at one of them pubs, down east it were – what were it called now? The Cock and Pheasant, that's it, down near the Mile End Road. "It'll keep me goin' till Mr Kean comes back for the winter," she told me. Full of grand ideas, she were, goin' to be a great actress one of these days. Mind you, I've 'eard that tale before, but she 'ad something and I weren't the only one to notice. If you arst me, some of them other young women weren't sorry to see her go.'

Daniel followed the old man's directions and tracked the pub down at last – George's Supper Rooms attached to the Cock and Pheasant – but the landlord was not particularly forthcoming. He looked Daniel up and down a shade contemptuously.

'Her brother, you say. Well, it's not the first time I've been told that. Our Katie keeps herself to herself, she don't have no followers if you know what I mean and she never mentioned no brother to me. You come back tonight and see her perform, then it's up to her, en't it?'

But that he couldn't do. He'd never been inside such a place. To meet her for the first time among a noisy audience would be unbearable.

He said rather desperately, 'If you could just tell her where I am living. I have a lodging in Paradise Alley, number fifteen, perhaps she could come there.'

'That's Ma Taylor's place, isn't it? One of them Methodys, she is.' The landlord grinned. 'No hanky-panky there, she'd not have it. I'll tell her, young man, that her brother Dan'l has come to town and then it's up to her, en't it, to decide whether she wants to know you.'

It was the best he could do, but after so many setbacks he came away with a feeling of failure and spent a miserable night wondering if she'd turn up, and if she didn't, what he could do about it. He wasn't going to give up now, he thought grimly, if she hated the sight of him, she must still acknowledge him.

Daniel was already up and dressed the next morning when Ma Taylor shouted to him from the bottom of the stairs.

'There's a young woman here askin' for you, Dan, says as how she's your sister.'

Daniel felt an overwhelming relief mingled with a kind of shyness. 'Ask her to come up, will you?'

He waited tensely, heard her come running up the wooden stairs, then the knock on the door. When she came into the room, he felt a sudden qualm of dismay, of disbelief, certain that there must have been a mistake. This slim girl with her dark, reddish hair, her flamboyant dress, her head held high, a wary look in the large eyes under their thick lashes, could not be the baby sister who had been snatched weeping from his arms.

'Sister?' he murmured tentatively. 'Little Katie?'

'Big brother Dan,' she said with a certain bravado, looking up at his six feet. And quite suddenly, there – in the slightly husky voice, the hint of laughter, the uplifted chin defying the world and all it could do to hurt and punish – he was seeing his mother, his beautiful mother, before grief and the struggle to live had worn her down.

Then they were clutching at one another, both talking at once.

'How did you find me?' Kate asked and Daniel tumbled into explanations and she laughed. 'Dear old Roddy, he saved my life. He and his wife, they were a marvellous couple. After months and months of hell, I thought I was in heaven.'

They seemed to talk for hours but he didn't tell her

everything. Kate had been born after their father's cruel death. It couldn't mean quite the same to her as it did to him.

In the next few days they saw one another constantly. There was so much time to make up, all those long years apart, but though they had come together at last so miraculously, Kate was still a stranger to Daniel, a lovely and exciting stranger about whom he seemed to find out something new every day. He did not at once go to George's Supper Rooms to hear her sing, though he hardly knew why. He knew so little about such places and what he did know, he disliked. He was afraid of being disappointed and if he was, then how could he face her, how could he bear to show her his disapproval when she had been forced to fight so hard to raise herself out of poverty and wretchedness? He wanted to care for her, cherish her, but knew he must tread carefully. She was proud of her independence, a little on the defensive even with him.

It was over a fortnight before Kate persuaded Daniel to go and listen to her. It was one Sunday afternoon, when she had taken him to a favourite place of hers, half-way across London through Marylebone fields where cricket was played, and out on to Hampstead Heath where there were trees and wild flowers, where squirrels raced and rabbits burrowed and they could look across the heath to London lying in a haze of summer heat.

She walked beside him, swinging her bonnet in her hand, her hair blown by the breeze. She was singing softly to herself, her voice low and sweet, and he listened enchanted in spite of himself.

> 'What is love? 'Tis not hereafter:
> Present mirth hath present laughter:
> What's to come is still unsure:
> In delay there lies no plenty
> Then come kiss me, sweet and twenty
> Youth's a stuff will not endure . . .'

'What is that?' he asked.

'It's one of Shakespeare's songs. Roddy made me learn it by heart. You know, Dan, till I joined the players, I didn't know anything. The orphanage just about taught me to read and write and add two and two, but I never saw a book. Roddy Crowne carried a crate of them around with him – poetry, plays, history. He made me read them and learn some of the poetry by heart. He used to say that at the worst moments of your life, the words would come back to comfort you. Do you think he was right?'

'How should I know? I never bothered with poetry and such.'

'Then you should.' She stopped, looking up at him. 'When are you coming to hear me sing? You only know the half of me, the private half. There is another side. Are you afraid, Dan?'

'Of course I'm not.'

'Then come.'

'All right, I will.'

'I'll keep you up to that.'

Then she took his arm and they walked on happily together and he felt unaccountably content, not yet realising how liberating an effect she had on him, widening his outlook, blowing away the restrictions of the past.

Kate did not let him forget and Daniel came back to his lodging early one evening in the following week to find her waiting for him, sitting cross-legged on his bed with his few books spread out around her.

She looked up, grinning at him. 'I've been trying to make head or tail of this lot but they're all too clever for me. No poetry, no romance, not a bit of spice among them.'

'Life's hardly a romance, is it?'

'It could be. You know what's wrong with you, Dan, you're too serious. Comes of living so many years with those Methodists of yours.'

'They're good people, Kate.'

'Oh Lord, I grant you that, but there's such a thing as being too good. If you can't have a laugh sometimes, if you can't have a bit of fun, if life's not an adventure, then you might as well be in your grave already. Living with the actors taught me that. It was grim sometimes, a real rough and tumble, especially when the rain came down, there was no shelter, the audience booed and no money came in for food, but some how or other we could always manage to laugh, to see the funny side and it does help, you know.'

She slid off the bed and picked up her bonnet, bending to look in the tiny mirror on top of the chest.

'I don't think Ma Taylor believes I'm your sister. She climbed up from the basement as I came in and gave me a very funny look. She thinks I'm your floozie.'

'If she did, she'd throw me out. She's very strict on morals is Ma Taylor.'

Kate laughed and put her arm through his. 'Then we must take care we don't shock her.'

They went down the stairs together and were met at the foot by Ma Taylor herself, her skimpy hair skewered into a knot on top of her head and her arms folded over her flat bosom.

'And where are you two off to, may I ask?'

'Daniel's coming to hear me sing,' said Kate demurely.

'Decent songs, I hope, nothin' nasty.'

'Oh no, it's very respectable. You must come with him some time.'

'That'll be the day! Mind you,' she went on unexpectedly, 'Mr Taylor now, he were right fond of a bit of singin'. Had a voice for it himself, too.'

'Was he your husband?'

'Aye, been dead and gone these twenty years. Fell down a manhole, he did.'

'Fell down a . . .?' Kate choked, turning a giggle into a cough.

'That's right and it en't nothin' to laugh about neither,' went on Ma Taylor severely. 'On his way home late one night, winter it were and dark as pitch. He were a coalman, see, and he were carrying a sack over his shoulder. It were one of his perks, they were allowed to pick up what fell from the sacks and the cover had been left off the sewer.'

'Was he hurt?'

'Broke his back,' she went on matter-of-factly. 'Oh he didn't die right away, lingered for three months he did and in such pain for the most part that I couldn't be sorry to see him go.'

'How terrible for you.'

'Well, that's life, en't it? All fun and games one minute, then something comes out of the blue and knocks you silly. Off with you then, have a good time and don't you be late home,' she added threateningly to Daniel.

'I won't.'

Down the street, the corner turned, and safely out of sight, they exploded into laughter.

'If you ask me, she's got a soft spot for you,' remarked Kate taking Daniel's arm. 'You'd better watch out.'

They walked on and she was silent for a moment and then gave him a quick look.

'I heard something yesterday about that man you told me about, that Everard Warrinder. His daughter is to be married.'

'Married!' It startled him. Could it be true – that girl he had seen at the inn who had rescued him from her grandfather's keeper? Could it be she? 'What was her name? Do you know?'

'No.' She was surprised. 'No, why should I? Has he two daughters? I thought we might go up to town and take a look.'

'No,' Daniel said quickly. 'No, it has nothing to do with us.'

'Yes, it has in a way. I'd like to see what he looks like for one thing and her too. It will be high society, lots of fine clothes. Oh come on, Dan, don't be a spoil-sport. We could go and spit in his eye.'

Daniel wished he could take it as lightly as Kate did, but then she didn't know the whole story, not yet.

'All right,' he said reluctantly. 'We'll go if we must.'

'That's more like my Dan.'

Of course she wanted to see the man whose skilful prosecution had brought their father to his hanging, but she had never known John Hunter, she had not sat beside her dying mother and heard those last few agonised words, and she did not have her brother's burning belief that such parasites as Warrinder should be swept away for ever if there was any justice in this country. Kate took life more easily, with a sturdy determination to better herself, to prove she was as good as they were or even better, and to show society that she was fighting her way to the top and meant to stay there.

The supper rooms where Kate performed had been built on the site of an old skittle alley at the back of the Cock and Pheasant. There was a platform at one end and rows of benches for the audience. Daniel paid his sixpence. Kate gave him a quick kiss and saw him in, before disappearing round the back somewhere. Daniel found himself sitting in a crowded house of respectable workmen and shopkeepers with their families. The rules were strict: no children under five, no drinks served in the supper rooms, though they could be obtained in the public bar in the interval, but nothing prevented most of the audience opening bags and tucking into pies, cakes, fruit and handfuls of nuts.

To Daniel it was a new experience and he was not sure he altogether liked it. Kate was already a favourite, there was no doubt about that. They applauded loudly when she came out in a dress he had not seen before, with a neck cut low to show off her pretty shoulders and a spreading skirt over a wide crinoline. She sang a couple of ballads about lovelorn maidens in a sweet, slightly husky voice, that had great appeal and caused some of the women to dab at their eyes in sympathy.

The applause and shouts of encore brought her back and she chose the song he had heard that day on Hampstead Heath, giving it full power of bittersweet melancholy. The audience sat silent, hushed into rapture, and when she came to the end with her arms outstretched to them, they gave her the favour of a moment's pause before they broke into applause.

Then the mood changed. Kate was followed by a man with a deep bass voice who bellowed out martial airs with great aplomb and after him came a couple of comedians whose cross-talk, delivered in a broad cockney with local allusions, had the audience doubled up with laughter, but left Daniel not understanding a word. There was a sketch with a great deal of knockabout humour and a butter-fingered, gormless individual who was always tripping over ladders, falling over pails of water and being slapped in the face with custard pies, to the extreme enjoyment of everyone.

During the short interval most of the men repaired to the saloon bar for liquid refreshment. It was very hot in the hall so Dan took a turn outside in the cool night air and was on his way back when he saw a hansom cab pull up. A man alighted and came towards the hall, his dress and manner so at variance with his surroundings that Dan was curious. It was growing dark by now, but as the man paused to pay his entrance fee, Daniel saw his face quite clearly. He was young and strikingly good-looking, except for an ugly mouth and an arrogant air that showed he obviously expected everyone to give way before him. Daniel followed the young man in and saw him take a seat at the back before returning to his own place, wondering what could have brought such a high-flyer to an entertainment such as this. When Kate came on again Daniel turned to look at the young man. He was leaning forward, his hands between his knees, watching every move Kate made. She was dressed more flashily this time, the actress rather than the innocent young girl. She sang more popular songs, leading the audience in resounding choruses with a great deal of verve and vivacity and the people rose to it. She was so young and yet she seemed to hold them in the hollow of her hand. Where did she learn such skill, he wondered, or was it something inborn, that circumstances had brought to light?

Afterwards Daniel waited for Kate under a lamppost which shed a pale light across the pavement. The street was almost empty when he saw her come out, laughing back to someone inside, then the young man he had noticed earlier stepped out of the shadows, putting a possessive hand on Kate's arm.

She pulled herself away and as Daniel moved to join her, he heard her say angrily, 'I'm not supping with you tonight or any night. I thought I made that clear last time.'

'Oh no, you didn't, you tantalising little devil. "I'll think about it," you said, "next time perhaps," don't you remember?'

Daniel had reached Kate's side by now. 'You let her be,' he said fiercely. 'The lady is not going with you. Isn't that obvious?'

'And who the hell are you?' said the young man haughtily.

'If you must know, I'm her brother.'

'Brother eh?' He gave an unpleasant laugh. 'I've heard tales like that before.'

'It happens to be true,' said Kate quickly. 'Please move out of our way. I don't need your escort. I'm going home with my brother.'

'Oh no, you don't!'

Daniel took a step forward. He had an intense desire to knock the ugly smirk off the young man's face but Kate had moved between them.

'No, Daniel, no, let him be,' and she took him firmly by the arm and they walked down the street together leaving her would-be suitor staring after them with a look of baffled rage on his face which boded no good to either of them.

'Do you get a lot of men like that?' asked Daniel a little brusquely.

'No, thank goodness. That one has tried it on before.'

'Who is he?'

'He's Viscount Raymond Dorrien and thinks he's the cat's whiskers because his father is some Lord Muck and very, very rich.'

'You wouldn't sup with a man like that, would you?'

'Good heavens, no. What do you take me for? Anyone with half an eye can see what he's after and I'm not what he likes to think I am.'

'I wish you'd give up your room and come and live with me,' Daniel said when they paused outside the dingy house

47

where Kate had her lodging, 'then I could look after you properly. I'm sure Ma Taylor could fit you in.'

'And watch my comings and goings like a hawk! No, Daniel, no, it's better as it is. We'd only quarrel. We're too different and I value my independence. I've been looking after myself since I was twelve. I rather think I know more about the wicked world than you do,' she went on affectionately and reached up on tiptoe to kiss his cheek. 'I like to be free but I like you too, Daniel, very much, so let's leave it as it is, shall we?'

'If you're sure that's what you want,' Daniel said doubtfully, watching Kate run up the dirty stairs and turn to wave to him before she went in. All the same he was going to keep a watchful eye. He was responsible for her, wasn't he, and any girl of eighteen alone in a great city was a potential victim of men like that well-dressed bounder tonight. In Daniel's opinion Kate was a good deal too sure of herself. Whatever she liked to say, she needed protection and he was there to supply it.

The staircase was very dark and she was fumbling with her key when two arms went around her waist, holding her tight, and a familiar slurred voice with its broken accent whispered in her ear.

'I've been waiting for you, my lovely, and who was that with you? Another of your admirers? But you sent him away, didn't you, like all the others . . . you came back to your loving Karl.'

'Take your hands off me, you idiot, you're drunk!' Kate said with exasperation, trying to wriggle free, and at that moment the key turned in the lock, she was through the door in an instant and had slammed it in his face. She leaned against it, shaking a little. Perhaps she should move away, but she liked her big room with a window that looked out high above the city streets, giving her an illusion of freedom and country air and Karl was not always drunk. He was a Polish immigrant driven out of his country by some violent pogrom and blown to England in the company of others. Whitechapel was a melting pot of refugees: Jews, Poles, Russians, Germans, all contriving to scrape a living and sometimes quarrelling viciously amongst themselves. Karl Landowsky eked out a precarious existence as some kind of an artist, living from hand to mouth, but when he wasn't drunk, he was a gentle, kindly creature. In the winter when Kate had suffered a heavy cold, he had made himself responsible, bringing her food and fruit out of his own scanty earnings. It was only when despair overwhelmed him and he drank too much that he imagined himself in love with her and let his feelings carry him away.

Men, Kate thought with a rueful shrug of her shoulders, were all alike from the callow youth in that great household at Bradford who had thought the pretty, terrified housemaid fair game, to Raymond Dorrien, son of a lord, who believed it is impossible for anyone in their right senses to resist his advances. But she had learned independence and self-reliance very early and very painfully and was unwilling to give it up to anyone, not even to this new brother.

Chapter 3

Margaret was married to her Freddie in the ancient round church in the Temple. It was eminently suitable as it was there that her father had his chambers and the church was packed to the doors with leading members of the legal profession as well as fashionable society. Christine had always loved the church. Once when she was a child as a special treat she had been taken to her father's rooms to be made much of by learned gentlemen, some of them still in wigs and silk gowns. She had stolen away while her elders were occupied, and crept into the ancient church shivering a little in the shadowy darkness but enthralled by the great sculptured effigies of the crusaders – Geoffrey de Mandeville, William Marshall, Earl of Pembroke – names going back to a fabulous past and who, at any moment, might rise from their stone tombs and come marching towards her in the full panoply of shining armour, heraldic surcoats and plumed helmets.

There was a great hue and cry when she was missed, some running to the river gate in case she had slipped on the slimy steps and fallen into the water, others hurrying up to the busy Strand where a venturesome child could be so easily crushed under pounding coach wheels, until, to her mother's exasperation, she was found curled up in one of the pews listening entranced to the choir rehearsing in some inner room, the boys' voices so sweet and pure that not even Mamma's sharp slap could wipe away the wonder of it.

There was no time to think about anything like that this morning. Christine was far too occupied with supervising four small bridesmaids who were greatly inclined to trip over their long dresses, drop their baskets of flowers or wave excitedly to families and friends.

The July day had begun badly with grey skies and a drizzle of rain, but when they emerged out of the church, the sun had broken through and they were met by that brilliant dazzle that sometimes follows summer showers, so that for a moment Christine could see nothing. They were held up in the porch while Mr Beard, who had recently taken up this new art of taking likenesses with a camera and had opened up a fashionable studio on the corner of Parliament Street, was making a great fuss of setting up his elaborate tripod, adjusting the big box camera and grouping the bride and groom in the most favourable position.

In addition to the guests, a large crowd had gathered to watch. Fashionable weddings such as this were not all that frequent in the austere precincts of the Law and this was certainly a sight worth waiting for.

Margaret looked enchanting in her flounced wedding gown of white lace caught up with knots of satin ribbon and rosebuds, her hair glimmering pale gold under the gauzy veil with its crown of orange blossom, while her new husband wore the full dress uniform of the Light Brigade – scarlet overalls, tight fitting tunic and richly embroidered jacket slung from one shoulder – completely eclipsing Gareth who was acting as best man since Freddie's younger brother was with his regiment in India. Gareth looked almost sombre in black broadcloth despite the white ribbons of the wedding favour in his buttonhole. Christine had not exchanged one word with him yet, nor had anyone else for that matter. He had travelled down from Scotland by night and only arrived in time to wash, dress and make his way to the church.

In that moment of stillness when the photographer held up his hand, whipped the cover off the lens and everyone froze for the 'take', Christine surprised a most extraordinary look on her father's face – a frown, a startled jerk of the head, a look of anger, or was it outrage? Then it passed, the photograph had been taken, he turned to his wife and Christine was free to follow the direction of her father's eyes.

Standing well in front of the spectators, still in the working clothes he had worn at the fair, hatless, his brown hair blown by the breeze, stood Daniel Hunter, his arm around a young woman who had pulled off her bonnet and was swinging it by its ribbons. Her hair was swept up into a loose knot, shining reddish in the sun, and her brilliant green gown of some cheap material was worn with such style that it made Christine look down with loathing at her bridesmaid's dress in palest pink. What on earth had persuaded Margaret to choose such an insipid colour? She wondered who she was, his sister? They were not at all alike. His wife, his girl? There was something familiar in the way she leaned against his shoulder. Christine was consumed with curiosity.

Clara, her fellow bridesmaid, nudged her sharply in the ribs.

'Do you see, Christine? That young man out there! The impudence! He's actually ogling you.'

'Don't be silly. He's doing nothing of the sort,' she said crushingly. She had never liked Clara, who was her first cousin and never seemed to think of anything else but looking out for a suitably rich and attractive husband.

Thankfully at that moment everyone began to move forward. The carriages had come into the square in front of the church. Margaret and Freddie were already driving away. Christine marshalled her little charges in front of her and was rewarded with a quick warm smile from Gareth as he lifted them into the carriage. The crowd had begun to melt away now and when she looked back, the young man and the girl seemed to have disappeared.

As the carriages began to move off one after the other, Daniel took his sister's arm and urged her away. The surge of relief that had swept through him when he realized that Christine was not the bride had made him angry with himself.

'Is he the one?' Kate asked hanging back, her eyes still on Everard Warrinder as he followed his wife into the brougham.

'Yes, he's the one all right.'

'He's wonderfully handsome.'

'I suppose that's what a woman would say. Come on, girl, let's go. We've seen enough.'

'I haven't, not yet. I don't often get a chance like this. Who's that coming out of the church now?'

Harry had just emerged through the door with a group of youngsters like himself, top hat in hand, his fair hair shining in the sun.

'He's Warrinder's son,' said Daniel reluctantly.

'He's a stunner, isn't he?' said Kate admiringly.

Guests were still standing in little groups and she watched as Harry moved amongst them, a word here, a laugh there, his glance roving carelessly over those who still lingered. For a breathless second their eyes met and clung together, then the moment had gone and Dan was tugging at her arm.

'I wager that one's game for a laugh,' she said. 'I wouldn't mind getting to know him better.'

'You're not likely to have the chance.'

'Oh aren't I? What do you bet me? You'd be surprised at what I can do if I really try. D'you see whom he is with? Viscount Raymond Dorrien. That chap seems to have his fingers in every pie.'

'I've told you before. You keep away from men like that,' he said sharply.

'Oh Dan,' she murmured affectionately, linking her arm through his and laughing up at him. 'You don't know me at all yet, do you? Don't be such a sourpuss. You were taking a good eyeful yourself, you know. Which of them took *your* fancy? The dark one? She had a saucy look.'

'She had nothing of the kind.'

'There you are, you did notice,' she said triumphantly.

And she was right, though nothing would have persuaded him to admit it. For an instant he had not been able to take his eyes from Christine, the flower-like face, the pink dress like the heart of a rose.

'Oh do come on,' he said abruptly. 'You're talking rubbish.'

*

The long exhausting day wore on. Weddings were occasions when the most unlikely people were gathered together, thought Christine, looking around her at a quiet moment when they sat down at table and everyone was comfortably eating. Her mother's brother, the Earl of Glenmuir, who hardly ever left Scotland, had made the long journey to see his niece married, leaving his pregnant wife behind him. He had years ago abandoned a promising diplomatic career to devote himself to his estates and had little or no sympathy with his sister who found Glenmuir unutterably boring compared to the bright lights of London, the fashionable round and the glamour of being the wife of a handsome and distinguished barrister who possessed something of the style and charm of a famous actor. She had fallen in love with Everard at eighteen and after twenty-five years of marriage could still feel a pang of jealousy when women crowded around him as they always did. She never doubted his fidelity, she didn't dare, it would have been far too unbearable, but like many highly strung men he was subject to moods. Something had upset him today, though his manner was perfect and only those close to him would have been aware of it. She wondered if there had been a setback in his new ambition to make a name for himself in politics.

Christine was wondering about her father too. Why had he reacted so unfavourably to Daniel Hunter, who was merely a casual spectator? Was it the young man himself or was it the girl who had disturbed him? Like her mother she would never dare to ask him but all the same she would have dearly liked to know.

The lavish wedding breakfast was nearly over, the champagne drunk, the three-tiered wedding cake duly cut with the bridegroom's sword followed by her father's witty little speech and Freddie's long and very boring one. Christine thought him the dullest young man she had ever known. Pleasant and good-natured enough but there it ended. How Margaret could contemplate spending the rest of her life with him was more than she could understand. He wouldn't even be a romantic Hussar for long. In a few months he would sell his commission, return to the family seat in Hampshire and devote himself to his father's lands, to the cows, the pigs and the sheep and no doubt to producing a bevy of children. Poor Margaret! How could she possibly endure the thought of such an existence? She said something of this when she was helping her sister change into the powder blue travelling dress of corded silk. They would be spending their honeymoon in Paris and then going on to Florence. That at least she envied them but nothing else.

'Won't you be terribly bored when you come home and settle down at Ingham Park?' she said kneeling at Margaret's feet and helping her pull on the new boots in pale blue kid.

'Bored? Of course I won't be bored. I shall have far too much to do. When Freddie's Mama died just after we had become engaged, his father said sadly that what Ingham Park lacked was a woman's touch and it would be my pleasure and duty to restore it.' Her eyes shone. 'Just think, Chris, I shan't ever have to consult Mamma any longer. I'll be able to do exactly as I please about everything.'

'If Freddie doesn't object.'

'Oh he won't,' she smiled confidently. 'I know exactly how to manage Freddie.'

'Oh well, if that's all you want out of life,' said Christine getting to her feet.

'All!' Margaret looked down complacently at her pretty new boots. 'All! I think I'm very lucky. You're so funny, Chris, you always want what you can't have, peculiar things like going to college or studying medicine. Nobody else I know wants to do anything like that.'

'Anyway Papa soon put a stop to it, didn't he?'

'You'll feel quite differently about it when you fall in love,' went on Margaret rather patronisingly.

'If I ever do.'

There was silence for a few minutes while Christine busied herself with checking the last few items in Margaret's dressing case. Betsy had gone down to see to the other luggage so they were alone in the bedroom. She glanced at her sister for a moment and then said a little shyly, 'Meg, are you looking forward to tonight?'

Margaret finished putting the tiny sapphire studs in her ears before she said, 'What do you mean? What's so special about tonight?'

'Well, you know,' Christine was a little embarrassed. She and her sister had never been all that close. 'Tonight Freddie will be making love to you, won't he?'

'Oh that!' Margaret picked up the hand mirror and turned it this way and that, adjusting a curl here and there. 'Mamma told me all about that. She said I probably won't care for it at first but I will get used to it, and I might even grow to like it if I'm lucky. Anyway it's only a small part of marriage, isn't it? Freddie and I will get on famously.'

It didn't sound at all like the *grande passion* she had read about in books and poetry – Romeo and Juliet, Abelard and Heloise, Leander swimming the Hellespont to spend only an hour with his love. She shut the case and locked it before coming to where Margaret was putting on the new bonnet with the pink roses under the brim.

'Freddie is on the reserve, isn't he? Does that mean he would have to rejoin the regiment if there is a war?'

'I suppose so, but there isn't going to be any war. Why should there be? How odd you are, Christine, always worrying about things that aren't going to happen.'

'Isn't it sensible to be prepared?'

But she got no further. The door was flung open and Clara appeared excited and breathless.

'The carriage is here already, Margaret. They're all waiting for you.'

After that it was all bustle and hurry. Freddie's comrades gave him a great send-off and they drove away under showers of rose petals. At the very last moment Margaret paused to toss her bouquet among the group of young girls all crowding around her, jostling one another, excited and happy. It sailed over Christine's head and was skilfully fielded by Gareth who thoughtlessly gave it to Clara who happened to be pressed up against him.

'Oh aren't I lucky!' she exclaimed. 'I'm the one to be married within the year!' and she took Gareth's arm, laughing up at him with such a provocative look that Christine was filled with a burning wave of resentful jealousy. No one had any right to Gareth, least of all Clara, no one except herself.

Then just as quickly she hated herself for it. Gareth did not belong to anyone, he was always supremely in control of himself. It was just that she was tired and Clara always grated on her anyway. She wished the day was over and she could go away and shut herself in her room but that wasn't possible, her mother would feel neglected and her father would frown, so the next couple of hours dragged tediously by being nice to everyone especially the elderly cousins who were almost strangers, bidding them farewell, seeing them on their way and afterwards comforting tiny fractious bridesmaids until their mothers carried them off. Peace at last descended on the great house in Belgrave Square and an army of servants began to clear the debris.

'How much simpler it would be if the young couple eloped,' said Lord Warrinder jestingly. 'It would save Everard a good deal of money and all of us a great deal of exertion. I hope, Clarissa, you're not expecting me to sit down to another feast tonight.'

'Certainly not. I thought a simple little meal about eight o'clock if that will suit you.'

'Excellent, my dear, excellent. You're going to miss Margaret but not all the chicks have flown. You still have Christine,' and he patted her on the head before disappearing with her father and Uncle Francis into the library, no doubt to enjoy a cigar and a restorative glass of brandy.

Christine would have liked to slip away too but her mother stopped her as she made for the stairs.

'See to everything for me, there's a good girl,' she said wearily. 'It's been such a tiring day, my head is splitting. I'm going up to my room to lie down for an hour or two before supper.'

'Very well, Mamma.'

She ought to change out of her bridesmaid's finery but felt too tired even to climb up the stairs. Except for the servants the house seemed suddenly very quiet. She walked through the drawing room and into the spacious conservatory, fresh and cool now and filled with the scent of myrtle and plumbago and other flowering shrubs. Beyond she could see the workmen beginning to stack the gilded chairs before dismembering the giant marquee.

A scattering of doves was on the lawn pecking at crumbs and insects. They flew up in a great whirr of wings as she pushed open the double doors and then stood still for a moment, glad of the evening breeze.

'I'm growing too old for this kind of junketing,' said a voice behind her. 'Come and talk to me, Christine.'

She turned round to see Gareth's great-uncle stretched out in a long cane chair half hidden beneath the gigantic palm that almost touched the roof.

David Fraser was in his eightieth year, a tall spare man, silver-haired and still handsome, who always contrived to make the ebony stick he carried seem like a fashionable addition rather than a prop to faltering steps.

'I thought you'd gone already,' she said pulling up a footstool and sitting at his feet.

'I thought I would wait for Gareth.'

'He went off with Harry and that friend of his from Oxford, but he'll be back, I expect.' She leaned against his knee with a little sigh. 'Isn't it nice to be quiet now it's all over?'

He put out a long hand and gently stroked her hair and they were silent for a little while until he said something so unexpected that she turned her head to stare at him.

'You know, my dear, when I saw you coming up the aisle today, I realized suddenly how very like your grandmother you are.'

'You mean Mamma's mother, the Countess of Glenmuir?'

'Yes, Isabelle de Savigny that was.'

'I never really knew her,' she said regretfully. 'She died when I was only three but Mamma has a miniature of her which was painted when she was about my age. She was beautiful which I most certainly am not.'

'It's not beauty, not likeness in that sense, Christine, but something more elusive, a charm, something different that makes men look and then look again.'

'And I have that?' she asked incredulously. 'You're not making fun of me?'

'Indeed I'm not. It has missed your mother and descended to you and I am afraid it does not always lead to happiness.'

'I used to envy her so much. I still do. When we were children and spent holidays at Glenmuir, I used to beg my uncle to tell me about her. She went everywhere with Grandfather, didn't she? Embassies in Russia, France, Vienna, Spain – sometimes it was quite dangerous. It must have been wonderful to be able to do that.'

'Interesting perhaps, and it certainly had its problems, but she always came up smiling,' he murmured, leaning back and looking into a past of which Christine knew so little. 'She was a lovely creature.'

'I believe you were a little in love with her.'

'More than a little, my dear, but she was the wife of my friend.'

'I've always felt that though it was very sad, it was somehow right that they should die together.'

'Perhaps, on that fateful return journey from Cadiz when the ship turned upside down in the Bay of Biscay. Survivors said your grandfather was almost the last to leave the ship and the boat was already overcrowded. Isabelle had always loved the sea and in the end it took both of them.'

She said nothing but put her hand on his as if to give comfort for a long past sorrow. Then he stirred and smiled at her.

'Tell me, Christine, you're very fond of Gareth, aren't you?'

'Oh yes, more than fond. For as long as I can remember he's been part of my life, like Harry, like a brother.'

'That's not quite what I meant but never mind.' He got up creakily from the chair. 'I don't think I'll wait any longer. Tell Gareth when he comes in, will you?'

'Yes, of course, and I'll ask Barton to call a cab for you.'

'Thank you, my dear. I don't think my old legs will carry me as far as the Albany tonight.'

He put his arm around her shoulders and they went into the house together.

Presently, when Christine came back from seeing him off, Harry was in the hall with Ray Dorrien who had been up at Oxford with him. She had never liked him and suspected that he had been the prime mover in the high jinks that had sent them both down with a stern reprimand, so she slipped away past them and through the drawing room to make sure the servants were carrying out their duties properly otherwise her mother would be upset.

'She's a real smasher, old boy,' Ray was saying, holding forth as usual about his latest craze. 'Didn't you notice her? She was outside the church and could knock spots off any of our crowd. She sings at one of those supper rooms downtown. Why not come with me tonight when all this flimflam is over?'

'Not a chance, I'm afraid,' said Harry who had begun to suspect that Ray Dorrien was not such a high flyer as he liked to pretend. 'My old man had me on the carpet over exam results. Wanted to know why I didn't get a First like he did. I've got to toe the line for a bit, play the good little boy, if I don't want to be packed off to some continental hole for a course on European law.'

'Fathers have to be tamed, old boy, it's the only way. I've got mine eating out of my hand.'

'Lucky you! You don't tame Everard Warrinder QC so easily,' said Harry drily.

'You never know till you try,' said Ray impatiently and looked up as Gareth came down the stairs. 'What about you, Fraser? Are you game for a lark?'

'Not my style, I'm afraid.'

'Too busy carving up your wretched patients, I suppose,' he said discontentedly. 'What a couple of spoilsports you two are. Might as well be a funeral wake as a wedding. I've had enough of it. I'm off.'

'What's up with him?' asked Gareth as the young man

moved away calling irritably for Barton and collecting hat and gloves.

'He's peeved because I won't join him in a kind of pub crawl in the East End. Are you staying to sup with us, Gareth? I know Christine would like it if you do.'

'If your parents don't mind.'

'They'll be pleased. Papa approves of you. "Why can't you be more like Gareth?" is one of his stock reproaches.'

'Oh my God, that's enough to make you my enemy for life!'

'Oddly enough it doesn't,' said Harry laughing.

So Gareth stayed to eat with them, a rather subdued meal as they were all feeling the effects of the tiring day.

'Sleep here tonight, lad, if you wish,' said Everard as they rose from the table. 'I doubt if you got very much rest on the night mail last night.'

'No, I didn't, none at all, it was far too noisy.'

'You were fortunate to arrive in time.'

'I know. It was taking a chance but the fact is I had a patient so gravely ill that until I knew he could be safely left in the care of a colleague, I felt I couldn't abandon him.'

'I doubt if there are many surgeons so conscientious,' remarked Lord Warrinder drily. 'Is it wise, do you think, to take your patients' troubles quite so much to heart?'

'I wouldn't be much of a doctor if I didn't.'

That was so like her Gareth that Christine felt her heart warm to him all over again.

'I think if you don't mind, sir,' he went on, 'that I would prefer to return home. I have been away for a long time and Uncle David is sometimes lonely.'

'You do what you think best. You're here for a while, I take it, you're not making a dash back to Scotland?'

'No, I have a month's leave.'

'Then we'll hope to see something of you.'

In the hall Christine said, 'Shall I ask Barton to fetch a cab for you?'

'No, I would rather walk.' He hesitated and then said

quickly, 'Will you walk with me, Christine? Just around the square?'

There was no one in the hall, no one to raise objections about it being far too late to go walking out with a young man, even an old friend.

'I'd love to,' she said. 'I'll just fetch a wrap.'

Gareth watched the slim figure in the swaying crinoline run up the stairs and wondered bemusedly what the devil was happening to him. He was in that state of fatigue when you no longer feel tired but instead are aware of a heightened clarity of vision, when even the simplest facts seem to possess a sharpened significance and Christine was part of it.

A year ago he had left a childhood companion, still in many ways a gawky schoolgirl rushing at things with coltish enthusiasms, and in the twelve months he had been gone she had subtly changed, grown up, matured. He had known it instantly when he stood beside Freddie and saw Christine come up the aisle, no child but a young woman, dark head poised, walking with grace and elegance, possessed of some indefinable charm. He had realized with a sudden stab that he wanted her for his own, that what he had taken for granted was no longer certain and if he did not stake a claim, others would and she could be lost to him for ever.

The stunning revelation had stayed with him all that day and he didn't know quite what to do about it. There had been other girls this past year, one or two, nothing that had mattered, his work was too absorbing, but this was different and he knew Everard Warrinder would probably look a great deal higher for his daughter. He had a small income of his own and more from his uncle but no country estate, no title to inherit like Freddie. Of course he meant to rise in his profession but that was going to take time and in any case wouldn't cut much ice with a distinguished barrister like Everard Warrinder, whose eyes were fixed on a great career at the very top. All these thoughts were racing chaotically through his mind as Christine came running down the stairs holding out both her hands to him.

It was a clear night, no hint of rain, the sky full of stars. As it happened there was no question of them parting where the road turned into the highway. Instead with this rare chance of being alone together, they walked round and round the square, the words tumbling over one another, talking of all that had happened to them in the months apart, light on their faces appearing and disappearing as they passed under the flaring jets of the gas lamps.

He found himself going on and on telling her all he had done and hoped to do and she listened pressed close against him.

'It sounds so tremendously worthwhile,' she said at last, sighing. 'I can't tell you how I envy you.'

'It has its grim moments, especially when a patient dies and you feel so absolutely useless . . . but you mustn't let me go on like this. I want to hear about what you have been doing.'

'Nothing really, just the usual round and it's going to be worse now that Margaret is married. I used to be able to escape to Bramber from time to time but now Mamma will expect me to do everything with her.'

'But you enjoy that, don't you, the parties, the balls, the theatres – Lady Clarissa has so many friends.'

'Yes, sometimes, but it's not enough, Gareth, it's so empty somehow . . .'

'What is it you really want, Christine?'

'I don't know exactly,' she confessed, 'that is why I wanted so much to talk to you. You see, Papa thinks I should be completely content to go on just as Margaret did but I'm not. I read and I hear about things outside our life – about poverty and children who are homeless, who need teaching and food and care when they are sick – oh I know it must sound stupid to you but I feel that I ought to do something to help when people like us have so much and others have so little. It's not just enough to give money as Mamma says, is it? We have recently become acquainted with the Nightingales and Mamma visits them sometimes when they are in London. Their daughter Florence is determined to learn about nursing the sick. She's so brave – she fought her parents over it and went off to some place in Germany to learn more about it. I'm not clever like her but I do so admire her courage.'

He was gazing down at the troubled face and thought of the vile conditions in the Edinburgh hospital, the crowded wards, the abysmal state of the nursing, the drunkenness and worse among some of the staff, the patients who died simply because there were so few who really cared, one nurse for some forty sick men and women.

'You wouldn't like it, Christine. Nursing is terribly hard work and the conditions are fearful. It's not the life for someone like you.'

'But there must be something I could do.'

He wished he could marry her now, carry her away into his own life, but it was not possible yet and it was far too soon to speak and trap her into promises which she might not yet fully understand.

He said, 'I promise I'll try to think of something and in the meantime I have a whole month before I need to return.'

'You'll come to Bramber, won't you? We shall all be going there in August.'

'I'll have to spend some time with Uncle David but of course I'll come. Dear Bramber! It has so many happy memories.'

'It'll be like the old days.'

'Maybe,' Gareth replied, though it would never be possible to recapture what had gone.

They had paused in front of the family house. The lamp outside the handsome front door spread a faint light over the steps.

Christine was aware of a curious feeling of tension between them that had never been there before. She was possessed with an inner excitement stemming partly from what David Fraser had said to her, giving her a new feeling of power as yet unrealised but deep within her, and also that sudden spurt of resentment at Clara's calm assumption that no man, not even Gareth, could resist her.

He said reluctantly, 'You had better go in, Christine, your

mother will be wondering where you are. Will Barton have locked up?'

'Not yet and in any case I could always go in through the servants' entrance in the area.'

They were standing very close together, silent at last, exhausted and yet content, and suddenly she whispered, 'Dear Gareth,' and reached up to kiss him on the cheek.

It was too much. Though he might possibly be putting her against him for ever, he could not resist the impulse that seized him. He pulled her into his arms and kissed her on the lips, gently at first, and then with a sudden fierceness that left them breathless. When he let her go, she stared at him, alarmed and exultant at the same time, and then turned and fled up the steps. The door opened to her knock and she went in without a backward glance.

'Damnation!' he muttered, cursing himself for a clumsy fool and yet not entirely sorry as he walked away.

In her own room Christine pressed her hands against her hot cheeks feeling again the pressure of that first scorching kiss, uncertain of her own feelings, aware of something quite new, but sure of one thing, nothing between her and Gareth could ever be quite the same again.

Chapter 4

Christine remembered that August as the very last time when summer at Bramber had the untroubled serenity of childhood, when even her society-loving mother was happy to relax, when her father lost the strained look he so often wore when his cases were difficult, when she and Gareth took out the horses for early morning canters on the Downs or went for long country walks, sometimes with Harry, sometimes alone except for the dogs. There were happy laughter-filled days like their picnic at Amberley Castle when a baby jackdaw fell from the nest high up on the parapet wall into the midst of their luncheon and Christine on Gareth's instructions fed it with tiny scraps of meat, then took it home where Tom offered to build a cage and teach it to speak. It was still summer but the countryside had a golden look full of the richness of harvest. Country neighbours called and joined in their expeditions, the men taking out the guns to pot a rabbit or an occasional hare and the women gossiping, pleasantly scandalous over afternoon tea. Ray Dorrien turned up unexpectedly one morning and since he had little else to occupy him lavished his attentions on Christine, much to her alarm. She had an uneasy suspicion that her father was inclined to look favourably on him. Lord Dorrien was wealthy, sat in the House of Lords and had considerable political influence.

She complained about it to Harry but her brother only laughed.

'Ray chases after every pretty girl.'

'I'm not pretty.'

'Oh yes you are, especially in Gareth's eyes. That's what spurs Ray on. He doesn't care for rivals.'

'Don't talk rubbish. I wish you'd warn him off.'

'Not my job. Give him one of your icy brush-offs.'

'They don't work with him. I suppose you think that funny.'

'I do rather,' replied Harry, grinning.

'Don't be so infuriating.'

She went off in high indignation, determined to avoid Ray as much as she could.

One night the young people made up a party and drove over to a summer ball in the Assembly Rooms at Brighton. It had been one of the warmest days of that August and the rooms were crowded and stiflingly hot so that Christine and Gareth escaped to walk alongside the sea rippling like black satin under a very young moon.

Gareth, despite his chosen profession so concerned with the practical, the more ugly side of life, had a romantic, almost a visionary streak inherited with his name from his Welsh grandmother. He kept it deep buried and did not often indulge it but that night, walking with Christine close beside him, he was keenly aware of the transitory nature of time, the moments that passed so quickly and would never come again. He passionately wanted to seize them, hold them in his grasp and knew that they could vanish almost before he realized them.

They had walked quite a long way trying to escape the other couples who, like them, were seeking the coolness of the night air and paused at last crunching over the shingle and looking out towards the sea. A gentle breeze lightly ruffled the surface and on the horizon a light from the guardship in the Channel came and went like a small star. In a very few days now they would both be returning to London and he must then go back to Edinburgh. He could not let the moment go without saying what was in his mind. He plunged in rather desperately.

'Christine, what would you say if I were to ask you to marry me?'

'Marry you?'

She was startled. He had been simply Gareth for so long, close as a brother, there was no intense excitement, no sweet ecstasy, no 'ringing of bells' as some romantic writer had described, but there was comfort and affection and familiar warmth. Ever since he had kissed her on the night of the wedding she had wondered whether the stir in her blood had meant that friendship was deepening into love, or whether she was just deceiving herself. In the half light she could see him looking down at her, his face strange, a look in his eyes she had never seen before that both alarmed and thrilled her.

He went on talking, almost as if he couldn't stop, not daring to give her time to say that to marry him would be too ordinary, too like slipping into worn and comfortable old shoes, a habit that could grow stale.

'Oh not at once, not immediately,' he was saying, 'it would not be possible placed as I am and I don't think your father would agree. But in a year perhaps. I have all kinds of plans and a promise of a good appointment. Uncle David will help, I know, but I couldn't bind you to anything, not a formal engagement, not yet, it wouldn't be fair, just a promise between ourselves until I can claim you openly for my wife.'

'I don't know, Gareth, I'm not sure,' she murmured and then was suddenly frightened lest she lose him. If she rejected him, others would not – Clara for instance, or one of those girls he met when he was away from her. Life without Gareth would be unthinkable.

He had captured both her hands and was drawing her against him.

'Just between ourselves, no one else, not even Harry,' he urged.

'Just between ourselves,' she promised.

He kissed her then, holding her tightly for a moment, then releasing her. She knew he was being scrupulously fair and reasonable but wished for once he would forget reason and good sense and sweep her away into some crazy world of love and ecstasy, only of course that would not be her Gareth.

'We must go back or the others will think we've fallen into the sea,' he said and took her arm.

Halfway back they ran into the rest of the party coming to look for them.

'Where the devil did you get to?' complained Harry. 'We've been hunting for you everywhere. We decided we'd had enough of that lark.'

'Too utterly boring for words,' drawled Ray Dorrien, 'all those tradesmen's daughters dressed up like little plump pigs!'

'It was so confoundedly hot we came out to look at the sea,' said Gareth easily.

'Is that all you came out for?' murmured Ray unpleasantly.

Christine shot him a look of pure dislike and Gareth said cheerfully, 'Well, there were the stars and a new moon. We turned our money over, didn't we, Christine?'

'I would have done if I had had any,' she said ruefully.

So amid laughter and jests they went to find the carriages and Ray's nasty little implication was forgotten.

'Heavens, this really is something, isn't it?' said Gareth, gazing up at the enormous three-tiered glass palace that housed the Great Exhibition in Hyde Park. 'They'll never believe me at the hospital when I tell them about it.'

It was a week later and he had decided that he simply must see this 'wonder of the world' as it was being called before he returned to Scotland, and had persuaded Christine and Harry to go with him.

'We've seen it twice already,' Harry had protested, 'and it's a five shilling day so the place will be packed to suffocation with trippers up from the country.'

'Not if we go early enough.'

And Gareth had been right. There were days at one pound, at five shillings, at half a crown and at one shilling, but when they alighted from the carriage soon after nine o'clock and entered Hyde Park, though there was a constant stream of visitors, it was not by any means overcrowded.

Glittering, gay and improbable, the great glass structure

designed by Joseph Paxton in the face of violent opposition and prophecies of disastrous collapse covered some eighteen acres of the Park and contained within its soaring arches three fully grown elm trees. They wandered happily from exhibit to exhibit, many strange and exotic from far-flung outposts of the Empire. They giggled at the sight of the Duke of Wellington, bent and beaky-nosed at eighty-two, who liked to walk in from Apsley House, and wandered around peering at some fantastic item through his eyeglass, impervious to the nudges and gawpings from the country visitors who had spotted the never forgotten hero of Waterloo.

Harry was gazing at an Eastern stand with a display of finely worked copper, of heavily damascened scimitars and curved swords in sheaths studded with gold and jewels.

'Aren't they fabulous?' he murmured, 'like some Persian fairy tale, all harems and dusky slave girls and yet they do exist. I wonder if I'll ever get as far.'

'Not as far as a harem, you won't,' said Gareth flatly. 'Those swords look quite capable of slicing your head off.'

Harry laughed and Christine moved on, her fancy caught by the silks and muslins of India, saris with gold thread and sequins, airy and insubstantial as a dream.

'Oh Dan, did you ever see anything so gorgeous? What wouldn't I give for just one of those?' said a fresh young voice and Christine looked up. Only a few feet away stood Daniel Hunter and the young woman whom she had noticed at Margaret's wedding. She saw the startled look on his face and had a feeling he would have moved quickly away if she had not smiled and held out her hand.

'So you did reach London after all, Mr Hunter. Did you have to knock down any more park keepers on your way? How long did it take you?'

'Most part of a week,' he muttered reluctantly, barely touching her fingers and drawing back.

The girl was looking from one to the other with frank curiosity and he went on, almost unwillingly, 'This is my sister Kate – Miss Christine Warrinder.'

Christine smiled. 'I met your brother when he won a most redoubtable boxing bout at the Chichester Fair,' she said pleasantly.

'Dan told me about winning the twenty guineas but he never mentioned you,' said the girl.

'It was a very brief meeting at the Three Tuns afterwards.'

Then Gareth and Harry had joined them and Christine began to make the introductions.

'Charmed,' said Harry gallantly, bending over Kate's hand. 'I think I heard something about you from a friend of mine. You are a famous singer, I understand.'

She laughed. 'A singer, yes, but not famous, very far from it. I sing at George's Supper Rooms in Whitechapel. I'm filling in time before I go back to the theatre.'

'So you're an actress too,' he said, intrigued. 'Tell me about it.'

She really is very attractive, thought Christine, she has such style and she speaks well, better than her brother, someone must have taught her very carefully. Harry looks smitten already.

Daniel was frowning. 'Gareth Fraser, did you say? Then you must be the doctor.'

'Well, yes, I am actually but how did you know that?'

'Miss Warrinder happened to mention you on the day we met,' he said a little awkwardly.

'Did she indeed? And are you boxing now or have you some other livelihood?'

Daniel reacted to the hint of condescension. 'I'm a teacher in a Methodist School.'

'I see. Isn't that very tough going?'

'Sometimes. It keeps me for the time being. I do have other plans.'

'May I ask what they are?'

Daniel stared at him and then said very deliberately, 'One day I intend to stand for Parliament.'

Gareth was startled and then amused. 'Is that all? Or do you aim to become Prime Minister one day?'

71

'You can laugh at me if you wish, Dr Fraser, but I will succeed, believe me, I will, and I shall have pleasure in forcing people like you to eat their words.'

'I don't doubt it.'

For a moment they eyed one another, Gareth, good-looking in his quiet way, conservatively dressed, very little sign of the fiery spirit that dwelled hidden inside him, and the tall rangy young man in his ill-fitting cheap suit, who could have been any kind of young workman with ridiculous ambitions except that there was something virile, powerful, determined about him.

Harry and Kate were standing very close laughing together over a huge stuffed tiger, Christine was looking at Daniel with a slight frown, and quite suddenly Gareth was aware of a *frisson* of danger, as if this young man was in some way a rival, as if this chance meeting spelled some kind of disastrous involvement for one of them. He shook himself free of it. He was being absurd. What possible link could there be between the Warrinders and this unlikely couple? He felt stifled suddenly, wanting only to get away.

'Well, we really mustn't stand here chatting,' he said pleasantly. 'We must move on. There is still a great deal to see. Are you coming, Christine?'

He nodded to the young man and then walked away with his arm through hers while Daniel watched them, angry with himself because this girl so far out of his reach had the power to stir him as no other woman had ever done and he didn't know why, because Gareth's quiet air of superiority had teased him into saying far too much. His dreams had always been strictly private.

'Kate,' he said irritably, 'Kate, we must be moving on.'

He wasn't going to waste ten of his precious shillings without taking full advantage of it.

'Coming,' she said but Harry had taken hold of her hand.

'I must go and join the others, they're waiting for me,' he said, 'but I'd like to come to hear you sing one night if I may.'

'Of course, if you wish, but won't you be going back to Oxford?'

He grimaced. 'I've finished with Oxford for the time being, scraped through Finals somehow. I'll be a pupil in Father's chambers during the winter. You'll still be at the Supper Rooms?'

'For a few more months.'

She smiled at him ravishingly and, entranced, he bent to kiss her fingers before hurrying after his sister.

'You two seemed to be getting on very well together,' said Dan when she joined him.

'Why shouldn't we? He's a nice boy. I liked him. He's not at all like that friend of his.'

'The Viscount Raymond, eh? They're birds of a feather, Kate. Don't make too much of it. They're not on our level.'

'No, they're not. They're several rungs above us but that shouldn't worry you, not with your principles. All men are equal,' she said teasingly. 'Aren't you always preaching that to me?'

'They're Warrinder's children.'

'Is that their fault?'

'Oh Kate,' he said, exasperated, 'you turn everything I say upside down.'

'No, I don't. I just see everything more clearly, that's all, not blinded by prejudice.'

'And you think I am. Is that it?'

'I think every time you look at Miss Christine Warrinder, you wish you weren't.'

And then Daniel laughed suddenly, tucking her arm through his. 'You're too clever for me. You bring me down to earth every time I go sailing up into the skies.'

'That's what sisters are for.'

'Come on, girl, let's get our money's-worth out of this lot while we still can.'

'Unusual kind of chap that and not afraid to speak his mind either,' said Gareth as they paused before a huge exhibit representing the might and power of the industrial north. 'I wonder what brought him away from his native haunts to London.'

'He told me his mother had died in some terrible mill accident,' said Christine.

'Did he? That might account for it, I suppose.' He smiled at her. 'You seem to have had quite a heart-to-heart. Was this when you met him at the Chichester Fair?'

'Yes. It was only for a few minutes while I was waiting at the inn for Harry.' She didn't know why she was so unwilling to talk about it.

'He probably hopes to make his fortune in London,' remarked Harry who had now joined them.

'Not as a teacher in a ragged school, he won't,' went on Gareth drily. 'The streets aren't exactly paved with gold nowadays.'

'His sister is a real corker, isn't she?'

'You watch out, young Harry,' said Gareth warningly. 'With looks like hers she probably has a string of admirers all thirsting for the blood of a rival.'

'I should worry.' Harry had a sublime belief in his ability to charm a bird off a tree if necessary.

Christine said nothing. She had found the meeting with Daniel Hunter oddly disturbing. He had still looked at her with a kind of suppressed anger, a resentment that she could not understand. She was on the point of asking Gareth not to mention the incident in front of her father, who had a way of probing into any casual relationship, when she was interrupted.

'Well, if it isn't Gareth Fraser!' boomed a loud cheerful voice. 'How are you, my boy, and how are you getting on? Forging ahead if I know anything about you.'

The speaker was a tall man, bursting out of his elegant frock-coat, his top hat slightly tilted, grey beard bristling.

'Dr Andrews! It can't be!' exclaimed Gareth, swinging round in surprise. 'I understood that you were in the United States.'

'So I was, so I am actually, only over here for a few weeks away from the daily round.' He beamed at Christine and

74

Harry as Gareth introduced them. 'Believe it or not this young man was one of my pupils – must be eight years ago – and one of the most promising. What are you up to now, my boy?' For some minutes they were both absorbed in medical jargon leaving Christine and Harry glancing at one another in amused resignation.

'Come and see me before I go back,' ended the doctor, clapping Gareth on the back. 'It's just possible that I might have a proposition to put to you, but now I must be on my way. I'm meeting John Dexter – remember him? He was a year or so older than you if I remember rightly. He is starting out in practice and in addition is taking on a clinic in the East End somewhere run by a couple of those devoted women of a Quaker persuasion or so I understand. Thankless work as I told him but by God it's badly needed down there, and John always had a touch of the medical missionary.'

What inspired Christine she never really knew but suddenly she found herself saying, 'Where is this clinic, Dr Andrews, and do you think they would be needing someone who would be willing to give some help?'

'And what would a pretty young thing like yourself want with a slum medical clinic, eh? It's the grimmest possible work, my dear. You wouldn't survive a day down there.'

'You don't know Christine, doctor. Once she gets her teeth into something, she's like a bulldog, she never lets go,' said Harry with a broad grin.

'Is that so? Well, it's Whitechapel way, I believe. Used to be run by an eccentric Scot who had been a naval surgeon and was largely financed, I understand, by the late Earl of Glenmuir.'

'But he was my grandfather,' exclaimed Christine, 'and the present Earl is my uncle so you see it is obviously meant to be – and it's just the kind of thing I've been looking for.'

'We-ell, in that case . . .' He was eyeing her curiously. 'I'll tell you what I'll do. I'll give Gareth what information I can worm out of John Dexter and that will give you plenty of opportunity to think it over before you make any rash decisions. Now I really must be off. Very glad to have met you and don't forget to keep in touch, Gareth. I'm over here for a month or so.'

He gave them his warm smile and hurried away.

'Marvellous man,' said Gareth. 'We all went in such deadly awe of him that it seems strange now to meet him on almost an equal footing. He's been in America for some months looking into the uses of this new drug Chloroform, which they have been widely experimenting with over there.'

'What does it do?' asked Harry lightly.

'Sends you into a sleep and when you wake up your arm or leg or whatever has been whisked away and you've not known a thing about it.'

'I say, that could be pretty marvellous on the battlefield, couldn't it? Only thing is you might wake up and find they've taken off the wrong leg.'

'That would be just your bad luck,' said Gareth heartlessly.

'Have you used it yourself?' asked Christine.

'I've seen it in use but not yet administered it myself. You'd think, wouldn't you, that a sick person would be only too pleased not to undergo the agonizing pain of an operation but it's not so. For the most part they're deadly afraid of it. They've no trust in the surgeon's knife when they can't see it at work. It's the most adventurous spirits that allow themselves to be guinea pigs.'

A little later when they were leaving the exhibition, Christine took Gareth's arm.

'Don't say anything about the East End clinic in front of Papa and Mamma, will you?' she whispered.

'Why? Do you think they won't approve?'

'I know they won't. Papa wouldn't even allow me to attend medical lectures. They'll stamp on it before it even starts but if anything does come of it, I'll get round them somehow. After all we don't know about it yet. They may have all the assistants they need down there.'

'I rather doubt that, but all the same I don't know as I much care for the idea of you working down there,' said Gareth frowning. 'You've had no experience.'

'I can learn, can't I? You had to.'

'That's different. I'm a man. It's not the same for you.'

'Don't worry, old man, she'll never stick it,' said Harry heartlessly.

'You shut up and anyway what's a man got to do with it? You have women as nurses, don't you? You can give me a long list of instructions and I'll follow them to the letter.'

'We'll see what Dr Andrews has to say about it,' said Gareth, privately deciding that he would paint such a horrific picture of what she might have to deal with that she would draw back, and not realizing how strong was Christine's determination to make something real and useful of her life.

In actual fact it was Harry who inadvertently put the cat among the pigeons. It was a family party who sat down to dinner that evening, with the addition of Gareth and his uncle. They had reached the dessert stage when the conversation turned on the general election expected to be held in the following year.

'I really don't understand, Everard, why you want to give up a very successful career at the Bar to go in for politics,' remarked David Fraser, putting aside the sweet pudding and helping himself to cheese. 'They're such an infernally dull lot, most of 'em. Not a spark of originality in any of them.'

'I'm not giving up the Bar, not entirely, but it's been an ambition of mine for some time, and since the member for the Whitechapel constituency is retiring next year and I was offered the candidacy, I jumped at it.'

'They are a deucedly radical group down there. It won't be a walk-over. You'll have a hard fight on your hands.'

'Oh I don't know. Times are changing. Chartism is dead. All those battles are over. Conditions for the working classes are improving. I shall be representing a good solid core of tradesmen and hard-working artisans. They don't want revolution any longer, fiery orators arousing the rabble and all that nonsense. They've had enough of it. They want good steady government, policies that will benefit their pockets.'

'I don't know so much. I don't think they're all like that,' said Harry out of a sheer spirit of contradiction in the face of his father's complacency. 'I should say you will have a very tough battle if the young man we met today has any say in the matter.'

'Indeed, and who was that?' asked his father amiably.

'Just a working-class chap, come down from the north I should say, and very full of himself and what he intends to become, Member of Parliament no less, with his sights fixed on Prime Minister ultimately.'

'What impudence!' said Clarissa indignantly. 'Talking to you like that! That's the worst of going to the exhibition on one of the public days. You never know what vulgar types you will meet. I hope you put him in his place, Gareth.'

'There was really no need, Lady Clarissa. It was just a casual encounter.'

'And what was this opinionated young man's name?' enquired Everard, casually beckoning the butler to refill his wineglass. 'Did he tell you?'

'Daniel Hunter apparently,' replied Harry, 'and he has a deucedly pretty sister.'

'What!' Momentarily Everard's hand shook and the wine spilled across the table. 'Sorry, my dear,' he muttered to his wife. 'Clumsy of me.'

There it was again, thought Christine. What was the link between Daniel and her father that disturbed him so greatly?

But now he had recovered himself. The butler had hurried forward, spread a clean napkin over the stain and refilled his wineglass.

'Silly of me. Something suddenly jolted my memory and then it was gone again. I must have been mistaken.'

'Well, if you're pelted with rotten eggs when you make your inaugural speech,' went on Harry irrepressibly, 'you can bet your bottom dollar that our friend Hunter will be in the forefront hurling them at you.'

'Don't talk like that to your father,' said his mother sharply. 'As if anyone would dream of treating him in such a shameful way. Come, Christine,' she went on, getting to her feet, 'it's time to leave the gentlemen to their wine and the discussion of questions which don't concern us.'

She swept from the room but in the drawing room found herself facing a rebellious daughter who made it quite clear that she agreed with her brother.

'But it does concern us, Mamma. I think we should know what Father is doing and why. If he is going to represent those poor people who live down in the East End, then he should go down there, mix with them, talk with them, listen to their problems. It's no use just making promises you know you can't keep.'

'Really Christine, don't talk so foolishly about things which you don't understand. Of course your father will go down there once or twice with his supporters but as for living down there, why the idea is preposterous. Members of Parliament do not need to do such things.'

'Then all I can say is that they should,' Christine said obstinately, but she realized it was no use arguing with her mother, who had never shown any real interest in matters outside her family and her social round. When the men joined them and the coffee tray was brought in she found herself regarding her father and mother with new eyes. Maybe it was because she had grown up at last with all childish things left behind her, maybe it was the new relationship developing between her and Gareth, but she seemed to be looking at them with heightened perception. Up to now she had accepted them without question as children do, god-like parents with whom you battled at your peril. Now she found herself wondering about them as people in their own right. Were they still bound together by love or was it merely habit and a sense of duty? Had her father ever strayed into another woman's bed, had her mother ever been tortured by jealousy? He was still so handsome, so attractive, He could still bowl women over in court and outside it. Once she had stolen into the criminal court and, safely hidden amongst the public, had admired his skill and brilliance in cross-examination. She was roused from her thoughts by Harry calling her over to join them in some new uproarious card game, which was watched with amusement by David Fraser till he dozed off in his armchair.

She did not hear her mother say quietly, 'I'm beginning to wonder, Everard, if Christine is seeing rather too much of Gareth. I am fond of the boy of course and it was all right when they were children but mightn't it spoil her chances of making a really good marriage?'

Everard Warrinder roused himself with an effort, his thoughts obviously very far away. 'I'm afraid we may have a problem with Christine. She is developing a will of her own.'

'I'm only too well aware of that,' said his wife drily. 'Ray Dorrien has been paying her a good deal of attention lately. Have you noticed?'

'Yes, and I gather his father would approve – but don't bully the child about it, Clarissa. Gareth is away a good deal. There is plenty of time.'

'She will be twenty-one next year.'

'I know, I know,' he said impatiently.

Clarissa, who was sensitive to her husband's difficult moods, said tentatively, 'What upset you this evening? Did it have something to do with Harry's mention of that pushing young man they met at the exhibition?'

'Oh that. No, no, that was nothing. It was just that the name reminded me of a very unpleasant case that came up some years ago.'

'You never told me of it.'

'Didn't I? It was that year you were so sick and the doctor advised a long stay at the sea.'

It had been three years after the twins were born when Clarissa had become pregnant again, but this time it had all gone wrong. The baby had only lived a few hours and she herself had very nearly died. It had been twelve months before she fully recovered, a year of great anxiety and distress for them both.

'I remember now,' she said thoughtfully, 'you looked quite ill when you came to join me and the children at Weymouth.'

'Yes, well, it's long over and forgotten,' he said putting his hand on hers. 'You were very patient with me I remember. These things happen in a profession like mine.'

'You should take more care of yourself. You take other people's troubles too much to heart.'

'Maybe, but it's the only way I know how to live and work. But now we shall be looking ahead to a new life and new interests.' He smiled at her with all the charm that still touched her heart. 'I think you're going to enjoy yourself planning political dinners and entertainments.'

Chapter 5

The medical centre was housed in what had been a warehouse, a gaunt ugly building, the walls roughly whitewashed, the stone floor scrubbed with strong carbolic. At one time it had been used to store bales of cheap cotton cloth which were sold to the sweat shops that abounded in Whitechapel, places where as many as thirty women stitched in underground cellars, fourteen hours a day, for a pittance, biting cold in winter and fetid with an enervating heat in the summer months. A stale smell still hung about the place, together with the reek of dirt, sickness and urine which battled with the disinfectant.

Christine's heart sank when she first saw it after a depressing drive through the worst slums she had ever seen: dark ugly rows of houses, the walls stained with leprous patches like some disgusting fungi, smashed windows with ragged curtains pinned across, children playing in the filthy gutters and hurling stones at the horses to the fury of her coachman, women standing in doorways, hands on hips, sullen and hostile. That first impression was to change. She was to learn that there were pockets where little houses were kept pathetically neat and clean, where a flower struggled to bloom, but also others that were far worse, broken-down hovels where it did not seem possible that even an animal could survive but which were home to countless vagrants and gangs of lost and abandoned children.

It had been a long hard battle with her parents and though she had come with the hearty recommendation of Dr Andrews, she was received with a good deal of caution. Martha and Deborah Hutton, the sisters who ran the settlement from the adjoining house, dispensing cast-off clothing, food, advice and very rarely a little money, looked at her askance. They had had their fill of fashionable young ladies who thought it added to their prestige to play the Lady Bountiful but who fastidiously drew their skirts away from the grimy fingers of children and could never be expected to soil their dainty white hands with any of the many distasteful tasks that arose daily. Dr John Dexter was only thirty but looked older, a stocky young man who combined an absolute devotion to the work in hand with an abrupt uncompromising manner. He was scathingly contemptuous of Christine's blundering attempts to help him for an hour or two that very first afternoon when his usual assistant was called away to the infirmary, and it took all her strength of will to carry on and not burst into indignant tears. She was greatly tempted to give up the whole venture except that she knew she would despise herself for ever if she did.

When she returned home that evening utterly exhausted, she faced up to it squarely and if anything was guaranteed to strengthen her resolve to go on with it against all the odds, it was her father's dry comment when she sat down to dinner with him and her mother.

'Well, Christine, how did your charity act go on? Weary of it already, I gather, from your looks.'

'On the contrary, Papa,' she said quickly, her resolve immediately hardening, 'I found it wonderfully interesting. The only thing is that one day a week is not really enough. They are so desperately in need of more help.'

'One day a week is more than enough,' put in her mother. 'It's one thing to give clothes and food to these poor creatures – but to go there yourself. If I'd had my way, you'd not have undertaken it at all, only your father was quite sure you would never keep it up.'

'Did you say that, Papa, did you?' He gave her a smile and a shrug. 'Well, you're quite wrong. I should hope I have more strength of will than that.'

'It's no more than some silly whim because Gareth is a doctor, I suppose, and the sooner you tire of it, the better,' went on her mother irritably. 'I don't know what Margaret is going to say about it when she comes to stay with us next month.'

'It doesn't really concern Margaret, does it?'

But Christine knew her mother too well to attempt to argue or try to explain that it fulfilled some inner need deep inside herself. She felt she had already learned a great deal. For one thing she would no longer take the carriage but travel by horse bus instead. She would provide herself with a simple dark grey dress like those worn by the two sisters, with a large holland apron and a scarf to bind around her hair. She studied assiduously the books Gareth had given her containing simple first aid instructions so that she would not be so lost when Dr Dexter asked testily for this or that, and succeeded so well that by the end of October she was able to write bravely to Gareth that Dr Dexter had actually given her a word of praise 'and that's something of a miracle from him, believe me. He's a very hard taskmaster but I don't regret it, not for a single minute.'

Sometimes, in an odd kind of way she thought she lived more fully when she was working down at the clinic than when she was visiting with Mamma, drinking tea in elegant drawing rooms, dancing at Clara's birthday ball or sitting in the box at the opera. It was on one of those evenings that, looking idly down at the auditorium in the interval, she was sure she could see Harry in the stalls and with him that striking girl who was Dan Hunter's sister. She felt a pang of alarm. Harry had been kept hard at work during the autumn in his father's chambers and was sharing rooms with one of the other fledgling barristers so that he was only rarely at home. She hurriedly drew her father's attention to something else, feeling sure that he would not approve, and made up her mind to tackle Harry about it at the first opportunity.

She had thought of Daniel Hunter more than once. He had been so intensely alive that she was curious, wondering where he lived and what he was doing in pursuit of his lofty ambitions. Then late one afternoon in November, to her great surprise he walked into the clinic.

The weather had turned very cold and dank fog was beginning to creep up from the river, eddying about the dark streets in smoky drifts. There had been so many patients that Christine had been called in to help: coughs, fevers, something called ringworm, all kinds of skin rashes that turned her sick and were the result of dirt and malnutrition. Some of the women came with horrific bruises and festering wounds that they swore were due to some foolish accident when more than likely they had been inflicted by a drunken husband or lover.

'Why do they put up with it? Why don't they run away?' she asked after they had been treating a young woman whose bruised neck and black eye suggested near murder.

'Families who live crowded together in one small room often end up tearing each other to pieces,' said Dr Dexter grimly. 'What can someone like you understand about such conditions? I heal them and they go back to it and it starts all over again mostly, because they still love the wretched man or they have children or there is nowhere else to go.' It made her feel woefully ignorant and foolish because she understood so little of such lives.

'I think perhaps we'll call it a day,' said the doctor wearily on that November afternoon, patting a small girl on the head and giving her a sweet from the bag he kept by him for all such emergencies. She trotted away, tears still running down her face but her cheek bulging with the toffee. 'If this fog keeps up we shall never get home tonight,' he went on. 'I think that's the last one.'

But he was wrong. He had rolled down his shirt sleeves and picked up his jacket when Deborah put her head around the door.

'There's another just turned up, doctor, and I fear it may be serious.'

He sighed and put down his coat as Daniel Hunter came through the door, looking around him somewhat doubtfully and leading a small boy by the hand. The child dragged back, obviously terrified. He looked about eight but as she found out later he was actually ten, pitifully thin and under-nourished, shivering with cold and fright.

'Come along, come along,' said the doctor brusquely, tired and a little impatient at the end of a long day. 'What is it this time?'

Daniel looked uncertainly from the doctor to Christine and then back again.

'The boy comes to my school. I found him in the yard when the others had gone. He is afraid to go home and I found out why. Show the doctor your hand, Dickie,' he went on gently, 'don't be afraid. He will make it better.'

The pleading eyes were too large for the white face and looked up at him imploringly, then the child held out his right hand wrapped round and round with a grubby piece of cloth.

The doctor carefully unwound the crude bandage and Christine drew a sharp breath. The small hand and wrist had been hideously burned. Inflamed and blistered, it was already suppurating and gentle though the doctor was, the child shuddered and flinched away.

'How did you come to do this, Dickie?' asked Dr Dexter quietly.

The boy looked desperately at Dan, received his nod and whispered, 'It were me step-farver. He put me hand to the fire.'

'Did he now? And why should he do that?'

' 'Cos he said I were a liar and liars should burn in hell fire.'

'And did you lie?' went on the doctor, deliberately going on talking as he held out his hand for tweezers and very slowly and carefully began to clear away some of the damaged tissue.

The child's frightened eyes watched his every movement.

'It were last night when he come home. He arst me where my muvver was and I told him I didn't know.'

Above his head Daniel said quietly, 'The boy's mother is terrified of the man she lives with when he comes home the worse for liquor and the boy knows it.'

86

It was a familiar enough situation but the cruelty that took out frustration so savagely on a small child horrified Christine. Little whimpers of pain escaped through the child's tight-shut lips from time to time but otherwise he made no sound and she felt tears prick at her eyes as she handed the doctor what he asked for, ointment, scissors, gauze, bandage.

At last it was all done and he straightened up.

'The boy is suffering from shock,' he said briefly. 'He needs care which he doesn't seem likely to get. I could ask one of the ladies here if he could stay in the centre for the night.'

'I'll look after him,' said Dan. 'He's too terrified to go home.'

'If you're sure you can do it,' said the doctor doubtfully. 'I can give you something to ease the pain. You should give it to him with a little warm milk. Is that possible?'

'I'll make sure he's cared for.'

'Very well and bring him back in a couple of days when I shall be here again so that I can watch it. The hand is in a very nasty condition.' He bent down to the child and said gently, 'You're a very brave boy, Dickie, and you won't be afraid to come back to see me again, will you?'

The boy shook his head and then suddenly turned, burying his head against Daniel's coat, shaken by a huge sob of pain and fright that he had suppressed for too long. Dan lifted him up, speaking soothingly, and the child pushed his head into Dan's neck still shaking.

'I'll have to see his mother first but I'll bring him back.'

'Good man,' said the doctor. 'Christine will give you the draught.'

She went with him to the door, handing him the small phial of laudanum. 'A few drops at a time, that's all. You must use it sparingly.'

He put it in his pocket, frowning at her. 'I never expected to see someone like you working in this place.'

'Does it surprise you so much?' She was nettled by his manner. 'I suppose because my grandfather is Lord Warrinder, you think I'm just another dressed-up society doll. Well, I'm not. I work here one day a week.'

'Why?' he asked bluntly. 'Why do you do it? Is it because of that doctor friend of yours?'

'Partly. I heard of the place through Gareth. If you must know I wanted to feel I was of some use, giving something instead of always taking.'

'I see.' He was still gazing at her as if he found it unbelievable. 'That Dr Fraser – are you going to marry him?' he asked abruptly.

She was taken aback for a moment. 'Perhaps,' she said at last. 'I think that's my affair.'

'He's your kind, isn't he? Not like that doctor in there.'

It had not occurred to her before but perhaps he was right. Perhaps Gareth was sometimes more concerned with acquiring knowledge than applying it practically. She was immediately angry with herself for her disloyalty.

She said sharply, 'I don't think you know what you are talking about.'

'Perhaps not. Anyway I mustn't stay here. I've got to get this boy home and into bed.'

He turned to go and suddenly she knew that she did not want to lose sight of him, she wanted very much to see him again. She said impulsively, 'I come here on Tuesdays. Will you come next week and tell me how Dickie is going on?'

'That doctor in there will tell you that.'

He gave her another long look as if he might have said more, then walked quickly away with the child still clinging to him, the small hands locked around his neck.

It was like a slap in the face. She wished she hadn't said it and then perversely was glad that she had.

Dr Dexter said impatiently, 'Are you coming, Christine? I have ordered a cab. I can give you a lift home.'

'Thank you. I'll be ready in a moment.'

And she was not quite sure why all the following week she was conscious of a pleasurable little feeling of anticipation at the thought of the following Tuesday at the clinic.

*

In actual fact Daniel had offered to look after the boy for the night forgetting that he had planned to go to the Working Men's Club. A notable speaker whom he particularly wanted to hear was coming down from the north but it was unthinkable to send Dickie home till he had seen his mother and found out what the circumstances were. He took the boy to his lodgings and then went out again to buy a gill of milk from the shop that sold everything, on the corner of Paradise Alley. It was watery enough, God knows, but it would have to do. He persuaded the boy to eat a little bread and butter from his own scanty store, gave him the milk with the laudanum and sat by him till he grew drowsy. Then he tucked him up warmly in his own bed and went down to look for his landlady. He had already guessed that Ma Taylor had a kind heart hidden away somewhere under that fierce exterior and he played on it, describing Dickie's plight and asking if she would look in on him once or twice during the hour or so he would be out.

'What next?' she demanded, folding her arms belligerently across her black bodice. 'Expectin' me to run up and down two flights of stairs, I suppose, and me with my poorly back! You've got an impudence, young man.'

He started to plead and she cut him short.

'Don't you try your charms on me, 'cos they won't work. I'm not sittin' up all night, mind you, I'm not losin' me beauty sleep for Jenny Colley's brat that she never ought to have had in the first place with the father goin' off somewhere and her takin' up with that great hulkin' brute that works down at the docks.'

She paused for breath and he said quickly, 'You're an angel, Ma, you really are.'

'Oh go on with you! I'm not that yet, I hope. You keep that pretty talk for that sister of yours, and where's she, I'd like to know, not been round to see you lately, has she? You keep an eye on her, Dan, she's a deal too sure of herself for this wicked world.'

He laughed and went out, quite sure he could rely on her doing as he had asked till he came back.

The fog had thickened and clung around him like a cold wet blanket but he didn't notice it, walking briskly and wrapped in a warm military greatcoat he had bought cheaply in the rag-and-bone market. He had already made contact with the Working Men's Association and had received a very guarded welcome. A new recruit who was filled with zeal and could express himself forcibly was valuable, but all the same in their opinion this Daniel Hunter had a great deal too much self confidence and was far too full of himself. Only time would tell if he had the right spirit.

Daniel had sensed their mistrust and was impatient of it but tonight might be different. He tried to think out what he could say if he had the opportunity to speak during the discussion that was sure to follow but irritatingly his thoughts kept going back to Christine. He had never expected to see her and found it disturbing. Even if she had not been Everard Warrinder's daughter, every instinct told him to put her out of his mind once and for all. She was not for him, never could be, and yet obstinately she would not go away. Something had sparked between them even as long ago as that moment at the summer fair and now maddeningly it was there again, stronger than ever.

He knew so little about girls. Living among Sam Jessop's austere community, his one aim in life being to escape that environment and get himself to London, he had neither the time nor the inclination to walk out with girls like the other boys, who liked to boast of their conquests. He had always been impatient with girls' giggles and their silly chatter, the plain fact that all most of them ever wanted was to kiss and cuddle in dark corners instead of a sensible discussion as to whether a strike was the only way to gain more pay and better working conditions, and there had never been anyone remotely like Christine. Oh hell, he thought, as he turned into the Club, isn't it time I forgot about her, the great lady condescending to show interest in the poor wretch who scrapes a living by teaching some forty ragged half starved brats in the slums? He was not at her beck and call, was he?

He'd not go next Tuesday, let her find out about Dickie from that doctor if she was interested.

He was late. The hall was already crammed and one or two men nodded to him as he squeezed on to a bench at the back. Then, after all the fuss of getting there, the meeting turned out to be a great disappointment. The speaker droned on, not about new strategy for the future, not about new proposals which needed to be put forward, but patting himself and his colleagues on the back for what they had already achieved, better rates of pay, shorter working hours, easier conditions for women and children who still slaved in factories and workshops. There was not a word about how these new rules were ignored or exploited, not a word about the infamous conditions in which so many people were forced to live, nothing about the thousands who slept rough night after night, the children who were picked up dying or dead from hunger and disease, nothing about the old woman who had starved to death in a house only a few doors away from his lodging and might never have been discovered if someone had not noticed the giant flies that clustered around the broken window.

The members of the Working Men's Association were mostly small shopkeepers, artisans, apprentices in a vast number of different trades, all good hard-working worthy people but if ever they had had fire in their belly, it had long since died down. Where was the spirit of only thirty years ago, when his father had fought long and bitterly for the right of every man to live a decent life and had died for his belief? He wanted to stand up, tell them about the horrors he had seen already in the few months he had been in London but tonight he was oppressed with a feeling of hopelessness. They would not want to listen. They did not want fiery revolutionaries who would only bring trouble. Of course poverty, sickness, suffering all still existed among the foolish, the hopeless, the ignorant, but it could be avoided if you shut your eyes to it.

Mr Brown, who was a stalwart member of the Committee, urged him to stay and share the tea and biscuits that his wife and Elspeth were already dispensing among the members but Dan excused himself, explaining about Dickie and making his escape.

As he went down the steps he was followed by another man somewhat older than himself. He had met Will Somers already, a fiery individual who was half Irish with a reputation for crazy notions which very rarely came to anything. They had a good deal in common and were both greatly impatient of the other more sedate and middle-aged members, but there was a wildness, an irresponsibility about Will that Daniel's more cautious temperament distrusted.

He paused at the foot of the steps and Will Somers caught him up and took his arm.

'Did you ever listen to such a load of empty platitudes in your life, and all of them there lapping it up like a lot of silly sheep with smug grins on their stupid faces?' Daniel grunted and Will went on. 'I've been hoping to meet up with you again ever since you stood up at that first meeting and let them have it.'

'It didn't do much good,' muttered Daniel. 'I might as well have kept my big mouth shut.'

'You made me sit up and one or two others, let me tell you. There's one that's not dead from the neck up, I said to myself, and I was right. You've still got the fire of revolution living inside you and that's what we need if we're ever going to get anywhere. There's someone I'd like you to meet. To hear him talk is like putting a flaming torch to a lot of dry tinder.'

'Who is this wonder man?' asked Daniel sceptically.

'His name is Karl Marx. He's a German actually and was thrown out of Paris for his fiery opinions.'

'I don't care for foreigners,' grunted Dan.

'They may be a funny lot, some of 'em, but they've more spunk than some of the English. Marx has a lodging in Soho and some of us go there in the evenings. Why not come with us?'

'Who goes there?'

Will looked around him and then said quietly, 'Revolutionaries, most of 'em, but they're all good chaps.'

'I thought their meetings had been forbidden.'

'So they were but it takes more than that to stop them. They went underground. Mind you, Dan, I'm not altogether with them. They have some pretty crazy ideas but I tell you one thing. They're planning a warm welcome for the new candidate who is going to be put up for the next election.'

'Who is it? Do you know?'

'They're saying it will be Everard Warrinder.'

'What!' Daniel stopped dead, staring at Will. 'Are you sure of that?'

'Pretty sure. He's a barrister apparently, one of those top lofty fellows, father a Lord, wife sister of an Earl and thinking to carve a political career for himself by slumming it down here at our expense. What about it, Dan? Will you come along with us?'

'Yes, yes, I will. Just let me know when you're going there.'

'Good man,' said Will, slapping him on the back. 'I always knew you had the right stuff in you.' He rubbed his hands gleefully. 'We'll make those stuffed shirts at the Club sit up!'

They parted a stone's throw from Daniel's lodgings and he looked after Will thoughtfully. He didn't have a regular job but his father was foreman in a big engineering works and a leading figure in the Engineers' Union, and Will lived at home picking up odd work from time to time. He was not entirely reliable and Daniel did wonder if he was right about Everard Warrinder. He'd go along with him, meet this Karl Marx and his hot-headed pals. Foreigners abounded in Whitechapel, all driven out of their countries for a variety of reasons and in Daniel's opinion not altogether to be trusted. Some of them ran the very worst of the sweatshops exploiting the only trade they knew, and most of them seethed with discontent. Cleverly manipulated they could be a very dangerous element.

When he reached home, Ma Taylor reported that Dickie was sleeping like a top.

'You'd better look out,' she said warningly, 'or you'll find that boy on your hands for good an' all. His mother's a lot too free with her favours for my liking and the boy's in her way.'

'I'll face that when I come to it,' he said cheerfully. 'Thank you for looking after him,' and he planted a kiss on her withered cheek.

'Well, I never!' she exclaimed, giving him a slap. 'Saucy young devil! I suppose I'm allowed to stop playing sick nurse and get to my bed, am I?'

He laughed and ran up the stairs. Dickie was sprawled across the bed, twitching now and again in his drugged sleep, and Dan looked down at him for a moment wondering what he had saddled himself with. He'd have to go and see the boy's mother tomorrow. He sighed and began to undress. He pushed Dickie gently to the other side of the narrow bed and got in beside him but not to sleep.

If Will was right and if Everard Warrinder was chosen as their next candidate for Parliament, then he would be among the first to show him plainly what he and a great number of other free spirits thought of him. What could he know of the poor wretches who swarmed in these crowded streets? What they wanted was one of their own kind, one who could plead their cause with passion and understanding. It had not occurred to him before but was that the reason why his daughter was working at that clinic, currying favour for her father? He worked himself into a furious anger at the very idea and was still seething with it when, against all his good resolutions to have nothing more to do with her, he went along there on the following Tuesday to outface her with it.

On that same Tuesday morning very early Margaret was sitting on her sister's bed in a pretty dressing gown watching her struggle to wrap up a large picture book in some brightly coloured paper.

'Isn't that a little premature?' she said lazily. 'It will be a very long time before the son and heir will be looking at books like that.'

'Son and heir?' Christine looked up, frowning. 'Whatever do you mean?'

'Hasn't Mamma told you? It is a bit early, I suppose. I'm pregnant.'

Christine sat back on her heels looking up at her. 'Oh Margaret, already? Are you pleased?'

'Yes, I am – very pleased.'

'Does Freddie know?'

'Not yet. He had to go on his last turn with the regiment almost as soon as we got back from Italy, but his Papa is overjoyed. Actually he was fussing over me so much,' she confessed, 'that I was glad to escape up here for a week or so on the plea of buying in baby linen.'

'Oh darling!' Christine knelt up and gave her sister a quick kiss. 'If you're happy about it, then I am. I must admit it suits you. You look prettier than ever.'

'Oh nonsense. I shall be looking all too matronly soon. It's you who's looking pretty, blooming in fact. I thought so at dinner last night. You looked radiant.'

'Don't be silly. I have always been the ugly duckling.'

'Well, she became a swan if I remember rightly from one of those boring old tales our governess used to make us read. I thought it might be Gareth only he's away – but Ray Dorrien couldn't take his eyes off you.'

'Don't mention him. Every time he comes near me, I get the shivers. Margaret, you don't think that Papa has his eye on him . . . ?'

'As a possible husband, do you mean? Papa would never force anyone on you.'

'I don't know so much,' said Christine gloomily. 'Lord Dorrien is horribly rich and Papa has his mind fixed on a future career in politics and that can be very expensive. I'm only glad that Harry doesn't see as much of him as he did.' She went back to tying up her parcel. 'This is for a little boy, one of Dr Dexter's patients. His brute of a stepfather put his hand into the fire to punish him because he told a lie. You should have seen the state it was in.'

'I hope I never have to,' said Margaret with a shudder. 'How can anyone do such a wicked thing?'

'Oh quite easily. I can't tell you some of the things I've seen already. If I did, Mamma would probably forbid me to take a step outside the house. The queer thing is I've grown quite accustomed to it. At first it turned me sick. Dr Dexter thought me a very poor creature because I had to run out and breathe clean air in case I disgraced myself by fainting, but now it only makes me angry that people can do such terrible things to one another.'

She finished tying up her parcel and stood up, smoothing her crumpled skirts.

'If you must go down and work in that frightful place, Chris, why do you have to wear such dreadfully drab clothes?'

'Well, chiefly because everyone else does and I thought I ought not to make it too obvious that I've so much more to spend on pretty clothes than they have.'

'But that's quite wrong. If you go down there wearing something attractive and colourful it will cheer them up, make them feel that one day they might have something like it.'

'Do you really think so?'

'Yes, I do, and I'm sure that I'm right.'

'Perhaps. I'll think about it. No time to change now though or I shall be late. You're staying a week or two, aren't you, so we can have lots of real talks and go out shopping together.'

'I'd enjoy that.'

At the last moment, mindful of what Margaret had said, Christine abandoned her dull brown coat and put on the short squirrel jacket her father had given her last Christmas with its matching hat worn jauntily at an angle. It was odd, she thought, jolting down to Whitechapel in the horse bus, how well she got on with Margaret now that she saw her only occasionally and Margaret was not at home all the time like a constant reproach.

She spent a busy morning at the centre helping to sort through the bundles of cast-off clothing with Deborah, the younger of the two sisters, who away from Bertha's uncompromising manner could sometimes be persuaded to share a joke and enjoy herself. Some of the idle rich were in the habit of salving their consciences by sending their footmen with great bundles of clothing and Christine was giggling at some of the wildly unsuitable garments. Among the warm winter blouses and skirts, there were ball dresses in taffeta and slipper satin lavishly embroidered with silver beads, morning gowns with frills of lace and knots of ribbon.

'What on earth do we do with this?' she asked, holding up an exquisite lawn nightgown hand-embroidered and trimmed with lace, designed for a wedding night and then discarded. 'Even my Mamma, who loves pretty clothes, would gasp at some of this extravagance.'

Deborah was gazing at the nightgown with something very close to envy, thinking of her own flannelette nightdress with long sleeves and buttoned close to the neck.

'Isn't it lovely though?' she breathed, wondering how it would feel to wear such a garment while blushingly waiting for a bridegroom, then she turned away quickly. 'It's really sinful extravagance, isn't it? Put it with those other unsuitable things. The rag-and-bone man will be glad to buy them and with the money we can buy suitable woollen underclothes which we hardly ever have given to us.'

Putting it with the others in one of the big cardboard boxes, Christine could not help thinking that some of the young women who came to the clinic, their fingers worn to the bone, their eyes sore with the fine stitching in a poor light, would gladly part with a few of their hard-earned pence so that just for a day or even an hour they could luxuriate in a dream of beauty and elegance.

They lunched frugally on a cup of tea and some bread and cheese before she went to join Dr Dexter in the surgery and asked him how Dickie had gone on.

'Who?' he said abstractedly. 'Oh you mean that child with the burnt hand. He's progressing pretty well, better than I'd expected. Young flesh heals quickly, you know. His mother brought him in and to tell the truth I was more concerned with her. Thin as a rail and coughing fit to burst her lungs. I gave her something for it and a chit to the hospital for further examination but she won't go of course. These young women never do. They believe the sickness will go away until the day comes when they collapse and then it's too late, no one can save them.'

She wondered what would happen to the boy if the doctor was right, an orphanage perhaps or one of those tough gangs who roamed the streets and had their own ways of picking up a living.

The afternoon wore away and Daniel did not come. It was ridiculous to think he would and yet she had been so sure. Annoyed with herself because the disappointment grew, she worked harder than ever, staying on after the door was closed and refusing the doctor's offer of a lift home.

'You really don't have to kill yourself over it, my dear,' he said half jestingly.

'I know. I just like everything to be left in order for when I'm not here.'

When it was all done at last, she came out into the dark street still carrying Dickie's parcel and glad of her fur jacket. It had turned cold and frosty with a sharp wind whistling down the narrow alley and blowing the litter in the gutter merrily along the street in front of her.

She turned a corner to where hackney carriages sometimes waited for hire and walked straight into the arms of Daniel Hunter.

He had come and then stayed outside, still undecided what to do. He saw the doctor leave alone, knew that Christine was still in there and waited impatiently, walking up and down. He saw her come out and walked deliberately in front of her. A faint light from the lantern hung high above their heads lit up the delicate face cradled in the luxuriant fur. For a moment they stared at one another, only a few inches apart, then she moved aside as if to pass him and he put up an arm and stopped her.

'You heard about Dickie.'

'Yes. I'm glad he is going on so well. I brought a little present for him. Will you give it to him?'

She held out the gaily wrapped parcel but he ignored it.

'You didn't tell me that your father is to stand for Parliament for this division next year.'

'Why should I?'

'I suppose that is why you are working down here, so that he can say my daughter is already one of you,' he went on savagely. 'The great lady condescending to make friends with the rabble, who will be ready to support him when he comes to visit the poor miserable wretches he will be representing after the fools have given him their vote, those who are permitted to possess such a privilege.'

'This is all nonsense,' she said, equally angry. 'My father is not like that. He is a proud man and he stands alone. He did not want me to come here. I had a hard battle to persuade him.'

He put a hand on her shoulder, swinging her to face him.

'Is that true? Or are you a liar like the rest of your kind?'

'Of course it is true and let me go. You're hurting me.'

He stood staring down into her face for a moment, his feelings a mixture of anger, frustration and a deep inner turmoil he didn't wish to acknowledge. Then, losing all caution, all good sense, he pulled her close and kissed her full on the mouth, clumsily, ineptly, but with a force that made her stagger. She was overwhelmed by it, by the hard strength, by the power of a passion that drew her irresistibly. For a wild moment she yielded to it. His hands were gripping her, something deep within her was stirred as never before. Then realisation flooded through her. She tore herself away, outrage surging up in her.

'Oh, how could you,' she breathed, 'how could you!' and slapped his face with all her strength before picking up her skirts and running away from him towards where the cabs waited, her parcel falling to the ground at his feet.

He leaned against the tall building beside him, unable to sort out his feelings, sure that he had made an utter fool of himself, quite certain that more than likely he had put her against him for ever but still not altogether regretting it. Her father was so damnably powerful. If she complained, it could lose him his job at the school. Mr Brown, conservative to the backbone, would be all in favour of bowing to authority. He squared his shoulders, thrusting the unwelcome doubt away from him. Let them do what they liked, he was still his own man. He took a step away, saw the package and bent to pick it up. There was no reason why Dickie should suffer. He began to walk back to his lodging, certain of only one thing. He must put Christine Warrinder out of his life now and for ever. He did not know yet how extraordinarily difficult that was going to prove.

At this hour in the evening Christine's cab made slow progress. She sat huddled in a corner torn between the feeling of outrage – how dare he treat her as if she were some slut he had picked up off the streets! – and a disconcerting certainty that it had not been at all like Gareth's kisses. For a few seconds she had been filled with a powerful urge towards him and was horrified and frightened at the same time. Of course it meant nothing, it was just the shock, the sheer unexpectedness of it that had taken her breath away, but all the same she wished passionately that Gareth was not so far away. She had a most desperate need of his love, his strength, his reassurance.

By the time she arrived home she had recovered herself a little and was even able to amuse Margaret with an account of the fantastic garments that arrived at the centre from the fashionable world.

'I could send you some clothes of mine,' said her sister. 'I shan't be able to get into them soon, and after the baby comes I know I shall hate them all. My father-in-law is so pleased with me he has given me permission to send all bills to him so we can have a gorgeous shopping spree and let ourselves go.'

'Lucky old you to be able to have everything new,' said Christine a little drily, remembering the mothers with the young children whom she had helped to undress and who had been sewn into their woolly vests all winter through to guard against the bitter cold of unheated attic rooms. But she said nothing. Why spoil Margaret's innocent pleasure?

When she went to the clinic on the following Tuesday, Deborah handed her a folded note with her name written across it in a firm bold hand.

'A young man left it for you,' she said. 'We kept it for when you came.'

She unfolded the sheet. Tipsy capitals raced across the page sometimes tumbling over the edge.

'*Thank you for the book. It's lovely. I liked the lion the best. He looked so kind and majestical.*' The last word was obviously a great struggle and ran down into a sort of tail to the one word, *Dickie*.

The spelling must have been Dan's of course but the painfully executed writing was Dickie's own. Foolishly she felt her eyes blur with tears and then was angry because Daniel had not brought the note himself. After all, he had behaved badly. The least he could have done was to apologise but of course that wouldn't have been his way, too damned proud to bend his stiff neck.

Later, when she was snatching a cup of tea with the doctor, he began to tell her of the increase in cases of lung disease that had come to his notice that winter.

'It's rife among the young women who work in those hellish sweatshops,' he told her. 'They breathe in foul air all day long, their lungs choked with the cotton dust and with sitting hour after hour over their stitching. It's little wonder if they are spitting blood after a few months. The mother of that boy Dickie, for instance. I warned her but she has taken no notice and yesterday I heard that she has had a haemorrhage. The boy found her lying on the floor, blood everywhere. Fortunately he had the good sense not to panic but ran to his schoolmaster. She is in the infirmary now.'

'Will she recover?'

He shrugged his shoulders. 'Maybe, but what she needs is good nursing and a long spell in clean air with plenty of eggs and milk – and where is she going to get that with her lover running like a hunted hare at the first whiff of sickness?'

'What has happened to the boy?'

'Taken refuge with the schoolmaster for the time being but if his mother dies it'll be the orphanage for him, poor little devil.'

'Isn't there anything we could do?'

'My dear girl, open the door to one and you'd have a thousand knocking at it. Charity is all very well and God knows what we should do without it, but what is really needed is a changed conscience in those who live removed from all this. We want new laws, rules to prevent people being exploited, help for those who cannot work, and where is that to come from?' He smiled suddenly. 'You didn't think I was a deep-dyed radical, did you? I keep it hidden. I don't want to be stopped from doing what little I can do by fools who think I may be plotting revolution. Perhaps one day there will be someone bolder than I who will speak out.'

She thought she knew someone who might do that very thing but it was not for her to say. Instead she smiled. 'When Dr Andrews told me about this place, he said you were a missionary at heart.'

'Did he? Well, he is a wily old bird.' He got up. 'Come along, my dear, no more talking of this never-never land. Let's get down to what we can do.'

Christine wondered if there was any way she could help the boy. It could not be easy for a young man to be burdened with a child but she knew if she did make any suggestion, it was likely to be thrown back in her face. Daniel's pride would not permit him to accept help from anyone, least of all from Everard Warrinder's daughter, and she wondered again why he should always speak of her father with such an angry bitterness.

When she came out she did not see the tall young man in the shabby military coat loitering in the angle of the factory wall. Daniel had made up his mind not to see her again and then found his feet taking him there and he looked at her hungrily as she paused for a moment looking to right and left before crossing the road, the boy who kept it swept touching his cap and flourishing his broom in front of her, beaming his thanks for the coin she dropped in his grimy hand. He watched till she disappeared and then walked briskly away. It was high time to put Everard Warrinder's daughter out of his mind once and for all. He had been telling himself that over and over again all this past week but her face still haunted him. Why, out of a hundred other faces, some more beautiful, more striking, more inviting, did it have to be that particular one? There was no answer and he found himself cursing the day he had won the fight at the summer fair and it had all begun.

Chapter 6

Christmas was upon her before Christine realized it. She would have liked to attend the children's party being organized at the medical centre, but instead had to cry off going there at all for a few weeks since the family were all going to Bramber until after the New Year, ostensibly to celebrate Lord Warrinder's seventy-fifth birthday. Not that the old man really wanted it all that much but it was Clarissa's idea and she was in her element organizing the festive house party. With a goodnatured shrug of the shoulders Lord Warrinder let her have her way. The old house would be bursting at the seams, thought Christine, helping her mother with sending out invitations and horrified to find that they included Ray Dorrien and his father.

'Why must we invite them, for heaven's sake?' she objected. 'They are not family.'

'Your father made a point of it. He enjoys the company of Lord Dorrien, who is a widower, while Ray was up at Oxford with Harry. It is very suitable.'

'I don't mind his father but Ray is an obnoxious young man. He will spoil everything. I suppose Papa needs to toady up to Lord Dorrien because of next year's election.'

'Don't talk such nonsense, Christine. Your father is far too proud a man to "toady", as you call it, to anyone. If he had, he might have gone further than he has done.'

She looked at her mother curiously. 'Have you ever regretted that he didn't?'

'No, of course not. Don't be so ridiculous. I would never

question anything he does and neither should you. Goodness knows there is quite enough to be arranged without you making silly objections to the guest list. I shall expect you to come down to Bramber with me at least a week before the rest of the family to make sure all the final arrangements have been made. Your grandfather has an excellent staff but we shall need to take extra from here and my cook.' She sighed. 'I miss Margaret. She was always such a wonderful help to me at times like these, but Freddie is only just back from his turn with the regiment and in any case she should not be doing too much at this time.'

'Will they be coming?'

'Of course, if the travelling isn't too much for her. Margaret was always very fond of her grandfather.'

Christine was only too well aware that there was nothing her mother enjoyed more than making a party work successfully and she had to admit when she went around the house very early on the eve of Christmas that the old place had never looked more gracious or more welcoming.

The green and gold drawing room which had been little used since her grandmother's death had been opened up. Every piece of furniture, every gold-framed mirror and valuable ornament, shone and sparkled while a giant fir tree, the new custom made popular by Prince Albert for his own children, stood at one end against the velvet curtains and was already surrounded by parcels of all shapes and sizes.

The gardeners had brought in barrow-loads of holly and ivy so that in the great hall the air was filled with the aromatic scent of the garlands which hung across the hall and climbed up the main staircase, their scent mingling with the sweet fragrance of the cedar logs slowly burning to ash in the immense stone fireplace.

In the kitchens the larders and pantries were bursting with delicious food, geese already plucked and stuffed ready for roasting, pheasants by the dozen, their tail feathers ready for decoration when they came to table, barrels of oysters, salmon poached whole with succulent shrimps, enormous pink hams from the home farm pigs, puddings, fruit and enormous jugs of thick yellow cream. Christine had a quick vision of the centre, with its pitiful hoard of party food for a hundred or so ragged children like Dickie who would fight for a plain bun and with luck an orange as the one precious treat of the whole year.

'Are we really going to eat all that?' she said to Mrs Gant who was just taking a huge black tray from the oven loaded with mince pies, smelling gloriously spicy, the pastry crisp and golden.

'Eat all that? Lor', Miss, it'll be gone in a trice and as much again before we're done. Why, when I was cooking for Lord Carlyon at his country house in Devon, we sometimes roasted lambs whole and sucking pigs too just for a birthday party let alone a Christmas and New Year affair such as this.'

'What about all those thousands who have nothing to eat at all?' muttered Christine.

'Well, Miss, there's some as has and some as hasn't,' said the cook comfortably, pushing in another loaded tray, 'and since that's the way of it, I see no reason for starving just because others do.'

It gave Christine a feeling of guilt because Mrs Gant was right and she knew she would eat and enjoy it like all the rest of the party and think nothing of it.

The first guests to arrive were Gareth and his uncle. She saw the carriage coming up the drive while she was out with Benjie and the two spaniels. There had been an early fall of snow and she raced across the white grass in her fur-lined boots to throw herself into Gareth's arms.

'Hey, hey, what's all this?' he exclaimed, but held her tight against him, kissing the tip of her cold nose before detaching himself. 'Help me with these parcels, Christine. Uncle David hasn't been so well. He shouldn't stand about in the cold.'

'The boy fusses over me like a hen with one chick,' grumbled the old man, returning her kiss. 'I'm perfectly well, my dear,' and he stubbornly refused her help as he slowly mounted the steps.

Presently more and more people arrived, all standing in the

great hall discarding scarves and shawls and fur-lined coats with the servants bustling around with trays of scaldingly hot tea, some of the cups surreptitiously laced with brandy for the gentlemen. It was a happy family party where everyone knew each other, though as usual Cousin Clara couldn't resist a few barbed words when she saw how much attention Christine was receiving as she flitted from one person to another.

'I wonder you didn't invite your new friend from the East End,' she whispered, accepting another cup of tea.

'If you mean Dr Dexter, he is on duty all over Christmas and the New Year,' said Christine coolly.

'I wasn't thinking of the worthy doctor.'

'Who then?'

'As if you didn't know!' and Clara gave her an arch look and went on her way to dig her sharp little claws into someone else, leaving Christine wondering how much she had guessed and where on earth she had heard it. She always felt slightly guilty about disliking Clara so much since in a way it was not really her fault she was so unpleasant. Clara's father had married Everard Warrinder's elder sister late in life and she had died in producing the one daughter. Finding himself saddled with a girl child instead of the hoped-for heir, he thankfully delivered her over to nurses and servants and proceeded to lead the bachelor life in London and Paris which his marriage had briefly interrupted. Clara had grown up with everything she wanted except the love she craved, and unfortunately she lacked the looks and charm which might have appealed to her father on his rare visits and could have tempted him to make her his companion. Deprived of the family affection she had longed for as a child, she retaliated by being difficult, waspish, spiteful, only too ready to find fault. When, out of pity, she was invited to join the young Warrinders at Bramber for the holidays, they had heartily disliked her, only very rarely inviting her to join their games and amusements and making fun of her slavish devotion to Harry.

Christine sighed and returned to her duties. Later that afternoon, rounding up guests and seeing them safely escorted to their rooms, she came across her brother who had hidden himself away in a corner. She smiled at his sulky look.

'What's wrong?' she asked, taking his cup from him. 'This is supposed to be a happy family party for Grandfather.'

'It's that abominable Clara. She has to be beastly about someone and I happened to be the nearest available.'

'Oh rubbish! I'm sure you are equal to anything she is likely to be poisonous about.'

'I don't know so much,' said Harry gloomily. 'This whole holiday is going to be hell. I wish I could have invited Kate Hunter. That would have made Clara sit up!'

'Don't be silly. How could you? She wouldn't have fitted in at all.'

'I don't see why not. She's worth a dozen of any of the girls here.'

'Probably, but heaven knows what Mamma would have had to say!' Then an idea struck her and she turned back to him. 'Harry, have you been seeing a great deal of her?'

'Not really, only now and then,' he said evasively. 'Anything wrong with that?'

'No, I suppose not but . . . Harry, you wouldn't . . . you're not . . . you know what I mean.'

'Oh for God's sake, Christine. She's not some floozie from the chorus. The least familiarity and she turns to ice.'

'But you do like her?'

'Yes, I do,' he said defiantly. 'I've never met anyone like her before. She's so immensely alive. She has had to fight her way up to be where she is. She lives in a real world.'

It was so like what she felt about Daniel that she was almost afraid. What was it about this brother and sister that appealed so strongly to them both? She would have said more but her mother called her and she was engulfed in the bustle of looking after their guests, and put the uncomfortable thought out of her mind.

The days passed pleasantly enough but with such a large house-party there was little opportunity to be alone with

108

Gareth. She would have liked to discuss the clinic with him, tell him about meeting Daniel Hunter again and the small pathetic Dickie, but even when they took the horses out or walked the dogs, Harry or Ray or Clara or any other of the younger guests would choose to come along with them, and as daughter of the house she had a great many duties.

'It's your turn now,' said Margaret complacently, 'to act as Mamma's dogsbody. I had to do it for years and years while you were growing up.'

Her pregnancy was not yet obvious but she sunned herself in Freddie's devotion. 'He treats me as if I were a very rare piece of eggshell porcelain,' she said to Christine with a giggle in the privacy of the bedroom. 'It can be absolutely maddening but also very relaxing and comfortable. I can avoid taking part in anything tiresome simply by sighing resignedly and looking frail.'

What was excessively annoying for Christine was to find Ray Dorrien constantly at her elbow with little attentions she did not appreciate. She could not understand why he persisted when she was as discouraging as possible without being downright rude. Then one morning she discovered the reason and was utterly appalled.

The holiday was almost at an end. Tomorrow was New Year's Eve and the next day most of the guests would be taking their leave and she heaved a sigh of relief, not because she had not found it enjoyable but because her mother's standards were high and her demands exacting.

She came down to breakfast very early and found her father alone in the morning room. They had been very late the evening before, the younger folk playing a wild game of charades till long after midnight and in any case most of the ladies in the party took breakfast in their bedrooms.

'Good morning, Papa,' she said and dutifully kissed his cheek.

'Ah, Christine,' he said, laying down *The Times* and folding his napkin. 'I have been wanting to have a word with you and now seems a good opportunity. When you have finished your breakfast, come along to your grandfather's study. He won't be down yet and we can be alone there.'

'Very well, Papa.'

She watched him go from the room rather apprehensively before she poured her coffee and decided she didn't want eggs or poached haddock. She hastily reviewed the last few days wondering if she had inadvertently done something to earn his disapproval. She slowly sipped the coffee and took a long time over buttered toast before pushing it all aside and going after him.

She crossed the hall and made her way to the pleasantly untidy room, piled with books and papers and smelling delightfully of fine cigars and old leather, where Lord Warrinder spent most of his time with Benjie lying on the rug at his feet.

Her father was standing at the window looking out on a garden that was only lightly touched with frost and she thought how handsome he still was in his early fifties, the tall slim figure, the thick dark hair scarcely touched with grey, the chiselled features. He could have made a wonderful actor, she thought, and perhaps a barrister pleading his client's cause needs some of those qualities of grace and showmanship.

'We should have a good day with the hunt tomorrow if the weather holds,' he said, turning to her, and she shook herself free of her romantic fantasies and prepared to face up to his reproach, though for once he was not frowning at her.

'Sit down, my dear,' he said pleasantly, 'I have something rather important to say to you.'

She perched on the edge of the chair facing him across the massive desk and wondered what she had done wrong this time.

'How would you feel about getting married?' he asked, taking her breath away.

'Married, Papa?'

'Yes. You will be twenty-one in a matter of months, it is high time we thought of your future and Lord Dorrien has approached me on behalf of his son. It would appear that

Raymond is very taken with you and I understand that he has already been showing you a great deal of attention.'

She was so astonished she could scarcely get the words out. 'Do you mean that Ray wants to marry me?'

'So I understand from his father. Is it so surprising? You've grown very pretty lately, my dear, it is little wonder if he is charmed and it would be an excellent match for you. Lord Dorrien approves of his son's choice of bride and is willing to give you both an excellent allowance. The family seat, Greystone Park, is a delightful place in Dorset I'm told, and there is a suitable house in town. You would be very fortunate.'

She stared at him appalled. He seemed to be pushing her towards a future which utterly revolted her.

'But I couldn't marry Ray, Papa, I couldn't. I don't love him, I don't even *like* him!'

'Oh my dear child, you don't want to make a hasty decision. You don't have to agree at once. You need time to think about it. I told Lord Dorrien that it depended on you. I would not wish to force you into anything but it is an offer with the most splendid prospects for you.'

'But I don't care about that. I don't care about his father's money, or his fine house. I don't have to think about it, Papa, I know now. I could never marry Ray Dorrien, never, never, never!'

'There is no need to shout at me,' said her father drily, 'but do let us be sensible about this. Is there someone else on whom you have set your heart? Gareth, for instance?'

She stared at him, unsure how to answer. Gareth had wanted it to be a secret between them so how could she blurt it out now without speaking to him first?

She said hesitantly, 'I suppose it is Mamma who has said that. She does not always approve of Gareth.'

'I have not yet discussed this with your mother, but remember, my dear, you have grown up with Gareth, it is quite natural that you should be fond of him, but childish affection is not always a good basis for marriage and he is still a long way from providing a suitable home for you. I feel sure that your mother would agree with me that you should give the matter very careful thought before making any hasty decision.'

'I'm not making a hasty decision. I know my own feelings, my own heart.' She raised her head, facing him squarely. 'I think I know why you would like this marriage. It's because of what Lord Dorrien could do for you, isn't it? He's important for your future and what happens to me doesn't matter, it never has mattered.'

'No, Christine, no. Is that what you think of me? Do you imagine that I would be ready to sacrifice my daughter – or indeed anyone – simply to further my own interests?'

He looked so angry and at the same time so deeply hurt that she quailed.

'I'm sorry, Papa, I'm sorry. I shouldn't have said that.'

'I think we'd better forget it. All I would say, and I'm thinking of your own interests, is do give the matter some thought for your own sake. God forbid that I should play the tyrant and force you into something against your will.'

'I will try . . .' she said in a subdued voice.

'Very well. You'd better go now. Your mother will be looking for you. We'll talk about it again later.' He sighed as she got to her feet. 'Why is it, Christine, that you have always wanted what is unsuitable, what is often against your own interests? Why are you always looking for the impossible?'

'Papa, I wish . . . I do wish . . .'

'Well, what is it you wish this time?' he said almost indulgently.

She wanted to get close to him, put her arms round him, make him understand, but she knew it was useless.

'Nothing really. I am being foolish. I'd better find out if anyone is up yet.'

Her father watched her go and regretted the barrier that always seemed to rise between them. It was true that this family alliance could be to his advantage but he also knew why Lord Dorrien sought it. He was an astute man but his great wealth had come largely through trade. His position in society was still precarious whereas Warrinders, untitled but rooted in

English county life, went back some hundreds of years. Everard's father was one of the most respected of the Law Lords, and his wife's brother was Earl of Glenmuir, whose ancestors had fought for Robert the Bruce. Any other girl but Christine would have been over the moon at the prospect of such a match with so many worldly advantages and yet . . . he got up and went to the window, pushing open the casement. The room had suddenly become suffocatingly hot. Once, long ago, he had been forced to make an agonizing choice and the memory of it still had power to haunt him. Christine had never been like Margaret, gentle and docile, she would fight him tooth and nail and he had problems enough without that.

In the hall Christine paused for a moment trying to face up to this new situation. Her father could be firm, often enough he had been unyielding, but he was not a brute. He would not lock her up on bread and water till she submitted, but there could be a subtle pressure from him and from her mother that would be very hard to live with and difficult to resist. She must find Gareth, tell him that the time had come to reveal their secret engagement. He must go to her father; even if it meant waiting for years and years she would be safe from Ray Dorrien – and safe too from Daniel Hunter, said a tiny voice inside her that she instantly crushed.

The thought sustained her through an exasperating morning during which she could never get Gareth on his own. The young men had arranged some rough shooting, going after rabbits or hares or wild duck, anything that ran or flew, she thought disgustedly, and although Gareth was not a great sportsman he enjoyed walking in the woods on such a fine frosty day and had elected to go with them.

'I must speak to you,' she whispered to him in the hall as he pulled on his boots and shrugged himself into his heavy coat.

'Come with us,' he said cheerfully.

'Yes, why not?' said Ray, putting an arm round her shoulders and drawing her close. 'Your company will make the day seem brighter and the sun warmer.'

She pulled herself away from him. It was all so forced, so unreal, she thought furiously. I don't think he wants this marriage any more than I do but it suits his father so he is willing to go along with it.

They would be tramping through the woods in groups. It would be utterly impossible to talk alone with Gareth. They were taking sandwiches and flasks and would not be back till tea-time. She must bear the time with patience. She would have liked to confide in Margaret except that for once her sister had developed a migraine and had decided to spend the day lying down in her darkened bedroom while Freddie joined the sportsmen.

The men came back as the day was drawing in, the sun like a flaming red ball sinking behind the black tracery of the trees. They tramped into the hall just as tea was being served, stamping their feet and bringing in with them great gusts of cold air, followed by the dogs, their fur already crisped with frost. There was a good deal of chaffing and laughter mostly aimed at those whose game bag was small. Gareth, who disliked killing any living creature, cheerfully bore the brunt of it.

'I'm afraid I could never see the point of shooting anything merely for the sake of it,' he said mildly. 'After all, none of us is exactly starving.'

'An easy excuse for a poor sportsman,' remarked Ray with more than a touch of malice. 'I hope Dr Fraser is a better hand with the scalpel than he is with a gun.'

'You shut up!' exclaimed Harry with unexpected fierceness. 'Gareth's as good a shot as anyone and next time your horse pitches you head first over its ears, you might be very glad that Dr Fraser is close at hand.'

This jibe at Ray's poor horsemanship was received with roars of laughter in this horse-loving society and Christine saw the dark blaze of anger on his face before he passed it off with a shrug and a smile.

It was not until they dispersed upstairs to dress for dinner that she could grab Gareth's arm and pull him into the small room on the first floor which had once served as a schoolroom and was now used by the girls as a retreat where they could be cosy together.

'What is it?' he asked when she had pushed him in and shut the door. 'What the devil is going on? You don't imagine I mind that nonsense with Ray, do you?'

'I do even if you don't, but it's not that. You don't know, you just don't know.'

'What don't I know?'

Quickly, vehemently, she told him what her father had said to her that morning.

'Ray Dorrien wants you to marry him?'

He was staring at her aghast. Ever since the summer he had been complacently sure it was all settled. Now suddenly he woke up to the plain fact that it was not certain at all, he could very well lose her to a man he didn't like but who could give her so very much more than he ever could, even in the future when he had established himself. It was the kind of luxurious life that her father would wish for her, that she might well want for herself.

'What did you say to him?' he asked at last.

'I refused of course. I told Papa that I could never marry Ray, never. I don't even like him.'

'How did he take it?'

'Rather well actually. He was unexpectedly understanding about it but I know he still favours the idea. You see, he has set his heart on going into politics and Lord Dorrien could do so much for him. I know that when he and Mama join forces over this, it's going to be terribly hard to stand out against them.'

'Perhaps they are right,' he said slowly. 'Lord Dorrien is wealthy. Marry his son and you could have everything you have ever wanted.'

'And Ray as a husband into the bargain! Dear God, Gareth, don't you know me better than that? Fine prospects, Papa said. I don't want their fine prospects. It's people who matter, not riches.'

'That's not what most people think.'

'I'm not most people.' She stared at him, her love and trust beginning to crumble about her. She had believed him a tower of strength and now at this crucial moment he was failing her.

'Papa asked if I was refusing Ray because I was too fond of you.'

'What did you say? Did you tell him about us?'

'How could I when you wanted us to keep it a secret? But now it's different. Don't you see that, Gareth? You must go to Papa, tell him that we want to be engaged.'

'He'll probably be very angry.'

'It won't matter if he is. Together we can stand out against him. In a few months I shall be twenty-one, I can do as I please, he can't stop me. I could walk out of the house and come to you.'

'You wouldn't be happy to do that and I wouldn't want it for you either. You'd hate to break with your parents. I couldn't allow you to do that for me.'

'Don't you want me, Gareth?' she said in a small unhappy voice.

'Of course I want you, now more than anything, but we've got to think of the right way to go about this. I want you to come to me openly. I want to make a home for you and that can't be for a year or two, not until I'm established. You must understand that.'

'I don't mind that. I don't mind how long we have to wait if only I am safe, committed to you. Don't you understand or does your work mean so much more to you than I do?'

'No, Christine, no, but it's all part of it. You're my love but I *am* a doctor and that's important too. I can't have one without the other.'

He took hold of her then, pulling her close to him. He still smelled of the forest, the spicy scent of bracken and winter bonfires and his hair was still damp from the frost.

'Hold me close, Gareth, make me believe it,' she whispered, her face pressed against his coat, her arms round his neck.

116

He tilted up her chin so that he was looking down into her eyes. 'You must believe it,' he said.

He kissed her then and was surprised by the strength of her response. She clung to him passionately, obliterating once and for all the memory of Daniel Hunter and his power to stir her into feelings she did not want to acknowledge.

'You will speak to Papa,' she urged at last.

'Yes, yes, I will, just as soon as this party is over and we are alone again.'

They parted then reluctantly and she raced up the stairs to find Betsy waiting in the bedroom with her evening dress laid out and worrying because it was growing late and Lady Clarissa was such a stickler for all the family to be in the drawing room at eight o'clock precisely.

In the strange way that circumstances sometimes work out, after all the fret and worry the Ray Dorrien affair blew itself out. Early the next morning all those who were going to join the hunt were gathered outside the house. It was a lovely morning, cold and frosty, but with the sun shining and the ground not too hard for the horses. The servants were carrying round trays of silver cups containing hot mulled wine. Christine was sharing one with Gareth. She was feeling unaccountably happy, not that she particularly liked chasing the fox but because she loved riding, it was such a glorious day and everything was right between her and Gareth. Tom and the grooms were busy with the horses, adjusting girths and making sure all the guests were satisfied, when Ray Dorrien came down the steps faultlessly dressed in elegant riding kit. He was in a filthy temper having just come from an explosive few words with his father, partly because his gambling debts even over these last few days had risen sky high and though Lord Dorrien was not tight-fisted, he had come up the hard way and knew the value of money, but chiefly because he had failed so dismally to make any sort of impression on Christine.

'Warrinder tells me his daughter doesn't care for you,' Lord Dorrien had said bluntly, 'and I can't say I'm altogether surprised. You've had experience with girls, a damned sight too much sometimes, so what the devil are you up to? This connection with Everard Warrinder could be valuable to me so you'd better pull yourself together.'

'Can I help it if the girl only has eyes for that confounded doctor fellow?' Ray had growled.

But his father was a man you argued with at your peril so he had said little more and swung out of the house in a murderous rage. It was not that he cared a rush for Christine, but marriage would give him an establishment of his own, he would control his own income and would have an entry into the cream of society. Christine would do as well as another to entertain his guests and bear him a child or two and he could go his own way among the company he liked best.

He sauntered down the steps while Paddy brought his horse. Paddy was a vacant-looking youth, not the village idiot by any means, but a little slow on the uptake. His mother was a widow and found it hard to make ends meet so Tom, with Lord Warrinder's consent, had taken him on as stable boy and had discovered to his surprise that the boy had an affinity with horses that was quite remarkable, even the most difficult-tempered responding to him.

'Take care,' Tom had warned Paddy that morning. 'Viscount Dorrien is a tricky so-and-so. He can be right nasty if you're not careful so mind how you go. Treat him extra polite like. Understand?'

'Aye, Master.'

Paddy now waited for Ray with some anxiety.

Ray took the reins from him. 'Give me a leg up,' he said curtly.

'Aye, Master – m'lord.'

No one knew quite what happened. Maybe the sun had melted the frost, making the ground greasy, maybe Paddy was over-anxious and Ray was clumsy. Whatever it was, the horse backed away, Paddy slipped and the next moment Ray was sprawling on the ground amongst the pile of dead leaves, mud on his face, green slime staining the fine new breeches and handsome coat.

'You damned clumsy idiot!' he roared, scrambling to his feet. 'What the hell do you think you're playing at!' and seizing the wretched Paddy by the collar he began to beat him mercilessly with his riding crop.

'What the devil's going on?' exclaimed Gareth. 'Oh my God, here take this,' and he handed Christine the silver cup and slid from the saddle.

'Stop, you damned fool,' he shouted to Ray, trying to grab hold of his arm. 'Do you want to kill him?'

'You keep out of this,' yelled Ray, his face livid with fury as Gareth, using all his strength, bent back Ray's arm till at last the riding crop dropped from his numbed hand.

Harry and his father between them dragged Ray back from the unfortunate Paddy who lay in a crumpled heap, blood already running from the savage weals across his face. Gareth dropped on his knees beside him.

'Is he badly hurt?' asked Lord Warrinder who had dismounted at once and come to join them.

'I can't tell yet, he's stunned at the moment.'

'Best take him inside and do what you can for him, Gareth. My housekeeper is a good one in emergencies like this. She will help you.'

Gareth and Harry between them helped Paddy to his feet and led him slowly towards the house. Christine gave her reins to a groom and went after them. Lord Warrinder watched them go and then turned to Ray Dorrien, who was sullenly trying to wipe the stains from his coat and breeches.

'I'm sorry,' Ray muttered. 'The fool was clumsy and I lost my temper.'

'That's hardly an excuse for half killing the boy,' said Lord Warrinder icily. 'I expect my guests to behave like gentlemen, not savages, and treat my servants like human beings. If you still wish to accompany us, I would ask you to remember that.'

Tom had brought Lord Warrinder's horse over and assisted him into the saddle, most of the others following him as he trotted slowly down the drive. Everard caught him up and rode by his side. Presently Lord Warrinder turned to his son.

'I understand that Dorrien has been taking an interest in Christine. She is your daughter, Everard, but she is also my granddaughter and I tell you now that I wouldn't trust a dog in that young man's hands. I should be glad if you would remember that.'

Ray was left glowering after them. 'To hell with his lordship!' he muttered furiously. 'I'll be damned if I'll run at his heels like some beaten cur.'

'Oh yes you will,' said his father, 'unless you want these toffy-nosed aristocrats to brand you a coward – and they will, so make sure you don't come off at the first fence!'

'Like hell I will!'

Tom was standing beside them, his face unreadable as Ray snatched the reins from him, hoisted himself into the saddle and gave his horse a vicious cut across the backside that sent them both hurtling down the drive after the others.

Tom looked after him with strong disapproval. No gentleman took out his bad temper on a half-witted boy or a dumb beast. They were saying this chap had his eye on Miss Christine. If she had any sense she'd turn him down flat, he thought, as he went towards the house to see how Paddy was progressing.

He found him in the housekeeper's room lying back in a chair looking white and shaken. Mrs Newton had supplied liniment and bandages and Gareth, with Christine to help him, had done what he could.

'How is he, doctor?'

'He'll survive but he's had a nasty crack on the head where he fell and there is a good deal of bruising. He ought to lie up for a day or two. I'll take another look at him tomorrow.'

'Very good, sir. I'll take him home myself. His mother is a sensible kind of woman. She'll see to him.'

Up to a short time previously Paddy had been the helpless butt of the village boys, mocked and bullied and laughed at. His few months in the stable yard with the horses and dogs had been like heaven. He opened his eyes, wild with alarm that it might now be taken from him.

'I'll be all right, Master,' he said desperately, 'I'll be back at work in no time, you'll see.'

'Of course you will,' said Tom comfortingly. 'I'll make sure o' that.'

'You go easy now, Paddy,' said Gareth warningly. 'You might have some dizzy spells. I'll have a word with your mother tomorrow.' He took Christine's arm. 'Come on, we'd better be off if we're to catch up with the rest of the party.'

'Will Paddy be all right?' she asked as they crossed the courtyard.

'Sure. His head's hard as a bullet. Lucky for him.'

'Now you know why I could never ever marry Ray Dorrien.'

'I wouldn't let you. I'd knock his block off first.'

She wanted to run and dance and sing. Her Gareth was back with her again, strong and reassuring. Everything was going to be all right.

'We'll probably miss the kill,' said Gareth as he lifted her into the saddle.

'I rather hope we will,' she said cheerfully, 'and I don't really mind if we don't meet up with the others at all. It's a heavenly day so let's just enjoy it together.'

They went trotting happily through the park side by side, unaware how that small unpleasant incident would have a more far-reaching effect on their lives than they would ever have believed possible.

PART TWO

Daniel

1852

Chapter 7

It was an evening in March and Daniel was making his way towards the Cock and Pheasant where he had promised to meet Kate after the performance. He had not seen her for a week or two and she had left a message with Ma Taylor that she had something important to tell him and would he have supper with her at her lodging in Vyner Street. He wondered what it was. He was always very conscious of his responsibility towards her, which often enough clashed with her strong determination to manage her own life.

It was a cold night with a sharp wind but even in these crowded streets there was now and again a taste of spring in the air. They must have a day out in the country soon, he thought, pack some food and eat it on Hampstead Heath or take a trip to Richmond and walk beside the river.

He was feeling remarkably pleased with himself that evening. Everything was going well, perhaps too well. Sam used to say that it was just when you were feeling puffed up with yourself that you took a false step. Still, the school was flourishing. Quite a number of new pupils had come along since Christmas, attracted perhaps by the games he had introduced on one afternoon a week in the school yard – in the teeth of Methodist opposition since they were inclined to believe that work and more work was the answer to all evils. There had been problems of course, particularly with the older boys, but he had a firm hand and was not afraid of administering physical punishment when nothing else worked. Mostly they had a healthy respect for him. Mr Brown and Mr Glossop were pleased with him and wrote cautious words of praise to Sam and Prue of their protegé's progress.

He had begun to find his feet in other ways too. He had been accepted among the members of the Working Men's Association, had even ventured to speak at their discussion groups and had short articles published in their news-sheets. The only thing he hid from them and from the Methodist Chapel was his attendance at meetings of the revolutionary group, not that so far he was particularly impressed. For one thing it was mostly foreigners who gathered in the dark cellar, talked endlessly of violence and revolution and never seemed to understand that the British were different. British people did not fly off the handle at injustices and immediately talk about manufacturing a bomb that would blow up their enemies. They did not rush into bloody confrontation which usually ended in their cause being put back for years and the leaders dead or in prison. He had felt like that himself once but he was learning to approach things differently. One day he was going to lead a party that would know exactly what needed to be done and how to put it into action, but that was a long way off and in the meantime he went to meetings, saying little but listening and learning.

His friendship with that wild young man, Will Somers, had deepened and he went with him to Soho where the strange fiery German, Karl Marx, who was not much more than thirty and looked like a bearded Old Testament prophet, lived with his family in two tiny rooms so cluttered with children, toys, dirty cups and saucers, broken furniture, books, papers and manuscripts that it was difficult to move. Marx was so desperately poor that there was never a fire and certainly no food to spare and when one evening Daniel tentatively offered a bag of tea he had obtained from Mr Brown's shop, poor Mrs Marx burst into floods of tears.

He listened fascinated to the theories expounded in a broken English he could scarcely understand and found Marx's friend, Friedrich Engels, easier to follow. He knew something of Engels, who worked with his father in Manchester.

126

When he described what he had seen in the mean streets of South Lancashire, the standing pools of offal and sickening filth, the hordes of ragged women and children swarming in rows of stinking hovels without a single privy, the pigs that throve on the garbage and rooted in the slimy puddles, Daniel knew exactly what he was talking about. He had lived in much the same conditions himself till rescued by Sam and Prue. Marx preached revolution, the complete destruction of the Capitalist system but if you did that, thought Daniel's more practical mind, what did you put in its place? Most of these fiery orators were hopelessly impractical. They could not manage their own lives, let alone the problems of a whole country. But out of all these burning discussions, these end-less arguments, there came ideas that grew and expanded and Daniel grew along with them.

The only person in his small world that he did not know how to deal with was Elspeth. As Mr Brown's daughter and a fellow teacher, he saw her every day. He was obliged to talk to her, to offer friendship. The only trouble was she seemed to want so much more than that. He was not conceited, he never thought of himself as being particularly attractive, and did not realize how much more exciting he seemed to her than the young men she met in her everyday life or at the Methodist chapel socials. He never realized how much effort she was making just for his sake. She gave up the chocolate and sweet cakes she loved for the sake of her complexion, she washed and curled her hair twice a week, she took pains that her white blouse and neat skirt were always clean and fresh. She would bring him a home-baked pie or a piece of cake for their frugal midday lunch and he would thank her awkwardly and wish she wouldn't. He had never possessed any of the small talk girls seemed to enjoy and would far rather have spent the scant half hour of leisure with a book. She had met Kate once and though she did not dare to say so openly took an instant dislike, thinking her flashily dressed and theatrical, anathema to a decently brought-up Methodist girl.

Kate for her part said shrewdly, 'You'd better watch out, Dan. She'll have you tied up in a parcel and at her feet in no time!'

'Oh what nonsense! It's only because I have to work with her. Elspeth's quite clever, you know. She is her father's right hand in the grocery business. She manages all his account books.'

'Make sure she doesn't manage you too!'

Of course it was all rubbish but all the same it troubled him. Poor Elspeth did not stand a chance beside Christine. He had not seen her since that last meeting but she still remained in his mind like an enchantment, desirable but unattainable for so many different reasons. Once or twice, though he did not like admitting it even to himself, he walked past the clinic in the hope of catching a glimpse of her, or offhandedly questioned Dickie, whose mother had come out of the infirmary but still occasionally attended the clinic for treatment.

He was thinking of Dickie as he approached the back entrance of the hall. The boy's mother could no longer work the long hours in the sweatshop so she did stitching at home, hours of eye-straining work sewing shirts for a few pence a day and Dickie tried to supplement it by running errands before and after school, more often than not falling asleep over his lessons. Something would have to be done about him.

He turned into the dark alley lit only by the lamp hung outside the door and saw there was a carriage drawn up and a young woman struggling with a man who was trying to force her into it. She was obviously unwilling and putting up a good fight; he hastened his steps and had almost reached them before he realized the young woman was Kate.

'What the hell is going on?'

He grabbed the shoulder of the man who was attacking her, swung him violently away and hit him with such force that the man fell backwards, stumbled over the stone kerb, made a grab at the carriage door, missed it and slithered down it into the filthy gutter.

Daniel had turned to his sister. 'Are you all right, Kate?'

'Yes, yes,' she gasped, trying to set her clothes in order. 'Thank God you came when you did. I've never been so grateful to see anyone.'

His victim was dragging himself up, pulling out a handkerchief to stem the blood running freely from his split mouth and Daniel saw that it was Ray Dorrien. A wave of anger swept through him, mingled with a scalding contempt.

'I thought I warned you before to keep away from my sister.'

'You'll pay for this, by God you will!' muttered the young man thickly.

'Come away, leave him,' said Kate urgently, pulling at her brother's arm.

'Should we?' he said uncertainly. 'Will he be all right?'

'I don't care if he isn't,' she said fiercely. 'Perhaps it'll teach him a lesson.'

He let her pull him away and they went quickly down the alley and out into the main street.

The cab driver, who had remained discreetly in the background, now came forward to help Ray to his feet.

'You feeling all right, sir?' he asked solicitously.

'No thanks to you,' muttered Ray sourly.

The cabby opened the carriage door and then gave a quick look around him.

'I know a couple of chaps who'd rough that young bruiser up nicely for you if that's what you'd like, sir.'

For a moment Ray stared at him while the proposition sank in. 'Where are they?'

'Not far, just round the corner, in the pub.'

'Very well. Take me there.'

With some effort he hoisted himself into the carriage. Ever since the New Year things had gone badly with him. His father was not pleased at the collapse of the marriage plans and had raised difficulties about settling his debts. Harry, who had always joined in with his plans and was good for a loan at any time, had become disconcertingly strait-laced and was always pleading the demands of having to work. To prove himself master of Kate had become very nearly an obsession, but what should have been a simple affair of carrying off that obstinate young woman and teaching her a very satisfactory lesson had been foiled by that infernal brother of hers. It was only natural that he should look for revenge and now the opportunity was being offered to him. He waited in the carriage while the cabby went into the dark doorway of some underground drinking den and returned with two roughly dressed fellows whom Ray eyed somewhat doubtfully.

'Joe here says as how you were lookin' for us, Guvn'r,' said one of them.

'Yes,' he said, making up his mind. 'Yes, I am. Get in. I want to talk to you.'

'I'm afraid you may have made a dangerous enemy,' said Kate as they walked quickly away towards Vyner Street.

'I don't think so. What could he do to me?'

'I don't know,' she said worriedly, 'but people like that have money and it gives them power.'

'I'll keep a sharp look-out,' he promised lightly.

'Mind you do.'

'What's the special news you have for me?'

'I'll tell you over supper.'

They went together up the stairs and said a cheerful good-night to Karl, whom they met on the landing. Daniel had met the Pole before. He occasionally attended the meetings of the Communist League though anyone less likely to start a world revolution it would be difficult to find.

Kate had laughed when he told her.

'Karl is the kindest of men. He wouldn't hurt anything, not even a spider. There was a huge one in my room one day and he refused to kill it. Instead he caught it in his handkerchief and carefully carried it outside.'

In her room she began to set out their supper. She had a little spirit stove on which she boiled water and made cocoa in two large china mugs. They drank it with pigs' trotters in a savoury jelly and two large baked potatoes, which they had bought from the man on the corner of Vyner Street who kept them piping hot over a little firepot and sold them with a dab of butter for a halfpenny each. To finish off she produced a large piece of ripe cheese.

'It's a feast,' said Daniel, sitting back in his chair and thinking how very attractive she looked in the mellow light of the little lamp with its round glass globe. 'What are we celebrating?'

'I thought you might have guessed. I'm going to leave the Supper Rooms and go back to the theatre.'

She had taken him by surprise. 'But why? How? When did this come about?'

'Well, it was partly chance and partly luck,' she said. 'I knew that Mr Kean's company were back at the Princess Theatre and I went to call on some of my friends and hear all their gossip. They were rehearsing *A Midsummer Night's Dream* and the girl who plays Titania, that's the fairy queen, you know,' he didn't know but nodded wisely as if he did, 'she'd damaged her foot while rehearsing coming up through the trapdoor. There just could have been an opportunity. I remembered that I had played the part with Roddy so I plucked up my courage and bearded Mr Kean in his own room.'

'What did he say?'

She grimaced. 'Mrs Kean was there and she had never cared all that much for me, and Mr Kean had been very displeased when I wouldn't go on tour with them last year but after a while they both became more friendly. He wouldn't let me play the part of course but he said he wanted someone who could sing the songs – there are quite a few in the play – and he'd liked my voice before. Anyway there it was, all in a moment I had been engaged to sing the songs, play a small part and understudy Titania.'

'Are you really pleased about it?'

'Am I pleased? I'm thrilled. He's not paying me very much, less than I get at the Supper Rooms, but then I couldn't expect that. I want to act, Dan. I've always wanted that more than anything. There'll be other parts and good ones, I'm sure of it.'

This passionate love of play-acting was something he found difficult to understand.

'Are you sure that it is what you want?' he asked.

'Of course I'm sure. I don't want to sing funny songs all my life, though I've enjoyed it these last months and I've learned a great deal from it. I've learned how to make people laugh and how to make them cry. I know I can hold an audience interested, just myself alone, and that's a wonderful step forward.'

She was so full of enthusiasm that he had to be glad for her.

'You'll have to give up your lodgings here and move nearer the theatre, won't you?'

'Perhaps. I hadn't thought of it, not yet. I like it here. Some of the company told me there were good rooms in Gower Street and that's only a stone's throw from Oxford Street and the theatre, but I don't know. I don't want to move in with all of them. I like my independence.'

She liked it too much for her own safety, thought Daniel, but that was an old argument.

He stayed on for a while telling her about his work and about Karl Marx and the Communists, which made her laugh and shake her head at such folly as wanting to turn the world upside down. Then she began to put the supper plates together and gave him a quick look as she put the remnants of the food away.

'Have you seen any more of Miss Christine Warrinder?'

'Good heavens, no. Why should I? What makes you ask?'

'I just wondered. You did tell me she worked in that medical clinic.'

'I have no need to go there for anything, thank the Lord.' He got up and began to help her with clearing the table. 'I really ought to go. When do you leave the Supper Rooms?'

'In two weeks and George is not at all pleased with me.'

'I'm not surprised. He knows he's on to a good thing with you.'

She shrugged her shoulders. 'You have to move on. You can't just stand still.'

She hugged him when they parted and he walked quickly through the dark streets to Paradise Alley, too absorbed in Kate's surprising news to notice the shabby fellow who slid quietly after him, observed where he went, took careful note of the dark silent house which Daniel entered with his own key, and then vanished into the shadows.

That same spring Christine found herself more contented with her life than she had been for a very long time. She had won a battle with her father over Gareth. After the unpleasant incident at the New Year combined with her grandfather's strong disapproval, any question of marriage with Ray Dorrien had been quietly dropped and there was a distinct coolness in the friendship between Everard and Lord Dorrien. When Gareth came to him with Christine he listened quietly but refused to allow a public engagement.

'It's going to take some time for you to establish yourself,' he said to Gareth, 'and until that time I would not have Christine publicly tied to you. We will see how you both feel at the end of this year.'

Christine protested but her father would not be moved. Still, it was what they both wanted, she was committed, and it put an end to wild dreams and foolish flights of fancy. She had won another little victory too for which she had to thank Dr Dexter, who had contrived to obtain for her admission to a series of lectures given by the Society of Apothecaries. Faced with a *fait accompli*, her father had given his permission for her to attend provided that she took Betsy with her, since she would be the only female in an entirely male company of students. However, that was easily circumvented and Betsy could be relied on not to say a word when she was dismissed at the gates of the college and with a few extra shillings in her pocket was free to spend a couple of hours pleasing herself.

A party to celebrate Harry's coming of age was looming in July. She too would be twenty-one but nobody seemed to remember that, she thought wryly. At first it was planned to hold a grand affair at Bramber but then Uncle Francis, who had come up to London on estate business, offered to open up Glenmuir House for the occasion.

'Would you do that?' said Clarissa to her brother, 'would you really? It would be marvellous if you would. We are not really large enough here and Bramber is a long way for guests to come.'

'Well, I don't seem to have done very much for my nephew or my niece,' he said, smiling down at Christine, 'and Harry is my godson after all. If you will undertake all the necessary arrangements, Clarissa, I'll give you *carte blanche* to do whatever you think fit at the house and Everard and I will settle the expenses between us.'

And so it was agreed, but even though Clarissa had already begun to make plans it was still a long way off, thought Christine contentedly, getting ready to go down to the clinic for her usual weekly visit and feeling most delightfully free. Margaret had not been so well lately. The doctor assured them it was nothing of importance but, alone at Ingham Park, she longed for her mother and Clarissa had gone to stay with her, ostensibly for a week but it looked like being for much longer. Her father was involved in a new and difficult case defending a client who had been charged with a particularly unsavoury murder. He very often dined out and when he was at home usually retired to his study after they had eaten together. Except for a few casual remarks he did not enquire too closely into how Christine was spending her time. The household ran smoothly under the able direction of the housekeeper and after Mrs Barley had paid Christine a morning visit to enquire about meals and find out who was likely to be in or out and whether guests were expected, she was free to do anything she pleased with no one to comment or question.

April had come in with showers and bursts of sparkling sunshine. Even down in Whitechapel there was a touch of spring. The flower women had their baskets crammed with bunches of violets. She bought one smelling sweetly of the woods and pinned it to her fur jacket. Billy, the crossing sweeper, thin and half starved as he was, waved his broom gaily as he swept the carriageway before her and she laughed at his capers as she tossed him a shilling. She was going up the steps of the clinic when someone tugged at her sleeve.

'Please, Miss,' whispered Dickie pleadingly. 'Please, Miss, will you come?'

'Why? What is it? Has your mother been taken ill again?'

He shook his head vehemently. 'No, t'ain't Mum. It's Mr Hunter.'

'Daniel? Is he sick?'

Again the boy shook his head. 'Not sick. He's been hurt – real bad.'

'I'd better go in and fetch the doctor.'

'He's not come yet. I asked the lady.' He tugged at her arm again. 'Please come, Miss.'

She hesitated, then said quickly, 'Very well. Is it far?'

'No.' He set off at once, almost running and pulling her along with him.

'When did this happen?' she asked breathlessly. 'Did he meet with an accident?'

'He didn't come to school this morning and Miss Brown, she sent me to find out. I think he tried to come and then couldn't,' went on Dickie, looking up at her, his eyes wide and frightened. 'There was an awful lot of blood. Do you think he's going to die?'

'No, no, I'm sure he isn't. I'll come and find out what is wrong, then we will fetch the doctor.'

They came at last to Paradise Alley and she saw the house that stood out so pathetically neat and clean amongst its wrecked and dingy neighbours. Ma Taylor was standing on the doorstep and she stared at Christine belligerently.

'And who might you be? I sent the boy for the doctor.'

'He's not here yet. I'm his assistant. May I go up to Daniel?'

'I suppose you'll have to,' she said grudgingly, then anxiety broke through the hostile armour. 'I knew as something were wrong when he didn't come down for his cup o' tea. Up with the lark he is always. So, I went up. Shocked me proper it did when I saw him.'

More and more disturbed, Christine ran up the three flights of stairs with Dickie scrambling after her followed more slowly by Ma Taylor.

Through the attic window a shaft of brilliant spring sunshine fell across the narrow bed on which Daniel was lying, still partly dressed, his eyes closed. He looked terrible. A towel stained with blood was on the floor beside the bed. A blow had split open his eyebrow and below it the eye was already turning purple. His mouth was swollen and bruised. As she came up to the bed, his eyes flickered open. They stared blankly for an instant, then slow recognition came into them.

'What the devil are you doing here?' he whispered.

'Dickie said you'd been hurt. I came to see how you were before I bring the doctor.'

'I don't want any doctor. I'll be all right presently. Just leave me alone.'

She took no notice. There was a great deal of blood on his shirt. She opened it and he gasped with pain as she gently touched the bruised chest. He had pushed a pad of torn rag against his shoulder and very carefully she eased it away. Blood started to flow again from what must surely be a slash with a knife from his shoulder to his breast. He would be very lucky if it had not reached his lung or some other vital organ.

'That wound will have to be stitched,' she said crisply, 'and the one above your eye.' She turned to Ma Taylor. 'If you could find me some clean linen I could bandage it until the doctor comes. I think he must have a cracked rib too. He is terribly bruised.'

'I'm all right,' said Dan again, trying to raise himself. 'It's only a flesh wound.'

'Don't be foolish. You're very far from being all right.'

Ma Taylor had bustled away and by the time Christine had taken off her fur jacket, she was back with some pieces of white sheet. Very carefully, using her newly acquired skills, Christine bound up the wound, supporting Daniel against her shoulder as she wrapped the linen around his chest as tightly as she could.

'It's the best I can do for the moment. Don't let him get up, it could start the bleeding again and he's lost enough already.'

She dipped a corner of the towel in the wash basin and very gently wiped the blood and dirt from his face.

'Let me be,' he muttered fretfully. 'I ought to try and get to the school . . .'

'Oh no you don't,' said Ma Taylor, pushing him back against the pillow with a surprisingly gentle hand. 'Dickie, you run along and tell Miss Brown that Mr Hunter has met with an accident and she must manage as best she can. Understand?'

'Yes, Missis. Is he goin' to be all right?'

'Right as ninepence if he don't do nothin' silly,' she said. 'Off you go now and be quick about it.'

With a worried look at Dan the boy clattered down the stairs and Ma Taylor turned to Christine, drawing her away towards the door.

'Been beaten up, that's what's happened to him, Miss, and I'd dearly like to know who done it. Must have been late last night. I was in me bed when I heard a sort of scuffle, but you hear a lot of things livin' round here and mostly it's best to keep yourself out of it. He must have dragged himself somehow up them stairs and never said a word, poor lad. He'd only to call out. I sleep light these days but that's never been his way. Not one to cause trouble is Dan. Keeps himself to himself.'

'Don't let him get up, will you?' whispered Christine. 'I'm going to fetch the doctor now.'

'Will he come?' muttered Ma Taylor with a lifelong experience of indifferent medical men who often enough refused to move without the certainty of a fee.

'He'll come,' said Christine confidently. 'We'll be back as soon as we can.'

By the time she reached the clinic there was a long queue of patients. The doctor listened to her while he went on cleaning a dirt-encrusted wound on a child's leg, afterwards clapping on a strong disinfectant and bandaging it firmly.

'The schoolmaster, you say. I remember him, an aggressive kind of chap. Can't it wait?'

'I don't think it can. I believe he must have been bleeding all night and there's other damage too.'

'What's the set-up like?'

'Clean and decent,' she said, well aware of the impossibly filthy conditions in which the doctor more often than not was forced to work.

'That's something to be thankful for at any rate. There you are, young man,' he said to the child, sending him off with a pat on the shoulder and a handful of toffees. 'And next time don't wait too long before coming to see me or I may have to cut off your leg and you wouldn't like that, would you?' He turned back to Christine. 'Better ask Deb to come down and hold the fort while I put together what I may need. Tell her to boil up some weak tea, some of those wretched women out there look ready to drop. You'd better come along with me, I may need some help. Is it far?'

'Ten minutes.'

'Good.'

Dr Dexter was brusque but extremely capable and in his own way could be kind. He turned back the blanket Ma Taylor had spread over Daniel and stood looking down at him for a moment.

'Well, young man, you've got yourself into a pretty pickle, I must say. You look as if a herd of elephants has been trampling all over you. Now where to start?'

He began to unpack his bag and put out the various items he would need while Ma Taylor hovered anxiously in the background.

'I don't want to trouble you,' murmured Dan.

'That's what I'm here for. Now shut up and brace yourself. This is going to hurt like the devil. Christine, give me a hand.'

He worked very quickly and very efficiently, putting something on the wound that caused Dan to gasp with shock, and then stitching it neatly and, with Christine's help, bandaging it firmly and securely before turning his attention to the cut above Dan's eye.

He carefully prodded his chest, said he was pretty sure there were a couple of cracked ribs and proceeded to bind bandage tightly round.

'I'm afraid they may give you some pain for a while so go easy, nothing too strenuous. Now let's take a look at the rest of you.'

He peeled down the muddied trousers and Christine gasped at the hideous bruises just beginning to darken.

'You would appear to have some very vicious enemies, Mr Hunter,' said the doctor, gently feeling him all over and causing little gasps of pain to escape through Daniel's tightly shut lips. 'They seem to have enjoyed kicking you around like a football. Not a great deal I can do for you there either. I'm afraid you'll be pretty sore for some time. Any idea who they were?'

'I'm fairly sure I know who set them on,' muttered Daniel.

'Want to make a charge? I'll bear witness to the state you're in.'

'Don't make me laugh.'

'Like that, is it? Well, you'd better watch out. Next time it could be worse.'

'I know.'

Not sure who Ma Taylor was, the doctor paused at the door to say, 'What he needs more than anything is rest and something to help the pain. My assistant will bring it for him. Nothing to eat today but plenty to drink. Some hot weak tea would be just right. Can you manage that?'

'O' course I can,' she said indignantly. 'I'll see to it.'

'Good. He's fortunate to have someone like you to care for him.'

'Dan'l is a decent lad.'

'Aye, but decent lads don't always get what they deserve,' he remarked drily. 'Come along Christine, there are a great number of patients waiting for us.'

They left together. Ma Taylor went down to the kitchen to

put the kettle back on the hob and Daniel sank back against the pillow in a haze of utter exhaustion.

Every part of his body ached, the wound in his shoulder throbbed agonizingly and the pain in his head was very nearly intolerable, but worst of all was the anger with himself for being such a fool, for letting himself be trapped by a couple of thugs in the pay of Viscount Raymond Dorrien. For the first week or two after that evening with Kate he had been careful, then in the way of things it slipped from his mind. He had spent the evening with Will Somers, had come home late and they had pounced upon him as he put the key in the lock. He had fought back vigorously. They must be nursing a few bruises of their own, he thought savagely, but there had been two of them and they had taken him by surprise. He'd gone backwards down the steps before he realized what was happening. The knife had been an additional touch of brutality. He had seen the glint of the blade and swerved desperately to avoid it, otherwise he might have been dead by now, just another body on the streets to be swept up like so much garbage. 'Bring a charge' the doctor had said. The very idea was ridiculous. He would have laughed aloud at it if it had not been so painful. People like the Dorriens with their wealth and their power were unassailable.

And through it all swam the face of Christine, bending over him, so close he could have touched her cheek, like one of his dreams only this was real, she had been there, had seen him in this wretched state of utter weakness, would probably be laughing at him for a fool with that clever doctor friend of hers, when he had liked to imagine facing up to her one day, saying 'Look what I can achieve despite Everard Warrinder, despite the stigma of a father hanged as a common criminal!' And yet in the midst of the slow burn of anger, the pain and the humiliation, he could still feel her arms holding him close against her breast, the gentleness of her hands wiping the blood from his face, the fresh scent of flowers as she leaned over him.

*

It was nearly six o'clock before Christine came back to Paradise Alley. Dr Dexter was conscientious and it had taken a long time to work through the long line of patients. As she went up the stairs she heard women's voices ahead of her in what sounded like some kind of argument. As she came into the room she saw a young woman whom she recognised at once as Daniel's sister standing beside the bed and on the other side was a rather plump girl in a dark brown coat and skirt, her plain bonnet pushed back from a cluster of tightly curled mouse brown hair.

They both turned to stare at her, then Kate took a step forward.

'I know you, don't I? You are Miss Warrinder. We met once before. Do you remember?'

'Yes, of course.' Christine turned to the other girl. 'And you must be Miss Brown from the school. Dickie has told me about you. Dr Dexter asked me to bring this.' She held up a small phial. 'It will alleviate the pain and help Mr Hunter to sleep through the night.'

'Ma Taylor told me you would be coming back,' said Kate. 'I've just been telling Miss Brown here that I am perfectly capable of looking after my brother and she really doesn't need to stay here with him but she doesn't seem to agree.'

'Daniel works at the school. My father and I feel responsible for him,' said Elspeth stubbornly.

'I don't need anyone,' said the voice from the bed with weary exasperation. 'If you will give me something to take away this infernal pain in my head, I'd be very happy to be left alone.'

'I think that settles it, doesn't it?' said Christine, suddenly feeling how ridiculous it was for three young women to be arguing over this one young man who obviously didn't want any of them.

'Very well, I'll go,' said Elspeth very unwillingly, 'but I shall come back after I've spoken to my father. Take care of yourself, Daniel.'

'It's a lot of fuss over nothing. I'll be back at school just as

141

soon as I can stand on my feet, Elspeth. Tell your father that, will you?'

'Of course I will.' With a defiant look at the other two girls Elspeth went reluctantly from the room.

'Thank goodness she's gone,' said Kate. 'I know she means well but she's like one of those burrs that get their claws into your clothes and can't be shaken off. What is the medicine you have brought?'

'It's a tincture of laudanum. The dosage is written on the phial. Shall I leave it with you?'

Christine put it down on the chest and moved to the bed. Daniel's face was grey and drawn with pain and fatigue. She put out a hand and gently smoothed back the sweat-soaked hair from his bandaged forehead.

'It was kind of you to take so much trouble,' he muttered. 'I'm sorry if I have seemed ungrateful.'

'Never mind.' She pulled the blanket closer over him and for a second their hands touched and she pressed his fingers gently. 'I must go now.'

Kate went with her to the door and out on to the narrow landing. 'Dickie told me what you did for Daniel and I'm grateful.'

'I did not do much, it was the doctor.' She gave Kate a quick look. 'I believe you see my brother sometimes.'

'Occasionally.' It was a guarded answer. 'He comes to hear me sing. I'm leaving the Supper Rooms, did he tell you? I'm going to join Mr Kean's company at the Princess Theatre.'

'Do you know who did this to Daniel?'

'Not for certain, but I can guess and it makes me feel very guilty. You see he had a fight with a man who has been pestering me for a very long time. He knocked him down.'

'And you think this is his revenge?'

'It looks like it.'

'Could I ask who it was?'

Kate hesitated and then shrugged her shoulders. 'Why not? He is – was one of Harry's friends.'

'Not . . . Ray Dorrien?'

Kate nodded and suddenly Christine laughed.

'Oh no, it's too absurd.'

'I don't think it's particularly funny.'

'But it is in a way. You see, at Christmas he spoke to my father. He wanted to marry me.'

'And you turned him down?'

'Yes – both of us, don't you see? No wonder he took it so badly.'

And suddenly in a relief of tension they were both laughing helplessly.

Daniel said wearily, 'What are you two giggling about out there?'

'Nothing really,' said Kate, 'just at the queer tricks fate sometimes plays on us. Thank you for all you've done, Miss Warrinder. We'll meet again perhaps.'

'I'm sure we will.'

Kate went back into the room, closing the door, and Christine went on down the stairs happy that now she had a purpose, someone who really needed her help. She would come again tomorrow, bring suitable food perhaps. Ma Taylor was a good soul but her means were limited and what would she know of an invalid's needs?

By the time she reached Belgrave Square her father was already half-way through dinner and he frowned as she came into the dining room, having only paused to take off her outdoor clothes and wash her hands.

'Wherever have you been, Christine? I have been worried about you. Mrs Barley said you had gone to that wretched clinic but you should have been home long before this. Dr Dexter has no right to keep you there so late.'

'He didn't keep me, Papa. I stayed willingly to help because we had an emergency.'

'I see. Well, I only hope that he saw you home.'

'Yes, of course he did.' It was not true but she thought it a harmless enough fib. 'You don't mind if I don't change, do you? I don't want to keep the servants waiting.'

'No, of course not. You'd better ring for Barton. I daresay the food will have been kept hot for you.'

'I don't think I'll bother with the soup and fish. What is that you're eating? Roast lamb? Will you carve it for me, Papa, please?'

The joint was still on the sideboard under its silver cover. Her father carved it for her and Barton came in with the servants, bringing dishes of hot vegetables.

There was a slight stiffness between them and they did not talk very much till the sweet had been served. He poured a glass of wine for her and she looked at the finely chiselled features and thought how handsome he must look in court in his wig and gown.

'How is your case progressing, Papa?'

'Pretty well on the whole. I think we may expect a verdict of not guilty in the next day or so.'

'That must be a great relief to the poor man.'

'And for me.' He smiled. 'It has been a difficult case.'

'It must be dreadful if after all your efforts you lose and your client is hanged.'

'It's not a pleasant thought and one blames oneself of course. Hanging is a barbarous death and to know oneself responsible for the condemnation of any human being can be very disturbing. It is one of the reasons why I prefer to defend rather than to prosecute.'

She remembered her mother saying once that her father suffered nightmares if a client was hanged, even if it had been deserved, and she wondered if it was true. She didn't dare to ask him directly but he was in an unusually friendly mood so she took her courage in both hands and did ask one more question.

'What would you do, Papa, if you were prosecuting in a case and then in the course of your investigations you were convinced that your client was in fact not guilty?'

He did not answer at once. He was looking down at the glass of wine in his hand almost as if in its ruby glow he was looking back into the past.

'It has never happened to me,' he said with an effort, 'but if it did, I should of course withdraw from it.' He swallowed the last of the wine and then went on drily, 'Why all these questions, Christine? Do you want to take up law as well as medicine and good works?'

'No, of course not. It's just that I wanted to know how it feels to possess the power of life or death over someone.'

'It's not quite like that. The judge has the final word. It doesn't rest on my shoulders.' He got up. 'And now if you'll excuse me, my dear, I have a few papers to run through before tomorrow morning. Ask Barton to bring coffee and brandy to my study, will you? I think you should get to bed too, you look washed out. Don't wear yourself out down at that clinic.' He kissed her on the forehead. 'Goodnight, Christine.'

'Goodnight, Papa. I hope all goes well for you in court tomorrow.'

She lingered for a little drinking her coffee and wished that she could feel closer to her father. It would be wonderful to discuss his cases with him, learn a little about how he worked, how he sifted out the truth from the mountains of evidence. But of course he would never allow her to do that. She wondered if he had ever confided in her mother and thought it unlikely. She suspected he had the poorest possible opinion of a woman's intelligence. She sighed and went up to her bedroom.

It had been an extraordinary day and she had been so busy that it was only now that she had the leisure to think about it calmly. She wondered if she should have told her father about Ray Dorrien but if she had, she would have been obliged to tell him about Daniel and Kate and a great many other things she would rather keep to herself. She had never forgotten his reaction to the very name of Hunter and until she knew the reason why she would far rather keep them apart.

She lay in bed with a warm little glow inside her at the thought of the next day. She would raid Mrs Gant's larder for some special delicacies to take with her. Now surely he would forget his prickly pride and accept some of the help she could so easily give. Dickie too, she must take something specially for him. She fell asleep in the middle of planning all the good things with which she was going to fill her basket.

Chapter 8

The morning post brought a letter from her mother. Margaret was feeling better but Clarissa thought it best if she were to stay for another week or two. She hoped Christine was looking after Papa and not getting into mischief. As if I were six years old instead of nearly twenty-one, thought her daughter indignantly, but all the same she breathed a sign of relief. Freedom from restraint with no questions asked was so delightful that she had no wish to see it ended just yet.

After breakfast she went down to the kitchen to talk to Cook and select some delicacies from the well-stocked larder, a small chicken, half a large cheese, a canister of the best tea, a dozen eggs, some of the rolls freshly baked that morning, a fruit cake rich with almonds, that last for Dickie.

Mrs Gant, a small neat woman, had been with the Warrinders since before Christine was born so she felt free to express an opinion.

'Really, Miss Christine,' she protested, 'I don't know what Mrs Barley will say, I'm sure, emptying my pantry like this.'

'I'll speak to her myself. Those poor people down at the clinic have so little and we have so much,' and she began to draw a graphic picture of Dickie and his sick mother, taking good care to say nothing of Daniel. Servants gossiping about her involvement with some young man, however innocent, would be certain to reach her mother's ears when she returned.

'It's not right, Miss,' went on Mrs Gant, 'for a young lady like yourself to be mixing with all that riff-raff down there.

There's poor relief and workhouses and infirmaries for people such as them, a good half of 'em artful lazy beggars I'll be bound. You ought to be out and about enjoying yourself instead of traipsing off down there to that clinic or whatever it calls itself. I'm surprised your Papa allows it.'

'He didn't at first and I *am* enjoying myself and if you were to realize how much all this will be appreciated, you would feel pleased about it too. Remember how you used to sneak cakes and buns to Harry and me for the tinker's half-starved children and the organ-grinder's monkey?'

'Oh go on with you, Miss, that was years ago and what Lady Clarissa would have said if she had found out about it, I don't know. The sooner Mr Gareth comes back from his doctoring the better, that's what I say. You ought to be thinking of getting married like Miss Margaret and looking forward to little ones of your own.' All this time Mrs Gant had been packing the various items into a basket. 'There now,' she went on drily, 'there's a right good feast for someone and while you're about it, you may as well take one of my raised pork pies. I made a couple but with the Master out so much, I daresay it'll not be needed.' She wrapped it in a white cloth and put it on top of the basket. 'But it's only this once,' she went on severely, 'can't have you doing this every day in the week, you know.'

'Oh it won't be every day, I promise, just this once. You're a darling.'

'Yes, well, I don't know so much about that.' She handed over the heavy basket. 'Now off you go. I have work to do.'

It was noon by the time that Christine reached Paradise Alley. She put her basket down on the step and looked around her. Nobody seemed to be about except a slatternly woman leaning against her open door and staring at her curiously.

'No use you knockin', Miss, Ma Taylor's popped out for a minute. You'd best go right up. Goin' to see yer young man, are you? He's a lucky feller, all sorts there've been goin' up there.'

She didn't care for the woman's sly grin but she pushed the door open, climbed up the stairs and then stood for a moment outside the attic room feeling suddenly nervous. The day before had been so full of drama with the urgent necessity to fetch the doctor and deal with the emergency that there had been no time to think about anything else, but this morning was different, and the ugly leer on that horrible woman's face had made her conscious of it. She was proposing to visit a young man of whom she really knew scarcely anything and it was against everything she had been brought up to believe decent and proper. Then impatience overcame her. What nonsense it all was. He was sick, wasn't he, and in need of any help she could give, so she braced herself, knocked at the door and at the answering murmur, went in.

The room was surprisingly clean and tidy and she saw at once that Daniel seemed a good deal better. The grey look of pain and exhaustion had faded and there was even a little colour in his face. He was lying propped up against pillows with a book in his hand.

'Is that you, Kate?' he said without looking up. 'You're back quickly.'

'It's not Kate,' she said feeling suddenly shy and she came further into the room.

He looked up then and saw her. She had no idea of the picture she made in that bare room. She thought she had chosen to dress suitably but the full-skirted gown of rich lavender silk, the tightly fitting jacket trimmed with purple braid, the velvet bonnet with one pale mauve rose under the brim, had a simple expensive elegance so far removed from what he saw around him every day that it both enchanted and infuriated him. The very fact that everything about her stirred him so deeply made him harsh.

He said, 'Whatever are you doing here? It's not your day at the clinic, is it?'

'No, but after yesterday, I wanted to know how you were.'

'I'm fine. Your Dr Dexter came very early this morning,

rebandaged me, told me I must have the constitution of an ox to survive but forbade me to get up for at least three days or the stitches may burst open. Kate is taking care of me between rehearsals at the theatre and evenings at the Supper Rooms so apart from being trussed up like a chicken and sore as old Harry, I'm very well looked after and I don't need anyone else.'

'So I see. I'm very glad.' The joy of filling the basket, the generous impulse that had brought her hurrying down there had suddenly fallen very flat. 'I thought things might be difficult for you while you were laid up,' she said in a small voice, 'so I raided our larder this morning and brought some provisions that might be useful.'

'Crumbs dropped from the rich man's table, is that it? Oh I know my Bible, it was drummed into me,' and because Daniel longed to say that just to look at her gave him pleasure, he said the direct opposite and lashed out at her. 'Is that how you think of me? The poor wretch to whom you take soup and a blanket when things go badly? Well, let me tell you, you're quite wrong. I don't want any of your Lady Bountiful act. I'm not one of those miserable creatures who crawl to the centre for a hunk of bread and a cup of weak tea. Kate and I stand on our own feet, we've always done so, we learned that early. We're beholden to nobody. Take your basket to those who need its contents and leave me alone. I want none of it now or ever.'

All this is one long angry stream and quite suddenly Christine's temper rose to meet him. She had acted out of pure kindness of heart and it had gone painfully wrong but to have it thrown back in her face in this hateful way was galling in the extreme.

'Of all the stiff-necked ungrateful pigs you must be the very worst,' she flashed at him. 'We did all we could for you yesterday, the doctor, me, Kate and your Miss Brown and all you could do was to rage and gripe against it.' She grabbed the basket and turned it upside-down so that everything tumbled out and scattered across the floor. 'Do what you like

150

with it. Throw it to the dogs if you wish, I don't care. I'm going and I hope I never have to see you again!'

She stormed out of the room and immediately he knew how much he regretted it.

'Stop!' he called after her. 'Wait a minute, Miss Warrinder . . . Christine . . .'

Somehow he crawled out of the bed, swayed drunkenly to the door and out on to the landing but she was already gone and he heard the front door slam. A great wave of dizziness swept over him and he had to hang on to the stair rail while it slowly receded. He heard footsteps coming up and thought with a leap of hope that she was coming back but it was Kate, very much out of breath by the time she reached the landing.

'Whatever's going on?' she gasped. 'That Miss Warrinder passed me going like the wind. Has something happened?' Then she grabbed hold of him. 'Are you all right, Dan? What are you doing out of bed? You know what the doctor told you. Here, lean on me, that's right. Careful now.'

She helped him back to the bed and he dropped on to it breathing heavily, angry at his weakness. After a moment she eased him into position so that he could lie comfortably and anxiously examined his bandaged chest.

'You seem to be all right. I don't think it's bleeding again. For goodness sake, lie quietly and tell me what happened. What are all these packages all over the floor?'

'She brought a basket of provisions for us,' he muttered. 'I . . . I told her we didn't need her charity and she took offence at what I said and ran out of the room.'

'I suppose you gave her one of your famous set-downs. Oh Dan, how could you be so unkind? I'm sure she did it all for the best.' She began to gather together the various articles scattered across the floor. 'Heavens, just look at all this – a chicken, a gorgeous pork pie, cheese, cake, tea, lucky the eggs didn't break – well, I'm not too proud to accept them, even if you are. They'll help my housekeeping enormously. We'll share them between us. That boy, Dickie, is coming to see you after school. We'll have a feast.'

Kate's happy-go-lucky attitude annoyed him but he had no wish to quarrel with her.

'Do what you like with it,' he said gruffly. 'I didn't mean to upset her. It's just that . . .'

'It got you on the raw, didn't it? You just can't endure anyone pitying you, can you?' said his sister sympathetically. 'I understand, and I daresay she will too when she has calmed down.'

But at that moment Christine was very far from calming down. She reached home still furiously angry, disappointed and hurt. There was no one in whom she could confide so she sat down and poured out the whole story in a long stormy letter to Gareth which, when it reached him some days later, alarmed him considerably. What on earth was she involved in down at that infernal clinic? He wished now that Dr Andrews had never mentioned the place, and thought of writing privately to John Dexter asking him to keep an eye on the people Christine met down there and then realized that if she found out what he had done, she would never forgive him.

By the time Christine had finished the letter, signed and sealed it, and given it to one of the servants to post, she had begun to feel differently about it. She had been clumsy. It just showed how little she understood about people but she would learn. She had wanted to show friendship and sympathy and it had all gone horribly wrong but she would go back, not immediately but in a few days, just to prove that she was not one of those silly women who took offence where none is really intended.

She passed the next few days very quietly, paid a morning visit on Clara who was now, it seemed, in hot pursuit of Ray Dorrien since Harry had proved a dead end. She was tempted to tell her about his latest villainy except that Clara would think she was acting dog-in-the-manger, unwilling to give up a rejected suitor. Let her find out for herself. She went shopping and bought the most exquisite handmade lace shawl for Margaret to salve her conscience at not going down with Mamma to visit her sister, and sent it off to Ingham Park with her love. She attended her medical lectures and revised all her notes. There was to be an examination at the end with a diploma but not for her, not for any female. However brilliant her work she would never be allowed to pursue the study of pharmacy any further, let alone practise it. She thought in frustration of signing herself Christian Warrinder. It would be such a slap in the eye for those fuddy-duddy examiners if she passed with honours and they discovered they were handing the diploma to a member of the despised weaker sex.

Her usual day for attendance at the clinic came round and she slipped out during their short midday break and made her way to Paradise Alley. Ma Taylor opened the door to her and greeted her austerely.

'If it's Dan as you're wantin', Miss, you'd better go on up. 'Oppin' mad he is to get back to his teaching but Mr Brown, he says no use startin' and then havin' to give up. Better to wait for a few more days. Keepin' an eye on some of those young varmints you need to be tough, I can tell you.'

'I'm sure you do. I won't be staying more than a minute. I have to get back.'

She edged past Ma Taylor and went up the stairs, not without some misgiving and wondering what kind of reception she was likely to receive. The door was open so she knocked and then went in.

Daniel was up and dressed. He was standing at the window which he had opened wide so that a fresh breeze blew through the room. He turned as she came in, a little out of breath from the stairs, her bonnet fallen back, dark curls of hair straying across her forehead. The unexpectedness of it shook him, then he pulled himself together.

He said abruptly, 'Kate says I owe you an apology.'

'For what?'

'For insulting you at our last meeting.'

'I think perhaps we were both at fault and to prove it, I have brought you these.'

153

'What are they?'

She put the books she had been carrying down on the chest.

'I noticed how much you like to read and these are by that Mr Dickens who seems to know such a lot about how the poor and the wretched are forced to live and work.'

'I don't read romances.'

'Oh don't be so prejudiced!' she exclaimed. 'Do you imagine you're the only one to feel for those who suffer? A great many people whom I know have read these and it has opened their eyes to conditions they never knew existed, never even guessed at. If you're going to do what you intend, don't you think you should know how people like me think and feel just as much as those you meet every day?'

'Perhaps.' He was startled by her vehemence. 'I never thought of it like that.' He came to the chest and picked up one of the books. '*Oliver Twist*, what's he? Some great lord's son?'

'No, he isn't, he's a homeless orphan whom nobody wants, nobody cares about, fighting his way up through a very cruel world.'

'Like me, eh?' He smiled at her suddenly. 'All right, I'll read them. I need something badly till I can get back to my work.'

'Good. Now I must go. It's going to be a long afternoon at the clinic.'

But she made no immediate move. It was as if the ice between them had broken and they were moving unsteadily towards something new. It was Daniel who broke the momentary silence.

'Miss Warrinder, I'm not sure if you know but this coming Saturday is Kate's last night at the Supper Rooms. She mentioned that your brother has promised to come. I suppose you wouldn't think of coming with him. It would please my sister so much if you did.'

He had taken her by surprise. 'I don't know. I didn't realize . . . I would have to speak to Harry.'

'There's something else,' he went on wryly, 'I nearly forgot.

A message from Dickie. He says I'm to tell you your cake is scrumptious.'

She laughed. 'I'll tell Cook. She will be pleased. She's proud of her fruit cakes. Now I really must go.'

'Till Saturday.'

'Perhaps.'

She gave him a brilliant smile and though he knew it was madness, though he was aware he was playing with fire, he was powerless against the leap of the heart, the feeling that his life had suddenly blossomed.

Running down the stairs she brushed against someone coming up, a young man who stood aside and swept off his hat with a flourish.

'Your pardon, Madam.'

It was an attractive face with a roving eye and a saucy look that was so completely unlike Daniel she wondered who he was as she went on her way.

'Fraternising with the gentry now, are we?' said Will Somers, coming into Dan's room with a knowing grin. 'Who's the charmer I met on the stairs?'

'She's the doctor's assistant at the clinic,' said Daniel curtly, 'she came to check up on me.'

'You don't say. A deucedly pretty one and out of the top drawer too if I'm not mistaken. They're usually hard-faced females of uncertain age with buck teeth and manners to match. Has her eye on you, has she?'

'Oh for God's sake!' exclaimed Daniel angrily. 'If it hadn't been for her, I'd probably not be here now. I was bleeding like a slaughtered pig till she got hold of that doctor.'

'All right, all right, sorry I spoke, but better not let the Red League find out too much about it. They might think you're sucking up to the enemy.'

'That lot!' said Dan with a certain contempt. 'They like to pour scorn on places like that clinic but if things go wrong, they're the first to be on the doorstep grabbing after any help they can get. What are you doing here, anyway? I thought you were working for a change.'

155

'So I am but I do get a break sometimes.'

'Has something come up?'

'Yes, in a way,' said Will, dropping on to the only chair, stretching out his long legs and grinning provocatively at Daniel.

'Well, spit it out, man, what is it?' said his friend, easing himself stiffly down on the bed. It was taking much longer than he had hoped to throw off the effects of that murderous attack.

Will leaned forward. 'Pa took me with him to a meeting of the Engineers' Union and it seems that they are putting up a candidate of their own at the coming election.'

Daniel sat up. 'Are they now? Who is it?'

'Fellow named William Nugent. You wouldn't know but he has been extremely active in the Union's affairs for some time – so much so he lost his job on account of it, and has now opened a pub at Stepney and is all eagerness to stand. He would be our first real live labour member if he were to be voted in.'

Daniel's interest was captured at once. This was what he intended to do himself in a few years, when he had shown what he could do, when he had proved his worth and won the right sponsorship.

'Has he a chance?' he asked.

'A slim one but it's worth going for.'

'Go on. What's the plan?'

'One of the first steps is to organize a protest rally against the man they're forcing on us. We've got to show Mr Everard Warrinder that he's not wanted for this district, then, at the right moment we produce our own man, the real Jack-in-the-box, one of our own, and that's where you come in.'

'Why me? What can I do?'

'Oh for God's sake, man, haven't you proved yourself already? You're a new voice. You can talk, people listen to you. You know how to put pep into it, get them worked up.'

'A rabble-rouser, is that what you think of me?'

'You said it, not me.'

'When will all this start?'

'We've got to think out the strategy. The first thing is to get some leaflets printed on the underground press and organize some distributors. We want to get to everyone, not just the rabble but all those sitting pretty, the shop-keepers, those who've got a nice bit tucked away. They are inclined to look down their noses at us at present, so we've got to push our man forward, get him known, and that's just what you can do. You've got what it takes to get to the heart of the matter. They'll listen to you even if they disagree. Will you do it? I wasn't the only one speaking up for you.'

'Yes,' said Daniel thoughtfully, 'yes, I'll do it if I can.'

'Good man. There's time. The election is not till the autumn. We can begin to put our plans into motion. It doesn't rest with me of course but my father has a big say on the committee and I thought I'd warn you, give you time to think about it.' Will got to his feet. 'Must be off. Have to earn an honest crust, I suppose.' He turned back on his way to the door. 'By the way our Mr Warrinder has just pulled off a notable triumph, apparently had the judge and jury eating out of his hand.'

'Another poor devil for the hangman, I suppose,' said Daniel sourly.

'No, you've got it wrong. His client walked out free as air. It seems our Queen's Counsel prefers defence to prosecution these days.'

'That could work to his advantage,' said Daniel thoughtfully.

'It'll be forgotten by the autumn. Nothing so fickle as the British public. Think it over, me boyo, it's your big chance. Wish I had your gift of the gab. Be seeing you,' and Will went off, whistling as he clattered down the stairs.

Daniel leaned back against the pillow and thought about it. It was a heaven-sent opportunity to show what he could do and it was what he wanted passionately – except for one thing. Everard Warrinder was Christine's father and very soon now he would be doing his level best to discredit him. In politics as in war almost anything was permissible. He knew one way he could do it but he shrank from it. It involved too many others and he was not even sure he could make it stick but he played with the idea for a while, indulging a sweet feeling of revenge for what had happened nearly twenty years ago. Then, reluctantly he put it aside. There was plenty of time and ammunition had to be kept in reserve till the right moment came to use it.

Christine tackled Harry when he looked in one evening that week and stayed to dine with them. She waited until their father had retired to his study and then turned to her brother.

'What's all this about you going to Kate Hunter's last night at the Supper Rooms?'

'How did you hear about that?'

'Her brother told me when I went to check up on his condition for Dr Dexter. Do you think I could come with you?'

Harry frowned. 'I don't know, Chris. It's not the kind of thing you would like. A bit vulgar if you know what I mean, not Kate of course, but some of the sketches.'

'Well, I'm not likely to faint dead away at a bit of honest vulgarity and I'd like to hear her sing after all you've said about her.'

'All right, I suppose there's no reason why you shouldn't but don't blame me if you don't like it. Better not mention it to Papa. I don't think he will approve. A taste of low life is all right for me but not for his cherished little daughter.'

'Oh shut up. I'm not all that cherished by him or by anyone come to that, and Mamma is still away, thank goodness. If he asks, I'll say I'm going to the theatre with you. He can't object to that.'

'I'll pick you up about seven on Saturday evening.'

'Harry, what should I wear?' she asked as an afterthought.

'Nothing too grand. It's not the opera and we're not sitting in a box.'

So when it came to dressing she chose an afternoon gown in deep rose pink, the wide skirts billowing from a tiny waist, fine lace edging the low cut neck but with long tight sleeves. Her father was in the hall when she came down the stairs and paused to look up at her.

'You're very grand tonight, Christine, where are you off to?'

'Harry is calling for me. We are going to the theatre with some friends of his,' she said hurriedly, hoping he wouldn't ask which theatre.

'I see. Well, don't let him bring you home too late.'

'No, Papa,' she said obediently. Then thankfully Barton was opening the door to Harry and the cab was waiting.

The hall was already packed when they reached it. Word had spread that Kate was leaving them and her faithful admirers had turned up in strength to give her a good noisy send-off. George himself, the proprietor, was presiding. He knew Harry as a frequent visitor and sailed up all smiles and bows, insisting on escorting them to seats in the front row with everybody staring curiously at the brother and sister in their elegant dress. Christine would far rather have slipped inconspicuously into a seat at the back.

The entertainment took her by surprise. It was crude in parts, the staging gaudy and tasteless. Many of the vulgar jokes and the coarse cockney humour sailed clean over her head, she did not understand a word of it, but the knock-about comedy and the sentimental ballads reminded her of the pantomime shows to which she had been taken at Christmas when she was a child. There was something irresistibly good-natured, lively and vigorous about all the performers and she was lost in admiration of Kate. It was not just her singing voice, which was sweet and true, it was her versatility and her power to hold enthralled this motley, chattering audience eating steadily at pies, cakes, fruit and nuts. In one of the sketches she played a saucy fly-by-night young woman holding the balance between two comic admirers and nearly brought the house down. A few minutes later she was singing the age-old

159

ballad of sweet Barbara Allen who finds out too late that her
cruelty has killed the man she loves.

> A cruel creature that I was
> To slight him that loved me dearly
> I wish I'd been a kinder maid
> The time that he was near me . . .

And the audience was hushed into tearful silence, forgetting
to delve into their bags for another apple. Where on earth
had this daughter of two mill hands from the industrial north
learned the art of holding an unruly audience spellbound by
the sheer force of personality? From whom had come that
magical talent?

'What do you think of her?' asked Harry in the short
interval, coming back to his sister with a welcome glass of
lemonade. 'Isn't she something?'

'Oh yes indeed, and how I envy her!' said Christine. 'To
be able to stand up on that stage alone and hold a crowd like
this in the hollow of her hand – isn't that wonderful? And yet
when you meet her she is so practical, so down to earth, so
sensible!'

'I told you so,' said Harry complacently, 'but you never
really believed me, did you? And now she's going to act with
a real theatre company, there'll be no holding her.'

The second part of the entertainment followed much the
same pattern as the first except that at the end they refused
to let Kate go. Back she came, singing encore after encore
and ending with a song of the sea with a rollicking chorus and
torrents of applause. Half laughing, half crying, she gathered
up the flowers flung to her on the stage.

Daniel did not join them until afterwards. He looked pale
and still walked a little stiffly as he threaded his way through
the jostling audience with his arm around his sister, who was
still in the glittering dress she had worn at the end of the
performance. It was almost a year since that first meeting at
the Chichester Fair and watching him come towards them, a
head taller than many there, Christine seemed to see him with

new eyes. He was no longer the angry boy at odds with himself and the world around him. He had gained in self confidence. He had the air of a young man who knew where he was going and was quietly determined to get there at all costs. He might be only a beggarly usher in a ragged school but there was something about him, a belief in himself, a strength and a purpose.

Then he had reached them and Kate was saying, 'It's so kind of you to come, Miss Warrinder.'

'Oh do call me Christine, please.'

'May I? Christine then,' and Kate leaned forward to kiss her cheek. 'Have you told them about the party, Dan?'

'Not yet. Kate has asked a few of her friends to come back to her lodging. She would be very happy if you would come too.'

Harry looked doubtfully at his sister. 'What do you think, Chris? Would you prefer me to take you home first? I can always come back.'

'Oh no!' she said quickly, unwilling to bring this fascinating evening to an end. 'I would love to come . . . that is if you think I'll fit in . . . '

'Lord, yes,' said Harry. 'Actors are a jolly crowd. They welcome everyone. We'll take a cab and follow after you, Dan.'

And so they did, making their way through the noisy bustling roistering crowd of an East End Saturday night.

There must have been about a dozen of them, some from the Supper Rooms, some from the Princess Theatre, who gathered in two attic rooms at the top of the house in Vyner Street. Karl Landowsky had joined in – the tall foreigner with his shock of tawny hair, who looked like a scarecrow and had the manners of a prince, had thrown open his room, which was almost entirely bare except for one chair, a small table and a long narrow bed covered with a handsome if somewhat faded piece of tapestry. What made up for it were the walls, covered from floor to ceiling with canvases in wildly brilliant colours together with charcoal sketches pinned up everywhere, a panorama of the life that jostled and fought its way through the surrounding streets.

The guests wandered in and out of the two rooms talking nineteen to the dozen and munching slices of pork pie or salami sausages, crunching pickled onions, tossing hot potatoes from hand to hand or gesticulating with a hunk of cheese and a muffin. Christine was bewildered and shy but utterly fascinated. She had never been to such a party or met anyone remotely like these people with their free and easy manners who said just what they thought and seemed to have no inhibitions.

'What a perfectly gorgeous dress,' remarked one young woman, looking her up and down admiringly. 'Did you borrow it from the theatre wardrobe?'

'Oh no . . . I'm afraid I don't act . . .'

'Don't you? You ought to, you have just the looks. Don't you think so, Byron? Don't you think she has just the looks for an actress?'

The young man who turned round was dark and slim and quite extraordinarily beautiful. He was to play Oberon in the *Dream* and looked every inch the Fairy King.

'By Jove, yes,' he drawled, 'you're right, darling, she's Juliet to the very life,' and he fell on one knee, gazing up at Christine so adoringly that she blushed with embarrassment.

'It is my lady, oh it is my love
Oh that she knew she were . . . '

he whispered with passionate fervour.

'See how she leans her cheek upon her hand
Oh that I were a glove upon that hand
That I might touch that cheek . . .'

The others had gathered round to listen and suddenly Kate was there too, slipping an arm around Christine and leaning towards Byron.

'Oh Romeo, Romeo, wherefore art thou Romeo?
Deny thy father and refuse thy name
Or if thou wilt not be but sworn my love
And I'll no longer be a Capulet . . .'

They ran on with a few more lines and ended in a roar of applause and then the group broke up again.

One of the actors had brought a guitar and he sat on Karl's table strumming it. Some of them began to dance to it while others wandered in to listen and Karl perched himself on the only chair and began to draw them, lightning charcoal sketches with a touch of impish humour. Soon they were all of them crowding around him laughing and eager.

Christine was left alone in the other room, glad of a moment of quiet, and presently saw that she was not alone. Daniel had not gone with the others but had moved to the high window and pushed it open a little. Christine joined him, grateful for the breath of air in the stiflingly hot room.

'You must be feeling very tired already,' she said quietly.

'No, I'm fine.' He smiled wryly. 'It's just that I never quite know where I am with Kate's actor friends.'

'I feel like that too but they are so friendly, so kind. I've never met anyone like that before, so free and easy to be with, so ready to accept a stranger from another world.'

'Your life must be full of parties of pleasure.'

'Oh no, it isn't, believe me,' she said earnestly. 'I suppose you would call anyone like me privileged, and I am of course compared with what people like you and Kate have had to suffer, but it's not all honey. There are so many restrictions. I have never been allowed to do any of the things I really wanted to do.'

She was standing beside him at the window looking out over the roof-tops. He could see the dark hair swept up with a rose the colour of her dress, catch the glitter of the diamond drop in the small ear, smell the perfume she used.

'And what things were they?' he asked.

'Oh nothing spectacular, things like studying with Harry's tutor, going to one of the colleges for girls, learning to be a doctor . . . even to work one day at the clinic meant a hard fight and Papa still doesn't approve. He doesn't take me seriously.'

'Is he so hard on you?'

'No, not really. He can be indulgent but only if we follow his wishes. You see Mamma has always done so and so has my sister Margaret. She has always been perfectly happy to paint a little, play the piano prettily, do beautiful embroidery, go visiting, but I was not and so more often than not we have been at loggerheads. Poor Harry too. He never really wanted to study law and become a barrister like Papa, he would have liked an army career but Warrinders have been linked with law for centuries so that was that.'

'I see.' It had never occurred to him that this privileged pair could want to rebel against their gilded life.

'That's why I'm so happy tonight,' she went on. 'For once I am pleasing myself. Papa wouldn't like it one bit if he knew I was here.' She turned to him smiling. 'That's quite enough about me. Tell me about you. I remember what you told us that day at the Exhibition. Are you following up your dream?'

'Not very far yet.' He gave her a wry smile. 'Perhaps a step or two.'

'When Papa comes down here to make his speeches, I shall come with him if he will let me.'

'I wouldn't if I were you,' he said quickly. 'It can be rough at election time, especially when feelings run high.'

'I'm not afraid.' She was very close to him and she put up a hand to touch his forehead gently. 'It's healed but it's left a scar.'

'They tell me it will fade in time.' He caught at her hand. 'When the election does come, we shall be on opposite sides. You won't hate me for it, will you?'

'Not if it is an honest fight and it will be, won't it?'

He bent his head and kissed the fingers he held. 'I'm not of very much importance but for my part I'll try to make it so.'

Long afterwards Christine was to think that it was at that moment she fell in love, but at the time all she was conscious of was how much she liked him and how glad she felt that the early icy resentment between them had vanished into friendship.

164

Then the others all came crowding back showing the sketches Karl had made, exclaiming over them, and after one last toast to Kate's success in her new life it was time to leave.

Daniel, watching the actors and actresses huddle into coats and shawls with hugs and kisses, calling out 'lovely party, darling' and 'see you at rehearsal on Monday' as they went through the door, noticed too how Harry lingered a moment holding Kate's hand and would have taken her into his arms if she had not laughingly eluded him, and he felt a sudden pang of alarm.

When they had all gone at last and Karl had said goodnight and shut his door, Kate flopped into a chair tired but very happy. He looked at her sombrely.

'Kate, is Harry Warrinder in love with you?'

'Heavens, Dan, what a question at this time of night. He thinks he is but he's only a boy, it doesn't mean anything.'

'Not so much of a boy. He's nearly twenty-one.'

'And he's Everard Warrinder's son, that's what you are thinking, isn't it? What does it matter, Dan? It's all in the past. He's not responsible for his father's sins.'

'It does matter. I don't want to see you hurt.'

She turned on him then. 'I'm starting a new life, one I've always wanted and I don't need a lover or a husband to complicate it but that doesn't mean that I can't have friends. You're my brother and I'm fond of you but I am still mistress of my own life.'

'So long as you remember the gulf between you.'

'Oh Lord, why are you going on like this tonight? We've had a lovely party and I'm dead tired and so must you be. Go home, Daniel, and stop worrying any more about your little sister. She's well able to take care of herself.'

'Shall I help you clear up?'

'No, I shan't bother with it tonight and Karl will give me a hand with it in the morning. You go home to bed. You look fagged out.' She gave him a hug and a kiss before pushing him towards the door. 'And take care,' she called after him, 'assassins may be lurking.' He laughed and went on down the stairs while she shut the door. She looked round the disordered room, then with a little shrug began to put what remained of the food into one dish, covering it over and storing it in her makeshift pantry. Then she piled together dirty plates, glasses and cups ready for the morning.

She was not quite so self-reliant, so completely sure of herself as she liked her brother to believe. She had made up her mind early in her life that she wanted to act, had always wanted it ever since those days in the orphanage when she discovered she had the power to make the other children forget their miseries, laughing or crying at the stories she acted out before them, and she was not going to let her ambition be threatened by a relationship with any man, whoever he was. She had seen it happen too often to other young women. There had been plenty who desired her ever since she was twelve and had fled from that hateful house in Bradford, and except for the abominable Ray Dorrien she had never found it difficult to escape their clutches. But Harry was different. She had known it for some time, perhaps from their very first meeting, and though she teased him and laughed at him, refused his gifts and only very rarely allowed him to take her to supper, she knew it would be only too easy to yield, to give herself up to all the raptures and torments of a love affair as so many of the other girls did.

Kate unpinned her hair and shook it out in a dark cloud around her shoulders. She peeled off the elaborate gown with its many petticoats and laid it carefully across a chair. She had to take care of her few fine clothes. She unhooked the tight-fitting corset, let it fall to her feet with a gasp of relief and stood in her cotton chemise and drawers staring into the small mirror that reflected little more than the slim shoulders and the swell of her breasts above the lace-trimmed shift. Harry had made a suggestion to her that evening so audacious, so absurd, that she had shaken her head laughingly but all the same it was tempting, so outrageously daring that it appealed to the wilder streak in her. But had she the courage to carry it through, could she meet the challenge

166

and win? Large eyes in a pale face stared back at her sombrely. 'You think I'm crazy,' she told that sober sensible side of her, 'but I could do it, you know, I could and succeed.' Then she laughed at herself. There was time. She did not have to make up her mind for weeks yet. She finished undressing, pulled her nightgown over her head, turned out the lamp and tumbled into bed to fall almost at once into a happy dreamless sleep.

Daniel was not so fortunate. For one thing the pain from his bruised ribs still nagged at him. In addition he had made a foolish promise to Christine that he knew he would never be able to keep. Elections were always rough. Parties dug up everything they could find, clean or dirty, to the detriment of the opposition and it was certain that when the time came, he would be in the thick of it. Then there was Kate. He had not yet told her the whole story of Everard Warrinder. He had almost done so when he was warning her about Harry and then had drawn back from it, not willing to spoil her evening of triumph. He thumped the hard pillow and tried to ease his aching body but the night had turned very warm, and the room under the roof was unbearably stuffy. He stared into the darkness and thought of Christine. If this was what they called falling in love, then it was high time to fall out of it. It was a madness that could lead to nothing but bitterness and regret, he told himself. It made absolutely no difference. He kept feeling her near, seeing her face, hearing her voice. Damn her for a witch! He'd been involved before he realised it and there was only one thing to do. Kill it before it went any further. It was dawn before he fell asleep at last.

Harry on the other hand was feeling distinctly pleased with himself until, on arriving at Belgrave Square, they were greeted not by a discreet Barton withdrawing the bolts and letting them in quietly, but by an irate father who wanted to know what the devil Harry meant by bringing his sister home at three o'clock in the morning.

'And don't try to tell me that the play went on till this hour,' continued Everard sarcastically.

'No, of course it didn't. We were invited to a party.'

'Were you indeed? One of your rowdy theatrical friends, I presume. Was that a fit place to take your sister?'

'You're quite wrong, Papa,' said Christine, valiantly coming to her brother's rescue. 'It was not at all rowdy but perfectly respectable. I enjoyed it all very much and you mustn't blame Harry. He offered to bring me home directly the curtain came down but I preferred to stay.'

'And I suppose it never occurred to either of you that I might be exceedingly worried as to what had happened to you.'

'As a matter of fact it didn't,' she confessed. 'After all, you knew I was with Harry and it was a lovely party. I'm sorry, Papa, if it caused you anxiety but do you need to ask all these questions now? It's late and I'm very tired and it is Sunday tomorrow.'

'It's Sunday today,' he said drily, looking from one to the other and then shrugging his shoulders. 'Very well, I'll say no more but I shall be glad when your mother comes back and the household returns to normal. The servants have left coffee and biscuits for you. You'd better take a cup and get to bed.'

'I think I'll take it up with me, and you really mustn't worry about me, Papa, after all I'm grown up now, you know. I'll say goodnight.' Christine leaned up to kiss his cheek before escaping into the dining room, followed a moment later by Harry.

'Thank goodness you got me off the hook,' he whispered. 'Any moment I thought he was going to ask me who my friends were, where we'd gone and what the play was, and that would have put the fat into the fire with a vengeance. He'd never understand about Kate or the Supper Rooms and how decent they all are.'

'If he asks any more in the morning I'll put him off somehow. It was a splendid evening, Harry, thank you for taking me.'

'Better please the old man by getting up bright and early

for church, like a good little boy,' grimaced Harry, taking the cup she had poured for him.

'I'll be there too.' She picked up her own cup. 'I'm going to carry mine upstairs with me. Goodnight, Harry.'

As she undressed she wondered whether she should write all about the evening to Gareth. He would see the funny side of it. Then she decided sleepily he might get the wrong impression. Better wait to tell him in person when he came down for Harry's birthday party.

Chapter 9

The Monday after the party and Daniel was back at school, surprised and a little gratified at the welcome he received. He knew that the children had played up poor Elspeth quite shockingly but in a curious sort of way his stern handling had won their respect and they seemed to appreciate his harsher rule and heavier hand.

A week later, on the Tuesday, which was Christine's day at the clinic, he walked round after school to meet her, carrying the books she had lent to him, his mind made up. She came out with Dr Dexter and they were laughing together over some incident in a free and easy manner which made him instantly jealous.

She stopped when she saw him and the doctor smiled and waved a friendly hand. 'Hallo there. Back at work, I understand. How are you feeling? No unpleasant after-effects?'

'I'm fine.'

'Good. I should go easy for a while if I were you, and come to see me if you have any trouble. Are you coming, Christine?'

'You go on, doctor. I want a word with Daniel.'

'I'll say goodnight then.' He raised his hat and walked away.

Daniel said abruptly, 'Don't let me keep you. I just wanted to bring back the books you lent to me.'

'So you have read them after all. Would you like some more?'

She was smiling at him and the words he had meant to say that would have rebuffed any further intimacy between them went clean out of his head. He smiled back in spite of himself.

'Yes, I would – very much.'

She thought for a moment. 'I tell you what I'll do. I'll bring them for you and leave them at the school.'

'I'm always free at midday. Perhaps we could . . . talk about them.'

'I'd like that. I'll try to find time but I never quite know when I shall be free. I must go now. They worry about me if I'm late home.'

He watched her hurry away and then walked moodily back to Paradise Alley. He'd acted against his better judgment but she wouldn't come of course. It was too much to ask. He must play a very small part in her social life. Why should she care a row of pins about him? He knew in a maddening kind of way that he would more than likely wait and hope from day to day.

Christine, jogging home in a dusty cab behind a tired horse, knew only too well that her days of freedom had come to an end. Her mother had returned, the house had settled back into the usual routine and she could not escape as easily. There was a constant inquisition as to what she was doing and where she was going, well meant but exceedingly irritating. There were calls to be made, visitors to be entertained, dinner parties to be arranged: the busy daily routine that she knew so well and found so utterly empty and meaningless. It was going to need some very careful manipulation if not outright deception, and she didn't really want to lie but Daniel was her own particular project, she wanted to help him, give him a little from her plenty. Gareth would approve, she felt sure. It filled a gap in her life and she never stopped to ask herself why she found the project so attractive.

Later that same week Daniel came through the school yard as the clock in the nearby church boomed twelve. Children still lingered. Elspeth had gathered the younger ones around her. Some of them brought their own bite of food with them and very often she brought slices of stale cake and buns to distribute among those who had nothing and could only stare

171

hungrily at the luckier ones. In another corner a group of bigger boys giggled, scuffling and cuffing one another. Dickie had not come that morning. Daniel knew his stepfather had turned up again and that could mean trouble. He must find time to go round and find out what had happened. Then he reached the iron gate and his heart gave a sudden leap. Christine was standing the other side of it looking around her a little apprehensively. In one bound he had reached her side.

'So you did come.'

'Yes, but I mustn't stay long. I'm supposed to be on my way to a concert with my cousin Clara and if I'm too late she will be bound to run to Mamma with some concocted tale or other.'

She was half laughing, her eyes sparkling as if to her this was indeed something of an adventure.

'There is a little garden beside a church where I go to eat my lunch occasionally. We could go there.'

'Only for ten minutes.'

'Ten minutes it is.' He took her arm. 'This way.'

There wasn't much to please the eye. A gravelled path, a few ancient dusty tombstones standing crookedly here and there in the rank grass. A few forlorn wallflowers had struggled up hopefully through the sooty black earth and a wooden bench wickedly vandalised had been re-erected on two stone blocks under a plane tree, but the sun of late April gave the flowers a shivering brilliance and out of the wind it was warm and smelled fresh and sweet of growing things.

In the end she stayed more than half an hour and on that first day they talked almost exclusively about Charles Dickens and *Oliver Twist*, which had come to Daniel as something of a revelation.

'I meet a Fagin every day when I walk through Whitechapel and my brightest pupil is the Artful Dodger to the very life,' he said enthusiastically. 'As for Dickie's stepfather who works in the docks, he could walk straight into the shoes of Bill Sykes. It's amazing. How does a man like that – rich, famous – know so much and write about it so well?'

'He wasn't always rich. They say he came up the hard way and worked in a blacking factory when his father went bankrupt. He never forgot the misery he experienced there. Papa told me he asked the police to let him accompany them into some of the very darkest of East End slums so that what he wrote should be the truth.'

'I'd like to meet him.'

'Perhaps you will one day, I know Papa has at some literary luncheon.'

She had brought more books for him, *David Copperfield*, *A Christmas Carol*, and her own favourite, *The Old Curiosity Shop*.

It was the first time they had really talked on equal terms and the words tumbled over one another, two minds discovering each other, the minutes flying by till the clock above their heads struck the half hour and she jumped up in panic.

'Heavens, I must run. I've got to get back to the Pantheon to hear Haydn's *Creation*.'

'I'll come to the clinic next week.'

'Yes, do,' she said breathlessly. 'Then you can tell me what you've read and what others you would like.'

Elspeth, shepherding her flock back into the school building, saw Daniel wave to someone from the gate, saw the back of a running figure in swaying silk skirts and short jacket and felt herself go rigid with shock and jealousy. He had never been one for casual flirtations and now there seemed to be someone, a rival maybe. That it could be Christine never once occurred to her. The gulf between them was surely too wide. Then she pulled herself together. She was going to win Daniel for herself some day and she certainly would not succeed by a vulgar prying into his affairs. After all this girl could be anyone – his sister perhaps, or one of her theatrical friends. She smiled serenely at him as he came up breathless, his uneaten lunch still in his pocket, the pile of books under his arm.

'Where did all those spring from?' she asked.

'Someone has just lent them to me.'

'You read too much, Dan.'

'Rubbish. No one can read too much. That's how we learn about people and about the world outside us.'

'I should have thought you could learn enough from the people all around you,' she said tartly.

'Not enough, Elspeth, not nearly enough. Sometimes I feel there aren't enough hours in the day for all I want to find out and experience.'

And often don't see enough of what is under your nose, thought Elspeth, rogues like Will Somers or that flightly sister of yours, but she wisely kept this to herself.

Christine slipped into her seat at the Pantheon Hall just before the conductor raised his baton.

'What on earth happened to you?' whispered Clara. 'I waited and waited.'

'I'm sorry,' she said quickly, 'but there was a hold-up. A horse slipped and fell in the street. We all had to get out and I had to walk most of the way.'

'Sh-sh!' hissed someone from behind them and they glanced at one another with a giggle and fell silent.

In the interval Clara peeled off her lavender kid glove and lifted up her left hand. An enormous diamond blazed on her third finger.

'Did your mother tell you? I'm engaged.'

'Really! How splendid. To Ray Dorrien?'

'Who else? Aren't you sorry now that you turned him down?'

Privately Christine thought the ring incredibly vulgar. Lord Dorrien was obviously showing off his wealth.

'Not in the least,' she said serenely. 'You needn't worry, Clara. It was his father's wish. Neither Ray nor I really wanted it. I hope you will be very happy.'

'Oh I shall. You can be quite sure about that,' she said confidently.

'When are you going to be married?'

'We haven't fixed a date yet. Certainly before the end of the year. You'll be one of my bridesmaids, won't you?'

'You never know. I might be married first,' said Christine mischievously, just as the crashing chords of the music swept them into silence and before Clara could think of an appropriate answer.

All during that May, a particularly warm and pleasant month that year, Christine and Daniel continued to meet once or twice a week, mostly at lunchtime and almost always in the churchyard garden, once when it came on to rain bolting into the church itself and taking refuge in one of the high old-fashioned box pews smelling of ancient wood and crumbling stone. She never went to Paradise Alley. It would have been impossible to escape Ma Taylor's eagle eye or the prurient curiosity of the slatternly neighbours. Christine raided her father's library for books which Daniel seemed to devour with a rapidity that astonished her, moving from Dickens to law and history and the witty astringent novels of that eccentric character Benjamin Disraeli, whom her father said was far too brilliant to be trustworthy but who had a way of stripping the hypocrisy and complaisance from the English ruling class while at the same time aspiring to be one of them. But as they became more familiar with one another, they widened out into other topics. Daniel didn't talk easily about himself but gradually she glimpsed something of those early days, the horrors of the orphanage, the brutal drudgery of the mill where only an inborn toughness and a strong determination had kept him alive when so many died, the sheer shining goodness of Sam and Prue Jessop who had rescued him. And in the same way, almost without realizing it, she revealed something of that country childhood down at Bramber with dogs and horses, tutors and governesses, privileged, rich, running wild with Harry and Gareth. Daniel grew to hate Gareth with an unreasoning jealousy because he had shared so much with her, occupied so much of her thoughts even now and probably didn't realize how fortunate he was.

There came a sudden break in their meetings early in June. Margaret's baby arrived a few weeks earlier than expected.

The telegram from Freddie sounded desperately worried and sent Clarissa hurrying to Ingham Park as fast as train and horses could carry her to be with her daughter in her ordeal. She was followed a few days later more calmly by Christine and her father.

There had been great anxiety but by the time they arrived Margaret was lying weak but blissful with her son, small but perfect, blessed with a fine pair of lungs and causing Freddie to swell with pride like a dog with two tails.

Freddie had resigned his commission but was still on the reserve and no one at that time except Everard, who had a sharper understanding of the political situation, thought very much of the plain fact that the vast Turkish Empire was on the point of collapse and that the ever growing power of Russia was stretching out greedily to seize part of the Ottoman possessions. It certainly never worried them at Ingham Park. They were far too busy planning a grand christening for John Everard – named after his two grandfathers said Margaret decisively, which made Christine wonder if she ever let Freddie have a say in anything. They stayed for over a week and riding round the estate with her brother-in-law, listening to him prosing on enthusiastically about his cows, his pigs and his horses, a new breed of sheep he was introducing and the repairs he was planning to his tenants' cottages, she began to wonder if she was misjudging him. In matters of this kind he was undoubtedly the master, and watching him with Margaret and the expert way in which he handled his baby son, Christine felt a sharp pang of envy of her sister, who had known just what she wanted and was wonderfully content with it. It made her feel restless and long to go back to town and to the life she had begun to create for herself there.

'Mamma is already planning the grandest of parties for Harry's coming of age,' she said to Margaret one morning, sitting on the edge of the bed. 'It's not much more than a month away now. Will you be well enough to come?'

'Of course I will. The doctor says I can get up tomorrow. I wouldn't miss it for anything. I'm already busily planning a new ballgown. I adore baby John of course but I can't tell you what a relief it will be to be slim again, and Dr Sinclair says no more babies for a year or two so I can go all out for a completely new wardrobe.'

'Won't Freddie mind?'

'Mind what?'

'Well, about having to wait before having another baby,' she said a little awkwardly.

'Oh that,' Margaret shot her a glance and smiled confidently. 'Oh I can manage Freddie. About the ball, it's your birthday too, Chris, have you forgotten? What are you going to wear?'

'Oh I don't know. It's never really mattered somehow. It's always been Harry who was important, not me. Mamma says I must wear white and I'm having a terrible battle with her over it. I don't want to look like an overgrown schoolgirl.'

'Tell me what you would really like and I'll back you up. Mamma always listens to me. Will Gareth come down from Scotland for it?'

'I don't know. I hope so. It seems such ages since I've seen him.' She got up and wandered across to the window, looking out on a green lawn bordered with golden roses. 'Lately he seems to have been so wrapped up in his work he doesn't seem to think of me at all. He takes me for granted.'

'Are you regretting that you refused Ray Dorrien now that Clara has got him hooked?'

'Heavens, no! She's welcome to him. I told Papa that if he really insisted, he would have had to drag me to the altar! It's just . . . oh I don't know . . . I'm being foolish, I suppose.'

'Christine, have you met someone else? Is that what is troubling you?'

She looked round, startled. 'No, of course not. There has never been anyone but Gareth for me. But you know what Papa insisted, no public engagement till the end of this year. It sometimes feels like a century.'

'And you would much rather see Gareth come galloping down from Scotland on a white charger and carrying you off like a romantic hero.'

'Perhaps.' She laughed and came back to perch on the side of the bed. 'With a sword in one hand and a medical chest in the other! You're so good for me, Margaret. You make me realize how silly I'm being. Tell me about your new ball gown,' and they settled down to a cosy chat on the rival values of silks and satins, of laces and ribbons.

The next day Christine went back to London with her parents and Clarissa plunged happily into organizing her son's coming-of-age ball in her brother's fine town house. She carried her daughter along with her into a multitude of preparations so that it was several days before Christine could escape back to the clinic. She wondered what Daniel must be thinking when she didn't turn up at their usual meeting place. Although she had left word with Dr Dexter that she would have to be away for some time, there had been no opportunity to contact Daniel and she had an uneasy feeling that he might believe she had simply tired of their meetings.

And she was absolutely right. That is just what he did think when one week went by and then two more without a word, until one evening he looked at the books piled up on his chest of drawers, picked them up and walked round to the clinic where he ran into Martha Hutton. Unlike her sister Deborah, Martha had never taken to Christine, considering her too rich and too spoiled, and heartily disapproving of her free and easy manner with Dr Dexter. She looked at Daniel coldly through her spectacles.

'And what would you be wanting with Miss Warrinder, young man?' she asked chillingly in answer to his question. 'She is a free agent, she comes and goes as she pleases. I understand she is away for a few weeks. I daresay she'll be back when it suits her. If there is something you wish to leave for her, you had better give it to me and I'll pass it on.'

'No,' he said, holding on to the books and instantly rebelling against her patronising manner. 'I'd rather return them myself.'

She shrugged. 'Please yourself but you might have a long wait,' and she turned her back on him and went up the steps of the house.

It was just as he thought. He might have guessed. It had amused her for a few weeks and now she was bored with him. Well, he was not dependent on her, for God's sake! He went back to his lodging, dumped the books and took himself off to the Workers' Association and was on his way up to their library when he ran into Will Somers.

'Hallo, stranger,' he said cheerfully, 'your classy lady friend let you down, has she? You're green, my friend. They're all the same that lot, sweet as honey till some toff turns up, then it's a wave of the hand, nice while it lasted, and they're off.'

'I don't know what the devil you're talking about,' growled Daniel, trying to escape from him.

'Oh come,' persisted Will. 'I'm not blind or deaf. Others have noticed too, some of the fellows at the League headquarters are wondering what you're up to. They'd like to be sure who it is you're hob-nobbing with, so cosy together in that old churchyard.'

'I am not aware that I am answerable to them for how I spend my free time,' said Daniel savagely, 'or to you either.'

'Perhaps not,' went on Will, who would dearly like to have known who it was that Daniel, who had so often expressed contempt for most young women, had found so attractive. 'Things are hotting up, old boy, you'll need to put your shoulder to the wheel pretty soon if we're going to get things moving.'

'They'll find me ready enough when the time comes,' said Dan brusquely. 'That Mr Nugent of theirs is not exactly a shining light. I have to find something worthwhile to work on,' and with that he broke away and went on up the stairs, walking unseeingly along the shelves till his angry frustration had died down.

It infuriated him that there had been talk about his meetings with Christine. He might have guessed that Will Somers would pry into it. He began to pull out books and examine them. None of the more modern volumes he wanted was there. The Association did its best but money was tight and they did not have the knowledge and expertise, not like

179

Everard Warrinder whose bookseller sent round a selection of the latest and most important every month for him to make a choice.

Frustrated and empty-handed he went down the stairs, wondered if he should hunt up Will and take him for a drink, decided against it and came through the doors into the street.

A small ghost with a white tear-stained face materialized out of the half-light and clutched at his hand.

Daniel looked down at Dickie with a tinge of remorse. He had meant to do something about the boy and then, wrapped up in his own affairs for the last few weeks, had done nothing.

He said gently, 'What is it, Dickie?'

The boy looked up at him piteously, tried to speak and choked. He tugged at his hand and with a feeling of foreboding Daniel went with him.

It was on the very next day that Christine rebelled against her mother and insisted on taking up her work again at the clinic.

'It's only one day a week, Mamma, I owe it to them and I'm not giving it up just for Harry's sake. It's weeks yet and there's been quite enough fuss over it already.'

Her mother grumbled but with a new determination Christine overcame her objections. Dr Dexter was glad to see her.

'We've been pushed without you. Summer is a bad time down here. They go down like ninepins with a multitude of infections which the cold weather seems to kill off.'

At lunchtime she slipped out and went round to the school. She couldn't see Daniel anywhere but Elspeth was in the yard and she called across to her, asking where he was.

'He had to go off somewhere, Miss Warrinder, but he'll be back this afternoon. Shall I tell him you called?'

'Thank you, if you will.'

Elspeth watched her walk away. Could she be the one after all? Was it possible? And she knew a spasm of angry envy. Why should *she* come down here looking for Daniel? Hadn't she enough already with her fine clothes and her privileges without grabbing after him too? She took very good care to say nothing to Daniel when he came back for afternoon school.

By the end of the afternoon when Daniel had still not made any effort to contact her, Christine felt disappointed, angry and miserable all at once. If that was how little he thought of her, if that was how much he cared, then let there be an end of it. She had put on her bonnet with every intention of returning home and making no further effort when she remembered the books. The last ones she had loaned him were among the very latest to come from the bookseller. If her father asked where they had got to, as he had done once or twice already, she could not go on thinking up excuses. With a sudden resolution she retraced her steps and walked briskly round to Paradise Alley.

June was in the throes of a summer heat wave. The early evening sun still beat down so that the mean crowded streets were stifling, filled with the reek of greasy food frying in rank fat, of decaying fruit and vegetables rotting in the gutters, of the fetid odour of unwashed humanity swarming everywhere. She tried to hold her breath as she pushed her way through market stalls and street sellers hoarsely shouting their wares.

Ma Taylor was outside with a large broom and a bucket of water sweeping the steps and broken pavement outside the house. She stopped when she saw Christine, leaning on the broom and staring at her as she came up.

'Well, you're a stranger and no mistake. If it's Daniel you're lookin' for, he's not here. He's gorn off to the infirmary.'

'Is someone sick? Is it Dickie?'

'No, t'ain't the boy, it's his Ma. Took bad she was. Seems the lad ran to Daniel late last night. In a right old state he were by all accounts. Out half the night Daniel were. I don't know the rights and wrongs of it but when he come home from school, he went off again without waitin' for a bite of food. Would you like to wait?'

Christine hesitated. 'Just for a few minutes. I did want to speak to him.'

181

'Come on in then, have a cup o'tea. I've got the kettle on. Then you can go on up to his room. He did say as he didn't think he'd be too long.'

Now she was committed. She drank a cup of Ma Taylor's dark brown brew and told her something about Margaret and the baby.

'So you see I've had to be away for quite a time.'

'Of course you have,' said Ma Taylor giving her a long look, 'it bein' your sister an' all. I thought as how there were something up. Dan's not been himself for a week or two now, face long as a kite. You go on up and I'll tell him the minute he comes in.'

The room was as she remembered it, very clean and tidy. The pile of books she had lent him was on the chest and beside them some sheets of closely written notes. Daniel obviously took his reading seriously. Pinned to the wall was Karl's charcoal sketch of Kate staring back at her, vibrant and challenging, and beside it there was one of herself which the Pole must have done at the party without her realizing it, for she was looking away from him, her face tilted, as if smiling at someone out of the picture. It was badly creased as if it had been fiercely crumpled and then carefully smoothed out again.

She stared at it for a moment. Under the roof the room was very warm and she felt the sweat trickle down her back under her light summer gown. Abruptly she pushed the window wide and was grateful for the welcome rush of cooler air on her face.

Daniel's own books were housed in a crude bookcase which he must have knocked up himself from an old wooden crate. She knelt down to look at them pulling one out at random. It was a worn and battered copy of Bunyan's *The Pilgrim's Progress* which had been well read and very carefully repaired. She was still looking at it when she heard someone coming up the stairs and hurriedly scrambled to her feet. Then Daniel was standing in the doorway staring at her as if he couldn't believe what he saw.

'You've come back,' he said.

'Did you think that I wouldn't?'

'I wasn't sure.'

Then quite without volition, almost as if they were sleep-walking, they moved together. His arms went around her, not kissing her, just holding her closely against him, and she had a curious feeling of inevitability as if it had been there always but just beyond their reach. Then the moment was gone and they drew apart.

'I was looking at your books,' she said a little shakily, 'I always loved *The Pilgrim's Progress* too.'

'Sam gave me that when I left to come to London. He had treasured it from a boy.'

He took the book from her and replaced it on the shelf.

'What has happened?' she asked. 'Ma Taylor said something about Dickie and his mother.'

'Yes. He came to fetch me last night. She is dead.' He passed a hand over his face as if trying to brush away something and then walked away from her to the window, staring out un-seeingly for a moment before he went on almost in a whisper, reliving the horror.

'When I got there she was lying on the floor. She was bruised and bleeding and obviously in great pain. Dickie was so upset it was difficult to get out of him what had happened. It seems she was pregnant and his stepfather believed she'd taken another lover when he was away working. They quar-relled violently over it and he began to beat her up. Dickie tried to stop him and he flung the boy off so viciously he was hurled against the wall breathless and bruised. His mother stumbled and fell and the man kicked her brutally till she lay still. Perhaps in his frenzy he believed her dead, I don't know, but it seems he snatched up his work bag and fled from the house. Dickie tried to lift his mother but she was far too heavy for him so he put a pillow under her head and ran for me.'

'What did you do?' she whispered, appalled at the raw savagery of that dreadful night.

He turned round to her then. 'Oh God, I shouldn't be telling you all this.'

'Yes, you should,' she said more steadily. 'I want to know.'

'There wasn't much more to tell. She was still breathing and I did what little I could, then I went to the infirmary. They came and took her in. There was no doctor on duty during the night and when he came in the morning it was far too late. She died at midday.'

'Oh poor woman,' breathed Christine. She could have wept for the pain and terror of those last few hours so utterly alone. 'What will become of Dickie?'

'That was what I was trying to find out. It seems his mother has an elder sister who'd never been very friendly. The police contacted her and she was there this evening. She will take the boy.'

'Perhaps that's for the best,' said Christine gently.

'I suppose so, except that he seems to be terrified of his aunt. God knows why. He clung to my hand as if I were his last hope and I offered to care for him for a few days at least but the Chief of Police said his aunt was the proper guardian. I did mention his coming to school and she said he was old enough to earn something towards his keep and she had no money to squander on useless book learning. All that seemed to concern her was laying claim to the few bits of things her sister had left.'

'Will they find the man who killed her?'

'I doubt it. He hasn't robbed anyone. He hasn't attacked anyone of importance, only beaten to death a poor girl who thought she loved him enough to bear him a child.' Suddenly Daniel brought his fist down bruisingly on the window ledge. 'Such things shouldn't be allowed to happen. Nobody did anything to stop it, nobody cared what happened to her. They turned her out of the infirmary though she was still suffering from the lung fever. She couldn't work yet she struggled to find the penny to send Dickie to school. There was no one to whom she could go for help, no one to protect her from the drunken brutality of the man who called himself her lover.

We have a poor law and do you know what happens? Those who should administer it grow fat and lazy while the destitute, the helpless, go on starving and dying without a single voice being raised in protest, or a hand stretched out to help. We need a new public conscience, new compassion, new laws, and I swear I'll find a way to set them in motion if it takes me all the hours of my working life.'

It was as if Daniel, like Bunyan's Christian, was fighting Apollyon, the foul fiend with the wings of a dragon and the mouth of a lion who used to creep out of the nursery cupboard and terrify her into a nightmare when she was a child.

She pushed aside her fantasy as Daniel turned back to her.

'I'm as much to blame as anyone. I guessed there was trouble but was too occupied with my own affairs to try and find out what was happening.'

'That's not true,' she protested.

'Oh yes, it is. "No man is an island" – I read that in one of the books you lent me and never realized how true it is till now.' Then he smiled. 'I shouldn't be saying all this to you of all people. I didn't mean to, you know. When Ma Taylor told me you were here, all I intended to say was how glad I was to see you, because I dreaded to hear that something terrible had happened to you or, even worse, that you no longer wanted to see me again.'

'It all happened so fast I didn't have time to let you know,' she said quickly. 'My sister's baby arrived before anyone expected it and everything at home fell into turmoil. I came to the school at midday today but I only saw Elspeth.'

'She must have forgotten to tell me.'

'I'd love to stay and hear more about everything, Daniel. It seems such a long time, but I mustn't. If I'm late home, Mamma immediately believes I have been abducted or murdered.'

'In that case I'll walk with you until I can see you safely into a cab.'

They went down the stairs together and suddenly they were back on the old familiar footing, only even closer because she had shared with him something that had moved him deeply. As they walked to where the cabs were lined up he told her about Kate.

'The young woman who acts the part of the Fairy Queen is still troubled with her broken toe so Kate is to play Titania till she has recovered.'

'She will love that. I must tell Harry.'

'Mr Kean has changed her name. In the theatre now she will be Kate Luce. I can't think why. I shall never understand actors.'

She laughed and pressed the arm linked with hers. 'It's all part of the magic. They like to hide their true identity.'

When he had helped her into the cab, she leaned forward to say, 'I may not be able to come very often for the next few weeks. We're all at sixes and sevens at home for Harry's birthday.'

'Isn't it yours too?'

'Yes, I suppose it is. I never think of it as mine somehow.'

He held her hand for a moment, then turned back the cuff of the kid glove and kissed her wrist, a little familiar gesture that sent a thrill rushing through her whole body. Then he released her hand, closed the door and the driver began to whip up his tired horse.

She sat quite still feeling the touch of his lips on her wrist, the pulse that beat there sending it vibrating through her. What was happening to her? She wasn't falling in love with Daniel, she couldn't be. Gareth had her love, had always had it. She was going to marry him, had already thought about their life together, yet now . . . she must forget about it, put it out of her mind. It meant nothing. It was just that she had felt sorry for him, had wanted to help and he had shown a touching gratitude.

Gareth would be coming down from Edinburgh for Harry's birthday. He would be there strong, reassuring, comforting. She longed for him suddenly. With him close to her all these odd fancies would be put in their proper place. She would tell him about Daniel and then they would both implore her father to allow them to be properly engaged. She would be twenty-one, he couldn't stop her, they could be married perhaps before the end of the year. Wasn't that what she wanted more than anything? And if that was so, why did she feel as if it was a prison door shutting her off from a wider kind of life which she was only now discovering for herself?

PART THREE

Everard

1852

Chapter 10

Christine had been right about having very little free time during the weeks running up to the birthday ball. Her mother made incessant demands on her and in between were consultations and fittings for her own new dress. With Margaret's help she had won her battle and thankfully would not be wearing schoolgirl white but tawny yellow organza lightly sprinkled with gold stars over a matching satin petticoat. All the same, it was surprising how often she contrived to meet Daniel, sometimes for only a few snatched minutes when she was on her way to somewhere else. Much to her mother's annoyance she had refused stubbornly to give up her days at the clinic and Daniel would come to meet her there after school closed, walking part of the way home with her through the warm summer evening so that instead of coming to a natural end as one part of her told her it should, their friendship grew and blossomed.

They still discussed the books she brought to him and she was surprised at the fresh thought he brought to them and the ready sense of fun he shared with her now that they were on equal terms. She asked him one day if he had news of Dickie.

'Yes, I have,' he told her. 'I have found out where his aunt lives. She is married to a man called Clem Walker and he runs a pawnbroker's shop down at Wapping close by St. James's Steps. He sells old clothes, old pots and pans, and I think the children who scavenge along the muddy shore while the tide is out take some of their findings to him and he hands out a few pence.'

'Is that what Dickie is doing?'

'I don't know. I didn't see him and they were unpleasant when I asked for him. They certainly don't send him to school. It's a filthy degrading business, Christine. The children wade barefoot in all the filth and slime as the water recedes. They call them mudlarks and if they fall sick or die it is nobody's business but their own. It's a crying shame,' he went on fiercely, 'that a boy like Dickie who wanted to learn, who had the ability to make something of himself, should be condemned to live like that.'

'We don't know that he is,' said Christine sensibly. 'Isn't there something we could do for him?'

'The law says the boy's natural guardian is his aunt and unless he was apprenticed to some proper trade then he cannot be taken away from her, and since they won't part up with as much as a penny a week for the school, they're not likely to find an apprenticeship fee.'

She knew he felt his helplessness keenly. Dickie was only one of hundreds of homeless orphans who scraped a living somehow in the slums of the city but he was a child they knew and one who had endeared himself to them.

Another time, walking down Cheapside, Daniel pointed out a large ramshackle building obviously undergoing extensive repairs.

'See that,' he said, 'in a few months that will be Mr Brown's new grocery emporium complete with plate-glass windows and a stock of the finest and most expensive items of food for rich city folk with greedy appetites.'

'Are you being serious?'

'Very serious indeed. Mr Brown has all the Methodist virtues, hard-working, honest, reliable and determined to get on in the world and he is succeeding. When the shop opens, he means to install his daughter as manageress and he asked me if I would like to give up the teaching and work for him in the shop with Elspeth.'

'Are you going to accept his offer?'

'No. I may be wrong but I think I can do better helping

192

children to get a little more out of their lives. Besides, my ambition is not to become a wealthy shopkeeper. I have other ideas.'

'Such as becoming Prime Minister?' she said teasingly.

He laughed. 'Did I really say that? I'm learning not to be so arrogant.'

She went on to tell him that one night her father had taken her and her mother to the Princess Theatre and they had seen Kate as Titania.

'She was superb,' she said. 'Most actresses play it like a pantomime fairy but Kate was quite different. She was unearthly, a being in a silver dress who had come from another world, a magical world.'

What she did not mention was that her father who had been leaning back and idly watching the familiar play had suddenly sat up at Kate's entrance and picked up the opera glasses, taking a long look at the glittering figure before he put them down and sat back frowning. She would dearly liked to have known what was in his mind.

The last time she saw Dan before the ball was a Tuesday, as usual, when he picked her up at the clinic and they took a cab to St Paul's because he said he wanted to show her something. When they alighted and crossed the busy road, he stopped suddenly, staring up at the dark ugly mass of Newgate prison, and his hand tightened on her arm.

'I wasn't much more than six,' he whispered, 'when I stood beside my mother and watched them hang my father for a crime he did not commit.'

'Oh no!' she exclaimed, shocked by the stark horror in his voice.

'And one day,' he went on as if she had not spoken, 'I swear I'll make those responsible acknowledge the injustice.'

A tremor seemed to run through him as if the throwback to the past was over and after a moment he turned back to her.

She would have liked to question him but didn't dare. One day when the time was right he would tell her. Instead she said, 'We'll have to hurry if I'm not going to be very late home. What is it you want to show me?'

Already Daniel knew far more about London and its history than she did. He had found some battered guide book, devoured its contents and enjoyed teasing her about the little she knew of her own city.

'It's not far,' he said, 'but we have to walk through the market.'

The great square of Smithfield had once lain in the midst of fields, a famous horse fair, a place where miracle plays were performed and where once had stood the smoking funeral pyres of Protestant martyrs burned to ashes for their faith in the time of Mary Tudor. The early morning meat market was long over but there were still great piles of rubbish. Very soon the giant drays would be rolling in piled with carcasses to be sold off the next day to early morning buyers haggling over the price.

They picked their way through the debris to the church of St Bartholomew the Great, filled with an ancient peace as the great door swung to behind them. He led her to the tomb of Rahere, who, so legend said, was once the King's jester and had led a riotous carefree life wasting his substance until, struck down by a grievous sickness, he vowed to St Bartholomew that if the saint cured him he would build a great hospital for the care of the sick and the poor of the city. He had fulfilled his promise, the hospital still stood, one of the finest in the world, Gareth had told her, and with it the church where he lay.

'I have loved this place ever since I found it,' said Daniel, 'though sometimes I wonder if we have moved very much farther forward since the Middle Ages. We need the vision of another Rahere. The laws are still harsh, children still die miserably and there is no compassion in the hearts of men.' Then he gave her a wry smile. 'There I go again, I'm preaching, aren't I? Climbing on to my soap box. You should shut me up.'

The church was growing dark with the shadows of evening and smelled of burned-out candles and beeswax. At the door she fumbled in her bag for a few coins and standing on tiptoe to drop them in the box she tripped on the worn paving and would have fallen if Daniel had not caught her in his arms. It was then that feeling the warm living body beneath the thin summer gown, all his good resolutions melted away. He pushed back the straw bonnet, tilting up her chin and kissed her hard and deliberately on the lips. Startled, she resisted and then relaxed, a strange sweetness running through her. Someone opened the door and one of the clergy came through, glancing at them in surprise and then smiling benignly at a pair of lovers stealing a quiet moment in the sanctity of the old church.

Daniel released her and she stood for an instant, shocked and disturbed, shaking a little as she retied her bonnet ribbons.

'Are you angry with me?' he asked.

'No, but I think we'd better go. It must be very late by now. I ought to take a cab.'

'Yes, of course.'

They came out of the church and crossed the market, threading their way through a small flock of sheep bleating loudly as they were driven in for the next day's dawn sale. Outside the prison in Newgate Street he stopped a cab and handed her into it.

'When shall I see you again?' he said, his hand on the door.

'Not till after Harry's ball, I'm afraid.'

'I have something for you.' He fumbled in an inside pocket, brought out a small package and put it in her hand. 'For your birthday.'

'I wish you were going to be there,' she said impulsively, 'you and Kate.'

'What would your Papa have to say about that?' he said drily.

He closed the door and walked quickly away, only too well aware that this summer idyll, these few short weeks which had possessed a bitter-sweet happiness for him, had come to an end. Soon, very soon, she would have to know and they would be split apart.

195

Christine did not open the package till she reached the seclusion of her own room. There she unwrapped the paper and saw a tiny box, one that might have been used for pills or, in an earlier age, where a lady of fashion would have kept the patches that adorned her pretty face. It had a dull sheen and must have been silver with an intricate scroll engraved on the lid. She wondered if perhaps it had belonged to his mother who had died so tragically and she was moved by the thought that he had given it to her. Of course it meant nothing. It was just that he had wanted to thank her for the happy hours they had spent together. In her heart she knew that this was not entirely true. The fact was they were still both of them two innocents caught up in a trap of emotions they did not entirely trust and not yet realizing how deeply and hopelessly they were becoming involved.

Christine took the little box with her among all the other things she needed when she and her mother moved to her uncle's house on the morning of the ball. After a busy day filled with a hundred last-minute tasks, she went up to her own room leaving her mother in the drawing room. Clarissa looked around her with a justifiable satisfaction. The spacious room was panelled in white and pale green lightly outlined with gold. Flowers spilled over from gigantic pedestals or gilded ormolu and tall Chinese vases, trailing strands of ivy and fern. Golden roses and tawny lilies provided touches of brilliant colour.

She walked around moving an ornament here and adjusting a flower there and stood for a moment beside the tall windows opening on to a small town garden where the gardeners had filled stone pots and urns with climbing heliotrope, plumbago and tuberose, with deep red carnations and sweet-smelling mignonette. Later, as the summer evening darkened, lanterns would be lit. In the dining room servants were putting finishing touches to the garlands decorating the tables, checking the candles in the candelabra and carrying in huge silver baskets filled with sweetmeats. She had been determined that her ball would be remembered as the last great event of the season before everyone departed for the country and as she went up the stairs she thought that even Everard's exacting taste would be pleased with the results of her hard work.

Betsy had already set out Christine's ballgown, the flounced petticoats, the silk stockings and satin slippers. It was too early to dress yet so Christine sent her to the kitchen for a cup of tea. On her dressing table lay her uncle's gift, a gold and emerald bracelet that had belonged to her grandmother, and a collarette of diamonds and pearls which her father had handed to her that morning. They were her first really valuable pieces of jewellery and she could not help taking a childish pleasure in them coupled with a tiny feeling of guilt when she remembered the poverty and wretchedness she had seen during the last year. However, if it was all sold and given away it would only be a drop in the ocean so why not enjoy it? As Doctor Dexter had said more than once it was not charity that was needed but a change of heart on the part of those in power. There was one exciting gift that she had never anticipated. Uncle Francis had told her about it that morning.

'It's a secret,' he had said with one of his rare smiles, 'that I've kept faithfully for twenty-one years and which was entrusted to me by your grandmother. She had never forgotten the misery in her youth of arriving from France a penniless refugee and I believe she sensed in you a grandchild who possessed something of her own independent spirit even though you were so young, so a sum of money was set aside to be given to you when you were twenty-one and for your sole use.'

'For me?' she had exclaimed. 'I can't believe it. Does Papa know?'

'Not yet. He will have to be told of course when it is handed over to you, but I thought she would have liked you to know today on your birthday morning.'

She lay on her bed and thought about it. Even now she couldn't quite take it in. She remembered her grandmother as a lovely person, full of fun and warmth, and though she was

197

so young she had sensed between her grandmother and grandfather a close loving relationship that she sometimes thought sadly lacking in her own parents. She did not know how much the legacy was worth but whether a few hundreds or a few thousands it would mean that she had a little income of her own with which she could do whatever she pleased and to someone like Christine who had all her life longed for independence it was a dazzling prospect. But now wasn't the time to plan how she could use it. The house was springing to life. She heard her mother's voice and the sound of servants running up the stairs. Some of their closest friends would be arriving early to take a light meal with them before the ball. She was already up and at the dressing table when Betsy came hurrying in.

'Lady Clarissa is asking for you, Miss. Master Harry has only just come in and you're not yet dressed . . .' she said breathlessly.

'Don't fuss. There's plenty of time. Most of the guests will not be arriving yet.'

In less than an hour she was dressed and took one final look in the long mirror. For almost the first time in her life she felt a flicker of satisfaction in her appearance. The dull gold of the gown gave the creamy skin of her face a warm glow. Her dark hair had been swept up with a cluster of golden roses, a few stray curls escaping round the small ears with their pearl and diamond drops, the collarette round her throat, the heavy bracelet clasped on the slender wrist.

'How do I look?' she said to Betsy who was standing by with the long white gloves and the tiny posy of rosebuds and maidenhair fern.

'Lovely as a dream,' breathed the maid, moved to unaccustomed poetry.

She wondered if Gareth would think so. He would be there with his uncle and she would walk straight into his arms and all those difficult perplexing worries about Daniel would vanish for ever.

On the landing outside she met Harry coming from his bedroom and he paused to look her up and down.

'By Jove, Chris, you look an absolute corker,' he exclaimed.

She laughed. 'Do I? So do you, come to that.'

And together brother and sister went on down the stairs to an evening that was to prove a great deal more memorable than either of them had anticipated.

Much later that same evening, when the ball at Glenmuir House was in full swing, Kate sat in her dressing-room at the Princess Theatre and wished she had not finally given in to Harry's pleadings. As long ago as her little party in April he had asked her if she would sing at his birthday ball and she had laughed at the very idea.

'Your parents would be horrified,' she had said. 'I can just see their faces – a common actress from a music hall standing up and daring to sing among all your grand relations and their friends! Harry darling, I love you for asking me but I couldn't do it. It's impossible.'

But he had gone on asking and refusing to take no for an answer and a certain independent spirit inside her had said why not? She was as good as they were, wasn't she? Why not seize the opportunity? What could they do to her? Listen in well-bred silence? Treat her with freezing contempt? She could face that. So she had at last given in to Harry, telling no one, rehearsing in private and taking care to say nothing to Daniel till the very last minute, knowing he would not approve, in which she was only too right.

'You are asking to be humiliated,' he said frowning, 'standing up there in front of a set of damned stuffed prigs!' but she refused to listen to him, buoyed up by her success in the theatre, by the fact that next month she would be playing a leading part in *The School for Scandal* and that Queen Victoria, who enjoyed a good play, had invited the Company to take one of their productions to Windsor Castle.

But despite all her bold resolution, now that the moment had come she was shaking with nerves. She was tempted to cry off, send word that she had been taken ill and had lost her voice, anything rather than face the critical eyes of the cream of society at Glenmuir House. Only two things sustained her, her own sturdy courage and her strong affection for Harry. She would not let him down.

She stood up, shaking out her skirts. She knew she had no ball gown that would stand comparison with the expensive silks and satins and gauzes of the ladies there tonight so she had gone in for theatrical effect. She had borrowed a costume from the theatre wardrobe in deep rich green with a scarlet sash tied in a huge bow with long ends falling behind her.

She had no jewellery of any value but it pleased her to wear the long jade earrings which Harry had persuaded her to accept. The dark red hair had been coiled into a coronet on the shapely head and the low cut gown with the tiny puffed sleeves showed off her white neck and beautiful shoulders.

The call boy put his head round the door. 'Yer cab's waitin', Miss.'

'Thank you, Bob.' She gave him her special smile that always made him shake at the knees, picked up the black lace shawl and swept down the stairs to the waiting hansom.

By the time she reached the house, the supper interval was over, speeches had been made by Harry's father, by his uncle and by Harry himself, and somewhat belatedly Christine had been included in the congratulations, the twin whose arrival had been so unexpected and, as she sometimes still believed, so unwanted. The guests had begun to return to the ballroom, the orchestra reassembled and Harry's spy, one of the younger footmen, made his way to him.

'The lady's arrived, sir,' he whispered.

'Thank you, Fred. Would you ask her to wait till I join her?'

'Very good, sir.'

The boy slipped quietly away and Harry crossed the ballroom to stand beside the musicians.

'Ladies and gentlemen,' he said, raising his voice, 'a dear friend of mine has consented to sing for us tonight as a special tribute to my sister and myself. I would ask you all to welcome Miss Kate Luce.'

200

There was a surprised silence for a moment as Harry walked towards the door at the end of the room, then everyone seemed to be talking at once.

Everard was frowning. 'What the devil is going on? Do you know about this, Clarissa?'

'No,' said his wife a little apprehensively. 'I do hope she is not entirely unacceptable.'

Gareth leaned closer to Christine. 'Is this one of Harry's famous jokes?' he whispered.

'I'm not sure.'

Things had not gone quite as she had expected with Gareth. For some inexplicable reason there had been a coolness between them as if they could not surmount the long months of separation. But this kind of affair was not conducive to intimate talk. She was sure that tomorrow, alone with him, everything would be different. In the meantime she drew a sharp breath as she saw Kate walking through the room on Harry's arm, her head held high, a glittering comb in the dark red hair catching the light. She saw her father start forward as if he would have said something and then sit back at a gesture from his wife, his eyes fixed on Kate.

There was someone else who also took particular notice. Ray Dorrien had been standing talking idly with a group of friends.

'My God,' he exclaimed, his eyes narrowing, 'so it's young Harry now, is it, the scheming little bitch!'

Clara looked up at him curiously. 'What do you mean? Who is she?'

'Never you mind,' he said, his mouth hardening. 'He's not going to get away with it, not this time, not if I can help it.'

If Harry's Uncle Francis had been taken by surprise, no one would have guessed it. He took Kate's hand and kissed it with a few words of greeting and led her to a suitable place in front of the orchestra, who had obviously been well primed by Harry.

If Kate was nervous, it was not apparent. She had known at a glance that she should not have come, that among this well-dressed company she stood out like some gaudy bird among a host of elegant doves, but she knew her talent and her limitations. She did not venture on operatic arias but sang what she knew best: the lyrics, the ballads that suited the tender and poignant quality of her voice. She had chosen her programme wisely, selecting one or two Shakespearian songs to start with, singing of

> 'What is love? 'Tis not hereafter
> Present mirth and present laughter . . .'

followed by the poignancy of,

> 'Golden lads and girls all must
> Like chimney sweepers come to dust . . .'

and with a teasing look around her,

> 'Men were deceivers ever
> One foot in sea and one on shore
> To one thing constant never . . .'

Then as the applause mounted and they asked for more she turned to the sweet melancholy of 'Barbara Allen' who died for love, to the tenderness of Tom Moore's 'The Last Rose of Summer' and the nostalgia of 'The Harp that dwelled in Tara's Halls'.

There was genteel clapping from the ladies, who thought her gown too farouche for words but were forced to acknowledge the quality of her voice, and hearty applause from the men, young and old, who surged forward calling for encore after encore as she sank to the floor in the graceful curtsey hammered into her by Mrs Kean.

Harry whispered 'Just one more, Kate,' and a little devil danced in her eyes. She turned to say something to the leader of the orchestra who nodded and both of them broke into the rollicking resounding song of the sea that had been a concert hall favourite for the last hundred years.

The chorus rolled around the room and was taken up by the younger gentlemen with a foot-tapping rhythm. She gave it all she had and at the end if the dowagers frowned behind their fans and some of the ladies contrived to look shocked, the applause was long and enthusiastic.

Then it was all over. She had tossed them kisses from her fingertips, had curtsied and waved them goodbye. Harry was urging her to stay and spend the rest of the evening with them but she shook her head.

'No, Harry, no, I don't belong here. I came only to please you and now I must go.'

The orchestra started to play as she moved to the door, talk broke out again and guests moved on to the floor. It was then that Christine saw her father get to his feet. He pushed aside his wife's detaining hand and went after them. With a feeling of apprehension she followed him. Gareth tried to hold her back but she jerked herself free and with a shrug he went after her.

By the time she reached the front hall the door had been opened and the light streamed out into the street. Kate was standing on the front steps while Harry put the shawl around her shoulders. Christine saw her father, usually so restrained, so conscious of his dignity, put his hand on Kate's arm and swing her to face him.

'What the devil do you mean by this absurd masquerade? Your name is not Luce, has never been Luce.'

'No, it is Hunter as I think you very well know, Mr Warrinder,' she said calmly. 'I am not ashamed of it.'

'How dare you force your way into my house in this vulgar manner?'

'I am here at your son's invitation.'

'Father please . . .' interrupted Harry angrily.

'Stand aside, boy. I'll deal with you later. You persuaded him to bring you here, didn't you?' He had her by both shoulders now and was staring down into her face. 'What does he mean to you? What is your relationship with my son? Are you his mistress?' And when she did not reply he went on furiously, 'Answer me, damn you!'

'I'm not in court nor am I on oath, Mr Warrinder, so I can refuse to answer,' she said coolly. 'May I go please? My brother will be waiting for me.'

Baffled, Everard let fall his hands and she gathered the shawl around her and moved down the steps. Harry would have gone with her but she gestured him back and went on to where Daniel stood by the waiting cab. Impetuously Christine flew down the steps after her, putting her arms round Kate's neck and kissing her cheek. For a few moments the two girls stared at one another then Kate murmured something and turned to climb into the cab.

'I'm sorry, Daniel. I would not have had this happen for anything,' whispered Christine. 'I'm so terribly sorry.'

He looked at her for a second lit by the street lamp into a dazzling vision of gold, jewels glittering in her ears and round her neck, and in that instant she seemed the very embodiment of all that was most alien to him, all that he was fighting against, utterly unattainable, completely out of his reach, and it filled him with a dumb cold fury. He turned his back on her and stepped into the cab to sit beside his sister.

Christine watched it pull away and then went slowly back up the steps. By this time her Uncle Francis had appeared in the doorway.

He said crisply, 'I haven't a notion what all this is about but I would remind you, Everard, and you too, Harry, that you have guests waiting for you.'

'Yes, of course,' said his brother-in-law. 'I'm sorry. We had better go in.'

'Before you go, Father,' said Harry, 'I want to know why you have chosen to insult my guest so outrageously.'

'I had my reasons but your uncle is right, now is not the time. I will speak with you tomorrow.'

He walked away and into the ballroom and after a frustrating moment Harry followed him.

'I can't imagine what all this commotion is about,' said Gareth, putting his arm around Christine. 'What on earth has Harry been up to? You must let me into the secret. Who are this brother and sister and what has upset your father? The young man's face is familiar but I can't place it.'

'It's a long story,' said Christine wearily. 'I'll tell you about it tomorrow.'

She felt a sudden revulsion against the whole affair and the alarming realization that there could be something deeper than she had believed between Harry and Kate. Was it that which had made her father behave in such an extraordinary manner or was it something even more serious? Above all there had been the devastating knowledge that despite all the days of friendship an impassable gulf still seemed to yawn between her and Daniel.

The music flowed out of the ballroom as they mounted the steps together.

'They are playing a Viennese waltz,' said Gareth, 'do you remember? We danced to it that night down at Brighton last summer.'

The night she had pledged herself to him and that now seemed so far away, almost in another life. He took her hand and they glided together among the dancers. There would have to be a reckoning. She knew her father well enough to be sure of that but she could brace herself to face it in the morning. For the moment she was back in her own world with Gareth, no more doubts, no more worries. She closed her eyes wearily and relaxed against him.

In the cab Daniel said, 'I told you what would happen. Why did you have to go there? Why did you have to make such an exhibition of yourself?'

'Oh for God's sake,' exclaimed Kate, 'I had given Harry my promise, I couldn't go back on it.' She turned away from him, tears sparkling in her eyes, tears of hurt and also of anger. 'You don't understand. It all went so well at first. They enjoyed it, I know they did. Do you think I can't sense an audience's reaction by now? And I did not stay though they urged me, Harry and his uncle, the Earl. I know my place. I was not a guest, simply an entertainer, so why did his father have to attack me in such a savage way?'

'He is afraid Harry may like you far too much.' Daniel's

205

voice hardened. 'I noticed you didn't answer him. Is Harry your lover?'

'No, he is not,' she said angrily, 'and even if he were, it would be my concern, not yours.'

'That's where you're wrong, Kate. It would be very much my concern.' He turned her round to face him as the cab jerked over the cobbles. 'Has he spoken of marriage?'

'He's only a boy still. He says a lot of foolish things,' she said, pulling away from him.

'It could never be, must never be. You do realize that, don't you, Kate?'

'Why?' she said stubbornly. 'Is it because my father was a working-class rabble-rouser and Harry's father is landed gentry? Actresses have married belted earls before now.'

'But not you, Kate, never you and Harry Warrinder.'

She stared at him in the shadowy darkness of the cab. 'There's something more, isn't there, more than the prosecution that hanged my father? There's some dark secret that you know and I don't. Isn't it about time you told me what it is?'

'Perhaps. I don't know . . .' It was locked inside him, never once spoken of to anyone, and while he hesitated unable to make up his mind, the cab came to a jerking halt, slipping on the greasy cobbles of Vyner Street.

He helped his sister out, groping in his pocket for the fare and a few pence for a tip.

'Are you coming up?' she asked as the cabby touched his cap and drove away.

'Not tonight. You're tired and it's back to work tomorrow.'

'That's true,' she grimaced, 'and this dress must go back to the theatre wardrobe before Mrs Kean finds out. It's served its turn. You mustn't worry too much, Dan, about Harry and me. As soon as the royal visit is over, it's pack our bags and off on tour till the Christmas season. By then anything could have happened.'

'Kate, I'm sorry.' He put his arm around her and drew her close. 'I want everything good for you, you know I do.' He kissed her cheek and she leaned against him for a moment.

'I tell you who was there tonight and looking daggers at me – Raymond Dorrien. He's engaged, did you know? Harry told me. His bride-to-be was there with him and if looks could kill, I'd be lying dead by now.' She gave a tired giggle. 'I think I've finished with him at last, thank goodness.'

'You take care. His kind have long memories.'

'She looked as if she'd keep him safely under lock and key.'

She gave her brother a little hug and went up the steps and into the house.

Daniel stood for a moment and then walked away, thankful that for the time being he had escaped telling her what weighed upon him and yet knowing that the moment would inevitably come – probably very soon.

Chapter 11

When the last carriage had rolled away soon after three o'clock there was more than one spending the night at Glenmuir House who found it difficult to sleep. Christine lay wakeful for a long time, knowing only too well that her father would question her obvious involvement with the brother and sister and determined to maintain her independence at all costs. Harry, his first flame of anger burnt out, was still determined to demand an explanation and at the same time was very conscious of the fact that he admired and respected his father and was also a little afraid of him, while Everard himself, usually in command of every situation, had to suffer a sharp reprimand from his wife.

When he came in from his dressing room she was already sitting up in the huge old-fashioned bed wearing a most becoming night cap of lace and satin ribbons that made her look far more like the girl he had married than the mature matron who had borne him three children.

She attacked at once.

'Francis is extremely annoyed with you, Everard, and I really can't blame him. How could you cause all that commotion in the hall with the servants standing around gaping at you, no doubt all ears? The sorry tale will be all over town before the day is out. Thank heaven the door was closed and only very few of our guests would have noticed the disturbance. I only knew of it myself when Francis told me. It really is too bad of you when everything was going so well. It's a miracle the whole evening wasn't completely ruined.

Whatever possessed you to do such a thing? It's so unlike you.'

'I was not willing to see Harry caught up in the toils of some scheming slut of an actress,' he muttered.

'I must say that in all fairness she didn't strike me like that at all,' went on his wife. 'I admit I was nervous at first and her dress of course was quite impossible but she had style and poise, the voice was well trained, and she behaved very suitably. It could have been a great deal worse.'

'Would you be prepared to receive her as your daughter-in-law?'

Clarissa looked at him startled. 'Now you're being ridiculous. Surely there's no question of that. Harry is very young still. He must have his fling like the other young men. It's harmless enough. If I remember rightly you sowed some wild oats yourself before we were married.'

'If I did, that has nothing to do with Harry.'

'Then why on earth treat the girl as if she were . . . were a . . . well, no better than she should be.'

'Why, why, why?' exclaimed Everard explosively. 'For God's sake, Clarissa, stop asking damn-fool questions. I'm not on trial.' Then he stopped at the sight of her shocked face. 'I'm sorry, my dear, I didn't mean to lose my temper. It's been a long day and we're both tired. I have certain plans for Harry and I shall speak to him about them in the morning. Shall we leave it at that?'

'Harry shouldn't have invited her without consulting us first of course,' went on Clarissa after a moment, 'but since he did, we can be thankful that it went off as well as it did.'

'Yes, I suppose so,' he said wearily, slipping off his dressing gown and getting into bed beside her.

'You won't be too hard on Harry, will you?' she whispered.

'That'll depend on him,' he said grimly. 'I shall have something to say to Christine too. She's been running wild ever since you spent those weeks with Margaret. What she needs is a husband to bring her to order.'

'Oh Christine,' sighed his wife. 'She has always been so difficult, sometimes I despair. She looked very pretty this evening, almost beautiful, and she received a great deal of attention but did she respond to it as any other young girl would? Oh no, she had eyes only for Gareth.'

'She could do worse,' said Everard shortly. 'Gareth has a lot of good sense. Try to get some rest, my dear. Do you realize it's close on four o'clock?' He leaned over and kissed her gently. 'You did very well, Clarissa. I was proud of you.'

She settled against him in the old familiar comfortable position, already drowsy, worn out by the anxieties of the stressful day, but he lay long awake, looking back into a past that he had always resolutely put behind him and which had now leaped into dangerous life at the worst possible time and could, if he were not very careful, not only wreck his peace of mind but his whole future.

The next morning Harry braced himself for an explosive argument with his father and found that it did not work out like that at all. To start with everyone was up late and inclined to be tetchy and out of sorts. After luncheon the Warrinders all returned to Belgrave Square, taking Aunt Grace with them, Uncle Francis's wife, who was longing to see Margaret's John Everard who had been left there in the care of his nurse. Harry exchanged harassed glances with Christine, both of them expecting the skies to fall on them at any moment and suffering from anti-climax when nothing happened. He was in his bedroom gloomily looking over the innumerable gifts which had poured in on him for his birthday and it was a relief to hear Barton's knock and be summoned to his father's study. He pulled himself together, marching down to brave the storm, and immediately had the wind taken out of his sails.

'Ah there you are,' said his father pleasantly, 'come in, my boy, and sit down. The house is at sixes and sevens today and we're all suffering from it, I'm afraid. Shall I ask Barton to bring us some tea?'

'Not for me, thank you, Father.'

'Right. Well then, let's get down to business.' He sat down at his desk and smiled at his son. 'For some time now I have been making some plans for your future and now seems the right time to discuss them with you.'

'Plans?' repeated Harry doubtfully.

'Yes,' went on his father briskly. 'I've kept my eye on you this past year since you came down from Oxford and have discussed your future with my colleagues in chambers. I think what you need is a broader experience of life and of course of the law. I am therefore arranging for you to spend a year in Paris, taking a course at the Sorbonne. It will give you wider knowledge, improve your French and I hope prove very enjoyable. I know that when your grandfather packed me off there at much the same age as you are now, I was only too delighted.'

'Paris?' said Harry, still not quite able to take it in. Despite all kinds of misgivings it was an alluring prospect. 'Do you really mean that I'm to spend a year in Paris?'

'Yes. You can stay with some friends of mine for the first month or so till you find your feet. After Paris we might consider some months in Leipzig perhaps. Does the idea appeal to you? It should. Some of your friends working with you in the Temple would give a great deal for the same opportunity.'

'Do you mean I shall be living there free to do as I wish?'

'Certainly within reason and you won't be cut off from us, you know. You'll be coming back to see your sisters and your mother, from time to time. In fact we may take a short break ourselves. There is nothing the girls like better than an opportunity to ruin me in the Palais Royal or the Champs Elysées. What do you say? Do you like the idea?'

'Yes, yes of course, it's wonderful. I never expected anything like this.'

'Good. Later on we'll settle down to discuss the details.'

'I'd like that, but before we do, there *is* something else . . . Father . . . about last night . . .'

'Ah yes. I think perhaps I owe you and the young lady an apology. I was misinformed, I'm afraid, about this young person whom you invited to sing for us. You really should have told your mother and me beforehand, you know, and your Uncle Francis,' said his father reprovingly.

'I know, I know, but at first she wouldn't consent . . . and afterwards . . .'

'You thought we might have raised objections. She is an acquaintance of yours and of Christine too, I take it.'

'Oh more than that,' burst out Harry enthusiastically, 'a very great deal more. She is a wonderful girl. I've never met anyone like her, so talented, and . . . so brave to get where she has with no advantages, nothing to help her.'

'Yes, yes, no doubt,' said his father a little impatiently, 'and naturally you have wanted to befriend her.'

'Yes, I have but it's more than that. I love her, Father . . . I hope, I very much hope that one day she will become my wife.'

For a moment Everard was silent, uncertain how to counter this absurd statement. To forbid it would very likely throw the boy headlong into her arms. He said gently, 'Do you indeed, and have you informed her of your intention?'

'Oh yes, more than once.'

'And what does she say?'

'She laughs at me,' said Harry honestly. 'She tells me I'm too young to think of such things and she has her career which is very important to her. Sometimes I believe she thinks far more of that than of me,' he added ruefully.

'I'm glad to hear that the young lady has so much good sense,' said his father drily.

'But I'll not accept no for an answer,' went on Harry. 'I'll wait and wait and one day I will persuade her, however long it takes.'

'I've no doubt you will try. At your age it's natural to have such dreams. The sad thing is that they are only very rarely realized.'

Harry frowned. 'You're not forbidding me to see her, are you?'

'Would it do any good if I did? No, you can tell her what we are planning for you and if she is as fond of you as you believe, she will be glad for you.'

'Oh she will, she will. She is interested in what I do. We talk about it sometimes. Thank you, Father, and thank you for suggesting Paris.'

'Yes, well, the best way to thank me is to start brushing up your French and getting ready to leave some time in August.'

'I will, I promise I will,' and Harry went away thankful at having got off so easily and with the surprising promise of a year's freedom in Paris into the bargain.

When he had gone Everard still sat at his desk staring in front of him hoping to God he had done the right thing. If he had been harsh, if he had forbidden Harry to see or speak with her again, he could have precipitated the very thing he most dreaded. Harry was twenty-one. He could have rushed into some crazy marriage and if what he believed was true that must never be, never, never! He got up and moved restlessly around the room. Somehow he must kill this unlikely friendship which had arisen between his children and this brother and sister, must kill it now before it did more harm and that meant not only Harry but Christine too. It had all begun when he allowed her to work at that damned clinic. Well, he could put a stop to that at least.

He rang the bell and when Barton appeared said brusquely, 'If Miss Christine is about, ask her to come here, will you? Then you can bring us a tray of tea.'

'Very good, sir.'

Christine didn't hurry to obey the summons. She delayed for a few minutes fiddling nervously with her hair and tidying her dress of flowered cotton. Her father detested sloppiness. When she ultimately knocked and went in he was standing with his back to her running his eye along the bookshelves at the far end of the room.

'You wanted to see me, Papa?'

'Yes, my dear, come in and sit down.'

She perched on the edge of a chair and watched him pull out a book or two and then replace them.

'Do you know what happened to a book by that fellow

Disraeli? It was called *Sybil* if I remember rightly. I am certain I ordered it.'

It was the last one she had lent to Daniel, a brilliant study of social inequalities which she knew would appeal to him and it had not yet been returned.

'I think I have it,' she said after a moment. 'I began to read it but of course if you want it . . .'

'No hurry. Finish it first, then you can bring it to Bramber. It will serve as good holiday reading.'

'Are we going to Bramber?'

'Certainly, just as soon as we can get away. Your Uncle Francis would like us to return with him to Scotland but with the election coming up, I shall have to spend time in the constituency and it's not worth making such a long journey for only two or three weeks. I think we shall all be glad to be free of London for a while.' He turned round as the door opened. 'Ah, here's Barton with our tea. Good.'

The butler placed the loaded tray on a small table beside Christine together with a silver basket of small cakes on a stand at her elbow.

'Is there anything more you require, Miss?'

'No, thank you, Barton. I'll pour the tea.'

'Very good, Miss.'

He went out, closing the door and Everard pulled up a chair and sat the other side of the table.

'Would you like your tea now, Papa?'

'Please.'

She took pains to pour it exactly as he preferred it, with very little milk and no sugar.

'What is it you want to see me about, Papa?' she asked, sipping her own tea nervously.

He drained the cup, put it down and then said abruptly, 'Was it you who introduced this young woman, this Kate Hunter, to Harry?'

Startled, she said quickly, 'No, it wasn't. I think it was Ray Dorrien. He had heard her sing and he took Harry to the hall where she was performing before she joined Mr Kean's company.'

'And like the young fool he is, he immediately believes himself in love with her. Well, I think I've settled that. Harry will go to Paris in August for a year's hard work. That should bring him to his senses.'

'Will he like that?'

'He'll learn to like it.' He got up and walked across to his desk and then turned suddenly to face her. 'As for you, Christine, I would prefer that you give up your work at that medical clinic.'

'But why, Papa, why?' she burst out. 'I like working there and by now I have learned to be really useful. Dr Dexter is pleased with me. I feel at last that I'm doing something worthwhile, something I've always wanted to do. Why must I give it up? Why?'

'Very soon now I shall be spending a good deal of time down there. Elections can be rough and I'm not expecting it to be easy. I would prefer my daughter not to be mixed up in it in any way.'

'But I wouldn't be. The clinic is not concerned with politics. Its purpose is only to help the sick and the poor and those who desperately need the little we can give them. Most of them have no idea who I am. I'm not Miss Warrinder down there, not your daughter, but just Miss Christine who assists the doctor and hands out medicines and food and clothes.'

'Maybe that's what you think but it doesn't work like that. Daniel Hunter knows who you are, he *and* his sister, and when the time comes he won't scruple to make use of you. He calls himself a radical. He is also connected with the Communist League and he will use every means in his power to damage my campaign.'

'I don't believe you. How do you know so much about him?'

'There are certain people down there who are already working in my interest.'

'Daniel wouldn't do anything like that. I know he wouldn't. He promised me.'

'Promised you?' He frowned down at her. 'What does this young man mean to you, Christine?'

'He's a friend, just a friend,' she said desperately. 'He came to the clinic one day bringing a small boy from his school who had been seriously injured. I was sorry for the child. I took an interest in him just as Daniel did. We talked together sometimes. He has so little and he works so hard. I wanted to help him, that's all.'

'He saw the chance to ingratiate himself with my daughter and he took it.'

'No, Papa, no, you're wrong. It was not like that at all. What have you against him and his sister? What have they ever done to you?' He made an impatient gesture but she swept on. 'Don't deny it. I've seen it whenever they have been mentioned from that very first time when they were in the crowd watching Margaret's wedding.'

'This is all nonsense . . .'

'No, it isn't. I've always known there was something. Is it because his father was hanged at Newgate that you're so bitterly against him?'

He swung round on her. 'How do you know that? Did he tell you?'

She had not meant to say it but now she had and must make the best of it.

'I don't think he really meant to say it at all,' she said slowly. 'It was one evening when he walked part of the way home with me. We came up to the prison and it was as if it burst out of him. He said he was a child when he saw his father die there. That was all. It was as if it were something deeply private and I couldn't question, I couldn't ask why. It must be nearly twenty years ago now. Do you know about that?'

'I know something. And I think because of it he has a deep grudge against anyone or anything connected with the law.'

'And you think that means you?'

'Perhaps. In any case it is a most unsuitable friendship and I am to blame for allowing it to happen. I should have foreseen something like this but I was preoccupied with a difficult case and your mother was away with Margaret.'

'Why is it so unsuitable?' she said passionately. 'Because he is not of our class – how I hate that word! Because his mother died in some terrible mill accident and he and his sister were thrown into separate orphanages and left to find their own way out into some kind of life. Is that the reason?'

'Not entirely.'

'If it is, then it isn't fair, it isn't just.'

'Life is very seldom fair or just as you will find out,' he said drily, 'and in the meantime I must insist that you do not see Daniel Hunter again.'

She stared at him for a moment and then said slowly, 'I will go with you and Mamma to Bramber if that is what you wish but I will not give up the clinic and I will not promise not to see Daniel again. You can't stop me, Papa, unless you lock me up and if you do, I'll find my way out somehow and leave home. I can make my own way. I can take care of myself.'

'So your uncle has already told you of this legacy, has he? I warned him it would lead to trouble. Why must you be so difficult, Christine?' he said in sudden exasperation. 'Why have you fought me all your life?'

She stared at him for a moment before she said, 'You and Mamma never really wanted me, did you? Harry was the important one. I was the troublesome late-comer.'

'You must not think that, Christine. It's not true . . .'

'Oh yes it is,' she went on steadily. 'I've lived with it ever since I was old enough to understand and I had to fight for some kind of independence otherwise I would have been nothing but I've never won, have I, never once, not till now.' She paused for an instant, aware for the first time of something vulnerable about him, a chink in the armour of his reserve, and she went on impulsively. 'I don't want to fight you, Papa, I don't want to do anything to harm you. I will do battle for you in this coming election if you will allow me. I'd like to come with you when you make your speeches down there.'

'What a strange child you are.' He smiled wryly. 'We shall have to see about that, won't we? In the meantime perhaps Gareth will change your mind for you. He came to me yesterday and he is coming to see you tomorrow. He would have dined with us tonight but his uncle is not well and he feels he should stay with him. He has asked if your engagement can now be made public and I have given my consent. I hope that pleases you at least.'

'He didn't say anything to me last night.'

'He will. You can be sure of that.'

'Thank you, Papa.' She hesitated and then went to him, reaching up to kiss his cheek. 'I was going to ask you myself but Gareth has done it for both of us.'

'Perhaps he will be more successful than I have been in keeping his wild bird safely eating out of his hand.'

'It's not like that at all,' she said earnestly. 'Gareth and I understand one another. May I go now?'

'Perhaps you should. It's nearly time to dress for dinner and your mother doesn't like to be kept waiting.'

'No, she doesn't, does she?' She gave him a quick smile and went out but he sat on, possessed by a weary feeling of defeat.

He who had never failed to bring difficult witnesses to book, whose cross-examination in court was the admiration of his colleagues, could not persuade, let alone control, his own daughter. How much did Daniel Hunter know and would he use it? He had no proof but dirt has a habit of sticking, proved or unproved. His election agent had suggested there were ways of getting rid of troublesome opponents – some trumped-up charge, a threat of imprisonment – but a scrupulous conscience would not allow him to use such methods. He must take his chance.

Barton came in to fetch the tea tray and said respectfully, 'Madam has asked me to remind you that the dressing gong has gone, sir.'

'Yes, I know. I'm coming now.'

He followed the butler out of the room and went up the stairs wondering what Clarissa would feel if she knew the truth. To her he had always been the perfect knight *sans peur et sans reproche.* He hoped for her sake she would never have to suffer the disillusionment.

*
218

Kew Gardens on a warm afternoon in late July was surely the ideal spot for lovers to plight their troth and Gareth certainly seemed to think so. He came early in his uncle's dashing carriage and carried Christine off from Belgrave Square, which was still full of relatives.

'I've a great deal to tell you, Chris, and I want you to myself,' he said firmly.

He wouldn't even allow her time to change her dress. She only had a moment to tie on a shady hat, fling a silk shawl around her shoulders and they were off. Once there he dismissed the carriage, told his uncle's coachman to return in a couple of hours and they went together into the gardens talking of everything under the sun except what was in both of their minds. There were families with children picnicking under the trees, couples strolling like themselves and in the giant hothouses elderly horticulturists were peering through eyeglasses at weird tropical plants and making copious notes.

She told him something, not too much, about Daniel and Kate and he shook his head judiciously over it.

'Of course Harry should never have gone ahead without asking your parents' permission but I must say I have never known your father to fly out as he did that night.'

'No,' she said with a worried frown, 'neither have I, but then he doesn't know Kate as Harry and I do.'

'Nor Daniel either, it would seem,' he said, looking at her quizzically. 'What part does that young man play in this drama?'

'Oh don't let's talk about them,' she said impatiently. 'I want to talk about us and for heaven's sake let's get out of this furnace. I shall expire at any minute if we don't, or one of those green monsters will bend down and gobble me up.'

Gareth laughed and took her arm. 'Not while I'm here, it won't.'

Outside the air was fresh and the gardens blazed with lilies, white, cream and tawny, heavy with fragrance. They walked on leaving the scattering of visitors behind them until they came under the shadow of the Pagoda rearing its unlikely

Eastern tower to the sky. White-painted seats were placed here and there and she sank down on one of them, untying the ribbons of her straw hat and fanning herself with it.

'That's better,' she breathed. 'Now what is it you were going to tell me?'

'First and foremost, I haven't yet given you your birthday gift. I kept it till now.' He felt in his inner pocket and produced a small leather box. He opened it, took out the ring, pulled the thin glove from her left hand and slipped it on to her third finger. 'Did your father tell you?'

'Yes, he did. He said he has agreed that we should be properly engaged.'

She stared down at her finger. It was a very pretty and costly ring, a sapphire surrounded with tiny diamonds, and with a little pang she thought of the small box in worn silver that still lay on the table beside her bed.

'How did you know it would fit?'

'I consulted Margaret.'

Six months ago she would have been speechless with pleasure, wild with delight. She would have childishly thrown her arms around his neck and kissed him. But they had been so long apart, so much seemed to have happened, now everything was different. He was watching her anxiously and in a sudden revulsion of feeling, a longing to reach back to the old hero worship, she almost hurled herself against him clinging to him, tears sparkling in her eyes.

He stroked her hair. 'What is it, darling? What's wrong?'

'Nothing, nothing at all. I'm just so happy.'

He tilted up her chin to look at him, not entirely satisfied.

'Christine, you are really happy about this aren't you? You have not had second thoughts.'

'No, no, of course I haven't.'

'You had me worried for a moment.'

He was holding her close against him, his mouth crushing down on hers with more real passion than he had ever shown before and she thought, of course I'm happy. It's what I've always wanted. Dear Gareth. I'm loved, protected, safe.

He held her very close for a few minutes and then released her.

'Now we must talk seriously about the future.'

'Is there all that hurry?' She leaned back. 'You're coming to Bramber with us, aren't you?'

'No, not this year. I'm afraid I can't.'

It was the first setback, the first warning that maybe everything was not all that it should be.

'Why? You've always come before.'

'It's Uncle David. His health is really far worse than he believes. He is suffering from a particularly vicious form of gout. He is in constant pain and is to take a course of treatment at one of the German spas and I can't let him go alone. You do understand, don't you?'

'Yes, yes, of course I do. I didn't realize . . .'

'He never fusses about himself but being away for some months I have noticed the difference in him.'

Uncle David had always held a special place in her affections. 'He is not going to die, is he?' she asked, looking at him in concern.

'I think the treatment, with me to care for him, will make all the difference and when it is over, in the autumn,' his face lit up, 'this is the really thrilling part. I have had the most wonderful offer. You remember Dr Andrews? We met him last year at the Exhibition. Well, he is still in the United States and he has invited me to join him for six months working on a special project. It's the most tremendous opportunity and when I come back in the spring we can be married because I shall be going to Bart's as one of their doctors on call and shall set up in practice.'

'But that's months and months away. Oh Gareth, I can't bear it. Can't we be married before you go? Can't I go to America with you?'

'It's not possible, dearest. We can't marry in a rush like that. Your mother will have set her heart on a grand wedding like Margaret had.'

'I don't care about that.'

'But she does. You wouldn't want to break her heart, would you? Besides I shall be working in the university. It is all men there, no place for a woman, even a wife. You would be isolated, completely on your own.'

'I wouldn't mind that.'

'But I would for you. It wouldn't be right.'

'Couldn't I take some course, do something useful?'

'There is nothing suitable.'

'It's always the same. There's nothing for women, only for men,' she said passionately. 'Do you know I was the top student in that pharmacy course? I had the highest marks of anyone but no one cared a button about it. I wouldn't be allowed to prescribe a remedy for a headache! Must you accept this offer?'

'But Christine, it's the opportunity of a lifetime. I'd be crazy to turn it down. My colleagues in Edinburgh are already green with envy.'

'There is always something,' she said angrily. 'First it was Scotland, then Uncle David and now America. It all means so much more to you than I do.'

She got up and walked quickly away from him but he came hurrying after her.

'Darling, you must listen to me. You've always known what my work means to me. You've always understood. Why have you changed so much?'

Because there is someone else who all the time you are away will be tantalisingly within my reach, because I'm afraid of falling in love with him and I know nothing can come of it. There were so many reasons but she couldn't tell him any of them so instead she waited for him to catch up with her.

'I'm sorry,' she said colourlessly, 'It's just that I'd set my heart on us being together and now it is all spoiled. Tell me about this wonderful work that you are going to undertake with Dr Andrews.'

So he went into details of the new experiments, new treatments, use of new drugs, changes in conditions they hoped to initiate, and she listened. She only understood about one word in ten but it did bring them closer together, except that the joy and gaiety and wonder of the afternoon had entirely fled.

A few days later Daniel came through the yard after school was over carrying the three volumes of Disraeli's *Sybil* with the intention of leaving them at the clinic for Christine. Ever since the night of the ball he had been going through a small private hell. A cherished dream had been brutally smashed. He had always known it could not last so why did it hurt so much, he raged to himself. Seeing her run down the steps that night in her golden dress, Gareth behind her supremely confident, sure of himself and of her, two beings from another world, had made him realize how deep the gulf was between them and yet he still could not quite forget the stricken look on her face when he had thrust her aside and turned his back on her.

He did not go into the clinic by the patients' door but knocked at the nearby house. Deborah opened the door to him and he held out the books.

'I would like to leave these for Miss Warrinder.'

'She is here today. Wouldn't you prefer to give them to her yourself? I'll call her.'

'No, no, please. I'd rather not . . .'

But Deborah, who hid a romantic heart under her plain grey dress and had a secret liking for the young man who was so different from most of the poor creatures who came begging for help, had already disappeared down the passage that linked them with the clinic.

He was greatly tempted to put the books down and run but a certain stubbornness of spirit kept him there with a sneaking desire to see her again.

True to her resolve Christine had defied her father's disapproval and had insisted on going to the clinic as usual, greatly strengthened by Gareth who was seeing as much of her as he could before he took his uncle abroad.

'I'll come with you,' he had said that morning. 'I'd like to see for myself what you and John Dexter get up to down there.'

In fact the two men, one so blunt, practical and plain speaking and the other so brilliantly clever, stuffed with theoretical knowledge but as yet without the common touch essential for work of this kind, got on splendidly together – so much so that Gareth took off his jacket, rolled up his shirt sleeves and offered to help with the long line of miserable patients suffering from a great variety of ailments in the stifling city summer. When Deborah looked in they were both absorbed in discussing suitable treatment for a particularly distressing skin rash and Christine gave them a quick look and crossed to her.

'What is it?' she whispered.

'It's that young man, you know, the teacher. He has some books he wants to return to you.'

'All right. I don't think I shall be missed for a few minutes. I'll come.'

She pulled off the silk scarf with which she covered her hair, untied her apron and followed Deborah along the passage. Daniel was still there just inside the door.

'I didn't want to trouble you,' he said stiffly. 'I just wanted to return the books you lent me.'

'Good,' she said with a smile. 'Actually Papa has been asking for *Sybil* and I was at my wits' end to think up a convincing lie.'

'Well, you needn't lie for me any longer,' he said and put the books into her hands. 'And now I must go.'

'No, please, not for a moment. I want to speak to you.' She put the books down on the chair by the wall and he saw the ring on her finger blaze for a second, caught in a ray of light through the open door. 'Not here,' she went on quickly. 'I'll walk a little way with you.'

'If you wish,' he said and went on down the steps.

Just beyond the tall ugly building that housed the refuge house and the clinic there was a tiny courtyard leading to an ancient church that lay back from the main road. A tree set in the middle lifted wilting foliage grey with dust in the long summer heat. It was there that Daniel turned to face her.

'Well,' he said, 'what do you want to say?'

'Why are you so unfriendly?'

'Why, why, why,' he said impatiently. 'Surely you know why.'

'Is it because of what my father said to Kate that night? I know it was unforgiveable but he didn't understand. He's not usually like that. He thought he was protecting Harry but he was wrong. He feels differently now.'

'Why should he, when he was absolutely right. I told Kate months ago that she must not encourage Harry. If she had listened to me she would never have gone there that night. There can never be anything between Harry and my sister just as there can never be any real friendship between you and me.'

'Why?' she said passionately. 'Why? You are as full of prejudice as my father is. It's people that matter, their hopes and dreams, not whether they are rich or poor, privileged or having to fight their way to what they want to be. I believed that you and I had risen above all those silly rules of class.'

'I thought so too for a while but I was wrong, hopelessly wrong,' he said bleakly. 'There is far too much that splits us apart. You stand there with your lover's ring on your finger and talk to me of friendship! Did you tell him about us and did you laugh together at the poor fool reaching out of the gutter for the stars? I don't want your patronage and I can't accept your friendship.'

'But why, Daniel?' she said again imploringly. 'We have shared so much these last months. Hasn't it meant anything to you?'

'It's meant too damned much. It's blinded me to the truth.' For a moment he stared at her, then quite deliberately he took her by the shoulders and kissed her so savagely that it took her breath away and she staggered back against the tree. He held her pinned there, his face only a few inches from her own.

'That's one of the reasons,' he said hoarsely. 'The other you will find out soon enough. Now go away and marry your doctor and forget the poor idiot who once crossed your path.'

He released her and walked away out into the crowded street already filling up with men and women returning from work and with children joyously released from school and darting recklessly under the horses' hooves, while she still stood there, her hand at her bruised mouth, shaken to the very depths of her being. Then very slowly she pulled herself together and went back into the clinic.

'Ah there you are,' said Gareth, 'we wondered what had become of you.'

'Someone wanted to speak to me.'

'We're just closing down,' said Dr Dexter. 'Thanks to your Gareth, I've got through quicker than usual. You're welcome down here any time, old boy.'

'I'll remember that. It's been an eye-opener. When I'm back from the States and Christine and I are married, I'd like to explore the possibilities further.'

'Your wife may have something to say about that,' said John Dexter drily.

'Don't you believe it! Christine is the one who'll keep me up to it. Isn't that so, my pet?'

He took her home then, too pleased with himself to notice how quiet she was. He refused to stay and dine with them as he and his uncle must make an early start for the Continent in the morning. When they parted Christine flung her arms around him.

'Do think about taking me with you when you go to America,' she said in an urgent whisper. 'Please, please, Gareth, let me go with you.'

'We've been over all that, darling. I wish I could. I'd pack you into my medical bag if I could but it really isn't possible. It won't seem so long, only a few months. I'll write, I promise, all the time.'

'Yes, of course,' she said dully, 'it's all right. I understand. We must make do with letters.'

There was one more curious repercussion from the birthday ball. Only a few days afterwards Ray Dorrien and Harry unexpectedly found themselves together at the stage door of the Princess Theatre and more or less had it shut in their faces. They both protested loudly but the stage doorkeeper was adamant.

'Now then, now then, gents,' he said. 'Miss Luce ain't seein' nobody, orders from above as you might say and you wouldn't want to cause her any trouble now, would you? They're rehearsin' every blessed minute for that there royal command and Mr Kean don't want no pryin' noses takin' a sneak look at what they're dishin' up. After that they'll all be packin' their traps and off on tour round the country till Christmas so it ain't no use you hangin' around.'

'Hell!' exclaimed Ray Dorrien, finding for once that all his handsome looks and the offer of a hefty bribe carried no weight at all.

Harry shrugged and moved away but Ray stopped him.

'I suppose you think you've beaten me to it, young Hal,' he said with a decided edge to his voice. 'How did you do it? Offer to put a ring on her finger?'

'If you must know I did just that but she'd have none of it,' said Harry coolly.

He had grown up during the last two years and no longer found his one-time friend's amorous exploits either amusing or to his taste.

'Playing hard to get is she, the little slut? What that young woman needs is a sharp lesson to show her she is nothing but a nobody trying to ape her betters, and I'm the right one to show her what's what.'

'You'll answer to me first,' said Harry fiercely.

'Oh come, boy,' went on Ray, putting a hand on his shoulder. 'You haven't exclusive rights, you know. It isn't the first time you and I have run neck and neck after the same girl and enjoyed the fun too. What's changed you, eh?'

'A very great deal,' said Harry shaking himself free, 'and if I understand rightly you're to be married soon. If I know my cousin Clara she'll keep you on a very short rein.'

For a moment an ugly look flashed across Ray's face and then was gone. He smiled and shrugged his shoulders.

'Clara will learn her proper place. I'll make damned sure of that.'

He waved his cane at a cruising cab and sketched a curt salute to Harry as he stepped into it.

Harry looked after him frowning, a little worried in case it should be more than an idle boast on Ray's part, then, remembering how closely guarded Kate was by Mr Kean's highly respectable company, it seemed very unlikely that any harm could come to her.

He had only seen her once since the ball and that was only for a few minutes on her way to rehearsal. She had been delighted at his news, promised to write to him while she was on tour and gave him a quick sisterly kiss. It was not nearly as much as he wanted and hoped for but after all in a week or two he would be off to Paris and she would be away travelling around the provinces. By the time Christmas came and the New Year, he thought with characteristic optimism, his father might have come to view things differently. He went on his way whistling.

Chapter 12

Dickie was crouched under a projecting corner of King James's Steps at Wapping, trying to shelter from the drizzling rain while he waited for the tide to recede and reveal the long stretch of slimy mud which was the hunting ground of the scavengers who daily searched for what they could pick up.

'You git out there with Jacko, boy, he'll show you what's what,' his Uncle Clem had growled on that very first morning as he stood shivering, stripped of the clothes his mother had painstakingly washed and patched for him to wear at school and given in exchange a pair of dirt-encrusted pantaloons cut off at the knees and a rag of a shirt. 'You won't need them good shoes neither,' went on his uncle, 'the water'd only rot 'em. Growin' boys eat food so mind you fill up that can there and earn yer keep.'

Jacko, thirteen and big with it, had shown a rough kindness telling him what he had to look out for: bits of coal, old iron, rope, bones, copper nails, old kettles, tin cans, coins if you were very lucky and, very rarely, old tools, all the debris dropped from the ships and barges that passed up and down the river, to say nothing of the bloated bodies of dogs, cats and rats which made Dickie shudder with a sick disgust. Hopelessly bewildered and still grieving for his mother, Dickie had found little or nothing during those first days and, returning with an empty can, received a box on the ear that sent him sprawling across the yard. Out of sheer necessity he had gradually learned and learned also how to fight and bite and kick when the other boys tried to snatch his miserable findings from him.

He discovered that his uncle ran a team of these children who brought him their findings regularly and he doled out the pennies and half-pence. It was only Dickie who received nothing.

'You're lucky,' said his aunt over and over. 'You've got a place to sleep and food in your belly and don't you never bring those stinkin' clothes into my clean kitchen neither,' so every night he had to scrub off the filth and slime from his legs and feet under the pump in the yard together with the filth-caked clothes, leaving them outside for the morning and putting on the ragged trousers and shirt his uncle had substituted for his own clothes which had disappeared into the shop. After that if he was lucky he might be given half a faggot or a pig's trotter with most of the meat already stripped away or, best of all and only very rarely, a hot floury potato, all depending on his aunt's whim. Accustomed to a life of near starvation, in his eyes, his uncle and aunt lived in comfort in a two-roomed cottage adjoining the large warehouse in which Uncle Clem carried on his business of pawnbroker and second-hand store and where Dickie slept on an old straw mattress with one thin blanket.

It was the smell he hated most, the nauseating reek that clung to him despite the scrubbing in cold water, and the sheer misery of every morning being forced to drag on the mud-encrusted filthy garments still damp from the previous day. He missed his school, he missed Daniel and most of all he missed his mother so that night after night that first week he cried himself to sleep, his face buried in the rough sacking of his hard bed and every day he grew more and more to hate and fear the couple who never ceased to remind him how grateful he should feel for every mouthful of food he ate and who, when business was bad, took their disappointment out on him with sharp slaps and blows from his uncle's stick raising weals and bruises on his bare legs.

It was fully light by now and the rain had stopped. He crept out from his niche and saw that the tide had receded and already the beach was filling up with children of all ages, boys and girls too with their long dirty hair and their skirts kilted high above their thighs. Here and there were old men and women grubbing slowly through the slime and pushed hither and thither by the bigger boys, careless of who was knocked over, and left to wallow helplessly in the mud.

August had been a dismal month, hardly a day without rain, but this particular morning a watery sun had broken through and a fresh breeze blew away the drifting river mist as Dickie felt in his pocket for his breakfast, a crust of stale bread with a smear of lard. He broke it in half thinking he would eat part now and keep the rest for later. It was then that he saw the dog. It was very small and painfully thin, the ribs showing clearly under the white coat encrusted with mud. It was sitting a yard or so away, its small body quivering with desire as it watched him eat the bread, its rag of a tail slowly wagging from side to side. Dickie broke off a piece of the bread and held it out. The dog came slowly and warily, snatched at the bread and backed away to eat it. Dickie squatted on his heels and held out another piece. This time the dog approached more eagerly and didn't move away but ate it and sat waiting in the hope of more. They finished the crust between them and when Dickie held out his hand, the little creature licked his fingers and crept nearer. It was the first friendly gesture since that dreadful day when he had seen his mother lying still and cold in the hospital, when Daniel had sadly walked away from him and his whole small world had crumbled into ruins around him. He gave a stifled sob, pulled the little dog close and hugged it. All that day it stayed close beside him and when he dug for treasure, it dug too with a wild flurry of paws and flying mud.

He liked to think afterwards that the dog brought him luck. To start with he had a more successful day than usual and in one of its frenzied diggings his new friend turned up a blackened coin that when scrubbed hard had the dull sheen of silver. For the very first time Dickie was tempted to keep it for himself. He was an honest child and up to then had always handed over everything he collected to his uncle. He stared at it uncertainly and then wrapped it in a bit of rag and buried it deep in his pocket.

In the early evening, the tide having pulled in and out again, he climbed wearily up the steps and along Wapping Wall to his aunt's cottage. He could see his uncle busy with a customer and as usual he washed off the muddy filth in the yard, dragged off the wet garments and pulled on the ragged trousers and shirt. His aunt was busy in the back room and there was a savoury smell of frying fish which the little dog sniffed appreciatively as it trotted at his heels.

His aunt's screech so startled Dickie that he dropped the tin bucket and its precious contents rolled all over the floor. He fell on his knees to pick them up as she grabbed hold of him.

'Take that filthy creature out of my kitchen,' she screamed at him. 'Now, this minute!'

'He's not filthy,' Dickie exclaimed indignantly, scrambling to his feet and facing up to her. 'I washed him under the pump.'

'I don't care what you did. Take it out of here, now,' she screeched at him and because he didn't move quickly enough, she hit out with the broom in her hand, lifting the little dog up and hurling it far out into the yard where it hit the ground with a squeal of pain and terror.

'You beast!' yelled Dickie, moved as he had never been by blows to himself. 'You wicked beast, you've killed him!' and abandoning everything he raced out of the door and snatched up the whimpering dog.

'Clem, Clem!' roared his aunt. 'Clem, come quickly!'

'What the bloody hell is goin' on?' grumbled his uncle, emerging from the shop. 'What's all this damned row? Can't you see I'm busy?'

'Look what that wretched boy's brought in, just look!' said his wife. 'I'll not have it, I tell you, get rid of it.'

'Orlright, orlright, keep your hair on!' said her husband. 'It ain't done you no harm as I can see.' He advanced on Dickie. 'Now then, young 'un, you give that there pup over to me, see. Yer aunt don't like dogs, not since her sister were bit by one. Foamin' at the mouth it were and she died after, ran

232

mad she did, it weren't nice to watch. Now you give it over to me. We'll get rid of it and no more said, eh?'

'No,' said Dickie defiantly, backing away from him. 'No, I won't. You want to kill it.'

'Now look here, boy,' said his uncle, rapidly losing his temper, 'I've been speakin' fair to you and I don't want no cheek, see. That stinkin' pup is goin' on the dunghill where it belongs, now this minute, and that's the end of it.'

'No,' screamed Dickie and would have run but his uncle was too quick for him.

With a swift movement he took the boy by surprise. He grabbed the little dog out of his arms by the scruff of its neck and hurled it over the paling and into the mountains high heap of muck and rubbish that piled up day after day for a month or more before the dust collector came to pick it up.

But Dickie, who up to then had accepted everything done to him, the lack of affection, the blows, the whippings, turned into a small fury defending the little animal that had humbly offered its friendship. He flew at his uncle, pounding at him with his fists, kicking at his shins, tears pouring down his face.

'Have a go at me, would you, you little devil. We'll see about that!'

A blow on the side of his head sent Dickie sprawling on the cobbled yard. His uncle picked up his stick and began to belabour him with it, his back and his bare legs till the boy crouched sobbing at his feet, his hands over his head.

'Maybe that'll teach you not to fight your betters,' he growled, dropping the stick at last. 'Now get to yer bed and stay there. No supper for you, my lad.'

He bestowed a last kick on the boy and then turned back to the shop where his fascinated customer waited for him in the doorway.

Dickie climbed slowly to his feet, stiff and sick, his whole body throbbing with pain but he didn't creep away to his straw mattress in the outside shed. He looked towards the shop and to the kitchen; neither his uncle nor his aunt were watching

233

him so he crept out of the yard and towards the great stinking mound of rubbish.

He scrambled over some broken furniture, climbed through an old wire frame, lost his footing in some indescribable muck and found the small dog. It had fallen into a wooden box and was feebly trying to scramble its way out. It whined pitifully when it saw Dickie and he lifted it out, hugging it against him, murmuring words of comfort.

Then he clambered over to the further side of the great heap, still keeping hold of the dog, and sat for a while out of sight of the cottage, his back against what had once been a bedstead and was now a tangled mass of broken wood and iron.

For the first time he thought seriously of running away. He didn't think his aunt would mind. She had told him more than once what a trial it was to have a feckless sister's brat thrust upon you whether you liked it or not. But where could he go? At eleven years old and in his limited world there wasn't much choice. He could join one of the gangs that roamed the streets but they were a rough crowd, had their own rules and did not welcome newcomers unless they had some special skill. There were the shops for whom he had run errands when his mother was sick but the few halfpence he earned wouldn't go far to feed himself and his new friend.

It was growing dark when he made up his mind to ask Daniel. Ever since the day Daniel had found him trying not to weep over his burned hand, he had seemed a god-like figure in his small world. Daniel would help him. Daniel would tell him what he could do.

He waited till it was completely dark before he went back to the cottage. Lights were out and all was quiet. Earlier his aunt had muttered, 'Where's that plaguey nephew of mine got to?' but his uncle had replied comfortably, 'He'll be back when he's hungry,' and they ate their fried fish with relish and retired to bed.

He went through the yard very cautiously, rescued the silver coin from his old working trousers, crept through to the shed and found a piece of string to serve as a lead for the dog. He was fearfully hungry but dare not risk getting into the kitchen to steal some food. He had very few possessions to put together. The picture book Christine had given him had been whipped away from him. 'You don't want that old thing, not a big boy like you!' A pretty scarf his mother had worn in brighter days had found a new home round his aunt's neck. There was a box of crayons Daniel had given him at Christmas and a few coloured glass marbles he had won from the other boys at school.

He put them together and then set himself to wait, nodding off to sleep and then waking startled with the pup nestling against him under the coarse brown blanket. It was about three o'clock when he sat up, that dead hour of the night when the world holds its breath, when old people lose their hold on life and everything seems to wait for the coming of the new day. He listened carefully but all was still very quiet. He crept across the yard and made his way slowly through the streets to Paradise Alley. There were few people about, a reveller or two, men coming off night shift and others hurrying to early morning work. Children slept huddled in doorways and he stepped carefully over bodies in the gutters, sick or drunk or even dead.

The house when he reached it was quiet, the door firmly shut. He settled down on the lowest step to wait. After a couple of hours or so the lodger who had the first floor front and worked at the docks came hurrying out and cursed as he nearly fell over him but people sleeping on doorsteps were too frequent to worry about. He had left the door ajar and with a quick look around him, Dickie went in, climbed the stairs and sat on the landing outside Daniel's door, so thankful to be safely there that relief spread through him and he fell asleep almost immediately with not the slightest notion that his simple decision was to have an unexpected effect on the life of the young man he most admired and loved.

A couple of hours later Daniel, coming out of his room at a rush, tripped over him and only saved himself from falling down the whole flight of stairs by a miracle. 'What the hell!' he exclaimed and turned round to be faced with Dickie, tousled hair, dirty face, filthy bare feet, trying desperately to quieten a small mongrel dog that was barking its head off.

'What the devil are you doing here?' exclaimed Daniel, taken by surprise.

'I've run away,' quavered the boy, frightened now but defiant.

'You have, have you?' A vision of trouble ahead loomed up in front of him. He sighed resignedly. 'In that case you'd better come in, hadn't you?'

He pushed Dickie in front of him into the attic room. It was seven o'clock by now and broad daylight. He could see at a glance what poor shape the boy was in, painfully thin, dark shadows under his eyes, a yellowing bruise all down one side of his face, the ragged clothes, the bare feet, one of them oozing blood.

He said gently, 'What made you run away?'

'Uncle Clem tried to kill my dog.'

'Your dog? Where did you find him?'

'On the strand. He didn't have anybody to care for him, 'cept me.'

It was not difficult to guess at what had happened. A child the couple didn't want but all the same one that could be exploited even to selling off the decent clothes from his back and the shoes from his feet. He felt pretty sure that they would not let him go easily and even if they did, what the hell was he going to do with him?

'I don't think that my auntie likes me,' said Dickie, his voice trembling a little. 'You won't make me go back, will you?' The near sleepless night, lack of food, and the cruel beating of the day before were all having their effect.

'Not if I can help it. We shall have to see.' Abruptly Daniel made up his mind. 'Now listen to me. There's some water in the bowl. You wash your face and hands while I go down and speak to Ma Taylor. Then we'll have some breakfast together. All right?'

Dickie nodded, the threatened tears drying up in the simple belief that his protector would somehow make everything come right, a belief that Daniel was very far from sharing as he went down to the basement kitchen.

'What were all that commotion I heard up there this morning?' said his landlady, fixing him with a stern eye as she took the kettle from the hob. 'Have you got someone up there with you?'

'Aye, I have, but it's not what you're thinking, Ma. Dickie has run away from his auntie.'

'Oh my lor'!' She put the lid on the teapot and slammed the kettle back on the grate. 'That'll cause trouble, you mark my words. That Clem won't let the boy go, not if he can see his way to making something out of him. He'll have the law on you for it like as not, abducting the boy or some such.'

'I'll have something to say to him first,' said Daniel grimly. 'The boy's a mass of bruises and hardly a rag to his back.'

'You be careful, Dan, he could do you harm.'

'Let him try. I'll have to leave Dickie here while I go to school but I'll be back soon as I can to work things out. I'll lock the door but you'll not let him in while I'm out, will you? You won't let Clem Walker take the boy back.'

'If he comes rampaging around here, he'll get a flea in his ear,' said Ma Taylor sturdily. 'What's that sister of Jenny thinking of to let him treat the poor kid like that? Never ought to be allowed to have children, that lot. They had one of their own once, a boy, and as soon as he were old enough he scarpered and I don't blame him neither. Joined one of them cargo boats and has never been seen from that day to this. But I warn you, that Clem Walker can be right nasty.'

By now she had filled two mugs with hot tea. 'You get that down him and then we shall have to see.'

'You're a treasure, Ma,' said Daniel gratefully, taking the two mugs and going upstairs with them.

Dickie, who had learned to look after himself when he was five years old, had washed his face, cleaned up the little dog as best he could, tried to drag Dan's comb through his tangled hair and was now sitting on the floor examining the ugly-looking cut between his toes.

'How did that happen?' asked Dan, putting down the mugs of tea.

'I trod on a bit of broken glass.'

'Didn't your auntie bandage it for you?'

'She said it wouldn't do no good 'cos we were always in the water and the river would wash it clean.'

And poison it like as not with all that filth, thought Dan. 'Leave it now,' he said. 'I'll put something on it for you presently. Drink up your tea while it's hot.'

He got out the heel of a loaf, some butter and hard cheese, his usual breakfast, and noticed how the boy tried hard not to wolf it, secretly breaking off pieces to share with the dog who accepted them gratefully. The pup was another problem he had to face.

'Now you stay here today,' he said when they had finished and everything had been put tidily away. 'I have to go to the school but when I come back we'll decide what must be done for the best.'

'Supposing Uncle Clem comes looking for me?'

'I don't think he will, at least not yet, and if he does, Ma Taylor won't let him in.'

He treated the damaged foot as best he could, put on something that stung and bandaged it with a piece of clean rag. He didn't much like the look of it and thought he might have to take the boy to the clinic but that would have to wait.

All that day while conscientiously dragging his reluctant pupils through reading, writing and the intricacies of simple arithmetic he tried to find a solution to the problem forced upon him. He said nothing to Elspeth but thought that later on when he'd given the boy some supper he'd walk round to the shop and speak to her father. Mr Brown had a great fund of common sense, a knowledge of the law and beneath the ruthless determination to get on, he had a kindly heart.

He stopped off at the cookshop on the way home and after a moment's hesitation bought three faggots with the wry

238

thought that if he didn't, half of Dickie's supper would undoubtedly find its way down that skinny little pup's throat.

Thankfully all was quiet when he reached Paradise Alley. No furious uncle or wrathful aunt had come thundering at the door or shrieking abuse and all three settled down to their supper, with Dickie, who had slept most of the day, in a lively mood and artlessly revealing to Daniel a great deal of what had gone on in that cottage down by Wapping Steps.

However this happy state of affairs was not to last long. Dickie's Uncle Clem had not been much disturbed when the boy didn't appear to pick up his breakfast.

'He's sulkin', he'll have gone down to the strand already,' he said to his wife. 'He'll be back like a shot when his belly is empty.'

It was not till the boys came late that evening with their day's findings that he realized that Dickie was not with them.

'He ain't been down there all day,' said one of the boys in answer to his question.

'Are you sure?'

'O' course we're sure,' said another, a weasel-faced boy who had always had it in for Dickie, who had resented him stealing from his bucket whenever he turned his back. 'Tell you what, Mister, he found somethin', money it were, that there dog dug it up and he were rubbin' and rubbin' at it.'

'Money? What d'yer mean? What kind o' money?'

'Dunno,' the boy shrugged, 'a guinea perhaps, it had a kind of shine to it.'

A guinea, a yellow Jimmy Goblin, and the damned little thief had the impudence to take off with what belonged to him. He weren't going to let him get away with that. His wife, when questioned as to where the boy would have run, said doubtfully, 'There were that schoolteacher at the hospital, too big for his boots he were, talkin' about us sendin' the boy to school, waste of good money I told him. He lives in Paradise Alley or so I've heard, a house kept by that Ma Taylor, one of them Methodys who think as the rest of us ain't good enough for them. That's where that plaguey boy will have gone.'

'I'll have him by the ears,' swore her husband. 'I'll have the law on him, abducting the boy, stealing from his proper guardians, you'll see!'

They had finished their supper and Daniel had just begun to think about walking round to the shop and consulting Mr Brown when the knocking on the door began.

'It's Uncle Clem,' whispered Dickie, shaking all over. 'You won't let him take me back, will you?'

'Not a chance,' said Daniel calmly. 'If it is him, then you make sure you stay up here and keep tight hold of that pup while I go down.'

By the time he reached the bottom of the stairs, Ma Taylor was already there, looking agitated and he put a reassuring hand on her bony shoulder.

'Don't you worry, Ma. You go back to the kitchen and leave this to me.'

'That's all very well but d'you hear what that great brute is shoutin' out there,' she said in furious indignation. 'This is a decent house this is, always has been. Listen to him and you'd think it were a bawdy house. I won't have it, I tell you!'

'I know,' he said soothingly, 'but nobody believes it. You leave this to me. I'll deal with him.'

He flung open the door and slammed it shut behind him so suddenly that Clem was taken by surprise and fell back a step or two. An interested crowd began to gather with no idea what the dispute was about but fascinated by the prospect of a fight in front of what was well known as the most respectable house in the Alley.

'What's all the disturbance about?' asked Daniel, his voice rising above the hubbub. 'If it's Daniel Hunter as you're looking for, Clem Walker, then here I am. What can I do for you?'

'And about time too!' Clem took a step forward. 'Where've you hidden the boy, eh? Where's that thieving nephew of mine? Thought he'd run away, did he, taking my good money with him. Well, he was wrong. You hand him over or I'll have the law on you.'

'Oh no, you won't. I'll have something to say first. We'll see what the law says about a man who beats his wife's nephew, who steals the very clothes off his back and his shoes from his feet.'

'It's a lie, a filthy stinkin' lie!' screamed Clem. 'Didn't I care for him as if he were my own kin and what does he do but rob the auntie who loves him and run off. You've got him hidden away somewhere and by God I'll get him back or it'll be the worse for you.'

'Very well. If that's what you want, then come and fetch him,' said Daniel recklessly.

He had not meant to lose his temper. He had intended to remain calm and sensible, to confront Clem Walker with reason and good sense, but the last month, ever since that wretched meeting with Christine, he had lived on a knife edge, sometimes raging against her, sometimes with a wretched conviction that it was all his own fault and not helped by Will Somers who had been deeply jealous of his involvement with Christine and never missed an opportunity to needle him about it. He braced himself almost joyously for what he knew must come.

'You bloody interferin' schoolteacher! Who the devil do you think you are, God Almighty?' roared Clem and charged up the steps.

He was a big man, accustomed to bullying all who opposed him, but Daniel had an unexpected wiry strength and had been kept in good practice by the boxing bouts he had encouraged with the older boys at the school. Clem found himself forced back down the steps, the crowd parting to let him through and then gathering around delightedly to watch the outcome of the battle.

It was quite a skirmish, the two opponents swaying back and forth and cheered on by the spectators for whom it ended all too soon with Clem, overweight and out of condition, forced to his knees, his nose pouring with blood, a painful crick in his neck, and Daniel standing over him, panting but triumphant.

'Had enough?' he asked.

'I'll get you for this, by God I will!' muttered Clem as he struggled to his feet, 'you and that damned little rat in there. We'll see what the Constable has to say when I bring a charge; abduction, robbery and assault, don't sound too good, do it? Don't think you've heard the last of it,' he went on viciously, ' 'cos you haven't, not by a long shot,' and he limped away to jeers and catcalls from those who had been watching.

Daniel might have won the first round but he had no illusions about what would follow. Clem had right on his side as Mr Brown took pains to point out when later that night he went round to consult him.

'It's a nasty business, Dan,' he said, 'especially with you teaching at the school an' all. It reflects badly, you see, parents don't like it.'

'But you've not seen the boy,' exclaimed Dan. 'Half-starved and covered with bruises. He's in a terrible state.'

'Very likely but you've got to remember he's only one of thousands. There are plenty like him. Fathers can beat their sons to within an inch of their lives, husbands can knock their wives about and it's their right. The law says nothing.'

'Then it should,' said Daniel stubbornly. 'I know it's only a drop in the ocean, it's one child in thousands, but it matters to me and making a stand, saving only one, is a step in the right direction.'

Mr Brown shook his head gloomily. 'That's all very well and I won't say I don't understand how you feel but I smell trouble and with the election coming up an' all, it's the last thing we want. You go easy, boy, think what you're doing, you could be right up against it.'

And unfortunately he was only too right. Clem Walker lost no time in doing what he threatened. The next day after morning school Daniel was faced with the local police constable, a decent enough fellow who was sometimes very aware that policemen were not popular in the East End. Ever since the force had been founded thirty-five years before and sent out

242

to patrol the streets, and despite the fact that petty crime had been halved, the great majority of working-class Londoners regarded them with the deepest suspicion. However, he knew all about the ragged school and knew the Methodists did good work in keeping children off the streets so his questions in this first instance were polite.

Daniel answered as well as he could while the Constable took painstaking notes in the fair round hand he had learned in a school much like this one.

'And what happened in Paradise Alley last night?' he went on. 'This Clem Walker is complaining of being assaulted.'

'It was he who assaulted me,' said Daniel drily. 'He wanted to take the boy by force and I resisted him. Dickie is sick, he's not even fit enough to come to school.'

'And the robbery?' went on the policeman, watching him narrowly. 'Did he make off with his uncle's strong box?'

'Strong box!' Daniel laughed. 'I'll show you what the boy made off with. I brought it to school to show the children.' He felt in his pocket and brought out a thin worn coin battered almost out of shape. 'It's a silver penny dated 1672 and must have been lying buried in the mud for close on two hundred years. The dog dug it up and the boy kept it as a curiosity.'

'Well, Mr Hunter,' said the Constable, closing his notebook and putting it carefully away; 'I shall have to report to the Sergeant o'course and it's more than likely that it'll be brought up before the magistrate at his next sitting.'

Daniel frowned. 'Will he force the boy to go back?'

'Hard to say. A child's proper place is with his relatives and not with a young man living alone like yourself if you know what I mean but there's no telling how Mr Goodall will view it. Just don't go knocking this Clem Walker down again. It won't do you no good. And now I'll be on my way. Good day to you, Mr Hunter.'

He walked away leaving Daniel staring after him. It was all so true. He did not know himself what he could do with the boy and yet his determination grew not to allow a delicate

243

child with a bright enquiring mind to go back to slavery and worse.

It was extraordinary what a furore this minor incident aroused. People took sides and opinions raged as to what the result would be. The whole affair was at its height when Christine came back to the clinic after the weeks at Bramber, long tedious weeks without Gareth who was at a German spa with his uncle, without Harry who had gone off to Paris and whose infrequent letters were filled with tales of the glamorous people he was meeting, actors, singers, artists, so that she wondered sourly if he had already forgotten Kate. Even a week at Ingham Park with Margaret did nothing to help. She and Freddie were so blissfully happy, so content with their baby son and their well ordered life that she had an insane desire to smash something, drop some kind of bombshell, anything that would shatter their complacency. Of course she knew what was wrong even though she would have denied it. She missed Daniel unbearably and could not get out of her mind that last ugly scene when he had walked away from her leaving her utterly bereft.

There was no one in whom she could confide, no one with whom she could discuss what was happening to her. Even to talk to Kate would have helped but she was far away, touring from theatre to theatre and out of reach except through letters which could chase after her and might never even reach her.

She lay and thought about Daniel in the long hours of the night, remembering how he could go from solemnity to laughter in a few seconds, his touching compassion for the poor and the wretched, the fresh vision he could bring to books and poetry she had known from childhood. If all this was love, then she was in it up to the neck and it frightened her. It had none of the safety, the serenity and dependability of Gareth's devotion, none of the quiet happiness Margaret enjoyed, and there was no future in it, since though her father and Daniel seemed to be implacably divided in every way, they were at

244

one in the impossibility of any real friendship or intimacy between Daniel and Christine.

Oddly enough almost the only moments in those weeks at Bramber which gave her any pleasure were those she spent with her father. She had a queer feeling that with Margaret gone and Harry away he was discovering her as a person for the first time and they grew closer than they had ever been. Clarissa had never cared for horses so it was Everard who rode with Christine in the early mornings and sometimes accompanied her on long walks with the dogs and she thought that she began to understand him a little more, a man who was deeply reserved, who found it desperately hard to give something of himself. His charm she had always been aware of and she began to understand how her mother had fallen in love with him all those years ago and why juries found it almost impossible to resist his pleading on a client's behalf.

When they returned to London he was tolerant even if he didn't approve of her work at the clinic and raised no strong objection when she began her weekly visits again.

It was Dr Dexter who told her about Dickie on the very first afternoon when, after a morning's hard work, they were taking a breather and drinking the tea Deborah had brought to them.

'Your friend, the schoolteacher, has got himself into a pretty pickle,' he remarked casually. 'It seems that Dickie has run away from his auntie and taken refuge with him. Now he is refusing to send him back.'

'How do you know?'

'The boy came in with a poisoned foot, very nasty it was, and he was full of it. He is in pretty poor shape, poor little devil, but his aunt and uncle are taking it badly. They want the boy back and are accusing Daniel of abduction, robbery and assault.'

'But that's ridiculous.'

'Of course it is but it seems our friend gave Clem Walker a bloody nose and that won't do him much good when it comes up before the magistrate.'

'Is the boy sick?'

'Not exactly but he was always frail and I gather he's suffered some pretty harsh treatment. It wouldn't take much to knock him over. I told Daniel that if they wanted a medical opinion, I would be willing to give it.'

She thought about it all that evening, remembering what Daniel had said when Dickie's mother died and his concern at the boy's obvious fear of his aunt when she took him away. She wondered if there was any way in which she could help.

That night at dinner she said casually, 'Papa, how much do parents have to pay if they want to apprentice their children to some kind of trade?'

'That's a custom which has largely died out nowadays, more's the pity, but I understand that bright lads are sometimes apprenticed to trades such as engineering and building. Why? You're not thinking of rescuing all the East End orphans and putting them to useful work, I hope.'

She smiled at him. 'No, not exactly, but I was reading about the old days and I wondered how much it had changed. What about shops? Do they take on young assistants? The girl who sold me a pair of gloves at Swan and Edgar's shop in Piccadilly the other day couldn't have been more than about thirteen.'

'In the drapery trade perhaps. Your mother could tell you more about that than I can. What is all this, Christine?'

'You're not wasting your money on some silly wild-cat scheme down at that clinic, I hope,' said Clarissa sharply.

'Of course not, Mamma. I was just curious about it, that's all.'

She thought about it all night and by morning had made up her mind. She had her own bank account now. The legacy from her grandmother gave her a small weekly income if she chose to spend it, and she could draw on it ahead if she wished.

At the bank that morning the elderly clerk counted out thirty golden sovereigns and said jovially, 'That's a very large sum. You're not going to spend it all at once I hope, Miss Warrinder.'

'Only in a very good cause,' she said, putting the money carefully away in her handbag.

She took a cab to Whitechapel and went in search of Mr Brown's shop. It wasn't difficult to find, the name in large letters having recently been written up above the window. Ezra Brown was definitely going up in the world. A boy of fifteen or sixteen in a clean white apron wished her a good morning and asked what he could do for her.

'Please tell Mr Brown that Miss Warrinder would like a word with him if he can spare the time.'

The boy was taken aback for a moment. Like everyone else he had seen the name Everard Warrinder staring him in the face on huge bills set up at strategic places in the city.

'Yes, of course Miss, at once,' he gulped and hurried out, returning almost at once with Mr Brown himself, smiling and bowing and inviting her to follow him into the small office at the rear of the shop.

Mr Brown proved a great deal harder to persuade than she had thought at first.

'It's true the boy is rising twelve but he's still very young to be taken on as an assistant,' he said doubtfully. 'I'm sorry for him of course. That Clem Walker is no more than a brute to treat the boy as he has done but I don't like the way Daniel is heading for trouble.'

'But don't you see?' she went on earnestly. 'When the case comes up and the magistrate hears how Dickie is being properly cared for and working his way through school by performing jobs for you during his spare time, it will make all the difference, won't it? If you were to speak up for him, you would be listened to, as you are such a worthy respectable person, and with your new shop you will be needing more people to work for you, won't you? Daniel has told me all about it and pointed it out to me when we were walking together one evening. When do you intend to open it?'

'At the end of the year, a grand opening for the Christmas trade.' He looked at her keenly. 'Why are you so interested in this lad, Miss Warrinder?'

He wondered for a moment if she were simply seizing the chance to make a show of generosity as the daughter of Everard Warrinder, the new candidate whose name flared on the hustings. It could carry quite a lot of weight.

'It's not on account of my father if that's what you're thinking,' she said quickly, sensing what was in his mind. 'He knows nothing about any of this and I'm not sure he would approve, but you see, Mr Brown, when I first came to the clinic more than a year ago now, Dickie was almost my very first patient and I couldn't help taking a special interest.'

And in Daniel too, he thought, remembering what Elspeth had hinted from time to time, not that anything was likely to come of that of course.

'If it's a question of putting you to any expense, then I'd be very willing to . . . to make an agreement to pay you so much annually like apprentices did in years gone by . . .'

'No, no, no!' he said, raising his hand and shaking his head, all his sturdy independence rising up against the suggestion of being paid for an act of generosity. 'If the boy behaves himself properly and works hard at his schooling and at his work here, then that will be enough. I'm not a rich man but I have a sufficiency.'

'Then you will do it! Oh that is so good of you.' She gave him a brilliant smile that made him glow at his own benevolence. She was not exactly pretty but she had a charm and elegance that he wished his own daughter possessed. It was little wonder if Daniel was taken with her.

'I knew you would help,' she was saying, 'you're just as good and kind and thoughtful as Daniel has described you to me. You won't tell him about this, will you? Not about me, I mean. He wouldn't want to feel obliged to me for anything.'

'But, Miss Warrinder, he should realize . . .'

'No, please, let him believe it is only from your own kindness of heart. There is something else.' She felt in her bag and brought out ten sovereigns. 'Will you ask your daughter to buy suitable clothes for Dickie?'

He shook his head. 'It is far too much . . .'

'Please take it. It will provide for him for the whole year. This is not my father's money but mine to spend how I wish.'

'Very well. Elspeth will be glad to do it for you.' He took the gold reluctantly and put it on one side. 'I will make sure it is spent wisely. Let us hope that all goes well and Clem Walker doesn't think up some other dirty trick.'

'Thank you for your help, Mr Brown,' she said and began to pull on her gloves.

'We shall no doubt be seeing something of Mr Warrinder now we are coming close to the election.'

'Yes. I would like to come with him when he makes one of his speeches but he doesn't want me to be mixed up in any of it.'

'Quite right too. Elections are not for young ladies like you and though he can be sure of the support of myself and my colleagues, there is, I'm afraid, a very strong radical opposition.'

'And Daniel is in the thick of it.'

'Yes, that's true,' he said in surprise. 'You know about that.'

'He told me.'

'I don't approve and I've told him so but these young men will have their wild ideas.'

'Perhaps he has cause. Thank you again, Mr Brown, and now I must go.'

'Maybe I shall have the pleasure of your custom when the new shop is opened,' he said, going with her to the door.

She smiled. The businessman anxious not to miss an opportunity. 'I shall certainly visit it,' she said.

'Phil, call a cab for the lady,' he said to the boy in the shop and bowed over her hand.

Mr Herbert Goodall, the magistrate, was a very successful tea merchant and had sat on the bench for a great many years. Fortunately he took an instant dislike to the blustering of Clem Walker and the tearful whine of his wife lamenting the loss of her dear nephew. He listened impartially to Daniel's impassioned pleading, took a good look at the thin-faced child who answered his kindly questions in a terrified whisper and then, as a firm believer in hard work and education for the lower classes, decided that the boy would do a good deal better in the employ of the highly respectable Mr Brown, even though as a staunch supporter of the Church of England he did not care for Methodists lumping them with all other ranting dissenters. So Dickie's fate was settled for the time being, with Clem Walker growling at the injustice, and Daniel fervent in his gratitude to his benefactor.

'Yes, well,' said Mr Brown a trifle uncomfortably. 'I'm glad to have been of assistance this once but don't make a habit of it, Dan. I'm running a grocery business not a home for waifs and strays.'

Daniel laughed and promised and then went off to persuade Ma Taylor to put a truckle bed in a tiny attic room hitherto used for storing unwanted rubbish, and even to tolerate the pup, now christened Penny after the coin Dickie had dug up. Dickie would in future take his meals with the Brown family but would still be under the eye of his beloved protector.

There were some who sneered at so much to-do over one small boy but all the same it had aroused public interest and Daniel's stock had risen among the more radical members of the Workers' Association. They began to consider him worthy of a place on the Select Committee, which considered proposals for all kinds of reform, and even the Communist League took time off from their new plan to blow up the House of Commons with a home-made bomb to congratulate him on a victory over injustice.

'They'd none of them be so pleased with you if they knew who it was who engineered it on your behalf,' said Will Somers as they walked away from the Mechanics' Institute one evening later that week.

'What the devil are you talking about? It was a very kind action on Mr Brown's part.'

'Oh very kind, and what part did that lady friend of yours play in his change of heart, eh?'

'What do you mean by that?'

'Isn't it obvious? Miss Christine Warrinder of course. Didn't you know? Phil Turner who works in the shop is the son of one of our neighbours. He was full of it. Daughter of the famous QC coming into the shop, large as life, his eyes fairly popped out, quite knocked sideways he was. It wasn't difficult to put two and two together.'

'And come up with the wrong answer. I don't believe you,' said Daniel curtly.

'Please yourself but the majority of those in there wouldn't be so glad to welcome you among the supporters of their own candidate if they knew you were accepting favours from the daughter of the opposition.'

'But it isn't true.'

'Isn't it?' went on Will mockingly. 'Why don't you ask her?'

It could be true, that was the worst part of it. It was just the kind of thing she might have done but why let him find out like this? Mr Brown had obviously been sworn to secrecy but how many others had known or guessed? All the rage and misery and loneliness of the past weeks swept over him again, weeks during which he had spent all his spare time doing everything in his power to point out the disadvantages of a die-hard Tory candidate such as Everard Warrinder. He would see her, tell her what he thought of her for going behind his back, making it appear as if he were hand in glove with the enemy.

She still worked at the clinic. He knew that from Dickie whose poisoned foot, hampered by malnutrition, was not healing as quickly as they had hoped. It was a day or two later when he took himself there and waited on the corner where they had met so many times before.

It was a cold blowy day and as she came through the door with Dr Dexter he saw her laugh as the wind caught at her green velvet skirts and whipped the silk scarf from her neck. The doctor caught it and returned it to her, laughing with her and then raising his hat and walking away. Now she was coming to where the cabs waited and he stepped out to confront her.

For a moment they simply stood staring at one another, then she said with the faintest tremor in her voice, 'If you're looking for the doctor, I'm afraid he has left already.'

'It is you I want to see.'

'Oh, why?'

There was a little gap between the tall buildings and he drew her towards it, away from the busy street.

'I think you know why,' he said furiously. 'Do you realize what you've done? There are people going about in this district who do not like me and are now only too ready to believe I am accepting favours from Everard Warrinder and at the same time blackening his name behind his back.'

'That's not true. Mr Brown promised he would tell no one.'

'Nor has he but do you imagine you can walk openly through these streets, daughter of a candidate whose life, family and opinions are being openly discussed and not be recognised? Not all of us are stupid clods, you know.'

'But this has nothing at all to do with my father. He does not even know of it. I did it for Dickie and for no one else. It was my own idea entirely.'

'Try telling that to those who would like to call me time-server for accepting favours from both sides.'

It was an exaggeration and he knew it but he felt bitterly about it and the words poured out.

'Why not come to me? Why not tell me what you were planning to do?'

'Because the last time we met you made it very clear that all friendship was dead between us and I knew you would not accept anything from me, not even for the boy.'

'How much did it cost you?' he said savagely.

'As it happens, nothing. I offered it but Mr Brown would accept no money from me.'

They were standing very close in the narrow opening, acutely conscious of one another, yet miles apart.

After a moment she went on with a kind of quiet desperation, 'I'm sorry if it has gone wrong. I meant it for the best, to help Dickie, to help you. Can't you believe that . . .?'

252

Her voice died away and he felt the anger and frustration drain away from him, leaving him empty and defeated.

'Yes, I believe it,' he said heavily.

She was looking up at him with a sudden appeal that he found desperately hard to resist. 'Daniel, must this go on? Can't we at least remain friends?'

'What would your father have to say about that?' He moved away from her. 'You had better go. If people saw us here together, God knows what inferences they might draw.'

'When my father comes down here before Polling Day, I shall come with him.'

'Much better not.'

She had an almost overpowering desire to put up a hand, touch his cheek, say, 'I love you, Dan, I realize that now and I know you love me. Why can't we just acknowledge it?'

He was staring into her face as if loath to let her go and then said abruptly, 'When are you going to be married?'

Startled she said, 'Not until next spring. Gareth is in the United States.'

'And has left you behind. What a fool he must be!'

'Gareth is a doctor,' she said defensively, 'and a good one. His work has always been as important to me as it is to him.'

'Is that so?' he said ironically. 'I only hope he realizes how very fortunate he is.'

Did he? She remembered the few hurried hours they had spent together before he sailed for America and wondered what she was going to tell him when he came back. Then she pulled herself together. Useless to think of such things now.

'I must go.'

'Not yet.' He put a hand on her arm but she pulled herself free and walked quickly away before she did something utterly stupid like bursting into tears or throwing herself into his arms.

He waited till her cab drove away and then walked back to his lodgings. He spent the evening writing a biting article for the radical news-sheet which had been suppressed but was still surreptitiously printed. He pointed out all the glaring faults of a candidate who might be a brilliant barrister but was one who had always set his face against reform, whose vicious attacks on the Chartists had led to their defeat – and who had seen a good man hang for his beliefs when it lay in his power to save him. He signed it with the *nom-de-plume* he had given himself – Spartacus, the slave in ancient times who had led a revolt against the injustice and cruelty of their Roman masters and been crucified for it.

When it was done he read it through wondering if he had gone too far. What would she think if it came into her hands? He was tempted to tear it up. Then abruptly he changed his mind, folded it and went out to drop it through the door of the underground cellar where the illegal paper was printed.

Chapter 13

Clara and Ray Dorrien were married in early November and Christine was one of the bridesmaids. She would have liked to refuse when the question came up in the summer but her mother had insisted.

'Clara is your father's niece after all, and it would look very strange, almost as if you resented her marrying Raymond.'

'But that's ridiculous. Of course I don't resent it. So far as I'm concerned she is welcome to him.'

'You could put it a little more graciously,' said Clarissa drily. 'There is another thing. Harry is coming over from Paris and will stand up with Ray as best man.'

'I can't think why. Their friendship cooled a long time ago,' she objected, but it did make a difference. She and Harry could have a private giggle over it.

The happy couple were married at St George's in Hanover Square and the ceremony with the reception afterwards was a very grand affair. The streets were lined with carriages depositing wedding guests in all their finery and yet, waiting in the porch and keeping an eye on two small bridesmaids and two mischievous boy pages, Christine was aware that somehow the whole affair had no heart. There was none of the warmth, the goodwill, that had pervaded Margaret's marriage to Freddie. The truth was that Clara had never endeared herself to her contemporaries. Her acid comments still rankled in many a heart; not even the plain fact that she was a considerable heiress had overcome her biting tongue and suitable young men were apt to shy off, looking for gentler qualities in their brides, till Lord Dorrien's eye fell upon her and he decided she was just the girl to keep his wayward son in order. There were one or two there that day who hinted that Clara might have got her just deserts in taking on Ray Dorrien.

Following her cousin's billowing crinoline of satin and priceless lace Christine exchanged a tiny smile with her brother. There had been a stag party of stupendous proportions the previous night and Harry, still comparatively sober, had had a hard job steering the bridegroom home and getting him to the altar in good time but he was there, a trifle pale, but impeccably dressed and even handsome in his own rather unpleasant way. Knowing them both so well Christine wondered how this ill-assorted marriage would work out. She foresaw a battle and idly wondered who would be victorious.

Clara's father, glad to get his daughter safely off his hands and in a husband's care, had spared no expense. The wedding reception dragged on, incredibly lavish and extravagant. Christine developed a headache and longed for it to be time to leave. At one moment she took refuge with Uncle David who though he now was obliged to walk with a stick was as erect and elegant as ever.

'How are you?' she asked, affectionately slipping her arm through his. 'It's so long since I've seen you.'

'Still on my feet,' he said drily. 'I don't intend to go shuffling into my grave yet awhile.'

'Don't say such things. You're still the handsomest man here.'

'You flatter me, my child,' he said patting her hand. 'It's a very long time since that could be said of me. Have you heard from Gareth lately?'

'No, not for a month. Why? He's all right, isn't he?'

'More than all right. He's coming home sooner than expected. He and Dr Andrews will be sailing at the beginning of December and he sounds very happy about it.'

Only five or six weeks away. She felt suddenly choked. He

would come home full of plans for their future and what was she going to say to him?

'Is there anything wrong, Christine? I thought you'd be as happy about it as I am.'

'Oh, I am,' she said quickly. 'It's just rather surprising. I'd not expected him to return until after the New Year.'

'Circumstances have changed apparently and for my part I am very glad of it. Months apart become serious at my age. No doubt his letter to you with all these details is already on its way.'

'Yes, of course it is.'

'Tell me, how is the election going? Is your father happy about the outcome?'

'He doesn't say very much to Mamma and me about it. But we intend to go with him in a week or so when he makes his big speech.'

'Better him than me. I've never had the desire to enter politics. I saw too much of the shady side of it with your grandfather. It can be a dirty business.'

'I'm beginning to realize that you're right.'

There had been an unpleasant little incident earlier that very afternoon between Lord Dorrien and her father which she had accidentally overheard.

Relations between them had been cool since she had rejected Ray's proposal and it sometimes made her feel guilty.

'I gather the gutter press have been having a field day with you, Everard,' Lord Dorrien had said. 'Do you know who is responsible?'

'I could hazard a guess,' her father had replied coolly.

She knew quite well to what he was referring. A copy of that news-sheet with its scorching article had found its way into the clinic. She had hoped her father had not seen it.

'I daresay you've made sure the fellow is suitably punished.'

'My dear Dorrien, that would be asking for trouble. There are few of us whose lives are so spotless that no mud can be thrown at us. To show resentment would be to acknowledge its truth.'

She moved quietly away before they were aware of her presence. She guessed who had written that article and it seemed only to widen still further the gulf between her and Daniel.

The eve of polling day was a cold bright day in late November. The morning mist had disappeared by noon when Everard drove down to Whitechapel, accompanied much against his will by his wife and daughter. They took their places on the dais of the large hall with his agent, with Mr Herbert Goodall, the magistrate who was also Chairman of the Tory Group, and also Mr Ezra Brown as representative of the Working Men's Association, smiling with pride and importance as he bowed to the ladies and ushered them to their seats.

As far as Christine could see the hall was packed with the most respectable and better off of the community, all those in fact whose status and position gave them a vote. On her advice she and her mother had dressed quietly. She wore her dark green velvet with a tightly fitting jacket trimmed with grey squirrel while her mother was in lilac edged with black braid and a bonnet in grey velvet with small curling ostrich feathers, nothing too rich or flamboyant. All the same there was a world of difference between their appearance of quiet elegance and that of the wives who had accompanied their husbands and who gazed at them with considerable envy.

Her father spoke extremely well, she thought. His voice had all the resonance and clarity of a well trained actor and with it he had a charm, an appeal that long practice with juries had taught him to use. He put over government policy and future plans with clarity and forcefulness, murmurs of agreement surging up from the body of the hall even if some of it was well above their heads. A few years ago Christine would have believed him impossible to defeat but now she could not help remembering how very little of what he said had anything at all to do with those outside, the homeless, the destitute, the starving, those with no vote, no voice to demand any of the

258

reforms they so desperately needed to make their miserable lives just one small degree more bearable. All those issues which Daniel had put forward so forcibly. She thought of the long queues who waited outside the clinic suffering the ills that come from poor food, filthy lodgings, polluted water and quite often from simple ignorance. Did her brilliant father ever think of those?

Nevertheless the afternoon went extremely well. Questions were asked and answered with tolerance and humour, arguments were dissected and shown for the folly they were, those few hecklers who persisted in leaping to their feet and trying to shout down the sober and more responsible were ruthlessly turned out by two stalwart supporters who guarded the door.

When it was all over and they were preparing to leave, someone came hurrying up on to the platform. He whispered to Mr Goodall who turned to Everard. It seemed that a large protest crowd had gathered outside, obviously bent on trouble, and he suggested that for their own safety it might be best for them to slip out by the back entrance where their carriage could be discreetly brought round to pick them up.

Her father shook his head. 'I'm not easily alarmed and I'm not running away,' he said. 'It would show a very poor spirit if I were to express fear of those whom I am aiming to represent.'

'But what about your wife and daughter?' persisted the magistrate anxiously.

'My place is beside my husband,' said Clarissa firmly.

'And like Papa, we have no intention of running away, do we, Mamma?' went on Christine cheerfully.

'As you wish of course,' but all the same Mr Goodall exchanged a worried frown with his colleagues which was justified the moment they came through the double doors and paused on top of the steps.

They were looking out on to an enormous crowd waving banners and screaming abuse at the tops of their voices so that it was impossible to make out what they were shouting, an unruly mob that seemed to increase every moment with the idle, the riff-raff, the layabouts, who would join in anything that spelled trouble.

The short winter's day was over and it was dark already. Here and there torches flared. In a sudden burst of yellow light Christine saw Daniel quite clearly and with him a man whom she thought she remembered as someone she had once seen going up the stairs to his lodgings. What motives had brought them into this mob?

Police were out, truncheons in hand, beating back the ringleaders to make a clear road to the carriage.

Everard put his arm around his wife. 'Come along, my dear, we'd better make a dash for it.'

They went down the steps towards the carriage, followed by Christine. As they reached it an egg flew past them and smashed harmlessly against the carriage window. A hail of missiles followed, rotten fruit, damaged vegetables, any handy rubbish, none of it doing much damage. Everard ignored it as he helped his wife into the carriage.

Someone was holding a torch high up so that for a moment Christine saw a portion of the crowd illuminated like a scene upon a stage. A voice shouted tauntingly, 'Everard Warrinder, liar and murderer!' Her father swung round in outrage to face his attackers. The man beside Daniel raised a pistol. She stifled a scream as with a lightning movement Daniel knocked the arm up and the pistol went off. Everard staggered and fell back against the carriage, the torch went out and was followed by something like pandemonium in the darkness. Mr Goodall came hurrying down the steps, women were screeching and men were grappling with each other and with the police, who were fighting their way through. They seized Daniel, who was staring down at the pistol in his hand, the man who had fired the shot having conveniently vanished in the scrimmage.

Everard had recovered himself. He was pale but quite steady. He thrust a hand inside his coat and it came out dark with blood.

'He got me in the shoulder, I think. I'm all right, it's not serious. Don't fuss, my dear,' he said irritably to his wife who was clinging on to him as if she expected him to fall dead at her feet.

'A doctor!' exclaimed Mr Goodall. 'Someone fetch a doctor quickly.'

The crowd, its appetite for drama somewhat satisfied by the shot and its desire for mischief dampened by the rough treatment of the police battling through them, had begun to disperse.

'We've got him! We've got the wretch who fired that shot,' said the Constable breathlessly, pushing through followed by two of his men gripping Daniel by the arms.

For a moment he and Everard Warrinder faced one another, then the latter said, 'You've got the wrong man, Constable. I saw it all quite clearly. He was not the man who fired the pistol.'

'But we caught him with it, sir, red-handed.'

'Maybe but it so happens that I know this young man. Keep hold of him for the moment. I would like to speak to him later.'

'If you say so, sir,' said the policeman, frowning.

Mr Goodall, extremely upset at the outcome of what he had hoped was a splendidly successful day, had now taken Everard's arm.

'You'd better come inside, sir, have that hurt seen to. Where's that damned doctor?'

'One of my men has gone for him, sir,' said the Constable, still very dissatisfied.

'Christine,' said her father quietly, 'take your mother home. I'll be all right. Don't worry about me. I will follow later.'

'No, no!' Clarissa was still clinging to him. 'I must stay with you. We don't know how serious it is.'

'Much better not. My dear, I'm not a child. Now do please go. I would feel much happier in my mind if I knew you were safe at home.'

She took a great deal of persuading but at last allowed her

261

daughter to help her into the carriage while Everard, leaning on Mr Goodall's arm, went back into the hall.

The Constable was prepared to follow but Daniel stood his ground and refused to move.

'I'm innocent. I've done nothing. You heard what was said. You've no right to hold me prisoner.'

'Oh yes I have,' said the policeman grimly. 'I'm not satisfied, whatever Mr Warrinder may have said, so in you go, young man, and no argument,' and he followed after his men who still had Daniel in their grip and pushed him roughly in front of them.

A few minutes later as Christine was still trying to reassure her mother Dr Dexter came thrusting his way through the now thinning mob.

'I was just leaving the clinic when I was told there had been an accident. What's the trouble?'

'My father has been shot,' said Christine. 'They have taken him inside.'

'Shot, eh? Is it serious?'

'He says not but go to him quickly please. I must look after my mother. Then I'll come.'

'Has she been hurt too?'

'No, but she's shocked and distressed.'

'I'll go in to him. Take care of yourself. I don't like the look of some of these fellows who're still hanging around.'

'I'll be all right.'

She felt a flood of relief that he was there, solid, calm and reassuring. It helped her to persuade her mother that her father would now be well cared for and she could go quietly home and not worry too much.

'I will stay and look after him, Mamma.'

'Oh how I wish he had never been persuaded into this affair,' lamented Clarissa. 'I knew from the first that no good would come from it. That wicked young man. He might have killed him.'

'But he didn't do it, Mamma. You heard what Papa said. He tried to prevent it.'

'Your father is always too generous. He cares nothing for his own safety. They must have been together, the two of them. What were they planning to do?' She suddenly stopped and looked keenly at her daughter. 'You know that young man in there, don't you, Christine? You recognised him.'

'Yes, I did, but only because he once brought one of the children from his school to the clinic,' she said quickly.

'If he is a teacher, then he ought to know better. I hope he and his companion are punished severely.'

'Papa wouldn't want you to upset yourself over it,' went on Christine soothingly. 'It could have been much worse and I promise you Papa is in good hands.'

'You'd better come home with me, my dear.'

'I'd much rather stay, Mamma. Papa needs one of us with him.'

Her mother must go but she was determined to remain. She wanted to be with her father but even more she wanted to know what was going to happen to Daniel. Surely they could not charge him with attempted murder and yet she was afraid. Whatever lay between her father and Daniel Hunter had suddenly become of vital importance. They were face to face now, bound together in some strange enmity and she had to know what it was and what the outcome would be.

'Very well,' said Clarissa wearily, still far from satisfied. 'I'll send the carriage back for you and your father.'

'You do that, Mamma.'

She watched the carriage pull away and then went back into the hall. They were now in a small cloakroom to the right of the double doors. Her father was lying back in a chair, his coat off, and the doctor was bending over him. Mr Goodall and Mr Brown were standing to one side looking anxious while outside in the body of the hall the police waited grimly with Daniel still pinioned firmly between his two guards.

'How is he?' she whispered.

'Not too bad,' said the doctor cheerfully. 'You're fortunate, Mr Warrinder. The bullet has gone right through the fleshy part of the upper arm so you are spared the worst. It's ripped an ugly furrow and there could be infection, I'm afraid. I'm putting something on it to help that but you would be well advised to consult your own physician when you return home and above all try to take things quietly otherwise you'll almost certainly run a fever.'

The first numbness had worn off and it was obvious that Everard was in considerable pain but he managed a smile.

'I'm greatly obliged to you, doctor. I gather you are from the clinic. I have heard of your work there from my daughter.'

'Yes, well, I do my best in somewhat difficult circumstances,' said the doctor drily, fixing the bandage and helping his patient back into the blood-stained shirt. 'Now, a little brandy might help if such a thing is available.'

'I have it here,' said Mr Brown eagerly. 'I sent one of the policemen to fetch it.'

'Splendid. Just a small measure, my dear sir, it will help you to pull yourself together and minimise the pain.'

Christine brought the brandy to her father. He swallowed it gratefully and lay back for a moment with his eyes closed.

'How are you feeling now, Papa?' she asked anxiously taking the glass from his hand. 'Are you in much pain?'

He pulled himself up with an effort. 'I'll survive. Has your mother gone home?'

'Yes. I managed to persuade her. She will send the carriage back for you.'

'Good. I don't think we need trouble you any further, Doctor. Christine, there is money in my coat. See that Dr Dexter is recompensed for his trouble.'

The doctor was repacking his bag. He said coldly, 'That's what I'm here for. I need no recompense.'

'Don't be offended. You may not but I'm pretty sure your clinic does. I'd like to show my gratitude.'

'In that case,' said the doctor gruffly, 'I'll accept it. I admit we live on charity, the State doesn't lift a finger. You may like to remember that, Mr Warrinder, for the future. Take care of yourself and good luck with the polling tomorrow.'

'Thank you. I think I may need it,' he said ruefully.

Christine went with Dr Dexter to the door and her father turned to his two colleagues.

'Please don't let me keep you here any longer. I've caused quite enough trouble.'

'I can't tell you how sorry we are that this terrible thing should have happened,' said Mr Goodall. 'I tell you frankly we never expected violence of this kind.'

'We can only thank God it was not worse,' added Mr Brown with equal fervour.

'These things happen. Irresponsible young men will act foolishly to draw attention to themselves however much we try to prevent it. While I wait for my wife to send back the carriage, I would be glad of the opportunity for a few words alone with the young man you have detained out there.'

Mr Goodall and Mr Brown looked at one another and then at the Police Constable who had just joined them.

'Is that wise?'

'I don't think he will attempt to murder me if that's what you are thinking.'

'I take it you don't intend to prosecute, sir,' said the policeman in an aggrieved tone, 'despite the fact that he was taken gun in hand.'

'No, I don't,' said Everard levelly, 'and for the reason I have already stated. If you wish to pursue the search for the person actually responsible, that will be your affair.'

'The prisoner denies any knowledge of him,' said the Constable stiffly. 'He simply states he saw the attempt to fire and did his best to stop it.'

'Exactly. I don't wish the case against him to be pursued any further. Have I your assurance on that?' When Everard spoke with the air of authority that had influenced juries and even impressed judges, there was no gainsaying it.

'It shall be as you wish, sir.'

'Good. Then show him in here and leave us alone if you please.'

They did as he requested. Reluctantly and with many

apologies and assurances of goodwill, Mr Goodall and Mr Brown departed, the latter with every intention of delivering a severe reprimand to Daniel and a demand for the exact truth of the matter.

Christine, returning from a few words with John Dexter about her father's condition, met them on the steps and bade them goodnight.

The Constable, who was deeply disappointed that his speed in apprehending the assassin had been thrust aside, stopped her in the lobby.

'Your father has asked to speak to the prisoner alone, Miss, and I don't half like it. I'm leaving two of my men on guard in case of trouble.'

'I'm sure they will not be needed.'

'That's as may be. You don't know human nature as I do, Miss, if you'll pardon my saying so. God forbid that any further harm should come to Mr Warrinder through any neglect on our part. I must return to the station to report the incident but I shall be back, you can be sure of that.'

She thankfully saw him go down the steps and looked around her. The two policemen were standing in a strategic position where they could keep an eye on what happened outside as well as inside. In the body of the hall the caretaker was busying himself with stacking the chairs and thinking about his supper. He hoped the great man would get a move on. It was bad enough getting himself shot but did he have to hang about chatting with that young chap who was altogether too full of himself? He made a great clatter with the chairs in the hope it would remind those concerned that he was waiting to lock up.

Christine stood in the lobby uncertainly. The door to the cloakroom was ajar. Should she go in? She knew her father had asked to be left alone with Daniel but did that mean her? It couldn't do any harm to try surely. She was about to push the door wider open when she paused, struck with what she heard, her father's voice, coolly ironic, saying, 'In that case I wonder you didn't fire the pistol yourself.'

'I didn't prevent you from being murdered out of any sympathy for you, believe me,' Daniel said fiercely, 'but simply because it would have damaged our cause, turned us into bloodthirsty assassins instead of reasonable intelligent people striving to work for better conditions for their fellows.'

'I thought your aim was bloody revolution,' went on her father with a hint of contempt.

'We are not revolutionaries,' said Daniel passionately. 'My candidate is a good honest man who has worked all his life, who understands the needs of the working man and the desperate poverty of those who through no fault of their own must see their wives and children starve with no redress, no hope, no alleviation of their misery except in the diabolic workhouses.'

'You're very eloquent on the subject.'

'Don't laugh at me,' said Daniel with a sudden violence. 'I have reason to be. What do you know of people like us? My sister and I were torn apart. For ten years we hardly knew that the other existed.' He paused for a moment and then went on, his voice hoarse with suppressed passion. 'Ever since I was seven years old I have cherished a dream, a great burning desire to see you on your knees begging for mercy as my mother once did for my father's life and then turn away as you did and laugh at the stupidity of such a plea.'

'I didn't laugh, Daniel, believe me. I didn't laugh.'

'No, you did worse, far worse. You made a bargain, you made a promise that you never intended to keep.'

'That's not true, I swear to you that's not true.' Her father's voice was suddenly so full of pain that Christine shivered. She knew she ought either to go in or go away and yet found she could do neither, only stand and listen.

'Up to then I had believed him guilty,' her father was saying, almost as if the words were being dragged out of him, 'and when I knew different, it was too late, much too late, it was impossible.'

'Of course it was impossible, ' went on Daniel relentlessly, 'it would have ruined you, smashed your career, wouldn't it, so you let it go and an innocent man was hanged till he was dead. I watched it, did you know that? I watched him turn and writhe in agony . . .' He was silent for a moment and then went on in a low voice filled with savage bitterness, 'If I were to tell all I know, you would be hounded out of the law, driven out of society.'

'If that is so, then why have you held your tongue for so long, or isn't it rather because all this is foolish surmise that has no truth in it. You have no proof.'

'Oh I could get proof. It would not be all that difficult. You have enemies, Mr Warrinder, who would be glad to listen to me. If it were only you who would suffer, then I would let it rip, nothing would hold me back but there are others who would be hurt, cruelly hurt . . . my sister for one . . .'

'And my daughter?'

'Yes, your daughter. God knows why but she has the greatest love and admiration for you.'

There was movement behind Christine and she looked round. The caretaker had come into the lobby and was talking quietly to one of the policemen. She was suddenly conscious of what they must think seeing her standing by the half-open door listening like some vulgar eavesdropper.

She felt the blood rush up into her face and moved away quickly into the hall, empty now, the chairs stacked and only one bench left standing along by the wall. She sat down on it, her mind in a whirl, tossed this way and that by what she had heard. She understood Daniel so much better now, understood his bitterness, but he could be mistaken, he must be, she had never doubted her father's courage and integrity, and it was not all. There was something more. What was it that still tormented them both? What else were they saying shut up together in that miserable room?

She didn't know how long she sat there on the hard bench. It was growing colder and she shivered. It seemed endless before one of the policemen came looking for her.

'Mr Warrinder's carriage is here, Miss.'

'Very well.' She got up stiffly. 'I'll tell him.'

As she went into the lobby the inner door was flung open and Daniel came out in a rush, brushing past her and the policemen, going down the steps and disappearing into the black night. Inside the room a flaring gas jet shed a harsh yellow light. Her father was bent over holding on to the back of a chair and she ran to him in alarm.

'Are you all right, Papa?'

'Yes.' He straightened himself painfully. 'Just reaction I expect. Is the carriage here?'

'Yes. I must take you home, put you to bed.'

He smiled faintly as she brought his heavy coat and draped it around his shoulders.

'Has that young man gone?'

'Yes. Papa, you're shivering. You'll take a chill. You've been here far too long already. We must go.'

'In a moment.' He turned to look at her. 'Christine, I asked you this once before. What does this Daniel Hunter mean to you?'

'I told you,' she said steadily. 'We have been good friends.'

'No more than that?'

'If you mean are we lovers? Then the answer is no and never likely to be.'

'Good. That's what I thought but I had to be sure.' He leaned on her arm and they moved slowly towards the door. 'I offered to help him. I could you know. I have friends.'

'What did he say?'

'Threw my offer back in my face.'

'What did you expect him to do? He has his pride just as you have.'

She helped him into the carriage, wrapping the fur rug closely around him and then leaning forward to kiss his cheek.

'All the same it was nice of you to try.'

The carriage started forward and Everard lay back with closed eyes. The wound in his shoulder throbbed relentlessly and seemed to add to the conflict in his mind. The dredging up of a past which he had believed long forgotten had been unbearably painful and he had no one but himself to blame. He could have silenced Daniel Hunter so easily, allowed the accusation to stand, have him brought before the magistrate, condemned to imprisonment, discredited, no one would have doubted his word, but that uneasy conscience of his wouldn't allow it. Even if it had been Daniel who had fired the shot, he still would have let him go free. Somehow he had maintained his icy coolness, his ironic air of detachment, while something within him had longed to unburden itself, to force that embittered boy to understand the truth that had been so painful, but he could say nothing. Instead he had let him go and wondered wearily if he'd been a fool, if he had put his whole future into the hands of an obstinate young man with a crazy dream of revenge. He shivered and at the same time felt the sweat break out on his face.

Christine felt for his hand and gripped it.

'Are you sure you're all right, Papa?'

'Yes, but I won't be sorry to be home.' He forced a smile. 'It's been quite a day, hasn't it?'

She drew closer against him, her thoughts divided between her father and the young man whose tormented face had thrust past her into the night.

And what of Daniel himself? He had plunged down the steps and into the darkness of the streets as if the devil were at his heels and in a way that was how it felt. He was angry with himself because he'd let his anger carry him away, had been quite unable to remain calm and cool with that astute man of law, Everard Warrinder. How dare the man offer to help him? He would starve in the gutter before he would accept so much as a crust of bread! All very fine drama but for the flicker of a second he had been tempted, till he thrust aside the devil's bribe. He walked on, mind churning, heedless of where he was going and bumped into a man who had stepped out of the shelter of a doorway into the faint glow of a street lamp.

'What the devil are you doing here?' he exclaimed angrily.

'Waiting for you,' said Will Somers airily. 'I had to know what had happened. So they let you go, did they?'

'Small thanks to you,' said Daniel. 'I told you from the start I'd not stand for any violence. It accomplishes nothing, only turns us into an undisciplined rabble. But you wouldn't listen, would you? You had to try and prove something and then couldn't face up to the consequences.'

'What happened to the pistol?'

'The police confiscated it.'

'Damnation, that cost me good money.' Will gave him a sly grin. 'It seems Everard Warrinder refused to prosecute.'

'They tried to persuade him but he saw what happened,' said Daniel curtly.

'And so he let you go free. All on account of his daughter's bright eyes no doubt.'

'Now look here,' said Daniel, seizing Will by the shoulders, 'you shut up about that. Christine had nothing to do with this, nothing at all, do you understand? What lies between me and her father is my affair. You can say what you like about me but keep your filthy tongue off her, understand?'

For a moment he glared down at Will, his face so savage that the other man quailed, then he thrust him roughly away from him and walked on through the black November night.

He walked the streets till near midnight. An icy mist crept up from the river and he shivered in his thin coat, returning to his lodgings by way of the school and the little churchyard where he and Christine had so often met during the summer. There had been moments during that night when he had almost believed in his enemy's sincerity, almost doubted his own strong convictions, then he thrust the weakness away from him. Everard Warrinder was a practised deceiver. What was it that he had read in one of those books Christine had lent him – that one may smile and smile and be a villain. Whoever wrote that knew what he was talking about.

He saw a faint glimmer of light coming from his room as he went up the stairs and he opened the door cautiously. A single candle had been lit and he saw a tear-stained Dickie curled up on the floor, Penny on his lap, and an old blanket round his shoulders.

'What the devil are you doing here? You should be in bed,' he said brusquely.

'They said you'd been arrested, that you would be sent to prison.'

'Then they said wrong because here I am just as usual. It's past midnight. You cut along to bed now like a good lad. It's polling tomorrow so no school. You can sleep late.'

'What is going to happen?' asked Dickie, yawning as he struggled to his feet. 'Will there be a fair?'

'Probably. All the world will be on the streets at any rate. Better leave the pup shut up here. He might get lost in the crowd.'

'I'm glad you're not in prison,' said the boy gravely.

'Yes, well, so am I.' Dan grinned and patted him on the head. 'Off you go now, goodnight.'

Dickie trailed away with his precious charge under his arm.

Daniel shut the door after him, too tired even to eat though he had taken nothing since early morning. He remembered suddenly that before all this had happened he had been due to sup with Mr Brown. Well, he would have to go round and make his peace with him in the morning. Methodists did not approve of violence in any form. If Warrinder had chosen to prosecute, it would have lost him his post as schoolteacher. As it was he would be lucky to escape a severe warning about his future conduct.

He took off his damp jacket, kicked off his boots and threw himself on the bed. For the first time he wondered what Christine had made of all this. How much did she know or guess of what lay between him and her father? Did she realize how close her father had been to death? In a wild mood Will Somers was capable of any madness simply to prove himself a man of action. Most of that night he tossed from one uneasy dream to another in a kind of waking sleep and it was not till the first pale streak of winter dawn that fatigue overcame him at last. He lay like a log till Dickie came knocking at the door, a mug of hot tea held carefully between his two hands, telling him that it was past nine o'clock and people were out on the streets already casting their votes.

Chapter 14

'My dear sir,' said Dr Murphy weightily, 'in my opinion you would be very ill-advised to venture out at all on this wretchedly cold day. Admittedly the wound is not too serious but you would be in grave danger of contracting a severe chill and could well end with a bout of fever.'

'Nonsense,' said Everard impatiently. 'I'm not a child to be knocked over so easily.'

They were all in the bedroom, Christine having followed her mother and the doctor. He was an elderly man whom she had known since she and Harry had measles together and with faces red as lobsters, but feeling perfectly well, had been a pest to their nurse and their distracted mother.

Clarissa had insisted on the doctor being called when they had returned late the previous evening. He had grudgingly acknowledged the efficiency of his colleague's emergency treatment, had given his patient an opiate and had recommended a day spent in bed or at least quietly resting in his room. But Everard had defied his advice, had brushed aside his wife's protests, had insisted on rising at his usual hour and was preparing to dress when Dr Murphy made his morning call.

'You must listen to what the doctor says,' said Clarissa with very real anxiety. 'You don't look at all well. The polling will go on perfectly well without you. There's no need for you to be there.'

'There is every need,' said Everard impatiently. 'I must be there when the results come through and I'll not allow it to be said that the foolish action of some hot-headed young man from the opposition has the power to put me out of action. I have loyal support down there and I would not disappoint them.'

The doctor shrugged his shoulders with a gesture that plainly said he washed his hands of it.

'Very well. If you must go,' said Clarissa with decision, 'then I shall go with you.'

'No,' he said quickly, 'no. I cannot allow that. It is not at all suitable and if there should be any violence – any kind of trouble – then I would not wish to expose you to it. Yesterday was quite bad enough.'

'Let me go with you, Papa,' said Christine impulsively. 'It's different for me. I've been down there so often. Some of them know me.'

'No, Christine, I'd much rather go alone. Now would you please all leave the room and allow me to dress. Perhaps, Doctor, to make it more comfortable you would make sure the bandaging is in order and arrange a sling.'

'If you say so,' said the doctor shaking his head, 'but I must confess I am inclined to agree with Lady Clarissa. I only hope you won't do yourself more harm.'

Outside the door Christine put her arm comfortingly around her mother.

'Don't worry too much, Mamma. I'm sure he'll be all right and he'll only fret if he stays here. I'll persuade him to let me go with him.'

'I don't know, Christine, I really can't understand why your father is so set upon it. It's as if he had to prove something to himself, which is ridiculous when you remember who he is. I know I shouldn't say this but I hope he doesn't win the election today.'

'I'm afraid it'll be a very near thing if he does.'

She was determined to go with her father, partly because whether he won or lost she wished to be loyally by his side and partly because she hoped that somewhere, somehow, she might contrive to see Daniel, to tell him that now she understood everything and he must realize that it made absolutely no difference to what they felt for one another. They were themselves and what their fathers had done to one another was in another time, in another world, and surely need not trouble them.

She asked Dr Murphy for advice just in case Everard should suffer any reaction and he frowned at her, still convinced of her father's folly.

'If he should be in pain, and he may very well be, persuade him to take a few drops of laundanum and try to shield him from too much agitation. Your father may not show it but his nerves are highly strung and the very fact that he will not permit himself to give way to them means that he wears himself out. I've seen it happen at the close of some of his more difficult cases. He will go on and on and it is only afterwards that he is in danger of collapse.'

It was a completely different view of her father. He had always seemed to her like a rock, so calm, so composed, not one who suffered inner turmoil. She had a feeling that during this past year she had been learning something new about him every day.

It was only after a great deal of argument that she at last persuaded him to let her go with him and after a light luncheon they set out in the early afternoon. The Tory headquarters had been set up in the Cock and Pheasant, the very place at whose supper rooms Kate had sung so successfully. It was a respectable hostelry whose proprietor was a staunch supporter of the government and whose public rooms were kept in very good order by two strong-armed stalwarts masquerading as waiters, who kept a strict eye on any person likely to cause a disturbance.

It was a slow journey since it was polling day all over the Capital and everywhere the streets were crowded. Down in the East End shopkeepers had prudently closed for the day and put up their shutters. In the case of any rioting their premises were only too liable to be looted.

The eating houses had closed their doors but street traders were everywhere, selling hot chestnuts, baked potatoes, faggots

276

and meat pies in greasy screws of paper, with new baked gingerbread, muffins, crumpets and huge slabs of plum duff, all washed down with a variety of drinks of very dubious origin.

Their coachman had the utmost difficulty in picking his way through the throng, shouting angrily at screaming children who raced alongside and were in horrible danger of falling under the hooves of his precious horses. Now and again a curious face pressed itself against the window to stare at them. One supporter boasting an enormous rosette recognised Everard and raised a cheer, while another saucy hussy tapped on the window and when Christine looked up rudely stuck out a long red tongue. It was already dark when they arrived at last, but they were given an enthusiastic welcome and to their driver's relief the carriage and horses were safely installed in the inn yard and he could retire to the public bar with a good pot of ale.

In the upstairs room Mr Goodall was waiting for them with Mr Brown and their cronies. They greeted Everard effusively, enquiring after his health and fussing over him while Christine looked around her. Someone pulled at her sleeve and she turned round to see Dickie, very neatly dressed, acting as messenger boy and bubbling over with self importance. She gave her father a quick glance and then asked him if he knew where Daniel was.

'He said he hadn't got no vote so he weren't goin' to come out in all this mob,' said the boy earnestly. 'He's lookin' after Penny for me.'

Then someone called him and the boy bolted across the room while Christine turned to Mr Brown.

'Dickie is looking very much better. How is he doing?' she asked.

'Not at all bad, Miss Warrinder. Performs his errands at the shop with never a penny out and is doing well at school so Daniel says. He'll be a credit to you one of these days, you mark my words.'

And Christine felt a little glow of pride that her small gesture had turned out so well.

The afternoon wore on very boringly. Her father was engrossed in conversation with Mr Goodall and his agent. They had been very solicitous for his comfort and he seemed quite at ease. There were one or two wives sitting together apart from their men. She recognised Elspeth and guessed the plump lady with her must be her mother. They smiled and nodded to her a little awkwardly and she smiled back, thinking that if she joined them her presence would probably have the effect of drying up the conversation and causing constraint.

It would be some considerable time before they could expect the first returns to come in and she wondered if she dared to venture out and make her way to Paradise Alley. It might be a hazardous thing to do in view of the election crowds but she had never lacked courage. No one was taking very much notice of her and she suddenly made up her mind. She beckoned to Dickie and he came racing to her side.

'Will you do something for me?' she whispered to the boy. 'If my father, if Mr Warrinder should ask for me, will you tell him I've just slipped out for a few minutes and will be back very soon.'

He nodded, giving her a wide grin. 'Don't you worry, Miss, I'll tell him.'

She felt in her small bag, found a shilling and put it in his hand.

'That's to buy a treat for Penny.'

'Oh thank'ee, Miss.' His eyes shone. 'He needs a proper collar real bad.'

'Then you get it for him.'

She smiled at him, took another quick look at her father and then slid quietly out of the room and down the stairs.

It was one thing driving through the streets in a carriage and quite another trying to make your way on foot. In no time at all she was engulfed in a pushing, jostling, excited group of men, women and children, to say nothing of a variety of dogs, all bent on enjoying the fun, supporting rival candidates, engaging in noisy argument and exchanging friendly

278

insults. She was shoved and buffeted from one to the other but refused to give up and for a while all went well. She was not far from her destination when she ran into a group of engineering apprentices headed by Will Somers who had erupted from the school, which had become Mr Nugent's headquarters, their dull but worthy candidate. It was then that the trouble really began.

Maybe Will Somers did not really intend it to go so far but he was the only one who recognised her and he was still smarting from Daniel's angry reaction to what he believed to have been a strong blow for the radical cause. Why not spite Dan and have a bit of fun at the young woman's expense? He stepped in front of her while his comrades hovered around them.

'Well, what do you know! Wonders will never cease!' said Will cheerfully. 'If it isn't Miss Christine Warrinder coming to wish good fortune to her father's rival!'

'No, no, I'm afraid you're wrong,' said Christine. 'I'm sorry but I'm on my way somewhere else.' She thought she had recognised him as the man who had shot at her father only yesterday and she felt a tinge of alarm.

'If you're looking for Daniel Hunter,' went on Will with a hatefully knowing smirk, 'then I'm afraid you'll not find him. He's out drumming up voters.'

'I'm not looking for Mr Hunter . . . or for anyone,' she said far too quickly, 'I've never experienced an election before so I was interested to see what happened. Now I'm afraid I really must go back to my father. Would you please be good enough to let me through?'

But by now they had closed in on her, sensing a bit of a lark, and Will said airily, 'It's *Mr* Hunter now, is it? I understand it was dear Daniel not so long ago.' She bit her lip at his impertinence but before she could answer him, he had turned to his friends with a wide gesture. 'Come on, lads, let's carry her to the polling station. Miss Warrinder presenting her good wishes to Mr Nugent who's going to show her father which of them holds the right views. That'll give us a column in tomorrow's daily rag!'

279

'No,' she protested, 'no, I can't do that. It wouldn't be right. You must let me go.'

But by now her arms were tightly pinioned and she was being half carried along between them. Christine was no coward, she did not scream or faint but fought back gamely to free herself. She realized now how foolish she had been. She had no idea what damage this might do to her father but she knew how angry he would be and so she desperately tried to get away. Then, as so often happens with mobs, the good humour turned vicious and as she fought to escape, they closed in on her and were joined by others, some of them women jealous of the fine clothes, the look of distinction. Someone tugged roughly at the ribbons of her velvet bonnet with its curling ostrich feathers, another made a snatch at the gold cameo brooch at her neck, while hands dragged at the over-mantel with its rich silk braiding, nearly tearing it from her shoulders. She tripped and fell up against a rough stone wall that grazed down her face. Blood trickled into her eye. They were laughing as they lifted her off her feet and carried her forward between them. She kicked out at her captors and a man whose knee she had bruised with the toe of her boot gave her a vicious slap across the face.

'Fight back, would ye, ye cocked-up bitch!'

For a dreadful paralysing moment she felt her senses swim and fought a terrible fear that she might faint. She clung to a railing with both hands lest she should fall and be trampled under the booted feet. She was in far too much distress to realize that the attack had suddenly lessened, that there was a movement away and someone was shouting. She shut her eyes for a moment to try and conquer the dizziness that threatened to overcome her.

Daniel had had a horrible day. It had begun with the necessary call on Mr Brown to ask pardon for missing the previous evening's supper party and was met with stiff reproaches. Although they had a certain sympathy with his radical views, pointed out Mr Brown severely, neither he nor Mr Glossop from the chapel were prepared to have any truck at all with violence. They had been utterly disgusted with the riot organized outside the meeting hall and it was only by the mercy of God that murder had not been done. He ought to go down on his bended knees to Mr Warrinder for his forbearance, few men in his position would have been so merciful. If he did not choose to mend his ways and toe the line, he could say goodbye to his post at the school and indeed to any respectable work of a similar kind so far as the chapel was concerned.

Smarting from the stern reprimand, aware of how much he owed to Ezra Brown and unable to offer any real defence without implicating Will Somers, which he was unwilling to do, he also had to endure deeply reproachful looks from Elspeth, who had gone to great trouble with her appearance at the party and had expected him to escort her and her mother to the Cock and Pheasant that afternoon even though he was supporting the rival candidate. It was altogether too much. He had gone back to his lodging, shut himself in and made up his mind to let the damned election go hang without him. But time passed agonizingly slowly. He could not concentrate on the books with which he had surrounded himself, not while so much was going on outside. Everyone living in the house, even Ma Taylor, had gone out on the streets. His restlessness increased till he could stand it no longer. He slammed the books shut, fed Penny, ate a hasty snack of bread and cheese, then locked the door and went down to the school where the voters for Mr Nugent were only coming in very spasmodically. By six o'clock he had had enough of it and was on his way home when he saw what looked like some sort of street battle. A policeman out on his beat was looking it over dubiously, obviously trying to make up his mind as to the best way of breaking it up.

'What's going on, for God's sake?' said Daniel.

'Not exactly sure, sir, but there's a woman in there. I heard her cry out.'

'Come on then. What are we waiting for?'

Together he and the young policeman, swinging his truncheon, fought their way through. Daniel caught a glimpse of Will Somers and was shaken by a wave of furious anger. After yesterday's disaster couldn't the fool keep himself out of trouble? Some of the youngsters knew Daniel and what with that and the policeman, who was bringing his truncheon down heavily on a few shoulders, they began to slink away.

Christine was still forced up against the railing, half strangled by the strings of her bonnet, her hair falling around her shoulders, mud and blood on her face and on her velvet skirts. She pulled herself upright with a violent effort when she saw him.

'If this is the way your supporters behave, I don't wonder you don't get any votes,' she said and collapsed forward into his arms.

'Hold on,' he said. 'It's all right. I've got you. You are quite safe now.'

Will Somers had caught sight of Daniel and taken very good care to vanish as quickly as possible. Deserted by their leader and their sport suddenly turned sour, his comrades were beginning to shuffle away looking somewhat shamefaced. The young policeman, emboldened by Daniel's support, was still laying about him. He had given Christine a good look, recognising her for what she was despite her dishevelled state.

'Do you want to bring a charge, Miss?' he said breathlessly.

'No, no,' she murmured. It was the very last thing she wanted. Her father would be furious with her and rightly so. 'It's over. Let them go.'

'If you say so, Miss. Go on,' he went on threateningly, 'clear off, the lot of you or I'll have you in one of the police cells quicker than you can say knife!' They were quickly melting away and he turned back to Christine. 'Anything I can do for you, Miss?'

'It's all right,' said Daniel quickly. 'I know this lady. I'll take care of her.'

'Very good, sir, and if you'll forgive me for saying so, Miss, you'd best not walk the streets alone on a day like this. It's not safe for a young lady like yourself.'

'I realize that now,' she said ruefully.

'I'll be off then,' he said, giving them both a curious look and then walking away with the regular measured tread which was part of his training for street work.

'Do you think he recognised me?' whispered Christine, trying to pull herself together and straighten her disordered clothes.

'Probably. He was right though. What in heaven's name brought you down here on a day like this?'

'I came with my father. He insisted on coming despite the pain he was in and I could not let him come alone.'

'I admire his courage,' he said drily. 'Shall I take you back to him?'

'Not yet, not looking like this. He will be so . . . so distressed.'

He frowned. 'I could take you to Paradise Alley,' he said a little doubtfully. 'There is no one there. Everyone is out on the streets. Then when you are rested, I'll take you back to the Cock and Pheasant.'

Reaction had set in. She clung to his arm feeling sick and faint as he led her through back lanes avoiding the crowded main street.

'That man who shot at my father yesterday,' she said hesitantly. 'He was there among them and he recognised me.'

Daniel's mouth tightened. 'Don't worry about him. I'll make very sure he says nothing of this.'

'Is he one of your supporters?'

'Yes, but it wasn't by my wish that he acted as he did. He believes in violent action but I don't and neither does the party. Nothing is ever gained by it. If he had succeeded in killing your father, it would have set our cause back for years, perhaps for ever.'

'Is that the only reason you stopped him?'

'Yes, of course.'

Christine sighed, overcome by a wave of fatigue. Nothing had worked out as she had imagined. She had wanted to find Daniel, had wanted to talk to him calmly and reasonably, make him realize that he must not let the bitterness and pain of the

283

past wreck the joy and happiness they had found in each other all this last year, and instead here she was at a hopeless disadvantage, sick and sorry because of what her own folly had brought on her and sensing already an edge of hostility in his attitude to her. If she were really sensible she would ask him to find her a cab and drive back to the Cock and Pheasant, except that she dreaded the questions that would be asked if she turned up looking like this, the inevitable repercussions, her father's disappointment in her for acting so irresponsibly on this day of all days. So she dragged herself up the long flights of stairs, leaned wearily against the wall while Daniel unlocked the door, stumbled into the darkened room and collapsed on the bed.

Penny barked shrilly and then came bustling around her feet and jumping up at her. Daniel busied himself with lighting the small oil lamp. He had lit a fire in the morning when he had intended to stay in and work at his books but it had already burned almost to ashes. It was very cold and she began to shiver uncontrollably. He knelt down by the hearth stirring the embers vigorously and then piling on kindling and a few pieces of his pitifully small store of coal.

'It will burn up in a minute,' he said getting to his feet.

He turned round and the light of the lamp fell on the disordered hair, on the pallor of her face marred with streaks of mud and blood. She looked so utterly forlorn, so completely unlike herself, that the strict guard he had put on himself splintered and broke.

'Oh, my love, my poor little love!'

Then he was beside her, raising her in his arms and piling up the pillows behind her, lifting her feet on to the narrow bed and tucking the rough brown blanket around her. He fetched a towel, dipped it in the jug of water and began to wash the mud and blood from her face. He untied the strings of the bonnet and took it away, then unfastened the brooch at the neck of her blouse and unhooked it.

'There, is that better? It'll feel warmer very soon now. I'll get the kettle on and make you some tea.' With a gentle hand he put back the disordered hair and kissed her forehead.

She closed her eyes and for a moment was back in her childhood being soothed and comforted by her nurse when she had fallen and hurt herself. Clarissa had never been the kind of mother who kissed and cuddled her children when they most needed it. A wave of relaxation and peace stole over her. She caught at his hand.

'Don't go away, Daniel. I want to talk to you.'

'In a moment. I'll put the kettle on first.'

He got up, fetched the small kettle, filled it from the jug of water and set it on the iron trivet hooked to the bars of the grate.

'It won't take long to boil,' he said and came back to sit on the edge of the bed. 'Silly child, what tempted you to come out on the streets alone like that? I'm surprised your father allowed it.'

'He didn't know. Dickie told me you had decided to stay at home and I was coming to find you. I wanted to talk to you.'

'What is there to talk about? Haven't we said it all already?'

'No,' she went on earnestly. 'You see I heard something of what you and my father were saying to one another last night.'

He drew back a little, frowning. 'Was it he who told you?'

'No, of course not. It was accidental. I didn't intend to listen and I only heard part but I understand now why you have drawn away from me. You can't forgive me for what my father did, isn't that right? But don't you see, Daniel, it was not he who condemned him. It is not he who has the power of life and death.'

'Isn't it?' He moved restlessly. 'I don't want to talk about it.' He tried to stand up and she pulled him back to her.

'But you must.'

'No! You think you know everything but you don't.'

'Then tell me the rest.'

She still held tightly to his hand, pulling him closer. She looked like a child with a clean scrubbed face, the dark hair straying across her forehead, vulnerable, appealing, as she had been so often in his dreams of her, and the feelings he had obstinately tried to crush, had refused even to acknowledge, suddenly burst into flame, a passionate desire rising within him in a hot wave. For this moment at least she was here, she was his, not as so often before fighting him but gentle, her eyes warming to his, her mouth waiting for his kisses.

'No talking, not now,' he said hoarsely and leaned forward.

His kisses began gently at first and she still resisted.

'No, Daniel, no, we should talk.'

'No!'

He brushed the protest aside, letting the tide of passion carry him away. He was kissing her with a mounting strength that alarmed and at the same time thrilled through her and while his kisses moved over her forehead, her eyes, her cheeks and came back to her lips, one hand unhooked her high-necked blouse and his mouth moved to her throat, to the swell of her breast above the white lace-edged petticoat and her body trembled with an eagerness, a longing she had never experienced. Almost involuntarily her arms went round his neck, drawing him closer, her hands tangling themselves in the thick hair.

Christine was not entirely ignorant of what happened between lovers. She had grown up in the country, had seen the villagers in furtive embraces, had known the birth of babies and puppies, but Gareth's gentle kisses had never prepared her for anything like this. She felt she was being carried away on a great tide. When he kissed her breast, she felt her whole body arch towards him. They were lost in a kind of delirium and she knew that if he went to the limit she would go with him in fear and trembling but with a longing for fulfilment. The sweetness, the breathless urge were all there and she gave herself up to it with joy. How long it lasted she didn't know, she had lost all sense of time, then suddenly, maddeningly, idiotically, the kettle boiled over with a loud spluttering hiss into the fire. Penny, who had been lying nose to the warmth, leaped back with a frightened squeal and the spell was abruptly broken.

'Damnation!' Then Daniel had broken away from her and stood up. He lifted the steaming, hissing kettle off the trivet and said prosaically, 'I'll make some tea.'

'I don't want any tea.' She was warm now, filled with urgency, glowing with awakened desire. 'Never mind that. Come back to me, Daniel, come back.'

But the moment had passed and could not be recalled. Daniel had recovered his senses. The strong puritan strain nourished by that strict Methodist upbringing sprang to life again. He was still trembling, he still wanted her passionately, but now other things had reasserted themselves. The wonder, the glory, had vanished. To lie with her now in this dingy lodging on the narrow pallet bed would seem like violation.

She watched him pour boiling water into the black pot and then fetch from the cupboard a cup and saucer for her and a battered mug for himself, while the turmoil in her blood slowly calmed down leaving her feeling strangely happy and peaceful. She was not sure whether she was glad or sorry that they had been driven apart but she was sure of one thing. This night had brought them together as nothing else had done and now surely they could look to the future. She swung her legs to the floor, shook out her crumpled skirts and began to hook up the neck of her blouse as he poured the tea and brought it to her.

'I've no sugar I'm afraid.'

'It doesn't matter.'

'Drink it and then I'll take you back to the Cock and Pheasant. Your father will have been looking for you.'

'What time is it?'

'It must be near eight o'clock by now. The returns will not be all in just yet.'

'Then there is time for us to talk,' she said, calmly sipping the hot refreshing tea.

'What are we to talk about?'

'You and me of course. It will be very hard to convince Mamma and Papa that I'm serious and I'm rather afraid that we'll never obtain their consent but we will have to face that probability. I am twenty-one. They can't stop me. I think my sister Margaret will understand and we can be sure of Harry. He will be on our side.'

He was staring at her as if she had taken leave of her senses. 'What in God's name are you talking about?'

'Now the past is all swept away,' she went on, 'now that we understand everything about each other, I am going to marry you, Dan. I'm going to share your life. Together we could do so much.'

For a moment he could say nothing, amazed at her glowing self-confidence, at her blind belief that what she was proposing was a perfectly simple matter when instead it was a minefield spiked with innumerable problems. Then he took a deep breath.

'Do you imagine for one moment that I would take you from your rich comfortable home and bring you to live in this – this garret? You must be out of your mind. Do you know what they pay me for trying to push a little knowledge into the heads of some sixty slum children? Seventy-five pounds a year – scarcely thirty shillings a week and that has to cover food, lodging, clothes, everything – it wouldn't keep you in pocket handkerchiefs.'

'I have money, Daniel,' she went on calmly, ignoring his outburst, 'quite a lot of money actually. My grandmother left it to me. My uncle told me on my birthday and it is mine. Papa can't touch it. We could live on that while you look for something better.'

'No, no, no!' he thundered. 'If I'm to take a wife, then, by God, I'll keep her. I'll not batten on a legacy from the Earl of Glenmuir even if he is your uncle!'

'That's nothing but old-fashioned prejudice. Can't we share it? What is mine is yours. Isn't that what marriage means?'

She stood up then, putting down her cup, and with the help of a little comb from her handbag began to tidy her hair and refasten the brooch at the neck of her blouse. Her calm assumption that he would at once agree to this impossible, this crazy proposal, took his breath away.

'You're not living in the real world, Christine,' he said despairingly. 'You've no conception of what it is like to live at my level. You've no idea of how it feels to be forced to keep to your bed because it is freezing and you have nothing with which to make a fire, to starve because money has run out and there is no more for a week, not the slightest notion of the hopelessness, the despair that you'll never fight your way out of it because always there is something else to drag you back. You come down to the clinic for one day a week, you work hard and feel happy at what you are doing and then you go back to Belgrave Square, to servants who run at your bidding, to food that appears at the stroke of a clock and for which you have done nothing, to rich clothes and fine friends, to ease and plenty. What do you really know about people like me?'

She was staring at him, the bitterness in his voice pricking the bubble of her belief in their future. She said in a small voice, 'Don't you care about me, Daniel? Don't I mean anything to you at all?'

'Oh Christ, you mean everything, you know you do, but I've got to be practical. I've got to think for both of us. How would you like to bear your first child in a room like this, without doctors and nurses, with nothing but an old soap box for a cradle, with none of the luxuries that surround your sister's pampered little prince,' he went on brutally.

'I could do it if there was no other way,' she said stubbornly.

'And what about me? Do you think that is how I would want it for you? Oh God!' he turned away from her banging his fist futilely against the wall. 'Maybe I've had a dream that one day when I've lifted myself out of this ruck, when I have got where I want to be, then, then I might come to you and defy the whole fashionable rich world you live in!'

'If your ambitions mean so much more to you than I do, more than I can ever give you, then why have you let me believe you care?'

'Why, why, why? God knows why! I regret it. All this past summer I've told myself I was running after a fantasy, an impossible dream, and I believed, God forgive me, I almost hoped that you were just . . . amusing yourself and when the time came as I knew it must, we could part . . . and it wouldn't hurt you too much.'

'But tonight, Daniel, was it the same tonight? Was it? Suppose the kettle hadn't boiled over, suppose we . . .' she paused and then went on in a whisper, 'suppose tonight you had given me a child . . . '

They stared at one another, both aware how very close it had been, could so easily be again now they had crossed a barrier. Then he said very quietly, 'I think you have forgotten something, Christine. You are engaged. You still wear his ring. What are you going to say to Dr Fraser when he comes back to claim you?'

What indeed? The thought made her tremble but she went on bravely.

'I shall explain to Gareth. He will understand. We have always said we would leave each other free.'

'If he loves you, he will never let you go. You belong to him, you grew up with him, he is part of your world as I could never be. Go back to him, Christine, and forget about me, forget I ever existed.'

'What has happened between us has happened,' she said stubbornly. 'You can't pretend it never existed.'

He looked at her broodingly for a moment and then turned away. 'We've forgotten one very important thing. I could never bring myself to take your father's hand in friendship.'

She made an impatient movement. 'I thought we'd put all that behind us.'

'No, in my mind it is still there and with it something else, something you don't know.'

She was suddenly frightened, aware that they had been talking around the crux of the matter and now she must face up to it.

'What is it?'

'I can't tell you, not now.'

'You must. We can't go on at cross purposes. What did my father do to you that you cannot forgive?'

He was staring down at the fire, kicking at it so that the dull coal blazed and spat. 'If I tell you, you will hate me for it.'

'Maybe I will but I must know. Go on. You can't stop now.'

'Very well.' He was still not looking at her. 'When my mother went to Everard Warrinder begging for her husband's life, he made a bargain with her.'

'A bargain?'

'My mother was beautiful, still was even then. She had a lovely voice.' He was staring in front of him as if he were looking back into the past. 'She used to sing sometimes to Kate and me, lovely old ballads . . .'

'Why are you telling me all this?'

'Perhaps because it explains it, I don't know.' He paused and then went on quickly. 'He promised that if she would . . . give herself to him, he would save my father's life but he never kept his promise and afterwards my mother knew she was pregnant. Kate is your father's daughter.'

Christine stared at him. 'I don't believe it, I won't believe it, it's monstrous, not my father. He would never have done such a vile thing, never,' she said in a choked voice. 'How do you know? You could only have been a child.'

'I was then, but I was eleven when she died and that was when she told me. People don't lie when they are dying.'

'She must have made a mistake.'

'Oh no. For all the months my father was shut away, she was only able to speak to him through prison bars. I know because she used to take me with her. At the end she worried about Kate. She wanted me to know, she begged me to protect her.'

'Have you told her?'

'Not yet, but that is why I was so glad when Harry was sent away.'

'Because he is her half-brother?'

'Yes. I don't think it runs very deep with him. I don't think he will suffer from them being separated and when they meet again, it will be different.'

'Does my father know?'

'My mother never told him but I think maybe he has guessed or why should he have been so angry at the ball, why did he send Harry away to Paris so quickly afterwards?'

And why too had he forbidden her to see Daniel again – but in that she had defied him. In a way it explained a great deal that had puzzled her but she still couldn't accept it, not her brilliant fastidious father. There must be some other explanation, there had to be, something that would make it more bearable.

'I didn't want to tell you,' murmured Daniel. 'But it has always been there between us.'

There was something else too, a dark shadow that had haunted him ever since the last night when he had spoken with Everard, an unexplained hint, a possibility only but it had been there and he could not entirely wipe it away.

There was a sudden clamour from outside, a sound of shouting, a rush of feet up the stairs, someone banged on the door and Dickie burst into the room.

'It's nearly time,' he gasped, aglow with excitement. 'I thought you'd want to know.' Then he saw Christine and grinned. 'You too, Miss, your father has been asking for you, they all have, more than once.'

'Oh my God, I must go.'

'Yes, of course,' said Daniel. 'Dickie, run to the school, find out what is happening to Mr Nugent and tell them I'll be with them as soon as I can.'

'May I take Penny with me?'

'If you like, but keep him on a string or he might get hurt or lost.'

'I will.'

The boy snatched up the excited dog and went clattering down the stairs two at a time.

Christine had pushed her hair under her bonnet and tied the ribbons. Daniel put the heavy overmantel around her shoulders and they went out together. He locked the door and followed her down the stairs. They were lucky enough to pick up a cab that was willing to take them to the Cock and

Pheasant. Excited crowds still thronged the streets waiting for the final announcement but they got through at last.

He helped her down and they stood for a moment looking at one another. Everything had been said yet they were reluctant to part.

'When shall I see you again?' she whispered at last.

He shook his head silently, then bent forward, kissed her cheek, gave her a little push towards the door and walked quickly away.

She crept up the dark stairs and paused in the doorway of the big upstairs room. Some good news must have come in. They were crowding around her father, all talking at once. He laughed and broke away from them. Maybe it was because of her heightened sensibilities that night but she saw him not as a father figure but as a man, still handsome, still extremely attractive; twenty years ago he must have irresistible. What had really happened between him and that poor woman who came imploring his help? It struck her suddenly like a blow that maybe they were not strangers, but already known to one another, and with it came another thought – had her mother known? – and immediately she doubted it. Surely she would have known if there had been any discord in their marriage.

She stood there watching them, still unnoticed, and could not sort out her feelings about him. She could not reconcile the father she knew and admired with a man who could callously suggest such a detestable bargain and then fail to fulfil it. If it were known, if it were to be blazened forth, it would ruin him. She knew quite enough about the society in which she lived to realize it would be utter condemnation. She shivered at the thought of the spite, the gloating of those who envied his success, his charm and maybe too resented his arrogance. She wondered if he had already thought of that and if it was one of the reasons that had brought him here today. He could have silenced Daniel and yet he had not done so and she knew that if it did happen, she might despise her father but she would still do everything in her power to protect him.

All these thoughts went chasing through her mind in the few minutes before she took a step forward into the light. He saw her immediately and came to meet her, anxiety and relief mingled in his face.

'Wherever have you been, Christine? We have been worried about you. Mr Goodall even sent someone out to look for you.'

For the first time in her life she lied to him. 'I'm sorry, Papa. I didn't mean to be so long. I went to the clinic.'

'Surely it is closed today?'

'Yes of course but I stopped to talk to Bertha and Deborah and didn't realize how late it was. It took time to walk back, the streets were so crowded.'

'You shouldn't have gone out at all. It was really very inconsiderate of you.'

She thought he had been genuinely anxious for her and put a hand on his arm.

'I didn't mean to worry you.'

'Well, never mind. You're safe and that's what is important.'

'You're looking very tired, Papa. Are you sure you're feeling all right?'

'Well enough. We should hear the final results very soon now.'

'How is it going?'

He shrugged his shoulders. 'Neck and neck it would seem at the moment.'

She knew Elspeth was staring at her curiously and was acutely aware of how untidy she must look. A tray of tea had been brought for the ladies and Mrs Brown said kindly, 'Won't you join us, Miss Warrinder? It must be a very tiring day for you worrying about your Papa. It's so brave of him to come down here after that dreadful incident yesterday.'

She yielded to their insistence and sat down with them, accepting the tea but taking little part in the conversation going on around her. The day had been too momentous. That last hour waiting for the final results passed in a kind of blur. She thought her father looked exhausted. The long day with the pain and the inevitable reaction had worn him out. She was thankful when a messenger came hotfoot at last. The final count was completed and Everard Warrinder had lost, not by a great many votes but sufficient. The safe respectable candidate whom no one had much regarded, who was neither Tory nor Radical but maintained a stolid middle way, had retained his seat. Nothing would change. Neither her father with his lofty ambitions nor Mr Nugent with his more humble plans to better the cause of the working man, had in the end got anywhere. So much for Daniel's passionate hopes and dreams. His time had not yet come.

Announcements were made, regrets expressed, hands shaken, and then at last they were free to leave. Their coachman, fortified by several hot meat pies and a tankard of George's best, brought round the carriage.

Sitting beside him and glimpsing his face as they drove through the poorly lit streets, Christine thought her father looked upon the point of collapse.

She said gently, 'Are you very disappointed that it has turned out like this?'

He stirred. 'Disappointed? Perhaps, but it happens. Win or lose – life is like that. You can never be sure. I've had my share of both.'

'Will you try again?'

'Who knows what the future holds for any of us?'

He was staring bleakly in front of him and in the half light his face looked greenish white with a faint sheen of sweat. Was he thinking of the past? Of the threat that Daniel could hold over him, or the daughter he had never acknowledged, could never admit was his?

Home at last, with Clarissa concealing her relief at the news and fussing over him because he looked so tired, Christine kissed them both goodnight and went upstairs. It was a relief to reach the safety of her own room with its fine furniture, its rich carpet, the warmth and comfort and luxury, with Betsy waiting for her with a tray of hot milk and biscuits, her silk nightdress laid out on the bed: all things she had taken for granted for so long that it was only now that she was struck by the stark contrast with the bare discomfort of Daniel's attic room. His words of scorn, his utter rejection, came rushing back so forcibly that she dismissed Betsy immediately and the girl stared at her in surprise before leaving quietly, shutting the door after her.

Left alone Christine dropped on to the stool before the mirror, staring at her face pale with fatigue, her unpinned hair falling in tangles around her shoulders. In the space of a single day she had become a different person. Was it possible for a few hours to change one's whole life, she wondered, and then knew it wasn't just the last few hours, it was the culmination of all those long summer days, the hours spent with Daniel, the feelings that had run between them, unexpressed but ever growing, needing only a spark to set them alight, and slowly, out of the tangle of the last few weeks, she began to wonder if after all she had been wrong. It had been she who had done the running, she who had gone ahead, blindly sure he felt as she did and was only held back because of her father, because she was who she was. With a slow tide of bitter humiliation she wondered if she had fallen hopelessly in love with a man who had rejected her for what she still thought were insufficient reasons. And then there was Gareth . . . she stared at the ring on her finger and then slowly drew it off . . . Gareth who was even now on his way to England full of plans for their future. Gareth who had been there for so long, part of her life . . . dear God, what was she going to say to Gareth?

Chapter 15

Daniel stood in the middle of Mr Brown's new shop in Cheapside and in the glow of the new gas lamps looked around at the handsome fittings and the well-stocked shelves. Every evening since the election as soon as school was over he had been up there, finding it a relief to work himself to the bone and return home too tired to do anything but fall into bed.

It was in many ways a risky venture in which Ezra Brown had invested most of his savings but Daniel had to acknowledge that in his way he was a man of vision. He was convinced that his daring conception of a city shop where you could buy not only tea, coffee, every kind of spice and all the dry goods but also cheeses with butter, thick gammon rashers cut from sides of well-hung bacon, prime ham sold by the slice, newly baked bread, bottled fruits, jam and marmalade, and a variety of choice confectionery, would have an immediate appeal to the wives and servants of prosperous businessmen, who could place an order in the morning, have it delivered by evening and pay when it suited them. He looked like being right, thought Daniel, judging by the number of people who stopped to peer through the plate glass window or dropped in to pick up the handsome leaflet listing all the goods in stock.

The failure of all his hopes at the election, the emotional turmoil of the meeting with Christine, angry reproaches from the select committee of the Working Men's Association and a violent quarrel with Will Somers had left him feeling drained and in a black mood of depression. He felt he was stuck in a rut from which he could not free himself. Maybe this was the right way to get on, he thought cynically, pandering to the greedy appetites of the rich and forgetting the heartbreaking needs of the poor and hungry. He turned back grimly to the job in hand.

'Daniel, come and look at what I've done.'

Elspeth's sharp voice roused him from his gloomy thoughts. Nearly every evening she had come with him and had worked as hard as he had at putting the finishing touches.

'Come and look,' she said again. 'I'd like to know what you think.'

She had been setting up a window display with tea falling from pretty painted canisters, golden coffee beans heaped beside the coffee grinder in wood and brass, all very tastefully arranged on a draped stand and to set it off a handsome japanned tray set with a teapot, coffee pot and several cups and saucers in expensive bone china.

'Not bad at all,' said Daniel, going outside to get the full effect through the glass. 'That ought to pull them in.'

'Do you really think so? Papa said it could be a waste of time but if it makes people stop to look, then it has caught their attention to what we are selling. Isn't that so?' and she slipped her arm through his asking for his approval.

'Where did the china come from?'

'Actually it's Mamma's pride and joy,' she said with a little giggle. 'I had a hard task persuading her to lend it and it is only for the opening, then she wants it back and I must think again.'

The gas lamps cast a warm glow over her, picking out a strand or two of gold in the brown hair and warming her pale cheeks. Her dark blue serviceable dress with its small white collar was plain but fitted her well, showing off a trim figure. She looked almost pretty.

Elspeth had changed in the last two years. She was no longer the plain plump girl with spots and little to say for herself. Though they had absolutely nothing in common he had been forced to realize she had a better grasp of business matters than he had. She had become her father's right hand since he had no son. If he had had any sense, thought Daniel stacking the last of the shelves, he would have fallen in love with Elspeth, only he never had had any sense, never since he had first seen Christine in the Chichester garden.

They went on working silently side by side with Elspeth only too well aware of his complete indifference. She felt again the prick of a burning jealousy of the young woman who obsessed him, that Christine Warrinder who wore another man's ring on her finger, who had everything she most envied and who wanted Daniel too. It wasn't fair and it maddened her. She knew they had been together on the election day because Dickie had innocently given away that he had found her there in Daniel's lodgings. She remembered how Christine had looked when she had joined them that evening, distracted, inattentive. How far had they gone? Had he made love to her? Surely he must realize that he was being played with by a rich young woman who had other fish to fry and when he did realize it, then she would still be there. She knew without it ever needing to be said that she would find it easy to persuade her father to accept Daniel as a son-in-law when the time came, if it ever did, she thought sometimes despairingly.

In actual fact Daniel had only seen Christine once since the election. Dickie had fallen all the way down the stairs and wrenched his ankle so badly that he had taken him to the clinic and she had been there standing by while Dr Dexter strapped it up, telling him cheerfully that he was lucky not to have broken it and if he rested it for a few days he would be right as rain.

Their eyes had met once and then fallen away but Christine had made no move towards him. It was he who had put the barrier between them and yet perversely he was angry because she didn't step over it and he did not guess at her reaction of sick humiliation at his rejection. She had made up her mind that however much it hurt she would never again be a beggar for his love.

On their way home from the shop that evening Elspeth said, 'Papa has invited Mr Warrinder to the opening. Do you think he will come?'

'I doubt it. It's flying rather high, isn't it? I don't suppose Everard Warrinder QC even knows what a grocer's shop looks like.'

'His daughter would come if you were to ask her.'

'Why on earth should she?'

'Oh go on with you, Dan,' said Elspeth, letting her jealousy run away with her for once. 'Dickie said you were thick as thieves on election night.'

'I don't know what you mean by that. All I did was to rescue her from being molested by a crowd of louts and escort her back to her father.'

'You did take her to your lodgings first though, didn't you?'

'Because she was in some distress and needed a few minutes to pull herself together. What else are you suggesting?'

'Oh nothing of course, but I can't think Mr Warrinder would approve of his daughter running off with you like that.'

'What the devil are you trying to say?' said Daniel, stopping dead in the street and facing up to her. 'Are you suggesting that I took her back to Paradise Alley in order to seduce her?'

'No, no, of course not . . .'

'In that case shut your mouth about things that are nothing whatsoever to do with you,' said Daniel angrily, walking on again so fast that she had to run to keep up with him.

'I'm sorry, Dan, I didn't mean . . .'

'Oh forget it.'

But she didn't forget it. His angry denial made her all the more certain there was more behind it. She began to play with a new idea, a little plan to get even with Miss Christine Warrinder once and for all and it became more and more attractive as she went on thinking about it.

Christine thought afterwards that those weeks running up to Christmas were among the worst she had ever lived through. She had gone ahead so blindly, so sure she was right. She had wanted to give Daniel so much, had longed to share his life oblivious of problems and difficulties, and nothing had turned out as she had expected. She realized that she had been hopelessly naive to think that it would. She found herself looking at her father with new and critical eyes, judging him and finding him wanting, which was made worse by the fact that he was in considerable pain and fever for several days after the election and she was obliged to share her mother's anxiety for him.

The wretched fact remained that however you felt life had to go on and she must dress and eat, smile and be constantly at her mother's bidding while there was no one in whom she could confide, no one to whom she could pour out the whole story, because the crux of it belonged to Daniel and must remain secret between them.

She spent a few days with Margaret, longing to find peace in that happy home, but even at Ingham Park there was a rift in the lute.

'Freddie will be called back to the regiment in the New Year for special training,' said her sister when they were spending a cosy afternoon together.

'Why?' Christine said lightly. 'We are not going to war, are we?'

'They're anxious that all troops should be kept in readiness. I don't understand it properly but it seems that Russia is threatening to grab part of the Turkish Empire and that's something that must be prevented at all costs.'

'But that old question has been debated about for ages and nothing has ever come of it. Britain would never go to war for something as trivial as that.'

'Lord Cardigan who is Freddie's Commanding Officer thinks there is a strong possibility. He spoke of it at the regimental dinner.'

'He is an old warmonger.' Christine steered John Everard's unsteady crawl across the rug. 'I don't think you need worry about it. It's just one of those rumours.'

'I hope you're right because Freddie would have to go and I would miss him quite dreadfully. When does Gareth come home?'

'Very soon now. We've been expecting him for the last month.'

'You must be looking forward to it. When are you going to be married?'

'Oh, I don't know.' Christine rolled a ball across the floor and the baby chuckled and crawled after it. 'It's been so long now I've stopped thinking about it.'

Margaret looked at her curiously, sure there was something wrong but not wanting to probe too deeply.

'You can be sure of one thing. Mamma will be making plans already.'

'Oh I hope not. I'd hate a grand affair like Clara had.'

'Are they home from abroad yet?'

'Clara wrote that they intend returning in time to spend Christmas with Lord Dorrien,' said Christine and began to talk about the baby, anything to keep her sister from asking more questions about Gareth.

The day after she went back to London, the invitation arrived from Mr Brown and Everard tossed it across the table to his wife.

Clarissa, whose provisions were ordered from Fortnum's lavish and expensive shop in Piccadilly, picked it up, glancing at it disdainfully.

'What impudence to write to you like that. You won't go of course.'

'Oh I don't know. Mr Brown is a very worthy hardworking individual and people like that should be encouraged. What do you say, Christine?'

'I'd be very willing to go with you, Papa.'

'You must be out of your minds, both of you,' exclaimed Clarissa. 'A shop in Cheapside, what next!'

'You forget, my dear, that but for a few votes, I could have been their member of Parliament by now. They made me very welcome. It seems churlish to turn it down in the circumstances.'

It was a cold winter's day with thin sleety showers that turned the roads slippery as glass when the carriage took them to Cheapside but the gas lamps had been lit and the new shop glowed with a warm welcome through the murk. Mr Brown came hurrying to greet them. Mr Goodall was there with a number of other prosperous tradesmen accompanied by wives and daughters. Methodists being mostly temperance there was no champagne but instead coffee was being served with cakes and biscuits, presided over by Elspeth and her mother. Everard, never at a loss, chatted easily to those whom he had already met, and Christine, looking for Daniel, saw him in the background keeping a watchful eye on the apprentices all in their best clothes and stuffing themselves with sweet cakes.

Mr Brown had asked Everard to make a few opening remarks and in a momentary hush he stepped forward with practised ease to make a witty and gracious little speech. In the applause that followed a belated visitor came hurrying through the door looking so stylish and elegant that it was a moment before Christine recognised Kate. The months of success had given her an added gloss, and with her had come Byron Farrar, the handsome leading actor in Mr Kean's company whom many of the guests, especially the ladies, had long admired. Their arrival caused quite a buzz of interest.

Kate gave Everard a tiny smile which he acknowledged with an inclination of the head and for a fleeting second as they stood face to face Christine saw the likeness between them and thought everyone else must surely see it too, until she remembered that it was only apparent because of her own secret knowledge. Then Daniel had come to greet his sister.

'I didn't really expect you, Kate.'

'I know but Mr Kean was good enough to allow Byron and me to miss morning rehearsal,' and she moved on to congratulate Mr Brown and accept a cup of coffee from Elspeth.

Everard put his hand on Christine's shoulder. 'I think we might slip away now, don't you? We've done our duty by Mr Brown.'

'Yes, of course, Papa,' she said and wondered if the wish to escape was due to Kate's arrival. She turned, intending to ask Dickie to run and tell their coachman that they were ready to leave and at that precise moment a heavy object came crashing through the window, smashing the glass, sending the whole display flying in all directions and hitting the packed shelves at the back of the shop with a resounding thud.

In the screams and commotion that followed, Christine found her father's arm protectively around her and her face pressed against his coat. Daniel, followed by another of the younger men, sprinted through the door in pursuit of the wretch who had hurled the missile and everyone began to recover and assess the damage. Fortunately it was not serious. The window, being heavy plate glass, had shattered but did not splinter into sharp fragments and on the whole there were few cuts and only one or two bruises from people falling over one another as they tried to avoid being hit by what turned out to be not a brick but a small paving slab that must have been hurled with considerable force.

Daniel and his companion came back dragging the evil-doer between them, all three of them plentifully splashed with mud and streaks of blood.

Dickie, white as a sheet, said in a horrified squeak, 'It's my Uncle Clem!' and suddenly Christine thought she understood and felt no small measure of blame for what had happened. Clement Walker had been furious at the verdict of the magistrate, which not only robbed him of the boy whom he hoped to exploit but had also had a damaging effect on his business. He must have nursed a futile anger all these months and had now taken his revenge on Daniel and on poor Mr Brown who had been guilty only of a kindly wish to help the boy at her own passionate urging.

She had to admire the calm way he was taking his misfortune, comforting his shocked wife and her extreme distress at the smashing of her beloved china.

'It's not the end of the world, my dear. Windows can be replaced, so can cups and saucers. I would like to assure everyone here that this unhappy incident will not interfere with the opening. Business will commence tomorrow and then be carried on just as we had planned.'

Two policemen had arrived by now and were taking down particulars from Daniel who had a long bleeding cut down one cheek. Christine would have gone to him but Elspeth was there first, dabbing at it with her handkerchief until he pushed her impatiently away.

Their coachman had appeared in the doorway and then came in looking anxiously around the shop.

'Are you all right, sir?' he said to Everard. 'I heard the crash so I moved the carriage and horses out of harm's way. They are just up the street.'

'Very wise of you. We are coming now anyway.'

'You go on, Papa,' said Christine quickly. 'I just want to say something to Mr Brown.' He was frowning down at her.

'If you must, my dear, but don't be long. I'll wait for you in the carriage.'

She saw him go and then flew across the shop to where she could see Daniel, who had just come in after giving what information he could to the policemen.

'All that was because of Dickie, wasn't it?' she whispered unhappily. 'I feel so guilty about it.'

'It's nothing to do with you. I'm the one he wanted to punish and it's Mr Brown who has suffered. I don't know how I shall ever make it up to him.'

She touched the long oozing graze on his cheek. 'Does it hurt?'

'Nothing to speak of. It's only a scratch.'

He caught her fingers and pressed them. She was very close to him and just for a moment they might have been alone, bound together so that there seemed no need for words. All her doubts and miseries vanished. He loved her. It had been there all the time. Even if they were split apart for other reasons it would still be there and a glow of relief and joy surged within her.

'I mustn't stay. Papa is waiting,' she murmured and broke away, only pausing to speak to Mr Brown and quite oblivious of Elspeth who had stood silently watching them.

'We are going to spend Christmas with my grandfather in the country,' she said a little hurriedly. 'I would be grateful if you would make up a hamper, a good selection of what you think we may need for the holiday. Could you do that?'

'Indeed I could if you're quite sure, Miss Warrinder.'

'Of course I'm sure. Papa agrees with me. Can you send it to Belgrave Square by Christmas Eve when we shall be leaving for Bramber?'

'It will be my pleasure.'

An order from such a customer would be worth its weight in gold and he bowed an acknowledgement as she hurried from the shop to where the carriage waited.

'What was all that about?' asked her father as he put out a hand to help her up the steps.

'I wanted to give Mr Brown a good Christmas order. I thought it was the least we could do especially after what happened.'

'Did you indeed?' said her father drily. 'I don't know what your mother will have to say.'

'Well, if she is annoyed because I haven't consulted her first, I'll pay for it myself.'

He smiled. 'Oh I think the housekeeping will be able to stand a double order. The real question is who is going to eat it. We're a small party this year.'

'There are all the villagers. They're always hungry. I'll distribute some of it myself if necessary.'

'My independent daughter playing Lady Bountiful, is that it?'

'No, it isn't. That's a hateful thing to say,' she said indignantly. 'It's just that sometimes I think we ought to share a few of the good things we have with those who have none of them.'

'I'm sorry,' he said solemnly, 'I stand corrected.'

And then they both laughed and for a moment were back on the easy footing that had grown up between them during these last months before Daniel had spoiled it for her.

*

In the meantime back at the shop the guests slowly began to melt away, expressing sympathy and regrets.

'I've seen that wretch before,' said Mr Goodall frowning. 'He came up before the bench, some question of ill-treating a child if I remember rightly.'

'You're right there, sir,' said Mr Brown ruefully. 'Try to do a bit o' good and this is the result.'

'Never you mind. I'll see you get justice,' said the magistrate. 'Can't have ruffians like that rampaging through the streets. There's such a thing as law and order. You'll carry on, I'm sure.'

'Take more than that to stop me.'

'That's the spirit,' and Mr Goodall shook hands and went away to his waiting carriage.

Daniel and the boys had already begun to clear up and Elspeth would have joined them but her father stopped her.

'Leave that, lass, and take your mother home. She's had a nasty shock. Daniel, take a look out and see if you can stop a cab.'

'I'd much rather stay and help you, Papa.'

'Not much you can do and Daniel will be here. We'll need to board up the window or there won't be as much as a pound of tea left by morning.' He put an arm round his tearful wife and helped her to her feet. 'Now don't you fret, my dear, you go home and Elspeth will make you a nice cup of tea. I'll be back very soon.'

Elspeth helped her mother out into the street where the cab had already drawn up.

'Now,' said Mr Brown briskly to Daniel when the women had driven off, 'it's high time to get to work. I've a load of orders already to get out by Christmas and I'll see they're carried out if it kills me. There's plenty of wood left from the shelving. It's out in the yard. Fetch it in with one of the tea chests. You and I, Dan, will fix up the window while the boys sweep up and put all the damaged goods into the chest. We can sell some o' them cheap down at the other shop, and mind you don't cut yourselves on any of that broken glass. We don't want more blood spilled than we can help. Carry on now and take care.'

He galvanised them into action and when Daniel came back with the planks of wood, they took off their coats, rolled up their sleeves and got to work nailing the wood firmly across until presently Mr Brown stood back and surveyed their efforts with satisfaction.

'That's done the trick. I doubt if any looters will get through that lot till we get the glass refitted. Pity about Elspeth's pretty little display but it can't be helped.'

'I feel it's all been my fault,' said Daniel remorsefully. 'I should never have involved you in that business of Dickie. I might have known something like this would happen.'

'Maybe,' said Mr Brown, 'but it's never any use crying over spilt milk. What's done is done. I tell you one thing though. Get on a bit, save some money and branch out into something new and you'll be the target of the spite and jealousy of those who spend their time envying others because they haven't the guts to strike out for themselves. That's life, my boy, and it works the same from the highest to the lowest and there's nowt to be done about it but pick yourself up and start again.'

'I owe you so much,' said Daniel awkwardly. 'If there is anything I can do to help out.'

'There is actually,' said Mr Brown thoughtfully, putting in another nail and giving it a sharp smack with his hammer. 'I've been meaning to have a word with you about it and now's as good a time as any. Elspeth wants to manage the running of this shop and she's quite a good choice for it, I'll say that for her. She's learnt a lot over the last two years but when all's said and done she is only a lass and young with it and the world being what it is suppliers, and customers too for that matter, look for a man in charge. If you would work alongside her for a few months, someone they could refer to, that would mean a great deal.'

'Does that mean you want me to give up the school?'

'No, not yet anyway, maybe you could carry on with both, see how it would work out. I'll be keeping an eye on the accounts and working between the two shops. I can't neglect the Whitechapel store, one must support the other if you understand me and this one is a costly venture that is bound to take some time to establish itself. I would be grateful and it would be keeping it within the family if you know what I mean. Elspeth likes you and I am sure you will get on well together.'

Daniel felt a wave of dismay. It was not that he disliked Elspeth but he would be forced into a far closer relationship than he would have wished and he would have been a fool not to realize that she liked him a great deal too much. It would mean very careful handling but all the same he did owe Mr Brown a great deal and one had to pay one's debts.

'I will do what I can and gladly,' he said with an effort.

'Good lad, I knew I could rely on you. Now I think we've done all we can for tonight. We'll cut along home. Come and sup with us, Daniel. A good warm fire and something tasty on the table will help us to sort ourselves out.'

He would have preferred to be alone but the thought of his icy cold room with no food unless he picked up a faggot or a hot potato on the way home was very uninviting.

'Thank you,' he said, 'if you don't think it will be too much for Mrs Brown.'

'Bless you, boy,' said Mr Brown heartily, 'you'll be welcome. It'll take her out of herself. You're one of her favourites, you know.'

Chapter 16

'There must be some mistake. I never ordered none of this,' said Mrs Gant when a large box packed with a great variety of expensive foods was delivered at the servants' entrance in Belgrave Square on Christmas Eve.

'There ain't no mistake, Missus, 'cos I've got the address written out plain, see,' and a paper was waved under her nose, 'and Master told me as how I was to take a cab 'cos Miss Christine were goin' off to the country to be with her Grandad,' said the delivery boy cheerfully all on one long breath.

'Well, I don't know what Lady Clarissa is going to say, I'm sure,' said the cook frowning, 'and I'll thank you not to speak of Miss Christine in that saucy way neither. You'd better bring it in, I suppose.'

The boy manhandled the heavy hamper across the threshold, pocketed the sixpence Cook rather grudgingly gave him and went off whistling, highly pleased with himself.

Clarissa, consulted later in the day, looked down at the collection of items ranging from finest coffee beans through to a prime ham and including rich cakes, biscuits, jellies, fruits and chocolates and then went in search of Christine.

'I don't know what you expect me to do with this lot,' she said. 'Was it your doing or was it your father?'

'It was my idea to give the order but Papa agreed with me. We'll take it to Bramber. I am sure some of Grandfather's poorer tenants will be pleased to receive something extra.'

'I can't see many of them enjoying Stilton cheese and port wine jelly,' said her mother acidly. 'That business down in the

East End seems to have turned both your brains. Your Grandfather will think I have taken leave of my senses.'

Christmas had usually been a time of big parties at Bramber but this year there was only themselves. Even Margaret and Freddie had decided to spend it at Ingham Park and much to his mother's disappointment Harry was spending Christmas with one of his new French friends and would not join them till the New Year.

It was a quiet lull after the stress of the last few weeks and Christine was glad of it. She knew her mother missed the dinner parties, the musical evenings, the balls and the theatres but this year she did not regret any of them. She could take out the horses whenever she pleased, sometimes alone, sometimes with her father or her grandfather. She went for long walks with the dogs and took pleasure in supplementing Lord Warrinder's customary Christmas gifts to his tenants with specially selected items from that well-stuffed hamper. She wondered what Mr Brown would have thought to see one of his jars of extra special fruit landing up beside the bed of a rheumaticky old farmer who eyed it suspiciously, but at least it was not being wasted. Sometimes, walking or riding, she thought how she would have loved to share her pleasure with Daniel and how ridiculous and unfair it was that it was not only the past that kept them apart but also the absurdity of class. Even her tolerant grandfather would have raised his eyebrows at such a guest and the servants, always far more class conscious than their employers, would have been at a loss, not knowing whether to treat him as one of themselves or as one of the gentry.

Gareth had still not arrived and though she knew that it was only delaying the inevitable painful meeting she was not sorry to have time to plan the kindest way to tell him that she could not marry him.

Two days after Christmas they had unexpected company. The carriage that rolled up the drive one afternoon brought Lord Dorrien with the happily married couple just returned from their honeymoon in Italy – or perhaps not so happy after all, judging from Clara's heightened colour and the scowl on her husband's face when they came into the hall.

It appeared they were on their way to Dorset and decided to break the journey at Bramber. Clarissa, who did not care for the country as much as her husband or her daughter, welcomed their coming and immediately despatched servants to prepare bedrooms and to warn Cook that she must provide a rather more extensive menu for dinner that evening.

Christine took her cousin to the room prepared for her, made sure the newly lighted fire was burning well and duly admired Clara's travelling dress of dark red corded silk, cut in the very latest Parisian fashion with an over-mantel of velvet lined with grey squirrel. They had never had much in common but she felt obliged to linger and chat a little.

'How did you enjoy Italy?' she asked as Clara examined her face in the mirror and began to unpin the heavy braids of dark hair. 'Papa took us to Venice one year but Mamma didn't like the heat and said the canals smelled disgusting so we've never been since. I can't tell you how I envied you visiting Florence and Rome.'

'I might have enjoyed them very much more if I had been with someone else,' said Clara unexpectedly, winding up her hair into a coronet on top of her head and sticking pins into it as if emphasizing a point. 'I tell you something, Christine, honeymoons are vastly overrated. You're stuck with someone morning, noon and night for a couple of months, expected to be always together – other guests whispering "Newly married" and making sure they keep out of the way, leaving you utterly alone together whether you want it or not.'

'Isn't that the idea?' said Christine. 'An opportunity to get to know one another intimately.'

Clara shot her a scornful glance. 'Perhaps it is if you happen to care for the same things but Raymond and I have such different interests. I wanted to explore the churches, the museums, the art galleries but Ray detested it, so that when he did come now and again it was on sufferance and completely ruined all my pleasure. All he wanted to do was to meet up with the other Englishmen out there, and there are plenty, you know, some of them pretty detestable, and drink and gamble and probably ogle pretty girls. I don't really know what they did, I was never invited to join them. I've never felt so thankful as when we stepped on the packet boat that brought us to Dover.'

Her outburst of appalling frankness took Christine's breath away. 'Are you already regretting that you married him?' she asked tentatively.

'Regretting it? Of course I'm not. It will be quite different now that we are back at home. I shall go my way and Ray will go his. Papa Dorrien is very generous. He has promised that I can completely redecorate the London house if I wish and it is very old-fashioned since it has been left just as it was when Ray's mother died. I shall enjoy doing that and then I intend to entertain, small select dinner parties, musical evenings – I shall invite all the most distinguished, the wittiest, the most amusing and glamorous people and they'll come because I shall make it the fashionable thing to do so. I've always wanted to have a *salon* but a woman on her own is at such a disadvantage, being married makes all the difference.' She turned glowing eyes towards her cousin. 'Do you think I shall be able to achieve that?'

'If anyone can, you will, Clara. You've never failed in anything you really set out to do. And what part will your husband play in all this?'

'So long as he plays the host when I want him to do so, I don't think I mind very much what he does. If he enjoys running after dancers and actresses, then let him, so long as he doesn't provoke a scandal.'

It was quite the bleakest prospect of marriage that Christine had ever heard and she could not help thinking that it was a kind of bravado, a determination on Clara's part to make the best of a rash and intolerable marriage and a brave way of hiding her disappointment and disillusion.

'Have you thought about children?' she ventured as Clara got to her feet and shook out her spreading skirts.

'Oh yes, of course, Papa Dorrien will expect that. He wants a grandson, I suppose, but there's time enough. I'll go through with it if I have to. I'm not a cheat. Do you think we ought to go down now? Your mother did say something about tea and we've had a very long cold drive.'

'Yes, of course. They will be waiting for us in the drawing room.'

They went down the stairs arm in arm, best of friends on the surface, but all the same it was not really a very pleasant couple of days and even Clarissa, the most gracious of hostesses, felt the strain.

To start with Lord Dorrien asked a great many probing questions about the election, which had the result of putting her father on edge, and then went on to express deep concern over the shooting incident.

'I did warn you, if you remember. You should have got rid of those subversive elements right at the start.'

'May I ask how?' said Everard ironically. 'Short of a general massacre I hardly know how they could have been traced.'

'I gather that you, let the fellow go free. Was that wise?'

'He was not responsible for the shooting so it would have scarcely advanced my cause to have him clapped into prison.'

'Will you try again?'

'Who knows where any of us will be in a few years' time,' he said briefly and changed the subject.

Raymond had obviously expected to find Harry at Bramber and was disgruntled to learn that he was still in France. To offset his ill humour Clara was all sweetness and light, which only had the effect of infuriating him further. Not for the first time Christine realized how grateful she ought to feel that her father had not pressured her into marriage with him. There was an ugly streak in Raymond Dorrien and it had shown itself already in the way he treated servants and dogs, indeed anyone whom he regarded as inferior and unable to hit back. Christine had an unholy desire that someone somewhere would have the temerity to do just that.

There were no more frank outbursts from Clara but one

morning when they were walking together in the garden, well wrapped up against a biting East wind, she began to ask about Gareth.

'I'd expected to see him here. Aren't you going to be married very soon?'

Christine felt desperately that if anyone asked that question again she would either scream or run mad.

'There have been delays on the American side,' she said edgily. 'But we expect him very soon now. He is a doctor, you know, he doesn't live like Ray on his father's wealth, and there is still a great deal to be settled about his work before we can think of being married.'

'I see. Well, he's your choice, a bit too much on the slow side for me,' and as if one thought had led to the other she ignored Christine's frown and went on blithely: 'By the way, what happened to that young woman Harry invited to sing at his birthday ball? Is he still her devoted admirer?'

'I don't know as he was ever that,' said Christine repressively, 'but he has been away for the last six months. Kate is the star of Mr Kean's pantomime just now and will be taking part in the new season of plays.'

'I always thought that Ray and Harry were rivals for her favours, wasn't that so?' went on Clara.

'I'm sure I don't know where you heard that and in any case don't you mind?'

'Goodness, no. Why should I? It's all in the past, isn't it?' She gave a brittle little laugh. 'I think I can make sure he doesn't stray too far in the future.' She shot Christine a quick glance. 'By the way, didn't she have a brother?'

'Yes. He teaches in a ragged school in Whitechapel. I see him occasionally when I go down to the clinic.'

'Heavens, are you still going down there every week? My dear, what a martyr to your principles you must be. I don't know how you can.' She shuddered dramatically. 'I couldn't stand it for a minute.'

'You never know what you can do till you try,' said Christine and put an end to Clara's probings by calling to the dogs. 'It's

315

blowing up very cold. I don't know about you but I could do with a hot cup of chocolate.'

'What a lovely idea. Let's go in and go on with our cosy chat over the fire.'

The guests left at last, to Christine's relief and she rather thought that her father was not sorry either, and it was early on New Year's Eve when Gareth finally arrived.

It had been a bleak morning with a light frosting of snow and Christine had been paying a visit to Paddy's mother, who was suffering from one of her usual winter bouts of bronchitis. Mr Brown's port wine jelly seemed just the thing for a rasping chest and an aching throat and she stayed for half an hour saying how pleased her grandfather was with Paddy's progress and that no doubt soon he would be promoted to head stable boy.

She was coming up the drive when she saw the carriage at the front door, saw the familiar figure jump down and then turn to help Uncle David, well wrapped up in shawls and scarves against the bitter wind. She panicked suddenly, grabbed the surprised Benjy by the collar and stood still, hidden in the shelter of the shrubbery. Last year she had raced to meet him, hurling herself into his arms, and now she couldn't. It would be false, it would be living a lie. She held back till they had gone into the house and the carriage had moved away, then she bolted round to the stables, went in at the servants' entrance and raced up the back stairs to her bedroom.

She stood in the middle of the floor panting, unnerved, and then told herself she was being ridiculous. All she had to do was to welcome him as usual, listen to all his news, talk, smile, laugh, and presently find a convenient time to tell him she had changed her mind, that she was no longer going to marry him and perhaps go on to say she had fallen in love with someone else. It should be easy. Engagements were not sacrosanct, they were broken every day and no one fell into despair or shot themselves over it. Only this was different. Gareth had been part of her life for so long, her prop and comfort in times of trouble, it would be hard to break the familiar ties, but to marry him feeling as she did about Daniel would be cheating him and she could not, she must not live a lie. All these thoughts raced chaotically through her mind as she pulled off her soaked boots, changed her gown, brushed her hair and pinned it up again. She gazed into the mirror, wondering if she looked any different, deliberately putting off the moment when she must go down the stairs and greet him as if nothing had happened.

Betsy burst in without knocking, eyes shining, voice bubbling over with excitement.

'Lady Clarissa sent me to find you, Miss. Mr Gareth is come at last with Mr Fraser. She thought you would like to know. They're all in the drawing room.'

'I know. I saw the carriage,' she said calmly. 'Would you mind setting my boots to dry and brushing out my gown, the skirt has become very muddied. I'm going down now.'

She gathered her courage, sailed past the puzzled serving girl and went down to face what she must and found at first that there was nothing to face. You cannot blurt out such a private decision in public and that first evening together was like a dozen others when Gareth had come from school or college or hospital, so much news to be exchanged, so many things to talk about. He told her there was a Christmas gift for her in his luggage, something very particular to America, and Uncle David had brought her Mr Dickens' latest bestseller hot from the press. Her father was demanding details of the work he had been engaged with and in his turn Gareth wanted to hear everything about the election. The words tumbled over one another. They talked all during dinner and afterwards in the drawing room when coffee was brought in. Christine sat close by saying little but watching Gareth's face, trying to analyse her feelings. She was still so fond of him, she warmed to him when he spoke enthusiastically of the medical experiments he had taken part in, the cases in which he had himself been involved, and yet she knew there was something lacking, some magic, some quickening of the senses, a stirring that was

317

physical as much as mental, and she thought perhaps, despite her affection for Gareth, that if she had never met Daniel she might never have realized how much she was missing.

He looked at her once and smiled. 'You're very quiet, Christine, what have you been doing all these months?'

'Oh I've just plodded along from one day to the next, no excitement, no thrills of discovery like you have had, I'm afraid,' nothing if you except falling headlong into a desperate love that was threatened and fraught with trouble, nothing except that she was now burdened with a knowledge of her father's past about which she could tell no one. Her whole life had been turned upside down so that there were days when she felt a completely different person and the future that had once stretched like a wide and sunny road before her was now become a dark forest through which she could see no clear path.

There was one awkward moment when he gave her the gift he had brought for her. It was a long gold chain intricately wrought with ancient signs and symbols.

'I saw it in New York when Dr Andrews and I were marooned there because of the hold-up in the shipping. It's from Mexico, Aztec work. The antique dealer swore it was genuine but it's possibly a good copy.'

'It's beautiful,' she murmured, letting it run through her fingers. 'You shouldn't spend so much money on me.'

'Who else should I spend it on?' he said smiling and threw it over her head. 'I see you aren't wearing my ring. Is something wrong with it?'

'Oh no,' she said quickly. 'It's . . . it's just that my finger seems to have got thinner, I was afraid of losing it.'

'We must get it altered to fit. According to the man in the antique shop, these chains were given by young men to their loved ones on their betrothal. All romantic nonsense, I expect, but it seemed somehow appropriate.'

The chain felt like a ring of fire round her neck.

A day later and she was thinking that she must soon find an opportunity to get Gareth alone away from the house, where they could be free of interruption, where they could talk sensibly and quietly, when Harry arrived very full of himself and his new life in France.

He hugged Christine, slapped Gareth on the back and said cheerfully, 'When are you two going to get spliced? I hope you'll give me fair notice. I wouldn't miss it for the world.'

'That's for Christine to say,' said Gareth, pulling her close to him so lovingly that her throat dried and she couldn't find an answer. 'Give us time to breathe, old man,' he went on, 'I've only been back a couple of days. Now what about these grand folk you've been staying with who own a chateau on the Loire?'

And Harry was well away describing, chiefly for his mother's benefit, the house party, the entertainment and his friend's pretty sisters.

'You ought to see their horses, Grandfather. They're the absolute tops, imported from Spain with Arab blood.'

'Well, I'm afraid you'll have to content yourself with my old hacks while you are here,' remarked Lord Warrinder drily and Harry had the grace to blush.

'I'm sorry, I didn't mean . . .'

'Oh go on with you, boy, tell us the rest. I only hope that in all this high living you found time to pick up a few useful details about French law.'

'Oh Lord, yes. I couldn't help it,' said Harry ruefully. 'The French are hard taskmasters. They rammed it down my throat.'

It should have been like old times and yet it wasn't, too many strains beneath the surface. The morning after Harry arrived, he came into Christine's bedroom after breakfast and plumped down on the bed.

'I wanted to ask you, Chris. Have you seen anything of Kate lately?'

'Yes, I have. She is making great strides in Mr Kean's company.'

'So I gather,' said Harry gloomily. 'I have only heard from her once while she was away on tour and she told me not to write as the letters would probably never reach her.'

Brother and sister had always been very close. She came and sat beside him on the bed.

'Harry, are you still in love with Kate?' she asked bluntly.

'I thought I was. I asked her to marry me – did she ever tell you that? She turned me down of course, said I was too young to know my own mind. It made me angry. I wouldn't take no for an answer and I swore that when I came home from Paris, I would ask her again.'

'And how do you feel now?'

'That's just it. I'm not sure, Chris. I still believe she's a thumpingly marvellous girl but things have changed. I've had time to think and now – oh Lord, it makes me feel the most awful rotter.'

'You've grown up, that's all.' They were the same age and yet she felt so much older and wiser in experience and she knew a huge wave of relief that his ardour had cooled and he need never know of that relationship which must keep them apart for ever. 'Kate is very determined to make a big career in the theatre,' she went on, 'and that hardly fits into marriage, does it?'

'Do you really think so?' said Harry greatly relieved.

'Yes, I do. Why don't you go and see her before you return to Paris? I haven't been to the pantomime yet and they say she is marvellous in it. Why don't we both go when we go back to town?'

'Chris,' went on Harry earnestly, 'what was all that about Papa being shot at during the election? He shut up about it like an oyster when I asked him but Mamma went on and on about Daniel Hunter being mixed up in it.'

'If it hadn't been for Daniel, it would have been very much worse. Some crazy rioter aimed a gun at Papa but Daniel knocked it up just in time so luckily it was only a flesh wound. The real culprit got away but the police grabbed Daniel, only fortunately Papa had seen what happened and insisted on them setting him free.'

'Good for Pa. He could have raised hell over it.'

'Yes, he could but he didn't,' and she wished passionately that she could pour out the whole story to Harry, only it wouldn't be fair on him and in any case most of it wasn't for her to tell.

'Odd, isn't it?' said Harry thoughtfully. 'But for that chance meeting at the Chichester Fair none of this might have happened.'

'Perhaps not,' but it had not been entirely chance. Somewhere along the line Daniel's obsessive bitterness against Everard Warrinder would have surfaced and brought them into a conflict that was still unresolved.

Later that morning Christine came down the stairs in boots, thick warm cloak, and scarlet woollen scarf wrapped around her throat. Gareth was waiting for her in the hall.

'Where are you two off to, the North Pole?' enquired Harry coming out of the dining room.

'Gareth and I are walking the dogs. Tom says the frost is too heavy this morning to take out the horses.'

'Shall I come?' suggested Harry and then saw the dismay written large on their faces. 'Oh go on you two lovebirds. I'll not play gooseberry,' he said and went off laughing.

'There are times when Harry's schoolboy humour makes me feel a hundred,' said Gareth as they went out to the drive and were joined by Benjy and the two spaniels.

It was bitingly cold but the icy wind had largely dropped and there were a few glimpses of wintry sunshine. They walked quickly not saying much, Christine realizing that the moment had come to stop pretending everything was the same as last year and dreading it. At any other time she would have delighted in the day, the stark black branches of the trees furred with glittering frost, the sharp clean smell of the winter woodland. She glanced at Gareth striding along beside her, swinging his heavy stick and smiling to himself as if at a happy future in which she could no longer play any part.

They walked through the park and then took a familiar footpath that led them up on to the wide sweep of the Downs. Sheep were scattered here and there and the dogs ranged widely over the fields, coming to heel now and then when she called them and then taking off again. The path climbed steeply upward through a thick scrubby hedge and then up on to the bare sweep of the rounded hill surmounted by a crest of trees. It was a walk they had done a dozen times before. It was steep in parts and the icy air took their breath away but they plodded on grimly. They reached the summit at last, panting but triumphant, smiling at one another as they dropped on to the split tree trunk set on two stumps which had served as a seat for as long as they could remember.

'I'm not quite so out of condition as I feared,' said Gareth breathlessly, 'though I must admit that months of American food have taken their toll on my waistline.'

The dogs had come and flopped around their feet. They were silent for a moment and Christine was nerving herself to what must be said now or never when Gareth swung round to her.

'Now I've got my breath back, I've got something very exciting to tell you. I've been bottling it up ever since Uncle David told me. The old man has been holding out on me. You see he owns a house in, of all places, Wimpole Street. It seems he leased it years and years ago when he once contemplated marriage. I don't know what happened, whether she called it off or he did, Uncle David keeps his own secrets and in any case he's never been the marrying kind.'

'He once told me that he was in love with my grandmother,' said Christine in a stifled voice.

'Did he? You were favoured. He very rarely talks about himself. It seems he kept the house and leased it to a series of doctors and the last one, whose family has grown in numbers, is now looking for a larger place so – do you know what? – he intends to give it to us as a wedding present. You do understand what that means, don't you? Now that Dr Andrews is settling in Harley Street and is going to take me on as his junior partner, we shall have our own house not too far away. Uncle David says it badly needs repainting and refurnishing but that could be left to your choice. How long do you think it will take – three months? We could be married at Easter.'

'No, Gareth, no . . .'

'In May or June then if you think Easter is too early. We shall have to consult your mother in any case. As soon as we go back to London, I'll take you to look over it. Then we can make decisions and the work can be set in hand almost at once.'

He had gone on almost in one long stream, so full of what he had been planning that she had felt it impossible to interrupt him, but now she brought her fist down hard on his knee.

'No, Gareth, no! You must listen to me.'

'What is it?' he asked and looked bewildered. 'What's wrong? Have I been running on too fast? Don't you like the idea?'

'It's not that.' She took a deep breath. 'I'm not going to marry you.'

It was said at last, clear and unmistakably. She saw the look of shock on his face followed by one of sheer disbelief.

'But you must. It has all been arranged for months now. Are you angry with me because I went to the United States and couldn't take you with me?'

'No, it's just because – well, we did say – do you remember? It was when we were at Brighton that summer, we did say we would leave each other free.'

'But that was over a year ago now. We've come a long way since then. Is that why you've not been wearing my ring? Is it?' She nodded miserably and he went on, 'But why, Christine, why? What has changed you? Is it something I have done? It can't be your father. He spoke to me only yesterday and was kindness itself. Your mother too.'

'It's not Papa or Mamma and it's not you, Gareth. It is my fault, mine entirely.'

'What has happened to change you?'

She shook her head dumbly and got up, walking away from him and he followed after her.

'Why is it your fault, Christine? Why? You must tell me.'

She turned away, staring unseeingly over the broad sweep of the Downs. 'I'm in love with someone else.'

'In love with . . .?' He frowned. 'I don't believe you. I won't believe you.'

'You must because it is true.'

For a moment he was stunned, then he said hoarsely, 'Who is it?' and when she did not answer him, he swung her round to face him. 'Who is this man?'

'I'm not going to tell you.'

'Why? Are you ashamed of him?' She shook her head and he went on relentlessly, 'Are you going to marry him?'

She jerked herself free. 'Stop questioning me.'

'I have a right to know. Are you?'

'No, at least not yet.'

'Why not?'

'There are reasons.'

'Is he married?'

'No, of course he's not.'

He paused in his questioning, looking so wretched she had an absurd desire to comfort him as she might have done a disappointed child.

'I still can't believe it,' he said slowly. 'Have you told your parents or Harry?'

'No. I had to tell you first.'

'And this man you say you love – does he know about me? Is he laughing up his sleeve at the poor wretch who has been living in a fool's paradise all these months?'

'No, he's not like that. He's too generous, too honest. He tells me that you and I belong together because you are part of my world and he is not, as if stupid class distinctions mean anything when two people love one another . . .' and then she stopped, suddenly realizing that she had spoken out of the bitterness and frustration of Daniel's rejection and knew that she had said too much.

Gareth was staring at her as the truth slowly dawned on him.

'It can't be, it's impossible,' he said slowly. 'It couldn't be that young man we met at the Great Exhibition, that vulgar pushing fellow with the ridiculous ambitions. You told me in one of your letters that he had turned up again at the clinic with a sick child. My God, it can't be true! You can't have fallen in love with a man like that.'

'Why can't I? You know nothing about him. You don't know how brave and loyal and good he is. You could never understand how desperately hard his life has been and the fight he has had to win through even to the little he has now.'

'Oh I've no doubt he has spun a very plausible tale,' said Gareth bitterly.

'Oh what's the use of talking to you,' she went on fiercely. 'You're the same as the rest, blinded by prejudice because he was dragged up in an orphanage, went to work at the cotton mill for fourteen hours a day while you were sent to Harrow and Cambridge. You don't want to listen, you don't want to understand. I'm not talking to you any longer. I'm going home.'

She began to walk quickly down the steep path but he followed after her.

'Don't run away from me. At least tell me about it. We've been close for a very long time, Christine. Don't you think you owe it to me?'

'Perhaps.' She slowed down and let him come up beside her. 'I did not want to hurt you, Gareth. I have wanted to tell you for months now but you were so far away and I couldn't put it down on paper. I tried. I wrote letter after letter and then tore them up.'

'I think I know what has happened,' he said, stifling his own bitter hurt, trying to speak calmly and reasonably. 'I know how deeply you have felt about the work you have been engaged in at the clinic. I know how generous spirited you are, you have even impressed that hard-bitten sceptic John Dexter, and there was this young man, intelligent, hard done by, struggling to make something of himself. I can understand the impact he must have made on your sympathies and who can blame him for exploiting it?'

'You've got it all wrong,' she exclaimed. 'It's not Daniel who has sought me or tried to impress me. He's too proud, too independent, he despises the class we come from. He fought hard and bitterly against Papa at the election.'

'Even to the extent of shooting at him,' said Gareth drily.

'That was not Daniel.'

'No, but probably inspired by him.'

'That's not true. Even Papa did not hold it against him.'

'And your father is not easily deceived, you would say. But tell me this, Christine,' went on Gareth ironically. 'If he is such a paragon of virtue, how did all this come about?'

And she couldn't explain, couldn't find the right words. How could she describe the slow growth of the feeling between them, the fire that nothing had been able to quench, that might so easily have flared into passion but for a boiling kettle, how tell him of the past bitterness between Daniel and her father that was such an insuperable barrier without betraying a secret that was not hers to tell.

She said lamely, 'I can't explain it but there have been times when we fought it and each other but it is still there and I could never cheat you, Gareth. I had to tell you however much it hurts.'

They walked on for a little in silence and then Gareth paused on a little hillock that looked down on to the parkland surrounding Bramber. In the cold still air the smoke curled up from the distant chimneys.

'I won't pretend it hasn't hit me hard,' he said slowly, 'but I have been trying to think what is the best for both of us. I'm not going to let you break our engagement, Christine, not yet . . .'

'But you must,' she interrupted. 'It's not fair on you that I should hold you to a promise that I have already broken.'

'But you haven't broken it, not yet. I believe you to be mistaken. You have let your feelings run away with you and have not yet realized the consequences and when you do, I'm going to be there. I'm not going to see you let down and made unhappy and not be there to give comfort as I've always done in the past.'

Whatever she had expected, it had not been this. That he should treat her almost as an irresponsible child admitting to some folly that in the fullness of time would surely pass. Not to be taken seriously was infuriating, and yet so like the Gareth who had always been a pillar of strength in the past that she did not realize how desperately hard it was for him to accept the disappointment, the shattering blow to his love for her, to the future he had been planning for them both.

'And what do we say to Mamma when she asks us to fix a date for the wedding?' she said.

'Leave that to me. I'll explain that the settling in with Dr Andrews, the fixing of my new duties at the hospital, will take much longer than I had anticipated so we must postpone our wedding for a few more months.'

'And supposing they guess that something is wrong?'

'We'll have to weather it.'

'Why are you doing this, Gareth? Why?'

'It's quite simple,' he said very quietly. 'I love you, Christine, I think I've always loved you and I can't contemplate losing you without a fight. I believe you are mistaken. If I'm right, then I'll still be there to pick up the pieces. If I'm wrong and I pray to God I'm not, then I must learn to accept as a great many other people have had to do that life has given me a raw deal and denied me what I want more than anything else in the world.'

'Oh Gareth, I wish . . .' but she couldn't go on. If only he'd shouted at her or hit her instead of being so unbearably understanding and kind.

They were nearly home when she stopped suddenly, turning to face him.

'I can't do it, Gareth, I can't go on pretending that nothing has changed.'

'I don't think it has, not seriously. How do you think I am feeling? Is it so hard to ask you to carry on for a little till we are both sure of what the future holds for us? Can't you do it for me, please Christine?'

The pain in his voice made her feel unbearably guilty.

'Very well,' she whispered. 'If you really want it, I'll try.'

Back at the house she knew she had to escape. She couldn't face a possible barrage of questions, not yet.

'I'm going up to my room. I don't want anything to eat. Tell them I'm not feeling well, anything you like.'

In the dining room when luncheon was served Clarissa said, 'She's not been looking herself for a day or two. I hope she's not sickening for the influenza.'

'You're the physician,' said Everard, pouring wine for Gareth. 'What do you think?'

'In actual fact,' he said carefully, 'we had a little disagreement this morning. I would like to postpone our wedding for a few months and she was angry with me because of it.'

'I'm not surprised,' said Harry half-jesting. 'You went gallivanting off rather too often this past year. I don't wonder at Chris taking umbrage at another postponement.'

Everard, who thought he knew more about his daughter than either of them, was not entirely satisfied but trusted Gareth to find a solution if a problem did exist.

Christine joined them in the drawing room after dinner that evening looking pale but composed. Her father looked up from his book as she came in.

'Feeling better, my dear?'

'Yes, thank you, Papa.'

She looked around the room. Her mother was working at her tapestry frame, Harry lounged on the sofa with a sporting magazine, Gareth was playing chess with her grandfather.

Lord Warrinder said testily, 'You're not concentrating, boy. You quite simply gave me that last game.'

'Sorry, sir. I'm out of practice. I'll promise to do better next time.'

For all his outward composure Gareth was finding it desperately hard to get through what was quite the worst day in his life.

Uncle David held out his hand. 'Come and sit by me, my dear and tell me all the latest gossip.'

He was the only one that evening who suspected that something was gravely wrong but he said nothing. Time to give sympathy and advice if Gareth should come to him as he still did from time to time.

'There's not much to tell really,' but Christine came gratefully to pull up a footstool and sit by his chair.

'Now tell me,' he went on, 'what's the latest drama down at that clinic of yours?' and he put an old veined hand comfortingly on hers.

The next day, the holiday over, the whole party packed up and went back to London.

PART FOUR

Kate

1853

Chapter 17

Kate, draped in a Greek-style robe of red, white and blue, her hair brushed out and gleaming like bronze under a gilded helmet, stood in the prow of a great ship and sang 'Rule Britannia', gallantly leading the audience into the chorus and ending with a resounding –

'Britons never, never, never will be slaves!'

– with a great stamping of feet and huzzas of applause.

The curtain fell and rose again half a dozen times. The pantomime had pursued its way through four hours of fairy tale with a flying ballet, slapstick humour involving two step-ladders and a pail of whitewash, an interlude with Harlequin, Columbine and Punchinello plus an endless stream of sausages and a thieving dog, ending for no reason at all with the entire company draped on the decks of a rather unsteady ship belting out a medley of sea shanties. There was little opportunity for anyone to show real acting ability but that hardly mattered since the audiences packed in night after night gaping at the scenic marvels, falling off their seats with laughter, cheering Kate to the echo and providing the necessary funds to finance Mr Kean's ambitious plans for a new season of classic plays.

Christine was in the stalls with Harry, which she much preferred to the stiff isolation of a box which Papa insisted on when the whole family paid an annual visit.

'Will you come round to Kate's dressing room or wait for me in the foyer?' asked Harry as they fought their way through the thronging crowd to the exit. 'I'm going to take you both to supper.'

'Are you? What fun. I hope you told Papa we might be late.'

'Of course I did, and where we were going. I think he rather approved. He simply said, "Don't keep your sister out till all hours", that's all. I didn't mention Kate.'

Christine laughed. She felt happy and carefree that evening. Harry always had that effect on her and she could relax in his company.

'Have you told Kate?'

'Yes, of course. I looked in at rehearsal this morning, only saw her for a couple of minutes. I told her you would be there too.'

Christine had a feeling that Harry preferred a third party to be present at this first meeting with Kate after long months apart.

There was quite a crowd gathered at the stage door but the old man had had his instructions and let Harry and Christine slip through while shutting the door firmly on the others.

Kate had risen to the dizzy heights of a dressing room to herself, even if it was not much larger than a cupboard, and when they squeezed in she was sitting in front of the mirror already three parts dressed. Daniel was perched on a stool in the corner laughing at something she had said as she wound the long reddish hair around her head and anchored it with a handsome glittering comb.

'Harry darling!' She raised her head for him to kiss her cheek and stretched up a hand to Christine. 'Did you enjoy the show? You've no idea what a booby I feel perched up there on the ship. Every time I move there is an ominous creak. I live in fear the whole thing will collapse one night and I shall end up in the middle of the orchestra pit.'

She was talking too loud and too quickly so that Christine wondered if she too was nervous.

Daniel got to his feet. 'If Harry is here, you won't need me to see you home tonight so I'll be off.'

'Don't go,' said Harry quickly. 'Come with us.'

Daniel shot a look at Harry's evening dress and Christine's silk gown.

'I'm not dressed for your sort of evening,' he said drily.

'Good Lord, I'm not taking the girls anywhere grand.

Vespers is very quiet, highly respectable, even Papa approves. All those fuddy-duddy types from the lawcourts go there, some even take their wives. Come on, man, don't be such a wet blanket.'

Across the room Daniel met Christine's eyes and read the invitation in them.

'You win,' he said. 'I'll come if you're sure I'll be welcome.'

'Fine,' said Harry heartily. 'I booked a table for four just in case.'

They picked up two cabs, Harry and Kate in one, Daniel and Christine following after.

'I'm glad you decided to come with us. It seems a long time since we've seen one another.'

'Yes,' he said. 'I hope you enjoyed your Christmas at Bramber.'

'What has happened at the shop?'

'It has been repaired and is making a good start.'

'Are you working there now?'

'No, only occasionally in the evening to help Elspeth with the books.'

They were stiff with each other but she slipped off her white glove and found his hand. After a moment he returned the warm pressure.

Harry was right about the restaurant. Vespers had an air of dignity as if nothing disturbing could possibly ever happen within its sedate portals. The waiter raised an eyebrow at Daniel but Harry's father was well known there and the rich can afford to have eccentric friends. They were ushered to a table discreetly shadowed by a gigantic palm. Harry ordered champagne and under its influence constraints fled away. Kate told them that two performances of the pantomime left her starving by evening, Christine set them laughing at the tale of a Bramber villager who, given a slab of gorgonzola cheese from Mr Brown's Christmas hamper, thought it had gone mouldy and fed it to his pigs, and Harry expanded about Paris, the shows he had seen, the famous people he had met. It was only Daniel who said little.

At one moment through the fronds of the palm Christine thought she recognised the couple at the next table. It was quite certainly Clara, dazzlingly dressed, so the man with his back to them must be Ray Dorrien. For some reason she felt a stab of apprehension and then dismissed it as absurd and they went on eating and laughing and talking together. It was growing very late when Harry filled up their glasses with the last of the champagne.

'Shall I order another bottle?'

'I think we've all had more than enough,' said Kate.

'We ought to drink a toast with the last glass,' said Harry, who was in the highest of spirits because the evening was going well, 'and I suggest we raise them to Kate Hunter who has worked harder than any of us on the good ship Arethusa!'

But they never even had time to lift their glasses before Ray had swung round. His chair crashed over as he thrust aside the palm and stood glaring down at Kate.

'So, Miss Kate Hunter who has been rehearsing so hard she can't see anyone, who has shut herself up in seclusion by order of the management, can still come roistering out with her boy lover!' Harry started to his feet but Ray went on relentlessly, 'You know what happens to lying bitches, don't you? They get what's coming to them!' and he picked up a glass of champagne and threw it in Kate's face.

She sat paralysed for the moment by the rage in his voice, the wine trickling down her chin.

Harry turned on him angrily and Daniel said thickly, 'You lying bastard! By God, you'll apologise for that!'

'I'm damned if I will.'

For a moment the tension held. At any moment it could have exploded into violence. Then Clara's sharp incisive voice cut through it.

'Raymond, I'm waiting to leave!'

'Coming, m'dear.' He threw down the empty glass, looked contemptuously from one to the other and then turned to follow his wife.

A waiter came hurrying, handed a clean napkin to Kate and began to mop up the spilled wine and shattered glass.

Daniel said, 'How long has he been pestering you?'

'Ever since we opened,' said Kate in a shaking voice, 'and I wasn't lying. We have been rehearsing very hard, that's why I told the doorkeeper to say I could not see anyone.'

'You should have told me.'

'I didn't want there to be any trouble. It was bad enough last time. He's married now. Why can't he leave me alone?'

'I think I know why,' said Harry, suddenly very serious. 'Ray has obsessions about people. He has always had them, even at Oxford. He must be the first always and if he wants something, whatever it is, he can't rest till he's proved that nothing and no one can stand out against him.'

'But that's ridiculous,' said Daniel. 'He's been running after Kate for near on two years. What does he want from her?'

'To prove himself her master.'

'He's got to be stopped.'

'He will be,' went on Harry confidently. 'Ray doesn't realize it yet but he's met his match. Clara won't stand for it. We know her, don't we, Christine? After all we grew up with her. I'd back Clara to win every time.'

'I hope to God you're right.'

The unpleasant incident had spoiled the happy atmosphere of the evening. Harry paid the bill. They gathered up wraps and shawls and left together, parting with promises to meet again before Harry went back to Paris.

Christine whispered, 'I'll be at the clinic next week as usual,' but Daniel only nodded. He had seen that she still wore Gareth's ring and it chilled him. He knew it was over, it had to be, and yet stubbornly he still hoped for a miracle.

He left Kate at her lodging in Vyner Street. The room still held her few possessions and she had paid the rent during the months away.

'I worry about you,' he said. 'It's a long journey home alone each night.'

'I'm going to move soon. There's a room coming up in a house in Gower Street where several of the company lodge. As soon as it is free, I'm going to take it.' She grimaced. 'The only trouble is it's a lot more expensive.'

337

'I could help you with that. Mr Brown is paying me for the extra work I am putting in at the shop.'

'No, Dan, you need all you earn. It's little enough, God knows. With any luck we shall all get a bonus from the panto as it's doing so well.'

'You must take care,' he said.

'Don't worry. I will.'

She saw him go and then wearily climbed the stairs. Daniel and she were a fine pair, she thought ironically, both yearning after the impossible. Damn Everard Warrinder! And damn the whole stupid chance that had thrown them together! It was all very well to be brave, to put on a good face, say it was all for the best, that nothing could ever come of it, but the plain fact remained that she had fallen in love with Harry with all the wonder and magic of first love. She had denied it, told him that it was impossible, laughed at him when he talked of marriage, but somehow deep inside her she had still hoped. Like Daniel she had looked for a miracle and only tonight knew with certainty that it would never come. Harry with his boyish charm, so alive with youthful ardour last summer, had grown up, had vanished into a wider world in which she could have no place. It was right, it was inevitable, it had to be accepted, but that didn't make it any less painful. Thank God she still had her work. One of the oldest actors in Mr Kean's company, a survivor from the great days of his father Edmund, had said one morning after watching her rehearse, 'Very pretty, my dear, very clever but it has no passion. It doesn't come from the heart. You should fall in love.' She wondered what he would have said now.

What none of them realized was that the foolish incident at the restaurant was only the forerunner of something else that would bring all their hopes and desires, all the past and the present, together into one shattering conclusion.

During the next few weeks Christine felt she was leading a double life, one that followed the usual duties of daughter of the house, shopping and visiting with Mamma, helping to entertain guests, explaining till she was weary of it that she and Gareth had decided to postpone their wedding for the time being, that it was all for the best, and no, she didn't mind at all, while all the time wondering what they would say if she were to blurt out the plain unvarnished truth.

It was all so absurd that sometimes she wanted to scream.'It's all so wrong,' she said to Gareth on one of the few occasions he found time for her.

'Please, Christine,' he said, 'please stick to what we agreed together. Don't you owe me something?'

He firmly believed she was suffering from an infatuation that would burn itself out. Part of her wanted to defy him, to stand up to Mamma and Papa, announce that she was going to marry Daniel and there was nothing they could do about it, but that would be forcing an issue on Daniel which he did not want to accept. So she kept up the farce and every time she went down to the clinic contrived a few minutes with him, although not at first. It was a couple of weeks after Harry's supper party before she came out of the patients' door and saw him waiting for her and after that she found herself living for their brief meetings, and despite all kinds of misgivings, so did he.

Once or twice she met him at the midday break in their old haunt of the churchyard. She told him about Gareth and he said, 'I see his point. I would not let you go either.' They kissed lingeringly under the ancient tree, stark and leafless now, and sometimes when it was cold and wet, they sat together in a musty pew at the back of the church and he told her about the articles he had begun to write castigating some of the evils he saw around him, some of which had been published in the radical news sheet.

'It's a start,' he said, 'but it doesn't have a wide enough circulation. If I could get one accepted in the *Daily News*, that would really be something.'

In their absorption in one another they did not realize that their meetings were being observed by the young woman who had succeeded Elspeth as teacher of the younger children. Eva was the niece of Preacher Glossop and gleefully took the opportunity of telling Elspeth all about Daniel and Christine when they walked home together from the Chapel after service on Sundays.

At the end of February Mr Kean's new production of *The Winter's Tale* burst upon an astonished public. For almost the first time in theatrical history the actors were dressed in authentic period costumes instead of everyday modern dress with a few antique additions which was the usual custom. Charles Kean, who was sometimes more of a schoolmaster than a leading actor and had received a classical education at Eton, sent his stage designer to the British Museum to copy original styles of dress from antique statues and vases and if his wife still insisted on wearing half a dozen petticoats under her Grecian robe, Kate looked utterly delectable as Perdita, the lost princess, slender as a lily, with flowers in her hair and wearing pale green muslin over flesh-coloured tights. She was greatly appreciated by the male members of the audience, including Ray Dorrien, who sat in a box beside his wife outwardly indifferent but inwardly smouldering with rage because his siege had got him nowhere. Flowers, chocolates, even a costly bracelet, had all been returned to him. Kate was not yielding one inch. He sat turning over in his mind a new and alluring plan to get even with her while his wife glanced at him now and then and decided it was time she took action herself. In actual fact he was finding Clara's sharp questioning of his comings and goings excessively irritating. One of these days he would have to make her understand that it was not a wife's duty to pry into her husband's affairs, but that could wait for a while. He had something more attractive to occupy his thoughts.

In the meantime Kate was doing her best to drown the hopes and dreams of the past year in hard work. Mr Kean's company were expected to be wholly devoted to their art. Time off for sleep and meals was totally ignored. Rehearsals had been known to go on till two or three in the morning and occasionally Kate slept on someone's sofa instead of taking the long journey home to Vyner Street. There was no time left to be regretful, no time to weep for lost love, she had been promised Viola in *Twelfth Night* and for that she was going to need every minute of her time.

The weeks went racing by in that cold spring until one afternoon, much to Christine's surprise, Clara called at Belgrave Square. Clarissa happened to be out so she politely offered her cousin tea in the drawing room and wondered why she had come since they had never at any time been particularly close.

Trivial matters being disposed of over tea and cakes, Clara came abruptly to the point.

'I believe you are well acquainted with that young woman, Kate Hunter, who is playing at the Princess Theatre.'

'Yes, I know her. Why?' said Christine cautiously.

'And you know of course that Raymond has been pursuing her.'

'I know he did some time ago. I rather thought he'd given it up after that unpleasant scene at the restaurant.'

'No, he hasn't and I don't like it. I find it excessively humiliating.'

'I can understand that you might but I don't really see what I can do about it.'

'Advise her to give in to him. Let him have what he wants and that will be the end of it. I know him. Once he has conquered, he will be bored with her.'

Christine stared at her, scarcely able to believe what she was hearing.

'You're asking me to tell Kate to . . . to have an affair with him, become his mistress?'

'Why not?' Clara got up, took a few paces away across the room and then came back, her face seeming to grow thin and pointed with spite and jealousy. 'She is only a common singer come up from nowhere pretending to be a great actress. I don't suppose it's the first time. She will have had other lovers, plenty of them I expect. What about Harry?'

'Harry would have made her his wife, not his mistress,' said

Christine indignantly. She stood up facing Clara. 'I never heard anything so outrageous in my life. Kate detests him. She always has done. Do you know what Ray did when her brother interfered and tried to prevent him pestering her? He set a couple of East End thugs on him and had him beaten up. Did you know that? If you can't control the man you have married, then I'm afraid it's just your bad luck.'

'If you won't help, then I'll find some other means. I'll not have him fooled by a scheming slut of an actress. I know what she is doing. She is playing hard to get, she wants more than he is prepared to give. She wants to crow over me, his wife, but I'll beat her yet. I'll show her two can play at that game and I'll win. If you're so friendly with her and her brother, then you had better warn them.'

'What do you think you can do?'

'Never you mind.' Clara picked up her gloves and her silver mesh bag. 'I'm going now but you'd better remember what I've said. Give my regards to Aunt Clarissa,' and she swept out of the room before Christine could ring for the butler to show her out.

Clara's ruthlessness worried her and she wondered what to do for the best. A few days later when they met briefly, she told Daniel but he was inclined to dismiss it as no more than the idle threat of a jealous wife.

'You don't know my cousin Clara,' said Christine earnestly. 'She might try and involve Kate in some kind of scandal.'

'I don't see how she can. Kate has never had anything to do with Ray Dorrien, has never accepted anything from him. The whole theatre company can bear witness to that.'

'I know but all the same do warn her.'

Then before either of them could do anything more about it, Christine was faced with an act of spite directed against herself.

The anonymous letter came when she was breakfasting with her father one morning. Clarissa very rarely got up early and often preferred to have a tray sent up to her bedroom so they were alone together.

Her father was drinking a last cup of coffee and slitting open his mail with a silver paperknife. She saw his face change as he ran his eye down the sheet of paper. He hesitated and then handed it to her.

'I think you had better read this.'

She took it apprehensively. It was a sheet of common paper torn from an exercise book, addressed to Everard Warrinder QC and written in capitals neatly set out on the ruled paper.

'I think that in the interests of common decency you should know that your daughter on election day spent several hours alone with her lover in his lodging in Paradise Alley and they have continued to meet there and elsewhere ever since that day.'

That was all. Nothing else. No signature, no indication as to where it had come from.

Who could have sent it? Dickie was the only one who had known she was with Daniel on that day. She felt sick at the spite that must have wormed it out of the boy and then kept silence for all these weeks.

Her father's eyes were upon her. He said abruptly, 'Is it true?'

She gripped her hands together to stop them trembling.

'Partly. I did go to Daniel's lodging but he is not my lover.'

'You did not tell me.'

'No.'

Barton knocked and came in, asking if they required fresh coffee and more hot toast.

'No, nothing more,' said Everard. 'You can clear the table and send word to the stable that I won't want the carriage for a while. I will ring when I am ready.'

'Very good, sir.'

Her father got to his feet. 'You'd better come with me, Christine.'

She followed him into his study dreading the coming inquisition but prepared to face up to it with as much courage as she could muster.

'Now,' he said when the door was closed and he had turned

to face her. 'The truth if you please. When did you go there and why?'

'After what had happened the day before,' she began, trying to keep her voice steady, 'after you had been shot and Daniel had been taken by the police and then released, I wanted to speak to him. I wanted to know more about what had happened and why you and he had spoken so long together. It was only natural. We had been friends, good friends. You know that. I told you.'

He gave her a long look and then moved behind the desk and sat down. 'So you have continued this unwise friendship against my express wishes?'

'Yes. Why shouldn't I? There was no harm in it.'

'I'll decide that when I know the rest. Go on.'

'I suppose it was foolish of me,' she said a little falteringly, 'since everywhere was so crowded but it wasn't far and you didn't need me . . .' She looked at him appealingly but he was watching her, his face stony, and she went on. 'I was wrong of course. The streets were horribly congested still and I was stopped by a gang of supporters of Mr Nugent.'

'Did they know who you were?'

'One of them did. They thought it would be a great joke to take me, your daughter, to the headquarters of their candidate but I didn't want to do anything that might harm you so I refused to go with them. Then they turned rough, they tried to hustle me along, it was very unpleasant. I don't know what I would have done if Daniel had not rescued me with one of the policemen.'

'And instead of bringing you back to me, he carried you off to his lodgings, I suppose,' said her father drily.

'That was my fault. You mustn't blame Daniel. I was upset. It had been very alarming and I didn't want any questions to be asked so when he said everyone was out and I could rest and tidy myself in his room, I went with him.'

'And stayed there for the next couple of hours.'

'It wasn't so long as that but we did talk, the time went by and I didn't realize how late it was and then . . .' the memory

344

of those fraught hours, of what had so nearly happened between them overwhelmed her and she faltered to a stop.

'And when at last he did bring you back to me, you told me a pack of lies.'

'I thought you might be angry with me.'

'Of course I would have been angry. I am angry now.' He tapped the letter that he had dropped on the desk. 'And these other meetings since that day?'

'I see him occasionally when I go down to the clinic, that is all.'

'You don't go to his room.'

'No, never, not since that day.'

'You've never lied to me before, Christine. Can I trust you? Is this the whole truth?'

She met his eyes squarely. 'Yes, Papa, it's the truth. There has been nothing else between us.'

'Very well, but how many other people beside the writer of this infamous letter know that my daughter seized the opportunity to spend hours alone with a young man who was among the most violent of the opposition, who had done his utmost to vilify me in their news sheets? Do you realize the damage you could have done to your reputation and to mine? How do you think Gareth will feel if I were to show him this letter?'

'Gareth will understand.'

'Gareth is not the man I take him for if he will be prepared to accept without question his future wife spending hours alone with another man.'

'I have told him all about Daniel.'

'Have you indeed? And what exactly have you told him?'

And suddenly she couldn't stand it a moment longer, the pretence, the excuses, the evasions, the lies.

She said steadily, 'I told Gareth when he came to Bramber that I was not going to marry him.'

'You told him what? But for what reason? What has changed your mind? And if this is so, why have you let the engagement run on? Your mother is already planning a June wedding.'

'I know,' she went on unhappily. 'But that was Gareth's wish,

345

not mine. He thinks I am making a great mistake. He refuses to believe me.'

'What does he refuse to believe?' Her father's eyes were on her probing, it seemed, to her very heart. 'What are you trying to tell me? What part does Daniel Hunter play in all this? I've asked you more than once what there was between you and you swore to me there was nothing but friendship. Was that a lie? Isn't it time that you told me the truth?'

'I wasn't lying, really I wasn't,' she said desperately. 'That was how it began but it has changed . . .'

'And is that what you told Gareth? That you have foolishly fallen in love with a beggarly teacher in an East End ragged school?'

'Yes, I did,' she said, stung by the sarcasm in his voice.

'And what did he say?'

'He thinks, he is sure that I'm mistaking infatuation for love, but I'm not, Papa, I'm not. I know my own heart.'

'Do you, I wonder. I'm much inclined to agree with Gareth. What are you planning to do? Give up your life here and live together on your grandmother's legacy? Oh I can see how the prospect might appeal to the young man. Who knows where it could end? If it goes on long enough she might even persuade her parents to accept him,' he said with a biting irony.

'You're wrong, absolutely wrong. Daniel is not like that. He wouldn't marry me if I went down on my bended knees to him and you know why, don't you? He can never forgive you for what *you* did to *his* father all those years ago. You let an innocent man go to the gallows because of your career, because of the prestige it gave you, and so I am tainted with your guilt. I must suffer for what you did.'

'And what else did he have to say about me, what other excuses did he give so that he could play the martyr and still keep you close beside him?'

The words were trembling on her lips. She wanted to scream them at him. He cannot forgive you for raping his mother at the moment of her greatest need and then abandoning her to

346

her misery, and then she knew she couldn't say them, because she still found it impossible to believe, because he was her father, loved and respected for so long, and she could not bring herself to rip aside the warm affection that had grown between them all this past year.

They were silent for a moment staring at one another and she had the queerest feeling that he was as much distressed about it as she was. Then he stirred, leaning across the desk and speaking with a slow emphasis.

'Listen to me, Christine. Marriage between you and Daniel Hunter is utterly impossible for many reasons. There is absolutely no question of it. You must understand that. I could never give my consent, never. I believe that Gareth is right. You have been too easily misled. You have allowed feelings of sympathy and compassion to influence you and you must be prevented from making a terrible mistake that could wreck your whole life. I am thinking that the best thing I can do is to send you to your Uncle Francis. Six months with his family at Glenmuir would do you all the good in the world, give you time to think, free from this young man's influence, free from the unhealthy atmosphere. I know you started this work at the clinic for the best of reasons but it has gone much too far. You must be free of it for a time so that you can pull yourself together, take a more balanced view.'

She was appalled at the decision in his voice. 'I won't go. You can't force me to go.'

'I can and I will. I am still your father and have authority over you. Believe me, Christine, for many reasons it will be for the best. As for this letter, I shall destroy it. Why distress Gareth unnecessarily?'

He got to his feet, tore the paper in half and tossed it into the fire.

'You can't do this to me, Papa, you can't. I won't accept it.'

'It will take a little time to arrange,' he said, as if she had not spoken. 'I must contact your uncle and find out how he is placed. Gareth must be consulted and your mother. I'm afraid she will have to forget all her plans for a summer wedding.'

'I won't do it, Papa, I won't. How can I let Dr Dexter down? How can I just abandon all my work at the clinic?'

'I myself will write to John Dexter, explain that in my opinion it is affecting your health. He is a sensible man, he will understand.'

'He will believe I'm one of those stupid women who start something and then give it up the moment it becomes inconvenient,' she said rebelliously.

'I daresay there will be plenty of opportunity to use what you have learned up in Scotland. There is poverty and sickness among the crofters and no doubt your Aunt Grace will be glad of your experience and skill in such matters.' She opened her mouth to protest once again and he raised his hand. 'No, Christine, no more argument. My mind is made up. Either you give me your promise not to see Daniel again or I shall be obliged to confine you to your room, something I've no wish to do. You are not a child. But you must understand that in this instance I mean what I say.'

To be shut up would be even worse and after all he could not prevent her writing and it would not be difficult to persuade Betsy to post any such letters secretly if he should insist on seeing them.

'Very well,' she said reluctantly, 'I promise.'

'And you will keep your promise?'

'If I must.'

'Good. I will not tell your mother yet about your broken engagement as it is not Gareth's wish but we shall have to think up some very good reason for the wedding being postponed for yet another six months.'

She stood up. 'May I go now?'

'Don't hate me for it, Christine,' he said more gently. 'Believe me, it is you I'm thinking of, not myself,' and when she did not say anything, he went on, 'You might tell Barton I'm ready for the carriage now. I am in court tomorrow and there is work to be done. I'm shockingly late already.'

She went out into the hall, gave the message to the butler and then went up to her own room, seething with anger against the writer of that wretched letter which had precipitated her into a situation she would have otherwise avoided at all costs. Oh God, why hadn't she had the courage to defy her father, throw a few garments into a holdall and walk out of the house? But it is not so easy to break familiar ties of affection and trust when you have nowhere to go and an unforeseeable future. What would Daniel do if she stood on the steps of Paradise Alley and said, 'Here I am. Do what you like with me.'

Neither Gareth nor her father had any conception of what she really felt for him. They thought it a sentimental attachment which time and change of place would easily obliterate and she had a violent and passionate desire to prove them wrong. She had given her father a promise but was she going to keep it? She was pulled this way and that by loyalties that warred against one another.

A week went by, each day becoming more and more unbearable listening to her mother's reproaches. If she said it once, she repeated it a dozen times.

'I really don't know what is the matter with you, Christine. You have everything a young girl could possibly want. You badgered your father into consenting to your engagement with Gareth and now you take absolutely no interest in the future and talk of a further postponement. You don't seem to know your own mind from one moment to the next. I always knew no good would come from you going down to that clinic and I'm glad your father agrees with me at last.'

Slowly, day by day, the tension grew till she could bear it no longer. Her father must understand that she had to see Daniel if only to explain. Letters were useless. She had written half a dozen and then torn them up.

One morning in late April when it seemed the cold spring was at last behind them and the trees in the square were turning a tender golden green, she made up her mind. She excused herself from accompanying her mother on a round of early calls on the plea of a bad headache, saw her leave, then dressed quickly and left the house, taking the usual horse bus and jolting down the familiar road. She went straight to Paradise Alley, aware that he often went back there at midday and hoping that she was right. For some reason the usually quiet street seemed alive with people. Little knots of women stood excitedly talking together and turned to stare as she went up the steps. The door was closed which was unusual at this time of the day. It opened to her knock and Ma Taylor grabbed her by the arm and pulled her inside.

'Don't want that lot out there listenin' to every blessed word,' she muttered. 'Got ears long as donkeys they have.'

'Why? Has something happened?'

'Has it? Oh my Gawd! You'd better come down to the kitchen.'

She followed down the stairs to the warm stuffy room. 'Is Daniel here?'

'No, he's at the police station and Lord knows when he will be back.'

'Why? What has he done?'

'It's not him, it's his sister, likely to be took up for murder she is!'

'Murder! I can't believe it.'

'True as I'm standing here.' Shocked and distressed but still enjoying the drama of it, Ma Taylor went on with her story.

'I don't know the rights and wrongs of it yet o'course, but it were late last night, long after midnight when one of them policemen comes banging at the door. Dan came down to answer it – he don't like me going when it's late like that – and there were that bobby large as life. "Are you the brother of that there Kate Hunter?" he sez and when Dan sez he is, then he goes on. "You'd better come along with me, young man, she's just murdered her lover!" I were that shocked I couldn't hardly get me breath. Couldn't sleep a wink all night for thinkin' of it. It can't be true, I sez to myself, she's such a lovely girl.'

'There must be some mistake. Kate would never hurt anyone.'

'That's what I sez to that policeman. "She wouldn't hurt a fly," I sez to him. "You wouldn't say that if you was to see the blood, Missus," he sez and then they were off, the pair of 'em, had a cab waitin' an' all. Dan brought her back here, near four o'clock it were, and she were white as a sheet. Then they were off again to the station early this morning and likely been there ever since.'

'Who was it? Do you know?'

'They didn't rightly say. Some toff as had been runnin' after her, I believe.'

Ray Dorrien! Surely it couldn't be. It was so unbelievable she couldn't think what to do for the best.

'When Daniel does come back, will you tell him I called and if he needs any help then he can come to me.'

'There ain't much you can do, Miss, and that's a fact. The law goes on its way regardless and them police won't never listen, you can't get a word in edgeways with that lot,' said Ma Taylor gloomily. 'And there's nowt anyone of us can do to stop it. But I'll tell Daniel you were here, Miss, don't you worry.'

'Bless you.'

'Will you take a cup o' tea now you're here? It's just brewed.'

Ma Taylor's invariable panacea for all troubles. 'No, thank you. I mustn't stay.'

Outside she felt the women's eyes turn to her again and hurried away to where she could pick up a cab, still far too shocked and upset to suspect what a catastrophic effect the death of that unpleasant young man would have on all their lives.

Chapter 18

It was after ten on that April evening when Kate had come back to her lodging in Vyner Street. She was feeling tired but very happy. Rehearsals for *Twelfth Night* had gone well. Mr Kean, and what was just as important Mrs Kean, had been very pleased with her. In the last few months she had proved her ability and had grown in confidence. The future had never looked more promising. She went happily up the stairs humming a few lines from one of the play's most haunting songs:

> 'When that I was but a little tiny boy
> With hey, ho, the wind and the rain,
> A foolish thing was but a toy
> For the rain it raineth every day . . .'

She reached the top landing and stopped abruptly. The door to her room was open and no one had a key but herself and old Ma Huggett, the owner of the house who squatted in the basement like a huge black spider and took little interest in the comings and goings of her lodgers so long as they paid their rent regularly.

She pushed the door wider open very cautiously, not knowing what she might find, and it came up against some obstruction on the floor. A candle on the table was guttering to its end but there was sufficient light to see that the body of a man was stretched on the floor. Was it some drunk who had somehow forced an entry and then collapsed? She touched him with her foot but he did not stir. She felt anger rather than fear that anyone should dare to invade her own private little kingdom. She stepped over him and with hands that shook a little found the matches and lit the lamp. She turned round with it in her hands and very nearly dropped it. The face of Ray Dorrien was staring up at her, deathly white, the eyes wide open and blood everywhere, blood that had soaked the pale buff of his trousers and some kind of bandage that had been tied round his thigh. She caught her breath in a stifled scream. Was he dead? He couldn't be. It was impossible. She put down the lamp and fell on her knees beside him, oblivious of the sticky patches of blood that stained the floor. She touched his face. It was still warm but he did not stir and there was no life in the eyes that gazed up at her. With a sick revulsion she put out a hand and gently closed them.

For a moment she could not move; numb with shock, she stared down at the man she had done everything in her power to avoid and had a sickening fear that he had conquered in the end. What was he doing here? Who had done this to him? She wondered for a dizzying moment whether it could have been Daniel who had found him there and taken an instant revenge, except that her brother would never have left her to face a homecoming like this. She got giddily to her feet and almost tripped over the bloodstained knife, her own bone-handled bread knife, that lay close beside him. Without even thinking she automatically picked it up and stood trembling with it still in her hand. She would have to do something, find help. Perhaps he was not dead. Perhaps there was still a glimmer of life. She must find a doctor and quickly. She was tempted to shut the door, shut out the hideous terrifying sight and run away from it but she could not do that. Daniel, she thought desperately, she must send someone to fetch Daniel, he would know what to do. She started down the stairs, so giddy and sick she stumbled from step to step. Halfway down she met a man coming up. He was carrying a candle and stopped on the small landing to let her go by. He was a quiet respectable middle-aged man who lived on the second floor and worked in a shoe factory. The candle lit her white face, the bloodstains on her skirt and the knife in her hand which she had forgotten to put down. She tripped on the last step and he reached out a hand to steady her. A decent girl, he had always thought, though she was an actress, not one of the tarty sort who brought men home and sat drinking and carrying on till all hours, but now he could see that something was terribly wrong.

'What is it, Miss?' he asked. 'Has something happened?'

She stared at him and suddenly felt so faint she could scarcely stand. 'There is a man in my room,' she whispered. 'I think – I am sure he is dead.'

She swayed forward and he gripped her arm.

'Hold on, I'm here. I'll come with you. It may not be so bad as you think.'

But it was. It was worse. He had once served as a hospital orderly and had seen some horrific sights but this was one of the worst, all the more shocking somehow in this quiet ordinary room. He knelt down, made a brief examination and then got to his feet.

'He's dead all right, bled to death, I reckon. That knife wound must have severed an artery. Someone has tried to help him. D'you see? There's an attempt at a tourniquet and a pillow under his leg to stop the flow and one under his head. But who would do such a thing?'

His calm assessment steadied her a little. The first sickening shock had begun to recede. She must not give way. She must try to be practical.

'What was he doing here?' he asked.

'I don't know.'

The desperation in her voice did not escape him. His observant eye had noted the elegant clothes, the handsome ring on the white manicured hand, the gold-topped bottle of champagne that stood on the table, and he formed his own conclusions. He could easily have been a lover preparing for a festive evening and there could have been a quarrel, jealousy perhaps – who can tell with lovers? In a frenzy she could have seized a knife and struck out at him, unluckily hitting a vital spot. To bleed to death took time.

Perhaps she had fled in terror at what she had done and then come back to find him dead and now must try and convince those who would question that someone unknown had struck at him. It was a plausible theory and one that the police would later seize upon as only too likely, but just now he voiced none of it.

'Do you know who he is?' he asked gently.

'Oh yes,' she said bitterly. 'He is Raymond Dorrien. His father is Lord Dorrien.'

'Dorrien?' he repeated. 'I've heard that name.'

'He is very wealthy.'

It strengthened his theory. These rich young men with nothing better to occupy them thought they could do as they pleased with the unfortunate young women who took their fancy. His sharp eyes had already noticed a scattering of gold coins, guineas by the look of 'em, on the floor. You did not often see gold in rooms of this kind. A dispute over money – what more likely? But he kept these thoughts to himself.

'I am afraid this is a case for the police,' he said. 'It's late but there's always a constable on duty at the station.'

She gave a shuddering sigh, feeling desperately alone with no friend to give reassurance, no one but this stranger.

'I have a brother,' she said. 'He lives quite near in Paradise Alley.'

'The police will send someone for him,' the man went on comfortingly. 'It must be reported. Will you stay here or come with me?'

She shivered. 'I don't want to be left alone with . . . him.'

'We'd best go,' he said and led the way down the stairs.

It was like a nightmare from which you cannot waken. For brief moments everything seemed wonderfully clear and then the darkness, the horror overwhelmed her again.

A sleepy constable who had already been on duty since nine o'clock and did not expect to be relieved till at least six in the morning looked up wearily as Mr Kennedy entered the station closely followed by Kate.

He stifled a yawn and said, 'How can I help you, sir?'

'I have to report a death in a lodging house in Vyner Street discovered by this young lady when she returned home earlier this evening. In some distress she asked for my assistance but I am afraid there was nothing that I could do. I regret the man in question is dead.'

The Constable straightened up. 'Dead? By his own hand?'

'By no means. He would have had to be a contortionist to stab himself in one of the most vital spots,' said Mr Kennedy drily. 'In my humble opinion the poor man bled to his death.'

The Constable looked from him to Kate, beginning to feel a keen interest. 'Do you know who he is?'

'Yes, I know,' said Kate with an unpleasant feeling that some kind of web was closing in around her from which she would never be free. 'He is actually Viscount Raymond Dorrien.'

'He's what! Are you sure?'

'Of course I'm sure.'

That really brought him wide awake. This was something very different from the usual round of petty thefts, pub brawls, wives screeching vengeance against vicious husbands, prostitutes soliciting for customers, moving vagrants on and bringing in paralytic drunks. A real murder case and not of some wretched thief but a gentleman, a bloomin' toff and it was in his patch. The young woman wasn't the usual tart either, neatly dressed, spoke like a lady, even if she did lodge in Vyner Street.

He said, 'I'd better come along and see for myself. I'll leave a note for the Sergeant. He's gone on his rounds but he'll be back in a jiffy.'

He asked for the address, laboriously wrote a short note, left it in a conspicuous place and took up his truncheon, slipping it in the special pocket made for it in his dark blue uniform coat.

It took a lot of courage on Kate's part to enter the room that had been her refuge for so long and had now assumed the chill atmosphere of a tomb. She shivered as the light fell on the upturned face of Ray Dorrien, turning it a greenish white.

'Gawd!' exclaimed the Constable. 'Someone's done for him all right! A sight to turn your stomach! We'll have to get the body taken to the mortuary.' He glanced around the room, saw the gold-topped bottle and the food that had been laid out beside it, a game pie, fine cheese, expensive fruit. 'Expecting him to supper, were you, Miss? Pity it's all going to waste.'

'No,' said Kate vehemently. 'No, I was not expecting him. He must have brought all this with him.' She wanted to scream, 'I hated him but he would never leave me alone!' but instead she tried to speak calmly. 'I came home about ten, very tired after a long day, and found him here.'

'Must have been a nasty shock. I'd better begin making some notes.' The Constable produced a pad and pencil. 'Now what about his family? His wife? His father?'

He had scarcely got started when the Sergeant arrived, a middle-aged man very full of his own importance, and with him came one of the newly formed group of detective inspectors, a man of superior education and a quiet unobtrusive manner who said little at first but nevertheless took command. The Constable was despatched to fetch Daniel, the Sergeant much against his will sent to summon the doctor despite the late hour.

Left alone the Inspector looked around him and said gently, 'I am afraid I must ask a few questions but it is not very pleasant in here. Is there anywhere else we can go?'

Mr Kennedy, who was finding the whole situation utterly fascinating, offered his own room on the floor below, which proved to be sparsely furnished and completely colourless.

It was then that the nightmare began in grim earnest and went on and on all through that dreadful night.

Over and over again, closely questioned, she went through the events of her day. The long rehearsals at the theatre until they finished at last at about six o'clock and since she was not playing in the comedy that night she had the evening free and decided to take the opportunity to see a friend who was playing with a rival company.

'At which theatre?' asked the Inspector, busily writing.

'The Haymarket.'

'Did you buy a ticket at the box office?'

'No. As an actor in another company we are allowed free passes.'

'So no one actually saw you enter the place?'

'I suppose not. I didn't speak to anyone.'

'Did you visit your friend backstage when the show was over?'

'No. I was far too tired. In fact I left before the farce that usually ends the performance.'

He looked across at her. 'So you could easily have returned to Vyner Street very much earlier than you said you did and no one any the wiser.'

'I could have done but I didn't.'

Too late she could see where he was leading her.

'Pity you haven't a witness who spoke to you at the Haymarket. However, shall we just run through it again step by step?' he said quietly.

'If I must.' Wearily she went through the whole rigmarole once again, certain that he was waiting to pounce on any inadvertent change in her story.

'And you had no idea at all,' he went on, 'that Mr Dorrien would be here waiting for you ready to make a night of it with you?'

'None at all and I resent your implication. I am not in the habit of making a night of it with any gentleman.'

'No, no, of course not,' he said with a half smile, 'it would not be at all the thing for any member of Mr Kean's highly respectable theatre company, would it? But a good-looking girl like you must have admirers. You're surely not going to tell me that you all live like nuns.'

He was laughing at her and a hot tide of resentment rose up in her. Because she was an actress, because they were still rogues and vagabonds in law, because she wasn't a so-called lady, any accusation could be levelled against her and no questions asked, it was only to be expected. She had never felt more vulnerable, more defenceless.

Only a couple of hours before she had come home happier than she had been for some time, the heartache from Harry's loss beginning to recede a little, buoyed up by a sense of achievement in her work, and suddenly without any warning she had been plunged into a nightmare situation. She knew without any doubt at all that Lord Dorrien and Ray's newly married wife would pursue every clue that might lead to his killer. She remembered the scene at the supper party and felt sure that jealousy, envy, spite, would play a part in putting the blame on her innocent head.

All this was racing chaotically through her mind as the Inspector went on gently probing, so there was little wonder that when Daniel came into the room with the Constable close behind him, the tension suddenly broke. Up to then she had felt nothing but anger that she should be involved in such a horrific situation but now suddenly the realization overwhelmed her that dislike Ray Dorrien as she did, he was still his father's only son, still a bridegroom of less than a year, and she burst into tears, clinging to Daniel, the words pouring out incoherently through her sobs.

'What have you been saying to her? Kate is not easily upset,' he exclaimed angrily.

'Merely asking a few necessary questions,' said the Inspector calmly. 'You, I take it, are her brother. Were you acquainted with Raymond Dorrien?'

'I knew him,' said Daniel briefly. 'He was one of those wealthy young men who have too much money and too little sense. He had been pestering my sister for close on two years. I myself had to warn him off at least twice.'

'Did you indeed? May I ask where you spent last evening, Mr Hunter?'

'Are you suggesting that I may have played a part in his death?' said Daniel belligerently.

'Not at all, merely asking a civil question,' was the smooth reply.

'It so happens that I spent the evening with my employer, a Mr Ezra Brown who is a pillar of the Methodist Chapel.'

'An unimpeachable alibi, I am sure,' commented the policeman with his maddening smile.

The Sergeant put his head round the door to say, 'The doctor is here, sir, and would like a word with you.'

'Right, I'll come. You too, Mr Hunter, if you please.'

Kate was still clinging to his arm. 'I'll come with you,' she whispered. 'We mustn't inconvenience Mr Kennedy any longer. This is his room.'

Mr Kennedy protested that they were welcome to stay as long as they wished but Daniel thanked him and he saw them go with regret. It wasn't often that his dull life was enlivened by anything so dramatically interesting. Since he was in at the start as it were, he might be called for further questioning. He hoped so. He would like to know the outcome. She was a very attractive young woman and even if she had stabbed the young man in a fit of rage he'd be sorry to see her hanged or imprisoned for life.

Upstairs in the room that no longer seemed to belong to her, Kate huddled against Daniel and heard the doctor reporting to the Inspector.

'A couple of hours earlier or even less and we could have saved him,' he was saying, 'but with the heart and brain starved of blood . . .' he shook his head regretfully, 'no one could last long. Someone has tried to help him. See that bandage there. If a doctor had been called then . . . but in shifting to try and help himself, the unfortunate young man caused it to slip and all was up with him.'

Time went slowly by. Decently covered with a blanket, Ray was taken away. The three policemen quietly conferred together. It was agreed that the Inspector, whose name appeared to be Joseph Blain, would himself inform Lord Dorrien and the unhappy widow.

Daniel said, 'Need we wait here any longer? My sister is exhausted. I should like to take her back to my own lodgings.'

The Inspector looked him up and down consideringly and then came to a decision.

'Very well,' he said at last, 'for the remainder of the night you may do so but I shall expect you both at the station early tomorrow morning for further questioning and a full statement. I would advise you, Mr Hunter, to engage a solicitor as soon as possible to undertake your sister's case.'

'Why? Are you accusing her of murdering Dorrien?'

'I'm not accusing anyone at this juncture. That will depend upon our enquiries and the result of the Coroner's inquest but there are circumstances that still need careful examination and she must be available at all times.'

Up to then the possibility had not occurred to Daniel, now it struck him with a sudden chill that Kate could be in deadly danger.

It was past three o'clock when they walked towards Paradise Alley, still pitch dark, no sign yet of the dawn, the streets empty except for a few vagrants huddled asleep in doorways, marauding cats slinking after their prey, a drunk who collided with them and had to be sent swaying on his way, a homeless dog loping after them hopefully in search of food.

'He thinks I killed him,' said Kate hopelessly, 'I know he does for all his polite manner. It is written all over him.'

'You mustn't think that. It's just their way of talking,' said her brother hearteningly, but the tantalising question hovered in his mind. Who was it who had driven in that knife and callously left Ray Dorrien to die?

Ma Taylor, who had been roused by the Constable who had fetched Daniel, was still up. She took them down to the kitchen, handed out mugs of hot tea and listened sympathetically before they climbed wearily up to the attic. Kate lay on the bed and Daniel made do with the chair and a blanket but there was little sleep for either of them during the last few hours of that wretched night.

He took her to the police station in the morning and left her there. Life had to go on and the school couldn't close simply because his sister was in trouble. The news had already spread, there was a buzz of excited talk and he had the utmost difficulty in maintaining order. He sent Dickie with a note to

361

Mr Kean at the theatre saying Kate was unwell that day and it was received with considerable displeasure. To miss rehearsal for any but the most pressing of reasons was heavily frowned upon. The unfortunate understudy was put through her paces and found wanting in almost every particular.

When Daniel came back to Paradise Alley after school he found Kate waiting for him looking strained and unhappy.

'The police have locked up my room while they are still making enquiries,' she told him. 'The Inspector said I will have to fetch the key from the Constable if I want anything.'

'We'll go together and collect all you are likely to need. Then you can stay here. I can manage. Ma Taylor will find me somewhere to sleep or I can borrow Dickie's room if I can fit in, it's no bigger than a cupboard.' He ventured a smile but it didn't get any response. 'Then we'll look for some decent new lodgings for you,' he went on. 'What about that room you spoke of in Gower Street?'

'I don't know, Dan,' said Kate slowly. 'After the Inspector had let me go, I went down to the theatre. I had to tell them something of what had happened and they were very kind but I could see what they were thinking. They've got to be prepared for the worst. What is the use of rehearsing me into an important part if I'm unable to take it up.'

'But of course you will,' said her brother. 'You mustn't let this upset you too much. The police can say what they like but they can prove nothing against you.'

She smiled and tried to buoy herself up with hope but in her secret heart she thought despairingly that she had been too fortunate this past year and now because of a damnable accident not of her own making she could be kicked back again into the gutter.

The next day *The Times* came out with a discreetly written paragraph but other papers splashed into screaming head-lines. One enterprising publisher had rushed out a lurid broadsheet with all the facts and a few extra ones from his own fertile imagination. It sold out almost at once and a reprint was ordered. Society was scandalised. A notable young man about town, one of their own, had been found murdered in a young actress's East End lodging. It was full of intriguing implications. There were some who said that Ray Dorrien had it coming to him and others who deplored such disgraceful goings-on. His young widow was saying to anyone who would listen that he had been fatally lured to his destruction by a scheming young woman out to get what she could from him. Lord Dorrien, grief-stricken at the loss of his only son, forgot how often that son had infuriated him and was on the warpath for justice at any price.

In the meantime the police were continuing their enquiries with very little result. Ray Dorrien appeared to have chosen his opportunity only too well. No one in Vyner Street had seen anything that evening that could lead them to believe in some unknown assassin who had been lurking there and seized his chance. The outlook for Kate became darker and more threatening every day.

The inquest was to be held the following week and until it was over she felt she was living in a fearful state of suspense. She went to the Princess Theatre every day but her work suffered badly. She could not concentrate on Viola's bitter-sweet lines when she lay under so dire a threat.

And it was during that week that Daniel made the not altogether surprising discovery that justice is not handed to you on a plate. It must be paid for like everything else so that the rich and the influential had an enormous advantage. Where could he find a solicitor when he had never had the necessity to employ such a person? He consulted Mr Brown who, though much shocked, was willing enough to give advice.

'There's a fellow belongs to the Chapel,' he said a little doubtfully, 'but he's not one for criminal cases, mostly deals with contracts and leases and such. But he will know the procedure. He'll cost you money, Daniel.'

'I realize that. I have a little saved.'

'If it comes to a trial which God forbid,' went on Mr Brown, 'you will need a barrister for her defence and their fees are high, they say as much as five hundred guineas down and a hundred each day for expenses.'

'I've not got that kind of money and am never likely to have,' said Daniel gloomily. Ma Taylor had told him about Christine's visit and her offer of help but he couldn't ask her for money, everything in him revolted against it.

'Doesn't the State do anything for those who have no means?' he asked with a feeling of hopelessness.

'Oh they'll put up some kind of a defence, some poor devil of a lawyer who is willing to act for the pittance which the State is willing to pay.'

Whereas Lord Dorrien could undoubtedly command the services of the most brilliant legal brain to prosecute the case and bring his son's murderer to justice. Daniel prayed that it would never come to a trial but his prayer was not to be answered.

The Coroner's inquest was held at the end of the following week and took place in the hall of the Working Men's Club which was large enough to accommodate all those who wanted to attend. The public benches were crowded very early. Almost the whole of Paradise Alley and Vyner Street took the day off to be there. It was their murder and a very sensational one. No one wanted to miss it. Some of Kate's fellow actors came to give support, among them Byron Farrar, who entered with such a lordly air and gave her such a brilliant smile that there were some who shook their heads and said more than likely that handsome piece already had other strings to her bow.

The Coroner was an extremely strict Methodist, quite unlike the easy-going Mr Brown, and it must be admitted a sore trial to his pleasure-loving wife and daughters. He regarded this unsavoury affair with a jaundiced eye, disapproving of young women who painted their faces, displayed shapely limbs on a public stage and were hardly better than the gaudily dressed females who accosted him when he returned from some godly occasion and received blistering reprimands for their pains.

He took his position extremely seriously and enquired into every tiny detail. The Constable gave his report followed by the smooth-tongued Inspector Blain, who put his view of what had happened with the utmost skill, impressing everyone. Kate was once more closely questioned as to what she had done on that evening and, reacting against the wave of hostility, she held her head high and answered crisply and clearly.

Lord Dorrien was there speaking movingly of his son and giving a strong impression of an innocent lad led astray by a designing female.

Daniel made a bad impression by losing his temper twice over the slur being put on his sister. Kennedy on the other hand was an excellent witness, giving a brief account of his meeting with her, the blood on her dress and the knife in her hand, which went a long way to damn her all over again.

A statement was read from Ma Huggett who said she had just set out her supper that evening, two pigs' trotters with a jar of pickled onions, when she heard someone come running down the stairs helter-skelter into the street but at the time thought little of it. She was used to her lodgers' queer antics but now it seemed to confirm the suggestion that Kate had fled from the house temporarily frightened at what she had done and had only returned later.

The proceedings dragged on until the afternoon. The Coroner shifted his papers together and peered at Kate over the top of his eyeglasses.

'It is not for me to pass judgment since it is not part of my office but I feel obliged to ask you . . . did you on the night in question deliberately and with intent to do harm stab the deceased so as to bring about his death?'

'No,' said Kate, her voice ringing out clear as a bell, 'no, I did not!'

Too cocky by half was the public verdict, she'll pipe down when she realizes what is coming to her, and Daniel had a strong feeling that some powerful influence was driving matters forward and that little attention had been devoted to the discovery of the real murderer.

The Coroner's jury, doubtful of the decision to which they were being pushed, brought in a verdict of death by knife wound delivered by some person unknown, but the very next day Inspector Blain, accompanied by the Sergeant, formally arrested Kate for the murder of Viscount Raymond Dorrien during rehearsal at the Princess Theatre. Three days later at the magistrate's court in a hearing that took precisely fifteen minutes, Mr Goodall, with a certain regret since he was a playgoer himself and had seen Kate perform more than once, assigned the case to the public prosecutor, the prisoner to be sent to Newgate there to await trial in due course at the Old Bailey.

Daniel went back to his lodging haunted by his last glimpse of his sister's frozen white face. She had made no outcry, simply stood there in her dark dress so forlorn, so terribly alone, that it tore at his heart. He had never felt so utterly helpless. The solicitor suggested by Mr Brown had proved worse than useless. He was a mousy little man, well-versed in cases concerning contracts, leases, bad debts, petty larceny and so on, but murder was quite outside his range. He had demanded his fee before he even started and was easily overcome by the astute Inspector Blain when he attempted to question the legality of the case being concocted against Kate.

'But don't you see,' said Daniel furiously when he made no further move, 'my sister was not there at any time during that evening till after he had been found dead.'

'I have already made it clear,' said the lawyer huffily, 'that simply to state a person was not present is not enough, you have to prove it.'

'But they can't prove without a shadow of doubt that she *was* there!'

The lawyer shrugged his shoulders. 'My considered opinion is that she should plead self-defence. He assaulted her and she fought him off.'

'With a knife in her hand, I suppose!' said Daniel contemptuously. 'Even I can see that a plea of that kind will get us nowhere.'

He was at his wits' end to know where to turn for help. That evening when he came home from the magistrate's court, he tried to stop himself thinking about it by putting together the clothes and other few necessities she would be allowed to have with her in Newgate. He put everything into a holdall and then sat for a long time on the bed trying to think what he could do. He had never trusted the police investigation. He had haunted Vyner Street trying to find a clue on which a case could be built. Someone must have seen something but questions got him nowhere. It seemed that the inhabitants on that particular evening had been both blind and deaf.

He knew now what his mother must have felt all those years ago, alone, friendless, without the money that can buy influence and provide a little comfort for those awaiting trial. In the end she had gone on her knees, paying with her body for help that had still been denied to her. Now he must do the same. He must go to the man he had despised for so long, swallow his bitterness, forget his pride and implore his help. He had one weapon against him and if necessary he meant to use it. He wrestled with the problem for two or three days unable to make the final decision. He took the holdall to Newgate and with the help of a small bribe saw Kate for a few minutes. She said scarcely anything but her face told him what she must be suffering in that vile place whose very walls seemed to reek of human misery. He thought about it all that night and the next day while he dragged his reluctant pupils through the bare bones of an education, and at last made up his mind. He set out in the early evening, his purpose burning inside him, to walk to Belgrave Square.

He had been there once before, months ago, when a foolish curiosity to see where Christine lived had taken him there. It was a handsome house with a flight of steps up to the white door with its fine brass fittings, the lamps on either side already casting a warm glow. Gleams of light shone through the windows though the curtains were already partly drawn. It was past eight o'clock but they would probably still be at dinner, Christine with them. He had not seen her since all this horror had fallen on them. No doubt her father had prevented it. After all, Ray Dorrien was one of their own class and he was married to Everard's niece. He could have gone to Everard Warrinder's chambers in the Temple but his colleagues would have been there and what he had to say was far too personal.

It was now or never. He steadied himself and then went boldly up the steps and raised the heavy brass knocker.

Chapter 19

When Christine returned home that day after Ma Taylor had told her the appalling news, it was to find the story had already begun to spread. Her mother came back from her day's visiting full of it.

'The most shocking thing, Christine,' she said, hardly waiting to take off her hat, 'they are saying that Ray Dorrien was murdered yesterday evening in the lodgings of that young woman whom Harry invited to sing at his birthday ball. It seems that very early this morning the police informed his father and Clara who understandably is quite distraught with grief and shock, poor girl.'

With rage more likely, thought Christine unkindly, because this will have effectively put an end to her ambitious plans of becoming a great society hostess with a wealthy husband obediently tagging at her heels.

'What was he doing there?' she asked.

'It seems he had intended to sup with her. Not the thing of course but you know what these young men are. When I think that it might have been Harry! I never particularly cared for Ray Dorrien but to die like that in his mistress's sordid East End room . . .'

'Kate was not his mistress,' said Christine fiercely.

'Oh really, my dear, I know you and Harry thought a good deal of her at one time but no one, not even Ray, would go as far as that without a good deal of encouragement.'

And that, Christine very soon found out, was the opinion of most people and she seethed with indignation on behalf of Kate and more particularly of Daniel. If she had not been bound by the promise she had given to her father she would have flown to his side, offering him all her own small resources if he needed them.

Of course they talked about it among themselves, especially after the day when Clarissa insisted on Christine going with her to see Clara and offer her their deepest sympathy. She was after all a close relative.

It was a most unhappy afternoon. Clara was not so much grief-stricken as filled with a bitter vindictive desire that Kate should be punished with the utmost severity of the law.

'Aren't you forgetting something?' ventured Christine gently. 'Up to now there is absolutely nothing proved against her and I'm pretty sure it was not she who invited Ray to Vyner Street. He must have made his own decision about that.'

'And at the same time arranged to be murdered, I suppose,' said Clara, turning on her with a bitter irony. 'You would say that. You're besotted on her just as Harry was, her and her wretched brother. If you had only done what I asked that day, none of this would have happened.'

'That's not fair,' flared Christine. 'Kate would never have agreed to become his mistress, never.'

'No, she did worse. She tempted him there and then when he was at her mercy, she punished him in the vilest cruellest way she could, leaving him callously to die. I pray every day that I see her hanged for it!' and Clara's overwrought nerves giving way at last she burst into a flood of angry tears.

They left her in the capable hands of Miss Motford, the elderly companion who had looked after the child Clara since she was nine years old and was both kind and firm.

'I don't precisely know what that was all about,' said Clarissa in the carriage on their way home, 'but I suppose the kindest thing one can say is that Clara is very upset and hardly knows what she is saying.'

'She knows very well,' said Christine, 'and she intends to do all she can to make Kate suffer for her own bitter disappointment.'

'Isn't that a little unkind?' said her mother mildly.

'Perhaps, but Clara knew all about Ray before she married him,' muttered Christine and then felt a twinge of remorse when her mother said quietly:

'Nobody knows anyone as well as all that.'

Thankfully she was spared the threat that had been hanging over her. She was not to be banished to Scotland after all. One morning that week her father silently handed her a letter. Her Uncle Francis had written saying he intended to take his wife and family for an extended holiday in France and Italy. When they returned in the late summer he and Grace would be delighted to welcome Christine any time she wished to come.

'I suppose you're thankful,' said her father drily. 'I could pack you off to Paris, you know. Harry would be only too pleased to have your company.'

'Oh no, Papa, please, not just now.'

'Have you kept the promise you made to me?'

'Yes, of course I have,' and she had. On that one brief visit she had not actually seen Daniel.

That evening they were joined by Gareth and on the surface it seemed almost like old times. More and more details had become known about the case that seemed to be occupying not only the police but half London, rich and poor alike.

'How can anyone die like that simply from loss of blood?' asked Christine. 'It doesn't seem possible.'

'It's only too possible if help is not at hand.'

'Must we discuss things like this over the dinner table?' complained Clarissa.

'But I want to know, Mamma.'

Gareth glanced at his host and receiving his nod went on in his best student lecture voice, 'It's very simple really. You see the body has one principal artery called the aorta which has branches extending to all parts. The blood flows down this artery from the heart and returns by way of veins – that's a very simple picture of the circulatory system. If the main artery is severed or damaged, there is a great outflow of blood, the patient becomes faint and fairly rapidly unconscious and, if help is not immediately forthcoming, ultimately dies of heart failure and brain damage. If Ray had been found in the early stages he could have been saved.'

'He must have suffered horribly with no one there to help him,' said Christine slowly.

'He must indeed. I would not wish such a death on anyone,' said Gareth. He turned to Everard. 'What do you think of this case, sir? Is the girl guilty? Surely no one could be so heartless as to leave an injured man to die?'

Christine watched her father's face. If what Daniel had told her was true, and surely he would never have said it if he didn't believe it, then Kate was his daughter, his own flesh and blood. His expression gave nothing away.

He said briefly, 'I couldn't express an opinion without knowing a great many more details. The police so far are not giving much away.' He paused for a moment before he went on. 'In the event of it coming to trial, Lord Dorrien has already asked me if I would act for him.'

'But you wouldn't, would you?' exclaimed Christine. 'You wouldn't take on a case against Kate?'

'As it happens, I told him that I have not taken up a prosecution case for a great many years. I prefer to defend clients rather than hunt them to death. If necessary, I advised him to engage the services of Sir James Dalfrey. He is a Counsel with a great reputation in such cases.'

'For heaven's sake,' said Clarissa, 'must we go on talking about poor Ray and this wretched young woman? There are more pleasant subjects.'

'Certainly there are,' said her husband with some relief. 'What is the latest news of your uncle's house, Gareth?'

'Very good. The tenants have moved out and we now have possession.'

'Not before time,' said Clarissa. 'From what I hear there is a great deal to be done before you can think of moving in. I can see I shall have to plan for a Christmas wedding instead of a summer one.'

Christine had a crazy desire to laugh. It was so ridiculous that they all, except for her mother, knew exactly what the situation was but not the smallest hint was given. The farce of their engagement still went on.

The day the news came through of Kate's arrest and committal to trial Everard Warrinder had been lunching with some of his colleagues in the Temple. They tossed the circumstances from one to the other with various legal niceties and jests while he sat silent, haunted by the past and tormented with indecision. The wine went round, the talk became more boisterous and the comments more ribald, especially among the younger members, till one of them turned to him. 'You're keeping pretty quiet, sir, what do you think? If I may say so it's a case right up your street,' and quite suddenly his patience snapped. He abruptly got to his feet.

'You sit there, all of you, talking about this young woman as if she were a common whore. She is nothing of the kind. She's an intelligent girl who has pushed herself up from nothing to become a highly gifted young actress with everything going for her. Why on earth should she have wanted to entertain a good-for-nothing womaniser like Ray Dorrien and if, as perhaps is possible, he forced himself upon her, why on earth would she have behaved in such a stupid and uncharacteristic way? It is obvious to me and should be to anyone that some kind of filthy trick has been played upon her and either the police are behaving in a more stupid way than usual or someone is making damned sure that they turn a blind eye and don't investigate too closely. Try looking at it from that point of view and see what kind of answer you come up with,' and he walked out of the room leaving his companions staring after him.

'Well!' exclaimed one of them at last. 'What's bitten him? She's certainly got under his skin. Not at all like old Everard,' and they laughed uneasily before changing the subject.

The next few days saw Ray's funeral down at his father's estate on the borders of Dorset. Clarissa insisted that they must all attend. It was only proper since whether they liked it or not he had been married to a close relative. They broke the journey at Bramber, picked up Lord Warrinder and then drove on to Greystone Park. Clara's father had returned from abroad to escort his heavily veiled daughter and there was a good turn-out of the rich and the fashionable, more for the sake of the father who was respected if his son was not. Surprisingly Margaret and Freddie had made the journey, the latter in full regimentals.

'Why the military glory?' whispered Christine to her sister as they came out of the church.

'He was on manoeuvres with the regiment and didn't have time to change. They're still going on about war with Russia.' Margaret looked worried.

'There won't be any wars, silly. I must say Freddie does look rather gorgeous.'

'Doesn't he? Baby John did his best to pull off his silver buttons this morning, nearly succeeded too,' said Margaret, full of pride in her son's strength. 'He's into everything now he's walking, nearly drives me and his Nanny crazy in case he hurts himself.'

By the time they were standing about the grave the early morning sunshine had turned to rain and it dripped dismally from the overhanging trees. After the coffin had been lowered and the earth scattered by the family, Clara found a moment to draw close to Christine.

'I told you, didn't I?' she whispered. 'I was right. They've arrested her and now she'll hang for it!'

A wind had sprung up. It shook the raindrops into Christine's face and down her neck. She shivered and moved away.

They did not go back to Greystone Park afterwards. Everard shook Lord Dorrien's hand and expressed his sympathy. Clarissa kissed Clara's cold cheek and saw with satisfaction that the flowers she had ordered were quite the finest displayed there. Then they drove back to Bramber, taking Margaret with them since Freddie had to hurry away to rejoin the regiment. They all stayed the night and then returned to

London in the morning. That was the day when Daniel came hammering at the door.

They had been quiet during dinner, all of them feeling the strain of the last two days. Margaret was just saying with pride that John Everard was so forward for his age that Freddie was going to buy a Shetland pony for his birthday and would be teaching him to ride before he could walk, when they heard the thunderous knocking at the door.

They had reached the dessert. Everard had waved away the compote of fruit and cream and reached for the cheese board when Barton came in.

'Excuse me, sir, but there is a person asking to see you. I told him you were at dinner and could not be disturbed but he was very insistent. He says his name is Daniel Hunter, that he is well known to you and that his business is extremely urgent. Shall I tell him to come back at some more convenient time?'

'No, Barton, show him into my study and tell him that I'll be with him in a few minutes.'

'Very good, sir.'

Clarissa waited till the butler had left the room before she said, 'I know who that man is. He's that wretched girl's brother, the one who attacked you at the election. How dare he come here like this! What impudence! Surely you are not going to see him!'

'I'm afraid I must, my dear.'

'But you've not even finished your dinner,' she objected.

'I have had sufficient.'

He drank the last of the wine in his glass, put down his napkin and rose to his feet.

'Excuse me. I'll join you all later in the drawing room.'

Christine would have given a good deal to follow him and hear what was taking place in his study but she must bear her soul in patience. Perhaps afterwards she could somehow intercept Daniel before he left.

Margaret whispered, 'What was all that about? I thought Papa looked very serious suddenly.'

'It is serious but I'll tell you about it afterwards.'

And the two girls, burning with curiosity in their different ways, meekly followed their mother to the drawing room.

Daniel, left alone in the handsomely furnished study, looked around him and knew against all his radical principles that this was just the kind of room he would have liked to possess himself, with its fine Queen Anne bookcases filled with row upon row of leather-bound books, the desk with its massive silver inkstand, the soft carpet under his feet, the fire that glowed extravagantly under the marble mantelpiece on this cool spring evening. On one wall hung a small painting of a woman, head and shoulders only, reddish hair in an old-fashioned style, the eyes looking down at a cluster of roses held in one hand. For a fleeting second it could have been Kate he was looking at but then as he moved to look closer, the likeness seemed to vanish. He spun round as the door opened and Everard came in. The last time he had seen him Everard had looked sick and pale, his shoulder bandaged, his shirt torn and bloody, his face drawn with pain. Now, in evening dress, he appeared handsome, self confident, immensely sure of himself.

'Good evening, Mr Hunter,' he said with an easy charm. 'Are you interested in pictures? That is a portrait of my mother painted when she was about eighteen.' He walked behind his desk. 'Barton tells me you want to speak to me very urgently. What can I do for you?'

He was a fool to have come. How could he force this man, so secure in his position, so well known and esteemed, to take on Kate's case, to use his skill and expertise on her behalf? Then he seemed to see again her white strained face, felt all the wretchedness of the case against her and his own helplessness and the words burst out of him in one long passionate stream.

'You've got to take on Kate's case, you've got to make them listen to you. I've told the police over and over again that she is innocent, that she was not even there, but they won't listen, they won't look elsewhere for the man who killed Ray Dorrien. They're blinded with prejudice because she is a nobody, a young woman living on her own, an actress with no important friends and he was the son of Lord Dorrien. That damnable Police Inspector smiles and goes his own way and won't move a finger. There must be some other explanation, there has to be, but they won't hunt around for it. They have what they call an open-and-shut case. But they'll take notice of you and you owe it to her. She's your daughter, you know she is, you've always known it,' he went on recklessly. 'If that portrait hanging there is your mother, then she is Kate's grandmother, the likeness stares out at you. You cannot deny it.'

He stopped, breathless, angry with himself because he had meant to be so calm, so reasonable, so logical and if necessary so threatening, and instead felt suddenly futile, a windbag shouting a lot of words into empty air.

Everard said drily, 'I'm not aware that I have denied anything so far. Calm yourself, boy, you're overwrought and I can understand why but you'll get nowhere by shouting at me.'

'I shouldn't have come,' muttered Daniel. 'I might have known it would be useless.'

'I wouldn't say that. As it happens I've been half expecting you.' He looked at Daniel with an experienced eye and thought the boy had probably gone through a minor hell in the last two weeks. 'Let's not jump to any conclusions too hastily,' he said and got up, moving to a side table that held a silver tray with decanters and glasses. He poured a small measure of brandy, brought it back to his desk and held it out to Daniel.

'Now,' he said, 'drink that and try to pull yourself together.'

'I don't want anything from you,' muttered Daniel.

'It's good cognac even if I say it myself,' Everard said with a half smile. 'Come, drink it. It will steady you.'

Reluctantly Daniel accepted the glass, took a small gulp and felt the spirit run fierily down to an empty stomach and then spread a comforting warmth through his jangled nerves.

Everard sat down again behind his desk.

'That's better. Now pull up a chair and let us talk reasonably.'

'I'd rather stand,' Daniel said stubbornly.

'Very well, if you insist on making us both feel uncomfortable.'

Daniel took another sip of the brandy, realized he was only succeeding in making a fool of himself and did as he'd been told. He brought up a chair and sat facing the man he thought of as his enemy. He put down the glass and leaned forward.

'I'm not lying, you know,' he said earnestly. 'Kate *is* your daughter.'

For a moment the memory of old pain was sharp, then Everard put it aside.

'Your mother could have been mistaken.'

'No, there was never anyone else. She always loved Kate very deeply. As a child I was jealous sometimes. That was why when she was dying, she begged me to care for Kate. She did not know that we were to be dragged apart and it would be years before I found her again but when I did at last, I tried to do as my mother would have wished.'

'Why did your mother never tell me?'

Daniel hesitated. He didn't want to say it but in justice he couldn't hold it back.

'I don't know, I've never known, but when I asked her she said only "He has a wife and children now". I could not understand why she didn't rage against you as I did. I have hated and despised you from that day to this.'

'I see.'

For a moment there was silence between them, then Everard said, 'Does Kate know this?'

'No, only that you were responsible for my father's hanging.'

'And for that she bears a grudge against me?'

'On the contrary,' said Daniel slowly. 'She has been full of excuses for you.'

'And you've told no one else about this, not even when you were campaigning against me at the election?'

'No. However much I despised you, however much I was tempted, it would have been like dishonouring my mother. I've told no one.'

'Good.' Everard sat for a moment quite still, staring down at his clasped hands while Daniel waited, hardly daring to breathe. Then he looked up and said abruptly, 'It is of the utmost importance that you still keep it hidden, that you drop no hint to Kate or to anyone. Do you understand?'

'Because of the damage it could do to your reputation?' he said with a touch of scorn.

'That too but not entirely. If I take up Kate's defence, I must appear completely impartial. It could hopelessly prejudice it if it were to be even hinted that I was trying to save my natural daughter from the gallows. Do you understand me?'

'Yes.' Daniel stared at him, still hardly daring to believe. 'Does that mean that you are going to take up Kate's case?'

'Yes.'

'I don't know what to say,' stammered Daniel suddenly overcome. 'When I came here I did not dare to hope, it was a desperate chance . . .'

'And if your plea failed, no doubt you intended to blackmail me. I'm afraid I have spiked your guns there,' said Everard with a half smile, 'my decision had already been made and now it has been settled between us, we had better get down to some details. Where has she been sent to wait for trial?'

'To Newgate and in the most appalling conditions. I was only allowed to see her for a few minutes. She said little but I know what she must be going through. They are so over-crowded that she has been pushed into a cell with others – thieves, prostitutes – God knows what. I tried to get it changed but no one there would listen to me. I even had to bribe the doorkeeper to take a few necessities in to her.'

'I think I can remedy that. I can at least make sure she is decently housed and receives decent food.' He pulled a pad of paper towards him and took up a pen. 'Now tell me everything that happened, every detail no matter how small or apparently insignificant.'

379

But before Daniel could find words to reply there was a knock at the door and Barton came in carrying a tray.

'Madam asked me to bring coffee for you and your guest, sir.'

'Thank you, Barton. Put it on the desk. I will deal with it myself.' He glanced at Daniel. 'You must have missed an evening meal. Are you hungry? Can we offer you something? A sandwich perhaps?'

He had eaten nothing since the morning but relieved though he was, he was not yet prepared to throw aside years of bitterness and resentment.

'Nothing . . . thank you.'

'Very well. That will be all, Barton.'

'Thank you, sir.'

The butler threw a disparaging glance at Daniel and went out, shutting the door.

Everard picked up the silver pot, poured the coffee into two elegant porcelain cups and pushed one towards Daniel.

'I prefer it black but help yourself to cream or milk.'

Daniel had rarely drunk coffee and when he had it was nothing like this. The fragrance of the rich brew made him realize suddenly that he was ravenously hungry. He sipped it, hot and strong, and it had a steadying effect.

'Now,' said Everard, 'let us get down to work.'

For the next half-hour Daniel found himself the subject of a professional cross-examination that left no point unturned, questions so subtly put that he was giving away more than he realized. Every detail of his early dealings with Ray Dorrien were examined, the thugs who had been set upon him and his own angry reaction.

Once his questioner looked up to say, 'From what you tell me, I wonder that you yourself did not come under suspicion.'

'Oh but I did and it was only a lucky chance that I spent the evening with Ezra Brown, who was doing his best to persuade me to give up teaching and take up a position in his new grocery store.'

'And marry his daughter into the bargain, I presume,' said Everard, leaning back in his chair half serious, half jesting. 'You could do worse. Are you going to accept his offer?'

He had hit the nail on the head and Daniel was quick in angry denial.

'No, never. Building up a store selling rich food to the wealthy is not the height of my ambition.'

'No doubt like my daughter, you would prefer to be handing it out to the undeserving poor,' said Everard drily.

'Do you need to laugh? Is that so worthless an ambition?' he said fierily.

'Not at all, very praiseworthy I'm sure, and don't be so touchy.' He looked down at the notes he had made. 'From what I can gather, there would seem to me to have been a serious laxity in police investigation. I cannot believe that no one in Vyner Street saw anything on that particular evening. How did Ray gain entry into Kate's room? Did he have a key? Has the lock been tampered with? Who else knew of his plan to wait for her there? And who was it who made some attempt to help him and then apparently abandoned him to his fate and made no move to fetch assistance? All these points I shall make it my business to search into.'

'It's going to take time,' said Daniel despairingly, 'and they are saying that Lord Dorrien is determined to have revenge for his son's death. Could he hurry on the trial? Could he try to get Kate convicted before the truth can be discovered?'

Everard smiled. 'You are not acquainted with the law. It moves extremely slowly and if by bad luck the trial should be brought forward before our investigations are complete, then I shall ask for a postponement until I have completed my case for the defence. It will not be refused.'

For the first time on that momentous evening Daniel relaxed, the tension within him slowly draining away. It was such a tremendous relief not to be hopelessly floundering in matters he didn't understand, all his protests falling on deaf ears, that he felt suddenly weak, almost too exhausted to fight any longer.

Everard was saying, 'Have you engaged a solicitor to safe-guard your sister's interests?' and he knew he must pull himself together.

'Yes, Mr Brown recommended someone but he was useless. All he keeps on saying is that she must plead self-defence, which is ridiculous because she was not there. When she came home, Dorrien was already dead, but he won't listen any more than the Police will. It is like battering at a stone wall.'

'I can recommend someone who is guaranteed to break down any stone wall set up by the police. He will demand further investigation on behalf of his client.'

'Mr Rouse demanded his fee before he would even discuss the details,' said Daniel hesitantly.

'Don't be anxious. That won't apply in this case.' Everard put down his pen and leaned back in his chair. 'There would seem little more to be done tonight but if anything further comes up that has any bearing on the situation, then bring it to me here or at my chambers in the Temple.'

'Yes, yes, of course.'

'And now I would suggest that you go home and get a good night's rest. If you'll forgive my saying so, you look as if you could do with it. Shall I ask Barton to call a cab for you?'

'No, I would rather walk.'

Daniel got to his feet and for a moment they stood facing one another, the handsome sophisticated lawyer and the young man who, despite his ill-fitting suit, his too-long hair, still possessed an awkward grace and a look of proud independence.

Everard said wryly, 'Last time we met you told me that the only thing that prevented you from shooting me was that it would damage your party and its fight against the present government. Do you still feel like that?'

It took Daniel aback for a moment, then he said, 'I'll tell you that after you have succeeded in proving Kate's inno-cence.'

Everard smiled. 'I see. We are to be friendly enemies working for the same cause.'

Daniel hesitated and then said sincerely, 'I never expected the evening to turn out like this. I am grateful, tremendously grateful, and I will work all my life to repay you.'

'I hardly think that will be necessary and don't thank me yet. I'm not God and far too much could go wrong.' He touched the bell and when Barton came in he said, 'Will you show Mr Hunter out and if at any time he comes himself or leaves a message for me, then make sure that I am informed immediately.'

'Very good, Mr Warrinder. Will you come this way, sir?'

Everard stood for a moment looking after him, wondering if he had been right. He had put the whole of his reputation, the future of his wife and his children in the hands of a young man of whom he really knew very little. Clarissa would call it an absurdly quixotic gesture on his part to give so much for absolutely no reward but then she knew nothing and despite his doubts it was a relief. By acknowledging to himself and to Daniel that Kate was his daughter, he was paying a debt. It was going to be unbelievably difficult but all the same he was glad the decision had been made.

Christine had made an excuse for leaving her mother and Margaret in the drawing room and had been hovering on the upstairs landing for some time watching out for Daniel's leaving. She heard the front door open and close, then pulled a shawl around her shoulders and flew down the stairs to the kitchen quarters. She whisked through to the astonishment of Mrs Gant who was just sitting down with the other servants for a last cup of tea and went through the area door into the square.

She could see Daniel ahead of her walking towards the main road and caught him up under one of the giant trees at the corner of the square.

'I had to speak to you,' she said breathlessly. 'Why did you come here this evening? What has Papa been saying to you?'

'You should not have come out like this, Christine!'

'Oh I know. They'll think I'm one of the servant girls running out to meet a lover. Perhaps I am,' and she gave a nervous little giggle. 'Daniel, you must tell me. What happened?'

They were very close together under the tree. He could only just see her face by the faint light of the street lamp. It was only a few weeks but it seemed like for ever since he had seen her and his arm involuntarily went around her.

'I still can't believe it,' he whispered. 'Your father has promised to undertake Kate's defence.'

'Papa has? But that's wonderful. How did you persuade him?'

'I didn't, not really,' he said slowly. 'I think he had already decided, but Christine, people like us, we can't possibly pay him. All that Kate and I have saved wouldn't pay for one hour's work by someone like him so questions are bound to be asked as to why he has taken it on. That's why it is very important not to drop a hint, not the very slightest clue as to who she is. You do understand, don't you? Not a single word to anyone, not to your mother or your sister or to anyone at all.'

'Of course I wouldn't,' she said scornfully, 'do you imagine I would ever say anything that might harm Papa? Daniel, I mustn't stay too long but there's something I must tell you. It's why I've not seen you for these last weeks. There was a letter.'

'A letter?'

'Yes, a beastly anonymous one sent to Papa. It said – it was written on common paper in horrible capitals – it said we had spent hours together alone in your room on election day.'

'Oh no. I never told anyone . . .' then he stopped. It was true he had said nothing but Elspeth had found out somehow, she had been spiteful about it. He was filled with an icy rage against her. 'Was your father very angry?'

'Yes and no. He wasn't unkind, more disgusted with whoever wrote it, but he has forbidden me to go down to the clinic again which is absolutely ridiculous. He even wrote to Dr Dexter himself and he has made me promise not to see you again. I couldn't help it, Dan, I had to agree but it won't be for long, I swear it won't. I'll get round him somehow. I'll make him understand, especially now.'

'And what about Gareth? Are you still engaged?'

'He didn't tell Gareth. He burnt the letter.' She sighed. 'It's all so crazy. Gareth and my father too, they will not believe me when I tell them how it is with me. They think I am like some silly creature who indulges in stupid fancies but it's not true. Tell me it isn't true.'

Her face was only a few inches from his own. The very fact that her father hadn't mentioned it this evening proved how confident he was in his power over his daughter. He could kill Elspeth for her interference because he was absolutely certain that the letter had come from her with the purpose of enraging Everard Warrinder against Christine and she had succeeded.

'Of course it isn't true,' he murmured and to prove it he kissed her, a long satisfying kiss. He had intended to remain cool, sensible and then couldn't stop himself. He wanted her, dear God how he wanted her, the turmoil of the last few weeks putting the edge on his need for her. For an insane moment he was tempted to push open the garden gate, pull her down with him on to the green turf and kiss and kiss, a fancy that vanished almost as soon as it was born.

'I must go,' she said breathlessly, 'they'll be looking for me, but we're together in this, Dan, we'll work together. I'll find a way, I promise I will, you and I and Papa, we'll save Kate.'

'You must be careful,' he said but she had gone already and he watched her run across the road and disappear down the area.

She smiled brilliantly at the faces turned to her in surprise as she went through the kitchen and when she had gone and the door closed beyind her, Mrs Gant shook her head in wonder.

'Well! What's biting our Miss Christine this evening, I wonder, runnin' out into the square like that?'

'Postin' a letter p'raps,' ventured the youngest scullery maid.

Mrs Gant snorted. 'Meetin' someone her Papa don't want her to meet, more like. She's a deep one is our Miss Christine.'

'Do you mean a lover?' whispered the scullery maid, eyes like saucers.

'I don't mean nothin' of the kind,' said Mrs Gant, 'and you can take them cups and saucers outside and wash them up and then get off to your bed, Annie. Talkin' like that about your betters, I never heard the like!'

Chapter 20

At Newgate Kate had been shut into a cell built to hold two and now housing seven including herself, all awaiting trial. To a young woman who had always deeply valued her hard won privacy, it was the utmost in misery and degradation.

For the first few days after the arrest she had been confined to the police station and had been treated with a certain decency. The young Constable was a kindly soul and though shocked at what she was alleged to have done, he could not help thinking she was different from the usual inmates, the petty thieves, prostitutes, vagrants and drunks, who more often than not screamed abuse at him and fouled the clean cells to such an extent they had to be scrubbed out the next morning if they were to meet with prison regulations. He let her have a cell to herself and though it was no more than four stone walls with a narrow pallet bed, a small stool and the necessary bucket in the corner, it was at least bearable.

Newgate, she found, was a very different kind of hell for which, it seemed, she was obliged to pay and pay again. A fee on entering the prison, another if you wanted a bed to yourself with very doubtful sheets and exorbitant charges made by the gaolers for any small addition to the meagre prison diet. The little she had saved rapidly began to drain away.

There was little difference in Newgate between prisoners already convicted and those up for trial. Innocent till proved guilty did not apply in that overcrowded gaol. The warder pushed her roughly along the corridors from the governor's office where she had been signed in. She was led through the men's quarters, a horrifying sight of some hundred and forty prisoners from boys of twelve to toothless grandfathers, sitting, lying, snoring, quarrelling, their eyes following after her as she passed through, trying to still the inner trembling until they reached the room assigned to remand prisoners. The door was opened, she was thrust inside and it slammed on her.

The six inmates stared at her, eyes greedily taking in every detail, the neat plain dress still comparatively unsoiled, the thick dark cloak, the shining hair now brushed back and tied with a ribbon. She was to get to know them intimately, the child of thirteen accused of smothering the baby she had borne secretly to the son of the house where she worked as scullery maid, the woman who in a fit of madness had stolen a silk scarf from a market stall, a prostitute who had been taken up for savagely biting a brutal client and a tall silent woman who did not finger Kate's clothes or crowd around her asking question after question. She knew she ought to feel compassion but was conscious only of a numb despair. She shrank away from them in revulsion and took refuge in the bed assigned to her against one wall, sickened by the stench of human sweat, strong carbolic and the foul reek from the bucket in the corner, horrified that she must eat and sleep, perform all the most intimate actions of life in this small room with six strangers. Her stomach revolted against the greasy soup and stale bread that was their supper and that night while all around her were sighs, groans, stifled sobs and restless movement, she lay on the bed with closed eyes and longed to die.

She saw Daniel for a few minutes but there was nothing that he could do to make it more bearable for her. One night when she lay sleepless the tall thin woman who had always kept her distance came and knelt beside the pallet bed. It was the dead hour of the night when even the sounds of misery and hopelessness that haunted the great prison had fallen into uneasy silence.

'They are saying that you murdered your lover, stuck him like a pig and let him bleed to death,' she whispered hoarsely.

Startled, Kate said, 'That is what I am accused of but I didn't do it.'

'Pity, but at least someone did and there's one brute less in the world. I did it, you know, I killed him with a coal hammer.'

Kate was staring at her in a kind of frozen horror while the woman went on almost dreamily as if something within her was compelling her to speak.

'I put up with it, you know, the beatings, the black eyes, the lies, the coming home roaring drunk, because I had the child. Pretty as a picture she were, not like me, not like him neither. "She's another man's get," he used to scream at me when he were in his cups. I used to steal the money out of his pocket when I could, all for her, never dreamin' . . .' She paused, staring into the darkness and then went on, 'She were just turned fourteen when they fished her out of the river, three months gone with his child. He swore it were none of his but I knew better. It was as if something burst inside my head. I took the coal hammer to bed with me and waited my chance. I hit him with it while he snored like the pig he was and if I swing for it I don't care, not now the girl's gone, not now I know he'll never do that to no one ever again.'

She spoke so calmly, so quietly, nothing but a flat whispered statement of fact but in the semi-darkness her eyes glittered with a kind of madness and in spite of her involuntary revulsion, the actress in Kate took note of that look and the tone of that voice. One day, she thought, when she played Lady Macbeth she would know exactly how to do it.

Each day the prisoners were given half an hour's exercise in the prison yard. It was a dank dismal place surrounded by high dark walls so that no sun ever penetrated but at least the air smelled fresh and after the stifling prison Kate drew in great gulps of it. It was almost impossible to believe that it was May already and outside in Cheapside the flower-sellers were doing a roaring trade, costers were crying their wares up and down the street and people would be walking with a new spring in their step.

The prisoners were kept constantly on the move, no talking together, no little groups to chat and laugh, but round and round monotonously. She had been there a fortnight that seemed like a year when one morning, when their time was nearly up, a prison officer came out and spoke to the warder who was watching them. As the dreary procession passed him, he said sharply, 'Hunter, you're wanted.'

Taken aback Kate halted, the woman behind bumped into her and swore loudly, then she stepped out of the line.

'Come with me,' said the prison officer.

Surprised and a little fearful she followed him up flight after flight of stone stairs till they reached what surely must have been the top floor of the main block. They walked down a corridor past several closed doors till he flung one open at the end.

'The prisoner, sir,' he said and ushered her in past him.

It was a cell like all the others, sparsely furnished but scrupulously clean and with a high barred window that being at the top of the building let in not only fresh air but even a faint streak of sunshine.

A man turned to her as she went in, a gentleman, she thought, youngish, formally dressed. He came to meet her with outstretched hand.

'I'm delighted to meet you, Miss Hunter. I've been one of your admirers ever since your remarkable performance in the Christmas pantomime. I am George Westcott and I shall be taking over your case from your former solicitor.'

She stared at him. 'But I don't understand. Did my brother engage you?'

'Your brother has been consulted of course,' he said smoothly. 'Shall we sit down? There is a great deal to talk over.'

He nodded to the prison officer who went out, pulling the door to, and she wondered if he were standing outside listening to every word.

The lawyer waited till she had sat down and then took the stool on the other side of the table and put down his portfolio of papers.

'Now,' he said briskly, 'first things first. I am from Simon, Westcott and Westcott – the "and Westcott" being me,' he grinned pleasantly, 'and since I have had a good deal of experience in criminal law, I think I can do a little better for you than your former solicitor.'

She felt bewildered by his easy confident manner. 'But Daniel and I, we have not sufficient means . . .'

'No need to worry about fees. All that has already been taken care of. I have also arranged for you to be housed in this separate cell. It is not exactly a palace, I'm afraid, and between you and me it is actually sometimes used for convicted prisoners waiting for the rope, but since it is not in use just now, I have been permitted to take it over for you. I have also arranged for your food to be brought in from outside. The warder will bring you a bill of fare each morning and you can then choose whatever you please for that day.'

'But all this will be very costly,' she said helplessly. 'I know from what I've had to pay already.'

He waved it aside as of no consequence. 'You need not concern yourself about that. Now, Miss Hunter, I have closely examined as many relevant details as I have been able to lay my hands on but I should be glad if it won't distress you too much to hear from you in your own words exactly what happened on that night when you came home and found Dorrien already dead.'

'Yes, of course I will if it will help.'

George Westcott had a pleasantly ugly face, his nose too large, his mouth too wide, but his eyes had a friendly way of crinkling up when he smiled and though she did not know why, he gave her a feeling of confidence which was very heartening.

He took notes of all she said in an extremely business-like manner, asked one or two shrewd questions and then shuffled his papers together and put them into his portfolio.

'There seems to me to be a great many points which have been neglected. I shall make it my business to enquire into them with this Inspector Blain. I wish we could have obtained bail for you but it is not permitted in a murder charge. Don't allow these wretched conditions to distress you too much. I am confident that before the trial comes up, Mr Everard Warrinder will have constructed an excellent defence.'

'Everard Warrinder!' she repeated. 'Do you mean that he will take my case?'

'Certainly.' The lawyer got to his feet and stood smiling down at her. 'You are very fortunate. He is one of the most brilliant counsels working at the Bar.'

'I know,' she said, 'I know who he is but he . . . there has been great trouble between him and my brother.'

'I assure you that it is so. He spoke to me himself only yesterday. Now if you will forgive me, I must go but I shall be seeing you again and Mr Warrinder himself will want to speak with you later on.'

He bowed over her hand and went out, pausing outside the door to speak to the prison officer.

She sat for a moment still dazed. It did not seem possible. All along she had been aware of an impassable gulf between Daniel and Everard Warrinder. It had inhibited her friendship with Harry and she suspected it lay like a barrier between her brother and Christine, so what had happened between them?

The prison officer broke in on her thoughts.

'Some people have all the luck,' he said sourly. 'It seems you are to have the use of this cell. You'd better collect your possessions from the remand prison.'

She felt guilty when she saw the looks on the faces of her former companions, envy mixed with a certain pleasure that at least one of them had somehow moved on to something better. They talked about it endlessly, the general opinion being that Kate Hunter must have some unknown and extremely powerful protector who was able to bend even the law to his will.

*

Everard Warrinder had made a wise choice. George Westcott was not one to let the grass grow under his feet. The firm of Simon, Westcott and Westcott had dealt with the legal affairs of the Warrinders for a generation and George himself had a great admiration for Everard. It was the kind of career he would have liked for himself but knew he didn't possess the self-confidence, the bravura, that carried so many barristers through to success in difficult cases.

Detective Inspector Blain suddenly found that his nice neat case was being attacked from all sides. It had seemed to him obvious from the start. A rich young man makes a fool of himself over a woman, they quarrel – only too likely – she attacks him, striking in a vulnerable place – maybe accidentally, that would be for the court to decide. Why go inventing stories about break-ins, unknown assassins, all fantasy fit only for the theatre? Now, however, he was being harassed by a number of unanswerable questions. No one in the street had seen or heard anything unusual on that fatal evening, he repeated more than once, but then he was new to the East End, an intellectual type with little experience of the sturdy breed that swarmed in those crowded streets, who kept themselves to themselves and still distrusted and disliked the police. Christine had a much better knowledge of them than he had and had made up her mind to put it to good use.

She had realized during her two years at the clinic that the patients who came for treatment could be difficult, uninformative, nervous of saying too much, even to the doctor, who seemed to live in a different world from theirs, and never, never say too much to the police in case you are drawn in whether you're innocent or not. They would often far more easily pour out their problems to her, especially the women, so it was Christine who made the first startling discovery almost accidentally.

For several days after the meeting between her father and Daniel she had been wondering how she could help. She thought she would go to Vyner Street, casually, a curiosity-monger, staring up at where a crime had been committed and with any luck someone might talk to her. It entailed a certain amount of deception. Her mother would most certainly not approve and her father would no doubt say that the proper wheels had been set in motion and she should not interfere. So far the promise he had given Daniel was not public knowledge. That would come when the date of the trial was fixed. After some thought she invented a series of lectures at the British Museum on Greek antiquities and Clarissa shrugged her shoulders at this impossible daughter of hers who was interested in all the wrong things. So Christine put on the plain dress she had often worn at the clinic, a simple bonnet from which she ruthlessly ripped the ostrich feather, borrowed a dark shawl from Betsy who was vastly intrigued and set out on her detective mission.

Down in Vyner Street, on that dull morning a barrel organ was grinding out a tune at the end of the street, with three small children capering around it and trying to attract the attention of the sad little monkey perched on the top. Outside the house next door a slatternly woman was washing down the front with a mop slopping layers of dirt from one step to the next. She looked up as Christine paused.

'Goin' up for a look-see at the chamber of 'orrors, are you? There ain't nothin' to see. The police have locked it up, interferin' busybodies. They do say it were enough to turn your stomach, blood all over. They took 'er up for it, ye know, the young woman what lived there.'

'Yes, I did hear something,' said Christine, 'but I think I'll go up and have a look all the same.'

'Please yourself, but you'll be wastin' your time,' said the woman, slopping her mop into the pail and sending filthy water splashing along the pavement.

On the top landing it was just as the woman had said, the door was locked and a police notice attached to it. On impulse she knocked at the door opposite where the Polish artist had lived whom she had met at Kate's party a year ago – what was his name? Karl Landowsky, that was it. There was no answer and she went slowly down the stairs again wondering why the police had not thought of questioning him. As far as she remembered, he had been on good terms with Kate.

The woman next door had finished her cleaning and was emptying her bucket into the gutter. The water swirled along over the bare feet of the children who giggled and screamed, kicking it up at each other.

'Still locked up, is it?' she asked, slapping the bucket down on the step.

'Yes. Do you know if the artist who had the room opposite is still living there?'

'The furriner d'ye mean? Funny feller, he were, drew a picture of me once in me apron an' all. I sez to him you might have waited till I got me Sunday one on. Pore devil, he met with a nasty accident.'

'What kind of accident?'

'It were one evenin' I was standin' out here, just come back from the boozer actually with a jug of ale for me old man, and he come runnin' down them stairs as if the devil were after him. He never looked to right nor left, but crashed right across the street and into one of them brewer's vans which were comin' down. You never heard such a commotion! The horses rearin' up and the driver tryin' to hold them and swearin' and cussin' as if it weren't his fault and at last when he got them quiet, there were the poor chap lyin' in the middle of the road white as death he were with a great bloody mark on his head that fair turned you up.'

'Was he dead?' breathed Christine.

'Not then, he weren't. Someone ran for the doctor from the next street and he didn't half carry on at being brought from his supper I can tell you, but he said as how the horse's hoof must have knocked all the sense out of him and he were properly con – con . . .'

'Concussed?'

'That's the word and bruised all over o' course. They took him off to the infirmary and none of us has seen him since. Could be dead by now, poor feller. Ma Huggett has been carryin' on alarmin' about the room bein' locked up and no rent comin' in.'

'Do you remember when it was that he was knocked down?'

'Ah now you're askin' – let me see now. It were a little time ago,' she frowned and then suddenly gave a whoop of triumph. 'O'course, fancy me forgettin' somethin' like that! I'm blessed if it weren't on the same evenin' as that pore young toff were knocked off up there. What with the police comin' and goin' and him bein' carried off to the morgue an' all it went clean out of me head.'

'Did you tell the police about it?'

'No, o'course I didn't,' she said contemptuously. 'Don't tell that lot nothin' or before you know where you are, you're bein' took up and asked what you were doin' and why. Best keep out of it I say and I stick to it.'

'Hasn't anyone been to the infirmary to find out how he is?'

'Not as I knows of. He didn't have many friends like – quiet sort of feller.' She stopped for a moment leaning on the mop handle and staring hard at Christine. 'Haven't I seen you somewhere before – at that there clinic, wasn't it?'

'That's right,' said Christine a little uncomfortably. 'I used to work with Dr Dexter.'

'That's right. I went there once. Had a horrible rash all over me hands and face and he give me somethin' to take and it went just like that, a bloomin' miracle it were. Well, mustn't stand here gossipin' all day, I've work to do. Nice to have had a chat,' and with a cheery wave she disappeared into the house.

Christine walked down the street, her mind full of what she had just heard. Was it possible that Karl Landowsky had found Ray in Kate's room, guessed at his purpose, tried to throw him out with terrible results and had run out for assistance only to be knocked unconscious? The very first necessity was to find out, but she was reluctant to go to the police. She would have to say who she was and it could have all kinds of repercussions. If she told Daniel and they went together to the

396

infirmary, they could well find their enquiries thrust aside as of no importance. Then she thought of John Dexter. He was someone who would be listened to and his questions answered. She would go at once. He was a man with a strong feeling for justice. He would be willing to help.

Deborah greeted her with pleasure.

'Are you quite better now? We've missed you. Your papa wrote saying you'd suffered a breakdown in health.'

'Papa makes too much fuss over nothing. I'm really quite well. Can I speak to the doctor?'

'We've been terribly busy. I shut the door and made him stop for half an hour otherwise he'd go on till he dropped.'

Christine smiled. She knew Deb tended to fuss over John Dexter, much to his exasperation. She found him in a corner of the surgery with bread and cheese and a large mug of tea.

'Hallo, stranger,' he said, 'what brings you here? Your father wrote that you had not been well.'

'I know,' she said, 'and I know what you must be thinking about me but it wasn't my wish, really it wasn't. My father just put his foot down and when he does, it's hard to fight against it.'

'We've missed you, some of 'em out there have been asking for you. Is this just a social visit?'

He knew all about the case of course, it would be difficult not to with half his patients chewing it over and asking his opinion. She told him what she had just discovered.

'Could you come with me to the infirmary?' she went on. 'Karl has not been discharged officially which means he is either still sick or dead. They will listen to you. We could see him, talk to him. He must have seen something and it could be of vital importance.'

'My dear girl, I can hardly desert a long queue of patients and go waltzing off at a moment's notice.'

'No, of course not, I do realize that but . . .'

'A day or two is hardly likely to make much difference,' he said thoughtfully. 'Tomorrow is the only free time I allow myself either here or at the practice. Can you come with me then – say about three o'clock?'

It would mean more deception, more evasions, but she could do it. 'Yes. I'll meet you there. What effect could this blow on the head have had on him?'

'Difficult to say. The degree of pressure on the brain can be quite impossible to judge with any certainty. It can cause complete loss of memory or it can mean only partial amnesia, that is the events leading up to the accident are wiped out of the mind.'

'I see. Does the memory ever come back?'

'Sometimes quickly, sometimes after months, sometimes never. We must leave that till I've had a look at this Polish friend of yours.'

'I'm very grateful.'

'No need to be, I'm interested. It seemed to me the police had chosen an easy solution that has as many holes as a fishing net and I would be glad to close some of them up. Now you must go and I must get back to work.'

'I wish I could stay,' she said ruefully, 'but it's not easy at home just now.'

'Papa rules the roost, eh? Well, it happens I'm afraid. Don't be late tomorrow.'

'I'll be there.'

She wondered if she should tell her father of her discovery but decided against it. Better to wait for a few days when she might know a great deal more. It was not so easy for her to get away the next afternoon. Her mother had taken tickets for a charity concert organized by a very eminent society hostess and was extremely annoyed when Christine said she had promised to go round the British Museum's Greek antiquities with the lecturer and his party.

'I really don't know what good you think this passionate interest in antiques is going to do for your future,' she said acidly. 'Gareth is not an archaeologist.'

'I find it far more interesting than sitting with a lot of silly women yawning their way through music they don't understand,' said Christine stubbornly.

So Clarissa stormed off to the concert and Christine met John Dexter outside the tall ugly building of the infirmary.

The doctor in charge was quite forthcoming. 'I remember the case. Physically he's quite recovered, actually asked for paper and pencil and has gone round sketching everyone. The poor devils are delighted, makes 'em feel they're still alive, I suppose. When he came out of the coma, he remembered nothing but some of it has come back quite quickly, all but the few days around the accident. Do you want to see him? We can't keep him here much longer, we need the bed. As it is some of 'em are sleeping on the floor. Go ahead, my dear chap. I'd be glad to hear what you think of him.'

Dr Dexter said, 'Do you want to come with me, Christine? It won't be too pleasant.'

'Of course I do,' she said indignantly. 'I haven't worked for two years at the clinic for nothing.'

He smiled. 'Come on then.'

It was far worse than she had imagined. The day was very warm and the long ward on the ground floor seemed totally airless and reeked with a variety of unpleasant smells. The long row of beds crammed together on either side were filled, some of the patients sitting up, others lying like corpses already. Flies buzzed over plates of uneaten food, overflowing slop pails stood unemptied. She had never sensed such a feeling of despair. She resisted the temptation to bury her nose in her handkerchief and instead held her breath, walking resolutely by the doctor's side. At the far end a man was lying on a pallet bed, his back against the wall, a pad of paper on his drawn-up knees, his eyes intent on what he was doing and for a moment she did not recognise him. He was very thin and gaunt in the coarse hospital clothes, his mane of tawny hair shaved close to his head and only the startlingly blue eyes reminding her of the charming artist she had met at Kate's party.

Dr Dexter said pleasantly, 'My friend Bob Relton has asked me to take a look at you since you are to be discharged soon.' He held out his hand. 'I'm John Dexter.'

Karl scrambled off the bed, bowing over the hand with a foreign formality.

'I am pleased to meet you,' but his eyes had shifted to Christine and he frowned as if trying to remember something.

'We have met before, yes?'

'Yes, Mr Landowsky, at a party at Kate Hunter's lodging more than a year ago now.'

'I remember – you and your brother.' He smiled apologetically. 'It is so good that I remember when I have forgotten so much.'

'Let me take a look at you,' said the doctor, so Karl sat on the bed while the clever fingers moved gently over the shaven head and he asked several shrewd questions.

'I understand that you still have some blank spots,' he went on.

'Yes, it is strange. The first thing I know before even I remember my name is that I can draw. My fingers itch to do something so they give me paper and pencil and then it came back slowly. I know that I spent some days with a friend who also comes from Cracow. He has done well in this country and he ask me to paint his wife, his daughter and then the little dog because it is the child's pet and he pay me. He gave me a draft on his bank, a cheque you would say, and I remember thinking that I must cash it to buy food and pay rent and then – pouf! it is all gone and I know nothing more till I wake up here with my head bandaged and hurting badly all over and they say I have been knocked down and the horses trample on me.'

'Have you somewhere to go when you are discharged?'

'Yes, if the landlady has not let my room,' he said ruefully. 'I must owe for several weeks and she is very angry if the rent is not paid.'

'It is not let,' said Christine quickly, 'and if it will help I will go and tell her that you are coming back.'

'I would not wish to trouble you . . .'

'It's no trouble. I would be glad to do it.'

They left soon after that and as they went through that evil-smelling ward, she looked back to see the tall lonely figure staring after them.

400

Dr Dexter said, 'I'd like to have a few words with Bob Relton before we leave. Will you wait for me, Christine? There are one or two points to be cleared up before we go to the police.'

'Must we go to the police?'

'Indeed we must. We cannot withhold what might prove to be important evidence.'

'No, I suppose not. I'll wait for you.'

'Good. I won't be long.'

It was a dismal street of tall dark buildings. A bench was set against the wall beside the door where she sat down to wait. When the doctor rejoined her about fifteen minutes later he looked very serious.

'Has it occurred to you,' he said as he took her arm and they walked back slowly to the clinic, 'that Karl could have attacked that unfortunate young man, wounded him badly – perhaps accidentally – and now is deliberately playing up the fiction of not being able to remember?'

'I don't believe it. I am sure he is not a liar,' she said indignantly. 'He is a good man. Kate always valued his friendship.'

'Very likely but the mind is capable of all kinds of strange behaviour, Christine. He may not even be doing it deliberately. If the mind does not want to remember something because it is too painful or too dangerous, it will simply shut down. It occurred to me that whoever did this to Raymond Dorrien must have had at least some blood on him so I asked Bob Relton what happened to the clothes he was wearing. It seems they had been so muddied and torn by the accident that they simply emptied the pockets and thrust the rest into the hospital furnace. But in the pockets apart from a few small items was a purse with some thirty guineas.'

'He could have cashed that bank draft he spoke of.'

'He could have done. He could also have scooped up some of the missing gold that was apparently scattered on the floor.'

'We could check, couldn't we, with his friend and with the bank?'

'No doubt the Police Inspector will do that very thing, but you can see that they must be informed or else Bob Relton and I will be in trouble. It's Thursday and he will be discharged on Saturday apparently. I'd like to be there when he comes back to familiar surroundings. It could make a difference.'

'You're interested, aren't you?' she said, looking at him curiously.

'Yes, I am.' He gave her an almost boyish grin. 'Shall I confess something? If circumstances had been different, if my father had not lost a great deal of money in an unfortunate speculation, I would have liked to go on studying as Gareth has done, go in for really comprehensive and intense research into the brain and its workings, but there we are. The money ran out and I must earn an honest living.'

'You know what Dr Andrews told us, that you're something of a medical missionary at heart.'

'Maybe. Perhaps it's a good thing the money did run out. I'm probably doing far more useful work in the clinic and in my practice than groping around in the fascinating intricacies of the brain.'

By now John Dexter was due back at his practice for evening surgery so after she left him Christine went straight to Vyner Street. She climbed down the dirty area steps and knocked at Ma Huggett's door. When there was no reply she knocked again louder and then cautiously pushed the door and walked in. There was a close stale smell as if some hundreds of meals had been cooked and eaten in the unventilated basement room and it was so dark and so crowded with furniture that for a moment she couldn't see anything. The sharp voice startled her.

'And whatd'you want bangin' away at my door like that, eh?'

She swung round and saw the fattest woman she had ever set eyes on. An abundance of flesh and a quantity of frills and flounces overflowed an enormous armchair while two small piercing black eyes stared at her from a face white as a curd cheese under the frill of a mob cap with one incongruous scarlet bow, balanced on the top of a mop of greasy grey hair.

'Well,' she went on, 'cat got your tongue, has it? If you're wantin' a room then I've none to spare. Them damned bobbies have made sure of that!'

Christine found her voice. 'I don't want a room. I've come to pay the rent for one, for Mr Karl Landowsky.'

'Him on the top floor, eh? The foreigner. Condescending to come back, is he? About time too. Three weeks he owes, five shillings a week and an extra shilling for being late with it. Rent on the dot is my rule and he knows that well enough.'

'He's been in the hospital.'

'What's wrong with him?' said the old woman suspiciously. 'Nothing catching, I hope.'

'No, he was injured in an accident. I'll pay for the three weeks owing' – she took out a sovereign and put it on the table beside the old woman and then put another half-guinea beside it – 'and that will cover the next two weeks. He's coming back on Saturday.'

'Oh is he? And who might you be, eh?' said the old woman staring at her curiously.

'Just a friend. Could I have the key so I could get the room ready for him?'

Ma Huggett had scooped up the money and it had disappeared somewhere in the folds of her voluminous skirts.

'No, you can't. I'm not handin' over the key to anyone to rummage just as they please. How do I know who you are or what you might be doin' up there? We've had enough trouble with the busies comin' round to last us for a lifetime.'

'Very well if that's what you say.'

'I do say and you shut that there door when you go out, see, I don't like strangers comin' through and pokin' their noses into my business.'

Christine had meant to open up the room, make it welcoming, refill the food cupboard, but that would have to wait till she and John Dexter fetched Karl from the infirmary. Somehow or other she must escape from home for still another day and if necessary face up to her mother's questions and her displeasure. She was not giving up now. It was far too important.

However, for once she was spared any new evasive explanations. Freddie had telegraphed that Margaret had taken a nasty fall when out riding with him and though not seriously hurt was very shaken up and distressed. As Christine had always known, Margaret was her mother's favourite and Clarissa immediately decided to run down and spend a few days with her. Her maid packed a small bag with necessities and Christine went in the carriage with her to the railway station.

'Give my dearest love to Margaret,' she said, seeing Clarissa installed in the first-class carriage with lavender water sprinkled on a large white handkerchief and the window tight shut against the smuts.

'Now Christine,' said her mother, 'don't be forever running in and out of the house and don't worry your father. He has not been looking at all well lately.'

'Don't be anxious, Mamma, and don't feel you need hurry back. Mrs Barley looks after us very well and Papa and I will do very nicely together.'

Christine kissed her mother and shut the carriage door, the whistle blew, the guard waved the green flag, the train glided slowly out of the station and she went back thankfully to the waiting carriage. She had a few days when she could please herself.

'My God, how good it feels to be free from that wretched place and back in my own home once again,' exclaimed Karl after they had brought him back to Vyner Street.

The room was bare enough save for the pictures that still covered the walls, but to an exile it was one small part of a foreign country which he could call his own.

Christine began to unpack the basket which Mrs Gant had put together for her that morning, milk, butter, a dozen eggs, ham, cheese, tea and coffee, enough to carry Karl over the weekend.

'I will make some tea, then it will really feel like home,' she said cheerfully. 'Now the rent is paid I daresay Ma Huggett will allow me to boil a kettle.'

'There is no need, I have a small spirit stove – but you must let me pay you for all this,' and Karl took out the purse which the hospital had returned to him together with some very ill-fitting clothes from their stock of second-hand garments.

'No, please,' she said quickly, pushing his hand away, 'there's no need. I have only done what Kate would have wished me to do.'

'Ah Kate!' exclaimed Karl looking disturbed. 'They tell me about the terrible thing that has happened to her and that it is I who perhaps have the secret of it hidden somewhere inside my head and cannot remember any of it.'

'Don't try to force it,' said Dr Dexter gently, 'you must let memory come back slowly. Listen to me for a moment while Christine makes us some tea. The police are going to question you very closely. I have spoken to the Inspector and warned him that you are my patient and must be treated with care.'

Karl leaned forward, his face alight with a new idea. 'Supposing I tell them that I *do* remember, supposing I say that I came home, saw this man whom I know slightly and realize he means no good for Kate. I try to make him leave and when he refuses, then I fight him and he is badly hurt. I run out to find help and all is over. I am knocked out and no one knows what has happened.'

'Very ingenious but it would be a lie, wouldn't it?' said the doctor, 'and it is never wise to lie to the police.'

'But it would free Kate, would it not? Afterwards what happens to me, it is not important.'

'And you think she would want to be set free at your expense? No, my friend, that will not do. This Inspector Blain is no fool, he will check all the details. Simply tell the truth as you have told us. The important point is that some time that evening you were here. You didn't go into your own room because the door was still locked, you must have seen Kate's door open, found Ray Dorrien bleeding, maybe dying, and run down the stairs to look for help. We must go on from there.'

'Maybe you are right. I am – what do you call it? – too melodramatic. I make the big gesture and it fall flat to the ground.'

They drank the tea out of three battered mugs, ate Mrs Gant's fat fluffy scones and then it was time to leave.

'What do you think?' asked Christine as they walked down Vyner Street.

'I think he is completely honest but what the truth is, I don't know. We can only wait and hope he remembers exactly what happened when he came back that evening and went up those stairs. It is one step forward but not far enough.'

And with that she had to be satisfied but it was still early and her unexpected freedom had gone to her head. Why not share this last discovery with Daniel before the police got hold of it? Would he be at his lodging or would he be working? She found her way to Mr Brown's grocery store and was greeted by Dickie in a huge white apron standing behind the counter and trying to look important.

'I'm on duty while Phil has his tea,' he said.

'Do you know where Daniel is tonight, Dickie?'

'Oh yes, Miss, he's at the Cheapside shop with Miss Elspeth. He is there every night now and all day on Saturday.'

She did not particularly want to meet Elspeth but still . . . She bought a slab of expensive chocolate, presented Dickie with it much to his amazed delight and then went out to find a cab.

Daniel had been working every extra hour he could when school was over. The solicitor's fee for doing precisely nothing, together with all the other expenses which had crowded in on him during the last weeks, had taken almost every penny of his small savings. Mr Brown was generous in paying him for the time he spent in the shop, which remained open till nine o'clock or even ten if customers still came. He was not enjoying it since it meant working side by side with Elspeth and he found it difficult to keep up even a pretence of friendship after Christine had told him about the anonymous letter.

They tended to snap at one another over foolish trivialities and Elspeth seethed with frustration because all the trouble over his sister, whom she had never liked, seemed to take him further away from her. One word of criticism, one slight hint that Kate might have brought it on herself was enough to bring an icy coldness between them.

It had been an exceptionally busy Saturday. They had been on their feet since they opened at eight o'clock and were both tired after a heavy week. They quarrelled over a customer's bill and she retreated behind the bead curtain that cut off the private room at the back of the shop. The very last thing she expected was to see Christine alight from a cab and come into the shop glowing with some kind of inner excitement. What was it about that infuriating young woman that he found so compelling? She could never find the right answer.

Daniel was still dealing with the difficult customer. He looked up as Christine came in and Elspeth, closely watching, saw the tiny intimate smile that passed between them. Then he had receipted the bill, the customer still grumbling was politely ushered to the door and he turned back to Christine.

'Can I speak to you for a few minutes?' she said. 'It is important.'

'I don't see why not.' He raised his voice. 'Elspeth, would you mind the shop for a few minutes? I won't be long.'

'If I must,' she said grudgingly, pushing her way through the bead curtain, 'but Saturday evenings are always very busy.'

Christine gave her a beaming smile. 'I won't keep him long, I promise,' and she took Daniel's arm. 'Do you *like* working here?' she whispered as they went out together.

'Not much but needs must when the devil drives.'

As usual on a Saturday evening Cheapside was thronged with people. It was the end of the week, no work till Monday, a week's pay burning a hole in their pockets. There were young men with their girls, older couples hunting for bargains, prostitutes touting for custom, pedlars by the dozen crying their wares and a rich succulent smell of food, from jellied eels to hot mutton pies, roasting chestnuts and baked potatoes.

Plunged into the midst of them, Daniel said, 'We can't talk here,' and took her firmly by the arm, dodging across the road through a stream of cabs, horse buses, carts and carriages, into the more dignified Giltspur Street.

'That's better,' he breathed as they emerged into the great space of Smithfield, quiet now since no market was held on a Sunday. They picked their way through piles of debris and came at last to St Bartholomew's Church.

'Let's go in,' said Christine, 'we can talk in peace in there.'

It was too early for any evening service and there were few people about, only one or two huddled forms who had found a resting place among the ancient tombstones. They sat in a pew at the back. It was very dark, the only light coming from a lantern hung high above them and all around the fragrant smell of old wood, of ancient stone, of beeswax and a kind of accumulated incense of hundreds of years of devotion and prayer.

'Now what is it?' he asked. 'I mustn't be long.'

She told him of all she had done that week, of finding Karl at the infirmary, of how Dr Dexter had helped and what it could mean, and knew that the driving need to tell him was only part of the reason that had brought her there. Far more potent was the longing to be with him again, to feel him close beside her.

'If only we could unlock his mind,' said Daniel. 'He must have seen something, spoken to Ray Dorrien perhaps.'

'Unless he himself was the attacker. He was very fond of Kate,' said Christine. 'We must face the possibility.'

'Perhaps we shall never know,' he said gloomily.

'John Dexter thinks his memory might come back quite quickly now he is back in familiar surroundings. We mustn't despair.'

'Sometimes it's difficult not to do just that.'

In both their minds was the memory of the last time they had been in this church, the day he had brought her there to see Rahere's tomb and he had kissed her for the first time.

Until Kate was safe from the charge made against her, Daniel could not think of himself or his own future. His bitter resentment of Everard Warrinder had been turned upside-down so that sometimes he no longer knew how he felt and the yawning gulf that had stretched between him and Christine seemed to have lessened.

In the dark seclusion of the ancient church they drew closer together, his arms went around her and he was kissing her with a fury made up of frustration, hopeless longing and the chaotic turmoil of the last few weeks. He pressed her back against the ancient pew, teasing open her lips so that she shuddered and then gave herself up to the almost unbearable joy of it, wanting more, so that when he unhooked the collar of her dress and pressed his lips against her throat, she pulled him closer, her fingers tangling in the thick hair until he kissed her again. The tolling of the half hour from the clock brought them back to reality. They fell apart staring at one another in the shadowy light and for a moment she was wondrously glowingly happy, then sanity returned.

'Mamma is away,' she whispered, 'but I must go. If I am very late, Papa will want to know the reason why.'

'Elspeth is going to be furious with me.'

They giggled together and then came back to earth again. She rehooked the neck of her dress and put on the discarded bonnet. He stood up, taking her hands and pulling her to her feet.

'I wonder what old Rahere would think of the goings-on in his very own church,' she whispered.

'They say he had a high old time before the sickness turned a sinner into a saint.'

Soberly they retraced their steps, he saw her into a cab and then went back to Cheapside to face Elspeth's acid comments and ignore them.

The cab crept along so slowly that Christine felt she could have walked faster but at last he pulled up in Belgrave Square. She hurriedly paid him and flew down the area steps and in by the servants' entrance. Mrs Gant had just begun to dish up as she flitted through the kitchen and up the backstairs to find

Betsy in her bedroom already putting out what she would need for the evening.

'Am I terribly late?' she gasped. 'Has Papa been asking for me?'

'Well,' said Betsy austerely, 'when Barton asked if he should serve dinner, the Master did ask if you were in and when Barton said that to his knowledge you had not yet returned, then Mr Warrinder told him to put it back for an hour as he didn't care to dine alone.'

'Did he sound angry?'

'No, just as usual, but then you're something of a favourite of his, aren't you, Miss?'

'I never thought so,' said Christine, her frowning face appearing through the folds of the gown that Betsy was lowering over her head.

'Oh go on with you, Miss. You've quite taken Miss Margaret's place in his regard. We've all noticed it downstairs.'

It surprised her to realize that what she had thought private to herself had become general knowledge even among the servants.

Dressed in her favourite green silk evening dress and with her hair brushed out and rearranged into ringlets by Betsy's skilful fingers, she sedately descended the stairs and found her father already in the dining room glancing through *The Times*.

He put down the paper as she came in. 'Ah there you are, my dear. I began to think I was destined to eat at midnight.'

'I'm sorry, Papa. I didn't realize it was so late.'

'You're looking very pretty tonight. Is it all for my benefit or are we to expect Gareth?'

'Not that I know of. Shall I tell Barton that we are ready?'

'If you will, unless you would like a glass of sherry first?'

'No, thank you, I'm far too hungry.'

'Very well.'

They sat down at the table and the servants began to carry in the silver dishes.

'And where exactly have you been gallivanting off to today?' he said lightly as the soup was placed in front of him. 'Your mother has been very annoyed with you this week. She says you have developed a most unladylike passion for Greek antiquities at the British Museum and I have been more or less commanded to enquire into it. Is it true?'

He spoke jestingly but all the same she guessed that he didn't believe a word of it and she would have to confess the truth, not that she was ashamed of it. On the contrary she was proud of what she had done.

'Not entirely true.' She glanced at Barton who had brought the wine for her father to taste and approve. 'May I tell you all about it after we have eaten, Papa? I should like to do that.'

'Very well. You may confess your sins over the coffee. Will you take wine, my dear?'

'Yes please, Papa.'

Barton filled her glass and they proceeded pleasantly through grilled sole with lemon sauce, roasted spring chicken and Mrs Gant's very special chocolate mousse while they talked about a great many things, particularly Margaret's accident, and she asked her father what truth there was in the rumours of Britain going to war with Russia which so much worried her sister.

'I've just been glancing through *The Times* and it would seem the situation is growing worse. Russia is threatening Constantinople and the Black Sea and beginning to cast greedy eyes towards India. The Cabinet have been debating whether to send in the Fleet to the Dardanelles as a precautionary measure and Palmerston is threatening to resign if Britain continues to show such a pusillanimous approach.'

'What does that mean?'

He smiled. 'Why have I wasted so much money on good tutors?'

'You should have let me go to Queen's College then I wouldn't have been so ignorant.'

'I prefer you as you are. If you must know, it means cowardly.'

'Will Freddie have to go?'

'If it gets as far as fighting then he will as he is on the reserve. Let's hope it doesn't come to it. We've been more or less at peace ever since Waterloo and I'm very much afraid the British war machine creaks a little with old age. If you have had sufficient, my dear, shall I ask Barton to bring our coffee to my study? Since we are on our own tonight, it will be more comfortable.'

'Oh yes, Papa, please.'

There was a cosy atmosphere in the book-lined room with a small cheerful fire to take off the chill of the evening. The soft light of the shaded lamps gave a warm glow to Christine's face as she bent over the silver coffee pot. He thought how much this daughter of his had changed in the last two years, shedding the awkward coltish rebellions that had caused so much argument and strife and yet with a resilience still that he liked in her. Was it Gareth's influence or had she learned it somewhere else? It was one of the things that worried him.

'Now,' he said pleasantly, taking the coffee cup she handed to him, 'let's have it. If it wasn't Greek antiquities and the British Museum, then what was it?'

'I've been to Vyner Street.'

'You've been where?' He sat up, putting down his cup and frowning. 'Christine, I don't want you mixed up with any of this very unpleasant business.'

'But I am, Papa, you must see that. I know Kate and Daniel and I knew Ray Dorrien only too well and I understand the people who live and work down there in the East End better than you do. I've had two years of it at the clinic. I've listened to them, I've spoken to them, I know how they feel and think.'

'I don't like it,' he said stubbornly. 'It could be dangerous for you.'

'Listen, Papa.' She pushed aside the coffee table, pulled up a footstool and sat close beside his armchair, looking up at him earnestly. 'I've found out more in the last few days than that Detective Inspector has in the weeks since it happened.'

She began to tell him all that she had done, about Karl Landowsky's accident, about going to the infirmary and enlisting Dr Dexter's help, and he listened, saying little except to ask a question or two.

'It's so maddening,' she said at last, sitting back on her stool. 'So much depends on what Karl can remember of that night and Dr Dexter says there is nothing we can do to hurry it. Minds cannot be bludgeoned into remembering, but at least it is a step forward.'

'And you say the police have been informed of this development?'

'Yes, John Dexter said it would come better from him as he could use his authority as a doctor when they question Karl.'

'He's right, and thank God he had the good sense to keep you out of it.'

'Because I'm your daughter?'

'That's one of the reasons. Since you've gone so far, Christine, you may as well know that I have put George Westcott on to the case.'

'That nice man who comes to Bramber and deals with Grandfather's affairs?'

'Yes, he is a very astute lawyer though he is only in his thirties. He has made sure that Kate is more comfortably housed in Newgate and he is trying to investigate the question of how Ray Dorrien got into her room when no key was found on him. The Inspector believes of course that she opened the door to him herself but we know different, so how did he get in? Was the door forced and by whom? It is apparently undamaged but George is taking a locksmith along there on Monday for an expert opinion. That's a possible lead. I scarcely think that Ray had the expertise to do such a very tricky job for himself.'

'Papa, there is something else that I ought to tell you. I have seen Daniel. I didn't deliberately go against your wishes but I had to know what had happened between you when he came here that night. You do understand, don't you?'

'What did he tell you?'

'That when the trial is fixed you will be defending Kate. It is true, isn't it?'

'Yes, it's true.'

'And I know why.' She paused and then said quietly, 'She *is* your daughter, isn't she?'

The moment had come which she had been dreading but she had to know the truth however hard, however painful it might be.

'Did Daniel tell you that too?'

'Yes. A long time ago now. On that election day. I didn't believe him. I can't believe it even now and yet I know it must be true.'

'What exactly did he tell you?'

She couldn't look at him. She was gripping her hands together so tightly that they hurt.

'He told me that his mother went to you imploring your help to save his father, that she had certain information that proved him innocent of the murder he had been accused of, that you promised to help and then . . . and then brutally and callously raped her, and afterwards you did nothing. You knew the truth but you let him die.' She paused and when he said nothing, went on passionately, 'But you couldn't do that, you could not be so cruel. I told Daniel that. I told him that if it did happen then there must have been some other reason, something we know nothing about. That's true, isn't it? Tell me that it is true.'

It was so humiliating, so inexpressibly painful that for a moment he could say nothing. Then he got up and moved away from her towards one of the windows where the curtains had not yet been drawn. Outside the street lamps glimmered in a faint mist like an arc of fairy stars but he saw none of them, only the lovely face looking up at him imploringly, remembering in the surge of long past memory the violent desire that had swept them together into an overpowering madness so long regretted.

He stood there silent for moments that seemed an age before he said slowly, 'There was no rape, no brutality, at least

I am not guilty of that. But I did let a man go to the gallows when I knew he was innocent.' He turned to Christine then, the words coming painfully. 'The explanation brought to me had come too late. Judgment had been given, sentence passed, an appeal would not have been allowed and even if it had, it would have failed. If I had made a public outcry, demanded a retrial so that justice could be done, it would have been the end of my career at the Bar. I hadn't the courage to make such a stand. I let him die and have regretted it ever since. You can't despise me more than I despise myself.'

She stared at him for a long moment before she said gently, 'I don't despise you, Papa. It must have been an agonizing decision to have to make.'

'It was.' For a time it had torn him apart. Clarissa had needed to be very patient with him.

'And you never knew about Kate?' went on Christine.

'No. I never guessed at such a thing. The very first time such a possibility crossed my mind was at Margaret's wedding. I glimpsed her standing with her brother and for a moment it might have been her mother standing there.'

It explained so much. 'Does Mamma know?'

'No, and she mustn't, Christine. It would hurt her inexpressibly. No one must know. You do understand that, don't you?'

'Papa, could anyone ever find out? Could they dig into the past and bring it up against you?'

'There are always envious people who muck-rake into the lives of anyone who achieves any kind of success and whom they want to damage. I have never cared very much for what has been said about me.'

'But they could do it?'

'Perhaps.' The worst of the storm was passing and he had recovered something of his usual calm. 'Is there any coffee left?'

'I am afraid it is cold. I could ask them to make us another pot.'

'Never mind. This will do.' He moved to the drinks table and poured brandy for himself and a small measure for Christine, then took it to her. 'I think we both need this.'

Brandy was associated with pain. She had only drunk it once when a tooth had been drawn, but now it had a warming, settling effect.

'Time for bed,' he said with an effort. 'I have an extremely heavy week in front of me.'

'Yes.' She put down her glass and then came to him reaching up to kiss his cheek. 'I know you haven't told me everything but I'm with you, Papa, all the way.'

'Bless you.'

For a moment he held her very close and then let her go.

He was very much aware that he had put himself in a hazardous position. His undertaking of Kate's defence would provoke a lot of questions. Those who disliked him would look for answers and not finding them readily might well dig deeper. He could be fighting not only for Kate but for himself. He took his glass to the drinks table, poured another measure of the brandy and then stood looking down at it thoughtfully. It comes to every man to make a critical decision at least once in a lifetime. Now he had made it and the future must take care of itself.

Chapter 21

During the next few weeks everything seemed to move forward with an almost alarming speed.

To start with on the Monday morning Inspector Blain together with the Constable and George Westcott stood on the landing outside Kate's door while the locksmith slowly examined the lock on the door. Being not only a locksmith but also an expert on clocks he had brought his spyglass with him, and with it firmly fixed in his eye seemed to be peering into every nook and cranny.

The Inspector shifted from one foot to the other. In his opinion it was a complete waste of time, a ploy thought up by that damned pettifogging lawyer who no doubt had to earn his expensive fees somehow. He was therefore considerably put out when Mr Erasmus Bolt stood up and delivered his verdict.

'That there lock were forced all right but by an expert. As nice a bit of work as ever I've seen. Hardly a mark to show for it and that takes some doing with them double locks, believe me.'

'Are you sure?' said the Inspector unwillingly.

'As sure as I'm standing here and locks is my business,' said Mr Bolt with a touch of indignation. 'I might almost venture to say there's only one as I knows of who could do such a tidy job and he were one of my prentices some years back. Jem Ryder, his name were.'

'Do you know where we could find him?' asked George Westcott.

'Ah now that's goin' back a bit. He were one of the best I had in the workshop but he went to the bad. I had to send him packin'.'

'For what reason?'

'Too clever he were for his own good, got mixed up with a bad lot and opened up a safe as we'd made ourselves. He pulled as nice a job as you could wish to see and got away with it but I knew who'd done it, could recognise his handiwork anywhere, so he had to go. Can't employ a prentice who robs his own master's work, stands to reason, don't it?'

'Indeed it does. Have you any idea where he could be found nowadays?'

'Can't say as I've seen him around lately. He usually shacks up with a big feller as goes by the name of Nick and I don't like to think what the pair of them get up to. Cunnin' as a weasel young Jem is and has the look of one too, little chap, thin as two planks nailed together. Is that the lot, gents?'

'Yes,' said George, 'and a good morning's work with our thanks.'

A couple of guineas changed hands and Mr Bolt went off well pleased with himself.

'Interesting, Inspector, don't you think?' said the lawyer pleasantly. 'At least it proves that our Mr Dorrien knew he would not be made welcome so he made sure of his own entry.'

'She could still have returned, surprised him there, quarrelled and stuck a knife into him,' said the policeman gloomily.

'Maybe she could but it's a step forward, especially if we can lay hands on this weasel-faced fellow who calls himself Jem Ryder.'

But that was easier said than done and discreet enquiries among the criminal fraternity didn't bring any immediate results.

In the meantime Christine was feeling hopelessly frustrated. There must be something more she could do, some way in which Karl's mind could be pricked into remembering what he had done that night, but John Dexter had warned her against badgering him.

Gareth said the same when she asked him what he thought.

'A bruised brain needs time to heal. You cannot hurry it.'

He had called one evening and her father had asked him to stay and dine with them. Afterwards when Christine was alone with him for a few minutes he asked her if she would come with him to look over the house in Wimpole Street.

'It is free now and Uncle David would like you to see it before any renovations are put in hand.'

'Gareth, does he know about us?'

'No, how can I tell him? He is old now and very frail. He has set his heart on doing all he can for us both. It would only upset him.'

'But he will have to know,' she said unhappily. 'I can't go on pretending. Don't you see that I can't? I should feel a cheat and a liar and he would guess, I know he would. He has always been a person who is very difficult to deceive.'

And at that Gareth suddenly and explosively lost his temper.

'My God, are you so besotted with this wretched man that you can't give so much as a thought to those who've known and loved you all your life? What does this Daniel Hunter give you? Nothing. He is using you, can't you see that? Through you he is insinuating his way into your father's regard, especially now there has been this trouble with his sister. I know he came here, no doubt whining and begging for help. It surprises me that your father has shown so much interest. I had always thought him to be an astute judge of character.'

'You don't understand, Gareth, you know nothing about it. What my father does to help him is because of something that happened back in the past.'

'I see and I'm not to know this deadly secret, I suppose. I am shut out, I must not be told.'

'It's not you only, Gareth, no one must know. Can't you trust me? It could cause all kinds of trouble. Don't you see that?'

419

'No, I don't. Can't you think of me just for a few minutes? I'm Gareth who loves you. I'm being as patient as I know how and you won't even do this small thing for me. Can't you come to please Uncle David, who has always been so fond of you? You seem to forget that it will be my home even if I have to live and work there alone.'

'I wish to God you could find someone else to love,' she said desperately.

He swung her round to face him. 'Do you really wish for that so much?'

'Yes, I do,' she said defiantly and then turned away her face, shocked because she knew in her heart that she did not want to lose Gareth and yet at the same time was unwilling to give him anything of her love.

'Very well,' she said at last. 'I'll come.'

So she went with him to Wimpole Street a couple of days later and Uncle David was there with the contractor who would be taking notes of what was required. The extraordinary thing was that going from room to room she began almost automatically to plan what needed to be done. It was a pleasant house, light and airy, with large sashed windows. She began to see the rooms furnished, the wallpaper, the curtains, the carpets, the kitchens that were in a shocking state, no servant worthy of her salt would contemplate working there till they were renovated. Presently she left Gareth with the contractor and climbed up to the second floor with Uncle David. This was where the previous tenants had placed their nurseries and she was suddenly overwhelmed with the realization that she was planning a house where she would live with Daniel, which was absurd. She was living in two worlds and one was pure fantasy.

Uncle David stood leaning on his stick and looking around him. 'We'll have to do something drastic about these rooms, especially as I am quite determined to live long enough to see your first son, Christine,' he was saying, smiling at her.

It brought home to her what she was doing and suddenly and unexpectedly she burst into tears.

420

'What is it?' he said gently. 'Am I being clumsy?'

'No, no, of course not, it's just that . . .' but she couldn't explain and she had to escape. 'I think . . . I think I'd just like to take another look at the kitchen quarters. Don't try to come down alone, will you, you might fall. I'll send Gareth up to you.'

She fled all the way down the stairs and bumped into Gareth in the hall.

'What's wrong?' he asked.

'Nothing. Uncle David wants you.'

She brushed past him and through the baize door that led into the servants' quarters and then out into the small town garden. It was overgrown, with ramblers climbing over the high walls, but there were some early roses and it was filled with sunshine and the scent of the lime tree. She took a deep breath and wished that everything was different and she had not made such a fool of herself.

Upstairs Uncle David had dropped wearily on to the window seat but he looked up as Gareth came in.

'Is there something wrong between you and Christine?' he said bluntly.

'No, of course not. Why do you ask?'

'She was very upset just now. I've sensed something amiss ever since we were at Bramber. What happened there?'

'Nothing.'

'Gareth, I may be old but I'm neither blind nor senile. Did she want to break your engagement?'

'Yes, but I won't release her from it.' Then it all burst out of him. 'She is obsessed by a young man she met through the clinic who calls himself a radical, whose father was apparently hanged as a Chartist rebel a decade or two ago and who scrapes a living as a teacher in a ragged school. It is so utterly ridiculous, so hopelessly unsuitable, and to make it worse it is his sister who is mixed up in this unsavoury murder case. She goes on blindly but I won't let her throw herself away like this, I won't.'

'Is he the young man who was in opposition to her father at that abortive election?'

'Yes. There is some connection between them but she won't tell me what it is. I wish I could understand what is driving her into this impossible situation.'

'I think I can. Has it never occurred to you that Christine has a great well of compassion, of sympathy, of thought for others, a great desire to be of use, and here is a young man who fulfils all these dreams in his need of her. It is easy to be carried away by such feelings when you are young and have a generous spirit.'

'But I need her too, desperately, all these last years I've thought only of her. I want her as a partner sharing my life with me.'

'Have you ever tried telling her how much you need her?'

'Not in so many words but surely she knows it already.'

'But does she? There's not been much evidence of it. For the last two years you have left her alone and open to other influences.'

'But all I've been doing has been for her.'

'Have you told her that?' Gareth turned restlessly away and his uncle went on, 'You have complacently expected her to work it out for herself. It is not good enough, Gareth. If you want her, you'll have to work for it and now I think you'd better go and find her. We've done enough here for one morning.'

David Fraser said nothing more but put the renovation work in hand and hoped that the two people he loved best in the world would somehow settle their differences and come together again. Gareth, smarting from his uncle's reproof, wavered between a great desire to strangle Daniel Hunter and an uneasy conviction that his uncle might be right and he had carelessly let slip away the person he loved and wanted passionately and did not know how he was going to win her back.

Kate would come up for trial at the Old Bailey in July and it gave an added urgency to the investigations that so far had not provided much on which a sound case for the defence could be built.

Clarissa had sent word to her husband that she was staying for a few more days at Ingham Park as Margaret had proved to be in the early stages of pregnancy and she wanted to make sure all was well before she returned home. She hoped Christine was behaving herself properly and not causing him any anxiety.

'Are you behaving yourself properly?' he asked, looking across the breakfast table at his daughter after giving her the news.

'Of course I am, Papa, you know very well that I am.'

That night of revelation had drawn them closer together. She was aware that there was a great deal he had not told her but one thing she knew for certain: whatever had happened it had been deeply felt and painful. Had he stepped outside the bonds of marriage? Was it a love affair? She ought to feel disgusted but she didn't. It made him more vulnerable, more approachable, and when the right time came Daniel would realize and understand it just as she did.

Still left comparatively free with nobody to question where she went during the day, she decided to go back to Vyner Street and find out how Karl was progressing.

She arrived at midday carrying a little bag of delicacies and found him just returning from his morning's work as baker's assistant, and still carrying the large basket, empty now except for the loaf which was part of his daily earnings.

'You shouldn't be doing that,' she exclaimed.

'Why not?' he said cheerfully. 'For the moment it is good. From six to twelve I carry the basket to customers. I smile and they buy. I am given free bread and a few pence with which to buy what else I need and so I keep my small savings and have the rest of the day to paint.'

She had brought butter and eggs and ham with the expensive coffee which he so much enjoyed, and he protested.

'I have no need,' he said with dignity. 'I earn sufficient.'

'I know but I like to do it so that I can share it with you.'

He smiled ruefully and gave in. 'You are like Kate. She too would treat me like a small boy who doesn't know how to care for himself.'

So she cooked eggs and made coffee and while they ate asked him what he had been doing.

He had touched up some of his hospital sketches and turning them over she thought how good they were, a poignant study of human helplessness and suffering.

'They ought to be exhibited,' she said in admiration.

He shrugged his shoulders. 'Who would want to look at what makes them sad?'

She went on turning over the sketches and came to one that was completely different. Two men whose heads were close together, one with hat pulled down to his brows, frowning eyes, brooding and surly, and the other a thin pointed face that reminded her of the stoats and weasels that Finch caught in the Bramber woods, hanging their corpses along the fence as a deterrent. She held the sketch up to Karl.

'Who are these two? They don't look like hospital patients.'

He took the drawing and looked down at it frowning. 'No, they are not. They are two faces I see in a dream.'

'A dream!'

'Yes, I wake one morning as if I come from nightmare but I can't remember any part of it. It is all confused except for these two faces. You know I have what you would call an eye for faces. I can see someone and then come home and draw him from memory and it will be exactly right. It was like that with these two faces. I could not wait till I had drawn them but who they are, I do not know.'

Perhaps the faces had leaped out of that damaged part of his brain. 'Could I borrow it?' she said. 'I'd like to show it to Daniel.'

It was late afternoon when she left Karl and made her way to the school. She did not wait at the gate, not wanting to draw attention to herself, but after about half an hour she saw the children come running across the yard followed by Daniel. He said a word or two to the young woman who worked with him and she walked quickly away. He had locked the gate before she moved to meet him and she saw his face light up.

'Why are you here? Has something happened?'

'I've something to show you.'

Sitting together on the churchyard bench she unrolled the sheet of thick paper.

He studied it for a long moment before he said, 'What is this?'

'Karl had a nightmare which he could not remember, only these two faces had stayed with him and he drew them before they faded from his mind. It seemed to me that they could have come from the blank part of his brain.'

'I know them,' he said slowly. 'They are the two thugs who beat me up. The big man is called Nick, I remember that. I don't know about the other, only that he was the one who kicked me viciously while Nick held me down.' He paused for a second. 'It's possible that Ray Dorrien used them again to break into Kate's room. We must show this to the Police Inspector and to the locksmith. He might recognise the smaller of the two. I wonder if Karl met them in Kate's room or coming away from it.'

'I don't know whether I'm being fanciful,' she said, 'but I have a feeling that they were frightened. Karl has an uncanny ability to convey mood but whether we can persuade Inspector Blain to see that or whether he will dismiss it all as moonshine, I don't know.'

Christine was right. The Inspector dismissed the drawing as the product of a sick mind and then was brought up sharply when the Constable who had been closely studying it suddenly looked up.

'I know that one,' he said, putting a stubby finger on the bigger of the two. 'Nasty bit o'work he is too. Used to do a bit of boxing but's gone flabby. We almost nabbed him once.'

'When was that?' said Blain, frowning.

'A few months back. He pinched a gent's wallet but he were seen. There were a rare old hue and cry but when we got him, there weren't a thing on him. He must have slipped it to a mate, see, and though the toff swore blind as he was the one who robbed him, we had no proof and had to let him go.'

Mr Bolt when shown the drawing was not so positive.

'Could be, could be,' he said, rubbing his nose thoughtfully. 'I'd say it's very like Jem Ryder, very like, but I wouldn't take me Bible oath on it.'

However it was enough for efforts to be redoubled to lay hands on the two men.

'What the police don't seem to realize,' said Daniel despairingly, 'is that with all this talk going the rounds, the two of them will go to earth somewhere and never be found.'

It was only too true as George Westcott pointed out when he was making his report to Everard. 'But we'll get them sooner or later, I'm sure of it. I've got a couple of good men on the alert. It seems they were last seen in some low-down boozing cellar called "Ned's Bar" near to that pub which has the concert rooms. Splashing their money about by all accounts. Did it come out of Ray Dorrien's pockets? Let's hope they're too cocky for their own good.'

It was at the end of that week that Clarissa returned at last from Ingham Park, so very disturbed at what she had heard that when her husband came home that evening she could scarcely wait for him to greet her and ask after Margaret before she came out with it.

'Freddie returned from London with some tale he had heard at his Club about that murder case. It seems that Sir James Dalfrey has been retained for the prosecution and that you, you of all people, will be undertaking the defence. Of course I told him it was all ridiculous. The very idea that someone like you would take up this wretched girl's case was utterly absurd but Freddie was very positive about it. It's not true, is it?'

'It's perfectly true, my dear,' he said calmly.

'But why, why? She is the sister of that abominable young man who did everything in his power to oppose you and but for the mercy of God might have cost you your life.'

'That's old history, Clarissa. It has played no part in my decision to act on her behalf.'

She stared at him. 'Everard, is there something behind this that I don't know? Has this girl some powerful protector who wishes to remain in the background but has retained you to act for her?'

He smiled. 'Good heavens, no! What a fanciful notion, fit for a sensational novel rather than a court of law. No, indeed. I happen to think that there has been a gross miscarriage of justice and I intend to do my utmost to set it right. As for fees, well, money is not everything.'

'I don't like it,' she said obstinately. 'Lord Dorrien, and Clara too, will press Sir James to the utmost. This girl has a very thin case I'm told. If you lose, it could do you a great deal of harm.'

'Have you so poor an opinion of my ability?' he said, smiling.

'No, of course not, but people are going to talk and ask why.'

'Let them. Now listen to me, Clarissa, I'm quite determined to go ahead with this and I should be grateful if you would not encourage any foolish gossip or speculation about my motives. Whatever you may feel about my decision personally, I rely on your loyal support.'

'Of course,' she said. 'Do you have to question it?'

'No, I know I don't. What would I have done without you all these years? Now let's forget about this. I want to hear the latest news of Margaret and that grandson of mine.'

The evening passed pleasantly enough but now and again Christine caught a puzzled look on her mother's face when she looked at her husband and was aware of a slight tension, as if they were careful not to touch on what was uppermost in all their minds. She wondered what her mother would feel if she knew that he was fighting for his own daughter. You thought of parents as remote beings untouched by the tumultuous emotions that tore their children apart. Now she knew differently. It had brought her father closer but she felt uncertain about Clarissa who had always seemed to live on the surface of life. What would happen to them both if she were to be suddenly plunged into the depths? Would it be sink or swim?

It seemed to her in these last few weeks before the opening of the trial that nobody could think of anything else, though at Belgrave Square by mutual consent it had become a forbidden subject. Summer had caught them unawares. The London streets simmered in a scorching heat while everyone connected with Kate's case was working day and night to build up an unbreakable defence with very flimsy material.

In Newgate the heat made life almost intolerable. In the overcrowded wards the air was thick with a thousand foul smells that even the buckets of carbolic that washed the floors could not kill. There seemed to be no freshness anywhere, even in the prison yard, and the dreary procession of prisoners dragged their feet in their daily walk through foul stinking air which seemed almost too heavy to breathe. Fever was rampant and the infirmary was crammed with the sick and dying.

Even Kate who was spared the worst could not escape entirely. The stone walls, the four-inch thick door with its heavy bolts closed in on her, sweating and dank, seeming to fill the air with all the misery and wretchedness endured by those who had suffered their last lonely hours within it.

It turned her so sick that she found it difficult to eat the fresh food brought in to her daily.

'She don't eat no more than a fly,' muttered the warder to his mate, carrying away a scarcely touched tray.

'You wouldn't neither with the thought of the noose danglin' in front of your nose night and day.'

'You don't think . . .?'

'There ain't no tellin', is there? But if she knocked off a toff like that, then it stands to reason them others like 'im are goin' to gang up on her, you mark my words.'

That was the day before Everard Warrinder came to see her. George Westcott had warned her.

'Don't be nervous,' George had said kindly. 'He is not at all frightening. He will tell you exactly what he wants from you when you come into the stand. He would like to establish a feeling of reassurance, of trust between you, so that you will not be too disturbed when you come into the court.'

All that was hard to believe when the only time she had been close to him he had been furiously angry, accusing her of unspeakable things on the night of Harry's ball, so that it seemed impossible to believe that now he was her only defender, prepared to convince the whole world of her innocence.

She had dressed carefully as far as the confines of the prison allowed, a simple summer gown in blue cotton with touches of white at neck and wrists, which she had made herself in those far-off days when the word murder had no particular significance.

She brushed her hair till it shone reddish bronze and then tied it back with a ribbon. She was ready far too early but found it impossible to sit quietly waiting and walked up and down the small room until she realized it only made her feel more agitated and she must appear calm and collected and not the brazen hussy he had once thought her to be.

She stiffened as she heard the heavy bolts drawn back. The door creaked open and she stood defensively on the other side of the small table waiting for him.

He came in with George Westcott who said in his pleasant voice, 'Good morning, Miss Hunter. May I present Mr Everard Warrinder who as you know will be your Counsel?'

He was smiling at her as he took her hand in a firm grip. 'We meet at last,' he said and then at his gesture George Westcott went out and they were left alone together.

For a few seconds they still stood as if sizing one another up. He noted that she looked very pale and had obviously lost weight from the stifling weeks in prison, but she had a dignity and resolution that pleased him. How strange that she was his daughter and he knew absolutely nothing of the formative twenty years that had made her what she was.

'He is wonderfully handsome,' she had said to her brother a long time ago when he had been pointed out to her and it was still true. She saw traces of Harry about him, the way the thick brown hair had a slight curl, though his was lightly flecked with grey, and the face was older, more mature, with a certain reserve, a certain coldness.

'Shall we sit down? It might be more comfortable,' he said with a quizzical look around him. 'If one can say the word comfort in a place like this.'

'It's paradise compared with where I was before,' she said. 'I'm grateful to you.'

'I wish I could have done more.' He pulled up a chair for her and sat opposite, putting the leather portfolio on the table and taking out a sheaf of notes. 'Now,' he went on briskly, 'I am afraid I have a few questions.'

'I am quite ready.'

He took her through the salient points once again, noting thankfully that her answers were clear and to the point in the trained voice of the actor, neither hysterical nor over vehement. He was unaware that beneath the table she had gripped her hands together to stop them trembling and felt the sweat prickle down her back under the cotton gown.

'I am going to put you on the stand,' he said, 'because I want the jury to see the kind of person you are and not at all what the newspapers and the broadsheets have been busily creating these last weeks.'

'In other words, not a brazen hussy on the make for what she can get but a decent hard-working young woman pestered by an arrogant detestable bully,' she said with a sudden bitterness.

He smiled. 'Exactly. You've hit the nail on the head and for that reason you must appear not too showy, not too provocative, forget the actress and the theatre and play yourself. You will find that I will make it easy for you, you have only to follow my lead, but Sir James Dalfrey is a very different matter. Make no mistake, he is a brilliant interrogator: gentle, almost understanding, then will come the sudden disconcerting pounce. Don't let him throw you into confusion. Take your time to answer any awkward questions. The court has patience and will wait and should he become too outrageous, then I will intervene.'

She listened carefully while he went on to instruct her in the court procedure so that forewarned she could prepare herself to face every contingency that might arise.

'Try to think of it as a difficult first night except that, I'm afraid, some of the lines will be unscripted. I think I have covered most points,' he went on, putting the papers together and tucking them into the portfolio before he got to his feet. 'I know the next few days will be the worst. Try not to worry too much. We are going to win.'

'Do you know what I've been doing to stop myself thinking, how I've kept myself sane? I asked Dan to bring me my Shakespeare and I have studied new parts. I could quote from Rosalind, Beatrice even Cleopatra without missing a word.'

'Bravo, and you will no doubt be playing those very parts in the not so distant future.'

'Do you really think so?'

'Indeed I do,' he said and wished he was as confident as he sounded. There were still too many gaping holes in the evidence.

'Mr Warrinder,' she said, nerving herself to ask the question, 'why are you doing this for me?'

'Didn't your brother tell you?'

'He told me that it was partly because of what happened years ago,' she said hesitantly, 'when you were responsible for my father's death on the gallows.'

'And is that what you believe?'

'I don't know. You see it all happened before I was born. I never knew my father. I have never felt the bitterness and anger that has tormented Daniel.'

He looked at her for a moment, tempted to tell her the truth, and then realized it would be the utmost folly at this stage.

'Let me say that I dislike injustice and I have felt that a desire for revenge at any price and a most bitter jealousy are partly responsible for this case against you and if I can counter that and set it right, then I will.' He took her hand and pressed it warmly. 'Goodbye till we meet in court – and try studying Portia. Think how well you will play the trial scene after this.'

When he had gone she dropped back on the chair, trembling a little now that the ordeal was over but feeling

431

unexpectedly comforted. She had a strong ally. She was no longer alone facing a hostile world. After a few minutes she got up and fetched her old worn copy of Shakespeare. She opened it at *The Merchant of Venice* and began to read.

The very next day one of the gaping holes in his case which Everard had been dreading was unexpectedly filled. Karl was hit on the head by an unknown assailant and very nearly killed.

He was coming home one evening just as it grew dark feeling very pleased with himself. That day he had sold a picture in the flea market, the money jingled in his pocket and he hummed a tune as he climbed the stairs. As he reached the top of the last flight, a dark shadow seemed to loom up above him. He dodged to avoid it and was hit a glancing blow by an iron bar that sent him sprawling. He fell heavily back down the stairs and lay in a crumpled heap on the small landing. His attacker followed him down the stairs no doubt with every intention of finishing him off, except that Mr Kennedy, disturbed by the noise, had opened his door to find out what was happening. For an instant he was aware of a thin foxy face twisted into a scowl, two wild eyes that glared furiously at him, then it had vanished and he heard the retreating footsteps go clattering down the stairs at a great rate. He considered chasing after the attacker, then realized it was probably useless and turned to the victim slumped across his own doorway.

Karl was slowly coming round. If he had not dodged, the blow would undoubtedly have killed him. As it was, there was blood streaming from a place above his eye and he groaned with pain as he tried to sit up.

Mr Kennedy knelt down beside him. 'It looks as though someone has had a go at killing you. I'd better call the police.'

'No, no!' muttered Karl dizzily, 'No police. I do not want to go back to that infirmary, not again.'

Mr Kennedy took out a handkerchief and mopped up the blood that ran down his face.

432

'But you must have help. You're in a very bad way.'

'No, no,' protested Karl. 'I am all right. I have had worse. If you can help me to my room . . .'

Still anxious, Mr Kennedy helped him to his feet, guided him up the stairs – with some difficulty since Karl was a good deal taller and heavier than he was – and at last got the door unlocked and helped him as far as the bed.

'Look here,' he said as Karl fell back against the pillow with a gasp of pain. 'I really ought to fetch a doctor.'

Karl dragged himself up. 'It is only bruising. It will pass.'

Mr Kennedy fetched water, bathed the wound and fixed a temporary bandage. He found the laudanum which Dr Dexter had given Karl for the headaches he had suffered since the accident, measured out a massive dose, covered him with a blanket and left him alone, not without some misgiving.

He had followed Kate's case with interest, knew something of Karl's connection with it and debated with himself as to what he should do. After sleeping on it he compromised and made up his mind to tell Daniel what had happened and leave him to make the decision. So in the morning on his way to work he called at Paradise Alley and ran into Daniel just coming out of the house. He described what had happened and Karl's resolute refusal to let him contact police or doctor.

'I sympathise,' said Daniel, 'he is very independent and he hated being shut up in the infirmary. I'll go and see him in my lunch-break.'

'It seems to me,' said Mr Kennedy judiciously, 'that someone is very anxious that he shouldn't tell what he knows.'

'My idea too,' said Daniel grimly. 'What wouldn't I give to lay my hands on that damned murderer!'

As soon as the children raced shouting into the schoolyard at midday, he hurried to Vyner Street and found Karl in a state of frenzied excitement. The heavy dose of laudanum had knocked him out till late in the morning. When Daniel came into the room he was sitting on the edge of the bed clutching his throbbing head with both hands. He looked terrible. The bandage had slipped, blood was still oozing from the wound on his forehead and had dried in streaks across his face.

He grabbed hold of Daniel in a kind of desperation. 'Those two men in that sketch – I remember where I saw them. It was here, that night,' he banged his forehead in an effort to clear his mind. 'I dream – it is confused – but when I wake it is still there. I must tell someone. I must go to the police.'

'Not yet,' said Daniel. He could see only too clearly that Inspector Blain would dismiss anything Karl might say as no more than the ravings of a sick mind. 'First you must see a doctor,' he went on, 'that wound needs stitching.' He thought for a moment and then made up his mind. He would take him to the clinic. Dr Dexter would know what to do and whether this second blow had somehow jolted the injured brain into remembering. He told Karl what he was going to do and the artist clung to him almost pathetically.

'Dear God, not that abominable infirmary!'

'No,' he said soothingly. 'I'll take you to Dr Dexter. You remember him. He helped you before.'

Luckily he found John Dexter having his own short break in a gruelling day. He took one look at Karl and then took charge in his own quiet reassuring way. He stitched the raw wound, examined Karl's head very carefully for any further damage and gave him a mild sedative.

'What do you think?' whispered Daniel while Deborah brought Karl a cup of tea. 'If he does remember, it could be vital evidence which is badly needed.'

'I think he will. At the moment it is a jumble, he is confused, but give him time and I think his mind will clear. The dose I have given him will soothe him, make him drowsy. Don't harass him with questions. Let him sleep. By evening who knows? I'm afraid it is something not even a doctor can foretell but there could be a great improvement. I would advise getting hold of that lawyer fellow, George Westcott, let him hear what he has to say before you go to the police.'

So Daniel took Karl back to Vyner Street, persuaded him to eat something and more or less put him to bed before racing back to the school. He was very late. Eva was full of reproaches at his leaving her to deal with his pupils as well as her own and the afternoon seemed endless. Afterwards he couldn't remember a word he said and thought he must have somehow automatically gone through the usual lessons. As soon as the boys were dismissed he took a cab to the dignified offices of Simon, Westcott and Westcott in Moorgate and cornered George Westcott just as he was leaving for home.

Karl was still in considerable pain but the feverish excitement had gone, his mind had cleared and he was able to tell them exactly what had happened to him on that April evening.

'I had cashed my money order at the bank and was coming home,' he said in his precise English. 'I do not remember the exact time but two men came out of the house just as I reached it, in such a tearing hurry that they collided with me and it cross my mind that they run away from something. I do not much care for their looks and one of them had a dark streak all down his jacket that look to me like blood. Then they are gone and I shrug my shoulders and think no more of it. I go up the stairs and see that Kate's door is open. I think maybe she has come home earlier than usual and I will go in and tell her about my good fortune in painting three pictures. I push open the door and it is horrifying.'

He stopped for a moment as if bracing himself and then went on. 'He was lying just inside the door where he must have fallen, his head against a fallen chair and there was blood everywhere on the floor, soaking into his trousers. I was so shocked I couldn't think for a second what to do, then he muttered something and I realize that though he look so sick, he is not dead and I kneel beside him. I say, "What has happened to you?" and he gasp out, "There were two men, one of them attacked me with a knife . . . I cannot stop the bleeding." '

'You're certain he said that – that there were two men and one of them attacked him with a knife?' said George busily writing in his notebook.

'Yes, I am sure and I remember the men I meet when I come in, but I have a small knowledge of anatomy from art classes long ago in Cracow. I think that the knife has cut into a main artery and that the loss of blood must be stopped or he will die. I look around for something to make a . . . a . . .'

'A tourniquet?' suggested George.

'Yes, that is it. I see a linen towel and I bind it round his leg as tightly as I can but it is not easy for the wound is high up in his thigh. Then I put a cushion under his leg so as to raise it and another under his head to make him lie more easily. I say, "Try not to move. I now go to fetch a doctor." I run down the stairs and across the road thinking only of the blood that is draining away his life, then something hit me, there is a lot of noise and confusion and pain, then all is black and I remember no more till I wake in the infirmary and for a time I don't even know who I am. Oh God, if only I had not run so fast, if only I had stopped to think, he would not have died and Kate would not be in the prison.'

'You must not blame yourself,' said Daniel gently. 'You acted for the best. It was simply an unhappy accident.'

'The really important thing is that now we know what happened,' said George Westcott snapping his notebook shut, 'even if we don't know the reason for the attack. Now listen to me, Mr Landowsky, you have already been cited to appear as witness for the defence, is not that so?' Karl nodded unhappily and the lawyer went on quietly and firmly. 'It is even more important now that you should tell what happened clearly and calmly as you have told it to us tonight. Mr Warrinder will help you through it.'

'And those two evil men who do this wicked thing?' said Karl.

'We'll find them, never fear. The search will be redoubled. It is obvious that the wretch who knifed Ray Dorrien tried to silence you and might have succeeded but for the good offices of your neighbour on the next floor. You must take great care of yourself. When it is known that you have recovered your memory of that night, you could be in double danger. He could try again. Tomorrow I will inform the police and the Constable will be asked to keep close watch.' George Westcott smiled and got to his feet. 'You'll have to make a statement to the police but I'll be there to make sure that Inspector Blain doesn't play any tricks and in the meantime don't trust anyone but Daniel here.'

He clapped Karl on the shoulder and went off well pleased with the evening's work.

'What kind of a fellow is this Polish artist?' asked Everard when George Westcott reported to him. 'Will he stand up to questioning?'

'Honest, straightforward and with an artist's eye for graphic detail,' said the lawyer.

'Dalfrey could play merry hell with that story when he's in the witness box,' went on Everard thoughtfully. 'He could insinuate that the man is inventing the whole story in order to save Kate.'

'That won't be easy when someone has obviously done their best to knock him out. I think you'll find he'll stand up to it. Anyone who has survived a pogrom in Poland, lost his home and parents and managed somehow to survive in England doesn't lack resilience. If I'm wrong, you are free to tell me to give up the law and take up chicken farming!'

Everard smiled. 'You're not likely to come to that. What we badly need is to lay our hands on those two wretched fellows hired by Ray to open up Kate's room. What did they quarrel about? Money? Cash for services rendered? Blackmail? Viscount Raymond Dorrien for all his father's wealth was well known for being tight-fisted. Harry was always complaining that whoever paid up for a night on the tiles it wasn't Dorrien, which makes one think, though I can hardly bring that up without further proof. Find them for me, George, particularly that little rat, Jem Ryder!'

The evening before the trial opened, Kate had an unexpected visitor. It was not yet dark outside but in the depths of the gloomy stone walls of Newgate shadows had already thickened and she had lit her solitary candle so that the light fell upon her book. To stop herself thinking she was doing what Everard had smilingly advised and was studying Portia's great mercy speech.

She tried one or two of the lines aloud to see how they sounded—

> 'But mercy is above this sceptred sway
> It is enthroned in the hearts of kings
> It is an attribute to God himself
> And earthly power doth then show likest God's
> When mercy seasons justice . . .'

Would the jury, those twelve good men and true with their prejudices and their narrow biased judgments, listen to the voice of reason and show mercy to her?

She was so absorbed she did not hear the bolts being withdrawn and looked up a little dazed as the warder raised his lantern high and showed in the visitor all in black like some ghostly apparition.

'Only five minutes, my lady,' he said and withdrew, pulling the door closed behind him.

Kate got to her feet as Clara raised her veil. She had only seen her once before but recognised her instantly.

'What do you want with me?' she whispered.

'I wanted to see you just once before they tear you to pieces, because they will, you know. Lord Dorrien will make sure of that and so shall I.'

Kate raised her head proudly. 'I am not afraid. They cannot touch me because I am innocent.'

'If you believe that, you're a fool.' Clara had never been beautiful but now her eyes looked enormous in the pallor of her face. She had believed she held a glittering future in her own two hands and this girl, this creature from the gutter, had robbed her of it. She would have liked to scream at her, strike her, destroy her utterly.

'You believe the great Everard Warrinder will save you but you're wrong. He is my uncle, did you know that? He is my

438

mother's brother. He'll never forget that and if he does, then he will bring ruin on himself. I'll make quite sure of that.'

'I don't believe you.'

'You will, Kate Hunter, you will when the time comes.'

For a moment across the table their eyes met and clung together, then Clara pulled down her veil and turned to the door. The warder opened it to let her through then closed it and shot home the heavy bolts.

Kate dropped on to the stool. Clara at her most dramatic was like a scene out of a melodrama. If it were not so deadly serious she could have laughed but instead, she sat there trembling, her fragile self confidence shattered. It took a long time to pull herself together and face the long sleepless hours of the night.

Chapter 22

The opening of the trial at the Old Bailey had something theatrical about it like the first scene of some historical drama at Drury Lane, with all the dignitaries of the court, the barristers in their wigs and silk gowns with their juniors and solicitors, the whole assembly rising at the entry of the Judge's solemn procession, all the majesty of the law destined to strike the utmost terror into the unhappy prisoner.

The public benches were crowded, a few actually queueing overnight for the best position. A small party had cut rehearsal at the Princess Theatre and had come to support one of their own, Byron Farrar foremost among them. Christine would have liked to sit with Daniel but as Everard's daughter she had a more privileged position and could only wave to him from a distance. Clara was sitting just beyond her looking fragile in filmy black beside the solid bulk of Lord Dorrien.

When Kate was brought in, her actor friends waved and called greetings, much to the disapproval of the court ushers and the jury, a body of mostly well-to-do tradesmen and honest artisans, churchgoing to a man and inclined to strict views on morality.

Across the court Everard's eyes met Kate's for an instant and for no real reason Clara's dire threats of the previous night seemed to vanish and she felt immeasurably strengthened. She had taken note of what he had advised but would not suppress her own personality entirely. Her dark green dress was stylishly cut, fitting closely to her slim waist and then flowing out into a full skirt. She wore no ornament, only a touch of white at the throat. She had swept up her hair into a coronet on top of her head which showed off the tiny gold studs in her ears and it shone bronze in the lights of the court. She faced the frightening panoply before her with a steady calm and Everard felt immensely proud of her.

That first day went on its slow tedious way. The prosecution set out its case with lengthy reports from the Detective Inspector, the Sergeant, the Constable and the doctor, and Sir James Dalfrey called some of his first witnesses.

Daniel watched and listened with a growing fascination. Quite apart from the burning personal interest, the whole rich majesty of the law which up to then he had raged against as hopelessly biased in favour of the rich and the powerful held him in a tight grip. At this early stage there was little excitement, no dramatic interruptions, but the learned cultured voices, the cut and thrust of argument held him spellbound. This was what he must learn if ever he was to achieve anything, no bluster, no ranting, no shouting, but the calm exposition of reason, the certainty that came from knowledge and experience. He could not withhold his admiration of Everard Warrinder. He looked so calm, almost indifferent, never raising his voice, and yet in a subtle way proceeded to cut away some of the ground beneath his opponent's feet.

There was for instance the manager of the Haymarket who swore on oath that Kate Hunter never entered his theatre on that night and therefore could only be lying.

'How many people does your theatre hold?' asked Everard rising to his feet.

'What's that got to do with it?' the man answered belligerently.

'How many?' persisted Everard patiently.

'A thousand or thereabouts.'

'And are you prepared to swear upon oath that you looked into the face of all that thousand or so on the night in question?'

'Of course not. That's ridiculous.'

441

'Is it? Do you keep the passes that come in from members of other theatres?'

'They are counted for that night as a rule,' he admitted reluctantly.

'And are you also prepared to swear upon oath that there were none at all from your rivals at Mr Kean's theatre?'

'Well . . . no . . . I couldn't swear to it. The box office manager might remember.'

'Thank you. That's all.'

He hadn't proved anything but he had sown a doubt in the jury's mind. There was no proof that she was *not* there so she could have spoken the simple truth and that was all he wanted to do at that stage.

A similar thing occurred with a member of the company, an actress, middle-aged and sadly run to seed, envious of a younger and more successful colleague. She had gone on at some length about the gifts that had poured in from Ray Dorrien and other admirers over the last two years.

'We've heard a great deal about these expensive items,' said Everard in his turn. 'What happened to them all?'

'How should I know? They do say she gave some of them away to her dresser and the boy who ran errands for her. None of them ever came *my* way, that I do know.'

'And what about the diamond bracelet you mentioned that everyone admired so much? Did she give that away too?'

'Not very likely, is it?'

'No, because you knew already that it had been sent back to Viscount Dorrien, and you told one of the stagehands that it made the Viscount so mad that he raced up to her dressing room, hammering on the door and saying he would get even with her. That's true, is it not?'

'It could be,' she said uncomfortably.

'And do you honestly believe that after that unpleasant scene, Miss Hunter would have willingly opened the door of her lodgings to him if he had come knocking at it?' said Everard with quiet irony.

'How should I know?'

'It would seem very unlikely, would it not?'

'Well, yes, I suppose so,' she admitted grudgingly.

The suggestion made by the prosecution of a young woman egging on a rich admirer to more and more costly efforts did not seem quite so obvious as it had done at first and the jury glanced at one another and let the doubt simmer in their minds.

The last witness that day was Mr Kennedy, who gave a brief factual account of the help he had offered when Kate had come to him and obstinately refused to be led by Sir James into expressing any personal opinion of the prisoner.

Everard tried a different approach. 'I understand, Mr Kennedy, that you were formerly a Sergeant in the Dragoon Guards and were employed in recruiting men to fill the ranks, a post that must have needed an excellent assessment of character.'

'Lord love you, sir, you're right there,' he said, expanding a little. 'You'd never believe the types who come up thinking they want to be Dragoons. Most of 'em wouldn't know one end of a horse from another while I'd as soon trust them with a broom as with a gun. More likely to shoot themselves or their next door neighbour.'

'I can well believe it, and as a matter of interest what was your opinion of the young lady who came to you for help that night?'

'Well, now you ask, we never did much more than pass the time o' day as you might say but I always thought that she were a very decent hard-working young woman for all she were an actress. No rowdy parties and no sitting up all night with gentlemen friends drinking and I don't know what else if you get my meaning.'

'I do perfectly. Thank you, Mr Kennedy.'

Daniel could see what he was trying to do all that day. Brick by brick Everard was building up a picture of Kate quite different from that presented by the news-sheets which would be confirmed when he called her into the stand to tell her own story and he had to admit his admiration for the strategy.

When the court rose at the end of that first day Christine waited for her father to join her in the carriage.

'How do you think it is going?' she asked him.

'Much as I expected. Sir James is reserving his biggest artillery for my witnesses. That's when you will see the feathers begin to fly.' He turned to her. 'By the way, Christine, I would prefer not to discuss the case at home this evening.'

'Because Mamma still disapproves of you taking it up?'

'Partly. In any case as soon as we have eaten I have work to do. It still worries me that Inspector Blain cannot lay hands on one or other of the two villains who opened the door for Dorrien that night.'

Daniel felt the same impatience with the efforts of the police, which seemed to lead nowhere. He had guessed that these two petty criminals were town birds. It would not occur to them to escape out of the East End into unknown territory. They lived in a shady world that had its own haunts and its own loyalties. To break into that world was almost an impossibility for a stranger but he had learned two things. The underground drinking den near the concert hall was popular amongst groups of petty thieves of all kinds who often enough fought among themselves but instantly ganged up against the police. Secondly he had an irrational belief that sooner or later Jem Ryder would show up there. There comes a time when a hunted man needs the company of his mates, so he took himself there night after night in the hope that his guess would prove right.

It was a vile place and his fastidious nose was revolted by the various disgusting smells of drink, dirt, human sweat, greasy food and the filthy sawdust on the floor where hungry dogs and cats rooted and fought and which was rarely changed more than once a week. He was aware that the two thugs, having once beaten him up, might recognise him, so he would sit hunched in a corner, his hat pulled down, a muffler half concealing his face, over a glass of beer that tasted horrible and which he strongly suspected of being doctored with something to make it go further.

Mr Brown had been extraordinarily kind in letting him off school during the trial. In any case many of the boys had already gone off strawberry picking or potato pulling in Kent and one of the young men from the Chapel was willing to take over for the last few days before the school closed for the summer. That anyone with Everard Warrinder's reputation should take up the cause of a young, comparatively unknown actress had surprised Mr Brown and he suspected that there was something behind it that Daniel had not told him, but all the same he had grown fond of the boy and was annoyed when his daughter attacked him over it.

'I'm sure I can't think why you should be so generous to Daniel,' she said irritably, when they had been discussing the case. 'What happens to that sister of his is no concern of ours.'

'Anyone in serious trouble should be our concern,' said her father sternly. 'Daniel has worked hard these last two years. The school has never done so well. Should I then turn my back on him?'

'He doesn't need you or me or any of us,' Elspeth went on bitterly. 'He is hand in glove with that Christine Warrinder and no doubt that is why her father has taken up the case.'

'From what I have seen of Everard Warrinder,' said her father drily, 'I should say he's nobody's fool. I cannot imagine even his own daughter influencing him against his will. What's wrong with you, Elspeth? Daniel has done a great deal to help you at the Cheapside store. I was under the impression that you worked well together and that you liked him. I've even thought once or twice that you and he might make a match of it.'

'If you have, then you're quite wrong. I wouldn't marry Daniel, not if he begged me on his knees,' she said violently, then unexpectedly burst into tears and ran out of the room.

Her father sighed. Girls! Elspeth was a good worker, sensible, wonderfully clear-headed up to a point, but changeable as a weathercock over young men.

*

Jem Ryder still failed to surface and the trial went slowly and inexorably on. Clara, called to the stand, spoke in a low trembling voice of the scene at the restaurant and her distress at her husband's obsession with an unscrupulous young woman. The prosecution's case against Kate, detail added to detail, looked black despite all Everard's skilful attacks on vulnerable witnesses. The vital evidence he needed was still missing.

Kate with his assistance told her own story well with a simplicity that convinced a great number of the public if not the jury. She was then severely mauled by Sir James Dalfrey. He had an insidious form of attack but she held her own steadily and only broke once.

'Your unfortunate victim was not the first to suffer at your hands, was he?' he began with a deceptive mildness. 'Harry Warrinder, the son no less of your learned counsel, was also, it would seem, a victim of your charms. In fact it would appear that at one time he and Raymond Dorrien were hot rivals for your favours.'

'I don't know what you mean by rivals. Must I say again that I never liked or encouraged Viscount Dorrien at any time.'

'But that wasn't the case with Harry Warrinder, was it? What did you feel for that charming young man?'

'Harry and I were good friends.'

'Good friends!' repeated Sir James with a smile. 'Is that what you call it? Good enough friends for his father to make a savage attack upon you when you sang at his son's birthday ball?'

There was a momentary silence. The judge frowned and looked across at Everard.

'Is this true, Mr Warrinder?'

How the devil did Dalfrey find that out? 'Quite true, my lord,' he said calmly. 'At that time I was under a misapprehension which I afterwards deeply regretted.'

'Regretted so deeply in fact that my learned friend took great care to remove his son out of your reach as soon as possible. Isn't that so?' went on Sir James.

446

'No, you are wrong. It was not like that at all. Harry had recently come down from Oxford. His father sent him to Paris to study French law. Harry told me about it himself and our friendship has continued ever since.'

'A little more than friendship surely. Did he not about this time ask you to become his wife?'

It carried her back to those unhappy weeks and she paused for a moment trying to steady herself.

'Yes, he did,' she said at last in a low voice.

'And you refused him. For what reason? It must have surely been a very tempting offer to a young woman such as yourself.'

'I thought him far too young to know his own mind.'

'Very right and proper, I'm sure, but a little difficult to accept. Isn't it far more probable that you refused him because you had another and far wealthier rival in mind?'

'No, no, no! That's a lie, a monstrous lie!' she said passionately, her voice breaking, for the first time near to tears, and Everard got to his feet.

'My lord, I must protest. These questions concerning my son's friendship with Miss Hunter are surely not relevant to the present case.'

The judge looked at Dalfrey. 'Quite so. Have you done, Sir James?'

'No more questions, my lord,' he said, well satisfied with the implication that she was little more than a greedy fortune-hunter.

It had been an ugly moment and could have rattled Kate badly but she had remained remarkably steady and Everard sighed with relief. As she stepped down from the stand, she stumbled and might have fallen if the warder had not taken her arm.

The judge, who was a kindly man and did not care all that much for some of Sir James Dalfrey's methods, said, 'Bring the prisoner a glass of water and give her a chair. Now, Mr Warrinder, shall we proceed? Your next witness if you please.'

The court heard about the break-in with the locksmith's

testimony and a description of the two men involved and then Karl Landowsky was called.

'We understand your witness is Polish, Mr Warrinder,' said the judge, 'does he require an interpreter?'

'No, my lord. His English is good but I would ask the jury to take into consideration that he has recently been involved in a serious accident which resulted in loss of memory and since his recovery from that has been viciously hit on the head by an assailant for whom the police are still searching and whom we believe to be one of the two men involved in the break-in.'

Karl, during his thirty years, had already suffered a great number of hazards. The richness and majesty of the British court impressed him and since it was unlikely to end in him being beaten up and thrown out of the country as had happened in Poland, he braced himself to speak out clearly and boldly.

He told his story well and so graphically that his listeners seemed to see the scene grow before their eyes. The sketch he had drawn of the two men was passed to the judge, to Sir James and then to the jury who handed it from one to the other peering at it, impressed in spite of themselves, and wondering if it was a true likeness or a figment of the artist's imagination.

That was the line that Sir James chose to take and it enraged Karl. He came of good Catholic stock to whom lying was anathema. He did not take kindly to the insinuation that he was deeply in love with Kate himself and was therefore prepared to lie like the devil in order to save her.

'I would suggest that these men you saw on your return that evening have sprung out of your vivid imagination,' said Sir James. 'I do not doubt that you entered the room, saw the pitiful state of the unhappy victim, tried to help him and were afterwards knocked down and severely injured, but when you recovered and knew the plight she was in, you then thought up a brilliant way of saving her. Why not invent two fictitious murderers and link them with the rascals who broke through the door? A most ingenious and plausible piece of fiction, I must congratulate you.'

And it was at that point that Karl lost his temper.

'I do not lie. Never. I may have to live as a beggar here in this country but my family in Cracow was honourable, a Landowsky does not lie, not even for a friend, not even to save a life.'

'Very high-minded, I am sure,' went on Sir James, gently persuasive, 'but to lie in order to save the woman you dearly love, that surely would be permissible.'

'I have suffered many times at the hands of those who robbed me of my parents, my brother, my home, but here in Britain I thought that truth would be respected but it seems that I am wrong.'

'There is more than one kind of truth,' said Sir James with his infuriating smile, 'and I am sure that in your own mind you have persuaded yourself that what you say is justified.'

'I am upon oath and you tell me that I lie,' said Karl furiously. 'I do not allow anyone to insult my honour,' and without any warning he vaulted across the barrier and made for Sir James, no doubt with the intention of taking him by the throat if two ushers had not seized hold of him.

There was uproar in the public benches, the Clerk shouted, 'Silence in court,' and the judge intervened.

'Mr Warrinder, I should be grateful if you would control your witness or else I fear we shall see murder done.'

Everard came down into the court and put a calming hand on Karl's arm. The two ushers released him and he stood quietly, ashamed now of his outburst.

'I am sorry,' he whispered. 'He make me so angry that I make a fool of myself. I spoil everything for you.'

'No, not at all. Do not upset yourself. Sir James was not actually accusing you of lying, he was simply suggesting that there was a possibility of another explanation. It is for us to prove him utterly wrong.'

'And we will?'

'We will. Never fear.'

Later Mr Kennedy was recalled to swear that the face shown on Karl's sketch was indeed the face of the man who had brutally tried to kill the artist only a few days before. It had the effect of strengthening the jury's belief in the foreigner's story, which had been sadly shaken by Sir James's insinuations.

The day came to its weary end at last with the situation still very much in the balance, though Everard, sensitive to the feeling of the court, was inclined to think it was very slightly more in favour of Kate than it had been. However the ugly fact still remained: unless they could lay hands on one or both of those two men they did not know who had killed Ray Dorrien or why.

It weighed heavily on Daniel as he trudged home through streets still filled with the heat of the day, his shirt sticking to him, no freshness anywhere, and he wondered how Kate must feel as they shut her up again within the sweating dark walls of Newgate. The thought of going to the reeking drinking hell-hole sickened him but it was his only hope so he clung to it. After a light meal which he didn't want he took himself there and watched and waited and hoped.

Arriving home at Belgrave Square hot, tired and depressed, Christine and her father walked into a surprise. Coming into the hall Christine gave a squeal of pure delight and hurled herself on to her brother.

'Oh Harry, darling Harry, how wonderful to see you and what are you doing here?'

'Here, steady on, old girl,' he said as he hugged her with one arm and held out his other hand to his father. 'How are you, Papa?'

'Well enough,' said Everard as Barton took his hat and portfolio from him. 'What has brought you home? Not trouble, I hope.'

'That's what Mamma said. I'm not still a schoolboy, you know,' said Harry half laughing as he disentangled himself from his sister and they all trooped into the drawing room.

450

'I've only just heard of this appalling case against Kate. I was on tour with Maître Drouet. He took me with him as an observer on his summer circuit, you know, and I picked up an English newspaper in Nancy, a day or two old of course. I was horrified. I pleaded a family crisis and came home as soon as I could. You might have let me know.'

'There was nothing you could have done,' said his father.

'You never know. Ray and I were pretty close at one time. I must say it was a rotten way for anyone to die and damnably hard on poor Clara, and I must say I think it's pretty splendid of you to take it up. Why didn't you write to me? I could have acted as your junior.'

'I have a very good hard-working youngster just now and in the circumstances you were hardly the right one, Harry. Dalfrey has seen fit to drag you in already.'

'As one of Kate's admirers, I suppose?'

'Exactly. It provided him with some very useful ammunition against me.'

'Because of the ball?'

'Yes.'

'Hell! Isn't that just like him.'

'I'm afraid it is. God knows how he found out about it but he has very few scruples about what he uses to further his own ends.'

'He'll have a hard job digging up anything against you.'

'Don't be too sure. There are few of us without a vulnerable spot somewhere,' said Everard drily. 'Ah, here's your mother. You look radiant tonight, my dear. Is it in Harry's honour?'

'You're late, Everard,' she said a little sharply. 'Has it been a bad day?'

'Passable. Will you put dinner back half an hour while Christine and I freshen up?'

The meal passed pleasantly enough with so much to talk about and was greatly enlivened by Harry, full of himself and his doings as usual, and the trial that was in all their minds was deliberately pushed into the background.

When Clarissa rose and took Christine with her, Harry said, 'I'd very much like to discuss the case with you, Papa, if I may.'

451

'We'll take coffee with your mother first or she will be disappointed. Afterwards I shall be going over my notes for tomorrow, we'll talk about it then.' He smiled. 'You never know. A fresh mind on it might find some legal loophole that I've missed.'

'I doubt that.'

They were all in the drawing room, one of the long windows open to the warm summer night, when the disturbance came. Christine had been giggling at Harry's imitation of Maître Drouet in action.

'He's a small man and he puffs himself out and gobbles like a turkey cock as he struts up and down. Not a bit like you, Papa, but he always gets his man in the end.'

'I'm delighted to hear it. He's charging me enough to tutor you,' said his father drily.

It was then that Barton knocked and came in looking a little agitated.

'Lady Dorrien is here and asking particularly to see you, sir,' he said to Everard.

'Clara!' He put down his coffee cup and stood up. 'What can she want with me at this hour? You'd better show her in, Barton.'

But Clara hadn't waited. She pushed past the butler, took one look around her and then faced up to Everard.

She was still in the black she had worn in the court but she had thrown back the filmy veil, diamonds glittered in her ears and her eyes were like dark holes in her chalk white face.

'You can't do it,' she said hoarsely, 'I won't let you save her. I want her punished, d'you hear me? I want to see her suffer!'

'Clara, my dear,' he said gently. 'You are overwrought. You don't know what you are saying.'

'Oh yes, I do,' she went on. 'I've thought of nothing else all day. You're obsessed with her, aren't you? All of you are and I know why, Uncle Everard, *I know why* and if she goes free, then I swear to God that everyone else will know, everyone, do you understand? I'll make absolutely sure of that.'

Her voice had risen on a note of hysteria, her body rigid,

her hands clenched, then quite suddenly it was as if all strength deserted her. She began to cry, huge shaking sobs.

For a moment they had all stood as if transfixed and it was Harry who saw her falter, leaped to her side and eased her into a chair, talking soothingly as if to a hurt child.

Clarissa said, 'Christine, run upstairs and bring my sal volatile. It's in the small cabinet.'

Then she knelt beside Clara, taking her hand, wiping the tears from her face with her own handkerchief.

'Poor child,' said Everard, 'she's suffering from nervous exhaustion and it's not surprising. She has been in court every day. I can't think why Dorricn has permitted it.'

'Clara always had a will of her own,' said Harry. 'I remember that from the old days.'

Then Christine was back with the sal volatile and Clarissa sprinkled some on her handkerchief and held it under Clara's nose.

After a moment Clara sat up, pushing Clarissa's hand away, the madness gone from her eyes. She looked frail and sick but she was herself again.

Everard had poured a small measure of brandy and brought it to her. 'Sip a little at a time,' he said kindly. 'It will do you good.'

She took the glass from him and then with a sudden defiant gesture swallowed the whole of it at a gulp, choked and threw the glass away from her, looking straight at him.

'I mean it,' she whispered, 'I really mean it. You do understand that, don't you?' Then she began to struggle to her feet. 'Now I'd better go.'

Christine put her arm around her shoulders, suddenly remorseful for the hard thoughts she had so often harboured against Clara.

'Did you come in the carriage?' she asked.

Clara shook her head.

'Harry,' said Everard, 'tell Barton to call a cab and you and Christine go with Clara. See her safely into the hands of that elderly companion of hers and advise her to call the doctor in the morning.'

Harry's hearty brotherly manner, harking back to childhood days when Clara was always chasing after him and Christine and more often than not coming to grief, had a soothing effect. She let him put his arm around her and help her down the steps and into the cab followed by Christine.

When they had gone Everard picked up the shattered glass and put the broken pieces on the tray.

'Poor Clara,' he said, 'she has missed out on almost everything. No mother, a father who has never shown the slightest interest in her, brought up by nurses and servants. We did our best but I'm afraid our own children never exactly made her welcome, did they, and now this happens to her. It's little wonder if she feels everyone is against her and longs to strike at them with any weapon she can find.'

'Clara has always been her own worst enemy,' said Clarissa. 'God knows, she is your niece and I have tried to be kind and received little thanks for it. What did she mean when she said she knows why you are befriending this girl? What does she know about the case that we don't?'

For a moment he hesitated. Was this the time to tell her the truth? But Clarissa's reaction was unpredictable and he dare not risk it, not now when so much was in the balance, so he compromised.

'You must not let yourself be disturbed by an hysterical girl, my dear. There has been a certain amount of speculation, I suppose, about my motives and she has seized on anything with which to attack me. It means nothing.'

'Clara may be upset but she's no fool, Everard, and she has Lord Dorrien at the back of her. He has never felt the same towards us ever since Christine refused to marry Ray. You will be careful, won't you?'

'Careful of what? A young girl's outburst arising out of spite and jealousy? You know me better than that. No doubt she is already regretting her folly in coming here.'

Presently Harry and Christine were back, reporting that Miss Motford had taken charge of Clara, had promised to get her to bed and call the doctor in the morning if she felt it necessary.

The incident was over but it had left an unpleasant taste in the mouth and that night while Christine brushed her hair and prepared for bed she did wonder uneasily if somehow a rumour had started about the relationship between Kate and her father and Clara had seized upon it, a weapon that in unscrupulous hands could be used with devastating effect. At the same time she felt she knew her father well enough to be sure that whatever the consequences he would not let it stop him from going his own way and doing what he believed to be just.

Chapter 23

A dogged persistence does sometimes bring results and it did that night for Daniel. It was extremely late. The air in Ned's Bar with the fumes of beer, raw spirits and a foul reek of rank tobacco had become almost too thick to breathe. Daniel had just begun to think that if he stayed a moment longer he would probably vomit when the door was jerked open and a big shambling figure lurched through it at a half run and ended up at the bar, bent over, cursing and gasping for breath. It was the bigger of the two men who had once attacked him, the one they called Nick.

There was silence for a moment, every eye in the place turned towards the newcomer till the barman said drily, 'What's up with you tonight?'

'Gimme somethin' to drink, for Gawd's sake! Bloody peelers nearly nabbed me, and for nowt, never went near the bleedin' toff but he yells out, "Stop, thief!" and there's the lot of 'em after me like a pack of damned wolves.'

'You gave 'em the slip, I hope.'

'Aye, dodged 'em all right, up and down them alleys, but I ain't got the wind I had once, shook me up proper, tripped up once, fair winded me.' He swallowed the brandy at a gulp and slapped the glass down for another. 'Got to be careful, see. It's Jem what they're after. I told 'im as it weren't no good tryin' to knock out that bloomin' foreigner but he would do it and then he didn't finish him off proper. They've been on to 'im ever since what with that Pole blabbin' the whole tale out in the court like nobody's business.'

'Holed up all right is Jem?'

'Aye, snug as a bug but we still gotter be careful and keep on the move. Never know who's watchin'. Got any grub handy? Neither of us has had a mouthful all day.'

All this was muttered in a half whisper so that Daniel only caught part of it but it was enough. He knew now that what he had to do was to follow Nick when he left, find out where Jem Ryder was hidden and then take his information to the police as soon as possible.

It was not too long before the barman disappeared inside and came back with what was obviously a parcel of food wrapped in newspaper. He handed it over with a bottle and Nick slithered through the door. Daniel waited a few seconds and then followed after him as unobtrusively as he could. It was a dark night, no moon, and it proved less difficult to shadow the man in front of him than he had thought. Nick shambled along, obviously never dreaming he was being followed. He took a devious route up and down alleyways that eventually brought him out at Wapping Steps by the river, past the enormous rubbish tips, past the cottage where Dickie's uncle lived, along a dark slippery stretch of shingle and mud until he reached a broken-down black shack that might have once housed a boat.

Nick paused then, looking around him cautiously, and Daniel flattened himself behind a great mound of stinking fishy rubbish dredged up from the Thames. He saw the door open, there was a glimmer of light, Nick whispered something as he slithered in, the door shut and all was black again. Daniel was greatly tempted to break in there and then and drag that skulking murderer out by the scruff, but knew that if he did, it would more than likely end up with both of them making a getaway and his own dead body floating down the river. Instead he took very careful note of exactly where he was and then made his way back as quickly as he could to the police station.

He was in luck. The Constable was there on duty as usual, with the Sergeant who had been given a blasting from the

Detective Inspector for inefficiency and who was still smarting from it. He was ready for anything that might prove him not a blundering ass but very much on the spot.

'You're sure of this?' he asked Daniel. 'I've got something better to do than go trekking down to those mud flats on a wild goose chase.'

'Of course I'm sure,' said Daniel, burning with impatience.

The Sergeant hesitated, half inclined to wait till morning when they would be backed up by the Inspector himself and one or two more recruits.

'If you do, you'll find the birds have flown,' argued Daniel. 'Nick was muttering about the need to keep moving on. At first light they could be up and away and we'll be back where we started. You get them now and you'll have one over that cocky Inspector Blain.'

'That's no way to talk of your superiors,' said the Sergeant pompously but it did the trick. He was not going to lose such a heaven-sent opportunity of showing what he could do.

It was still dark when they set out but by the time they reached the lonely strand, the first streak of silver glimmered along the horizon. Everything was very still and quiet. Cautiously they circled the shack, noting that it had only one small window at the back.

'I'll knock and demand entrance in the name of the law,' said the Sergeant, 'while you two watch that window in case they try to make a getaway.'

'Nick couldn't get through that opening but Jem could,' whispered Daniel, 'and he's the one that matters.'

They took up their places as the sky slowly brightened a little. The Sergeant began to hammer at the door but nothing stirred. He paused a moment, then knocked again louder, but still no response so he stepped back and threw his considerable weight against the rotting timbers. They gave way with a crash and he burst into the shack. Then all hell seemed to break loose.

There were shouts, scuffles, crashes, then Nick came hurtling through the doorway with the Sergeant almost on top of him and they grappled together on the slimy ground.

The Constable gave a shout of warning. Jem Ryder was wriggling through the tiny window, crazy to escape and seemingly unaware of the two waiting in the shadows. Clothes were ripped, rotten timbers cracked and split as he forced his way through and fell head first into the mud. Daniel leaped on him but he was strong and wiry. He wriggled under him like an eel and a long thin blade shone dangerously for a moment in the strengthening light. Daniel felt the knife slice into his shoulder and down his arm but he took no notice. He had the little man by the shoulders and was trying to pin him down but he fought as savagely as a cornered rat. They were rolling over and over on the muddy ground when the Constable seized his chance. He delivered a vicious kick that knocked all the breath out of the little man and with a grunt of satisfaction the policeman knelt down and clamped the heavy handcuffs on his wrists.

Daniel staggered to his feet and realized for the first time that blood was beginning to soak through the sleeve of his jacket where the knife had sliced down his arm, but as yet he felt no pain. He had got Jem Ryder at last and that was all that mattered.

He pulled out a handkerchief and stuffed it inside his coat to try and soak up the blood. He would not feel safe till the two were locked up in a police cell. Nick seemed to have given up the fight. He stumbled along, pushed and prodded by the Sergeant, swearing and cursing under his breath, but Jem was another matter. Twice he tried to get away but hampered by the heavy handcuffs he did not get very far. The third time Daniel tripped him up and as he fell he hit his head on a piece of rotten timber sticking up like the tooth of some prehistoric monster and knocked himself half-unconscious. He let them drag him along between them. When they reached Wapping Lane the Sergeant commandeered a cruising cab and bundled them in. At the station they were both charged with obstructing the police in their lawful duties and locked up in a cell.

'Now what?' asked the Constable breathlessly for Jem Ryder had resisted furiously to the very last moment.

459

'Inspector Blain must be informed,' said the Sergeant. 'He'll decide what is to be done.'

'And take days over it more than likely,' said Daniel. 'It's Mr Warrinder who must be told, and as soon as possible. The court opens at ten o'clock and today the prosecution will be summing up their case. If he knows we've got Jem Ryder he can ask for a postponement. I'll go myself. I'll ask for a message to be conveyed to him.'

'Not looking like that, you won't,' said the Sergeant. 'You're bleeding like a slaughtered pig. That wound needs stitching, my lad.'

It was only then that Daniel became conscious of the pain, the blood-soaked sleeve and a curious feeling as if he were not really there. He pushed it away from him. This was no time to give up.

'Dr Dexter will see to that. The clinic opens at eight. I'll go there now.'

'It's not the correct procedure,' grumbled the Sergeant. 'I shall be blamed for rushing things. These wretches must be properly charged and questioned.'

'To hell with procedure! You can tell the Inspector what you damned well like. I am going straight to the top.'

At the clinic John Dexter took it in his stride.

'This suspect of yours is putting up a good fight, I'll say that for him,' he remarked ironically as he peeled off the blood-stained jacket and shirt. 'First he knocks the Pole on the head and nearly kills him and now he slices you up with a knife. What next, I wonder!'

'Nothing, I hope, we've got him safely under lock and key, thank God.'

'That's one blessing. Now sit down and hold tight. This may sting like the devil.'

He washed the wound with something astringent that made Daniel gasp, then carefully stitched the long slash and bandaged it tightly.

'You're going to need a sling and something else to wear,' he said, holding up the bloody jacket, 'or else the court usher will think you have come from a massacre. I'll ask Deb if she can find you something from the settlement store cupboard, and in the meantime sit yourself down and take it easy. If you carry on much longer like this, you'll end up a stretcher case.'

So while Deborah rummaged through the cupboard for something suitable he could wear, Daniel was given one of the doctor's draughts, which tasted foul, followed by a cup of hot strong tea and only then realized how very badly he had needed both.

It was nearing midday before John Dexter would permit him to leave, wearing a shirt and tweed jacket that had once covered the portly form of a gentleman at a shooting party in the Highlands, while Deb promised to do what she could to sponge out the bloodstains and brush off the accumulated mud from his own clothes.

When he arrived at the Old Bailey Sir James Dalfrey was well into his summing up, the jury and the public were listening in rapt silence and the court usher refused point blank to let him in though he protested he had a vitally important message for Mr Warrinder.

'Write it down,' the usher said pompously, 'and I'll see it reaches him,' and then reluctantly was obliged to supply Daniel with pencil and paper.

He simply wrote, 'We've got Jem Ryder locked up in a prison cell,' and thankfully through the partly opened door saw it travel to George Westcott, on to the junior barrister and finally end up in Everard Warrinder's hands. He glanced at it, looked searchingly across the court, caught Daniel's eye as he leaned wearily against the doorpost and nodded.

The relief was so tremendous that he felt suddenly weak. He dropped down on the bench that ran along the wall, leaned back and closed his eyes. He was still sitting there when a little later the public began streaming out and with them came Christine with Gareth close behind her.

'Daniel!' she exclaimed and sat down beside him regardless of the people pushing along beside them. 'I didn't see you in the court this morning and I wondered where you were. Was it you who sent that note to Papa? He has asked the judge for a postponement to give him time to consider fresh evidence. Is it true?' She touched the arm held stiffly in the improvised sling, her voice full of concern. 'You're hurt. Is it very bad? You're looking dreadful.'

'It's nothing. The important thing is that we've found Jem Ryder. That was what was in the note I wrote for your father.'

'Oh how wonderful! It could make all the difference. How did you find him and where?'

The crowd had thinned by now and with an effort Daniel hoisted himself to his feet. 'Do you think I could have a word with your father?'

'Yes, of course, we'll go to the other exit and meet him.' She took Daniel's arm protectively and moved away, forgetting Gareth so completely that he was left staring after them.

It was the first time he had seen them together and was aware of the instant rapport between them, the intimacy of look and touch which he had never quite believed in, and he was tempted to walk away. Then with a surge of angry jealousy he walked quickly after them and caught them up.

There could not have been a greater contrast between the two young men, Gareth in his well-cut suit, every inch the successful young doctor, and Daniel in the ill-fitting tweed jacket with a muffler at his throat and the awkwardly contrived sling. They were walking on either side of her rather like two dogs stiffly on the alert and needing only a spark to set them at each other's throats.

Everard Warrinder came to meet them.

'My dear Daniel, this is splendid news. Did Christine tell you that I've asked for a postponement? Judge Mackie is a decent old boy and has given me four days to consider the new evidence.' Then he frowned. 'What's happened to you, boy? Were you attacked? Is it serious?'

'Not in the least, no more than a flesh wound. It would seem that Jem Ryder is a lot too handy with knives,' said Daniel drily.

'I'd like a few details of how you found him if it won't be

too much for you. You're not looking too good. What do you think, Gareth?'

And Gareth, who would have liked nothing better than to see Daniel drop dead at his feet, could not entirely subdue his doctor's instincts.

'Since he has got this far, I should say he will be all right. There could be reaction of course. I came from the hospital and have my bag with me. I could give him something that might help.'

Nothing would have induced Daniel to confess to any weakness before his rival. 'Thank you, no,' he said icily. 'Dr Dexter has looked after me very well.'

'Good. Then that's settled.' Everard swept them all into the ancient tavern where all the legal luminaries from the Old Bailey gathered at one time or another and in a secluded corner Daniel told them how he had tracked down the two criminals and with the help of the Sergeant and the Constable had taken them prisoner.

'At some cost to yourself it would seem,' said Everard. 'Where are they?'

'At Whitechapel police station. The Sergeant wanted me to wait for Inspector Blain but I came straight to you from the clinic.'

'Thank God you did. We're going to need as much time as we can find to get to the bottom of this business.'

'They are not talking, either of them. They are refusing to say a word.'

'I daresay we can find a way of overcoming that. I'll get word to George Westcott and then go down there myself.'

'I'd like to come with you.'

'Is that wise? Shouldn't you rest that wound of yours?'

'To hell with that! She is my sister.'

'Very well. Gareth, will you take Christine home and tell Clarissa what has happened and that I don't know when I shall be back.'

'I'd like to come with you, Papa,' protested Christine, her eyes on Daniel.

'No, my dear, it's not at all suitable. This is an off-the-cuff visit for my personal satisfaction. Come along, Daniel, no time to waste, we will take a cab.'

When they had gone, Gareth said quietly, 'Is the carriage still here?'

'Yes. Franks will have been waiting for Papa. Tell him to go home, will you? I'd like to walk a little.'

Gareth did as she asked and then came back to join her. They found their way through side streets without saying very much till they had crossed the busy Strand and walked down to the Temple. It was quiet and cool there under the trees.

'So that's the famous Daniel Hunter,' said Gareth as they walked along beside the river. 'Very impressive, acting the hero, wounded in the cause of justice.'

Christine turned on him fiercely. 'Don't laugh. It's so easy and so cheap to laugh and it is unworthy of you.'

'I'm not laughing, believe me,' he said, a burning jealousy that he had never felt before rising up in him bitter as gall. 'I'm trying to understand what magic he possesses that has taken you so completely away from me. Do you know what Uncle David said that day when you came to look at the house?'

'Did you tell him about us?'

'I didn't have to. He had guessed already as far back as New Year at Bramber.'

'What did he say?'

'He said it was because you feel that Daniel needs you so much that you want to help him, you have an overwhelming desire to give back to him all that he has missed, and though I believe he may be right about you, I think he is totally wrong about Daniel. I think he possesses a proud independent spirit. He may not have money or success or any of the things most men look for, at least not yet, but he has grown up in a harsh world that has taught him to go on alone and though he will use you as he uses everything, he will continue to fight his own battles, if necessary without you, without anyone,' and even as he was saying it he knew despairingly that it was not entirely true. What had drawn these two together would need something far more drastic to drive them apart.

She stopped to stare at him. 'I don't believe you. You're quite wrong. You are only saying that because you can't accept the truth.'

'No,' he said with a quiet desperation, 'I've thought about it a great deal and I think I'm right. I wish I wasn't because I believe you may suffer a great deal of pain and disillusionment.'

She walked on quickly, knowing in her secret heart that in a way he was partly right. There had been times when Daniel seemed to escape from her into some world of his own in which she could play no part, and she had rebelled against it.

After a moment Gareth came up beside her, making a strong effort to swallow the surge of love and jealousy that had shaken him, taking her arm, trying to restore the trust and friendship that had always been between them.

'If your father wins this case,' he said gently, 'and I think he will, what are you going to do?'

'I don't know. I think he feels differently about Daniel now but all the time I have had a feeling that there is something hidden, something in the past I don't know about that will keep Daniel and me apart.'

'Something you can't tell me?'

'No, because the little I do know is not mine to tell.'

Gareth sighed. 'There are times when I have a tremendous longing to grab hold of you and shake you into realizing how foolishly you are behaving.'

'I know you do. I'm sorry, Gareth.'

'And at other times,' he smiled wryly, 'well, I suppose I can still provide a shoulder to cry on.'

'Oh God, what a wretched muddle I'm making of my life. You should go right away and forget about me.'

'There are moments,' he said with a quiet intensity, 'when I wish someone would teach me how to do just that!'

*

465

Everard Warrinder very soon realized that neither Nick nor Jem Ryder was going to be easy to deal with. The most they would admit to so far was the break-in to Kate's lodging and that oddly enough was due to the fact that Nick was inordinately proud of his mate's skill as a locksmith.

'Proper wizard with 'em is Jem. He could open up the Bank of England if he could get near enough to it,' he boasted.

'A pity he didn't use his expertise to better advantage,' said Everard drily.

Out of the mixture of lies and evasions, he gathered that of the two Nick was by far the most vulnerable and likely to break under the pressure of separate questioning. He was apt to be carried away by his own eloquence, not realizing till too late where it was leading him.

'You do realize, don't you, that breaking and entering is a punishable offence,' Everard pointed out.

'Oh come orf it, Guv'nor, we weren't doin' no 'arm, never touched a bloomin' thing. It were just to please this toff who was wantin' to give his girl a nice surprise and a bit extra on the side if you get my meanin'. He knew what he wanted all right, brought champagne an' all and some very tasty food. She were a good lookin' piece too. I'd seen her once when she were singin' at that there supper rooms.'

A gold mesh purse had been found hidden away in that black shack on the strand when it was searched by the police. Jem swore he had picked it up in the street but it had almost certainly belonged to Ray Dorrien. The blood-stained jacket that Karl had noticed had long since vanished into some rubbish tip but it seemed a skilful use of knives was one of Jem's accomplishments.

'He learned it from some feller at one of them fairs,' muttered Nick uneasily. 'He could throw a nifty blade could Jem.'

It had all begun to add up and pretty soon Everard had formed a fairly clear picture of what had actually happened on that night but to persuade either of them to admit to it was going to need all his skill when the court reassembled and the trial was once more on its way.

He opened the defence that day by having the two men brought in to the court and recalling Karl and Mr Kennedy. The jury to their astonishment were faced by the living prototypes of the artist's sketch already shown to them. Similarly Mr Kennedy, still on oath and asked if he recognised the man who had brutally attacked his neighbour, pointed a dramatic finger at Jem.

'That's the one. Couldn't never forget that face,' he said. 'Gave me nightmares for a week afterwards.'

'He's a bloody liar!' yelled Jem.

'Silence!' thundered the clerk of the court.

'You'll have your chance to speak later,' said the judge sternly. 'Put up your first witness if you please, Mr Warrinder.'

So Jem was led away still muttering and Nick was called to the witness box, a big loose-limbed fellow running to fat who stood looking around him, nervously twisting his battered hat between his two hands. In all his life of petty crime he had never before stood in a court such as this.

Everard led him very gently through the preliminaries until gradually he began to recover his spirits, even began to enjoy it, all these grand folk in their wigs and fine gowns hanging on his words as if he were some bloomin' oracle.

'Where did you meet Mr Dorrien?' asked Everard.

'Well, it were like this, see. We was in Ned's Bar one night and this fine gent, he comes up to us askin' for a bit of 'elp and me and Jem didn't see no 'arm in it, seein' as how we'd worked for 'im before.'

'It didn't occur to you that if it was necessary to break into Miss Hunter's lodging, it meant she might not exactly welcome Mr Dorrien?'

'Oh Lord love you, Guv, you know wimmen,' said Nick scornfully, 'blow hot, blow cold they do, never know where you are from one minute to the next.'

'How much did he pay you?'

'Five Jimmy Goblins on that night . . .'

'Jimmy Goblins?' questioned the judge.

'Guineas, my lord.'

467

'I see. Carry on.'

'And ten more,' went on Nick, 'when we'd done the job, see.'

'But when it came to it,' said Everard, almost casually, 'you thought that what you'd done was worth more than a paltry ten guineas, didn't you?'

'Well, wouldn't you? 'Tisn't everyone as could do a neat job like that,' said Nick indignantly, looking around him rather wildly for his absent mate and then plunging on. 'Jem were proud o' what he could do with them locks and seein' as the toff had plenty, we thought as how we might ask for a bit more like.'

'Very natural I'm sure. How much more?'

'Fifty guineas.'

A gasp of outrage ran all around the court. A man could keep wife and child for a year on fifty guineas.

'Rather a large sum, wasn't it?'

'Oh come on, Guv, a chap like that Mr Dorrien wouldn't think nothing' of spendin' twice that on a night with his girl.'

'I daresay,' said Everard drily. 'What happened then?'

'He turned nasty.'

'How nasty?'

'Shoutin' at us, sayin' as how we'd made a bargain and he weren't payin' a penny more and if we didn't like it then we could clear off and get nowt. He had his purse in his hand by then and Jem, he made a grab at it but the gent jerked back and it fell on the floor. He lost his temper proper then, cussin' and carryin' on and sayin' as how he'd have the law on us till Jem sez that if the police started askin' questions, it wouldn't look too good for 'im bustin' into a young woman's lodging and that made him more mad than ever . . .'

Nick was well away now, reliving the scene to his fascinated audience and Everard only needed the occasional word to help carry him along.

'He was threatenin' to throw us out and sayin' as how we could go beggin' for our money. He grabbed hold o' me and started to force me through the door. I were a fighter once, y'know, Guv, ex-boxer, Battlin' Nick they used to call me, but that were a few years back and I'm not the man I was, while that Mr Dorrien, he must have worked with the Champion, up to every trick o' the trade, he was. He got me in a stranglehold till I could hardly get me breath and he were goin' to throw me down them stairs. I were as good as gone when I sees Jem . . .'

Nick stopped suddenly, staring around him as if he had suddenly realized where he was and where his story was taking him.

'Go on,' said Everard gently, 'what was Jem doing in all this? Didn't he try to help you?'

'Aye, he did,' muttered Nick. 'There was a knife handy and he took it up . . .'

'And of course he could see what was happening to you, couldn't he?'

'That's right. Never one to let a mate down is Jem. He didn't mean no 'arm, Guv, I swear he didn't, it were accidental like . . .'

'What was?'

'He came up beside me. He's a small man is Jem and the toff he was a big feller – at any minute he were goin' to throw me down them stairs, I'd be lyin' dead with me head split open, I thought, and it was then that Jem struck out . . .'

'With the knife?'

'That's right. He got him in the thigh just as the gent lunged forward . . .'

Nick stopped staring in front of him as if reliving that terrifying moment.

'And then what did he do?' asked Everard very quietly.

'Jem pulled out the knife and a great spurt of blood followed it. Mr Dorrien, he just stood for a moment and then he went down clutching at his thigh and the blood it were suddenly everywhere. Never seen nothing like it. For a minute I were knocked sideways. Never could stand the sight o' blood. Cut me finger once and fainted dead away. Jem sez, "We got to get out o' this," and I sez, "Ought we to do somethin' for 'im?" but he were pickin' up the money. "We'll take what's owin' to us and clear off. His doxy'll be here any minute, she'll see to 'im." He pulls me out o' the room with him and we got down them stairs somehow. When we come out there were a feller comin' in but he didn't say nothing and we come away . . .'

'Leaving the unfortunate Mr Dorrien to bleed to death.'

'That weren't our fault, Guv,' said Nick indignantly. 'We weren't to know how bad he were and there was that chap goin' in, and his girl, she'd be there any minute . . .'

'If you had fetched a doctor,' said Everard, his voice hardening, 'his life would have been saved and an innocent young woman would not have been arrested for his murder.'

'T'weren't no murder, I keep tellin' you, it were accidental like. You ask Jem. He never meant no 'arm. It were the gent himself acting vicious that did the trick,' went on Nick desperately, looking around him like a cornered animal and only now realizing how his own eloquence had betrayed him.

After that the result of the trial was a foregone conclusion. Jem Ryder, called to the witness box, denied emphatically that he had done anything until, faced with Nick's involuntary confession, he grudgingly admitted that he had in fact threatened Ray Dorrien with a knife.

'Threatened him, that's all it was, and that I'll swear to me dying day: I had to stop him throttlin' Nick, didn't I? "You let him go or else," I sez and that toff he lunged forward and threw himself on to the knife,' a statement that brought some jeering laughter from the public benches, quickly suppressed. Jem glared round at them. 'Go on, laugh,' he said, 'very funny but it's true as I'm standin' here.'

Even Sir James Dalfrey's agile brain could find no holes in this sorry tale and he asked no more than a few questions that did nothing to destroy the obvious truth.

Everard outlined his defence with cool precision, the judge summed up and the jury were out for precisely fifteen minutes, returning with an unanimous verdict of 'Not guilty.'

There was a loud cheer from a group of actors who had rushed to the court from the theatre and an agonized scream from the front benches, followed by a small commotion as Lord Dorrien half-carried the fainting Clara out of the court.

Dalfrey, who to do him justice was not a bad loser, came across to shake his opponent by the hand. 'To tell you the truth,' he said cheerfully, 'I'm not sorry to see it go this way. A pity to lose so charming an acting talent to the gallows.'

Everard crossed to the dock and took Kate's hand as she stepped down.

'Am I really free to go?' she whispered.

'Free as air,' he said smiling at her.

Dazed with relief she impulsively threw her arms round his neck and hugged him.

'How can I ever thank you?'

'It's your brother you should thank, my dear, he brought me the clinching evidence at a good deal of risk to himself.'

Then she was holding out both hands to Daniel and exclaiming over him because he still carried his arm in a sling.

Harry came hurrying to kiss her cheek, Christine hugged her and then her theatrical friends surged around her, kissing and congratulating her.

They carried her with them to the street outside where a small crowd had gathered and gave her a cheer. After the long stifling weeks in Newgate, the hours of torturing anxiety, she felt suddenly wildly elated. She was free, the sun shone, the air smelled sweet and the dark future had become filled with dazzling promise.

'We knew you would come through,' said Byron Farrar with his lordly air. 'Mr Kean gave us a few hours off so we've made our preparations. You are coming back to Gower Street with us to celebrate.'

'Oh no, I couldn't,' she said. 'I couldn't just run off like that. There are so many people I ought to thank.'

'Time for all that tomorrow. We've got a cab waiting and there is champagne.'

She laughed at the sheer craziness of it and George Westcott appearing suddenly at her shoulder, she turned to him for reassurance.

'You tell me what I ought to do.'

'Go off and enjoy yourself,' he said promptly. 'Drink champagne and be happy.'

'Come with us, sir,' said Byron expansively. 'The more the merrier.'

'Not quite the thing for an old sobersides lawyer like me.'

'Where's Dan?' exclaimed Kate distractedly. 'I'm not going without Dan.'

'I'm here,' said her brother. 'You go on. I'll follow later.'

'You will come?'

'Yes of course I will.'

He watched the actors pile into two cabs and drive off towards Gower Street. Kate was happy to be with her friends. They were part of her world, one in which he had never really fitted. Relieved and immensely grateful that she was free and the nightmare was over, he was suffering from an intense reaction. For weeks he seemed to have lived with it night and day and now suddenly there was nothing. He felt curiously isolated as if he didn't belong anywhere. The wound that he had neglected ached intolerably. He could see Everard Warrinder in a little group with Harry and Christine and Gareth and knew he did not belong with them any more than he did with Kate and her actor friends.

He turned his back on them and began to walk towards the city. It was then that Christine saw him. Franks had brought the carriage and her father was stepping into it.

Gareth said, 'Coming, Christine?'

'In a moment. Harry,' she whispered hurriedly, 'tell Papa and Gareth to go on and that I'll follow after them with you.'

'What's all this about, Chris? Where are you off to?'

'I want to speak to Daniel. I'm worried about him. Say we won't be long. Please, Harry.'

'Very well,' he said a little reluctantly. He liked Daniel, thought him a damned good chap, but all the same he didn't altogether like it. 'What are you up to, eh?'

'Nothing. I just want to make quite sure he's all right. I

thought he looked pretty sick in the court and I know that knife wound has been troubling him.'

'You take care now.' He was still doubtful but they were very close and they'd shared a good deal in the past. 'I'll wait for you in the Wine Bar but don't be too long.'

'I won't. Bless you,' she said and hurried after Daniel. He was not walking quickly and she soon caught him up.

'I thought you had gone with Kate,' she said breathlessly.

'No. They're not really my friends. She'll be better without me.'

'But you can't be all on your own, not today of all days. Come back with us.'

He shook his head. 'I'd scarcely fit into your mother's drawing room, would I? You go back to them, Christine. It's where you belong and your father will be asking for you.'

'He'll be asking for you too.'

'No, he won't, not now. My part in all this is over.'

She knew him in this mood, withdrawing into himself, stubbornly refusing to give an inch and she knew exactly what she was going to do to break down his rejection and to prove Gareth wrong.

She let him walk on but did not return to Harry. This was a busy street and it was not difficult to stop a hansom cab.

'Where to, lady?' said the driver genially.

She thought for a moment. Where could she buy food, wine perhaps, something with which to make a little feast.

'Cheapside,' she said with decision, 'and as fast as you can make it.'

She stopped him outside Mr Brown's shop and went in. Phil Turner was at the counter that day and came hurrying to ask her what he could do for her. Daniel had more than likely been half-starving himself this last week so she bought ham and cheese, bread still warm from the oven, and rich fruit pastry.

'What wine do you have?'

'We don't hold much stock here,' said Phil doubtfully, 'but there's a wine merchant further along the road. I could run down there if you say what you would like.'

Christine had never bought wine in her life and felt at a loss. 'It will take too long.'

'The master did draw off a few bottles of sherry from one of the casks,' suggested Phil hesitantly.

'That will do. Bring me one of those.'

He went to fetch it and almost collided with Elspeth who had been watching them through the bead curtain.

'What is that Miss Warrinder doing out there?' she hissed at him. 'She ought still to be in the court.'

'It's all over,' said Phil, 'didn't you know? Everybody as has come into the shop has been talking about it.'

'What is it?'

'Not guilty,' he called back over his shoulder as he returned to Christine, packing her purchases neatly into a small box and carrying it out to the cab for her.

When he came back Elspeth grabbed him by the arm. 'Where is she off to with all that food?'

Phil, who had suffered more than once from Elspeth's sharp tongue, was not giving anything away.

'She didn't say, simply got in and the cabby drove off.'

She was going to Daniel of course and Elspeth began to torture herself with wondering what was going to happen in that attic room, hugging and kissing and congratulating each other no doubt, now it was all over, and she burned with jealousy.

'I hope she paid you,' she said sharply. 'The Warrinders are much too grand to have an account with us.'

'Of course she did,' said Phil indignantly, *and* gave me a handsome tip at the same time – but that titbit he kept to himself.

Paradise Alley was simmering in afternoon sun. A ginger cat stretched itself luxuriously on the steps as Christine paid off the cab and carried her box in, suddenly realizing that she had no key and she was going to look pretty silly sitting on the top of the stairs waiting for Daniel to come back. She was saved from anything so ignominious by Ma Taylor calling up from

474

the basement, 'Is that you, Dan?' and then climbing up to exclaim at the sight of Christine.

'Well, I never did. If it isn't Miss Warrinder. Where's Dan then? He's not been took bad, has he?'

'No indeed. It's great news. We've won the case. Not guilty. Kate is free.'

'Just think o' that! What a blessing and Dan worrying himself near to death over it. Looked fit to drop he did when he went off this morning.'

'He'll be here in a minute. Can you let me have a key to his room? I've brought something for him.'

'Goin' to have a little party, are you?' said Ma Taylor with an approving nod. 'That's the ticket. Cheer him up proper that will. He's been that down in the dumps all these weeks.' She groped among the keys hanging in a bunch at her waist. 'Now you let me have that back, won't you? Where's his sister off to then?'

'She has gone with her friends from the theatre. They were all in the court this morning.'

Christine took the key and went on up the stairs. The attic room was neat and tidy as usual but looked somehow bare and comfortless. It was also very hot under the roof. She pushed the window wide and began to set out her purchases on the small table, the bottle of sherry in the middle with two mugs. She took off her bonnet, peered at herself in the tiny mirror on the chest and set herself to wait. Time was flying by and she knew she ought not to stay but they had both of them worked so hard for this moment of triumph and she wanted so much to share it with him. Harry would wait for her. He had never yet let her down.

There were books piled up by the bed and she picked up one of them, a new radical publication which he had filled with annotations and comments. As she turned the pages she came upon a cutting from the *Daily News*, a paper which prided itself on its trenchant criticisms of government failings. The article was a scathing comment on the shameful way a new scheme providing clean water for part of the East End had been put off time and time again on the plea of expense. It was a scheme dear to John Dexter's heart, who was convinced that the periodic epidemics of cholera and typhoid stemmed from the polluted water which was all that thousands of men and women living in dank cellars and crowded ramshackle houses were forced to drink. The article was not signed but bore all the marks of being written in a cold fury by Daniel himself. She was deep in it when she heard the footsteps on the stairs and hurriedly returned it to the book.

He flung open the door and then came to a sudden stop. She was standing under the window, a stray gleam of late sun gilding her hair and turning her muslin dress into a vision of green and gold that took his breath away.

It was a moment before he said abruptly, 'What the devil are you doing here?'

'If Mahomet won't come to the mountain, then the mountain must come to Mahomet,' she said gaily. 'A fusty old governess of mine was fond of quoting that. I thought we might celebrate the victory together.'

'If I'd wanted to do that I could have gone with Kate and drunk champagne. I thought I made it clear that I'm not in a party mood.'

'If that's how you feel, then toss it all out of the window, though it would seem rather a pity. I'm hungry if you are not.'

For a long moment he still glared at her, then suddenly he began to laugh. 'Oh God, Christine, what am I to do with you? All right, you win. What's in that bottle?'

'Sherry,' she said dubiously. 'It was all I could get and Joe said it was Mr Brown's best and drawn from a cask at the back of the shop.'

'Let's try some then.' He took up the bottle awkwardly, prised out the cork and poured a measure into the two mugs. 'Let's drink to Kate's future and to your father, who has secured it for her.'

They clicked mugs and took a gulp. Christine wrinkled up her nose in disgust.

'Oh heavens, it's awful, isn't it?'

'Is it? I wouldn't know.'

'It's nothing like we have at home.'

'Your father probably orders the finest vintage direct from Spain,' he said drily. 'Awful though it is, let's have some more.'

This time he slipped his right arm out of the sling and leaned forward to pick up the bottle but not without an exclamation of pain.

'Is that wound still troubling you?' she asked anxiously.

'Now and again.'

'Let me see.'

'Certainly not. It's nothing.'

'Don't argue. I know about these things. Have you had it looked at again by Dr Dexter?'

'Didn't want to trouble him.'

She made him sit on the bed, helped him off with his jacket and opened his shirt. There were traces of fresh blood on the bandage where it must have stuck and then been jerked away, while the flesh around the wound was pink and a little swollen. He winced when she gently prodded it.

'There could be infection. You must go back to the doctor.'

'Tomorrow will do. Let's drink our sherry.'

They took another gulp, then he put down the mug and pulled her down beside him on the bed. The wine, potent if over-sweet, on an empty stomach had made him feel light-headed. He rocketed from the depths of depression to a wild recklessness.

After all these weeks working so closely with Everard Warrinder in a common cause, the resentment, the bitter anger had slowly begun to ebb away in spite of himself. There was a charm about the man which he had fought against but found increasingly difficult to resist. He was prepared to believe there could be some other explanation of the un-happy past, and in the same way the gulf that had yawned between him and Christine had vanished.

He pulled her into his arms and began to kiss her with a kind of exultation. He had rebuffed her and yet she had come to him. It moved him inexpressibly and he was filled with an overwhelming tenderness that grew into something deeper, threatening to run out of control. He tried to be sensible, to draw back, to put her away from him, but it was too late. The flame was lit and would not be put out. He was dizzy with it. He had not intended it and neither had she but now it had become inevitable. They could not draw back and suddenly it was Christine who was in charge, Christine who stood up and silently began to unhook her simple summer gown, let it drop to her feet with the crinoline and the silk petticoats until she stood shyly, infinitely desirable, in her white lace-trimmed chemise.

He had dreamed of a moment like this a hundred times and had awoken to frustration. Now it was reality. He stripped off shirt and trousers. For a moment they stood mouth to mouth, flesh against flesh, then he lifted her on to the bed. He was inexperienced but gentle, almost reverential at first, his hands straying over her body, his kisses following after them, until she trembled and drew him closer, the tension growing and growing until when he invaded her body at last it was on a great wave of shuddering desire that overcame pain and shock and she was lifted into a joy and ecstasy that left her lying content and fulfilled, his hand still on her breast, her head against his shoulder. She felt so happy she did not want to move. She had no feeling of guilt, only a certainty that what she was doing was right. She would have liked to stay drowsing in the comfort of his arms, waking to the joy of another day together, but that could not be yet. The summer afternoon was merging into evening when they stirred.

'I mustn't stay too long, Harry is waiting for me,' she murmured and struggled from the bed.

While they dressed they kept on stopping to laugh and kiss again, to sip more of the dark brown sherry, to feed each other with pieces of ham and cheese on buttered bread and he began to tell her about his article being accepted by the *Daily News* on the strength of what he had been writing during the months after the election in the radical news sheet which was always in danger of being confiscated by the government.

'The paper has asked me for more and I'm beginning to learn what they want. They don't pay much but it's a start.'

They went on talking eagerly as they ate, making plans as if everything was now settled between them instead of a future still filled with problems.

'There are local newspapers springing up all over the country,' he was saying, 'there is the *Northern Clarion* in Lancashire, which is looking for new writers who have experienced what they write about and Sam Jessop has written saying why don't I go up there and join the staff. The Methodist Chapel is founding a school like Mr Brown's down here. With his recommendation I could teach and write at the same time. It could be a living.'

'Will you go?'

'I don't know. Till Kate was safe I couldn't think of anything else and now I don't like to leave her alone in London.'

Her eyes glowed with enthusiasm. 'If you did go, couldn't I come with you? I could teach perhaps or I could start a clinic. We could be working together.'

Crazy impractical dreams most of them but that evening, in a new-found happiness and confidence in one another, nothing seemed impossible. He wanted to go with her when she left but she shook her head.

'It's too soon and Harry will be waiting for me. You must stay and take great care of that wound of yours. Promise me that you will go to the clinic tomorrow.'

He saw her into the cab and driving through the City she heard one of the great church clocks strike seven and found it amazing that it was only a short time since she had followed him from the law courts and now her whole life had changed, become more real, more magical, more utterly fulfilled than she had ever thought possible. Neither of them had intended it but the mood of exultation, the long pent-up emotions of the last few weeks had carried them away beyond her wildest dreams so that now she felt a new person, no doubts any longer, sure of herself and of Daniel.

When the cab drew up at the Wine Bar, Harry was outside waiting for her, both deeply concerned and angry.

'Do you realize how long you've been?' he burst out. 'I could have drunk the place dry. What the devil happened to you?'

'I'm sorry, Harry, I really am, it was just . . . well, I had to stay a little while and the time went by before I realized it.'

'I hope to God you've got a good story for Papa,' he grumbled as he climbed into the cab beside her. 'He'll be wanting to know what on earth we've been doing for the last couple of hours.'

By the time they reached Belgrave Square, dinner, which had already been set back on their account, was just about to be served.

'We were thinking of sending out search parties for you,' said her father drily. 'What happened to the pair of you?'

'I went home with Daniel,' she said serenely. 'His wound had been affecting him pretty badly and nobody seemed to be taking much thought for him at all. I was worried so I made sure that he had food and reminded him that he must go to see Dr Dexter now that the anxiety is all over. He does not take sufficient care of himself.'

Nobody saw fit to ask if Harry had gone with her so he took good care to say nothing to the contrary and only Gareth wondered.

'I'm sorry if he felt neglected,' said her father as they sat down to table, 'I assumed he had gone with his sister and her actor friends. He could have come back with us.'

'He said he didn't think he would fit into Mamma's drawing room,' said Christine.

'Oh really, I'm sure I don't know why he should say that,' said her mother. 'Anyone would think I was an ogre. Of course he would have been welcome after all your father has done for him.'

'Daniel has his pride, my dear,' said her husband. 'Now this is all over I must try to do something for him. He is intelligent and has done a lot to educate himself. There must be openings for talent of that kind.'

'He writes, Papa, very well too. Even the *Daily News* has accepted one of his articles and they are asking for more.'

'That's interesting. There are openings for enterprising journalists and I have friends in that line although not, I'm afraid, with the *Daily News*. I rather think it is now largely financed by Lord Dorrien and I'm not on exactly the best of terms with him at the moment.'

Gareth said little that evening but he noticed a difference in Christine. She was quiet, loving, gentle, but her eyes held a serene content, an inner happiness that disturbed and tormented him. When he was leaving he took her aside for a moment.

'What really happened this evening?' he asked bluntly.

'I told you. I was worried about Daniel.'

'Is that really all?'

But that evening in her new joy and confidence nothing could disturb her.

'Yes, of course. Dear Gareth, you really mustn't worry about me so much. I'm not worth it.'

'You are to me.'

He put his arms around her and kissed her hard on the mouth.

'That much and more,' he said hoarsely and left her.

She watched him run down the steps, her hand at the lips he had kissed, sorry that she could not respond as he would have wished.

She believed that nothing in the world could destroy the happiness of that wonderful evening but she was wrong. It could and did all too soon.

Chapter 24

The more scurrilous publications and news sheets did not ordinarily penetrate the dignified portals of Belgrave Square except via the servants' quarters but someone made very sure that the *Daily News* was delivered one morning in August some weeks after the trial. Barton looked at it dubiously, then folded it and put it with *The Times* beside his master's place.

Everard frowned at it in surprise. 'Where did this come from?'

'Delivered by hand, sir,' said the butler.

'Must be some mistake.'

However he took it with him unread when he went to his chambers in the Temple, where matters were being cleared for the usual summer recess, and one of his colleagues, seeing it lying on his desk, said cheerfully, 'Someone on that rag has his knife in you, Everard. What are you going to do about it? Sue them for libel?'

The article appeared in a column normally devoted to criticism of the government or society scandals or any subject likely to arouse controversy.

It had been extremely skilfully written. It was simply headed 'Trouble in Legal Practice' with a large question mark and then set out a hypothetical dilemma where a well-known counsel is faced with a problem rising from past indiscretion. A hitherto unknown child is accused of a crime – what does he do? Does he acknowledge his bastard? Or does he defend saying nothing, especially when it could be linked with a long-past incident when he conducted a very successful prosecution while at the same time indulging in a liaison with his victim's wife.

It mentioned no names, there were no dates, no precise details, but the implication was obvious and anyone reading it would know to whom it referred.

If he sued the paper, it would be to acknowledge its application to himself and if he didn't, if he let it go and brazened it out, it could be a slur on his name for the future that could be exceedingly unpleasant for his wife and his family. At the same time the hideous fact stared him in the face that it was substantially true even if the hidden facts were quite different from those hinted at in the article.

He sat staring at it for a long time uncertain what to do. At his club where he lunched alone as he often did, he knew some of his acquaintances were talking about it by the uneasy glances they threw at him, by the way they deliberately avoided any mention of it. Clara's threats that he had dismissed suddenly took on a new significance and he was well aware that this attack must have been instigated chiefly by Lord Dorrien, who had somehow dug into the past and despite the proved justice of the verdict on Kate still could not forgive him for acting against him. But where could he have obtained his information when there had never at any time been any hint of it? He thought of Daniel and then dismissed it. Once perhaps, when the boy was still seething with rage against him, but they had shared a great deal since then and there had been a change in his attitude. Daniel would have been far more likely to throw it in his face than choose this sly way of getting back at him. One thing he knew quite certainly. Clarissa would want the truth and in all justice and however painful he could not deny it to her.

Clara had seen it when her father-in-law tossed the paper to her across the breakfast table. She ran her eye down the column. To cause pain to the man who had successfully thwarted her bitter jealousy went some way to soothe her rage and disappointment.

483

'Can we follow it up?' she asked eagerly.

Lord Dorrien shrugged his shoulders. He was not prepared to indulge this whim of hers too far.

'It'll no doubt give him some uncomfortable hours,' he said briefly. 'Let's leave it at that.'

Daniel did not see the article till the early evening. It was the last day at the school before it closed for the summer. Mr Brown was talking of expanding it, taking over a derelict building close by and converting it into classrooms since attendance had grown considerably over the last two years. Daniel spent some time discussing the plans with him and then went off to call on his sister. Kate had a problem which she wanted to discuss with him. Mr Kean's season at the Princess Theatre was drawing to a close and the company would be going on their annual tour. She had been asked to accompany them but the manager at the Haymarket intended to put on a revival of *She Stoops to Conquer* in the autumn and had offered her the leading part, no doubt hoping to reap an advantage from the publicity of the trial, but it was a good part in a lively old comedy and very tempting.

In the meantime Daniel was feeling wonderfully happy, more content with himself than he had felt for months. Ever since that magical evening, he had known everything was going to come right. Nothing now could surely come between him and Christine. There were a hundred problems of course. They could not marry yet, not for months, not for years perhaps, but he had a complete certainty he could overcome all opposition. They had only met once or twice since that momentous evening and they had sat on their old seat in the churchyard and discussed all kinds of plans, some of them shooting up to impossible heights, others severely practical. He knew very well he would be up against stiff opposition from her father and was all for facing him with it straightaway but Christine still shook her head.

'I know I can persuade him to understand and see my point of view but we must wait a little till I find the right time. If we rush it, we will spoil everything.'

It was in this happy mood that he arrived at Gower Street to find Kate waiting for him with a copy of the *Daily News* in her hand and looking very disturbed.

'Daniel,' she said, almost as soon as he came into the room, 'Daniel, have you read this? I don't take the *Daily News* but someone delivered it personally as if they wanted to make absolutely sure that I saw it. It's horrible. I couldn't believe it.'

'What is it?'

She handed him the paper where the article had been heavily outlined in red ink.

He read it quickly and felt sick. The spite was so obvious. Someone had leaked a mere suspicion and a clever journalist had exploited it into a malicious attempt to discredit Everard Warrinder.

Kate was watching him. 'Did you know about this?' she said urgently. 'Is it true?'

'I told you about the past, about the prosecution of John Hunter.'

'Oh that, yes. I could never feel as strongly about it as you did, Dan. I never knew him. He was only a shadow in my life and after we were separated and all those years when I was fighting for existence even the shadow disappeared. But what of this? You must tell me. Am I Everard Warrinder's daughter?'

'Yes,' he admitted and looked away from her.

'You've known all this time and yet you never told me?' she said incredulously.

'I thought it would distress you to know you were illegitimate, that it would destroy what memories you still had of your mother. She was dying when she told me and it was only then because she loved you so much and worried about what would become of you.'

'Oh my God,' said Kate dropping into a chair, 'I can't believe it. Now I know why you were so against my friendship with Harry, Harry who is now my half-brother. Now I know why his father was so angry with me at the birthday ball and why he made certain of sending Harry away from me. He had to make sure he destroyed the affection that had grown up between us.'

'Does it still distress you?'

'No, not now so much,' she said thoughtfully. 'It did for a long time but I grew to realize that Harry had outgrown me as I've outgrown him. I'm still very fond of him. Do you know, Dan, that when Mr Warrinder came to see me in Newgate, the first thing I saw was Harry in him, an older, more mature, wiser Harry, but quite unmistakeable. After all these years feeling myself so completely alone till we met again,' she said slowly, 'it feels very strange to find I have a father and one I can admire, one I can love. I think in a way, even though it can never be acknowledged, I'm rather proud of being Everard Warrinder's daughter.'

'Oh Kate, for God's sake,' exclaimed Dan, 'this is not like one of your dramas in the theatre where everything comes right in the last act. This could have frightening consequences for Mr Warrinder. I wish I knew where the information came from. Someone must have leaked a few hints and a muck-raking journalist has put two and two together.'

'I didn't tell you but Ray Dorrien's wife came to see me in Newgate. She terrified me. She swore that if Mr Warrinder won my case she would ruin him. She couldn't do that, could she?'

'Lord Dorrien could and he has an interest in the *Daily News*.' Then he stopped suddenly as the idea struck him. 'Mr Warrinder can't think that I am responsible for this, can he? I swore to him I would tell no one and I meant it. I've kept the secret all these years for our mother's sake and for yours. He can't believe that I sold this story to this wretched newspaper for money. They would pay well for this, far more than for any articles I write. There's Christine too. She knows that I've had work accepted . . .' the thought that she might think him guilty of this abominable attack on her father appalled him. 'I must go there now, at once. I must tell them it is none of my doing.'

'If you go, then I will go with you.'

'No, Kate, this doesn't concern you . . .'

'But it does. I want to tell Mr Warrinder that it makes no difference to how I feel about him. If this is going to be talked about, and it's bound to be, then I am in the middle of it.'

'All right. Come if you must. We'll go now at once. We'll take a cab.'

Clarissa might not have seen the article at all that day if she had not attended a meeting of the society giving aid to impoverished gentlewomen and taken a reluctant Christine with her. At the end of the afternoon one of the members who cherished a poisonous envy of Clarissa, who in her opinion already had far too much – daughter of an Earl, handsome husband, an exquisite taste in clothes – made a point of asking her very sweetly if she had seen the *Daily News* that morning.

'It's not the kind of newspaper we take,' she said shortly.

'Indeed. Well, I should take a look at this morning's edition if I were you. Here, have my copy.'

Clarissa would have brushed the offer aside but Christine with a slight feeling of foreboding accepted it with a word of thanks.

In the carriage Clarissa said irritably, 'You shouldn't have encouraged that woman. She is a pusher, always trying to pick acquaintanceship with people she thinks might do her some good. You'd better see what rubbish she was referring to.'

It was not easy to read the poor print in the jolting carriage but Christine was able to gather enough to feel horrified.

'I don't think you should read this, Mamma, not till you have spoken to Papa,' she said.

'Why? Is it an attack on him?'

'Yes, in a way.'

'Give it to me. Let me see.'

She took out her gold-framed lorgnette and ran her eye down the column, quickly gathering sufficient to make her crumple the paper fiercely in her hands.

487

'It's all lies, of course, stupid vicious lies. You notice they don't mention any name, they dare not. This is Clara and Lord Dorrien attacking your father out of spite because they lost their action. He must deny it now at once.'

'I don't know whether he can, Mamma.'

'Nonsense, girl, of course he can.'

When Barton opened the door to them, Clarissa said at once, 'Is Mr Warrinder home yet?'

'Yes, Madam. He is in his study with Mr Harry.'

'Tell him I'd like a word with him alone, will you, Barton?'

'Very good, Madam.'

Christine followed her mother up the stairs with a sinking heart. Clarissa did no more than remove her stylish hat and gloves, take a quick look at herself in the mirror and then went down the stairs to the study, the crumpled newspaper in her hand. Christine went after her.

Everard rose to his feet as his wife stormed into the room. She ignored Harry and went straight to him holding out the newspaper.

'This disgusting attack on you. It's all lies, isn't it? You'll force them to apologise and withdraw it at once.'

'So you've seen it already. I'm sorry about that.'

'Some wretched woman at the meeting this afternoon made quite sure that I did. What are you going to do about it?'

'Nothing.'

'Nothing!' She almost shrieked the word at him. 'Nothing! But why?'

'For one thing it does not mention me personally so I have no right to demand a retraction without admitting that the cap fits, and secondly, because in the main it is not lies but the truth.'

She stared at him as if she couldn't take in what he had said. 'You mean that what it says here about this . . . this liaison with some woman is true . . . that this girl whom you have been defending is actually her daughter and *yours* . . . ?'

'Yes.'

'Oh my God! I can't believe it. I won't believe it. Not you, Everard, not you . . . it isn't possible.'

She looked so stricken that Harry sprang to her side.

'Don't take it so badly, Mamma. You only know one side of it.'

'Leave me alone, Harry, don't interfere. This is between me and your father.'

'No, Clarissa. An explanation if we must have it concerns Harry and Christine too.'

Many married men had affairs with other women and in most cases their wives had to accept that it happened. The important thing was not to be found out. But to Clarissa, who had loved her husband passionately, believed in him absolutely, it seemed for the moment like the end of the world. She dropped into a chair and buried her face in her hands. He came to her side.

'I am sorry, Clarissa,' he said gently, 'that you should have learned about it like this.'

'I suppose you would have gone on lying to me for ever,' she said fiercely.

'Not lying,' he said, 'simply keeping silent and not wishing to hurt you with something that was long over.'

'I want to know,' she said stubbornly, 'I want to know everything now.'

He sighed. 'Very well, if you must.'

It was at that fraught moment that there came Barton's knock at the door and he came in looking a little anxious.

'Mr Hunter and his sister are asking if they could see you, sir,' he said.

'Tell them to go away,' said Clarissa stormily. 'The impudence, to come knocking at our door now of all times!'

'No,' said Everard with decision. 'No, Clarissa, they have as much right to an explanation as anyone here. Show them in, Barton.'

'If you say so, sir.'

'Why, Everard, why?' exclaimed Clarissa as the butler went out. 'They are strangers. They have no real part in our lives. I don't understand.'

489

'You will soon enough.'

They came in a little hesitantly, aware at once that something was very wrong.

With a sudden flare of anger and dislike Clarissa tossed the paper at Daniel's feet.

'After this I wonder you have the face to come here, you and your sister.'

'But that's why we have come,' said Daniel steadily. He picked up the paper, put it on one of the small tables and then turned to Everard. 'I wanted you to know I had nothing to do with this. I swear I didn't. I have never spoken of it to anyone, never, not even to Kate. You do believe me, don't you?'

'Why should we believe you?' said Clarissa bitterly. 'You tried to kill my husband once. You could be looking for another way to destroy him.'

'Be quiet, my dear. For God's sake let us all keep calm about this. Yes, I do believe you, Daniel. There are plenty of people who make a living by muck-raking into the past and selling what they come up with.' He looked around at them with a faintly ironic smile. 'It seems to me that I am now the one on trial.'

'No, Papa,' said Harry impulsively. 'No, you don't have to feel like that. You don't owe us any explanation. We know you, we believe in you, we love you. I vote we ignore this filthy article, simply take no notice of it at all, go on as usual, and then it will die a natural death as all such spiteful attacks do in the end.'

'Thank you, Harry. I'm grateful for your loyalty and I agree with you about ignoring it publicly but I think your mother will not be happy to leave it like that. I had hoped that what happened was safely buried in the past and could be forgotten but some quirk of fate has taken good care to tangle it up with the present and there is now no escape. I can only tell you what actually happened and then it will be for you to judge me as you wish.'

In the pause while they looked doubtfully at one another, Barton knocked and came in again, looking apologetically at Clarissa.

'Mrs Gant is asking whether dinner should be served at the usual time, Madam.'

'Oh I don't know,' she said distractedly. 'Tell her to hold it back for at least another hour. I'll let you know when we are ready.'

'Very well, Madam.'

Barton withdrew and reported to the kitchen that there was a proper to-do going on upstairs and goodness knows whether any of them would be sitting down at table at all that evening.

'It's that there article in the newspaper,' said Mrs Gant. 'I knew there'd be trouble as soon as I set eyes on it, and I've a nice piece of turbot with anchovy sauce too, with roast leg of lamb to follow. Oh well, we can keep it warm, I suppose, and if it spoils, then it spoils, but I tell you one thing, Mr Barton, that if I had the wretch who wrote that nasty muck about our Mr Warrinder in my kitchen, I don't know what I wouldn't do to him! Horse-whipping is too good for that sort!'

Upstairs in the study Harry had placed a chair for Kate and Daniel stood close beside her. Christine felt she knew better than anyone how painful this was going to be for her father, a deeply private man who had always found it difficult to express his inmost feelings. She saw her mother's eyes fixed on him as if almost terrified of what she might hear and with a sudden sympathy she pulled up a footstool and sat close beside her chair.

Everard had gone to the windows and drawn the curtains as if to shut out the outside world. The lamps glowed softly and they all seemed to be waiting in a hushed expectancy for what he was going to say.

'I should perhaps explain,' he began without looking round, 'that I knew Mary Hunter before she married John Hunter, long before I met and married you, Clarissa. It was during my first years at the Bar and it so happened that I had a number of cases working alongside my chief in the north, mostly in Lancashire. Mary was a singer with a troupe that went from place to place throughout that part of the country. She was eighteen and I was twenty-two. She was beautiful, full

491

of life and warmth and gaiety, with a steadfast courage that had lifted her from a poor childhood to a life that was far from rich but was at least independent and she was proud of it. We lived together for almost a year and were very happy.'

'Did you never think of marrying her?' asked Clarissa in a stifled voice.

'No, never, the idea never occurred to either of us. She could not have fitted into my life as I couldn't have fitted into hers, but we were young, spent most of our leisure time together and never even dreamed of such a thing. At the end of the year I was called back to Bramber for my mother's serious illness. Mary would never accept any sort of gift from me but on that last day I bought her a little antique silver box from a junk stall. "I shall keep my memories of you in it," she said and we laughed about it.'

That same silver box now stood on Christine's dressing table and she suddenly felt like weeping for that unknown girl.

'After my mother recovered,' he went on, 'I remained working in London. We exchanged a few letters but she was constantly on the move and I was never sure if she received any of them. Some months later I was called north on another case and went in search of her. We had been very happy together and I was concerned to know whether she was still doing well. I sought out some of her old comrades but they had split up and gone their different ways and nobody could tell me what had happened to her. At last I tracked down an elderly woman who sometimes made costumes for the troupe and she told me that very soon after I had gone, Mary had married a man who had, it seemed, always been in love with her. "Lucky for her," this woman went on. "She was pregnant. Didn't you know?" It was a shock. I hadn't known. Mary had never hinted at such a thing and I was distressed to think she could have been alone and in trouble when I would certainly have done what I could to provide for her and any child.'

Daniel's hand, resting on his sister's shoulder, suddenly gripped it so hard that she looked up at him in surprise.

'Are you all right?' she whispered.

'Yes, of course,' but there was a taut look on his face as if he was holding himself back by some strong effort and she was worried about him.

Everard had dropped down in the chair behind his desk and sat for a moment staring at the massive silver inkstand that had been a gift from his father when he had taken silk, the youngest QC at the Bar.

'That winter,' he said with an effort, 'I was back in London and we met, Clarissa, if you remember, at your brother's coming-of-age celebration.'

'And you married me because my father was Earl of Glenmuir and your father's friend and everyone said what a lovely couple we were and how very suitable it was,' she said with an extreme bitterness.

'It wasn't quite like that, my dear, as you know very well. When I saw you first that night I thought I'd never seen anyone more radiantly beautiful and could hardly believe my luck when you rejected a number of very eligible suitors and chose to smile at me.'

'Why didn't you tell me then?' she said with a catch in her voice. 'Why didn't you tell me that you had already loved and lived with another woman?'

'Because it was over and done with, part of growing up and this was real life. I had a flourishing career and we were wonderfully happy, weren't we, when Margaret was born and then later Harry and Christine came along. We'd been married close on six years when the loss of your last baby made you so desperately sick, much at the same time as the whole country was in turmoil over the Chartists and the Reform Bill. It was a time of revolution everywhere, Italy, France, the whole of Europe was in revolt and the Cabinet were desperately afraid that we might have revolution here. There were riots in the north, soldiers were called out to keep order and the lawcourts were crammed with cases of arson, wanton damage and even murder. I can't remember a worse time publicly or privately. For an agonizing few weeks I thought I was going to lose you as well as our child, and then when the doctors at last pronounced you out of danger they insisted that you should leave London and live for a year at least in a warmer climate and as near the sea as possible. I took a house at Weymouth for you and the children but there was no question of my going with you. I was far too busy, and I was only able to make one or two rare visits.'

He paused and then got up and moved to the drinks table. He poured a small measure of brandy and glanced around at the others but they shook their heads so he took the glass back to his desk and stood for a moment with it in his hands as if uncertain how to go on.

Christine knew that this was the moment he dreaded most of all and her heart went out to him. Why couldn't her mother leave it at that? Why force him to go on? But Clarissa was sitting forward in her chair, her hands tightly clasped on her knee, her eyes never leaving him.

He swallowed the brandy at a gulp and braced himself to go on. 'The government was hunting for a scapegoat and they found it in John Hunter. He had been a mill-hand himself at one time and had become a powerful leader with a burning belief in the cause of his fellow workers, a charismatic personality who had an irresistible appeal and up to then had escaped all attempts to silence him. So when towards the end of the year he boldly led an enormous rally to Westminster demanding workers' rights, the opportunity was seized to arrest him and charge him not only with treason but with the brutal murder of one of the policemen who had taken him prisoner. They had secured a notable victim at last and on the strength of my experience in the northern towns I was appointed to the prosecution.'

'Gosh, you never told any of us about that, Papa,' exclaimed Harry.

'Since you were only three years old at the time I don't think you would have appreciated it,' said his father with a faint smile. 'I did not know then that John Hunter was the man whom Mary had married. It was a difficult case with witnesses

494

that were either mistaken or deliberately lying but it was an important one for me and I worked hard at establishing it. The trial was already days old when Mary came to see me one evening.'

'You mean she came here, to this house?' whispered Clarissa.

'Yes. She had changed of course. Six years is a long time and her life couldn't have been easy, moving from place to place with her difficult husband, but she was still beautiful, still full of courage, and I was distressed for her. She swore to me that he was innocent of the murder, that I was being deliberately deceived by witnesses who were bitterly jealous of him. She said she could find proofs and simply to comfort her I told her to bring them and I would do what I could. But the days passed, she did not come, and there was never any doubt that the verdict would be hanging.' He turned away from them then and was silent for a moment as if summoning strength for the moment he most dreaded.

'You may find it difficult to understand,' he went on at last, 'but though I had won my case and received a good deal of congratulation, I was unhappy about it. Over the course of the trial I had felt a certain admiration for the prisoner's courage and strength of purpose and when I came home that night felt no pleasure in knowing he was condemned to a horrible death. That was the night Mary came back to me, bringing with her certain proof of how the truth had been twisted, destroying much of what I had so carefully built up. I could not make her understand that it was too late. "You can save him," she pleaded. "You can bring an appeal, ask for a retrial." She wept hopelessly and despairingly and I tried to comfort her. I'm making no excuses, I meant only to console, but when I took her in my arms the memory of how much we had once shared overwhelmed us both as if the years between had all been swept away . . .'

'Oh God,' murmured Clarissa, 'I can't bear it, I can't. How could you forfeit even for one moment what we had been to one another – how could you?'

495

'I wish to God I could answer that but I can't . . .' he hesitated for a moment and then went on, 'I'm sorry, my dear, I would never have told you if you had not insisted. There's not much more to tell. I could see now where the fault lay and God knows I did try to get the verdict changed to imprisonment but it was impossible. Any thought of an appeal was utterly rejected as bringing discredit on the government. They had wanted a scapegoat whose death would deter others and they had got it, innocent or guilty hardly mattered. To have forced it into the open, to have demanded a retrial could have meant the end of my career at the Bar. I had to let it go. I let an innocent man go to his death and it has haunted me ever since. Mary and I lived through those agonizing few days somehow and then one day she disappeared. I knew she had found it hard to forgive me. I tried to find her but she had gone out of my life and she brought up Daniel to hate and despise me for what I had done.'

'It must have been very soon after that when you came to Weymouth for the last month we stayed there,' said Clarissa slowly.

'I'm afraid I must have been pretty unbearable to live with.'

'Why didn't you tell me then, Everard? Why didn't you?' she asked painfully.

'I couldn't. It was too deeply buried in me and you had been so very sick. I couldn't bear to hurt you. I never dreamed for one second what the result of those few days might be . . . it has been an extraordinary experience to find I have a daughter about whom I have known nothing.'

'You must have loved her mother very dearly that you were willing to risk your career, throw away your happiness and your family's future in order to save her daughter.'

There was so much pain and disillusionment in Clarissa's voice that Everard made a move towards her.

'You must not think that was in my mind. I could not forget that I had once let an innocent man die and without realizing it had condemned Mary to a life of poverty and loneliness. To do all I could for Kate in her need seemed the very least I could do.'

'And now that she is here, what do you expect from me? That I should welcome this girl into my home, cherish her as my daughter? I can't do it, I can't, it is impossible, you cannot ask it from me . . .'

Clarissa was letting the wild words carry her away, though she scarcely believed in them herself. Everard, for once at a loss, made a helpless gesture and it was Kate who rose to the occasion with a dignity that silenced Clarissa's outburst.

'I am sorry, Lady Clarissa, that you should feel so bitterly about me coming here. Until today I had not the slightest inkling of any of this. I want nothing from you or from Mr Warrinder but there is one thing that I came here to say. You see, I never knew John Hunter, he was just someone in the past, like a heroic figure out of history, but this is different. I'm proud to be Everard Warrinder's daughter. I think I understand now why my dead mother loved him and I am happy to have a father whom I too can love and respect. I'd shout it aloud to everyone if I could.'

Everard smiled. 'I'm afraid it is not going to do you much good, my dear.'

'It's warm in my heart and that's what matters. You have given my life back to me. I can never thank you enough for that.'

'I don't want thanks. It's enough to know that we are not enemies.' He sighed and looked around at them. 'You wanted the truth and now you have it,' he went on wearily, 'but there is one thing to be said and in this I believe that Harry agrees with me. I'm determined to do nothing about this newspaper article. This is a deeply private matter and if I can prevent it, I don't intend to let it be dragged through the press with all their vulgar publicity. I shall simply ignore it and carry on as usual and endure what consequences there may be. I'd be grateful if you could help me in this, especially you, Clarissa.' He moved across to her and would have put a hand on her shoulder but she flinched away from him. 'You are my wife

497

and whatever you feel about me in private, I expect you to support me in every way in public.'

'I don't know that I can,' she said distractedly. 'However I try, it will be there always in my mind. I shall read it in every face, hear the pity in every voice. I shall never be able to escape from it, never . . .' Her voice choked into a sob, she stumbled to her feet and ran from the room.

He would have followed her but Harry stopped him.

'Not you, Papa, not yet. She is very upset. You must give her time. I'll go to her. She will be better with me.'

'Go with him, Christine,' said her father, suddenly sounding helpless and lost, but she shook her head.

Harry was her mother's darling. She had always known it. He would have far more influence with her than she had. They had too often been at cross purposes.

'She will be far happier with Harry,' she said gently.

For a moment no one moved, then her father looked around at them and made a valiant effort to bring everything back to normal.

'We would seem to be the sole survivors,' he said, 'and I suppose something will have to be done about Barton and serving dinner if it is still eatable. We must make a show of sitting down to it if only to stop the servants' gossip. God knows what they have been saying already in the kitchen. What about you, Daniel? Will you and Kate join us?'

'No,' he said, 'no, better not. It will only cause more talk. Kate and I are still strangers here.'

'Scarcely strangers after what we have been through together,' said Everard. 'Don't lose touch though. Come and see me again. Christine was telling us that you have had articles published not only in that radical sheet of yours but in other newspapers. If that's what you want to do, I could be of use to you. I have several connections in that line of work.'

'Thank you,' said Daniel stiffly. 'I would be grateful.'

'Kate too. Are you going back to Mr Kean's company, my dear?'

'He has asked me but there have been other very tempting offers. I still can't believe that I am free to choose.'

'Come, Kate, we must go,' said her brother brusquely, aware that if he stayed a moment longer he would burst out with the question that burned on his lips and he mustn't, not now, not yet, with Christine standing there sublimely unconscious of the black shadow that threatened to destroy everything between them.

She came to the door with them, hugging Kate and saying she would call to see her soon in her new lodging and holding up her face for Daniel's kiss, whispering, 'Come back soon, Dan. Papa means what he says. It's going to be all right for us, I know it is.'

He plunged down the steps taking Kate with him. What was he going to do? How was he going to tell her that if what he believed was true, then they could never come together, never be married, never achieve any of the wonderful things they had planned.

Christine came back into the study to find Harry had come back saying Clarissa had decided to go to bed and didn't want any dinner.

'Nonsense,' said her husband, 'of course she must eat. Christine, go and ask Mrs Gant to send up a tray, something light and suitable, and then tell the kitchen they can serve what's left of the meal.'

In the end Christine sat down at table with her father and Harry. Dinner was served as usual but they did not really do justice to it and the kitchen staff much later that evening enjoyed half the turbot, a good part of the roast lamb and the entire chocolate mousse which had come back untouched.

'It's always been Miss Christine's favourite too,' said Mrs Gant, giving Annie a lavish second helping. 'I'm sure I don't know what things are coming to.'

When Christine went up to her room she looked in on her mother. Clarissa was not in bed but sitting in her dressing gown staring in front of her and looking as if she had been weeping.

'Where's your father?' she asked abruptly.

'I left him downstairs with Harry having a nightcap. He'll be up soon. Is there anything you would like, Mamma? Can I fetch you a hot drink?'

'No, nothing. You go to bed.'

Christine hesitated and then knelt down beside her mother's chair.

'Don't be too hard on him, Mamma. It's so long ago. It's over and done with and he loves you very dearly.'

'Does he? Tonight I find it hard to believe. You don't understand, Christine. How could you? You're far too young. I feel betrayed. All these years he has been holding back something vitally important to him. Why did he never tell me when it meant so much to him?'

'Perhaps it was for that very reason. He was afraid that if he did you might have turned away from him as you have done tonight.'

Clarissa looked startled as if the very idea was new to her, then she said brusquely, 'Nonsense! I've never known your father to be afraid of anything. Go to bed, child. You look tired.'

'I think we all are. Goodnight, Mamma.'

She kissed her mother's cheek and went back to her own room. A little later Harry came up and banged on her door with a cheery, 'Goodnight, Chris, sleep tight,' as if the discovery that his father was not quite the paragon he had always been held up to be had pleased rather than distressed him.

Presently she heard her father come slowly up the stairs and could not resist opening the door a crack with the intention of giving him a hug and a goodnight kiss. She saw him go to the bedroom door, find it locked and stand for a moment before he moved away towards his dressing room. She had a passionate desire to give her mother a good shaking, not realizing that Clarissa, petted, spoiled and indulged, had always skimmed along on the surface of her supremely contented life and the shock of coming face to face with a sudden grim reality, to find her perfect husband could be guilty of a

500

lapse even if it was so long ago, had been overwhelming. She was torn between a passionate desire to punish him and at the same time a certainty that he would come begging for her forgiveness so she locked the door, but it did not work out as she had hoped. She heard him come and waited breathlessly but he did not knock, did not plead with her. After a moment she heard him walk away and sat on, tears of anger and self pity pricking at her eyes and thickening in her throat.

Chapter 25

The school was badly in need of its annual summer clean-up and Daniel had offered to paint the walls of the big classroom, which were not only filthy but also covered with crude caricatures of himself, insulting comments and graffiti of every imaginable kind which often made him laugh and which no boy would admit to even under the threat of the most dire punishment. He had made the offer to start on the cleaning partly to put off for as long as possible working with Elspeth at the Cheapside shop, which Mr Brown had suggested would carry him nicely through the summer, and partly because he could think more clearly when his hands were busy slapping on paint.

That extraordinary evening at Belgrave Square had given him a more sympathetic picture of the past but it had also presented him with a problem that he was finding unbearable as well as insoluble. He had tried to put it out of his mind by writing a scathing follow-up to his article on the failed water scheme with a graphic description of the miserable houses which lay within ten feet of a stagnant lake where dead cats and dogs were thrown and into which oozed a disgusting stream from a broken sewer, but, that written and sent off, the problem still remained and while he painted that afternoon he put it to himself plainly once again.

When his mother had parted from her lover – and he still found it difficult to see the young Everard Warrinder in the man he knew – she had been pregnant and had made a hasty marriage with John Hunter, and there lay the problem. Was he, Daniel, that child or wasn't he? Was the John Hunter who had loomed so large in the first six years of his life, who even after his death had still filled his childish mind as someone to love, admire and try to emulate, was he not his father after all? Had he simply adopted and cared for his wife's love-child?

If it was true then he must face the horrifying fact that Christine was his half-sister and he shuddered away from it as if their loving had become a kind of sacrilege. He had been brought up in a strict narrow religion. He had broken away from it but those early teachings were always there at the back of his mind. Incest, the unforgivable sin against God's law which produced its own terrible retribution. Memories that he had forgotten crowded in on him. In the grim circumstances in which some of the mill folk had been forced to live, whole families shut into one small room, it had happened often enough, fathers coupling with daughters, sisters with brothers. He had a shocking memory of a child with dribbling mouth, lolling head and empty eyes and remembered the whispers he was not meant to hear. He and Christine had loved one another in all innocence and had rejoiced in it but suppose, just suppose it bore fruit. The very thought sickened him. He must put it out of his mind, refuse to accept it, cling to a belief that he was the son of that good honest man John Hunter. He would go to her father as he had planned, tell him boldly that they loved one another, that Christine was of age and he could not prevent them from marrying, except that he knew she would be happier if he were to give his consent. Having made the decision at last, he acted on it the very next day, going not to Belgrave Square but to Everard Warrinder's chambers in the Temple.

The clerk who admitted him looked him up and down disparagingly. 'Mr Warrinder never sees anyone without an appointment,' he said disdainfully.

'I think he will see me. My name is Daniel Hunter.'

'Is that so?' The clerk frowned at him. 'Wait here,' he said and went off, returning almost at once with a slightly more condescending manner.

He showed Daniel into a gracious room where the long windows looked out on the Temple gardens, where the wall was stacked with massive leather-bound legal volumes, where the atmosphere was one of dignity, elegance and learning that made him feel woefully inadequate. He stiffened against it.

Everard rose from behind his desk. 'Come in, Daniel. I'm delighted to see you. So you've taken me at my word. Splendid. What can I do for you?'

'That isn't the reason why I have come.'

'No? Well, never mind. Sit down.' He indicated one of the handsome leather chairs. 'Make yourself comfortable. Would you care for some coffee?'

'No, thank you, and I prefer to stand.'

'As you wish.' Everard went back to his chair behind the desk while Daniel stood facing him, twisting his hat awkwardly between his hands.

There was little apparent sign of the emotional upset of that disturbing evening except that now and again a shadow of weariness seemed to cross the handsome face, but the charm was still there and the friendly interest. Daniel had to brace himself against it.

'If it is not my help in finding new literary outlets for your work, then what is it that has brought you here?' he said and leaned back with an easy smile.

'I am going to marry your daughter,' said Daniel bluntly.

'Are you indeed?' That brought him upright, the hands toying with the pen on his desk suddenly very still. 'Go on,' he said, 'when exactly did you come to this momentous decision?'

All the fine speeches that Daniel had rehearsed in private about forgetting class distinctions, about ignoring the disadvantages of one of them having money and the other almost none, fled out of his mind; instead he went blundering on, the words tumbling over one another. 'Christine and I love one another. I fought against it for two years because of the difference between us, because I felt I could never forgive you for what you had done in the past, but now it has become

504

different. We have come to a decision and whatever you say we are determined to go through with it even though I know it will be very hard for you and for Lady Clarissa to accept . . .'

'Not nearly so hard as it will be for Christine if I were to give my consent to this foolish marriage.'

That brought him up short. 'Why do you say that? Why is it foolish? Christine is not a child. She has thought long and hard about this, as I have done. We've come to our decision slowly but it's all the stronger for that.'

'And like the two idealistic idiots you are you feel you can no longer live without each other. Is that it?'

'Don't laugh at us,' said Daniel furiously.

'I am nowhere near laughing, believe me. Oh for heaven's sake, Daniel, don't stand there glowering at me. Sit down and let us consider this situation like two sensible adults.'

Daniel looked at him uncertainly. He had expected an angry explosion with which he was prepared to do battle, not this reasonable almost friendly approach. It was oddly disconcerting. After a moment he reluctantly pulled up a chair and sat down.

'I am serious about this and so is Christine,' he said belligerently.

'I am sure you are, very serious and so am I.' He leaned across the desk and Daniel was immediately aware of the trained legal mind which could so easily demolish all his arguments and he was suddenly very afraid.

'Have you taken serious thought,' said Everard quietly, 'about what this will actually mean for you both? You are intelligent, you have ability, you are prepared to work hard, but to achieve any success will necessarily be a slow process. To you that will not be hardship, you have grown up with it, you've learned to manage your resources, but think just for a moment what it will mean to Christine, who from childhood has never lacked for anything, who has a personal maid to run errands for her, who has never been obliged even to wash out a pocket handkerchief, who has not the smallest idea how to live on a restricted income or how to shop wisely or make a few shillings go a very long way, all of which she will have very painfully to learn. Even with the legacy left to her by her grandmother, even if I were prepared to give her the allowance I have given to Margaret, it would not amount to more than a fraction of what she spends each year on dresses and pretty trifles.'

'Christine will learn,' he said stubbornly, 'she wants to learn. We don't need any of the advantages or the riches you have given her.'

'It's not riches, Dan, it's the small things that make life tolerable that you mind the most. What will she do when a child comes along? What will you do when you are forced to abandon all your most cherished dreams and be prepared to undertake any kind of drudgery simply to put food into their mouths?'

Daniel had a sudden vision of his mother coming home from the mill and stitching, stitching far into the night simply to earn a little extra for him and his baby sister, her bright spirit, the joy she had taken in singing, very nearly destroyed. He remembered Prue Jessop spending every Sunday scrubbing and cleaning because there was never time during the working week. Could he bear to see Christine fighting a helpless battle against poverty, becoming old and worn in the relentless struggle to live, losing her bright spirit, her eager questioning mind, all the qualities that had endeared her to him? He wanted to reject the grim picture Everard had drawn, he wanted to deny the truth and could not.

'Why are you saying all this to me, why?' he said at last. 'What can you know about it, you who have never suffered any of these things?'

'Not personally perhaps, but in thirty years at the Bar I have seen a good deal of life's tragedies, the cruelties that an endless fight can inflict, men driven to despair and to unbelievable savagery because they must give up their hopes and ambitions if they are to live. I once defended a young woman who had drowned her two children because she could not endure to see them slowly starve to death.'

'Did you save her?'

'She did not hang for it but she was still imprisoned and I think she might have preferred to die. I would not like to see Christine suffer a fate like that.'

'She would not. I would work my fingers to the bone before she should suffer any ill.'

'Of course you would but it might not be enough. In cases such as that love flies out of the window and bitterness, regret, even hatred take its place. No, Daniel, I will never condemn Christine to such a life. I will do everything in my power to prevent her marrying you.'

'We don't need your consent,' he said fierily. 'We don't want your money or anything from you. We will make our own lives.'

'No, Daniel, no!' Everard got up, walked away restlessly and then came back to face him across the desk. 'There is something further against your marriage, something that has been in my mind for some time.'

Daniel got slowly to his feet, pushing back the chair. He had hoped he was wrong, that this moment would never come but now it had. He said, 'I know what you are going to say. When you abandoned my mother, she was pregnant, wasn't she, and it is possible, just possible, that I am that child. But there is no proof of it. I am John Hunter's son, he is part of me, I feel it, I have always known it. I owe nothing to you.'

'Feeling is not enough. The possibility is still there and it has haunted me. The woman who told me that Mary was pregnant took pleasure in taunting me. "You have a fine son," she said, "but you'll never have any pleasure from him." It could be true. I tried to find out more but could discover nothing and until life in its own unpredictable way brought us together there was no reason why I should.'

A feeling of sickness seemed to rise in Daniel's throat. He said with difficulty, 'When my mother came to plead with you . . . did she say nothing then?'

Everard turned away as if he found the memory of that time still too painful. 'We thought only of ourselves,' he said at last.

507

There was silence for a moment, then he shook it away from him and went on.

'There is more, Daniel, we must look at this from all angles. I have my enemies as you already know who have been working against me. I had hoped that the snake was scotched but what if it is only temporary? What if they should dig deeper? Do you want the finger pointed at Christine? Think what it could mean to her and to you. Is that what you want? Go away, Dan. Leave her. I still believe, have always believed, that her feeling for you is largely one of compassion, of tenderness, but not the love that should be the basis of marriage. I strongly opposed the friendship between you two. I think you know that. Your sister's trial has thrown us all together but now we are back to everyday life, I am sure she will see that I am right. Her first love was always Gareth and I am certain that deep within her that love is still there and with you gone from her she will realize how very important he is to her. If you will accept my help, I could make it easy for you.'

'Gareth!' Daniel repeated in a savage outburst of pain and jealousy. 'Dr Gareth Fraser, so eminently suitable, who neglected her till he thought he was losing her and now does all in his power to get her back. I'm not afraid of him and you can't buy me off, Mr Warrinder. I'm not to be got rid of so easily. I won't give Christine up, not for any reason, I swear I won't!'

'You feel like that now but when you are calmer, you will think again. You will realize that I'm right.'

'Never! This time you are mistaken. I love Christine and I'll marry her. I'll fight you every step of the way and I will win!' He brought his fist down on the desk so forcibly that everything jumped and a paperknife fell with a clatter to the floor. Then, unable to trust himself any further, he turned and ran out of the room.

A moment later the clerk came hurrying in looking disturbed. 'Are you all right, sir? I heard the crash and that young man went by me like a hurricane.'

'He lost his temper with me, Simmons. It takes the young like that sometimes. I'm pretty sure that when he comes to his senses, he will see reason. I won't see anyone else this morning and I'll be leaving soon.'

'Very good, Mr Warrinder. Are you off abroad for the holidays?'

'Paris perhaps, for a few weeks with my son. It depends on my wife.'

He sat for a while thinking how best to deal with the situation. In his judgement, after the first violent resentment had died down, Daniel would begin to realize the truth of what he had said. He hoped he was right. Tonight he must tackle Christine and guessed he would meet formidable opposition. He could expect no help from Clarissa. Relations were still strained between them and in any case there had always been a latent antagonism between mother and daughter. He knew that Christine had deliberately deceived him in letting him believe that he was right in assuming that there was no more than friendship between them and he blamed himself severely for permitting the situation to get out of hand. Christine had never been like Margaret. Time and again she had fought him. He must do everything in his power to protect her from what he believed to be a fatal mistake.

Daniel walked away from the Temple trembling with anger. He doesn't really believe that I am his son, he told himself, any more than I do, but because there is some doubt he will use it as a wedge to drive us apart and I won't let him do it, I won't!

But Christine, hearing it for the first time, would be shocked and distressed. He ought to warn her so that when her father spoke to her she would know how to answer him. He would go to her at once. He strode along the Strand, skirted St James's Park and found his way through back streets to Belgrave Square.

Barton was taking his luncheon with Mrs Gant so by chance it was Betsy on her way through the hall who opened the door to his loud knock. She knew who he was of course. The servants had all been enthralled by the trial and followed it avidly so she gave him a broad smile when he asked if he could see Miss Warrinder.

'Miss Christine is out, sir, she has gone to help Mr Gareth choose curtains for his new house. She won't be back till late this afternoon. Shall I tell her you called?'

'It doesn't matter.'

After the morning it was like a death knell to his hopes. Of course there was no reason why she shouldn't be helping Gareth. He was an old friend, God damn him! He seemed to hear her father say again, 'He was her first love,' and he could be horribly right. Jealousy burned through him but as he tramped back to Whitechapel, he calmed down, the anger slowly fading and he began to see their romantic dream in the bleak remorseless light of everyday.

'We'll be married in spite of you,' he had said boldly and meant it, but supposing they did, then where could he take her? To Paradise Alley with the sluttish street all gaping at her thinking the worst?

Most of his small savings had gone on the expenses of the trial. He had nothing but the wage which Mr Brown generously continued to pay during the summer months. It was scarcely enough for one, let alone two. She would offer to pay for everything and the thought was bitter as gall. There was the half promise of work in the north which had tempted him but where could they live? At best for a week or two in Sam and Prue Jessop's tiny back room, at worst in some wretched lodging house which he could face alone but the very thought of Christine in such a place was unthinkable.

All the rest of the day and through most of the night he battled with it knowing that Everard Warrinder had been right. They had been living in some cloud-cuckoo-land and the reality was bitter.

Two years ago he had tramped into London filled with high ambitions to become a leader like John Hunter, to win his way through to becoming the voice of the people and he had gone some small way towards it. Love, marriage, had never entered

510

into it. He knew too well that it could be a trap from which a poor man could never extricate himself and now it had happened to him. He had fallen in love, but not sensibly, not with a working girl like Elspeth, but with someone far out of his reach, who had spoiled all other girls for him and for a dazzling breathtaking moment he had believed the dream could become reality. His mind wrestled with it, backwards and forwards, her father's arguments fighting with his own hopes and always hanging over it the doubt, the frightening doubt about their relationship. Even if they told themselves it didn't exist, even if they shut their eyes to it, it would still be there gnawing away at them. Her father was right. One could face up to life's big disasters, it was the small nagging things that destroyed confidence, that broke the spirit and turned love and trust to rancour and hatred.

'Go away, Dan, leave her,' her father had said, but he didn't know how much they had shared, the joy, the laughter, the overwhelming moment that had brought them together, the sense of comradeship, even the quarrels. He could not just walk out on her without trying to make her understand.

The next morning he went back to the school. He might as well finish what he had begun. He painted steadily all the morning, still uncertain whether to write or go to Belgrave Square and risk having the door shut in his face. He was on top of the ladder leaning forward at a precarious angle when the decision was taken out of his hands. The door was flung open with a crash and Christine was there, panting a little as if she had been running, her bonnet pushed back, her hair blown about by the wind.

'It's all lies, isn't it? What Papa told me? It's all lies,' she said as if the words had been on her lips all the way there and now she could no longer hold them back.

'Wait a moment, I'm coming down and shut that door. The wind is blowing everything over.'

She obediently pushed the door to as he climbed slowly down, pot of paint in one hand, brush in the other. He put them down carefully.

'How did you know I was here?'

'Ma Taylor told me,' she said impatiently. 'What does that matter? I had to talk to you. Oh Dan, I can't tell you how awful it was. Papa told me that you had been to see him and we had a dreadful quarrel over it.'

She would have put her arms around him but he waved her back.

'Better not touch me. I'm covered with wet paint.'

He pulled out one of the benches that had been stacked with the desks in the middle of the room.

'Now come and sit down and tell me what happened after you came back from choosing Gareth's curtains for him.'

'How did you know about that?'

'Your maid told me when I called.'

'I had to go with him,' she said defensively. 'He was in such a terrible muddle and he has no one to help him, no mother or sister, and Uncle David is not very much interested in things like that nowadays.'

'You don't need to make excuses. I understand. Go on.'

'Well, it was after dinner. Papa called me into his study. He told me all about you coming to see him and then he went on and on about how wretchedly poor we would be and what was worse that I could become like a millstone round your neck holding you back from what you really wanted to do and in time you'd hate me for it and then he went on to say something quite beastly. He said when a young woman marries someone in a different social class, she was always pulled down to his level and I was so sick and so angry because it is not like that with us and I told him I didn't believe any of it and in any case it makes absolutely no difference to how we feel about each other. It doesn't, does it?'

'It could,' he said soberly. 'What happened then?'

She paused and then went on more quietly.

'He told me then about your mother being pregnant and that you could be my half-brother, like Harry and Kate. It's not true, is it? He's only saying that to keep us apart, isn't he?'

'No, I don't think so, Christine. I think it has always been

512

in his mind and that is why all along he has tried to keep us apart. He has, hasn't he?'

'If it is really true, why didn't he tell me before?'

'It wouldn't have been easy for him, would it? And he has never really believed you were serious.'

She was staring at him, her eyes widening in a kind of horror. 'I don't believe it,' she whispered. 'I don't want to believe it.'

'Neither do I but I'm beginning to think that we must.'

'No,' she said vehemently. 'No, it's not true. I would have known if it were. We were so happy that day. I didn't imagine that, did I? Everything was right between us, wasn't it? You felt it too. Well, can't we go on from there? Can't we simply shut it out of our minds, forget it?'

Guilty lovers must have said that time and time again.

He took both her hands in his, drawing her towards him.

'No, Christine, we can't. I realize that now. I wish to God we could. I have thought and thought about this but the doubt will always be there in our minds and in the end it could destroy us.'

She stared at him and then pulled her hands away. 'I see it all now. I understand. You're using it as an excuse just as Papa has done. You're afraid that I'll be a drag on you, holding you back from what you really want to do, all those grand notions of yours – they mean so much more to you than I have ever done . . .'

'No, Christine, no, you're wrong. I've worried myself sick because I can give you so little, no real home, none of the things you should have, that you have grown up with. Your father made me see myself for what I am, a selfish brute dragging you down to my level, spoiling your life. Gareth was your first love, he told me that, and he is still there, isn't he? He's still important to you.'

'Leave Gareth out of this,' she said fiercely. 'You didn't think like this when we made love together. I thought then I'd found something real, something precious that would last for ever, but it wasn't like that for you, was it?' Her voice choked for a moment but she went on bravely. 'Supposing I were to be pregnant?'

'Oh my God, you're not, are you?'

She saw the look of horror on his face and could have laughed if she had not felt so desperately unhappy.

'I don't know. I could be. That frightens you, doesn't it? Don't worry. I'll never come begging to you. Gareth was right. He told me I'd find out one day that you didn't really need me, that you were self-sufficient, you would go ahead pursuing your own way even if it hurt me like hell. I wanted to prove him wrong, I thought I had, but he knows you better than I do.'

She was crying now, angry tears, that she wiped away impatiently.

He said, 'No, Christine darling, you mustn't think like that. I never dreamed for one moment that such a thing could come between us tearing us apart.'

'But you're not sorry, are you, not really sorry, not in your inmost heart. It's such a wonderful excuse, isn't it? Nobody could blame you for it. Oh dear God, why did it have to happen like this? I don't know how I can bear it. I don't know how I can go on living . . .' and she turned, running blindly away from him towards the door, colliding with Elspeth who was just coming in.

'Christine!' he said and went after her. She was in the mood to do anything, dash into the road, throw herself under a passing vehicle. Elspeth grabbed at him as he passed her and he flung her off. 'Let me go, damn you!' But by now Christine had reached the gate and was out in the street holding up her hand to a passing cab, hurling herself into it. He stared after it with a feeling of utter despair and then went slowly back into the room.

'Run out on you, has she?' remarked Elspeth sweetly. 'Well, I'm not surprised. I always knew no good could come of it.'

Daniel pushed the bench back to its place in the stack and took up his brush before he could trust himself to speak.

'What are you doing here?'

'I'm free this afternoon so I thought I'd come and see how you were getting on and Papa asked me to tell you that the plans have come for the extension to the school and he'd like to discuss them with you tonight over supper.'

'Tell him I'll come later. I'd like to finish this today if I could.'

She had come up beside him, putting a hand on his arm, her voice softening. 'There's no need to work so hard, Dan. There's plenty of time.'

'There's every need,' he said moving away from her. 'Your father is paying me and I like to fulfil my obligations.'

'Well, at least come and eat with us. We hardly see anything of you nowadays. Mamma has remarked on it.'

'It's kind of your mother to think of me but I'd rather not. I'll come along later.'

'I suppose we're not good enough for you, that's the real truth, isn't it?' said Elspeth tartly. 'You'd far rather sup with that Miss Warrinder up in that attic of yours. Love's young dream, I suppose. What else do you do up there? Can't you see what a fool you're making of yourself, running around after her like a little dog, doing all she says while she carries on with her own life, squired around by some of her rich friends and then running down here to her common working-class lover. She ought to be ashamed of herself. I wonder what her Papa has to say about it . . . if he knows!'

'Shut up,' said Daniel. 'It's none of your business.'

'You can't shut me up like that. It *is* my business if it affects all my father has done for you. Someone has to try and make you see sense. I thought all this trouble with your sister would have made a difference but it hasn't, has it? Don't think for one minute that she'll marry you. That sort are far too clever for that. She'll have her fun and then leave you high and dry . . . there are names for girls like her, you know, for all her high and mighty ways . . .'

But she had gone too far. Goaded beyond bearing Daniel dropped his brush, swung round and slapped her across the face. 'Don't dare to speak of her like that!'

515

'I shall speak any way I like,' Elspeth gasped, one hand flying to her scarlet cheek.

'Not to me, you won't. Now get out of here, get out! Can't you see when you're not wanted?' and he took her by the shoulders and pushed her towards the door so roughly that she stumbled, falling against the stack of benches.

She glared at him furiously as she picked herself up, then deliberately kicked over the pot of paint and stalked to the door.

He stood looking down at the spilled paint that would take him at least another hour to clean up. No doubt she would go complaining to her father and he would find it hard to find excuses for his behaviour. Mr Brown had been good to him. He could hardly explain how she had goaded him into it.

It was then that his resolution began to harden and he knew the decision had to be taken. He would have to leave London, put all this behind him, try to make a fresh start. To remain within reach of Christine and yet never to see her would be an impossibility. There was too much against them. He could not fight it any longer. He would have to try and make Mr Brown understand and then pack up. He had little enough, God knows, but he had made a few useful connections through the Working Men's Association. He could not afford to toss aside the recommendations they could give him if he were to stand on his own feet and not sponge on the generosity of Sam Jessop . . . For a moment he stood still, too sick at heart to move, then slowly he began to pull himself together. There was Kate to think of. He must see her, find out how she was placed, then he must write to Sam. He found some old rags and began to clear up the spilled paint.

It was a relief that evening to find that Elspeth had not gone complaining to her father after all and he was spared having to think up lame excuses, but all the same it was very difficult to make Mr Brown understand why he was willing to throw up a safe job and return to the north.

516

'You are giving it up just when you will be enjoying the benefits of all the hard work you have put in during the last two years,' said Mr Brown, surprised and not a little hurt. He had liked Dan and felt he had done a good deal for him. 'With the school enlarged, more pupils coming in and another teacher working under you, you would be in a far better position. Think again, I beg of you, Dan, don't toss aside what could be the making of you for some wrongheaded radical ideals.'

What could he say? That he had fallen in love with Everard Warrinder's daughter who was also his half-sister so that his only hope was to go away where he could not see or hear of her if he were to remain sane? He could see the shock and horror grow on Mr Brown's honest face if he did.

Instead he talked a great deal about teaching not being his first aim but only a stop gap and that now he had been successful in having articles accepted in a major newspaper he wanted to return to the industrial north where workers still lived in appalling conditions that could provide good fuel for his pen.

'And what do you hope to achieve by that?' asked Mr Brown, who had no trust in such windy ideals.

'I don't know yet but I can speak at meetings, I can do something towards waking up the social conscience.'

And end up like your father like as not, thought Mr Brown gloomily. 'And how are you going to live?' he went on practically. 'Sam Jessop is a good fellow but has always been far too kind-hearted for his own good. He and Prue haven't much behind them.'

'Do you imagine I don't know that? All I would ask from them is a bed for a night or two till I find my feet. Then I shall make my own way.'

Mr Brown shook his head over his obstinacy but now Daniel had made up his mind he wanted to get away as soon as possible. He was tormented with anxiety about Christine and sorely tempted to go to Belgrave Square and demand to see her except that it would do no good, only prolong the agony, and she was not alone. She had her father, she had Gareth.

517

On the morning he went to see Kate he ran into George Westcott who was just leaving her new lodging in Gower Street.

'What was he doing here?' he asked her as he went in. 'Has he become one of your admirers? He's such a solid worthy lawyer that he has never struck me as a theatre-goer.'

'You'd be surprised. He's very intelligent and very knowledgeable about plays,' she said defensively, 'but he called this morning for another reason.' She gave him a quick look. 'I hope you won't be angry with me, Dan.'

'Why on earth should I be angry? What's all the mystery? He hasn't made you a proposition, has he, or asked you to marry him?'

She laughed. 'Good heavens, no. Can you imagine it? He's a born bachelor. He came to tell me that Mr Warrinder would like to settle an allowance on me, so much each month, which he will take care of for me.'

His first reaction was one of anger. Did Warrinder believe him incapable of looking after his own sister? 'What did you say?'

'I refused at first but Mr Westcott went on to say that after all Mr Warrinder had done for me, it would be like throwing his generosity back in his face, that he knew the acting profession was a precarious one and it could help when times were difficult so I said I would think about it.'

It was true enough and in one way it was a relief. He had been worrying about leaving his sister unprovided for but with George Westcott looking after her affairs the burden of responsibility was lifted a little.

'I've never accepted anything from anyone before,' she went on, 'but this is different. It's hard to reject kindness so generously offered.'

'It's not kindness,' he said harshly, 'it's only what he should do. Mother fought and died horribly to keep the two of us alive. He owes it to her to look after you now.'

'Don't you think you're being a little unkind?'

'I don't feel very kindly disposed towards Everard Warrinder at the moment.'

'You and Christine?'

'Yes.' He was tempted to pour out the whole wretched story and then held back. Why should he burden her with it?

'You think I should refuse this offer, don't you, Dan?'

'No, I don't. Accept it. Why not? In one way I'm glad of it for you as I have to leave London very soon,' and he began to tell her about going back to the north and what he planned to do there but said nothing about Christine. She didn't know everything that had gone on between them but she had guessed a good deal and she grieved for him.

'When do you go?'

'Very soon now that I've settled everything.'

On his way back he called at the Cheapside shop to speak to Dickie. The boy was working there regularly now and was proud of his new status. He was thirteen and had shot up in the last year but Daniel was still his hero and he was deeply distressed that he was going away.

'Come and see me tonight,' he said to the boy. 'You can choose one of my books as a memento if you like.'

'Oh yes please. May I bring Penny?'

'If you wish.'

The little dog still had a starveling look despite good feeding and shadowed his master everywhere.

Outside the shop Daniel unexpectedly bumped into Will Somers, looking exceptionally prosperous and well dressed. He had not seen him since before the trial and their friendship had never recovered from the arguments that had followed the shooting incident at the election.

'Hallo, stranger,' said Will. 'I hear you're deserting us, going back to your old haunts. Bit of a come-down, isn't it?'

'I don't happen to think so,' said Daniel. 'Things are stagnating down here. Everyone is too wrapped up in themselves, too smug, too complacent, but up there are still some live wires. I hope to have plenty of first-hand experience for my newspaper articles.'

'You're not the only one who has been getting into print,'

said Will. 'I've been writing a few columns for the *Daily News* myself, spicy items, you know, destined to make some of those overfed tabbycats in the government and the law feel the pricks.'

'What the hell do you mean by that?'

'Well, you have to possess a nose for it of course and I flatter myself I have just that and it works, old boy, by God how it works! An Editor will pay more for items like that than for three columns about the stinking water sewers that seem to occupy your pen.'

Daniel was staring at him. He said slowly, 'It was you who wrote that filthy piece of scandal about Kate's trial, wasn't it?'

'Didn't write it actually, old boy, just dropped a few little hints and one of those journalistic johnnies was on to it like a flash and wrote it up. Made a damned good job of it too, didn't he? Must have made Everard Warrinder lose that "holier than thou" look of his all right. How's the daughter, by the way? Still in the running is she or has her Papa put his foot down on it?'

'By God,' exploded Dan, 'it was you all this time, wasn't it, poking your dirty fingers into things that don't concern you. I could kill you for that,' and he grabbed hold of Will by the shoulders and shook him savagely.

'Here, look out,' cried Will Somers, trying to pull himself out of Daniel's grasp. 'What have I done? It's not my fault if the pretty little bitch has chucked you over. She's probably got other fish to fry.'

'Don't you dare to speak of her like that!' said Dan furiously.

'I'll speak how I damned well please. Anyone with half an eye could see what she was after. Had you properly on the run, didn't she? You were being nicely fooled, my boy, didn't you realize?'

'Oh I realized it all right and so will you,' said Daniel, so infuriated by Will's taunts that he was lost to all good reason.

He hit Will so hard that he fell back against a tall stone wall and suddenly, without quite knowing how it came about, the two of them were fighting in grim earnest, there in the middle of the crowded street, swaying backwards and forwards, with passers-by either gaping at them or quickly hurrying by. But it couldn't continue. Someone had already run for a policeman and by the time he arrived, Will had collapsed up against a lamp post, blood streaming down his face, only half conscious, while Daniel stood glowering down at him. Dickie had come running out of the shop and was staring in horror with Phil and Elspeth close behind him.

When the Constable arrived to back up his subordinate, Will had been hauled to his feet and the policeman with the help of a passer-by had firm hold of Daniel. They were both marched off to the police station near Newgate where Will received rough medical treatment for a bruised mouth, a split eyebrow and a lump on the head while Daniel was charged with assault.

'You'll come up before the Bench tomorrow, my lad, and you'll be lucky to escape with a fine,' said the Constable heavily.

'I can't pay any fine,' muttered Dan.

'Then it will be a month or so in the lock-up. That'll soon cool you down.'

'Got a solicitor, have you?' said the policeman with rough kindness, locking him into one of the cells. 'He might get you off.'

Dickie, who had sneaked after them and was listening with all ears, was wondering how he could help his idol. He didn't think Mr Brown could do much but there was Miss Christine. She had always been ready to do anything for Daniel and he knew all about where she lived because he'd gone there once simply to gape at the great house where Daniel went in and out so freely. He dodged out of the station and considered how he could get there as quickly as possible and then did what all the street boys did with the utmost danger to life and limb. He waited for a suitable vehicle and then as the carriage went on its stately way he ran behind it till he could jump on to the cross bar, clinging agile as a monkey. It took him close to Piccadilly and from there he ran all the way to Belgrave Square, hammered at the door and when Barton opened it demanded to see Miss Christine.

'Certainly not,' said the scandalised butler. 'Be off with you, boy, at once.'

'No, I'm not going, not till I've seen Miss Christine. You go and tell her. It's important. It's about Daniel.'

'I don't care what it's about. Now you be off, I tell you, coming to the front door indeed! I never saw such impudence.'

'I won't go. You'll have to throw me out first,' said Dickie, raising his voice and pushing his way across the threshold.

Then a door suddenly opened and he nearly fell backwards for there was the great man himself saying 'What on earth is all this racket, Barton? We can't hear ourselves speak.'

'It's this impudent boy, sir . . . '

'It's because of Daniel,' said Dickie recovering his breath. 'He's in terrible trouble.'

'Daniel?'

'They're going to send him to prison and he didn't do nothing, not really, he just knocked someone down . . . and the Bobbie grabbed him and took him off . . . '

'You'd better come in,' said Everard frowning. 'It's all right, Barton, I'll see to this. Come along, boy, don't be frightened. What's your name?'

'Dickie, sir,' he said in a tiny voice and followed Everard gingerly into the study.

'I don't know what's going on, George, but Daniel Hunter seems to have got himself into trouble with the police. Now, Dickie, you had better tell us as clearly as you can what happened,' said Everard kindly enough.

The boy stared from him to George Westcott, who had called in on Everard that day to report on his interview with Kate.

'Dan had just gone out of Mr Brown's shop,' he began hesitantly and then poured out his story rather incoherently but quite enough for his listeners to grasp that the quarrel had been about that infamous article in the *Daily News*.

'What can we do about it, George?' said Everard thoughtfully when Dickie had stammered to an end.

'Well, I could go down there now, offer bail for him so that he needn't spend the night in a cell and then pay his fine in court tomorrow. I don't think it is likely to go any further. It's not a very serious offence. He hasn't killed anyone.'

'Fortunately,' said Everard drily. 'We'd better do that then. Wait outside in the hall, Dickie, and then this gentleman will go with you and we'll rescue Daniel from the pretty pickle he seems to have got himself into.'

So Dickie waited in the hall and presently George Westcott came out, Barton called a cab and they set off together.

In the meantime Daniel had been shut into the cell and was feeling extremely sorry for himself. It was too absurd to have put himself in danger of going to prison when he was on the point of going away, and all because he'd lost his temper with that rat Will Somers. He should not have let his spiteful jibes catch him on the raw. He ought to have learnt sense by this time.

It was early evening by now and he was feeling tired, sore and very hungry when the door was unlocked. The Constable said, 'There's a gentleman to see you. Come on, look slippy,' and he was led back into the charge room to find George Westcott waiting for him.

'How did you get here?' he asked a trifle ungraciously.

'Your faithful follower, Dickie I believe he calls himself, came to Belgrave Square and demanded that Mr Warrinder should do something about it.'

'Dickie did?'

'Yes, with great determination too. You obviously inspire hero worship,' said George drily. 'I have gone bail for you so you're free to go but you'll have to turn up in court tomorrow. I'll meet you there and pay the fine.' He saw the obstinate look on Daniel's face and went on before he could protest. 'Now don't get up on your high horse. Accept Mr Warrinder's generosity and be grateful for it. There is something else too.' He took a folded paper from an inner pocket. 'I have been

523

instructed to give you this draft on Mr Warrinder's bank. You will no doubt find it of use for the future.'

Daniel took it and looked down at it. The sum was considerable. It would keep him in modest comfort for a year at least. Very slowly he tore it in half and held it out.

'Tell him I'm grateful for payment of the fine. I would have been hard put to it to find the money in a few days but I don't want anything further from him.'

'He will be sorry. He means well, you know. He is concerned for you.'

'Perhaps.' He paused and then went on a little hesitantly. 'When I saw my sister, she told me of your visit. You will spare a thought for her occasionally, won't you?'

'It will be a pleasure,' he said, a smile giving a warmth to the rather solemn features. 'I understand you're leaving London so I'll take the opportunity of wishing you good fortune.'

'Thank you.'

'I'll see you in court tomorrow,' he said, nodded to the Constable and left, leaving Daniel grateful and just a shade resentful because of it.

The policeman let him go with a surly growl. 'Some of us have all the luck. Mind you turn up tomorrow, ten o'clock sharp and don't get into any more street fights. You may not get off so lightly next time.'

Outside, Dickie was waiting. 'Is it all right?' he asked.

'Yes, thanks to you. Now you run along to the shop and come and see me afterwards.'

'I wish you weren't going,' said the boy wistfully.

'So do I sometimes. Cut along now or Miss Elspeth will be angry with you.'

'Oh her! I'm not frightened of her.'

'Then you ought to be. Off you go now.'

Dickie was just one more of the many things he was going to miss in the months ahead.

PART FIVE

The Reckoning

1853–1854

Chapter 26

Ever since Christine had come back from the meeting with Daniel at the school she had shut herself into her room away from everyone. For a day she even locked her door against Betsy, saying all she wanted was to be left alone and refusing all offers of food.

'Go away,' she said to her mother when, exasperated, Clarissa remonstrated with her through the closed door. 'I'm not ill, I don't want Dr Murphy and I don't want to talk to anyone – can't you understand that?'

It was something her mother found difficult to accept but Christine had always been an impossible child, from the very beginning, so she shrugged her shoulders. Left alone for a few hours she would probably come to her senses.

'It's so utterly absurd shutting herself up like that,' she complained to her husband in the evening. 'You had better go and talk to her. You seem to have more influence with her than I have. I know she has been upset by all this wretched business. God knows we all have. Sometimes I hardly know how to face it. Wherever I go I seem to feel people's eyes on me, watching me, wondering how I feel and what I think about it. It's worrying enough without Christine choosing to behave in such a ridiculous manner. Has she quarrelled with Gareth? Only the other day she spent time with him choosing furnishings for the new house. Any other girl would be happily planning for their future.'

'This has nothing to do with Gareth.'

'You seem very certain about that.' She looked at him with

a sudden unpleasant suspicion. 'Surely it has nothing to do with that wretched young man, Daniel Hunter. It couldn't have. He's so totally unsuitable, the very idea is ludicrous. If only you had never taken up the case of that sister of his, none of this would have happened. We could have gone on with our lives untouched by the past.'

'Could we? Sometimes I have wondered.' He felt as if a wall of glass had risen up between him and Clarissa. They could see each other quite clearly but could no longer communicate. 'It is useless to go over all that again,' he said wearily. 'It happened, it is over and we must learn to live with it.'

'But we will never be able to go back to what we were before, never!'

'That's for you to decide, Clarissa. As for Christine I am afraid that it is my judgement that has been at fault and I bitterly regret it. You may as well know that Daniel Hunter came to me a day or so ago asking for permission to marry Christine.'

'He did what!' Clarissa was shocked. 'I can't believe it. I hope you told him just what you thought of his impudence.'

'I certainly told him that I would not give my consent to their marriage under any circumstances but I have begun to think Christine is more deeply involved with him than I had believed.'

To Clarissa the very idea seemed unimaginable. 'Surely she cannot have been so foolish. It's all because of that clinic giving her all the wrong ideas. I can't think why you ever allowed her to go there.'

'It's too late to regret that now. Love is no respecter of persons, my dear. Young women have fallen in love with unsuitable partners from the beginning of time. I'll go up and see if Christine will let me talk to her.'

But he was no more successful than her mother had been. When he knocked on her door, saying gently, 'Let me in, my dear. Can't we talk together about this sensibly?' all she said was, 'What is there to talk about? It is your fault, all of it, I've nothing to say to you.'

She walked up and down her room hour after hour with the wretched feeling that her whole life had been turned upside down and she could not yet reconcile herself to it. It seemed to her that all these months, nearly two years now, she had thought, lived, dreamed of nothing but Daniel, going through resentment, hurt pride, comradeship, shared laughter and finally through to love, cutting through the trauma of the past into the hopeful present, full of joy. She had spent hours planning their life together and now he had rejected her. He had listened to her father's arguments, let himself be convinced, his love not strong enough to carry them through all the obstacles. That was what was so unbearable. The humiliation, the bitter disappointment of that rejection, sliced through her. It was only very gradually that the realization of that other damning reason against their marriage began to swim to the surface and with it came panic and a devastating feeling of betrayal. Why had her father not warned her? Why had he not told her of the taboo on their love, except of course that he had never even dreamed of such a possibility, any link between the daughter of Everard Warrinder and the beggarly teacher in an East End ragged school being quite unthinkable.

When they had made love it had never once occurred to her that she might become pregnant. Now it did and she was panic-stricken. Her monthly period was well overdue but she had not been concerned. It could sometimes be variable. Now suddenly it had a frightening significance. Incest – that forbidden word never mentioned in polite circles – had a terrifying sound, unheard of, undreamed of, belonging to history and now suddenly very close. Byron had slept with his sister, they had said, and had to flee from England under a frightful shadow of guilt. She remembered her governess's shocked face when she had innocently asked her one day what it meant.

It couldn't possibly happen to her, could it? How could she tell Clarissa or even her father about the hours they had spent so joyously together? There had been one or two cases among young girls of her acquaintance who had been spirited away abroad on the plea of ill-health or foreign travel and had returned nine months or a year later while whispers went from one to the other and somewhere a baby was put out to be fostered or more conveniently died.

It was then that the idea began to grow in her mind. She must go away, right away, till she was sure, till she had somehow learned to live with the possibility. But where? If she fled to Bramber, her grandfather would be full of kindly questions. It would not be fair to burden Margaret, who was expecting her second child and worried to death by the threat of war and Freddie's involvement. Then she thought of Glenmuir. As far as she knew, Uncle Francis was still abroad. Letters had reached them from Rome and Florence and Venice but the household would still be there. She knew the housekeeper, she would be made welcome, and far away from everyone she could make plans, learn to face whatever the future had in store for her.

The decision having been made, she had to plan the journey and think how to escape from the house without anyone knowing where she had gone and asking a lot of stupid questions. She had travelled to Glenmuir many times before but it had been arranged by her father. The train to Edinburgh, an overnight stop, then coach to Fort William where her Uncle Francis had always met them for the final few miles to the West Coast. She had always loved the castle on its rocky headland, looking across to Mull and Iona with the sharp salt breeze and the wild waves that at high tide surged up to the very walls.

Fortunately she had money, having drawn on her own account some days before and then never used it. She hoped it would be sufficient. She remembered that the express left at eight o'clock on its day-long journey. She pulled out a large carpet bag from the back of the wardrobe and began to pack it with necessities, changes of underwear, a thick tweed skirt and some blouses. She could not take too much since she would have to carry the bag herself. She wondered whether to tell Betsy what she intended and then decided against it. There would be all kinds of questions asked when it was found that she had gone and it was not fair to involve the girl in it. By six o'clock that evening everything was ready except for last-minute additions and for the first time in that week she felt hungry. When Betsy knocked and asked if she could come in and help her dress for the evening, she said she still did not want to come downstairs but she could bring her something to eat on a tray. A wave of thankfulness swept through the whole household. It would seem that Miss Christine had at last come to herself again. Mrs Gant took great pains to prepare a tray of delicious food guaranteed to tempt the most capricious appetite and her father heaved a sigh of relief and made sure that a glass of her favourite white wine, chilled but not too sweet, was added to the tray.

'I'll go up later and have a word with her,' he said to Clarissa. 'If you agree, my dear, I'm thinking of a trip to Paris. We could leave Christine with Harry for a few weeks. It will do her good to be away for a time and they always get on well together.'

However when he went up to her room later he was met by Betsy.

'Miss Christine told me to tell you, sir, that she feels very tired and has already gone to bed.'

'Very well. Tell her I'll see her in the morning.'

It was five o'clock and still dark when Christine stole quietly down the stairs carrying the carpet bag, warmly cloaked because railway carriages could be draughty and were unheated. No one was about so early. She slowly drew back the well-oiled bolts and opened the front door. Outside the chill of an early mist touched her face with clammy fingers. She went slowly down the steps into the growing light. A cab had stopped a few doors up the square delivering an early traveller. She waved to the cab and he came towards her. She lifted in her bag and climbed into the carriage, urging him to hurry. As he whipped up his horse she looked back fearfully but the house was still very quiet and she sighed with relief.

It was not until after eight o'clock that her absence was discovered. Betsy knocked as usual and receiving no answer tried the door and found it unlocked. She knew at once that the room was empty. The bed had been neatly made but the wardrobe door was wide open, one or two discarded gowns were lying across a chair and essential items had vanished from the dressing table. She took an anxious look around her and then ran down the stairs to where Barton was serving breakfast to his master in the morning room.

'Miss Christine's gone, sir,' she said breathlessly.

'Gone? What do you mean, girl? She may simply have decided to take an early morning walk.'

'Oh no, sir, I think she must have packed a bag. Some of her gowns are missing and all her toilet articles.'

'Are you sure? I'd better come and see for myself.'

He put down his napkin and went quickly up the stairs but it was only too obvious that Betsy was right. Christine had fled out of the house taking very little with her and leaving no indication as to where she had gone. The servants were closely questioned but no one had seen anything of her until Annie, her face and hands smudged with black from cleaning the kitchen stove, muttered something under her breath.

'What's that?' said Mrs Gant sharply. 'Speak up, girl. Mr Warrinder won't eat you.'

'I saw her when I were sweeping down the area steps,' she whispered. 'She come through the front door with that big bag.'

'Was she alone or did she meet someone?' asked Everard, trying to control his anxiety.

'Oh no, sir, but there were a cab just two or three doors away and she waved to him. When he come along, she got in.'

'Did you hear what she said to the driver?'

Annie thought hard. She had been greatly intrigued and had come part way up the area steps to watch and wonder.

'Somethin' about a station,' she ventured at last.

'I see. Thank you, Annie.'

The girl went bright scarlet at being thanked by the god-like

532

master whom she hardly ever saw and Mrs Gant said sharply, 'Don't just stand there, girl, get back to your work and don't you tell nobody about Miss Christine, do you hear, not one word. What happens here is our business and don't concern nobody else in the square.'

Everard's first thought was that she had defied him and fled with Daniel and must be brought back at once before anything worse happened. He knew from George Westcott that Daniel was heading back to the people he had lived with as a boy. It was a forlorn hope but he took the carriage to Euston Station and realized at once that to hunt for a couple among the teeming crowd of men, women, children, luggage and dogs was worse than useless, so he ordered his driver to take him to Mr Brown's shop in Cheapside, was fortunate enough to find him there and could make a cautious enquiry.

'I'm afraid you're too late, Mr Warrinder. Daniel went off yesterday and sorry I was to see him go. He could have had a good safe job down here but you know what young men are, always restless and full of grand notions. I only hope that he won't regret it. I could give you his address though I doubt if he will be there long. Elspeth, write down Sam Jessop's direction for Mr Warrinder.'

He took it without much hope. Daniel had obviously travelled alone but it was still possible that in a moment of madness Christine had decided to follow him.

He returned home to find Clarissa torn between anxiety and a very real anger at her daughter's wilful disregard of their feelings, and he told her what had happened and what he feared.

'I could go up there myself or I could ask the police to telegraph and it's just possible they could locate her as she comes off the train but I don't want to do that. It will cause too much talk. She is our daughter not a criminal.'

'We don't even know that she has followed him,' said Clarissa. 'Not even Christine could be so wantonly foolish. She could have gone to Bramber. You know how fond she is of your father – or even to Margaret. Surely we can wait for a few hours. Christine is very fond of you, Everard. I cannot really believe she would do anything deliberately to hurt you.'

'I'm afraid she is not very fond of me just now. There is Gareth too. He must be told but not yet. We'll wait a little and hope she recovers her senses. I trusted Daniel and I still don't want to think badly of him. There has to be some other reason that has driven her away, there has to be.'

At least she had taken clothes and money with her which must surely mean that she didn't contemplate throwing herself in the nearest river but that was poor comfort and did nothing to still his anxiety.

In the meantime Christine was discovering that undertaking a long train journey to the wilds of Scotland could be a daunting experience. To start with, after she had bought her ticket, which cost a great deal more than she had expected, it was only just after six. There were still two hours to be got through in the dingy waiting room where people came and went all the time and several dubious-looking passengers stared curiously at the unusual sight of a good-looking young woman in an expensive fur-collared cape who was obviously travelling alone. She longed for a hot drink but the one trolley dispensing tea from an urn had a long queue and she didn't dare to abandon her luggage so she sat huddled into a corner, nervously watching the door in case her flight had already been discovered and her father had come chasing after her.

Installed in a first-class carriage her troubles were far from over. Other passengers had thought to provide themselves with a food basket and by midday she was nearly fainting with hunger and thirst. At one or two of the infrequent stops there were wagons selling food and drink but she did not have the courage to venture among the wild scramble of passengers all fighting to buy before the train pulled out again. It was not till York that an elderly passenger took pity on her and asked if he could fetch her anything. He came back with a mug of tea, weak but hot, and a cheese sandwich so dry that only extreme hunger forced her to eat her way through it. Now and then the train went roaring through tunnels which covered her in black smuts if she wasn't quick enough to pull up the window and there was an inexplicable stop of three hours somewhere near the border. Outside the windows on either side stretched hills, purple and brown as the evening began to draw in, beautiful but looking to her tired eyes like the middle of nowhere. People got out and walked up and down the line speculating about breakdowns and that it might be necessary to continue the journey by road so that her heart sank, and then thankfully the guard was shouting 'All aboard!' and slowly the engine began to pull out and gather speed. But it did mean that they did not reach Edinburgh till near midnight and she took a cab to the Waverley, the only hotel she knew. The receptionist on duty at this late hour looked warily at this forlorn young woman trailing a large carpet bag, her face still grubby from the smuts she had tried to wipe away, and asking for food and a room.

'It's verra late and the kitchens have closed down,' he said unhelpfully. 'Would you be wanting the room just for the one night?'

'Yes,' she said wearily. 'I have to go on to Fort William.'

'That's no' so easy, Miss. The coach leaves from the Canongate very early and if ye've no place booked, I'm afraid ye'll have a day's wait for another.'

That would mean a further day and night at the hotel and she had a dreadful feeling that the money she had left would not cover it.

'But I have to reach Glenmuir,' she said at last rather desperately, 'it's very important.'

'Glenmuir?' he repeated, giving her a sharp look. 'Would that be the castle?'

'Yes, of course. The Earl is my uncle.'

'Is he now? Why didna you say so before? His lordship is staying here, has been for a couple of days. He's away just now, supping with friends. Would I be telling him you are here when he comes in?'

She had believed him to be still abroad and didn't know

whether she was glad or sorry, but it would at least save her from the ignominy of not being able to pay her way and she was so desperately tired.

'Tell him please that it's Miss Warrinder – Christine Warrinder.'

After that of course nothing was too good for her. She was found a comfortable room, a can of hot water arrived, she could thankfully wash the smuts and grime from her face and hands and presently sit down to the tea and toast she had requested, kitchen or no kitchen.

It was after midnight when a knock came at the door and her Uncle Francis came in, smiling and holding out his arms in his friendly way.

'Christine, my child, this is a very unexpected pleasure. Why didn't you let us know you were coming? Are you alone?'

'I thought you were still abroad,' she said and then overcome with weariness and the difficulty of explaining why she had wanted to escape, she quite uncharacteristically burst into tears.

He put his arms around her, holding her close, murmuring soothing words and supplying a handkerchief till she pulled herself together and blew her nose.

'I'm sorry,' she said, 'I didn't mean to be so foolish but it's been such a very long day. I just wanted to get away from everyone. I thought you were all still away and wouldn't mind if I came here.'

'Some business cropped up and brought me back sooner than I had intended. Grace won't be returning for another week or two so you will have to be content with your old uncle for company. Does your father know that you've run away?'

'He will by now but he won't know where. Don't tell him, Uncle, please don't tell him, not yet.'

'Certainly not now. It's past midnight,' he said diplomatically. 'Tomorrow you can go with me to Glenmuir. It will be an early start but you won't mind that, will you?'

'I don't mind anything,' she said fervently. 'Not now I'm here.'

'I'll say goodnight then.'

He gave her a hug, kissed her cheek and went away thought-fully. There was obviously far more to this than she had told him but he wouldn't press her. She would tell him in her own good time. However in the early morning he telegraphed to his brother-in-law before they set out for Fort William and Glenmuir.

Everard received the telegram late in the afternoon, having spent two agonisingly anxious days. Francis had written sim-ply, 'Don't worry. Christine safe with me. Advise leaving her with us for the time being. Letter following.'

The relief was enormous. 'Should I go up there?' he said to Clarissa. 'It's burdening your brother with what is really not his concern.'

'Wait till you get his letter. Francis has always been very understanding.'

'What about Gareth? He will be asking about her. He has the right to know something of all this.'

'Tell him whatever you feel he should know, Everard.' They were in the drawing room and Barton had already brought in a tray of tea. She lifted the silver pot before she went on, 'You know I'm beginning to realize that Christine is far more like you than Harry is or Margaret, so full of complexity that I sometimes wonder if I have ever really understood either of you.'

'Isn't it a little late for that?' he said drily. 'Have I been so difficult to live with all these years? You never told me.'

'I don't think I fully realized it till now. It's very disconcerting.'

He smiled and took the cup from her. 'In that case perhaps I should begin apologising for it.'

But the shared anxiety had at least brought them a little closer than anything else had done during the last few weeks and he was grateful for it.

At much the same time as Christine fled to Scotland, Daniel found his way into the offices of the *Northern Clarion*, two dirty rooms in an even dirtier street but crackling with life and energy due to the new Editor, Joe Sharpe, who was in his early thirties, swore like a trooper, had no fancy manners whatsoever, but was determined to turn the *Clarion*, founded by his father, into the authentic voice of the industrial north. In some thirty or so years it had risen from a single sheet to a good-sized newspaper, radical, controversial, often on the point of closure, but definitely a survivor, something to be reckoned with in the near future. He welcomed Daniel with open arms, had read his contributions to the workers' newssheets, which had a wide circulation, and also those the *Daily News* had accepted and had been impressed. Here was a man after his own heart, one who was not afraid to speak his mind and damn the consequences. He was also John Hunter's son which was something he could usefully exploit.

'Can't pay you much,' he confessed at this first meeting, 'we only just manage to keep the presses rolling.'

'I'm all right. I've got a temporary job teaching at the Methodist school.'

Joe grinned. 'Have to mind yourself there, no bad language, no drinks on the side, no skedaddling after the local girls, eh?'

'Never was much in my line.'

'The *Clarion* was one of the first to report your father's speeches,' went on the Editor. 'There was a man who could raise fire in his listeners. They're all so bloody smug these days, bleating about how much better conditions are for the workers. If I had my way, I'd force some of these pretty gentlemen to wade through the cesspools, swallow some of the filthy water and take a very good look at some of the hovels our workers still live in.'

'Do you keep old copies of the newspaper?'

'Aye, we do as it happens, got them back to the first numbers. Nearly lost the lot in a fire a while ago but someone managed to pull the sacks out just in time. They're all there, a bit scorched round the edges but still readable.'

'I'd like to look through some of them if I may. They'll give me an idea of what the *Clarion* is looking for.'

'Go ahead. Any time you like.'

So that was how Daniel, scanning through early copies, read John Hunter's speeches and thrilled to them and then one day accidentally came across a half sheet turning yellow, partly burnt and crackling in his hand. It reported an early meeting of the Chartists but that was not what caught his eye. At the end there were congratulations to their leader on the birth of a fine son, born a month prematurely but doing well, a particularly happy event since his wife had suffered a painful miscarriage shortly after their marriage.

Daniel stared at it. There it was, the proof set out in this piece of yellowing scorched paper. No doubt now. He was John Hunter's son, just as he had always known. Why had no one thought of looking up the information before? Except of course it had never been necessary and in any case who would think of digging into the archives of an obscure paper as the *Clarion* was then. He cut the piece out carefully and put it in his pocket. What should he do about it? Write to Everard – to Christine? What difference would it make now if he did? He still couldn't support her. It was not easy to live on the occasional pittance from the newspaper and the Methodist Chapel up here was not so rich as those down south. The salary he received was only half of what Mr Brown had been willing to give him towards the end of his two years.

The cutting burned in his pocket for the next couple of days before it became too much for him and he sat down one evening to write to Christine, explaining how he had discovered the truth and going on to tell her something about his life, stressing the good things and avoiding the loneliness, the heartache, the long hours of the night haunted by memories of all they had shared. He tried to make it sober and factual but despite his intention it breathed his love and longing for her and an unexpressed hope that now there was nothing to keep them apart, perhaps one day . . . When it was done, he read it through, was half inclined to tear it up and then abruptly signed and sealed it, sending it off before he could have second thoughts. Afterwards he waited and hoped.

539

Surely she would write, if only a few lines to say how she was, but the days went by and there was nothing. Maybe she was right to make the break final but it was hard to accept and he tried to drown it by long walks around the worst areas of the city, by taking extensive notes and coming back to write fiery articles which impressed Joe Sharpe even if he didn't always print them.

Christine had been at Glenmuir for nearly a fortnight when Gareth arrived. There had been a brief note from her mother reproaching her for causing them so much anxiety and a much kinder letter from her father merely saying she hardly needed to steal away like a thief in the night since he would not have raised any objection to her going to Scotland and ending with a more loving note than she had ever received from him. 'Don't stay away too long, Christine. I find I miss you very much.'

She nearly cried over that but then she was inclined to cry over all kinds of stupid things in those first few days. Her father had written more fully to his brother-in-law giving a guarded account from which Francis gathered there had been a most unsuitable love affair and wisely said nothing about it. In the meantime Christine was free to do as she pleased. There were the two big friendly wolfhounds, Fergus and Tara, only too ready to accompany her whether walking or riding. There was Donald Macrae, who saddled a horse for her and followed at a discreet distance till he felt sure she was competent to look after herself. She did not see much of her uncle. The highlands were in turmoil. More and more land-owners were evicting their crofters from their ancient homes in favour of the more profitable sheep and the Earl of Glenmuir, with some thousands of acres of hill pasture and a great many tenants, was resisting all temptation to follow suit and was being called in to help settle disputes and sometimes act as peacemaker. They would dine together in the evening. She would tell him about her day and afterwards he would fall asleep in his big armchair in front of the slow burning logs, the dogs stretched at his feet, and the thoughts she had tried to dismiss during the day would come flooding back. Where was Daniel now? What was he doing? How was he living? More and more she bitterly regretted the cruel hateful words she had flung at him at their last meeting.

She was still obsessed with the fear that she might be pregnant with his child and yet up here, far away from London, she felt as if she were in another world, wrapped in a cocoon where she was safe and nothing and no one could touch her, a cocoon that was rudely torn apart when she came down to dinner one evening and her uncle greeted her cheerfully.

'See who is here, Christine. You'll have a companion to walk and ride with you now,' and Gareth got up from his chair and came to take her hand and kiss her on the cheek.

It was such a surprise that it was a moment before she snatched her hand away.

'How did you know that I was here?'

'Your father told me. I had a few days free and thought I might as well come up here to join you.'

'And you're very welcome,' said Francis heartily. 'It has been lonely for Christine and Grace is not expected to return till the end of next week.'

After dinner and during the evening Gareth and her uncle kept the conversation going while Christine remained silent and wished passionately that Gareth had not come. She knew exactly what he was thinking and it infuriated her. He might not say, 'I told you so,' but she thought she could see it in his eyes and in his easy confident manner. If he thought she was now ready to fall into his arms, then he was very much mistaken.

In actual fact she was misjudging him. Gareth's reasons for coming were far more complex than that. He knew how she must be feeling, the sense of loss, the pain of rejection. He knew he should wait longer, a month or two perhaps, for her to recover from the shattered illusion but he couldn't wait. He'd wasted enough time already by not being bold enough, by not laying his claim to her and letting another steal her from him. Now the time had come to throw all the power he had into persuasion, to make her realize where her true happiness lay, force her to acknowledge that her obsession with Daniel was simply an episode, part of growing up, and it was now over with no harm done.

The next morning before he went down to breakfast he took out a letter which was addressed to Christine and had come the morning he was to leave. Everard knew it came from Daniel and hesitated between opening it and burning it unread but he was a just man. He had trusted Daniel and knew no reason to doubt that trust so he had handed it over to Gareth with one or two other trivial items of correspondence. 'You may as well take them to her,' he said. 'They will travel quicker by you than by the mail as I understand letters are only delivered to Glenmuir once a week, if then.'

Now the decision lay with Gareth and he stared down at the letter undecided. Whatever was in it would be bound to bring it all back, revive the pain and bitterness that was over and done with. Surely it would be better for Christine if he were to destroy it and say nothing. He was horribly tempted to read it, even went so far as to break the seal and draw out the flimsy sheet. His eye fell on the first few words – 'My dearest Christine, I have the most wonderful news . . .' Then good intentions fled. He could not stop himself but read on about the discovery that swept away the barrier between them, the unexpressed hope that it made all the difference, they were free now to love as they would . . .

In sudden violent disgust at what he was doing he tore the single sheet in half and dropped it into the fire that except for a few days in high summer always burned throughout the rooms of the castle. Instantly he regretted it and would have snatched it back but the flame had devoured it and it was gone for ever.

The decision had been made for him. She need never know and it was for the best, he told himself, in an effort to stifle the feeling of guilt. She would wait and wait and hope and it could all be for nothing, wasting her life when he could give her comfort, security, love. He would do everything in his power to make it up to her. He went downstairs full of firm resolutions not to waste precious time.

His host said apologetically that unfortunately he had to be out on business most of the day but Gareth must treat the castle as his own and please himself. If he wanted to ride, Donald Macrae would find a suitable mount.

'I'm afraid Christine went off very early,' he went on, 'she often does, but Donald will be able to tell you which direction she has taken. I like him to keep a watchful eye on her.'

So after breakfast he went down to the stables and was greeted cheerfully by the young Scot who, primed by his master, had already brought out one of the horses and was busily saddling up.

'Do you know which way Miss Christine went?' asked Gareth.

'Aye, I do that,' he said, giving him a leg up into the saddle. 'D'ye see yon path climbing up through the trees? If you follow that – mind you there are a few twists and turns so ye'll need to keep your wits about you – you'll find it comes out on the headland. Miss Christine likes it up there. There's a grand view over the sea and the islands and a wind to blow all the cobwebs away.'

It was a fine brisk morning but the sun shone and out of the wind there was still a good deal of warmth in it. He followed the path as best he could and after one or two false starts at length emerged on to the heights and into a dazzle of sunshine. For a moment he could see nothing, then his horse whinneyed and he saw that Christine had tethered her mare further along in a sheltered spot where the horse could crop the thick short grass. He trotted quietly over, dismounted and tied his bridle to a convenient branch.

He smiled when he caught sight of Christine. She was standing high up on the headland wearing what must be an old pair of breeches belonging to one of her cousins, a thick shirt and a leather waistcoat. It took him back to days at

Bramber when she used to love to shock Clarissa by riding with him in Harry's old breeches and certainly it was very practical up here among these twisting highland paths.

'I thought you might come after me,' she said as he climbed up the slope, the turf short and springy under his feet. 'How did you know where to come? Was it Donald?'

'Yes, it was.'

'He fusses over me like some old Nanny.'

She was only a few feet away from him by now, her hair blown by the wind into wild tangles and a glint of battle in her eyes.

'How much did my father tell you?' she demanded.

'Everything, I believe,' he said a little breathlessly. It had been a stiff climb. 'He is very distressed for you.'

'I doubt that. Why have you come here? Is it to gloat?'

'No,' he protested. 'How could you think that of me?' but she went on unheeding.

'Why not? You have every reason to do just that. You've been proved right, haven't you? It must make you feel very pleased with yourself. You told me once that when it came to a choice, when there was nothing for it but to defy my father, defy the whole world, then Daniel would think twice about it, would see me as an unwelcome burden, a stumbling block in the way of his ambitions. He would listen to my father's arguments and reject me without another thought . . .' her voice broke into a dry sob.

'No,' said Gareth, 'no, Christine, you're not being fair to him.' He thought of the letter the fire had devoured and quickly quelled the feeling of guilt. 'There is another reason, a very vital one . . .'

'Oh I know what you mean. Father's fear that Daniel is the child he fathered on his mistress. I don't know whether to believe it or not. You see it was such a wonderful reason to tear us apart, wasn't it? And yet . . . and yet . . . Anyway that's why I came up here. I wanted time to think, to be away from everyone. I wanted to face what must be faced alone.'

'Has it been so very hard to face?' he said gently and would have taken her hand but she snatched it away.

'You don't know the half of it. There is something else, something that Father couldn't tell you because he doesn't know, no one does. Don't you understand yet? Can't you guess?' She gulped and then went on quickly. 'I could be bearing Daniel's child.'

'What!' For an instant the shock paralysed him, then he said hoarsely, 'It isn't true.'

'Oh yes, it is. You don't want to believe it, do you? Not about me, not about the girl you have chosen for your wife, but it's true. We were lovers and it was wonderful. I was so happy, so sure of him and of myself. It seemed that nothing could ever come between us. I believed in him and I thought he believed in me and then this . . . this . . .'

She turned and ran away from him, stumbling, half falling down the path that ran down the other side of the headland.

Such a black rage shook Gareth that for a moment he could not move, rage against Daniel who had taken Christine in her innocence, rage against himself for letting her go, rage against her for going so much further than he had ever imagined. Then he went crashing down the slope after her.

The path descended steeply into a sort of valley between the two headlands, a green haven sheltered from the wind, incredibly beautiful but they had no eyes for it.

As he reached her she stumbled and almost fell. He caught hold of her and swung her to face him, shaking her in a fury of anger.

'Is it true? Is it or are you just tormenting me?'

She could have lied and he would have believed her but she couldn't, not to Gareth. The old loyalty, the old bond, still held. Instead she almost spat the words in his face.

'Yes, it is true, and I'm glad, glad that whatever happens, at least I have that to remember.'

And that was the last straw that pushed him over into a dark tide of passion that he had never expected in himself, so powerful that it swept all before it.

'Oh my God!' He was staring down at her, his hands gripping her shoulders so cruelly that she cried out.

'If you have a child, then I swear to God it will be mine and not his,' he said furiously.

He kissed her with a ferocity that terrified her. She tried to pull herself away but he held her with a grip of iron. He pushed her down on the grass and fell on top of her, pinning her to the ground. She was frightened then. She began to plead with him.

'Let me go. Please, please, Gareth, let me go.'

But he was deaf to her pleading, deaf to everything except the rage that possessed him. One hand was tearing at her clothes, unhooking the boy's breeches. This was the Gareth she had once dreamed of as a schoolgirl, sprung from some fierce Welsh ancestor, sweeping all before him, only she wasn't a child any longer and he was no wild Celtic chieftain but a rising young doctor who was always so calm and cool no matter how desperate the situation.

The sun burned down on the quiet valley, the wind shrieked but they were sheltered from its bite, above their heads gulls screamed, soaring and then plummeting to the rocky beaches far below and she felt her body arch and tremble into a climax that came with a fierceness that left her gasping. Then it was all over.

The tide of passion slowly ebbed and Gareth rolled away from her, deeply ashamed and yet in a way wildly triumphant. It was the last thing he had ever imagined, something he did not understand in himself and now she was his and he would never let her go again.

She was lying quite still, her clothes disordered, her eyes closed. He leaned across and kissed her very gently on the lips.

'When are we going to be married?' he murmured.

Her eyes flickered open. 'Married! After this!'

'Particularly after this.'

She struggled to sit up, still very shaken. 'No, Gareth, no. I can't think, not now. I never imagined such a thing.'

'Neither did I.' He looked at her and then away. 'I suppose I should apologise but I'm not going to because I'm not sorry. I have captured my wild bird and I'm not letting her go.'

'And if I say no? If I refuse?'

He smiled. 'We'll see about that.'

This was a Gareth she didn't know. Always before it was she who had led, now it was he who was master. She rebelled fiercely against it but in a queer sort of way after the turmoil, the misery, the anxiety, it was almost a relief to let herself be carried along on the tide of his will, even if only temporarily.

He stayed for a few more days and Francis, who really knew very little of all that had gone on in London, assumed that Christine was still pledged to him and that they would be married just as soon as the differences between them had been sorted out.

At his particular request Gareth accompanied him down to Arisaig where a group of evicted crofters was gathering to take the boat to Oban, from where they would be shipped as emigrants to Canada and Nova Scotia.

'God knows it has made me feel ashamed of my fellow countrymen to see such suffering,' said the Earl. 'There are just a few of us who've been feeling the same and we've organised some relief, little enough, God knows, extra food for those who have none, medical treatment though most doctors are refusing to lift a finger for the poor devils.'

Christine insisted on going with them and when her uncle said, 'It is scarcely a sight for you, my dear,' she was angry with him.

'You forget that I've had two years working at an East End clinic.'

There was little enough they could do except rebandage wounds that had been suppurating, treat burns where some wretched crofter had tried desperately to save something precious from his burning bothy, hand out a few remedies that might relieve pain and sickness on the long voyage, pass over sacks of oatmeal and flour that could provide porridge and bread for the children.

The sheer misery, the pitiful sight of old people who were left behind weeping because there was not enough money to

547

pay for their voyage, the men who flung themselves down kissing the ground they loved and were leaving forever, the helpless cries of women and children.

How small seemed her own miseries in the face of such suffering and she felt ashamed of her selfish absorption.

'I will discuss details of our marriage with your father,' said Gareth on the morning when he was leaving.

'No, Gareth. You are taking too much for granted.'

'Very quiet, I think, don't you?' he went on unheeding. 'You will have to help me there or your mother will be planning the wedding of the season.'

'Gareth, will you please listen to me?' she said desperately. 'You can't do this. I'm *not* marrying you.'

'Oh yes you are. No argument, we've had enough of that, and don't stay up here too long. I wish you were coming with me now.'

'I must have time. This is my whole life.'

'It's mine too. No more than a week, Christine, promise me.'

'I'm promising nothing,' she said and had a desperate feeling that the only way to escape the indomitable will of this new Gareth would be to take a running jump off the headland into the sea, but despite everything life still had meaning for her.

Chapter 27

Christine stayed on at Glenmuir for another ten days after Gareth had left and would have liked to stay longer with her kindly uncle, who did not ask awkward questions and sometimes took her with him when he was dealing with the evicted crofters so that she felt she was at least doing something useful, but she knew she could not run away for ever. The future had to be faced.

This time her uncle made sure that she travelled with every comfort. He insisted on taking her to Edinburgh himself, staying at the Waverley overnight and the next morning seeing her installed in a first-class carriage, Ladies only, with a lavish luncheon box on the seat beside her and a pile of newspapers and magazines on her lap.

'Now you take care,' he said. 'I have telegraphed to your father the time of your arrival so he will be there to meet you at the other end.'

'I'm so grateful to you,' she said. 'I don't know what I would have done if you hadn't been at the hotel that first night.'

'I expect you'd have managed somehow. You're a resourceful puss, aren't you? Ask Everard to let me know that you have arrived safely, will you, and now I'd better get out or I shall be carried along with you whether I like it or not.'

He kissed her and stepped out on to the platform. 'Grace will be back next week and will want to know all about you so don't forget to send us an invitation to the wedding.'

'If there is a wedding,' was on the tip of her tongue but the train jolted forward and there was only time to wave goodbye with a dismal feeling that she was being carried away from a safe harbour to face a sea of trouble.

All during the tedious hours of the day-long journey she wrestled with her problem. Was she going to give in to Gareth's insistence that they be married at once or wasn't she? She was still haunted by an unreasoning anxiety that she might be bearing Daniel's child. Ever since parting with him her mind had been in turmoil which the stormy meeting with Gareth had done nothing to still. She felt unutterably weary as if she had been fighting a losing battle for far too long. It would be only too easy to give in and yield to pressure. She was aware that she must somehow put Daniel out of her mind and knew she could not. It was there always like the ache of an unhealed wound. She shuddered away from returning to Belgrave Square, taking up her old life with everyone saying nothing but thinking the more after that frantic dash for freedom. Perhaps with Gareth she could take up a new life. There would be so much to do, she would have no time to think, no time to ponder on what might have been and there would be the comfort and reassurance of a man whom she had known all her life – but did she really know him? That day on the headland had revealed a different Gareth, some-one she had never dreamed of, with a new and unexpected violence with which she would have to cope. This way and that went her thoughts in a wearying indecision.

At long last the train steamed into the London station only a few minutes late and her father was there waiting for her. She had thought she hated him for the way in which he had destroyed so effectively the future for her and Daniel but when she saw him in the rush and bustle of arrival, when he held out his arms to her, relief flooded through her and she went straight into them and knew that in spite of everything she loved him still.

The first greetings over, sitting beside her in the carriage, he took her hand in his. 'Now listen to me, Christine. Gareth has told me that he would like to be married just as soon as it can be arranged but I made him understand that it depends

550

on you. That is why I'm asking you now before you meet your mother, before any pressure is put upon you. Do you want this marriage to go ahead because if you are unhappy about it, I will not allow you to be forced into it whatever the circumstances.'

He was offering her a way out and she was grateful but there was a great deal that he didn't know. All that long day she had fought her problem and now somehow it had resolved itself. Gareth meant safety, a busy practical life, settled, secure, no aching worries and anxieties and at that moment it seemed like a wonderful haven in which to take shelter.

She said at last, 'I've thought and thought about it, Papa, and now at last I've made up my mind. I shall marry Gareth whenever he wishes.'

'Are you sure about this?'

'Quite sure but I would like it to be very quiet, no crowds, no fuss. I was thinking that I'd love to be married in the old church at Bramber if Grandfather will agree.'

'I think he'd like it above everything but I'm afraid that your mother will be very disappointed.'

'I know she will but I can't help that. After all it is my wedding.'

So that's how it was. They were married by special licence with her mother complaining bitterly about the undue haste.

'What are people going to think?' she lamented over and over again. 'First you run out of the house without a word to anyone, causing your father and me untold worry and anxiety and now there is this hasty marriage. Why must you do this to us? I don't know how I'm going to face it, the sly looks, the questions that will be asked. As if things weren't bad enough already.'

But Christine was determined and supported by her father had her way. She married Gareth in the ancient church at Bramber with all the tenants and villagers piling in to watch and with a small gathering of close friends who came back with them to the Grange. Clarissa had to content herself with turning the church into a veritable bower of flowers and galvanising the staff into serving a memorable wedding feast.

Harry arrived from Paris just in time to stand beside Gareth at the altar and afterwards, getting her alone for a moment, he said, 'Everything hunky-dory, Chris? I did rather wonder when I got Papa's telegraph about the wedding.'

'Everything's fine,' she said steadily.

'And Dan?'

'That's all over.'

Then just for a few seconds she leaned against him, her face hidden, and he held her very close till she was able to smile again and rejoin the guests.

Later Lord Warrinder, at Christine's particular wish, took himself off to friends in Scotland leaving the house to the young couple for a few weeks. They could not embark on a trip abroad since Gareth had already taken too much time off from the hospital and it had been her choice to stay at Bramber. Nothing there reminded her of Daniel. Except for the fleeting moment of that very early encounter in the park, he had never been there with her. All its memories were bound up with childhood with Harry, Gareth and their friends, so there, she thought, it would be easier to put Daniel out of her mind.

By the end of their stay she knew quite surely that she was pregnant. It had come so quickly she could not help wondering sometimes whether the child could indeed be Daniel's. Perhaps she would never know. It was not as if the baby would be brown, or yellow or black! Christine had never been maternal, never longed for babies of her own as Margaret had. She could have wished it otherwise but it had happened and must be endured and she was determined not to fuss and not to give up anything because of her condition. She had her first argument with Gareth over it.

'As soon as we return to London, I'm going to put you in the care of Dr Howard Speir, who is a first-class gynaecologist,' he said decisively.

'I'd much rather have dear old Dr Murphy,' she said obstinately. 'I've known him since I was a child.'

'He's an elderly man, not up in modern methods and I want you to have the best. There is another thing. I do wish you'd give up this daily riding or at least go at it more gently.'

'Good heavens, why? I'm perfectly well and it is something I enjoy.'

During the weeks at Bramber she had gone back to her old ways, hunting out Harry's old breeches and riding out over the downs. Sometimes she needed desperately to escape even if only for a few hours.

'You must be sensible,' he went on. 'You take too many risks. You rush at things, Christine, almost as if you wanted to break your neck. I don't intend to lose our child through your carelessness.'

'How do you know it is your child?' The words were out before she could stop them and she regretted it instantly when she saw the look on his face.

'Must you say that?' he said with a suppressed anger.

'I'm sorry,' she said quickly, 'I'm very sorry. I didn't mean it.'

She wished now that she had never told him of that night with Daniel that she could not forget. She had flung it at him in a mood of frustration and bitter disillusion and it had provoked a storm in him which she had never imagined possible. He had never referred again to that morning on the headland but she sometimes thought that it was still in his mind when he made love to her, so that he had to prove himself over and over again. She was fond of him, deeply loyal, and genuinely wanted to make a success of their marriage, but try as she would their relationship lacked the vital spark that had flared between her and Daniel and which was still so much alive, however much she strove to put it behind her.

While she was fighting her battle at Bramber Daniel was doing much the same while trying to knock a little learning into the heads of fifty unruly and unresponsive boys, until the day he took some copy into the newspaper office and found the Editor with his nose in *The Times*.

'What's so interesting?' he asked.

'This bloody business of Russia grabbing at the Turkish empire. Old Pam is threatening to resign again if something is not done about it. If we do go to war, and we probably will, you know who will suffer! Not the nobs – oh dear no, they'll all be sitting pretty, it'll be the poor bloody infantry!' He looked up suddenly. 'If it does come, Dan, what d'you say to going out there with them and sending back reports on what it feels like fighting for Queen and country in some hellish spot far from home? It'd be a grand scoop for the *Clarion*, might even steal a march on *The Times*.' He pushed a pile of newspapers across his desk. 'Here take these. Have a look at the news for yourself.'

'Thanks, I will.'

But what caught his eye first as he picked them up was something that held him rigid, staring down at it, hating to believe and yet knowing that it had been inevitable.

'The marriage took place quietly in Sussex between Christine, daughter of Everard Warrinder QC and Lady Clarissa Warrinder, and Dr Gareth Fraser, only son of the late Lieutenant Colonel Edward Fraser . . .'

'What do you think, Dan? Would you go?' said Joe sharply.

He looked up frowning. 'Go where?'

'To the bloody war if it comes off.'

'Yes, of course I'd go.' He'd go anywhere just to get away, just to forget what might have been.

'Good man,' said the Editor. 'We'll keep you to that when the time comes.'

It was September when Christine and Gareth returned to London and they moved at once into the half-furnished house in Wimpole Street. There was still a great deal to be done and Christine went to work with energy, glad of the excuse to fill her time.

Her father, calling in one day, found her surrounded with samples of curtain material and catalogues of baby furniture and thought she looked tired.

'Why don't you stay with us at Belgrave Square instead of camping out here in discomfort. Then you could finish all this at your leisure.'

'It's better if I'm on the spot. Nothing has really been done about the nurseries except repainting and they are going to be needed.'

'Already?'

'Yes, already,' she said with a grimace.

'Is that what you want?'

'Not particularly but there it is. Uncle David, bless his heart, is so pleased that he says I can order whatever I please in the way of furniture and so on and he will foot the bill.'

'Your mother will want to have a hand in it.'

'I suppose she will. Well, I don't mind listening to advice. I don't necessarily have to take it.'

It greatly disturbed her that there was still a coolness between her father and mother. Before the trial and its consequences there had been a strong hint in high places that Everard would be honoured in the New Year and Clarissa had wished above all to go with him to Buckingham Palace and see him receive the recognition which his work deserved. But now, without anything officially being said, the suggestion had been quietly dropped and Clarissa resented it bitterly, just as she resented Kate. She would not receive her at Belgrave Square and for the sake of peace Everard did not insist. He simply went his own way, meeting Kate now and again for a quiet luncheon, and if acquaintances raised their eyebrows at his interest in a rising young actress who was making such a success at the Haymarket, he had after all saved her from the gallows.

Christine had her second quarrel with Gareth when she insisted on going down to work at the clinic.

'It's not at all suitable,' he stormed. 'You're my wife now and you've quite enough to do supervising the work at the house.'

'If you expect me to sit at home and spend all my time having little tea parties and indulging in babytalk and scandal, then you can forget it. You've always known how I feel about things like that. I'm bored with this baby already. You told John Dexter how interested you were in his work and now you're going back on it.'

'You weren't pregnant then. Believe me, it's you I'm thinking of, Christine.'

'It's months yet and I'll be sensible. I won't do anything foolish.'

They argued about it for a couple of days and then she found an unexpected ally in Dr Andrews' wife.

Molly Andrews had proved very different from what Christine had expected. She was younger than her husband, not yet forty, large, plump and with no nonsense about her. She dressed plainly, had no interest in fashion or scandal, and was always very welcome at her husband's dinner parties where the guests were mainly medical men with whom she could talk almost as an equal. Her one great regret was that they had no children and for that reason perhaps she took the young couple under her wing. She had known Gareth when he was still a student doctor and was delighted that he had married a sensible young woman and not some fashionable bird-witted chit. She sympathised with Christine from the first and when she and her husband were dining with them and the question of the clinic came up, she took her part.

'There's a great deal of nonsense talked about pregnancy,' she said. 'It's a perfectly natural condition and Christine is a fine healthy girl. Don't stop her doing what she longs to do. I've known far too many young women who've retired into a sort of semi-invalidism and it's the worst possible thing for mother and baby. George agrees with me, don't you, dear?'

So Christine won her point and they settled down into a quiet routine. Gareth was working very hard at Barts and in Dr Andrews' busy practice in Harley Street while Christine finished the redecoration of the nursery floor. She took Uncle David on a tour of inspection since he had paid for the lovely pale blue and white of the bedroom and the glowing colours of the playroom with a frieze of animals stalking round the walls and brightly checked curtains.

It was during that morning that she asked him if he would like to leave the Albany and move in with them where she could make sure he was properly cared for.

'The house is quite large enough and you could bring all your special treasures with you.'

'My dear girl,' he said, 'you and Gareth are only a few months married. You don't want an old codger like me sitting at your table like some confounded ancient death's head. I do very well, you know. Edwards has been with me ever since I was a dashing young blade shuttling between England and the Continent. He knows all my fidgets and how to deal with them. I'm hanging on till I see your son before I think of shuffling off.'

'Don't talk like that and it could be a daughter.'

'If it is, then call her Isabelle just to please me.' Then suddenly serious he said, 'You are happy, Christine, you and Gareth together, aren't you? I have wondered sometimes.'

'You find out that you mustn't ask for too much and then everything is fine,' she said lightly and went on to tell him of other changes she was planning.

Uncle David might be old but he saw people very clearly and he had hit the nail on the head. On the surface all was well but they had never entirely recovered the old feeling of companionship and trust. Sometimes she blamed herself and at other times found it difficult to understand his reactions, like the stupid quarrel over the newspaper. It was after the New Year and she had spent a morning with Kate, who was now back with Mr Kean's company and being occasionally squired around by George Westcott, much to Christine's amusement.

'Don't you find him deadly dull?' she said. 'He used to come to Bramber sometimes to see Grandfather and we all groaned when he stayed to dine with us.'

'He's not dull at all,' said Kate, 'he's immensely restful and after the hectic life of the theatre, it's sometimes very soothing.'

It was that morning that Kate showed her a copy of the

Clarion with an article by Daniel and she asked if she could borrow it.

'Of course you can. I have others too. Dan sends me any he thinks I might find of interest.'

So it happened that when Gareth came home that evening, he found his wife on the sofa utterly absorbed in reading them and flew into an unexpected rage.

'Where on earth did that rag come from? I don't approve of its politics and would prefer not to have it in my house.'

'It's my house too, Gareth, and I borrowed them from Kate. Daniel has been writing several articles in it during the last few months.'

'How long has this been going on?'

'There's nothing going on as far as I know. I only borrowed them this morning.'

He looked at her keenly. 'Has he been writing to you?'

'You'd know if he had. You see all my mail.'

'Are you implying that I spy on you?'

She knew nothing of that burned letter and so could not understand his sudden angry flare.

'No, of course I'm not. What's the matter with you, Gareth? Are you jealous? You needn't be. There's surely no harm in being interested in what Daniel writes.'

'No, no, of course not,' he muttered. 'You do as you please.'

But all the same there seemed no point in provoking another quarrel and so after that she kept the newspapers out of his sight and read them in private.

In actual fact in political matters things were going from bad to worse that spring.

At the end of March the British government at last yielded to pressure and together with France declared war on Russia. Tsar Nicholas withdrew his ambassadors from London and Paris and the whole country was swept by war fever. Soldiers who had often been the most despised members of the community during the forty years since Waterloo suddenly became the heroes of the hour. Cheering crowds gathered to watch the troops marching to the various ports for embarkation and in April Margaret left her new baby daughter at Ingham Park and brought her small son to London to see his father riding at the head of his men.

They had an excellent view from a window in the Strand from which they were able to see the procession as it advanced slowly down the Mall past Buckingham Palace where members of the royal family would give the salute. Owing to the crowds in the streets that day they had to come very early and so had a long time to wait.

Christine should not have been there at all. Her baby was due in a matter of weeks, perhaps even days, and according to her mother she should be spending the time in decent seclusion and not flaunting her condition in public. From the very first she had refused to shut herself away but this morning for once she rather wished she had followed Clarissa's advice. It was exceptionally warm for April and the window had to be tightly shut since John Everard, who was nearly two and a lively child, had already been hauled back in the nick of time from falling headlong into the street below. Christine loosened the ribbons on her fashionable hat and took out a handkerchief.

'Are you feeling all right?' asked Margaret, eyeing her sister a little anxiously.

'Yes, of course. Don't you start. Mamma was bad enough. I think she is afraid I might give birth in the middle of the procession.'

They could hear now the distant sound of a military band and catch a glimpse of the first detachment of marching men.

'Will that be Papa?' asked the little boy, hopping up and down in excitement.

'No, darling, not yet. Look out for the horses. When you see them, then there will be Papa.'

Christine stirred uncomfortably in her chair. She had found these last months very nearly intolerable and longed for it all to be safely over and for her life to go back to normal.

'They're coming, they're coming! Look, Auntie,' shrieked the boy and she roused herself to lean forward beside her excited nephew.

It certainly made a very impressive spectacle, detachment after detachment of men marching to the stirring drumbeats of the band, their handsome uniforms, red and blue and green, every accoutrement spick and span and gleaming in the spring sunshine. After them came the cavalry brigades on their magnificent horses, helmets and breastplates polished to a dazzling brilliance, horse trappings jingling and glittering.

'I can see Papa,' yelled John Everard. 'There he is, do you see him, Mamma? He is riding Blackie.'

Margaret opened the window a fraction so that her son could put his head out and wave furiously as the company trotted slowly by to the increased martial music of the band.

Freddie really does look rather gorgeous, thought Christine, riding stiffly erect ahead of his men, one gloved hand on hip, the other on the reins. For an instant his eyes flickered towards his small son and Christine saw the pride on her sister's face mingled with the shine of unshed tears. She had a sudden vision of the future that lay before these marching men in their rich panoply, the heat and dust and sickness, the wounds and fury of battle, the glory inevitably mingled with blood and death.

She said quickly, 'They are all saying that this is only a precautionary move on the part of Britain and the whole affair will be over by Christmas.'

'They always say that in case the men become disheartened,' said her sister. 'Freddie told me that Lord Raglan and the other Commanders take a very different view.' She pulled the little boy back from the window and shut it. 'They're all gone now, darling.'

'Didn't Papa look wonderful? Is he going out there to kill people?' he asked, eyes shining at the prospect.

'I expect so but only if they try to kill him first. Now come along, Johnny, it's time to go home and you can tell Grandpapa and Grandmamma all about it.'

The streets were slowly clearing but it still took time to thread their way through to where the carriages were waiting. Margaret turned to her sister.

'Are you coming with us, Christine? I think Papa will be expecting you.'

'I don't think I will. Tell him I'm feeling rather tired, will you? You are staying for a few days at Belgrave Square, aren't you? I'll see you later on.'

'Very well. Look after yourself now.' Margaret kissed her sister and they parted, the two carriages going their separate ways.

It was after three by the time Christine reached Wimpole Street. She felt too exhausted to eat much, so contented herself with some tea and toast. Afterwards when she felt more rested, she went up to the second floor to make sure that the nursery curtains, which had been unsatisfactory, had now been altered and rehung. To her surprise she saw the new Nanny was already installed. Janet Renfrew was the younger sister of John Everard's Nanny and had been highly recommended by Margaret.

'We weren't expecting you till next week,' she said a little sharply.

'I know, Madam,' said the young woman. 'I do hope it does not put the household out but Lady Clarissa told me she thought it might be best if I came here at least ten days before baby is expected.'

'How like Mamma!' said Christine with a certain annoyance. 'She does so love to fuss. Very well, Nurse Renfrew, since you are here, you may as well make yourself comfortable. If you don't know London, you can go out and about and see something of it if you wish.'

'Thank you, Madam, but I am sure I shall find plenty to do here.'

'Please yourself.'

It was while she was finishing her tour of inspection that she heard Betsy calling to her up the stairs.

'There is a gentleman asking to see you, Miss Christine.'

Betsy could never get used to calling her Madam. They had known each other too long.

She went out on to the landing. 'Who is it?'

'It's that Mr Hunter, Miss, and he says he would like to see you urgent as he hasn't very much time.'

The shock paralysed her for an instant. Then feeling flooded back, surprise, excitement and an intense unexpected pleasure.

'Tell him to wait for me, Betsy. I'm coming now.'

She started down the stairs, tripped in her haste and nearly fell, only just saving herself by clinging to the handrail, twisting her back with a wrenching pain that shot through her and left her breathless for an instant. Then she recovered, took a deep breath and went down more carefully. Now was not the moment to do anything foolish. Daniel had come to see her at last and she was shaken by such a confusion of feelings that she was trembling when she reached Gareth's consulting room on the ground floor and Daniel came to meet her with outstretched hands.

He was in uniform. That was almost the first thing that struck her because it seemed so unlikely, a dark blue uniform with red pipings. He looked older, broader, altogether very sure of himself.

For a moment neither of them said a word, their eyes simply devouring each other, then she withdrew her hands gently and let herself drop on the leather-covered couch.

'I never imagined that you would volunteer,' she said, 'not you of all people.'

He smiled, tossed aside his military cap and sat down beside her.

'Neither have I, not really, not in a line regiment. I am an orderly in a medical unit. The *Clarion* is sending me out there as their war correspondent and it seemed a good way to find out at first hand the reactions of the ordinary soldier not only to the war but to his conditions of service.'

'I've been reading your articles in the paper for some time now. Kate lends them to me. I would have liked to show them to Papa but the trouble is that Gareth doesn't approve. He doesn't care for the paper's politics.'

'And you don't want to quarrel with him.'

562

'There doesn't seem much point but it doesn't stop me reading them.'

The words were unimportant. Beneath them they were busily assessing the changes wrought by the months apart.

Perhaps Papa was right, she thought, he is forging ahead without me, something which perhaps he could never have done shackled with a wife.

She is more beautiful than ever, he told himself with a kind of despair. She has a new warmth, a new gravity, and she is bearing his child, God damn him!

'How do you come to be in London?' she was asking.

'I'm on my way to Southampton where we are to embark but I begged leave to spend a few hours in London. When I arrived this morning, everything was disrupted because of the military procession and in trying to avoid it, I found myself near Wimpole Street so I thought I would take a chance on finding you at home.'

It was not quite the truth but it would serve. Everything sensible in him had told him it was folly but he could not go away on what looked like being a pretty serious assignment without seeing her just once again. And there was something else. Had she received that letter of his? Did she know the truth or didn't she? He had not intended to speak of it but now he couldn't hold it back.

'I hoped against hope that you would write to me but you never did.'

'I might say the same about you.'

'But I did write once, soon after we parted. I had discovered something very important that I wanted to share with you.'

She frowned. 'What do you mean? What was it?'

He hesitated, then fetched out a wallet from an inner pocket, took out the scrap of yellowed scorched paper and gave it to her. She read it through once and then again very slowly before she looked up at him.

'But this means . . .'

'It means that my mother lost the child she might have borne to your father and that I am the son of John Hunter as I always knew that I was.'

563

He took the paper back from her and put it carefully away. 'You wrote to tell me of this?'

'Yes. I waited for an answer, waited and waited, then one day I saw the announcement of your marriage and I told myself that you had made your choice and that must be the end of it.'

'I never received that letter.'

'Perhaps your father intercepted it and thought it wiser not to pass it on.'

'Where did you send it? To Belgrave Square?'

'Yes.'

'I was in Scotland with my uncle by then. Papa would never have destroyed it unread and if he had read it, he would have told me what it contained.'

'You seem very sure of that.'

'I am sure. I know him.'

'Then what happened to it?'

'I don't know but I intend to find out.'

'Does it matter now, Christine? It is over. I did wait, I did hope but reason told me that I could not have expected you to wait and wait till I could come to you when Gareth was there ready to give you a fine house, love, a child, all that you should have when I could do none of those things. It might have been better and spared us useless bitterness if I had never discovered the truth.'

'Don't say that. It's wrong, all wrong,' she said fiercely. 'We have been deceived. Oh it's not Papa's fault, it's not anyone's fault except whoever it was who read that letter and made sure I never received it and I'm going to find out who that was.'

She gasped as the pain she had felt before knifed through her again. It could have been her mother of course. Clarissa had never liked Daniel and she could be ruthless if she believed that what she was doing was right.

Daniel said anxiously, 'Are you feeling all right? You're looking very pale.'

'It's nothing. I bruised myself when I came down the stairs

just now. It will pass. I'm angry, Daniel, terribly angry that I was never given that letter.'

'Don't be. It won't do any good. It is over and done with and we can't bring it back however much we might wish we could. Don't waste time regretting it. I have to go very soon. There is so little time and I have to see Mr Brown and then get the train to Southampton.'

'Dan, will you write to me from wherever they send you?' She had gripped his hand feverishly, her eyes full of pleading. 'Please write. It will mean so much to me to be able to follow you wherever you have to go.'

'I don't know what kind of conditions we will be living in but if you really want it, then I will write whenever it is possible.'

'Perhaps you had better send them through Kate.'

'Why? Will Gareth be jealous?'

'I don't know, perhaps not, but I want to make quite sure of receiving them.'

'Very well, I promise. I wish to God I could stay longer. There is so much I want to hear, so much I have to tell you, but it is impossible.'

He got to his feet, pulling her up gently to face him, taking both her hands in his and kissing them. For a moment they were standing very close, then his arms went round her and he was kissing her till they were both breathless. He tore himself away, snatched up his cap and she heard him go through the hall and the front door slam before she fell back on the couch shaken by a mingling of pain, anger and a helpless frustration.

It seemed only a few minutes before Gareth came in followed by Betsy, carrying a tea tray which she put on the small table beside the couch.

Christine was still shaken by the emotional turmoil, by the revelation that had come out from her meeting with Daniel, and would have welcomed some time alone. The last person she wanted to see just then was her husband.

'You're home early,' she said with an effort to appear as usual.

565

'Yes. Betsy told me you had a visitor and that's why you are down here instead of in the drawing room. Who was it?'

'No one of importance.'

He swung round on her. 'Don't lie to me, Christine. It was Daniel Hunter, wasn't it? The carriage passed him as we came down the street. I couldn't mistake him.'

'If you know, then why ask?' she said coldly and began to pour the tea with a hand that shook a little, trying to ignore vicious stabs of pain that seemed to be increasing rather than lessening.

'Did you know that he was coming?' said Gareth taking his cup.

'No, of course not. He was passing through London on his way to join a medical unit for embarkation at Southampton and he called to say goodbye.'

'What in God's name does he know about medicine?'

'If you must know he is going to act as war correspondent for the *Clarion*.'

'That radical rag. Oh well, I suppose it's a leg up for him.'

'Don't sneer,' she said fiercely. 'I happen to think that it is very courageous of him and I fully intend to read whatever he sends back.'

'You won't find it easy to buy copies down here.'

'I'll put a special order through our newsagent,' she said defiantly.

Gareth brought his cup back to her to be refilled and said with an apparent indifference, 'How long was he here? Did he have anything else to say to you?'

It was then that the thought shot through her mind that it could have been Gareth who had obtained possession of that letter, Gareth who had destroyed it and deliberately kept from her the knowledge that could have made all the difference to her life, and it burned within her so strongly that she could not leave it unsettled. She had to know now.

'Gareth,' she said, 'I have something I must ask you, something very important that concerns us both . . .' then suddenly without any warning her whole body was convulsed by such a

566

violent pain that she cried out, arching her back against the agony.

'What is it?' Gareth was beside her at once putting his arm around her and holding her close. 'What have you been doing to yourself?'

'Nothing,' she gasped as the pain very slowly ebbed. 'Nothing at all. I did trip as I came down the stairs this afternoon but it was nothing. I didn't fall.'

'You shouldn't have gone with Margaret to watch the procession. It has been too much for you. I told you not to go.'

'But I felt perfectly well then. It can't be the baby, can it, it's not due for another fortnight.'

'I don't know but we'll very soon find out. Don't be alarmed, my love, I'm here with you. Everything is going to be all right.'

He was all tenderness, all kindness, wonderfully reassuring, and for the moment nothing else mattered.

Betsy was sent to fetch Jane Renfrew and between the two of them and Gareth, Christine was slowly taken up the stairs, undressed and put to bed while Mark, their manservant, newly promoted from footman at Bramber, was despatched to summon the formidable Dr Howard Speir.

'There's surely no need yet,' she said wearily, leaning back against the pillows. 'Perhaps I have just wrenched my back. He won't like being summoned too early.'

'Damn it, that's what he is being paid for,' said Gareth. 'I want the best and I intend to have it.'

Afterwards, looking back on that night and the following day, Christine could remember nothing clearly, only bouts of wrenching pain and other moments when it receded and she lay gasping and sweating with someone bathing her forehead with a cool towel and speaking soothingly. Then as the hours wore on she was possessed by a frightening certainty that something must be terribly wrong and no one would explain or tell her anything as if she were some kind of an idiot. Once she was certain that she saw Dr Speir with Gareth and even George Andrews all conferring together in hushed voices in the shadowy room and longed to scream out to them but when she opened her mouth all she could manage was a dismal croak. Then Nurse Renfrew was there, lifting her head and trickling something liquid between her dry lips. At one time she thought she saw her mother bending over her with tears in her eyes which was so unlike her that it seemed impossible. Behind her was her father and she clung to his hand wanting to say, 'Don't go away, Papa,' and couldn't get the words out.

Time passed, whether minutes or hours she couldn't tell, but when she could bear no more she was given a whiff of something, was it ether or chloroform she wondered vaguely, and what seemed a very long time afterwards she was shaken by a feeling that was not exactly pain but as if she were being wrenched apart followed by relief and a queer sensation as if her whole life were draining away.

What could have happened? It must be something dreadful. 'Is it dead?' she whispered.

'No indeed,' said Dr Speir's hearty voice. 'You have a fine son, Mrs Fraser. Take a good look at him.'

Someone lifted her head and she was staring at a little red crumpled face, two tiny clenched fists, a fuzz of dark hair and she hated it. It was an incubus born out of violence, the child of a near-rape on a Scottish headland and she closed her eyes against it.

There were voices whispering all around her.

'She has come through a very bad time. It happens like that sometimes.'

'Will she be all right now?'

'Please God. She's weak but she's holding her own. Let her sleep.'

Then she seemed to drift away and when she opened her eyes again the room was very quiet, the lamp carefully shaded, only a flicker of firelight. Someone who held her hand was sitting close beside the bed. She felt the warm pressure like a lifeline holding her back from the darkness.

'What time is it?' she whispered, her voice a mere thread in the silence of the room.

'Just after midnight,' and she realized it was her father close beside her bed.

'Where is Gareth?'

'He was exhausted. I sent him to lie down. Do you want him?'

She shook her head, frightened that he might go away and leave her alone.

'Don't go, Papa. Hold on to me.'

'Don't be afraid, my love. I won't leave you.'

After a time, very slowly normality began to return. The baby had not yet registered. She was still groping in the past . . . Daniel and what he had told her, something important that she had to know.

'There was a letter,' she murmured after a long pause.

'A letter?' her father repeated, humouring her. 'What letter?'

'One from Daniel – a long time ago now. Did you read it, Papa, before you burned it?'

'No indeed. I remember now. It came after you had gone away. I gave it to Gareth to give to you at Glenmuir.'

She breathed a long sigh. So that was it. Now she knew and later when she was strong again it would be an issue to be settled between her and Gareth. Wearily she drifted away again into a half sleep that slowly deepened but she did not relax her hold on his hand.

Everard looked down at this daughter of his who had become so very dear to him and wondered about her as he had done more than once since her marriage. He thought there could be trouble ahead and knew no way in which he could give advice or help. Once, badly cramped, he tried gently to withdraw his hand but she held on all the tighter even in sleep so he remained sitting there till the first streaks of light came through the slats of the Venetian blinds and Gareth came in half-dressed, his hair tousled, his eyes heavy with troubled sleep.

'How is she?' He bent over the bed, putting his hand on her forehead.

'Sleeping now and I hope and believe on the mend.'

'It's after six o'clock. You go and get some rest. I'll take over here.'

Everard drew his hand away cautiously and stood up. 'I must wash and shave. I'm due in court but fortunately not before midday. Where is Clarissa?'

'In the drawing room. I couldn't persuade her to lie down. The servants are up. They will bring you tea and anything else you need.'

As he passed him, Everard put his hand on Gareth's shoulder. 'You'll need to deal very gently with her. You know that, don't you?'

'I realize it only too well but sometimes it is difficult to know how.'

He took his father-in-law's place beside the bed and Everard went along to the drawing room, finding his wife huddled over a small fire lit against the early morning chill and looking quite unlike herself in a plain woollen dressing-gown, her hair falling untidily around her shoulders.

She looked up as her husband came in and he said quickly, 'It's going to take time but she is doing very well now.'

'Thank God. I thought at one time . . .' her voice choked.

'So did I.' He sat on the sofa beside her. 'Do you know, Clarissa, all these hours when I was sitting beside Christine, she has been holding on to my hand. I dared not move and I had the queerest feeling that I was holding her back, keeping her with us and the years seemed to roll away. I kept thinking of when you lost the baby and were so grievously sick. You may not remember but I sat by the bed all night then, holding on to you as if by doing so I could keep you beside me.'

'I do remember,' she whispered, 'oh it's all very vague and shadowy but it was rather like someone who is drowning and clings on to a thrown rope. If I once let go then the dark sea would swallow me up but so long as you were there holding on to me, then I was safe.'

'I still am there,' he said gently.

He leaned forward to kiss her cheek and she turned her face to him so that their lips met in the first kiss for a very long time. For a moment they clung together, then Betsy knocked and came in followed by another of the servants carrying a tray loaded with tea and toast and freshly boiled eggs.

Everard got up stretching himself. 'Oh Lord, I'm stiff. After we've eaten, I must spruce myself up and go into court to defend a client who has been treating his wife's lover a little too brutally for comfort.'

'Will you get him off?'

'God knows. I am pleading justification. The lover is really a very nasty piece of work. At the moment I don't feel capable of defending a client who has stolen sixpence from a blind beggar but maybe inspiration will strike, as Harry is so fond of telling me.'

Christine was young and resilient. She made a much quicker recovery than the doctors had expected. Within a week or so she was clamouring to get up and was impatient when they advised the utmost caution. That first sick revulsion against the baby vanished on the day Nurse Renfrew put him in her arms and she felt the tug of the small mouth at her breast. Gareth had insisted that for the first months at least she should feed him herself and after a day of rebellion she found a kind of sensuous dreamy content in the close intimacy of it. During those early days she had found herself gazing into the small face searching for likenesses and finding none. Once when her sister had come on a visit she asked her what she thought.

'Do you think he takes after me or Gareth?'

Margaret looked solemnly at the baby lying in his cot before she said judicially, 'I think if he is like anyone then it is Papa. He has the same straight elegant nose and the slightly peaked eyebrows,' and Christine laughed.

'Perhaps he is going to grow up to be another famous QC or even a judge.'

'What name have you chosen for him?'

'David of course. We both agreed about that. David Gareth Everard – what a mouthful for someone as tiny as he is,' she went on tenderly.

They had been discussing the christening which eventually took place about six weeks later on a day in June, when quite a number gathered at the church and came back afterwards to Wimpole Street with congratulations and gifts.

Harry came over from Paris to take up his duties as Godfather. 'Not that I'll ever be much use spiritually,' he said wryly to his sister, 'but I'll be able to give a bit of good advice about what not to do when he starts growing up.'

David Gareth Everard disgraced himself at the service by screaming at the top of a powerful pair of lungs as soon as the holy water touched his forehead.

'I bet that's caught the devil on the hop!' muttered Harry wickedly under his breath and Christine stifled a giggle.

Uncle David, who was beginning to look rather like a skeleton loosely strung together with wire but was still indomitable, held his namesake on his knee and smiled benevolently when the baby hand clutched at the black silk ribbon of his eyeglasses till Christine whisked him away.

It seemed a pity that such a pleasant and peaceful day should end as it did.

The guests left early and Gareth and Christine settled down to supper and a quiet evening. That week the first letter had come from Daniel and was duly delivered to Christine by Kate. It was brief and mainly factual. Her father had already told her that the ultimate aim of the war was to invade the Crimea and take Sebastopol, the great fortress where the Russians were entrenched, but there was a long way to go before that could be achieved. Daniel wrote how his unit had accompanied the troops to Malta, then on to Constantinople and were now temporarily settled on the shores of the Black Sea where the summer heat was terrific.

'I've been appointed acting Sergeant,' he wrote, 'only because except for the two doctors in charge, I seem to know more about the ordinary everyday ills than the others who are medical students all sprung from among what we used to call the "Nobs". It comes from having a working-class background. Where I grew up, we couldn't afford doctors so we had to learn to treat ourselves and use a lot of commonsense . . . I think of you often. Has the baby arrived yet? Write to me even if it's only a line to say you're well and happy,' and he gave the special army address from which mail would be distributed.

She had read it more than once and in fact had taken it out that very morning, intending to ask her father where exactly these exotic places were that Daniel had mentioned, and left it lying on her dressing table when she was called to the nursery for a final decision about the beautiful christening robe worn by Margaret and herself and now loaned by Clarissa for the occasion.

Gareth who since her confinement had been sleeping in another room on Dr Speir's advice came into the bedroom to fetch something and picked it up. He saw at a glance what it was and felt a moment of anger that she had not told him about it. He looked at the first few lines, then quickly folded it up and put it into the drawer where she kept her pocket handkerchiefs.

He thought about it once or twice during the day and had almost decided to let it go and not make an issue of it when Christine herself innocently brought it back into his mind.

'Margaret was telling me today that she has heard from Freddie,' she said lazily. 'They have now been moved out to a place near Varna on the Black Sea which sounds quite pleasant except that it is terribly hot and the food is dreadful. Margaret has discovered that Fortnums are making up food parcels and sending them out to a collecting post for distribution. I thought I might go with her so that we can choose what seems most suitable in the circumstances.'

He was not sure what made him say it but the words were out before he could stop them.

'Are you also thinking of sending a food parcel to Daniel Hunter?'

She looked at him, frowning. 'What makes you say that?'

'He has been writing to you, hasn't he?'

'Have you been spying on me?'

'There was no need to spy as you call it. You left the letter on your dressing table. I saw it when I went in to fetch my cuff links.'

'And did you read it?'

'Certainly not. As a matter of fact I put it in one of your drawers. Why didn't you tell me you intended to write to one another?'

'I didn't want to provoke a quarrel.'

'Why should it if it is so innocent?'

'Oh it's innocent enough. They are not love letters if that's what you mean, but you would want to read them, wouldn't you, just as you read that letter Papa gave you to bring to me at Glenmuir.'

'What letter? What the devil are you talking about?'

'Don't pretend you don't know. The letter which you destroyed because in it Daniel wrote how he had discovered the truth about his birth, that it was all a mistake and he was no more related to Papa or me than you are.'

'How do you know about that?'

'He told me when he came here that day. How he wrote to tell me about it and wondered why he had no answer. I thought at first it was Papa but afterwards I realized it must have been you who destroyed it because you knew it would make all the difference in the world to how I felt.' She turned to look at him. 'I am right, aren't it?'

'Not entirely.' He sat up in the armchair, realizing that the moment he had dreaded had come and he couldn't escape from it. 'At first I never intended to destroy it but I believed I had a right to know what he had written to you. I thought it was for the best, Christine, I swear I did. You and I had been so close, we had been everything to each other till Daniel came between us. If I had told you, you would have gone on hoping and waiting for years perhaps, ruining your life, wasting it, when I could give you so much. We had planned our life

574

together, you know we had, Uncle David, your father and your mother, everyone expected it . . . I could not bear to lose you, to see it all thrown away for nothing, for some dream that could never come to anything. You must understand that.'

'Oh yes, I understand even if I don't agree and you were utterly ruthless about it, weren't you, you trapped me by raping me on that Scottish headland.'

'That's not true,' he said passionately. 'It was you who drove me to it. It was never planned, never deliberate.'

'Maybe not,' she said wearily, 'but it happened all the same. You cheated me. I could have had a choice and it was denied to me.'

'I hoped you would never have to know.'

'Wasn't that the act of a coward?'

'Maybe, I don't know. I was fighting for you, for our love, for our whole life together. Is it so hard to forgive?'

'It's easy enough to forgive but not so easy to forget. Daniel was right. He said it's over and done with and we can't bring back what is past however much we may wish we could. There's no help for it, is there? We're married, Gareth, you and I, and we've got to make the best of it.'

'There was a time when you wanted that more than anything else.'

'I know but one changes, one grows up, there are other influences. I was wrong to let you go on believing we could ever find it again. It's useless to regret what you can't change.'

'You make our future sound very bleak.'

'I feel bleak at the moment.' She got to her feet. 'I really am very tired after all the fuss today. I think I shall go to bed.' She smiled faintly. 'You do realize that your son wakes me up at some unearthly hour demanding food.'

'Don't go, not yet.' He got up, taking her arm, turning her round to face him. 'Don't condemn me for so little a thing.'

'It's not little to me.'

'Tell me it's not all lost between us.'

'Not all lost, different that's all. Once I would have trusted you completely. Now I don't know.'

'I love you, Christine. I couldn't bear the thought of losing you.'

'I know.' She kissed his cheek and slipped away from him.

He dropped into the chair with a feeling of despair. He had wanted her so much that he had taken a chance and now it had blown up in his face because he had misjudged the strength of what lay between her and Daniel, but he'd win her back. He'd never let her go. If it came to an issue between him and Daniel Hunter, then he would win, he must win. He did not realize how very soon and how unbelievable it would prove to be.

Chapter 28

The dignified gentleman in an elegant frockcoat with a carnation in his buttonhole might have been a member of the diplomatic corps instead of one of Fortnum's shop walkers, thought Christine with a giggle. He was discussing gravely with Margaret what should be included in the food box to be sent out to Freddie.

'Tea, coffee, chocolate, of course, Madam, but I would hesitate to include too much potted meats since the great heat could turn them rancid and we cannot be certain how long the box will take to reach your husband. We for our part make sure the packages travel as quickly as possible to the collecting point but after that I am afraid army efficiency leaves much to be desired. We can include cheeses of course, well cured bacon and ham, brandy, and I understand tablets of soap are very acceptable.'

Christine had already made up her mind to send a similar box to Daniel but she wouldn't do it now. It could cause too much comment and though she could swear Margaret to secrecy, it would be better if she didn't know.

'Do you think it will really reach him?' said her sister gloomily as they came out into Piccadilly.

'I'm sure it will and he will be so pleased. It will seem like a breath from home.'

She went back the next day to give her own order and was amused at the raised eyebrows when she gave the direction – Sergeant Daniel Hunter, the number of his medical unit, the northern regiment.

'Shall I place it to your account, Madam?' asked the shop assistant shutting his order book.

'No.' This was not Gareth's affair but her own. 'I will pay for it now in cash.'

'As you please, Madam.'

When she came out into the sunshine of early July she thought of the time when Daniel had been beaten up and she had taken a basket of provisions and more or less had them thrown back at her. She didn't think his stubborn pride would refuse her help this time. They had come a long way since then.

Ever since the christening and its aftermath life for her and Gareth had settled again into a calm routine. He was working hard and she busied herself with the baby and the household. They would discuss daily happenings in the evenings which were still rather quiet as she didn't yet feel up to social occasions or organising dinner parties, they took pleasure in the progress of their baby son, but they still slept apart following Dr Speir's strong recommendation of no intimacy for at least another three months, but with all this they never regained the old bond of loving trust. Once they had told one another everything, argued, quarrelled and come together again happily, now they watched what they said, careful not to provoke argument, and that magic that had been theirs in the days of growing up had gone for ever.

All that summer it seemed that the army sweated it out on the plains round Varna and no steps were taken to pursue the plan of campaign. The Prime Minister vacillated, reluctant to order any extension of the war, Ministers argued fiercely for and against while William Howard Russell, the forthright Irish correspondent sent out by *The Times*, attacked the British Army organisation for hopeless inefficiency coupled with a total inability to deal with the various crises that arose every day. Up in the north where people were more inclined to take the *Clarion* than *The Times*, they were reading Daniel's far more trenchant report about the provisions that always arrived late and were often inedible because of the heat, the epidemic of cholera raging through the troops and killing at least fifteen men a day, the makeshift hospital where the orderlies wolfed the food sent in for the patients, where blankets and mattresses had run out so that sick men were lying on rotting floorboards that housed an army of fleas, lice and a colony of hideous bloated rats. The whole country seethed with indignant anger. There were demonstrations demanding the continuation of the war. The Chancellor raised income tax from sevenpence to one shilling and two-pence in the pound, infuriating the better off, and *Punch* came out with a cartoon showing the Prime Minister blacking the Tsar's boots.

Christine was not sure where the idea first sprang from that she might go out there herself when of course the very notion was absurd. No one, least of all Gareth, would have allowed her to do any such thing though it was true that wives and sweethearts often accompanied men in the ranks and a great number of Officers' ladies had gone with their husbands and were apparently having a wonderful time in Constantinople, where the British Ambassador held great state with balls and soirées and made sure that reports from the war front were kept as far away as possible.

When she was staying down at Ingham Park for a couple of weeks in August Margaret told her one day that the wife of Freddie's batman had been invaluable in looking after the needs of both men.

'It must be a tremendous adventure,' said Christine wistfully. 'Did you never consider going out there with Freddie?'

'No, never. The very idea terrifies me, besides how could I leave the children? Then there is the Park. My father-in-law is wonderfully efficient in running the estate but he relies on me too. I've learned a great deal over the last three years and I think I can say I know almost as much as he does about the needs of the sheep and the cattle and the pigs,' she went on modestly.

'Lucky old you,' sighed Christine. 'I feel so utterly useless. The house runs itself and Nanny looks after David so efficiently

I have hardly anything to do with him except feeding him and that will come to an end very soon. I feel life is passing by and I'm doing nothing. Any return to the clinic has been stamped on by Gareth and at the moment I don't think I can fight him over it.'

'You wouldn't want to go away and leave the baby, would you?' asked Margaret, a little shocked.

'I might. You see I happen to know that Dr Andrews has been approached about working out there. He is a wonderful organiser and fearfully efficient and if he took a team, it might do a little for the medical services which, according to what Daniel writes, haven't moved an inch since the days of Waterloo. If he did go, Gareth would accompany him and that would be my opportunity.'

'They'd never let you go with them.'

'I don't know. I can be pretty forceful if I really try and I do have an ally in Molly Andrews. I can't see them going without her. If it does happen, Margaret, and it is a pretty big if, would you take care of Baby David for me? Oh I know Mamma would take him on if I were to ask her but a young baby would disrupt their household at Belgrave Square whereas down here – well, your Clary is only a month or so older than David and with the two nurses and your ample nurseries . . . would you do it for me?'

'Of course I would,' said Margaret, 'I would do anything, but he will be only a few months old. How can you bear the thought of leaving him?'

'I shan't like it but he is too young to miss me and after all, at the moment he sees more of his Nanny than he does of me. I don't suppose anything will come of it anyway,' she went on rather despondently.

But Christine was wrong. Outraged public opinion together with strong pressure from their French allies had its effect. Orders went out at last for an invasion of the Crimea. The troops began to embark at Varna for Calamita Bay in readiness for a combined assault across the River Alma against the great redoubts that protected the fortress of Sebastopol.

580

'Calamity Bay might have been a more appropriate name,' wrote Daniel with bitter irony, describing the landing of some eight thousand men into sheeting rain with no protection and obliged to find shelter where they could in the angle of a wall or wrapped in their greatcoats while their French allies were snug and warm in the small tents supplied to each man. As usual army inefficiency had made sure that most of the equipment, tents, medical supplies, mattresses, blankets, had all been left behind.

That was when Dr Andrews finally made up his mind. He had already been in touch with the War Office, who insisted that medical arrangements under the supervision of Dr John Hall were more than adequate and they wanted no civilian interference.

'I know John Hall,' he said wrathfully, 'he is an old-fashioned martinet whose ideas have stuck in the same groove for the last thirty years. He believes that decently equipped ambulances are pampering the men and disapproves of chloroform since if a man screams in agony when his leg is being hacked off it proves he is still alive.'

Together with a couple of like-minded friends he began to make plans for travelling out there with or without official recognition and Gareth was to go with them.

He came home to Wimpole Street one evening full of it and Christine listened to him quietly before she dropped her bombshell.

'I shall come with you.'

Stopped in mid flow, he looked at her in amazement. 'Come with me! Don't be foolish. We can't take a woman. And in any case I wouldn't allow you to risk your life like that. What about the baby? What about the house here?'

'It's in very good hands and David is as happy with his Nanny as he is with me, indeed almost more so. He has already been weaned and is progressing very well on the bottle.'

'I know why you want to go,' he said with a quiet anger. 'It's because of Daniel, isn't it? I know you've been writing to him. I know you are sending food parcels.'

'Only two so far, and what if I have? He needs them just as much as Freddie does, probably more, and who else is to send them? I did tell Papa about it and he agreed with me.'

'You didn't feel the need to tell me.'

'Only because I knew you would raise some stupid objection. I paid for them myself by the way. They didn't come out of my housekeeping allowance.'

'As if that had anything to do with it.'

'Listen, Gareth,' she said patiently, 'there are, I believe, something like sixty thousand men out there in the Crimea. There isn't much chance of me meeting Daniel, is there? We can't arrange a secret rendezvous on the beaches of Balaclava or wherever it is you are planning to go.'

'Don't make silly jokes.'

'I'm not. I'm trying to convince you how stupid your suspicions of me are. You don't seem to realize that I am also very fond of you. I don't want you to go into this venture alone. I want to share it all with you, good or bad.'

'I wish I could believe that.'

'You can, Gareth, believe me you can. I can't sit back here in idleness leading a comfortable life while you may be going through hell out there. Tell me one thing. Is Molly going with her husband?'

'Yes, she is,' he said reluctantly, 'but she is older. It's different for her.'

'Why is it different? She is only a woman. I've had quite a lot of experience of sickness and we'll be companions for each other. I shall go and see her tomorrow. I shall ask her what she feels about it.'

'She'll say the same as I do. The whole idea is preposterous. What is to happen to the baby? Who will take care of him?'

'I've already settled that with Margaret. She will make him welcome at Ingham Park. He will be safe with her in the country where no harm can come to him and Papa and Mamma will keep a watchful eye on him.'

'You've got it all wrapped up, haven't you?'

'I've thought about it and I'm determined to go through with it.'

'Not if I can help it,' he said firmly.

But Gareth was fighting a losing battle as he very soon realized. The next day Christine took herself round to Harley Street to speak to Dr Andrews' wife. Molly listened to her in silence before she spoke.

'You're quite sure about this, aren't you, my dear? It's not going to be an exotic picnic, you know, putting on your prettiest gown and swanning it at one of the Embassy balls in Constantinople.'

'I know. That's not what I want. I want to be with Gareth. I want to share something of what he will be going through.'

'Have you thought seriously about what it's going to mean? It won't be feeding sick men with egg custard and bathing their feverish brows. It will be bloody wounds, hideous amputations, men screaming with pain, and death only too frequent because George is determined to take his unit right into the battle zone and it will be all hands to the plough.'

'I know it won't be easy,' she said steadily, 'but I have had some experience. Please let me come with you, Molly, it's very important to me.'

Molly was looking at her keenly. 'What about your baby? You must think of him, you know.'

'My sister Margaret will take care of him. It will be a wrench leaving him but at the moment I think Gareth needs me more than he does.'

'Very well. I'll speak to George. The decision lies with him, you know. If he agrees, you and I will get together and decide what we need to take with us. We shall be loaded up with medical equipment and a box of useful provisions so personal luggage must be kept to the minimum.' She gave Christine her warm friendly smile. 'Speaking personally I'd like a companion with me and you and I agree about most things, don't we?'

At first Dr Andrews was against the idea. 'She's a plucky lass, I grant you, but she had a bad time when that baby was born.

We can't risk being burdened with someone falling sick and having to be shipped home.'

'She is a good deal tougher than she looks, George, and she has a brave spirit. I'd welcome a companion and together we could do a lot to ease life for the rest of you.'

His wife was persuasive and he had great trust in her judgment of character. 'I only hope you're right,' he said and gave in. It cut the ground from under Gareth's feet. He could not stand out against it and even found himself reluctantly enjoying the fact that they were now working together on a shared cause.

Christine went on a shopping spree with Molly, buying plain sensible hard-wearing clothes and plenty of warm underwear.

'They say the winters can be cold and it will be October before we reach there,' said Molly, choosing plenty of woollen knickers and flannel petticoats.

Of course Christine met opposition. Clarissa was horrified and said so very forcibly.

'I thought she'd outgrown that wilful streak of hers now that she is married,' she said to her husband. 'Can't you do something to stop her? She may listen to you.'

'She is no longer my responsibility. Only Gareth can do that and it seems that he has agreed.'

'He is far too soft with her. She does just as she pleases. Abandoning her child and going off like that flibbertigibbet Mrs Duberly, who went flaunting off with her husband as if it were a summer picnic.'

'From what I hear it will be very far from being a picnic,' said Everard.

At the very last moment they had an unexpected addition to their company. One of the doctors had been obliged to withdraw on account of his wife's sickness and to Christine's surprise and pleasure John Dexter took his place.

'I wanted a change,' he said briefly, 'and when Dr Andrews told me there was an opportunity to join him, I jumped at it.'

'It's not a holiday excursion,' said Gareth half jesting.

584

'I'm aware of that but it's something different, new problems to face. It's the stimulation I need. I was growing horribly stale.'

It was September by the time they set out, travelling through Paris to Marseilles and then taking ship to Constantinople and the Golden Horn. Fortunately it was a peaceful voyage, the weather was fine and they all enjoyed it. The saloon boasted an old battered piano and one evening Christine put on the one pretty dress she had packed and after they had dined, amused them by playing and singing in her small light voice some of the songs she had learned from Kate. Afterwards John Dexter showed an unexpected talent, thumping out some old music hall tunes in which they all joined, forgetting for the moment the grim future that lay ahead of them.

When they retired to their cabin and were already undressed, Gareth came up behind her as she brushed her hair and kissed the back of her neck.

'I'm glad you are here, Christine,' he whispered.

'Are you?' She twisted round to face him. 'Are you? Then I am glad to be here,' and she let him take her in his arms.

That night for the first time since David's birth they made love and it was gentle and satisfying. For a little while they were happy and contented with one another and Gareth could forget the uneasy certainty that some time in the weeks ahead the issue would have to be fought out between him and Daniel.

Christine was charmed by her first glimpse of Constantinople through the gauzy mist of early morning, magnificent white houses surrounded by gardens still full of colour, a fascinating skyline of domes, long slender towers and minarets etched against palest blue, but she found that the reality was very different. The splendid houses of the rich surrounded by courtyards with heavily barred gates lay beside filthy hovels; the streets were piled high with decaying garbage through which rats scurried and squeaked, market stalls selling fine jewellery, exquisite silks and damascened silver

585

and copper were surrounded by beggars crawling through the gutters showing their hideous sores and begging for alms.

The very day they landed they were greeted by news of the great British victory won on the banks of the Alma. The troops had fought like demons, splashing through the river, capturing the two great redoubts and driving the Russians into retreat. That evening the British Ambassador was holding a grand party in celebration which Dr Andrews stubbornly refused to attend.

During the day while Molly and Christine went on a sightseeing tour, the men had sailed across to the Asiatic side of the Bosporus to take a look at what had once been the old Sultan's palace and was now to serve as a hospital for the sick and wounded. They returned seething with anger that the army board could allow such a hellhole to be used for such a purpose.

'It's no more than a cess-pit,' raged Dr Andrews, 'the floors inches deep in the filth and decaying refuse of years, sewers beneath the building that have not been cleaned out for a century and spread a poisonous effluvia throughout the whole building, while fleas, lice, rats are everywhere. A healthy man would have a fight to live a week, a sick man would scarcely last a day. Someone should take his excellency by the scruff and walk him through it from cellar to roof, that would teach him not to be smug and to put his wealth to better use!'

His openly expressed criticism did not go down well with the other English residents.

The news of the battle changed their plans. The army instead of following up their victory had been ordered to march south to Balaclava, there to prepare for an all-out assault on the south side of Sebastopol, and it was there that action could be expected so the very next day the party took passage across the Black Sea to Balaclava.

Daniel had received Christine's last letter, written a few weeks before they left England, just before the battle and in the general chaos had put it in his pocket unread. He did not open it till all was over and they had set out on the wearying march to Balaclava. A cart had been provided for the medical unit but he had given up his place to one of the soldiers sick with the pain of his wounded shoulder and trudged beside the cart. It had been his first experience of a battle and he found it hard to rid his mind of the horrors he had seen. It would have been easier to fight, he thought. Grappling furiously with an enemy did not give you time to think. He knew he would remember forever walking across that battlefield after the storm and stress were over, where men and horses lay huddled and still under a starlit summer sky, a few lights here and there as men like himself went from one to another with their lanterns, carrying water to moisten the cracked lips of dying men, a death-like silence everywhere broken only by the moans and despairing cries of those in agony for whom he could do nothing. Worst of all as the darkness deepened were the ghouls who stole out of the shadows and stripped the corpses of everything, even down to their muddied boots and sweat-soaked socks.

His next despatch to the *Clarion* was already growing in his mind. A victory but won at the cost of more than two thousand dead or dying, some of whom could have been saved if the surgeons had not run out of ether and chloroform, of splints, of lint and bandages and blankets, if the wounded had not been piled on to rickety carts that jolted them over the rough cart tracks to the ships that would carry them to that very hospital at Scutari condemned by Dr Andrews.

He read Christine's letter during their midday halt and seethed with futile anger. How could Gareth have allowed her to accompany him to this appalling place? He understood so well her brave determination, her longing to be part of it, but then she did not realize what she would have to face, the dirt, agony, suffering, death and very probably sickness. The cholera had abated but men still fell out of the ranks, struck down with a terrifying speed and more often than not dead by nightfall. He read the letter twice, aware of a perverse pleasure in the thought that she might be somewhere near and

587

not thousands of miles away. The bugle sounded, the men were already on the move. It was time to resume the march. He folded the letter carefully, putting it away in an inner pocket and took up his knapsack, trudging on through the warm sunshine and clouds of dust that sudden showers turned into liquid mud with no idea that by different ways chance was bringing them closer together and to an unexpected meeting.

The little town of Balaclava had once been the summer playground of the rich with its white houses spreading up the slopes, the walls covered with climbing roses, with vine and clematis, the gardens gay with flowers, the orchards of peaches, nectarines and figs. It presented a charming picture as the ship slowly approached the almost landlocked harbour, the water shining like a lake of silver. But as they dropped anchor the pretty illusion vanished abruptly. The water was choked with refuse of every imaginable kind while here and there the corpses of cholera victims insufficiently weighted floated hideously to the surface. Christine shuddered away as a distorted face, greenish white, bumped against the ship's side and then floated obscenely away.

When they went ashore they were met with the news that the army were expected to march in very shortly and any kind of accommodation was likely to be scarce. They required a base not only for personal luggage but for the large amount of equipment that they had carried with them. It was the ever resourceful Molly who by the end of the day had located a small villa on the outskirts of the town whose inhabitants had fled in terror and whose owner was only too pleased to let to these wealthy English milords. A servant went with the house, a Turkish widow who spoke a little English since her late husband had been in service with a wealthy Englishman who had made his home in the Crimea. Accommodation was limited and Christine, unpacking in the tiny room she would share with Gareth, was very aware that the pleasure and excitement of the journey was over and she must brace herself to face the work she had come so far to share with him.

The next morning after a sparse breakfast of coffee and stale bread she set out to forage for food with the Turkish widow, whose name was Anna, as guide and interpreter. The villa was only a couple of miles from the slopes above Balaclava from which could be seen the bastions and ramparts of the town of Sebastopol and it was among these hills that the army would be encamped. The men had gone up there to reconnoitre and find out what the conditions were for establishing a frontline field hospital while Christine found her way to a flourishing market where fruit and vegetables were in abundance but any kind of meat was in short supply. She managed to buy a few scrawny chickens, a couple of dozen eggs with a large cheese, and was busy filling the baskets with bread, vegetables and fruit when she heard the distant bugles and the insistent beat of the drums and realized that the first contingent of the army must be approaching. She was debating whether she had better make for the villa when Anna plucked at her arm, eyes shining with excitement.

'It is the soldiers. We wait and we look,' she whispered.

'All right,' she agreed rather doubtfully. 'We had better stand back. Leave the road clear for them.'

They came, those first divisions, marching bravely, heads up as befitted a victorious army, but she could not help noticing how exhausted they looked and though they had spruced up their uniforms, many of them were badly worn, thick with dust and stained with dark patches that could have been blood.

The first troop passed, then a brigade of cavalry, the regimental colours bravely blowing in the sea breeze, then carts filled with sick and wounded men, and walking beside one of them unbelievably was Daniel. Some obstruction ahead halted the ranks for a few seconds. He pushed back his cap to wipe the sweat from a face tanned by the burning sun of Varna. He was staring straight in front of him and she wanted to call out to him but the words strangled in her throat. All around her the market people were smiling, cheering, welcoming the soldiers with baskets of fruit and flowers. The order came to move on. Those in front marched slowly forward. She could not let him go. 'Daniel!' she whispered but he heard. He turned his head and saw her. Their eyes met. She took a step closer but he could not move out of the ranks. He stretched out his hand, their fingers touched and clung, then he had gone on and she was looking after him with idiotic tears in her eyes. It had been so totally unexpected that for a moment she could not come to terms with it.

Anna was looking at her curiously. 'You know him?'

'Yes, an old friend,' she said briefly. 'There will be more of them soon. I think it best we go back to the villa.'

She said nothing about seeing Daniel to anyone. Far better not since meeting him again seemed pretty remote and she did not want to disturb the warm relationship that had developed with Gareth. In any case the next couple of weeks were extremely busy and were enlivened by an unexpected visit from Freddie. She could hardly believe her eyes when she opened the door and there he was in all his splendour. Then he was hugging her and they were both talking at once.

'Margaret wrote in one of her letters that you might be coming out here but I never thought it would really happen. Quite a number of people have come flooding out here,' he said wryly, 'as if the army were some kind of a peepshow. I came up here on the offchance that one of them might be you.'

He was brought in, greeted by Gareth and introduced to the others.

'We're short of medicos, you'll be very welcome,' he said. 'We're encamped about a couple of miles above the town. Luckily we have tents but as usual they are in short supply and most of the men are sleeping rough. It's a place called Kadikoi, a few villagers and a church that is being rigged up as a field hospital. We're expecting the order to attack every day. They call us out at daybreak and keep us on the alert for four or five hours, dashed uncomfortable it is too, but we survive.'

He gave them a brief account of the battle which he had come through unscathed but Christine thought he looked tired under his tan, and his uniform, though clean and well-brushed, showed signs of wear and tear. He had come down to the town to collect mail and a few extra provisions that had come in on one of the ships and could not stay long. She went out with him to where his horse was tethered.

'We'll be up there with you all very soon,' she said. 'Take care of yourself, Freddie.'

'And you take care too,' he said, leaning down and touching her cheek. 'Must think of young David you know.'

Then he had ridden away and she thought what foolish things we say in a time like this and did not know whether it was better to be miles away in England and waiting for news or here on the spot in the thick of it all and with ever-present danger just around the corner.

Two days later when the men had already gone ahead to make what preparations they could nearer the scene of action, she and Molly were wakened very early in the morning by Anna.

It was still dark but she was saying excitedly, 'It begins already. Do you hear? The guns!'

The low rumble was like distant thunder. This is it. It has come at last, thought Christine, her stomach tight with apprehension and excitement.

'We'd better eat something and take some food with us,' said Molly practically. 'Heaven knows when we shall get back here. Are you all right, Christine?'

'Yes, of course,' but she could eat nothing, only drink the tea that Anna had made for them.

It was still only five o'clock but the streets were full of confusion, carriages, rickety cabs, carts everywhere swarming with people. All those sight-seeing English visitors were crowding into them with baskets of provisions like trippers going to a picnic, thought Christine with disgust. Molly commandeered one of the cabs and for a scandalous fare the driver agreed to carry them both to Kadikoi. When they arrived there, they found most of the visitors had climbed up one of the grassy slopes and were making themselves comfortable, spreading rugs and opening up baskets of food as if it were no more than a village outing instead of a bloody battle which would be fought to a finish in a confusion of agony, slaughter and death.

For a few minutes she and Molly stood looking across the ground towards the ramparts of the citadel they were about to attack and where the guns were smoking already and it seemed to her like some grand theatrical scene, finer than anything presented at Drury Lane, against a backcloth of a slowly brightening sky. The sun had just begun to break through and shone on rank after rank of men in their brilliant uniforms and glittering weapons, on gorgeously arrayed Hussars and Dragoons, on horses standing motionless as if on parade. It seemed impossible to imagine that in just a few minutes all this splendid array would be involved in a chaos of frenzied fighting, of mangled bodies and horses screaming in agony, of blood and death, till night fell with a result that no one now could foretell.

Overcome with a sudden dread, she shut her eyes for a moment against the scene in front of her and Molly touched her arm gently.

'We're not watching a play in the theatre like those fools up there,' she said with her calm common sense. 'We are here to help our men and try to save what we can out of the wreckage.'

'Yes,' she whispered, 'yes, I know,' and together they moved down to where the dressing stations had already been set up, to where the surgeons were already making preparations and the orderlies were unpacking rolls of lint and bandage, unrolling blankets, putting stretchers ready to hand. Somewhere along this line, thought Christine, Daniel is doing all this just as Molly and I are, and it comforted her to know that she was sharing it with him and with Gareth.

There were other women helping beside themselves. Some of the wives of men in the ranks were already battle-hardened and extremely resourceful. They had looked askance at

Christine and Molly to start with but in the imminence of battle class distinctions were forgotten and they were united in a common cause.

The unspeakable horrors of that day and night were something Christine tried to blot out of her memory, though there were some she knew she would remember for ever. At first she had wanted only to shut her eyes and ears against the incessant clamour of the guns, the roar and confusion of men fighting for their lives, the screams of terrified horses, the smoke cloud that mercifully hid some of the carnage and the grim aftermath when darkness began to fall at last and men stopped killing each other. The surgeons worked on and on, amputating shattered limbs, probing and bandaging ghastly wounds, line after line of the wounded waiting with heart-breaking patience, some of them still on their feet, some clinging to a comrade, most lying on the stretchers brought in by the orderlies in a never-ending stream.

It must have been near to midnight when Christine came out of the church hospital carrying a canteen of water and went down the long line of stretchers with men still waiting for treatment. Flares had been lit casting eerie shadows and the doctors were working by the shifting uncertain light of lanterns. She moved from one to the other moistening cracked lips, whispering futile words of comfort, trying to ease cramped positions as best she could. The last in the line lay so still, his eyes closed, the smoke-grimed face turned away, that she thought he was dead already but as she knelt beside him and tried to lift his head a little, the eyes flickered open, he muttered something and in the dim light she realized that it was Freddie. One arm hideously mangled lay across his chest. There was blood everywhere and she could only guess at how badly he was injured. She trickled a little water between his lips but he could not swallow and she gently wiped the blood and water from his mouth and leaned forward to listen to the muttered words.

'Had it, old girl, full in the chest. They killed poor Blackie, damn them!' and a long shudder ran through him.

Blackie, Freddie's favourite horse that he had loved second only to his wife and children. She stayed with him till his turn came at last and he was lifted to John Dexter's operating table. Steeped in blood to the elbows, his leather apron horribly stained, the doctor set to work. After a brief examination he gave Christine the chloroform-soaked handkerchief that had already served a dozen men.

'Hold it over his mouth and nose. I've got to take off this arm.'

Trembling she did as she was told, shutting her eyes so that she could not see though it was done with incredible speed and the doctor turned to the wounds in the chest. He probed, swabbed and bandaged. Two of the orderlies carried the unconscious Freddie into the hospital and John Dexter answered the unspoken question in Christine's eyes.

'Not a chance,' he said.

'How long?'

'Mercifully not more than a few hours.'

She went back to Molly who was brewing beef tea on the small portable stove they had imported for their own use and she began to carry it round to those patients able to take a few strengthening mouthfuls while she thought of Margaret and of dear kind-hearted Freddie who had never willingly hurt anyone, of John Everard who had proudly watched him riding at the head of his men, of little Clary who would never know her father.

When she went back to Freddie, the effect of the chloroform had worn off, his eyes were open but he was beyond pain, beyond almost everything. She knelt beside him and took his hand. He was saying something and she leaned closer.

'My horses . . .' he was muttering. 'Brownie and Rufus . . . don't let them be shot, Christine . . . they never did any harm . . .'

Tears pricked her eyes. How like Freddie to think not of his own pain but of the dumb creatures he had loved. She wiped the trickle of blood from his mouth. The effort to speak had exhausted him. The hand she was holding in hers relaxed and with a long shuddering sigh he died.

Molly found her still crouched beside him, stiff with cold and misery, and was unexpectedly brusque.

'He's gone. There's no more you can do for him but there are others crying out for help. Go outside for a few minutes. The night air will revive you. We've enough work here to carry us through the night.'

It was what she needed. She stumbled to her feet and went out into the night, walking a little way up the slope. It felt cold and refreshing after the stifling reek of the hospital. Flares were still burning, throwing grotesque shadows, and she leaned against a wooden fence, the tears running helplessly down her face so that she was hardly aware of the arm that went round her, turning her so that her face was hidden against Dan's shoulder and he held her close till she stopped shaking and lifted her head.

'I should be ashamed,' she whispered, 'but it is Freddie.'

What was one amongst so many? There was nothing he could say, nothing he could do but hold her against him and then bend his head to kiss gently the trembling lips before moving away. After a moment she pulled herself together and began to walk back to the camp.

Gareth, wearied beyond belief, arms and back aching with the strain, sickened by the smell of blood and sickness, had stopped for a brief rest leaning up against one of the pillars that supported the awning over the operating table when he saw them. The two figures outlined by the flares against the night sky were like an illuminated picture, standing so close together, his arm around her. He saw how reluctantly they parted and was filled by a black ungovernable rage of jealousy.

He grabbed hold of her as she came back passing between him and the hospital, pulling her round to face him.

'It's not the first time, is it? Where have you two been meeting? Where?'

'What?' She was still dazed with grief, still half blinded by tears. 'What are you talking about?'

595

'Don't pretend you don't know. You've had such splendid opportunities to meet, haven't you? Down at the villa while I have been away up here.'

'I've not spoken to him before tonight.'

'Don't lie to me.' He shook her so roughly that she stumbled and half fell against the wooden post, the rough wood grazing her cheek.

'I was telling him about Freddie.'

He stared at her. 'Freddie? What about Freddie?'

'He died a few minutes ago.'

'Oh my God! I'm sorry.' He was overcome with remorse. 'I'm truly sorry. I didn't know.'

'It doesn't matter,' she said tonelessly.

'It does matter. I thought . . . never mind what I thought . . . oh my poor love, I know how you must be feeling.' He would have taken her in his arms to comfort her but she pushed him away.

'I must go back to Molly. There is so much to be done,' and she walked quickly away from him and up the steps of the hospital.

He stood staring after her, hating himself for his insane suspicion, realising that with a few angry words he had destroyed the warmth that had grown between them during these past weeks and he could have wept in utter exhaustion and despair at his own folly. Then he shook himself free of it and went back to the operating table, going on grimly throughout the night till daylight came at last.

Daniel, still anxious about her, had seen what had happened and very nearly intervened, filled with a futile anger that Gareth should treat her like that until common sense told him it could only make things worse. He went back to his own unit very aware that sooner or later, unless he was very careful, there was going to be a confrontation between them that would probably help nobody.

Chapter 29

It was a week after the battle and Christine was trying to write to Margaret. It was desperately hard to find the right words. Her sister would be hungry for every painful detail. That would have to wait until she had returned home but she could tell her how with the help of Freddie's batman, Corporal Wells, she had rescued his two horses. Brownie and Rufus were now housed in a half-ruined stable attached to the stone cottage where Gareth and the others had set up their quarters. All the cavalry horses were desperately short of fodder and thin as scarecrows but Ben Wells contrived to steal some food and visited his two charges regularly. One day she would bring them back to Ingham Park where they would grow fat and sleek again.

She signed the letter quickly and folded it ready for despatch with a short note to her father. She and Molly had returned to the villa partly as a brief respite from the hospital, mainly to see what they could find in the way of fresh supplies. The aftermath of the battle, the numbers of men sick and wounded, had thrown everything into confusion. Supplies of every kind, blankets, clothing, food, medicines, had gone hopelessly astray or had vanished mysteriously into a flourishing black market. You could buy almost everything if you had money. Maybe it was only a drop in the ocean but they had to do what they could for those immediately under their care and that was where Molly was now, scouring the market for sheets, blankets, preserved soups and potted meats, arrowroot, beef tea, jellies, biscuits, wine, even at a scandalous price.

When she returned they would load it up and get it transported to Kadikoi.

It had turned intensely cold and fuel was short so when the knock came Christine had to disentangle herself from a thick rug before she could answer it. Outside stood Daniel, holding the halters of two mules, one of them already partly loaded. She was so surprised that it was a moment before she could find her voice.

'What on earth are you doing here?'

'I met your Mrs Andrews in the market on the same errand as myself. We agreed to share the two mules she had been bargaining for in return for my help with the loading and my company on the journey up to the camp.'

'How fortunate for us.' They were being hopelessly formal with one another, afraid to show any familiarity.

'You'd better come in,' she said. 'We haven't much in the way of food but I could boil up a cup of coffee for you.'

'Better not, don't you think? In any case there are thieves everywhere and I'd hate to lose either of these mules. It took long enough to bargain for them.'

'If you're sure.'

'I'm very sure.'

'Then I'll bring it out to you here.'

So when Molly came back she found them standing close together in the porch drinking black coffee and quite obviously on intimate terms.

'A mug of coffee is just what I need,' she said, her sharp eyes missing nothing. 'There's a bitter wind down by the harbour. As I expect he has told you, this young man has offered to help us load and will accompany us to Kadikoi. He tells me that we are in deadly danger from villains who will stop at nothing to steal the lot especially with nothing but two women in charge.'

Within the next hour the goods were loaded up and they set out, wearing their thickest boots and kilting their skirts high to avoid pot holes of appalling mud; Daniel leading the two mules and trudging silently behind them.

And that's how Gareth saw them as they came at last into the camp and stopped outside the hospital.

'You look as if you had just arrived from Siberia,' he said as he came to meet them.

'We feel like it,' said Molly. 'There's an arctic wind across those hills.'

Daniel had already begun to unpack the loaded mules. 'Shall I carry them into the hospital for you?' he said to Molly.

'I'd be grateful if you would.'

'Where did you pick him up?' asked Gareth with a sharp look at Christine.

'In the market on much the same errand as I was,' said Molly, aware of the edge in his voice and wondering why. 'He's been a tremendous help. Should I offer him something do you think? His pay can't be much as a Sergeant in a medical unit.'

'No,' said Christine quickly, 'No, Molly. He may be acting as orderly but he is also war correspondent for the *Northern Clarion.*'

'Is he now?' said Molly. 'How very interesting. I'd no idea you knew him so well.'

Then Daniel came back and she thanked him as he shouldered his own load, nodded to Christine and Gareth and went back to his own part of the camp.

Christine knew what Gareth was thinking and it irritated her. Did he believe she was carrying on a clandestine affair with Daniel? The very idea was ludicrous in the circumstances. Surely he knew her better than that, she thought angrily, forgetting the strain under which they were living. Underfed, overworked, nerves always at a stretch, it was easy to become the prey of wild imaginings. Ever since Freddie's death they had been on edge with each other and there was no opportunity to be alone together, no moments of quiet intimacy. At night she shared Molly's bed and Gareth slept with the others in the stone cottage.

There had been a lull in the fighting during the last few days, only occasional skirmishes, but it could not last. On

November 5th, when in London the children would be setting out their guys and begging passers-by for pennies, the Russians launched a determined attack on what was called the Inkerman Ridge and they woke to the roar of the guns and knew that the army were massing once again to recover the lost ground.

It was a strange day, icy cold with a white mist dense as any London fog lying in patches over the hills, so that moving round the hospital Christine could hear the clash and roar of battle eerily muffled by the fog which became even more dense as darkness fell. That night the orderlies found it difficult to locate the wounded, often guided only by despairing cries for help. A dreadful rumour ran from one to the other that the Russians, instead of taking prisoners, were bayoneting wounded men to death and efforts to bring in as many as possible were redoubled. Coming out for a breath of the cold night air Christine saw Daniel for a moment in the light of one of the flares, carrying a lantern, water canteen and medical pack slung across his shoulder, before he disappeared into the fog.

Some hours later, the stream of wounded having temporarily dried up, Gareth, working alongside John Dexter, stirred restlessly.

'What the devil do those orderlies of ours think they are up to? There must be dozens of men still out there.'

'They are doing their best. You can hardly see a hand in front of you.'

'I think I'll go out there myself. Take a good look around.'

Dr Dexter was surprised. 'If you do, you'd better keep a sharp look-out. The Russians are not likely to stop and ask who you are.'

He couldn't explain the compulsion that was driving him out there, only knew he had to go. Carrying a lantern and an emergency medical pack, he set out across the slopes. The Crimean winter had set in early. The grass under his feet was crisped with frost. Well, at least it might stop some of the bleeding and save a few lives, he thought to himself. He had gone some considerable distance seeing no one when he heard a scuffle, a muffled shout and a figure lurched out of the mist and went by him at a rush, hands clawing at his face. A Cossack by the look of him, going about his murderous business no doubt, and he turned quickly in the direction from where the sounds had come. He nearly fell over the man who lay face downwards and he put his lantern carefully down, knelt on the grass and gently turned the body over. Blood was welling from a wound in his chest. He could not see how serious it was so he moved the lantern nearer and by the small yellow glow was looking down at Daniel Hunter.

He lay very still and for a moment Gareth thought he was dead or at least very near it. He had always known there would come a time when they would meet face to face but not like this. For the space of a few seconds he knew a terrible temptation. If he were to walk away and leave him, he would undoubtedly die before further help could reach him and no one would know, no one could blame him, he would be simply another casualty of the war. Christine would mourn for a little but he would be free of him, free from all jealous doubts for ever. Then as he knelt there, shaken by the appalling thought, Daniel's eyes flickered open. He saw recognition come into them and he knew he could not, the instinct to save life was too strong in him and he could not deny it.

'You . . . of all people,' Daniel muttered feebly.

'Never mind that.'

He was already opening the tunic and then the shirt. The bayonet wound did not seem to be as fatal as he had thought at first. He plugged it with a swab of the medical bandage. Then he raised Daniel's head and gave him a sip from his own brandy flask.

'What happened?'

'I tripped in the fog . . . one of those confounded trenches . . . I've done something to my leg . . . I couldn't walk . . . and then the Russian loomed up . . . I thought he would spit me like a chicken but I managed to throw the lantern in his face . . .'

His voice died away on a wave of pain and Gareth gave him another sip of the brandy.

'I saw him as he broke away. You've probably scarred his face for life. Don't talk any more. Save your strength. I'm going to take a look at that leg.'

In the poor light it was difficult to make any proper examination. He did not think it was a break, more likely a bad fracture, but it was obvious Daniel couldn't walk. To go back to the camp, collect a stretcher and help would take too much time. Under cover of darkness battlefields were dangerous places. Another of the Cossacks could well finish him off or he could become weaker from loss of blood.

'You'd better leave me,' muttered Daniel, 'somebody will probably turn up. I'll survive.'

'Shut up, I'm thinking.' He stripped off the extra coat he had dragged around his shoulders before setting out and put it over Daniel. 'Now don't try to move,' he said brusquely. 'It will start the bleeding again. I'm going to look for some help.'

Gareth took the lantern and crunched away through the frosty grass. By now the moon had risen, shedding a wan light over the slopes strewn with the aftermath of the battle. Here and there in and out of the mist shadowy figures moved stealthily. No doubt the night marauders who came out last of all, stripping dead bodies, leaving them naked and pitiful before they could be gathered up for burial. He stumbled over men and horses and discarded equipment but there was no one who could help carry a wounded man back to the camp. Then he had an idea. He searched for a Russian gun, much like those issued to the British infantry but this one had its bayonet already fixed. Put together like that it was a good five to six feet. If Daniel was strong enough to use it as a prop or crutch he thought he might perhaps be able to get him back. Daniel was tall but not heavily built and he himself was strong enough.

He turned back and found that Daniel had struggled into a sitting position and was leaning against a tuffet of the coarse grass. He was shaking with cold and reaction but he managed a weak smile.

'I was sure you had deserted me.'

'I thought of it,' said Gareth drily, 'but changed my mind. Christine wouldn't like it.' He showed him the gun with its fixed bayonet. 'Do you think that with the help of this and your arm round my neck, we could somehow get back to the camp?'

'I can try.'

It wasn't easy. Gareth hoisted Daniel to his feet and he stood swaying, propping himself up with the gun. Then, with an arm around Gareth's neck and Gareth's arm supporting Daniel around the waist, they set out. It was not all that far but with stops every few minutes, it took a very long time. Once Daniel stumbled and fell heavily. He lay so still that Gareth thought it was the end but after a few moments he stirred and struggled to sit up. It took some time but at last he was on his feet again and they plodded on, Daniel keeping going by sheer effort of will over exhaustion and pain. It was long after midnight but there were still people about as they staggered in across the rough ground. Daniel would have collapsed if it had not been for the willing hands that supported him and, at a nod from John Dexter, carried him into one of the operating tents while Gareth stood breathing heavily, not far from collapse himself, his neck and arms aching, his back feeling as if it would break in half but aware also of a certain curious feeling of satisfaction that against all odds he had succeeded.

John Dexter looked at him a little anxiously, 'Are you all right?'

'I'm fine. He's the one who needs you. He's been bleeding like a pig from a bayonet wound and has a damaged leg, fracture or break, couldn't be sure out there. Go on, man, don't just stand there. I'd hate to think of all that effort going to waste.'

Some time later, sitting on a bench drinking black coffee that tasted like mud but was blessedly hot, Gareth saw John Dexter come out wiping his hands on a rough towel.

'What's the verdict?'

'Better than you might think. He's weak of course from loss of blood but luckily the bayonet didn't touch anything vital. If gangrene doesn't set in he should do all right. The leg is fractured in a couple of places. Not a damned splint left anywhere of course but I've set it and bound it up as best I can. Molly has found a mattress for him in the hospital. Come and take a look.'

Christine was kneeling beside Daniel as Gareth came in with John Dexter and she looked up at them anxiously, Freddie's death still weighing on her.

'Will he be all right?'

The doctor bent down to take his pulse. 'Good strong beat. He's tough, that one. With any luck he'll survive. At the moment it's sheer exhaustion as much as anything. Let him rest. Tomorrow we'll have a better idea. He's a lucky fellow. If it hadn't been for Gareth, he'd be freezing to death out there.'

She frowned. 'Gareth brought him in?'

'He did. Quite the hero. Let him tell you about it.'

'Shut up, you idiot,' said Gareth but Christine had turned to him with a look in her eyes he had not seen for a long time and Molly, who had come bustling up, took in the situation at a glance.

'There's nothing either of you can do for the moment so why don't you take a few hours rest. I'll be here for some time yet, Christine, so why don't you and Gareth share the tent. You've done enough, both of you. Nobody can go on for ever.'

'If you're sure . . .' murmured Christine.

'Go on with you, girl. No point in carrying on till you drop. That's not going to help anyone. I'll look out for Daniel here.'

So she and Gareth walked away together and outside the hospital she turned to him.

'Tell me about it.'

'For God's sake, there is nothing to tell. I'd have done the same for anybody.'

'I'd still like to hear about it.' She took his arm. 'What made you go out there tonight?'

604

He remembered that inexplicable urge and felt like saying Fate except that it sounded too melodramatic.

'It was just that the men had been slow in bringing in the wounded and I wanted to take a look for myself.'

The little tent was icy cold and comfortless but moments of privacy were few and far between. They sat close together, blankets around their shoulders, and talked about the latest report on the progress of their little son and how very hard it was going to be for Margaret, widowed so young.

'What do you really intend to do about those two horses?' he asked suddenly. 'The poor brutes look half starved.'

'I know. Corporal Wells does his best but he says all the cavalry horses are suffering. As soon as things settle down here, we can arrange for them to be shipped home. Freddie would like that and I can't let him down.'

They had not been like this, talking together so intimately, since before Balaclava and after a time, growing warmer in their huddle of blankets, stirred by what had happened and by his battle with himself out there on those frozen wastes, the need to love and be loved grew in Gareth. He began to kiss her, to unfold the layers of clothes they all wore against the cold, to find her breast. At first to kiss and caress seemed enough but when she responded with gratitude and affection, the need grew stronger and more passionate and at last would not be denied.

She yielded to his urging, laughing because it was all so unromantic, finding one another in a flurry of blankets and half-unbuttoned garments and giving herself to him freely and generously. Afterwards, when exhausted he fell asleep, she lay wakeful, thinking of Daniel and how strange it was that the angry clash between them which she had dreaded should end not in a fiery battle but in Gareth saving his rival from a cruel death.

It was the last moment of peaceful privacy they or anyone else would know for a very long time. A few days later when Daniel was already improving and chafing against the weakness that kept him chained to his mattress and after hours of

605

torrential rain, a storm broke over them with an indescribable and unparalleled violence.

It began very early in the morning. Soon after five o'clock Christine went outside to fill the big iron kettle from the pump and was struck by a gust so strong that it flung her against a stone wall and sent the kettle spinning down the road. Somehow she managed to scramble after it, refill it and fight her way back to the hospital, spilling half of it as she went. A few minutes later one of the windows blew in with a great scattering of glass and sheets of icy cold rain. One or two of the patients were cut by the flying fragments and for the time being there was little they could do to stop the rain pouring in except cover those nearest to it. Outside the hurricane increased in force. Hospital tents were blown clean away, taking valuable equipment with them. A huge marquee set up for those patients waiting for removal to Balaclava was ripped away, leaving men drenched to the skin and hopelessly trying to retrieve clothes, beds and blankets. The shed where the horses' fodder was stored was blown completely away with all its contents nobody knew where. Officers, men, orderlies, everyone was running hither and thither desperately trying to salvage what they could from the wreckage. Now and again tremendous gusts shook the hospital but luckily it had been sturdily built and withstood the hurricane's ravages. However, worse was to come.

By mid afternoon it seemed that the tempest had begun to blow itself out. Molly went out for a few minutes to assess the damage and Christine was preparing to boil up some of their stock of beef tea to give everyone a hot drink when it seemed that the dying hurricane braced itself for one more terrifying onslaught. There was an ear-splitting crash, a low rumble like thunder, a horse screamed in terror, men were shouting and the whole building trembled in the blast. After the first shock, Christine ran to the door. Outside there was a scene of chaos and she saw that the stone cottage and its adjoining stable had vanished and in their place lay a vast heap of stone, brick and rubble in which men were frantically digging.

For an instant she stood petrified, then Molly was there, taking hold of her, saying, 'Don't worry, my dear, don't worry. They will get him out. It's going to be all right.'

'What do you mean? What's happened?'

'It's Gareth. He was trying to save the horses and the whole place collapsed on top of him.'

'Oh no, no!'

Molly tried to stop her but she pushed her away and ran through the rain and choking dust to where the men were still digging and began to tear at the great blocks of stone.

'Leave it,' John Dexter said, 'leave it, Christine. We'll get him out.'

But she took no heed, tearing at the rubble, bruising her hands, breaking her nails.

They found them both at last. The horse, Rufus, was dead already, but face downwards in the mud, a great wound on the back of his head, cuts and abrasions all over him, was Gareth, miraculously still breathing. With infinite care in case there should be internal damage they carried him into the hospital, where Molly had somehow managed to salvage a mattress and some blankets in the little corner they reserved for themselves.

Then Dr Andrews and John Dexter were both there bending over him. Daniel had started up from his mattress but Christine pushed him back.

'There is nothing you can do,' but he gripped her hand for a moment and it gave her a kind of strength.

The two doctors got to their feet looking very serious.

'He's not . . . not going to die?' She could scarcely get the words out.

'No, no, my dear,' said Dr Andrews, 'he is deeply unconscious but breathing normally. So far as we can judge, there is nothing broken but I fear it's far too early to tell. He has a couple of cracked ribs. We can bind those and dress the wound in his head, then we shall see.'

They did what they could, stripped off his wet clothes and rolled him in blankets. The wound in the back of his head was bandaged, the other cuts and abrasions treated, then they could only wait and hope.

'Call me the instant he recovers consciousness,' said Dr Andrews and went away to help in the other salvage work.

Christine sat beside him for most of that day and night, taking her share with Molly in preparing what food they still had left in store but returning constantly to watch over him. She felt stricken with guilt because it was she who had persuaded him to save Freddie's two horses, she who had pressed him to let them be housed in the stone byre and she guessed that it was for her that he had risked his life so unnecessarily and yet so bravely.

Towards morning he stirred, muttered restlessly and opened his eyes, staring at her in a daze for a moment.

'Where am I? What happened? I was trying to free Rufus . . .' He tried to sit up and fell back with an involuntary groan of pain. 'Oh God, my back!'

Molly slipped away and returned a few minutes later with Dr Andrews, who had been up all night and looked grey with fatigue but who still managed to be cheerful and reassuring.

'How are you feeling, my dear boy? You frightened us to death last night.'

'It hurts like hell,' muttered Gareth.

'Let's take a good look.'

The examination was long and very painful and at the end of it Dr Andrews was thoughtful.

'So far as I can judge, there's very extensive bruising of the spine,' he said. 'How bad it is difficult to tell at the moment because of the inflammation. You're going to have a few very unpleasant weeks, my boy.'

Gareth said bluntly, 'What does that mean? Paralysis?'

'No, no, only temporary, but we must take great care.'

Christine followed him to the door. The hurricane had been followed by the snow. It had been falling all night and lay everywhere, covering the scene of devastation with a mantle of purity and adding to the misery of men who had no warm clothes, little food and only what shelter they could contrive out of the wreckage.

'Tell me,' she said, 'what can I do to help him?'

'There is little any of us can do at the moment, my dear. I can't even give you anything to ease his pain except a little laudanum from my own private store. What he needs is proper hospital treatment and so far as I have been able to find out there's no likelihood of that for some time. The storm would seem to have wreaked worse havoc at Balaclava than it has here. There's no hope of any transport for a couple of weeks, if not longer. Now listen to me,' he said taking both her hands, 'keep his spirits up, don't let him believe he cannot be cured. I'll be here every day to ease him in any way I can and as soon as it is at all possible we will arrange for him to be shipped home and you must go with him. Back in London there are excellent treatments for conditions like his. Do you understand me? Don't let him believe for a single moment that his condition will leave him crippled for life. You're a brave lass. I know you can do it.'

It was only too true. They were marooned in the encampment, only a few miles from Balaclava but unable to communicate, shut in by the snow, no transport, no carts, no horses to be found anywhere. Down in the town everything was in chaos. Ships in and outside the harbour had been hopelessly wrecked. Supplies intended for the winter, urgently needed clothing, sacks of flour, cases of meat, medicines, ammunition boxes, bales of blankets, horse fodder, all floated in the water or lay burst open and rotting on the quayside scavenged by hundreds of rats and mangy dogs.

The next three weeks passed in a kind of blur in which they survived as best they could. Daniel had made a quicker recovery than anyone had believed possible. The wound healed and one of the men clever at carpentry knocked him up a crutch out of some of the wrecked timber. With it he managed to get about the hospital even if he was unable to venture outside and he proved a tower of strength, helping in any way he could with the patients who were bedridden.

Sometimes it struck Christine how extraordinary it was that the two men who meant more to her than anyone lay within a few yards of each other but did not communicate at all except through her. Daniel took good care to speak to her no more than he did to Molly but she was conscious always that he was there, a source of strength that helped to keep her going.

The pain lessened a little but Gareth was still unable to move and though they never spoke of it, she knew what he dreaded. He was a doctor, it could not be concealed from him: although Dr Andrews and John Dexter sat by his bed and spoke encouragingly of complete recovery as soon as he could return to England, he had seen too many cases of spinal injury not to fear the worst and a future that he dare not contemplate.

Afterwards Christine wondered how they survived those appalling weeks but they did and she thought she would never again eat a good meal or sleep in a soft bed without being thankful for it.

Towards the middle of December the icy rain stopped, the sun came out and conditions began to improve a little. Transport arrived with food and a load of blankets and army greatcoats for the men, who had been reduced to rags. Dr Andrews began to talk of getting Gareth down to Balaclava and John Dexter said that now the army were settling in for the winter, it was about time he returned to his practice and offered to travel with them so that he could take care of Gareth on the voyage.

It was an enormous relief to Christine. The troopships that carried the sick and wounded to Constantinople were places of horror, men crowded on the open decks often in freezing cold and lashing rain with only one surgeon and a couple of orderlies. Dr Dexter's authority could make all the difference and he would oversee their arrival at Constantinople and arrange for their voyage to England.

The day they were to leave came at last. They did their best to pad the rough cart in which Gareth must travel so that the jolting journey would not do too much damage and at the last moment Daniel asked if he could come with them. He had despatches he needed to telegraph through to the *Clarion* which were greatly overdue and it could only be done in Balaclava. He had discarded his crutch for a stout stick, offered to do any errands Dr Andrews might require and would return on a later transport. So they set out with Molly waving them goodbye and Brownie, Freddie's sole remaining horse, trotting behind the cart.

In Balaclava, after Daniel had left them, they discovered that the ship would not sail for another couple of days. They debated whether they should go to the villa but John Dexter, by sheer force of authority and a good deal of judicious bribery, had persuaded the Turkish Captain to let them have a tiny cabin for himself and Gareth, hardly big enough to turn round in, but at least his patient would be dry and warm and he was afraid that if they did not take possession now, they would probably lose it to someone offering an even larger bribe.

'You go to the villa,' he said to Christine, 'and when you come on board, I'll move out.'

'But what will you do?' she asked anxiously.

'Oh I'll find somewhere to bed down. I'm not difficult to please. You give yourself a couple of days off.'

It was very tempting. 'I do have things to pack up,' she said doubtfully, 'and it would be marvellous to have a bath, but . . .'

'No buts,' he said. 'I order it as your doctor. No use wearing yourself to a shadow. You've a long hard voyage in front of you.'

So gratefully she did what he said, took a cab to the villa and was greeted by Anna with shrieks of pleasure, since she had gloomily concluded that they had all perished in the hurricane. She willingly agreed to bank up the fire, put on kettles and pots of water, drag the big tub in front of the sitting room stove and then go out in search of food.

It was heaven to strip off soiled clothes that had often been lived in day and night, to soak in hot water with sweet-smelling

611

soap, to wash her hair and with it to wash away some of the agonies and anxieties of the last few weeks. She put on clean clothes and dried her hair in front of the fire, revelling for a few hours in the luxury of it. Her only disappointment was to find that having eaten so little for so long, she could only manage a few mouthfuls of Anna's delicious cooking.

She slept late the next morning, making up for the long wakeful nights, and spent the day packing up the few clothes and other items she had brought with her, happy to be clean, quiet and alone, the tension that had gripped her for so long gradually unwinding.

In the early evening she was stretched on the huge old sofa in front of the fire when the door opened.

'Is that you, Anna?' she murmured sleepily.

'No.'

She sat up abruptly. It was not Anna standing there but Daniel.

'Goodness, you gave me quite a shock. How did you get in?'

'I met Anna going out and she let me through. Am I disturbing you?'

'No, of course not. Come and sit down.' She shifted up on the sofa but he took one of the chairs by the fire.

'I came to see how you were and to ask a favour from you.' He took out a bulky packet. 'I've been at the telegraph office all day but it's in a hopeless state of chaos like everything else down here. Could you take these and send them on to the *Clarion*? The address is on the outside.'

'It could be a longish voyage,' she said doubtfully.

'I still think they'll reach the Editor more quickly than if I leave them here where they'll probably gather dust in some forgotten corner. I'd hate to waste all the time I took to write them.'

'In that case of course I'll take them.'

He put the package on the small table. 'You won't forget.'

'Never, I promise you.'

'Thank you and now it's just to say goodbye and wish you and Gareth a good journey with, I hope, a happy result

612

when you reach England and he can receive proper medical treatment.'

He sounded so absurdly formal that she had to smile a little.

'You don't need to go yet, surely? Stay a little. Have you had any supper?'

'Not yet. I'll pick up something in the town.'

'There's no need for that. Have something with me. Anna has left some of her delicious Turkish kebabs. I don't know where she finds the food but she does somehow.'

'If you're sure . . .'

'Of course I'm sure. There's always far too much for me. I'll fetch it. She leaves it to keep warm by the cooking stove.'

When she brought it in he came to sit beside her. She thought he had probably not eaten all day so she piled his plate with the tasty skewers of meat. What it was they didn't care to enquire too closely, goat of course and chicken and chunks of mutton perhaps from the burst sacks on the harbour quay. There was crisp home-made bread to eat with the kebabs and a creamy curd cheese. Afterwards she made coffee in a large jug and brought it in steaming hot from the stone kitchen.

'There's no milk, I'm afraid, but lots of sugar. I don't like it Turkish style, it's too thick and muddy and you can't drink enough of it.'

As they ate and drank, Daniel loosened up and began to tell her how he had first started on the *Clarion*. He told her about Joe Sharpe, the foul-tongued but good-hearted Editor and the responsibility he felt to report the truth as accurately and as vividly as he could.

'What he pays me for these despatches, he is putting into the bank for me so it will be useful when I get back after all this is over.'

'But what are you living on now?'

'My sergeant's pay. It's not much but it's sufficient and what other men can live on, so can I. In that way they feel I am one of them and so they talk more easily about everything.'

Time seemed to fly by and then Anna was back, looking in

613

to say she was going to bed and giving them both a beaming smile.

When she had gone Daniel got to his feet. 'Time I was off too.'

'You can't get transport back to the camp till the morning,' she said. 'Where did you sleep last night?'

'On the ship actually. I bedded down with some of the men, picked up some useful copy for my next despatch. Russell of *The Times* drinks with the officers, I try to get the views of the men in the ranks. It provides a good contrast.'

'You don't need to go, Daniel. You could sleep here and help me with my baggage in the morning.'

'No, better not.'

'Why? It's only a few hours. I have to leave very early to board the ship.'

'It isn't that . . . '

'Then what is it? You're not afraid of what people might think, are you? There's no one here who knows us.'

'Your servant believes we're lovers already.'

'Oh heavens, who cares what Anna thinks.'

He suddenly pulled her to her feet, kissed her fiercely and then pushed her away from him. 'That's why I can't stay. Your husband is lying out there sick almost to death. It's impossible.'

And abruptly she was furiously angry with him. 'Do you think I don't realize that? Do you imagine I don't know that I must do all I can to nurse him back to health, but he won me away from you by a trick. He owes me something.'

'He saved my life,' Daniel said stubbornly. 'But for him I would have died.'

'Gareth is a dedicated doctor, I hope he always will be, but he must pay his debts. It's little enough, God knows, a few hours together. We've hardly exchanged half a dozen words since the day I saw you marching through the town. Don't we deserve more than that?'

For an instant they stood glaring at each other, then she dropped on the sofa, all anger gone, only conscious of an overwhelming despair.

'If you go now, you go out of my life for ever. We both know that, there's no escaping it. It's got to be and I don't know how to face it . . . '

The tension of the last few weeks overcame her and tears were running helplessly down her face.

'Don't, my love.' He sat beside her holding her close against him. 'Don't weep like that. If it will help then I will stay a while longer.'

She took the handkerchief he gave her, sneezed and blew her nose. 'I'm sorry to behave so stupidly,' she said with a watery smile. 'What we could both do with is some of Papa's best brandy but I'm afraid we must make do with more coffee.'

Perhaps it was inevitable. Neither of them intended it but in the last weeks, though they had kept away from each other, they had been acutely aware of what had bound them together from the very first and was still there, strong as ever. Now, alone, away from Gareth's jealousy, away from prying eyes with the certain knowledge that in a very few hours they would be driven apart, the tension between them grew until it could have only one result.

It was very late when he got up to put some more wood on the dying fire.

'You can sleep down here,' she said. 'I will go up to the bedroom.'

'It will be too cold for you up there. You take the sofa, I'll make do with a chair.'

'It's very large. There's room for us both,' she said in a strangled voice.

With a sudden gesture he pinched out the candles that were all the light they had and in the glow of the burning wood he crossed the room and lifted her from the couch into his arms. The passion, the hunger that had been crushed, battened down, resolutely stamped upon, flared up and overwhelmed them, every nagging doubt, every hesitation vanished, and they came together with joy into its fulfilment.

*

She was woken very early by Anna coming in with a tray of tea, poking the fire into a blaze and lighting the candles.

'The gentleman, he is outside,' she said cheerfully, 'he splashes cold water on his face and he says drink your tea while he finds a cab.'

Christine pushed aside the blanket Daniel had tucked around her and began to gather her clothes together. She took the hot tea upstairs with her so that when he came back she was already dressed and ready. Without his stick he was limping very badly but with the help of the driver he carried the luggage out to the rickety cab.

'Come with me,' she said, but he shook his head.

'We made our farewells last night.'

He took both her hands, kissed them and stood for a moment looking deep into her eyes, then he turned and limped painfully away. She had parted from him once before in torment and frustration and now they must part again, and this time it was even harder because they were older, had both suffered in different ways and knew it had not diminished what they felt for each other.

Then she shook herself free from the sharp finality of their parting and told the driver to take her to the harbour.

On the ship John Dexter was already looking out for her.

'How is he?' she asked.

'Well enough but asking for you.'

There was no help for it. It was her future. She must face it and make the best of it.

'I'll go down to him.'

In the cabin Gareth said, 'What have you been doing these last two days?'

'Taking a hot bath, eating and sleeping,' she said cheerfully.

'Have you seen Daniel?'

'Yes, he came to say goodbye. He has gone back to Kadikoi.'

He shifted restlessly and she leaned over him anxiously. 'Are you in pain?'

'No more than usual. I can stand that. It's the thought of the future that haunts me.'

'When we reach London and you have proper treatment you will feel different about it.'

'Do you really believe that?'

'Of course I do and so should you. You always used to tell me that a patient's belief in himself is half the battle.'

'What arrogant fools we doctors are,' he said drily.

There were shouts from the deck. The ship shuddered as the anchor came up.

'It looks as if we're on our way. I'll call John and then we can make you really comfortable.'

'Wait a moment.' He had caught hold of her hand and pulled her close. 'Kiss me first.'

She hesitated only for a fraction but he saw it and turned his head away. 'It doesn't matter.'

'Oh darling, what a fool you are!' She turned his face towards her and kissed him hard on the lips. 'There, that's a promise for our future. Now I must go and find John.'

Epilogue

JUNE 1856

It was a warm sunny day in June and Daniel, along with some hundreds of the public, was watching the revue of the Guards in Hyde Park, one of the many events to celebrate the peace treaty signed in Paris in March without any great advantage to anybody except that people had stopped killing each other. He found it almost impossible to believe that this splendid array of men in their handsome uniforms could be the same as those he had seen a little more than a year ago struggling heroically to survive a Crimean winter, half starved, uniforms in rags, frost-bitten, dying of hunger, of wounds, of cholera, officers and men in the ranks alike. The cannon fired off several resounding salutes, all the neighbouring windows shook and the Queen arrived with her escort, riding a horse appropriately named Alma. He pushed dark thoughts behind him and began to note down what she was wearing for the benefit of his female readers who were interested in such details, a scarlet military tunic with gold braid, a gold and scarlet sash, a navy blue skirt piped with white, a round felt hat adorned with white and scarlet plumes. There was nothing, she assured them in a short emotional speech, that she enjoyed more than meeting the gallant heroes who had fought for her so magnificently and returned victorious.

The revue over at last, he turned his attention to the more distinguished of the visitors who had risen from their chairs, mingling and chatting together before they departed to their carriages. One group in particular attracted his notice at once – Everard Warrinder, a little older but still handsome, Lady Clarissa, elegantly dressed as always, a blonde young woman in the lavender of half-mourning who must be Margaret, holding a small wriggling boy by the hand – this of course had been Freddie's regiment – and with her a slim figure in black silk with a velvet jacket, white flowers on her large straw hat. He wondered if a time would ever come when he could look at Christine without inner turbulence, without an infuriating and suffocating feeling of loss that not even a few weeks living the high life in Paris at the expense of the newspaper had done anything to alleviate.

He hesitated, undecided whether to speak to them or quietly disappear. For over a year now he had deliberately cut himself off from Christine, from all of them, with the certainty that it must be done if he were to survive and work. To see her again, to talk to her, would only revive what was gone and could never be recaptured, even if it still obstinately went on living within him.

Then the decision was taken out of his hands. Someone had come charging across the grass, had seized his hand and was pumping it up and down. Harry, every inch the successful young barrister, was saying 'By Jove, if it isn't Daniel! This is marvellous, old boy, where the devil have you been hiding yourself all this time? Come and tell us what you've been doing. Papa has become a devoted reader of the *Clarion*, we all have.'

It would have been churlish to refuse, to make some lame excuse and walk away when once they had all been so closely linked, when he had shared so much with them. He followed Harry across the grass and they all turned to him.

Everard was shaking him by the hand, Lady Clarissa was smiling at him, he was bowing over Margaret's hand and bending down to say to the small wide-eyed boy, 'I knew your Papa. He was a very brave man,' and then there was Christine.

Her hand lay in his for a moment, their eyes met and locked together. She had seen him before Harry, before anyone, though he looked so different in the fashionable plaid trousers, the dark green coat, the hat with its curving brim that gave him a rakish, dashing look.

'My son David,' she murmured and the little boy was looking up at him with Gareth's eyes before he shyly buried his face in his mother's skirt.

'And this is my daughter Isabelle.' That took him by surprise. The baby in the nurse's arms must have been eight or nine months old, two bright hazel eyes staring at him seriously from under the frill of the muslin bonnet. He put out a finger to touch the rounded cheek and the baby seized it, pulling it to her mouth with a chortle of laughter.

'You're highly favoured,' said Christine. 'She doesn't do that for everyone.'

Then they were all talking together for a few minutes. He told them that he had been in Paris reporting on the treaty and the personalities involved for the newspaper.

'Are you intending to work full time for the *Clarion* in future?' asked Everard.

'Only as their London correspondent. I hope to be taking up a roving commission with the *Daily News*.'

'So you will be based in London.'

'Only part of the time. I am hoping for some foreign assignments. I am told there is trouble brewing in India.'

'There are trouble spots everywhere,' said Everard drily. 'You must come and dine with us. We'd all like to hear something of your experiences.'

Then Christine suddenly took charge.

'Papa, could you take Nanny and David home with you in the carriage? I'd like to stay and speak to Daniel for a few minutes.'

'I want to stay with you, Mamma,' said the little boy, obstinately clinging to her hand.

'No, darling, you must go with Grandpapa. I promise I won't be long. I'll be back to have tea with you.'

Everard, who understood the situation better than anyone, said cheerfully, 'Come along, Davie. If you're very good, perhaps Nanny will let you toast muffins for tea. You'd like that, wouldn't you? Don't forget to leave your address with Christine, Daniel, so that we can get in touch with you.'

The party broke up with promises of everyone getting together again very soon before the others moved away to where the carriages were waiting and the two were left alone together.

'Is this wise?' said Daniel. 'What is there to talk about?'

'A very great deal. Shall we walk a little?'

She took his arm as she had done so often before, when he used to walk part of the way home with her from the clinic, days that seemed to have happened in another world. There was still a great number of people everywhere so they made their way towards the Serpentine before she spoke.

'Why did you stop writing to me? I waited and waited but there was nothing after I'd let you know that we had arrived here and I had sent your despatches on for you, nothing except one brief note of thanks.'

'It seemed the wisest thing to do. We could never have gone on seeing one another. Gareth had made that quite clear and he was right. It would not have been fair to him or to you so I made the break. It was not an easy decision.'

She was staring straight in front of her. 'Then you don't know.'

He frowned. 'Know what?'

'Gareth is dead.'

'What! Oh my God, I can't believe it! I did wonder when I didn't see him with you today but I never dreamed . . . when was it?'

'Months ago now. Soon after Isabelle was born.'

'I did not see a mention of it anywhere.'

'Oh they didn't write much. Just another casualty of the war, not even very heroic. He only tried to save two horses, one of which died and the other . . . well, I do know that Margaret was pleased when I took Brownie back to Ingham Park. His horses had meant so much to him, she said, it was like part of Freddie.'

'I'm sorry, Christine, I'm very sorry, it must have been hell for you.'

'It was worse for him.'

They had reached the Serpentine and sat on one of the benches set up beside the water. It was quiet there, only a few strollers.

He said gently, 'Can you tell me about it?'

'I will try. You see the trouble was there was no possible cure. Oh we tried everything, every doctor, every kind of treatment. John Dexter and Dr Andrews, when he came back, were tireless with new ideas, new methods, but the damage had been too severe, it could not be mended and he was in constant pain that they could do little about except give him drugs that in the end had little effect. He tried very hard at first to conquer it. He said, "If I can't practise medicine, I can at least study and do research," and for a time he did until the pain became too unbearable.'

Daniel felt helpless to express what he felt and he took one of her hands in his, trying to convey his sympathy by the warm pressure of his fingers.

'The worst of it is,' she went on steadily, 'I believe he intended to die.'

'You mean . . . '

'Yes. I think he killed himself and I think Dr Andrews thought so too. Oh he signed the death certificate that his heart had given out under the constant strain but he knew and so did I.'

'But how,' said Daniel, 'how could he do such a thing, paralysed as he was?'

'Gareth was a doctor. He knew about these things and he still had access to his drugs cabinet. It was there adjoining his consulting room just as it had been when he locked it before we went away and Mark, our manservant, who was devoted to Gareth, would have done anything he asked him to do.'

'You mean he took something?'

'Yes, probably an overdose of the painkiller he had been prescribed, because at the end, at the very last, I believe he had guessed about us.'

'About us? You mean about that night in Balaclava?'

'Not specifically and I'm only guessing but I know in my inmost heart that I'm right. That last evening I'd been reading to him as I often did. Then Nanny brought in David and Isabelle to say goodnight to him and unusually for him he took the baby into his arms, looking into her face, talking to her. She has always been very individual and even so young she was already her own little person. When Nanny had taken the children away, he asked me if I ever heard from you and I said I would have told him if I had. He seemed quite happy, quite peaceful and loving when I kissed him goodnight but in the morning he was dead, apparently in his sleep.'

'Isn't it possible that is what really happened and you are tormenting yourself for nothing?'

'No, it's one of those things you know and can never drive out of your mind.' She turned to look at him and he saw that her eyes were bright with unshed tears. 'I have told this to no one and would not, could not, only to you. You understand, don't you? You know what it means – Isabelle is your child, not his, and I think he knew that night.'

He stared at her, finding it so unbelievable that he could not take it in. 'Are you sure? Do you mean that she is . . . ?'

'Your daughter. Oh yes, I'm absolutely sure. To me it is obvious though I don't think anyone else has noticed her likeness to you because they don't expect it. To them she is Gareth's child, come out of those last dreadful weeks in the Crimea. You don't need to feel worried or responsible. She will grow up with the same privileges and advantages as David. Only I will know, and now you.'

He was distressed that she had been forced to bear so much alone.

'You should have told me about it. You should have written.'

'How could I? I didn't even know where you were. I've lived with it for months now but I had to tell someone and that one had to be you, but now it is done and if I am to go on living, then I must put it behind me. I must learn to think of other things.'

A light breeze blew across the water. She shivered and stood up.

'It's growing chilly. Shall we go on walking?'

'Yes, of course.'

He was still disturbed by what she had told him, but after a moment she turned to him.

'I'd like to hear about you. Tell me what you have been doing.'

'There is nothing much to tell.'

'You're looking very prosperous.'

'You mean these clothes. I've learned that if you want to get to the bottom of the matter, you must conform a little, assume

626

a character so that you are accepted, but I've not sold out to the establishment, I'm still at heart a fiery radical.'

'Does your leg still trouble you?'

'Only when I am very tired.'

'Where are you living now you're back in England?'

'Kate wanted me to stay with her but she has her own life and it's not mine. I've taken over my old lodging in Paradise Alley till I can find something more suitable. Ma Taylor is very puffed up about it. I have an idea she goes around boasting of her war hero. Mr Brown has offered me a future partnership in his Cheapside shop . . . '

'And Elspeth?'

'She is, I understand, walking out with someone who is very much more suitable than I ever was.'

'I'm glad because I have a proposition to make to you.'

He smiled. 'That sounds a little ominous.'

'Actually it has only just occurred to me. I have a house, a very large house. The children live on the second floor. Uncle David has one large room to himself. He's very old now but not at all difficult to live with and his manservant is a treasure. But there are still a number of unoccupied rooms. Why don't you take one of them? Make it your home in London and if you dash off abroad as you say you are hoping to do, it will always be there waiting for you.'

'Christine, are you crazy? How could I possibly move in with you? Your mother, your father, Margaret, everyone would be horrified.'

'Who cares if they are? I'm not crazy, only very practical and if it offends your pride you can pay me for your board and lodging. You see I have now to look to the future. My children are going to need a father.'

He stopped on the path and turned her round to face him. 'Christine, are you asking me to marry you?'

'Once upon a time you wanted it very much but of course if you have changed your mind . . . '

'Have you thought all this out in the last few minutes?'

But she went on unheeding, 'Of course there would have

to be a decent interval, we mustn't scandalise society and you needn't worry about Papa. I told him what you had told me about your mother and he was as pleased and relieved as we were.' Then she stopped. He was still staring at her and her courage suddenly failed her.

'Oh God, I'm being incredibly stupid, aren't I? I am assuming far too much. It's eighteen months since that night in Balaclava. A great deal could have happened since then. You think I'm being callous, uncaring about Gareth, don't you, but you see I was prepared to devote my life to him, I did everything I could, and when suddenly the need was gone, I was lost, I had nothing left but a dream, an impossible dream, I realize that now. I was expecting far too much and I should not have burdened you with it . . . ' her voice choked and she walked quickly away, not wanting him to see the foolish tears that threatened to overwhelm her.

He paused only for a moment and then went after her, grabbing her almost roughly by the shoulders, turning her back to him.

'You fool, Christine, you dear dear idiot, don't you realize what you've done to me? I came here today knowing nothing of any of this, not even expecting to see you or anyone I knew, and you've turned my whole life upside down. Gareth is dead, you are free, I have a child – is it any wonder that it's knocked me off my feet? You must give me time to realize it, to recognise how my life has changed. I thought I knew where I was going, now I'm lost. I have new responsibilities to face, new plans to make . . . '

'I'm sorry. You always used to tell me that I took far too much for granted and did not think things out before I spoke.'

'Just give me time to get my breath back, that's all I ask.'

'Very well, but while you do, I think it is only fair to tell you that John Dexter has already asked me to marry him.'

'Has he, by God, I'll have something to say about that.'

A respectable couple strolling nearby were scandalized to see a young woman, a widow by the look of her, being violently embraced by a man and showing every sign of thoroughly enjoying it. They shook their heads sadly at the shocking laxity in modern behaviour.

When at last he released her, Christine said breathlessly, 'Oh heavens, I forgot the children. I promised to have tea with them.'

'I'll come with you to your carriage.'

It had been a long hard road but it seemed that at last they had come to the end of it. They walked hand in hand.

When he helped her into the carriage, she said impulsively, 'I'll come to see you at Paradise Alley. It will be like old times.'

He smiled indulgently. 'If that's what you want.'

'I do. Tomorrow?'

'Tomorrow, it is.'

He shut the door, watched the carriage move away, then suddenly he tossed the stylish hat in the air, caught it, jammed it on again at a suitable angle and strode away towards the park gates with a new spring in his step.